THE TICKET-OF-LEAVE MAN;

OR,

WEALTH, POVERTY, AND CRIME.

THE TICKET-OF-LEAVE MAN IN HIS COUNTRY HOME.

PROLOGUE.

THE SEVERED HAND.

A TICKET-OF-LEAVE MAN! A garotter, a burglar, and perhaps *a murderer*! Such, at least, are the attributes ascribed to the man who having offended against society, is released by subsequent good behaviour on a ticket-of-leave.

People shrink from his path, and carefully bar their doors at night if he is known to be in their neighbourhood. Policemen hunt him from his situations, and so prevent his getting an honest living; the judge gives him a long term of punishment when he is brought before him for the same offence for which the Honourable Edgar Smythe or Jones gets off with a forty shilling fine. Nobody cares to help him, nobody pities him, nobody inquires whether he has a wife, children, a sister or mother.

No. 1.

No! society is against him, and it is, "Hunt him down to the hulks or the gallows."

So, every hand being against him, the ticket-of-leave man turns his hand against the world.

He must live in prison or out; and thus he waylays travellers whom he thinks possessed of too much money; in the night, with crowbar, jemmy, and dark lantern, he breaks into the rich man's house—the poor man's he never disturbs—and with the spoil he obtains by these nefarious practices leads a jolly life along with his blowens and pals.

Reader, come with us to the Central Criminal Court; there you shall see the ticket-of-leave man as he too often figures.

The court was crowded; it was the trial of a man for the worst of crimes—murder. There was a general hush when the prisoner was brought in.

Every one looked with curiosity upon him.

He is quite a young man, and certainly far from what you would have expected in a convict and murderer. His features were good-looking and intelligent; and when he calmly glanced at the judge and jurymen, the sympathies of the crowd went with that pale, weary face.

What further increased the interest was the presence in court of a young boy, very fair and refined in looks; he was understood to be the prisoner's nephew, who, since the accusation of murder, had prayed to be allowed to share his uncle's cell. His earnestness had gained this, though he was frequently away, on all of which occasions he was strenuously gathering evidence in the convict's favour.

It was understood that he had a mass of evidence which his sagacious perseverance had enabled him to collect, and people who admired his brave devotion waited in eagerness to hear the boy's appeal.

So it had been rumoured that he would address the court, and that the substance of his statement would criminate another instead of the prisoner.

The counsel for the prosecution opened the case. It was observed that when he first caught sight of the prisoner, he became deathly pale, and was some time before he could commence his speech.

He stammered, too, as he went on, and failed, at first, to deliver himself with his usual address.

But, after awhile he recovered himself, and though still pale and avoiding the eye of the prisoner, he soon made the case as black as could be against him.

The victim, he said, was murdered under circumstances of great atrocity, rendered more horrible from the fact that she had once been his betrothed.

At the mention of this the prisoner was observed to tremble visibly.

The counsel went on.

The young girl had left her village, and remained in London, the match having been broken off by the fact of the prisoner's committing a burglary, and, as was suspected, a former murder.

A gentleman, it seems, had met the unfortunate woman in the street, and taking compassion on her forlorn position, took her home. The prisoner by some means found her out and effected an entry into the house during the night.

Then a most barbarous murder had been committed. From the testimony of the housekeeper, it would be shown that the prisoner was seen lurking near the house—that in the night she was aroused by screams of the most dreadful nature, accompanied by imploring appeals for mercy.

Rushing from her room when the cries of murder were so terrible as almost to petrify her, she was suddenly encountered by a man, masked, and with a lantern, who, it would be shown, was the prisoner.

She had only a momentary glimpse of him, when she was knocked down and beaten senseless.

What followed could then only be conjectured. The gentleman who owned the house was absent: returning in the morning, he found the shutters unopened, but the door on the latch. A key admitted him.

He found, then, what he (the counsel) could scarcely describe. The housekeeper lay senseless and bleeding on the stairs.

He kept no other servants, and, making an immediate alarm, he gained the assistance of a constable, and the injured woman having been lifted to her bed, they searched the house.

In the room occupied by the unfortunate woman who was made the victim of the prisoner's rage was a dreadful sight.

The bed-clothes were soaked with blood, and in the greatest disorder.

A print of a bloody hand was on the bed-post.

The walls were spattered, the floor stained with blood. A handful of hair—the young woman's—was lying in the clotted pool, and in the bed lay a mutilated clenched hand—the hand of the victim.

Here the prisoner became so deathly that he was obliged to be supported by the officers and the faithful boy.

A shudder ran through the court, and the counsel went on.

Everywhere there were marks of a dreadful struggle. The unfortunate girl had evidently been assailed while in bed, as portions of her night dress, all marked with blood, were found, and her clothes were undisturbed.

It was supposed she had resisted, and that the severed hand had clutched the bed-post, when the murderer, to hasten his work, must have cut it off with his deadly knife.

Here the prisoner groaned in anguish; his emotion was taken in proof of his guilt, and he became now the object of universal execration.

The counsel went on to say that the particulars of the horrible deed could only be conjectured, as the principal evidence was wanting.

The body had been carried away.

This, however, only made the case much worse; he likened the prisoner to a second Greenacre, and described him as mangling the wretched victim of his revenge, and conveying away the bleeding portions of her body.

He showed them how notorious the prisoner's antecedents had been—how he had already been guilty of a former murder for which he was yet untried—how desperate had been his deeds—how he had associated with the most notorious wretches, and how by deeds of violence he had lived, and evaded or resisted justice.

Amidst a buzz of sensation the counsel ceased.

No one in court then was not convinced of the prisoner's guilt.

The housekeeper gave her evidence, and was carried away fainting.

Next came the "gentleman," Mr. Ralph Merton.

He was ghastly, and perspired ceaselessly while he gave his evidence; at times he faltered, and had to moisten his lips with water. Then again he could scarcely stand.

There was a newly-made scar on his cheek, as if the flesh had been recently torn away by something sharp; on that scar the eyes of the boy were fixed during the whole time.

When Mr. Ralph Merton had sat down, the counsel rose for the defence.

He told the court that he had a tale to tell that would enlist their sympathies, and convince them not only that the prisoner was innocent, but that he had been for years the victim of other men's crimes.

He drew the picture of his peaceful village home, where, with the young murdered girl—his sweetheart—he had been happy, till there had come one who stole away her affections, and, having brought her to London, seduced and deserted her; the man, he said, was now in court, and had assumed a prominent part in the prosecution.

The counsel for the prosecution here became greatly agitated.

The prisoner had been charged with a former murder. He was prepared to show that that deed rested where least expected. He had evidence, too, to show in the present case, in which the "gentleman," Mr. Ralph Merton, would show in a different light.

That "gentleman" had lived at the same village with the prisoner; at that village he knew the unfortunate murdered girl; his friend it was who had formerly seduced her—from that friend he had gained her by violence.

He would call the "gentleman."

Ralph Merton was made to stand up.

He would ask him where he was on the night of the murder?—where he got the scar on his face? and would show them that if the wretched woman had been really murdered—and till the body was traced that could not be proved—some other hand than the prisoner's had committed the deed.

He called for the production of the cut-off hand.

Amidst profound sensation it was produced.

He bade the court look at it, and then look at the face of Ralph Merton. He would call before them the boy-nephew of the prisoner, whose evidence would show what false statements had been made.

And to support his evidence, he would open the bloody hand, in which they would find a proof of who was the actual criminal.

But first he would give them a history that would draw their tears for the falsely-accused prisoner at the bar.

The sensation and excitement increased in court. Ralph Merton trembled like a leaf; the counsel for the Crown was pale as death; the prisoner, too, was agitated—but by anguish, not fear.

But the excitement was at its height when the boy stood forward and called for the woman's hand to be opened.

People swayed forward in eagerness to see what horrible proof that blood-clotted portion of the missing woman contained.

But ere we describe what evidence was shut up within those clenched fingers, we will briefly dilate upon the history of the prisoner—a history which drew tears from many of the audience, and which showed what terrible sufferings and wrongs had been endured by the ticket-of-leave man.

The recital will also disclose what startling, thrilling, and appalling deeds he was connected with, or witness of.

CHAPTER I.

GOES BACK A PERIOD.

Two young beings sat together on a lawn before a manor-house that stood in a little village in Wiltshire.

One was a pretty-faced, blooming girl, young and neatly attired, but with a slight air of coquetry about her.

The other was a manly, honest-looking young fellow, whose frank face was overcast as he spoke.

"Ah, Mary, it be all acos o' that Lunnon gent that you've come over like this. You used to be glad once on a time to speak to such folks as I, but now you've got proud, and we're not good enough for you nauther."

"I'm sure, Dick, you have no right to talk to me as you do: if the gentleman speaks to me, must I toss up my head and go by?"

"Nay, it's what you do to me sometimes; but I know what it be: this Lunnon mister have put fine notions in your head, and been telling you I be not good enough for you. But I tell you what it is Mary, lass, if you listen to him you'll rue the day: he means you no good, and if you cling to him it'll be your ruin, and honest Dick tells you so."

Pretty Mary tossed her head in anger. In her heart she deeply loved the young countryman, but the attentions of a young swell from London had called into play her coqueting disposition, and, without meaning anything, or knowing of her danger, she was being led into a snare that, as her lover told her, menaced her ruin.

Some further vexed discourse took place between the pair, during which they forgot that they were the subject of observation of the villagers.

While Richard was accusing her of levity, two individuals approached whose presence—that of one, at least—caused Mary's cheek to crimson, and her eyes to sparkle with a pleasure she was hardly conscious of, but which further aroused the jealously of the young countryman.

With these two, who now approached, the reader shall make an intimate acquaintance.

One of them was Ralph Merton, the son of the worthy squire; but so unlike that worthy individual, that it seemed scarcely credible such a son could belong to such a father.

Dissolute, heartless, and scarcely honest, his doings had long been a source of uneasiness to his parent; for, even at his then early age, he had wickedly deceived two young girls of the village. His father had sent him to London, in order that better habits might be knocked into him.

He could have scarcely acted more foolishly,

Arrived in the metropolis, Ralph broke loose from the restraints of the gentleman who had him in training, mingled in all the vices and gaieties of the London capital, and returned an artful and finished scoundrel.

He was not exactly the sort of person you would have liked to have trusted either with your sweetheart or your money.

His features, once passible, but sinisterly changed by his course of dissipation and profligacy, showed that mixture of cunning and ferocity which spoke plainly, to any one who had the penetration to read, what his real character was.

He was one who would gain by artful hypocrisy if he could; and if not, would try other means to attain his object.

His companion was a little more refined in his appearance.

He was elegantly dressed (thanks to his unpaid tailor), and had a profusion of false jewellery about his person; his features were good-looking, and sufficiently rakish in their expression to make them captivating to simple-minded damsels.

Henry Warner was a young fellow of fast habits, whose acquaintance Ralph had made while in London, where the former was completing his studies for the profession of a barrister.

When in town the pair had been fast friends. Warner, an adept in sharp practices, had soon initiated Ralph into the mysteries of living like swells at the expense of other people.

They swindled everybody and paid nobody— sharing one common purse, and showing with *eclat* in all low haunts of the metropolis.

Ralph had been back some time at his native village; his friend had but lately arrived from London, but in the brief space of his sojourn here had already marked out as his victim the unsuspecting Mary.

Both, with an air of polished elegance, raised their hats, Warner cordially shaking hands with the young girl.

"Your villagers," he said, "are improvising a dance; see, the music is about to commence. May I have the pleasure of your company as my partner?"

Mary looked at Richard; if he had given her but a glance she would not have accepted the offer; but he had turned away from her, and with a gloomy countenance kept his eyes sullenly on the ground.

The young girl hesitated a moment, and then, half in pleasure, half in fear, accepted the arm of Warner.

Then the young countryman rose.

"You've chosen, Miss Mary," he cried, "and for your woe. When your heart was free, Dick Parker loved to be in your thoughts; but so long as you turn to another, you'll have nought to hear from Richard, except this, that if you don't mind you'll find yersel' in a snare that you won't get out of without sheame."

He turned angrily to the young Londoner.

"And you, Mister Lunnoner, beware! If you do harm to Mary, I'll follow you all over the world but what I'll make you pay for it—mark me! I will!"

Warner smiled superciliously, and the young countryman would have gone beyond words, had not a pleasing-faced boy stepped from the villagers, and taking him by the arm, led him, with soothing words, away.

But Mary was left with Warner, while Ralph looked spitefully but exultingly on her anticipated fall.

CHAPTER II.

THE PLOT AT THE "BLACK SHEPHERD."

QUIET and distinctively rural as was the straggling village where the hero of this tale, whose daring career has gained him so great a notoriety, was born, the tavern known as the "Black Shepherd" numbered sometimes amongst its visitors men whose character and profession were not such as would render them agreeable companions for the more honest portion of the community.

It had borne a very questionable repute even before the suspicious circumstance occurred there of a traveller having been found dead in his bed. He was believed to have been the possessor of a considerable sum of money; and as this, together with his watch and other valuables, had been found wanting, very ugly rumours got afloat respecting the inn and its owner.

In fact, it was whispered that the landlord had murdered the traveller, and possessed himself of his booty.

To be sure there had been an active investigation. Two sharp-nosed detectives from London had been down to fathom the case; but as the search of the house and examination of the landlord resulted in the grand discovery of nothing, the detectives returned to London, the traveller was buried, and mine host of the "Black Shepherd" continued his business as usual.

With this exception—that there were always lurking about him low, rusty-looking personages, whom he used to treat liberally, even while it seemed he feared and hated them.

It was night, and the back parlour of the "Black Shepherd" contained a tolerable number of guests. There were one or two militiamen, a commercial traveller, a few country bumpkins smoking long clay pipes and swiping beer from quart stone jugs; Richard Parker, by whose side was seated a boy, not twelve years of age—the same who had led him away when a collision had been imminent between him and Warner—and the identical two, Ralph Merton and his friend Hal, on whom at times the young countryman gazed with wrathful scorn.

The pair sat together at one corner of the room conversing in a low tone, as they discussed the measure of ale and gin placed on the table before them.

"And so," said Ralph, "tin's out."

"I'm sponged quite as dry as you," returned Warner, "in fact, don't know how I shall get back to London."

"What! so dried up as that?"

"'Pon honour."

"So am I, Hal."

"Can't you bleed the governor?"

"No go; he won't shell out anyhow."

"Well, you've used the old flint pretty freely."

"That's just it; and so he's put the screw on: but I tell you what, Hal—some money I want, and some money I must have."

"Hush: some of those yokels will hear you."

"Look here," said Ralph, sinking his voice to a whisper, "there's no chance with the governor; I've tried his drawers—picked the locks—that's one of the dodges you learned me."

"Well—any scraps?"

"Not a fluke; he's put it somewhere, or else it's all in the bank, where I can't touch it."

"Ah! fine things, those banks; tell you what, Ralph: I mean to be a director of one some of these days. Capital investment—lead splendid life—give banquets—people come and deposit their money—high interest—never such a chance—gold pours in—some day a smash—directors wanting—money *non est*."

"Never mind that, now," interrupted Ralph, "just hear what I've got to say, and then let's hear if you're ready for a go-in."

"Well, let's hear."

"Well, as I've said, there's no chance with the governor."

"No."

"And old Boniface here, keeps his till almost empty If I knew where he kept his hoard I'd have a try at it. I think I know a trick that would frighten him."

"Yes."

"But that's not it just now. But there's the parson."

"Ah!"

"He's got a fatter living than most of his cloth; and those charitable speculations he has been mixed up in have put a little in his pocket. You are listening?"

"To every word."

"Hal; I've found out that he keeps a devil of a dose of money in his house—and what's more, I've found out *where he keeps it*."

Ralph looked at his friend to see how he received this communication. Warner looked slightly puzzled, but merely nodded his head.

The squire's son continued—

"It's a haul worth taking, to say nothing of the services of plate, and testimonials he has had presented to him. Why, the one he got from the African Society—the old scoundrel—is worth a cool five hundred."

"I hear."

"Well—suppose that was lifted with the tin; two fellows up to a little could easily do the job. What do you say, are you game?"

"What! *rob* the parson?"

"Speak lower, for Heaven's sake—yes."

"Wha—how!"

"Get in at night when they're all asleep. I know the way about the house; I haven't been there for nothing. Once get hold of the booty, we shall have cash enough to cut a shine again."

"But this is burglary."

"Oh, the devil; never mind *what* it is if it puts the money in our pockets. Come, what do you say?"

"Why, I don't half like the idea."

"Stuff, you've done other things—don't stick at this"

"Bah! I don't mind a little in the quiet line, and I never care how much I run in debt for, but this is something out of the way."

"Look at the chance! and the job's so easy too: come, you may as well join; you'll want some shiners; there's that little bit of stuff, blue-eyed Mary, the girl that that mealy-mouthed fellow opposite is so fond of; you'll have to treat her to-morrow, if you haven't given over your plans."

"Given over? I rather think not; what, leave the fair-lipped Mary to that clown?"

"I thought not. You'll be in for this?"

"But—but—I hardly see how it's to be done."

"I'll tell you. You see that boy by the side of Mary's lover?"

"Yes."

"That's his nephew."

"Well?"

"His sister's child; they say the parson is the father any way; she was seduced by somebody while she was in his service, and he, like a true Christian, turned her out, to starve, or steal; when he pretended to find it out, there was some fuss made about it, as she accused him of being its parent; of course her tale was not believed—the parson's oath settled the case; and while she was almost hissed out of the court, he was presented with congratulations, testimonials, and all that sort of thing."

"Of course!"

"Of course! and so, of course, when she came to his door-step, and asked him to support her child, and he had her driven to jail as a vagrant, why, she took poison as soon as she came out, and left her child at his door—that was that boy; the parson had him put in the poor-house, but the girl's brother, Dick Parker, over there, took him out, although he was himself only a boy, and worked hard to keep them both."

"But what the deuce has this to do with—with ——"

"Our night's work—a good deal; ever since, he has borne the parson a grudge, and more than once he has been locked up for suspected poaching on his grounds; now I've a little plan all ready cut and dried, by which this fellow shall be useful to us, without knowing it, and when the job's done, it shall seem his handiwork."

Warner made no reply; scamp as he was, he did not like the proposition so coolly submitted to him, by his more villanous associate.

"Can't something else be done," he asked; "it don't seem right to put it on that fellow."

Ralph laughed at him.

"What! are you turned Methodist? Faugh: a year or two abroad will do him no harm, even if he's convicted; he'll be better looked after and have less work than now; but that's not our look-out. I have made sure of the job, and if you won't help me, why, damme, I'll take some one else."

"Are you certain we shall not be taken?"

"Trust me. I could walk all over that house blindfold."

"But, suppose old Parson Wordly should see us, and raise an alarm?"

"We must silence him!"

Warner shrunk back.

"Silence him?"

"Yes."

"How?"

"Why, knock him over. I have a neat little pistol, the sight of which will, I fancy, be quite enough for him; he's a knowing card, and though he is so fond of Heaven, doesn't want to go there just yet. Now he won't make any noise, and if he does——"

"And if he does?"

"Well, I don't see any particular harm in putting him out of the way."

"Doing what?"

"Giving him a settler."

Warner turned pale.

"Look here, Ralph, I don't tumble to this at all. There's no knowing what it may lead to."

"Never mind what it leads to; so long as we are safe——"

"But——"

"Oh curse your 'buts,' will you stand game or not? if you've a mind to fill your pockets; be in this job. All that plate——"

"I was just thinking that may betray us."

"It might—but it wo'nt. I have a little crib-hole made by gipsies under a hill. I have often had a jolly carouse there by myself; I will get the things there; I'll have a fire—silver melts; we'll bury the spoil; in a week or two we can be off."

"I'll join—we can't be hanged for it."

"No, nor suspected—ha!"

"What's the matter?"

"Be careful—I had forgot."

"What?"

"The landlord's private room is behind this."

"Good God!"

Warner broke out in a perspiration.

"If he has heard us."

"If he has——"

The face of Ralph shewed his meaning.

"It's all right" he whispered, suddenly; "see, here he comes."

CHAPTER III.

HOW RALPH WORKED HIS VICTIM.

The door opened, and Mike Marlow, the landlord entered. He was a man of middle age and middle height, but with a coarse squatty face, short neck, and rough straggling hair.

His eyes had a sinister leer, and there was a perpetual, repulsive-looking smirk upon his countenance.

He carried in his hand a huge jug of ale, which he set before the pair whose conversation has just been recorded.

They looked at each other.

"Was that ordered?" asked Ralph.

"Well, no" returned the landlord, "but I thought as how your measure would be about run out, and so it is" he added, removing the empty measure.

"But the last is'nt paid for."

"Oh, I don't mind that; I know gentlemen like you is my best customers, and so to hell with him as would stint such because they beant flush of cash say I." "Besides," he continued, "I know as how if you ain't got it now, zounds, you'll soon be able loike to pay the same."

Still Ralph and Warner looked at each other.

"Bless'd if you are not a first-rate fellow," said the squire's son, while Warner kept his glance fixed on the table.

"Ees: and so now, gentlefolk, drink: there—a dash more of the white in it, and I hope you'll sing out when you want some more."

"Oh, thank you, this will be quite sufficient."

The landlord grinned and turned away.

"Drink us a pleasant health, will you landlord," cried one of the villagers, handing him a mug of ale.

"Wi' all my heart. Here's a merry day for you to-morrow on the green, and here's a health to pretty Mary Westland—she's to be belle to-morrow, and God bless my ould heart a stunner she be."

The face of the young man pointed out by Ralph flushed, and Warner looked up with a smile.

The landlord poured the contents of the mug down his throat, and, bowing awkwardly, left the room.

"It's all up," said Warner.

"What is?"

"Why, the game."

"What for?"

"He's heard us."

"The landlord?"

"Yes."

"I don't think he did. No: I watched him close enough, and I didn't see him change; besides, he was in the front all the time."

"What made him bring in that?"

"Oh, it's his way; he knows I always pay him, some time or another."

"Well, let us drink up and go: I don't care how soon I am away from here."

"It is all right: don't be frightened. Here, toss off; now, if you're ready."

Warner, who really needed something to revive him, drained the mug, and the pair rose to go.

Outside they paused.

"We must separate to meet again when the job's on; you know where to be: one o'clock, that's the darkest time, and best. Bring the flasher with you."

"And you?"

"I am going to wait for this fellow: I'll settle it with him, and then get my tools ready."

"For God's sake let us be careful."

Ralph smiled, and the pair shook hands and parted.

The squire's son loitered near the inn till Richard Parker came out, accompanied by Charles, his sister's son.

As soon as he saw them Ralph turned down a lane, and waited till they overtook him.

Richard's glance, as he came near, was none of the most amiable. The attentions of his friend, the London swell, to his sweetheart, pretty-faced Mary, had been far from relishable.

He loved her with the honest love of a true Englishman, and disliked both the Londoner and his manner.

The boy who, in all things, shared Richard's feelings, looked even more sullenly on the squire's son.

Both believed him to be, in a great measure, the most culpable of all; for he had introduced his friend to Mary, and fomented an acquaintance between them, which had already led to deep misery.

When, therefore, Ralph, with a smiling face and friendly manner, approached and held out his hand to Richard, the honest fellow, and the boy, drew back, and endeavoured to avoid him.

But Ralph was not easily disconcerted.

"Why, Richard," he said, "how is this? Come, bear no malice."

"I bear no malice; but I don't wish for your company—neither me nor mine."

"Oh, come, don't let anything that's gone by interfere between us. I have a word or two to say to you."

"I want no words——" began Richard; but the other stepped towards him and whispered—

"It is of your sister and her seducer."

The face of our hero flushed, then became pale.

"What of *her*—of *him*?" he asked.

"Come a little way with me, and I will tell you enough that will enable you to clear her name, and have vengeance on her murderer."

"Ay, such is the word! My poor sister! she was murdered!—murdered! If you can tell me anything that is *true*, I will go to the end of the earth to hear it."

"You need not go so far, Richard. Come with me a little way, and I will tell you what will surprise you."

Here the boy interposed.

"Oh, Dick, don't go, he does'nt speak truth. Look at his eyes how spiteful they are; he is bad; don't go."

"It is of your mother, my sister——"

"Then I will go too."

"No."

It was Ralph who spoke.

"May he not go?"

"No; what I have to disclose will convince you what you have to do. Send the boy home. If you are what I take you to be, you will take instant means for clearing your sister's honour."

"Shew me the way."

"Send the boy home, he is not discreet. I will not keep you, boy. It will be for you to judge how soon you will return."

The boy threw himself in his brother's arms.

"Oh, Richard, don't go; or if you will, take me with you."

"Go home," said Richard; "I will be there soon."

"Richard——"

"Go home."

He almost pushed the boy out of the way, and turned away with Ralph Merton.

With tears in his eyes Charles watched his young protector disappear with the squire's son. Boy as he was, he had sufficient judgment to see that Ralph Merton was a bad man; and he feared for Richard.

So, when they had turned out of sight, he forced his way through a hedge, and, keeping them in sight, followed at a distance.

Not far did Richard walk in silence.

He was eager to hear what Ralph had to relate concerning his sister, and he abruptly questioned him.

"Let us sit down on this trunk of a tree," said Ralph; "we can talk more easily."

In the darkness they sat down.

"Your sister was a pretty girl when first Parson Wordly took her?"

"She was," muttered Richard.

"And a virtuous one?"

"Till she fell."

"Which she never did."

"How?"

"A wife could do no sin."

"A wife?"

"That's what your sister was."

"Wife to whom? to *him*?"

"To Parson Wordly. Sit down Dick; don't get agitated, and I'll tell you more—how you can prove it."

"Tell me that, and I will deal with him."

"You shall: you see your sister Jane was a rather meek girl, and after he'd married her, and, as you thought, seduced her, he told her it was all a sham. Well, she threatened to disclose all if he did not make it right, but you know what happened."

"Ay! she died!"

"And her boy was made a bastard pauper; in place of which, Dick, he's the parson's heir, spite of all the fuss of his *new* wife and child. Now, Dick, there's only one thing you want to enable you to prove all this, and that is—the certificate."

"If I could get that!"

"You can."

"Master Merton, show me how, and I will do anything you may desire."

"Well, you're not afraid?"

"Afeard, of what?"

"Well, of a little bit of a scrimmage, walking in the dark in somebody else's house."

"I should fear nought if I could get that which would right my sister."

"That's right. You know the parson's study?"

"I do."

"The window opens on the lawn."

"Yes."

"And is easily reached. In that room, Dick, in a little bureau that stands in the corner, the parson keeps your sister's certificate. If you're not a coward you can get in there."

"Break in?"

"Yes—how else? They won't let you in. Break in, of course. When you're in open that bureau top drawer; pull out a little drawer at the back; you'll find some papers—the certificate is amongst them."

"But, if they should find me out while I'm getting in?"

"Say what you've come for. Bah! man, never be a coward. Let that boy have his rights; and your sister—think of her; she's dead, and can't help herself."

"Ay, so she be."

"But you can help her boy—redeem her name, which now the village perts scoff at."

"Ay, so I will."

"That's right. Give me your hand. I thought you were true. I'll do all I can to help you, by Jove!"

"Master Merton, what makes you so willing loike to see parson down?"

"Didn't he spoil my marrying Miss Watts, with her five thousand pounds? Dick, I hate him, and will do all I can to make him sweat. You're not shirking?"

"Noa. I'll get the paper; then see what he'll say."

"You're a real brick!"

"When shall I try?"

"To-night."

"To-night?"

"Yes; about one or two o'clock rather. They'll be all asleep; you can slip in in the dark, feel your way to the bureau, take a chisel, wrench the top open; when you've got the papers hook it quickly."

"I'll do it. But there be the great dog—if he should hear I."

"Dick, I'll manage to see to him presently."

"Thank'ee, Master Ralph. Look'ee, if so be that I get the lines, and it be as you say, I'll not forget your kindness when Charley be parson's heir."

"Never mind that, my good fellow; let's be off now. Hark! what was that?"

A sound like the breaking of a branch beneath the tread.

"It be some one listening," cried Richard, starting up.

They both looked in every direction, but as no one was to be seen in the darkness, and as no further sound was heard they concluded there had been no one there.

After a few more instructions from Ralph, Richard took his departure.

Ralph drew a long clasp-knife from his pocket, and, opening the blade, crawled about on all fours to see if he could come across any hiding eavesdropper.

Fortunately—for there was murder in his heart—if any one was there he failed to discover them, and he slowly left the spot.

No sooner was he out of hearing than the boy, Charles, slid down from the branch of a tree where he had been crouching.

"Poor Richard," he muttered. "That man means something wrong. I'll try, if I can, to keep Dick out of harm's way."

He bounded across the lane, and striking across the fields ran towards his home, arriving there breathless and hot about two minutes before his guardian.

Ralph had, in the meanwhile, continued his way slowly homeward, musing as he went.

"The job's made straight now: if any one gets in for the scrape it will be Dick. Ha! a nice talk that about the marriage. Well, it will keep suspicion from us, and when that job's done I'll see if I can't steal a march on my friend Hal with pretty-faced Mary."

The squire was up waiting for his son; he praised him warmly for his virtuous abnegation in reaching home so early, and expressed a hope that he would soon break himself of the bad habits he had contracted in London.

"You know what it will be Ralph," said the venerable, kind-hearted man; "when I see you as a lad should be, I'll be no niggard with my gold; you have but to go the straight course, and all will be well. I can't live for ever, you know."

"You've lived too long already," thought Ralph, but he replied by a sanctified speech that would have done credit to a canting Spurgeonite.

The fact was his father had lately dropped hints about disinheriting him, and thus he had found himself necessitated to play the hypocrite, for a time at least.

Master Ralph had a little part to play this night, and he played it to perfection.

His first move was to discourse with his father on the follies he had been guilty of, and the regeneration which he hoped was about to take place.

Then he became suddenly unwell, and in a faint tone asked for a drop of cold water.

The good squire, touched by his son's illness and humility, and overjoyed at his asking for so modest a drink, ordered the servant to bring in a large tumbler of wine, which, with his own hands, he administered to his son.

After this, as Ralph pretended, he felt a little better and thought sleep would benefit him, he helped him to his room, and saw him safely in bed.

Having exhorted him to pray, and wished him a fervent "good-night," the noble old man retired to his own chamber, and falling on his knees, with tears in his eyes, thanked the Almighty for bringing about such a reformation in his son.

But while he was praying, what was Ralph doing? He had jumped out of bed as soon as his father was gone, and commenced arranging in a small bundle a dark lantern, a line, and several implements of housebreaking, all of which he took from inside the mattress.

His next act was to load a double-barrelled pistol. These arrangements were barely concluded when he heard a careful step approaching his room.

He put the things under his pillow, and jumped in bed.

The door opened, and his father entered.

Ralph pretended to be fast asleep.

"God bless him," murmured the old man; "I have been harsh to him, but now that his heart is touched he shall find me the kindest of fathers."

He caressed with his hand the forehead of his son, and assuring himself that he would be better in the morning, again softly departed, and went to bed.

It might have been thought that Ralph would have been moved by his father's earnestness, and induced to redeem his past errors, and avoid evil for the future.

But wickedness was too deeply engrained upon his system, and not for one moment did he think of turning from his intended crime.

Half an hour passed.

The house seemed silent: no one moving: all asleep.

Ralph leapt from the bed.

Hastily he dressed himself, and walked to the window; a beech tree grew beneath, extending its branches to the panes, and thence to an outbuilding that reached the skirting wall.

Ralph had often descended that way, and he intended to do so now.

First he opened the door and listened.

All was dark and still, and he returned, treading on tiptoe lest he should be heard.

THE MURDER.

The crafty plan he had hit upon was to leave the room by these means: get over the wall: effect the burglary, and after having stowed away the plunder, return by the same means to the house; so that his absence would never be guessed.

His object in inveigling Richard into the trap was as cunning.

He himself could enter by means of a key, and, unsuspected, depart the same way; but Richard would leave enough tracks to identify him, even if he were not caught in the act.

This last result seemed most likely, for Ralph did not doubt that the unsuspicious youth would prove but a bungling burglar, and make noise enough to betray himself.

More than once he smiled as he thought how skillfully he had concocted his plan.

He never thought of the misery his villany would entail on the harmless Richard Parker.

Once when he was about to depart, he thought he heard a step near the window.

He waited and listened, but as nothing came of it he prepared for the venture.

Taking his parcel from under the pillow, he crammed it in his coat-pocket, and with his pistol in his vest, he opened the window and looked out.

It seemed safe enough, and he ventured to the tree; it gave with his weight, and almost precipitated him to the ground.

But he clung like a monkey, and scrambled from branch to branch till he got to the out-building. As he dropped to the roof he caught sight of the shadowy form of a man leaning against a shed.

With palpitating heart he lay flat on the roof.

After assuming this position for a few weary, anxious minutes, he crawled along the top, to the end, and again cautiously peered about him.

Here a second surprise awaited him.

The man was gone!

Rendered extremely uneasy, Ralph, in great trepidation, looked along the ground, but without again catching sight of the object of his fears.

The minutes fled, and the delay was becoming dangerous. He made up his mind to face the worst, and drawing his clasp-knife, hastily flung his line to the wall, and making a slip coil that could easily be drawn round an iron rod on the roof, took the other end in his hand, and crossed to the wall.

As he did so, the shadow of the mysterious man again flitted before him.

Grinding his teeth, Ralph jerked his rope violently back, and leaping from the wall, made a rush to the lane adjoining his father's property.

Thence he hurried to the fields, and crossing them, arrived at the appointed place where Hal was to be waiting for him.

The shadow still haunted him. He could not conjecture who it could have been, and his perplexity became increased as the fear of his absence being discovered grew upon him.

He entered the copse without seeing Hal; looking round for him, he was again startled by seeing a cloaked figure leaning against a tree.

He got his pistol out, and slid behind the trunk.

It was a case of murder now if it were anyone waiting to follow Hal Warner and himself.

He put his pistol on full cock, and placed it behind the ear of the cloaked man.

As his finger was on the trigger, the individual turned, and he recognised his friend Warner.

"Hal!" he cried.

"I—what—that pistol?" said Warner, evidently frightened.

"I thought you were somebody else," exclaimed Ralph, coolly putting back his pistol; "What the deuce have you got that cloak on for?"

"It's a paletot. I put it on to drop on the way, in case we were seen."

"Humph," growled Ralph. "Are you ready?"

"Quite."

"Come on, then; it's time."

One o'clock chimed from the village church.

Ralph grasped Warner's arm, and the pair hurried towards the residence of the clergyman.

CHAPTER IV.

MIDNIGHT MURDER.

THE room in which Richard slept with his young nephew was a small one, and, like the rest of the house, not very luxuriously furnished.

He had had a hard struggle to get on, and what money he had saved was carefully put by till the occasion of his marriage with Mary.

He lay down with Charles that night, though intending not to sleep. No words had passed between them, for Richard was absorbed in his own thoughts, and the boy was intent upon fustrating the design, whatever it may have been, of Ralph Merton.

Thus mutually striving to deceive each other, the pair lay side by side—each pretending to be asleep, but each fully awake.

Busy and troubled were Richard's thoughts. His sister's dishonour had preyed on his mind, and his excitement knew no bounds now that the artful tale of the squire's son promised him the means of clearing her fame and establishing the rights of her disgraced child.

Thoughts of Mary, too, obtruded themselves into his mind. He could not cease to love her, though his heart was grieved by her coquettish conduct; but, his affection returning, he began to think that he had been hasty and unkind, and he repented of the words he had spoken.

But he resolved on the morrow to speak more explicitly, and to make her a plain proposal, which, if accepted, would, he felt, make them both happy.

The morrow! it was to be a day of pleasure, mirth, and festivity—yet there stole over him an ominous presentiment of some terrible calamity.

One o'clock chimed as he lay thinking. He listened to his nephew's breathing—it was regular and light. He slid softly from the bed, and hastily put on his clothes.

From his drawer he took a sharp chisel: it had his initials carved rudely upon it, and, as he held it in his hand, a chill crept over him, and something seemed to impel him to return it to its place, and abandon his enterprise.

But he thought of his sister, and the opportunity of bringing down in his pride the haughty, sinful parson, and, with strengthened resolution, put the chisel in his pocket and opened the door.

A moment he paused to look at the boy.

To all appearances the boy was quietly sleeping. He passed out and shut the door.

In an instant Charles, who had been watching and listening, leaped to the floor, and began hurriedly to dress himself; but Richard heard the bound on the old boards, and, returning suddenly, confronted his nephew.

They looked at each other in silence—Richard was confused but resolute, the boy equally determined.

Then Richard spoke.

"Where are you going, Charles."

The boy would have hesitated at speaking an untruth. He answered boldly—

"To follow you."

Richard was a little subdued at the boy's earnestness, and at one moment thought of taking him with him.

But the remembrance of the hazard he ran stayed him: whatever danger he himself ran, he would not expose his sister's child to any.

"Charles," he said, "where I am going you cannot come. Remain up for me if you like—I shall not be long."

"I would rather go with you. Dear Richard, I know you are engaged in something that Ralph Merton is concerned in. He is no good to anyone, and I am sure he is not your friend."

"You must not come—there may be risk."

"Then I will share it with you."

"No. Bide thee here: I will be back soon."

But the boy rushed forward and clung to him.

"Don't go," he cried, "unless you take me too.

If squire's son has set you to anything, depend on't he means you some harm. He would play you a trick and laugh at you afterwards."

"I tell thee, Charles, I must go. Stay back; and when I come again I shall, mayhap, have somewhat to show thee."

He endeavoured to pass out, but the faithful boy would not suffer him.

"I know where you be going, and what for," he exclaimed, vehemently; "I hearn the tale Bad Ralph told; it's some villany of his that he wants to lead you into. Oh, Dick, stay with me, you will be safe here."

"No, I will run the risk to get that thee heard him speak of."

"He told you lies; how could he know it was there? Oh, he be a devil indeed; don't thee go; put it off till to-morrow; see what he says in t'morning."

"Charles, for your mother's sake, I must and will do't."

"For her sake, I won't let you go. Unless you hurt me, you shall not go."

He hung desperately round Richard's neck. The young countryman wrestled. Boy as he was he possessed a good share of strength; he held Richard fast, and when he found his efforts were like to prove unavailing, wound his arms round his uncle's neck, and shed tears.

Not even that stayed Richard; he wrenched his arms apart and thrust him back; then pulling the key out of the door, he shut it, and locked the boy in.

He heard him kicking at the panels, and calling on him to return; but he closed his ears, and hastened from the house.

But in the open air he still seemed to hear the imploring voice of Charles, but he hurried on: over the fields and stiles he passed, and arrived breathless at his destination—the house of Parson Wordly.

It stood on the crest of a slope, surrounded by a thick shrubbery and copse. To the side where the new-mown lawn spread out Richard crept, and made his way to the parson's study.

The night was a dark one, and thus, in some measure, favourable to the enterprise. it was not, however, such an one as the professional burglar would desire—a night when the wind shakes every shutter, and the heavy rain drowns every sound.

It was not without a tremor that Richard prepared for his task. He knew what risk he ran; it was, at the least, burglary, and for that crime the country justices would send him to the sessions, his case, well weighted down with evidence, seemed in every way damnatory.

The parson, too, was no friend of his, and would rejoice in the opportunity of sending him over the water!

He had escaped one peril.

The watch dog—a huge hound which the fat parson kept loose at night to tear the flesh of any who ventured into his grounds—was silenced.

Ralph had kept his word—he wondered how; he was not aware of the cunning practices of tha gentleman.

With some little nervousness Richard took from his pocket his chisel and commenced operations.

There were no bolts or bars here to encounter, or Richard would have failed. The parson trusted to his dog and his servants. The room, too, contained little of value, and he knew that even if an entry were effected, there was no passing from that to another apartment.

The door was stout, and had heavy locks.

Dick went to work in a very unprofessional manner. His first act was to cover his hand with his cap and dash in a pane of glass.

The crash was less than he expected; but still the noise startled him, and he crouched down for a few moments.

He heard no sound following; fortunately for him the household was fast in slumber. The servants slept from over work, and the parson snored off the effects of a gluttonous dinner.

Our hero being now assured, put his hand in through the broken pane and thrust back the hasp.

Then he slid the window gently up, and bounded in. It was pitch dark inside, and Dick, who felt no fear, grew timidly nervous; there might be some one else in the room for all he could know to the contrary.

In which case it would not be very jolly to be seized by the collar, or have a pistol put to his ear, just as he had got the paper.

"I'm in for it," he thought, "and if the devil is here I will not turn back."

So he groped his way to the wall, and along the wall to the corner, stumbling over two chairs, and almost knocking his wind out against a heavy table.

At last he reached the bureau. Feeling for the drawer named by Ralph, he took out his screwdriver, and inserted the blade in the crevice.

It was not a very expeditious tool, nor in very experienced hands; but it answered his purpose.

A wrench, and the lock snapped, the drawer coming out bodily.

He now searched for the secret drawer, and after a good deal of splitting up of wood, got his implement in a slit.

He gave a vigorous wrench, and the secret drawer came out broken.

So far Ralph had been correct; now for the proof of the rest. He inserted his hand, and found a lot of papers in bundles and packets.

Grasping all, that he might be sure of the precious document, he drew his hand forth; but at that instant there rang through the house so frightful and piercing a cry of woman's agony, that he shook all over, and dropping the papers to the floor, stood appalled and chilled.

A second cry, more wild than the first, sent the blood back to his heart, and made the flesh creep on his very bones.

There was foul work going forward. He rushed to the door, as a third scream, fainter, but still fearful in its terrors, vibrated from room to room.

He will see what was the cause of those cries of agony.

Ralph and his friend Warner had reached the house long before Richard. Provided with a key, they gained easy access, and were soon at work, commencing their depredations in the lower offices, where they packed up the most valuable of the plate.

They next proceeded to the ante-room, where testimonials of silver and gold ornamentature were placed; these Ralph, without much ceremony, broke up, so as to take away only what was most precious, Warner assisting, though with many fears and apprehensions.

After gathering a goodly amount of booty, Warner, who was getting more nervous every instant, proposed that they should hasten away.

"We've got enough," he said; "let's go while we are safe."

"Pshaw! Let's have enough: it's only one venture; besides, what we've got is no good just yet: we must stow it away. We want some coin."

"Where is there any kept?"

"In the parson's room; he wouldn't sleep comfortable if he had it anywhere else: plenty there—gold and notes too."

"But is it worth the risk? If he wakes he will be sure to recognise us."

"Not he; he's a rank coward, too; so if he sees us he will pretend not to be awake."

"And then inform against us to-morrow."

"What a precious soft-heart you are; haven't I told you I'll manage the job. How can he know us in our masks. Put yours right and let's trot."

Warner adjusted his mask. Ralph took up the lamp, and having carried the plate where they could easily make off with it, they ascended to the parson's chamber.

Parson Wordly was one of those men who made his religion a cloak for every sin: sensual and gluttonous, he had grown fat on his living, and had—it was rumoured—more sins on his head than even his cloth would cover.

Amongst other little practices, he was in the habit of introducing the confessional amongst the bodies of his flock, and many a lady, married and single, had his artful insinuations brought from her high estate of virtue to be the victim of his sleek, seductive infamy.

Many a simple village girl, too, had his accursed wickedness ruined and disgraced.

The gentry of the neighbouring localities were well acquainted with his sensual practices; but as he was one of their set, and kept a good house, with liberal wine, they were not disposed to pay heed to any statement brought against him.

Lately he had married a young lady, the daughter of an officer's widow; though the bridal months had not long been over, his piggishness of disposition had already shown itself in the shape of coarse insults and ill-treatment.

The young wife, too proud to speak of her bad usuage, was yet not meek enough to bide by it. At the present time she slept in a chamber apart from her husband, her maid, a young girl, sleeping with her.

And so the parson was left to sleep alone, saving such times as he could inveigle secretly to his room some pleasing concubine.

There are many such ministers of the gospel—sleek, bland-looking, smiling-faced, gluttonous wine-bibbers, whose only aim is the indulgment of their sensual propensities.

Parson Wordly was awake when the two amateur burglars entered; he had been revolving in his mind a measure for the entanglement of a fresh victim when he heard the door tried.

As Ralph had said, he was a rank coward. His fears instantly conjured midnight murderers and thieves, and he lay quiet, though with palpitating heart and trembling limbs.

The door opened, and his visitors entered.

One peep he took at them 'ere he closed his eyes; the sight of two men with masks, dark lanterns, pistols and knives, was quite enough for his nerves but, apprehensive of what might result if he made his consciousness known, he lay as if alseep.

In that hour of fear he thought of his many sins and prayed inwardly more fervently than he had outwardly done for years.

Neither of the robbers spoke. Ralph, who seemed to know his way to every corner of the house, went straight up to the chest of drawers.

Parson Wordly heard the drawer open, and the chink of gold followed.

It was hard to lose his money, but it was worse to lose his life; so he continued to lie still.

Presently he heard the crumpling of notes.

"I shall have you now," he thought, "all the numbers are taken."

The noise of their movements ceased, and he began to perspire at every pore.

Were they creeping murder him?

It was a horrible thought; and he had much difficulty in keeping himself still.

Some time passed—still no sound: it began to grow oppressive, such an anxious silence; but after the lapse of some minutes he began to think they were gone.

Under this impression he ventured to unclose his eyes.

The round orifice through which the bullet of a pistol is dropped was right before his left peeper.

He shivered inwardly, and closed his peepers instanter.

He was in horrible fear lest he had been seen.

Luckily for him he had not. Ralph, who held the pistol, had at that particular time turned to motion Warner out of the room, and so the movement of the parson escaped him.

He lingered a little while to convince himself that all was right, and then softly went away.

Relieved from his deadly fear, the parson's teeth began to chatter: he would have given much to have been able to give the alarm, and so had them stopped; but his cowardice was too great to permit him to rise from his bed.

A long passage led from his room: near the end was the chamber where Mrs. Wordly slept, with her maid; it opened from an anteroom of larger dimensions.

As they were passing the door a sudden thought seemed to strike Ralph.

"*She* sleeps in there," he said.

Warner merely glanced at the door, and passed on. But Ralph stopped.

"I've a good mind," he muttered. "She was proud enough when I made her an offer: I might teach her different now."

"Come along," interposed Warner, who was apprehensive of deeper crimes should Ralph enter there.

"Not till I've been in and scared her," returned Ralph.

"Hark! Do you hear that crash?"

"It's that lubber breaking in. What a noise he makes. Come in and look at her."

Warner would rather have gone on, but he felt compelled to obey the dictates of his less scrupulous associate.

"We shall get into trouble," he muttered.

"Come on; we shall not stay long."

Ralph opened the door, and entering, placed his booty on the floor. Warner followed him into the inner chamber.

A wax light was burning, and side by side, but in different beds, lay the lady and her maid. Ralph approached the former, and bending over her, seized the coverlet in his hand, and tore it from her.

"She looks pretty, don't she?" he muttered.

Ere Warner could reply, the lady, awakened from her sleep, suddenly started up, and seeing two masked men in her chamber, uttered a faint scream.

Ralph's hand instantly closed over her mouth.

"Make a noise," he muttered, "and I choke you."

Her struggles ceased almost as he spoke: she had fainted; but that scream had aroused her maid, and as they turned to hasten from the room, she sat up in bed, her voice for a moment frozen at the unexpected spectacle.

"Come away," cried Warner, seeing the murderous look in Ralph's eye; "let's be clear before she scares the house."

He dragged him from the sleeping apartment, but in the ante-chamber, Ralph's mask, loosened in his struggle with Mrs. Wordley, fell off; he turned round to pick it up, and in doing so revealed his face to the maid, Anna, who had left her bed for the purpose of giving the alarm.

She recognised him instantly, and with a loud shriek, uttered his name.

He had hastily re-placed the mask, and was hurrying from the room, when the sound of his name brought him back.

Leaping behind the astonished girl, he shut the inner door. Shut up with that lawless man, momentary fear took possession of Anna; but before she could collect her energies for action, Ralph had seized her in his brutal grasp.

"So," he hissed "you know me."

"Oh, Master Ralph, Master Ralph!" was all the girl could say.

"Master Ralph! That name is your doom."

"Help! What would you do?"

"I will shew you," he cried, drawing his clasp knife. She shuddered, and as he opened the blade, gave a second wild scream. Ralph who was impeded by her struggles, finished opening the knife with his teeth.

Then Warner interposed.

"Not that, Ralph; let her go, for God's sake let us have no murder."

"There's no other way—she's recognised me."

"Make her swear not to reveal——"

"Fool! do you think we should be safe? No, this is the only way."

It was a terrible moment. Aware of her impending fate, the girl, who was no coward, wrestled with her assailant, and cried loudly for help.

But no help came.

Her supple form in its dim outline became uncovered as she struggled for dear life; her limbs were twined round Ralph's—her bosom was against his breast.

But he had the fatal knife against her throat, and was about to draw it across, when Warner dragged his arm away.

"Not that," he again gasped; "come away—come away."

But Ralph struck him aside.

It was all over then with the unfortunate girl, and she knew it.

A third wild scream she uttered—the shrieks that Richard had heard. There came no more, only faint gasps. The miscreant had thrown her down, and plunged his weapon into her quivering flesh.

She lay against the door. Ralph closed his knife, and picked up his spoil; then he dragged Warner, who was nearly fainting, from the room.

"This way," he cried, as Warner was making for the door.

Warner followed, scarcely in possession of his senses, the deed he had witnessed had so much appalled him.

Ralph stopped at the door of the study, and opened it, as Richard was beating against its panels.

"Fly for life!" he cried; "you have been heard—away!"

He contrived to knock Richard's cap off, and insert some of the parson's bank-notes in the lining; then he dropped the knife in his pocket.

"The papers!" exclaimed Richard, scared by the late cries and the wildness of Ralph's manner.

"Never mind them now; if you hesitate you are lost."

"But you—those screams——"

"Away, fool! unless you want to be transported. Hark! the alarm-bell—away!"

He helped to thrust him from the window.

Though the alarm-bell was pealing, he stayed to laugh wildly.

He had sent Richard off, but sufficient tracks to hang him were behind him.

His chisel lay in the room, his initials on it—the track of his boots would be seen; he had in his pocket the bloody weapon with which the deed had been committed, some criminating notes in his cap, and on his jacket and cap were marks of blood.

"Enough to hang him, and clear us," he muttered, as he led Warner away.

Unimpeded, they reached the corner where the plate had been stowed. Unopposed, they crept from the house; it was almost away from any other dwelling, and so, while the alarm-bell was ringing, and the frightened servants were hurrying from their rooms, the murdered girl lay at the door, at the other side of which stood her mistress, wildly screaming for the help that did not come.

CHAPTER V.

THE EVIDENCE OF THE BLOODY KNIFE.

THE terrifying tumult quickened Richard's pace. At every step he took a dread of impending danger increased on his mind. His thoughts began to grow more collected as he left the house behind, and he now weighed things that till then he had been too confused to regard.

The presence of Ralph, coupled with the shrieks he had heard, and his excited manner, suggested some deeper deed than any he had intended; debating as he ran how best to proceed, he suddenly came upon his nephew Charles.

The brave boy had broken away through the window, and was now hastening to seek Richard. His joy at meeting him was excessive; the hasty treatment he had received was forgotten now that he saw him safe.

"I am so glad to see you, Dick," he said. "I began to fear evil would come to you."

"And I am glad to see thee, Charles, lad, for there be that that I don't like the looks of come about sin' I left you."

The boy looked up in alarm.

"What has happened?"

"Nought that I know of, but——"

"But what?"

"Ralph wor there."

"Ralph!"

"Ay, lad. What makes thee so scared?"

"Dear Richard, let us haste home. If he was there you are not safe."

"Oh, I'm safe now; but there's more than that."

"What more?"

"Thee knows what I went there for. I had just got my hand out' paper, when such screams, Charles, as made my hair stand on end came through the house; then Ralph came in where I was and thrust me out."

"Some deep plan is working against you. That bad man—what was he here for?"

"I don't know, lad; I didn't think on't, or I would not have run away like a coward."

"Better than to have stayed."

"I don't think so, lad; and blessed if I don't go back now."

The boy held him by the sleeve.

"Dont go, Dick—come home; you'll be safe there may be."

Strong in his energy, he dragged him away.

Suddenly Dick paused.

"What is it?" said the boy, feeling him start.

"D—n it, I've done a foolish thing; I've left my chisel there, and it's marked with my name."

Without a word, the boy started away from Dick, and soon bounded out of sight. In a few minutes he returned, panting and white.

"I have been there," he said, sorrowfully.

"Thee has not got it?"

"No."

"Did thee see anyone?"

"The house is aroused: they were in the room, and had got the chisel."

Dick leaned against a tree, and broke out in a cold sweat.

"There's something wrong," he muttered, "something wrong."

But the boy said nothing; he hung his head, and with bated breath led his uncle home.

He breathed more freely when they had shut the door. Dick staggered upstairs as unsteady as a drunken man, and Charley got the light.

But no sooner had he glanced at Dick than he uttered a frightened cry, and setting the candle on the table, rushed towards him.

"What be the matter?" said Dick, turning ghastly pale.

"Oh, Dick! poor, dear Dick!"

"What be the matter, boy? Open thee eyes and look."

"I cannot: hide it away, hide it away!"

"Hide what?"

"The blood, the marks. Oh, Dick."

"The blood? the marks?"

"Yes, on your arm; stains fresh of murder."

Horrified, Dick looked at his sleeve. There, fresh and damning, was the purpling stream of recently shed blood.

He uttered a deep groan and fell back in a chair.

"It be his doing," was all he could say.

"Ay, it's his work; but what will it be to you?" cried the boy, shedding bitter tears. "Why did you go? I knew something bad would come of it."

"Thee wor right, lad. Hillo! what's this?"

He had thrust his hand in his pocket and found the knife.

"This be not my knife," he continued, as he drew it forth.

Both shrank then: the blood lay clotted on the blade, and was thick on the handle; it stained his hands as he held it, and he groaned aloud.

"How came it there?" he cried. "Speak, Charley —thee don't utter a word."

"He put it there," returned the boy, sadly.

Dick trembled in every limb.

"He? And what can he have done that for?"

"To fix the guilt of his crime on you."

"Crime? What crime do you think he have done?"

"Murder."

Trembling visibly, Dick let the terrible knife fall; it lay at his feet, looking grim and accusing, while he hid his face in his hands and groaned aloud.

Even the boy seemed dumbfounded and appalled at this new danger.

"Oh, lad!" cried Richard, "what can be done? What will they do?"

"You will be accused of murder, if murder has been done," returned the boy, almost fiercely.

With staring eyes, Dick gaspingly regarded him.

"Why, what am I to do?"

"You must escape. Yet where? If you run away it will look worse. They would find you, too, wherever you went."

"And so they would, lad."

"You must stay and meet the charge. Be hero; I will go and see if I can follow Ralph."

"No, don't go; I can't stay by myself. Don't leave me, lad. Hark! what be that?"

"Somebody comes. Oh, God!"

A voice came from beneath the window, then a loud summons at the door.

Dick bounded from the chair.

"Who be it?" he cried, wildly.

"The officers and the squire's servants."

"Ask them what they want."

Pale and shivering, the boy put his head out of the window.

"What are you here for?" he asked, striving to speak calmly.

"We want Richard, boy"

"What for?"

"He's been doing murder up at the parson's."

"Who is murdered?"

"Oh, he knows well enough—parson's girl it be; thee needn't parley there while Dick hides—we shall find him."

"He doesn't hide—he is here."

A shout rose in response that chilled the heart of Richard.

The boy went down the stairs.

When he opened the door, they rushed in pell-mell, and with great display of action, looked round for the murderer.

"Where is he?" said one.

"We'll drag him out," said another.

"He is upstairs; come up—there be something up there we want to show you."

His words surprised them, but they hurried up the stairs and broke into the room where Dick was.

He was standing in a dejected attitude awaiting their coming, the blood-clotted knife still lying at his feet; his looks were more in favour of his guilt than of his innocence, and the men, stopping short at sight of the knife, advised him to give himself up quietly.

"Yes, I'll go with you," returned Dick. "Take me before the magistrate; I'll tell all to him."

Rather roughly they seized him, and one of the constables, darting forward, picked up the knife.

"This be a bad business, Dick."

"Yes, it's all up with him now. Come along."

"Let's put these on, first," said a third, producing a pair of handcuffs.

Dick recoiled, and the boy stood forward.

"You needn't put them on, Mister Constable," said Dick; "I'll go with you quietly."

"You'll have to, but we must make sure."

"Yes, we mustn't take a murderer a before magistrate without irons."

"You are fools," cried Charles, standing by his uncle; "if you want to put irons on the murderer you must find him elsewhere."

"No doubt, my young sprig; but on the irons go."

Dick resisted: conscious of his innocence, he could not bear that indignity. By the exercise of his utmost strength he broke away, and, hurling to the floor the one who had the irons, stood at bay at the farther end of the room.

There was a general commotion instanter; none dared, singly, to attack the enraged youth, but they advanced in a body towards him.

They were surprised to see him stand so quiet.

"Come, come," said one, "it's no use kicking; the job's done, and you must be scragged for it."

"I will make no resistance if you don't handcuff me; but I'm innocent, and I won't have them on."

"You looks innocent. Bill, just hold that youngster; he looks as if he meant mischief."

The individual addressed as Bill, and who was a puffy-faced, red-nosed constable, advanced to the boy with the intention of taking him by the collar. He was quite surprised when a well-sent thrust in the waist from Charley's fist sent him on his back.

He was up again in a few moments, and himself and another constable, using their staves, collared the boy, and held him fast while Dick, after a brief resistance, was secured and manacled.

"Now," said the chief constable, in triumph, "drag him away, lads, to the lock-up."

"The lock-up!" exclaimed Dick. "Take me to the magistrate first."

"Oh, we can't disturb a gentleman at this hour. You'll see him soon enough."

"But I have something to tell him."

"Very likely; but it will keep, I dare say."

"I tell you if you take me to him he will order my release."

The constable winked, and placed his finger along the side of his nose.

"A likely tale," he returned. "Off with him, lads."

Dick saw that further appeal was in vain, and with deep dismay he gave himself up to his fate.

"I never thought to wear these," he groaned, raising his menacled hands: "but it is my own fault; it all comes of being led by that bad man."

At this juncture Charles, who was still held, made a step towards the window.

"He's there," he cried—"the real criminal. Go with the constable, Dick; I'll be after the villain."

He darted from the two men, and bounded from the house.

The constable looked out: a muffled form was seen for an instant amongst the trees; then the boy crossed the path in the same direction.

"It be Ralph," said Dick, as they dragged him away.

CHAPTER VI.

DICK ON HIS TRIAL.

The news of the murder of the parson's maid-servant travelled over the village with wonderful rapidity. The excitement was great, but it became more intense when it was known that Dick Parker was taken up for the deed.

Wise people then began to shake their heads, and say—they never expected much good of Dick, etc. It was astonishing how soon he got a bad name.

Anyone who had asked his character the day previous, and now heard all that was said against him, would have been surprised that such a villain could have lived so long undiscovered.

At the hour appointed for the hearing of the charge people flocked to the court-house, eager to see the desperate criminal, now the free subject of comment and notoriety.

The time had gone terribly hard with Dick: locked up by himself, he began to give way to desponding fears. He had not seen his nephew since his imprisonment, and awaited with feverish anxiety the coming investigation.

At eight o'clock the surly gaoler entered.

He brought his breakfast—a jug of water and a piece of hard bread, which he placed on the stone floor, with as much ceremony as he would have bestowed on a dog.

A murderer was rather a rare sight there, and he took a hard look at the criminal, retiring with a glance that said plainly enough that, in his opinion, the hardened wretch before him was just the sort of man to do murder, and that the sooner he was hanged out of the way the better.

Dick ventured to speak as the man reached the door.

"Will it be long before I see the magistrate?"

"Not very long, my bird. What, are you in a hurry to get the rope round your neck?"

Dick's eyes flashed fire, and he stepped towards the gaoler; that worthy fled outside, and barred the door with more speed than he had shown for years, and Dick was left alone.

His breakfast untasted, he sat moodily on the hard bench. The hours passed wearily. He wondered what people would think when he told his story, and whether he should be believed.

If he should not be! It was a horrible thought. There were many proofs against him, and only his word to criminate Ralph.

If his innocence should not be credited, he would be hanged as surely as he now sat there.

A faintness came over him, and he drank off a draught of the brackish water.

Ten o'clock came, and the door of his cell was unbolted.

The constables had come to take him before the Bench. They grasped him anything but tenderly, and regarded him with a look that showed they, at least, had no sympathy with murderers.

Dick bore all patiently; he was only glad when they got him into court.

Here, in the criminal's dock, he was placed exposed to the gaze of the eager audience and the frowning magistrates.

If he had entertained any strong hopes of acquittal, they would have left him when he looked round in the court.

Mr. Merton, the father of Ralph, was on the bench beside his brother magistrates, and the parson sat near, regarding Dick with a look that showed the prisoner he had made up his mind to do all he could towards getting him out of the world.

Dick looked round for his nephew. The boy directly after entered, and took his place as near to him as they would allow.

It must be owned that Dick's appearance was anything but prepossessing: haggard and pallid from agitation and want of rest, and the tell-tale marks of blood on his jacket-sleeve, gave him a worse aspect.

At the first look the magistrates decided him guilty.

The head magistrate, Mr. Hewart, commenced the investigation. He was a purse-proud, hard-natured man, whose sympathies were wholly given to his class.

The poor he regarded as so much scum, not to be thought of in regard to justice or right.

Having scrutinised the prisoner through his glasses, he coughed slightly, and spoke.

"What is the evidence to support the charge of murder against this man?"

"If you please," began Dick.

"We will hear you afterwards," returned Mr. Hewart.

"But I've somewhat to tell thee."

"Silence!" cried the magistrate, frowning him down.

"I'm not the guilty one——"

"Keep the man quiet," said Mr. Hewart. And Dick was instantly seized by the constables, who forced their knuckles into his throat, and seemed disposed to throttle him, if necessary.

Decidedly, a court of justice is no place for a poor man.

"Now, Mr. Constable, we will hear the charge."

Charley kept close to Dick, and the constable commenced his story.

He detailed how the alarm-bell had drawn him to the house, the finding of the murdered woman, and other circumstances with which the reader is acquainted.

"The door of the parson's study wor open," he said, "and I went in. It wor all in disorder—a bureau had been broken into, papers were strewn about, the window-panel was smashed, and sash left open. I found this on' floor, beside the bureau.

He produced the chisel belonging to Dick.

The court examined it, and Mr. Hewart read aloud the initials of Dick's name.

"With this the bureau was wrenched open?"

"It wor, sir."

Ralph's father spoke.

"Is there any evidence to connect the prisoner with the burglary? The chisel might have been used by another."

Mr. Hewart smiled sarcastically; but Dick hastened to speak.

"It be my tool, and I used it there; but I did not do the deed of murder."

Mr. Merton laid down the chisel, and, after a dead silence of a few moments, the constable proceeded.

That admission of Dick's had gone heavy against him.

The constable then detailed finding marks of footsteps on the carpet and on the ground—marks made by a hob-nailed boot, the nails being circular on the sole, and square on the heel.

"Let us see the prisoner's boot," said Mr. Hewart.

The constable pulled his boot off, and it was seen that it corresponded with the tracks described.

The boy Charles became paler, but made no remark.

"These evidences made you suspect the prisoner?"

"They did, sir. Me and my brother constable went to his house. We found him in his room, looking scared enough: his jacket wor marked with blood, and this were on the floor."

He exhibited the blood-stained knife.

A shudder ran through Dick's frame.

The magistrates looked stern.

"This is proof positive," said one.

Here Dick excitedly spoke—

"It's no knife o' mine: I never did the murder. I can tell'ee who did it."

"Silence!" cried Mr. Hewart.

"Silence!" echoed the usher.

The constables jerked their prisoner, and everybody *looked* silence.

"What was the prisoner's manner when you took him into custody?"

"Queer enough, sir: he shook all over."

"Had you any trouble with him? Was he violent?"

"Very much so. He struggled hard, and fought so that it wor all we could do to get the handcuffs on him. He wor desperate, an' no mistake."

At this false rendering of the truth, Dick looked wildly round, and would again have spoken, but

the constables who anticipated some such attempt at speech jerked the words out of his mouth.

But Hewart continued his questioning.

"Did he make any observation?"

"He said he would tell all, and that it was all his own fault, and come of listening to bad advice."

"Ha! just so!"

Poor Dick! everything looked black against him. The boy, Charles, now spoke.

"If this be a court of justice perhaps a witness may speak."

Everybody looked at the boy in profound surprise, but Hewart dropped his spectacles and glanced at him as if he would have annihilated him then and there.

The constables got ready to pounce on him, and drag him off, at the slightest sign from the magistrate.

"Who is that boy?" asked Mr. Hewart.

"It be prisoner's nephew, sir."

No. 3.

"Oh!"

"I am his nephew. I have evidence to give if you will hear it."

"Indeed! Well, we will hear you. Let him be sworn."

The oath was taken, and the boy commenced. His tale was brief. He told the magistrates that after Ralph had gone away with Dick, he followed, and heard Ralph persuade him to break into parson's house at night.

Mr. Merton, who had been rather in favour of the prisoner, at this drew himself up.

"And pray on what pretence did he induce him to break into Mr. Wordley's house?"

"He told him the certificate of my mother's marriage to parson wor locked up in bureau."

At this the face of Mr. Wordly became rather pale.

"A pretty story, indeed!"

"It be true. Ralph, be bad enough to do murder."

"It is true," cried Dick. "I broke in, and opened the bureau; there were papers there, and I had just got them, when I heard such terrible screams that I was scared and dropped them."

"No doubt."

"Then Mister Ralph came; he had a mask on, and when I asked him what he was doing he told me I should be took, and pushed me out of window. I know then he put knife in my pocket: he be a villain, God knows. Oh, sir, I am innocent of blood."

"Of course. A lame attempt at putting the guilt on another. The prisoner's statement, like the boy's, is not worthy of comment."

"Heaven knows it to be the truth," cried Charley. "When the constables took Dick, I saw Mister Ralph watching behind trees; he wor there to see him taken."

"That will do, boy; the influences which have been at work to get you to tell that tale are easy to see: you are young, or we might put you on your trial for perjury. The guilt of that wretched man is clear enough."

"It be a lie," cried Dick; "Mr. Ralph knows all about it—let him be called. Let him face me if he can."

"He is here," cried the usher, as with an unabashed look the murderer entered.

He bowed to the Bench, and then glanced coldly at the prisoner.

"Mister Ralph," said the head magistrate, "the prisoner has told us a story about you having induced him to break into the house where the murder took place."

"Thee knows it be true," interrupted Dick, but he was instantly jerked to silence, and the clerk of the court read over the statements of Dick and Charles.

To the surprise of both the latter, he denied the whole affair.

"A fabrication from beginning to end," he said. "I certainly did pass them as I was going home, but I never saw them after."

"Why, thou lying villain——"

"Silence!" roared the court.

And Dick was silenced.

"I have refrained from speaking in my son's behalf," said Mr. Merton, "but this I can affirm, that he was in bed at an early hour in the evening; he was unwell, and I found him fast asleep when I entered his chamber to see how he fared."

Here the Rev. Mr. Wordly was seen to smile a peculiar sort of smile; immediately after he stood up to add his evidence.

"Robbery," he said, "was added to murder. Property and money to an immense amount have been carried off; and there is no doubt the dreadful deed was committed in the vain hope of preventing detection. My wife's evidence might be added; she distinctly saw the prisoner, but the terrible events have made her too ill to attend."

"We can dispense with her evidence on such grounds. Prisoner, if you have any of the blood-gained plunder about you, I recommend you to give it up."

But Dick only stared wildly at the speaker.

"Has he been searched?"

"No, sir."

"Let him be so at once."

Dick offered no opposition, and they rummaged in every pocket. The Rev. Mr. Wordly, watching Ralph's visage, saw him smile when Dick's cap was turned inside out. He was not surprised when he saw the notes produced from inside the lining.

He had his own suspicions of how they came there.

At this fresh criminating evidence Mr. Hewart sternly exclaimed—

"It is unnecessary to raise any points of law: his guilt is palpable."

Scarcely had he ceased speaking when a confused hubbub was heard outside the justice-room; then a voice, not the most melodious in its tones, was heard to exclaim—

"Tell yer I will go in! Yer ragamuffin, will yer show fight? Here's for you — one! whist — over you go!"

There sounded a hearty thwack, followed by a heavy fall. A wild hurrah was the next that came.

The magistrates looked at one another.

The usher looked dumb.

This invasion of the sacred rights of the court was appalling.

"Bring in that man," said Mr. Hewart.

The constables left for the purpose, but were roughly pushed aside, as a voice exclaimed—

"Never sweat, old pine-apple! I'm coming in in a jiffey. Look, round goes the wheel. No thimble-rigging, remember; take your chance in this corner."

And the owner thereof abruptly presented himself to the astonished court.

The intruder was a knowing-looking young fellow, with a face brown from exposure, and hardened to a look of devil-may-care indifference. He was dressed in a costume not altogether elegant or intact, and had a rowdy-looking hat stuck on the back of his head.

This last (the hat, not the head) was officiously knocked off by the constable, who was almost petrified at the audacity of the man who had no respect for the majesty of the law.

Gazing confidently round the court, he winked good-humouredly at the magistrates, and, touching his forelock to the parson, let his roving glance settle with an indignant expression on the face of Ralph.

"You're there, yer scamp of the world, are yer?" he cried. "A neat trick you've been up to; but I'm the lad that'll make yer spin round like a teetotum. Gentlemen all, now's yer time. Walk up, walk up!— I ax pardon— what shall I say for myself; none on yer knows my good-looking mug. But here I am, like Barry in the circus— here I ar', I say; an' p'rhaps you'd like to know what I ar' here for, may-be, pos—i—tyveli—e?"

So amazed were the functionaries of the court by his strange behaviour, that they were at a loss how to act, and one of the magistrates was about to speak, when the intruder, with a theatrical wave of the hand, abjured him to silence, and continued:

"You're a-going to speak, I see it by your hie; but don't. Yer was going to ax me what I ar' here for. Now don't interrupt a gemmen—back, you scaramouches. That's my way of speaking. No, gemmen, says I—well, where was I, as Jim Jubbins said, when the rain washed him out of a mag—ny—fy—cent garret into a hor—din—ar—y cellar of mean di—men—si—ons."

At this point the head magistrate found speech.

"Take that madman from the court. I'll commit him if he speaks again."

"Yer'll commit a herror first, if yer do—get back yer thin-weazened, lick-staff devils! Now, yer honner, if yer'll only hear—and them as don't hear won't never understand—I's a going to tell you a tale what, as Richard the Third says to Julius Cæsar Pompey, will make yer blood stand on end, and friz yer 'air like quills on the blubbering por—cu—py—ine. I ar' come here, I ar', to stop that ar' long-nosed, leather-faced, hookywalker scaramouch there—to stop his little game, so I ar', I ar'."

"Oh, you have," said Mr. Hewart. "Pray let us know who you are—*you are*?"

This was said in attempted mimicry of the intruder.

"Sure I will, and no mistake," returned that individual, in his sing-song tone. "Make way there for a gemmen, yer idle wagabones, what's got all the world on his shoulders. My name, as I was about to say when that ere gemman with the hook-nose what makes a ladder for his specs, which isn't of first-class make—I'd sell him better any day for fifteen-pence—seven-and-a-half, going (the specs, not the nose, for that arn't worth nothing—not at no price)—going, seven-and-a-half, six, five—here, the lot for twopence. No buyers, then yer shan't have 'em. Hand up the next article, Jemima, and mind what the baby's drinking out of."

The next article was his hat, which he took from one of the constables, wiping him over the face with it by way of testifying its soundness. Turning the article over and over, he was about to commence in his volubility of speech, when Mr. Hewart, with a threat of imprisonment, demanded his name.

"My name, as I was saying, says I—them as knows me don't never want to ax, and them as doesn't doesn't never want to know; but as yer honner were so peelite, I'll tell yer without fail. Roving Rob I'm called, and if yer wants a leary blade as can put yer up to a move or two, and show yer which way to look for Sunday when yer've got bird-lime in yer eyes, why, I'm the one. Blessed if I didn't think I should have comed too late; but, howsomedever, as my chum, Joe Jobbings, the tinker, used to say, says he, 'It's never too late to mend,' which ar' a maxim yer all ought to know—if you'd like to see which way the wind blows, why——"

"Silence!" cried the magistrate. "Speak again, fellow, in answer to my questions. What are you here for?"

"Why, as I was saying, last night, a little arter the hours when rips goes toddling home, an' prigs what hasn't got no home of their own gets into somebody else's—well, as I was saying, last night, about that wery identical time, I sees that gemman wot stands over there, and who answers to the name of Mister Ralph, as they says in the bills when a poodle's lost, stolen, or strayed, or impro—pi—er—ly mislaid—I sees that blessed gemman—true as yer sitting there—clambering over his blessed par—i—ent's wall, arter he had got out of his window and comed along of a tree, which, if it had known what a vill—i—an it bore, would have tumbled down and broke his blessed neck."

Pausing a moment to take a look at Ralph, he continued.

"This black-looking gemman I follows, when he sneaks along the lane, and falls in with a pal standing ele—gant—ly agin a tree, in a cloak; an' together, like two birds of a feather, they goes to the identical house of that identical old gemman what's a-working his mouth as if he had got the gripes, with a santified look, and a white choker round his identical neck—he needn't turn up the whites of his blessed hies, that's him I mean, and he knows it, he does, though he pretends not to know nothink at all about who I means."

"Confine yourself to your statement," interrupted Mr. Hewart, while the Rev. Mr. Wordley looked uneasily at his feet.

"Well, so I will; as I was a-saying, says I, I sees them two, and they lets themselves in, and arterwards I sees their shadders on the blind, and, thinks I to myself, when I sees their motives of packing up plate, and silliver, and gold, thinks I, lawks shouldn't I like to be all along of yer, gemmens, and a-helping yer of doing that interesty—ing and joyful—wery—operat—i—on, shouldn't I; well, p'raps I shouldn't rather—lawks no, nevertheless, notwithstandy—ing."

Ralph looked hardened, but changed colour slightly; his eye met the curate's, and a look instinctively passed between them that made him feel very uncomfortable.

"Well, out they comes arter I'd heard such blessed screams, that I thought they had got into a Turki—esh harum, and was a-wringing of the necks of all the blessed women, one arter the other, like they does chickens vot they sends to market, tender and juicy. I see yer *hie* a'coming round this vay, an' so I'll let you have more some other blessed day. Thinks I, I doesn't care a farden rushlight who they be; I'll just step in and see the blokes, and share of the booty, but out they comes, as I says, with a rush, and carries in their hands what looked suspish—i—ous—ly like plunder, at which I makes a grab, but being on top of a blessed slippery dyke, lost my equy—ly—bry—um, and souses myself head and tail, all over, like a blessed pickled cowcumber, in the mud and water."

In spite of the serious charge which occupied their investigation, the magistrates (Mr. Hewart excepted) could not repress a smile at the fellow's oddity. I said in spite; but the fact of a fellow creature being on his trial for murder made but little check to their mirth when opportunity offered.

As for the audience, they were already in a roar.

And Roving Rob continued his sing-song recital.

"Well, when I gets up, all covered with clay, with my hies bunged up, and my blessed mouth full of toe-biters, I hears such a rub-a-dub-dub in the house that, thinks I, there's some blessed critters put out of the vay, and as I'm a henemy to sich sights, I'll just take a twist arter them coves what's got the swag, and so I does, but find 'em I doesn't; but there's what I've come here to say, I ar' to tell yer that that 'ere blessed young man am as hinnocent as a blessed hinfant, and that him as did the job is that ugly mug a-standing there, and a-trying to look all manner of ways at once, which he can't nohow—though who the blowke was that was with him I can't say, unless it wor that in—di—vid—ual that's a-nobbing on to that young man's sweetheart, and that's all I ar' come to say."

Delivering himself of the last sentences with infinite gusto, Roving Rob gave a jerk of his thumb towards Ralph, and stood the wonder of all present.

"I do not understand," Mr. Merton said, in his mild tones, "what is the meaning of this extraordinary being's strange tale. I presume, however, my son will not suffer from the uncorroborated testimony of an idle stroller."

"Be assured of that," returned Mr. Hewart; "we will give the vagabondising dog a taste of gaol if his answers about himself are not more satisfactory than his story about your son."

Sternly regarding Roving Rob, he said—

"What is your occupation?"

Rob jerked his head aside as if he did not understand the query.

"I ask you what you live on?"

"Why, since yer ax I don't know as I mind telling I lives on acorns, huckleberries, mouldy crusts, for which I ar profoundly thankful, not to say nothink of any kinds of broken victuals, such as cold legs of mutton, ribs of beef, wine bottles, which they've forgot to open, and thereby left the wine in, and such sorts of scran which, if you've any about yer, I'm not proud, and seeing as how I'm precious hungry why I'll not be above accepting of."

"No doubt. Now, perhaps you will answer my questions: what is your profession?"

"Anything yer like; I professes to be a gemmen, which I isn't, likewise professes dancing. Just clear away there yer blockheads, and see how soon I'll show his honour how to dance a clean jig."

"Scoundrel: I'll commit you for contempt."

"Oh, no, yer wouldn't be hard on Roving Rob, the pedlar, as gets his living by honest means—leastways he doesn't cheat no oftener nor his obliged, which is more than some of you gemmen can say—no disrespect to yer cloth, and no offence meant."

"Oh! a pedlar—a hawker of goods."

"That's my case, as the corpse said to the sexton, when he dug up his coffin, and was agoing to walk away with it."

"You sell goods, then, at the vi lages?"

"That's the point, as the needle said to the snail; I goes from place to place without having never a home to display my wares, like them as catches young salmon, and glad am I, when, like green peas, I can shell out."

"And pray, Mr. Pedlar, are you supplied with a license."

The countenance of Roving Rob fell, but in an instant he recovered his assurance.

"Does your honour think I'd rob the excise by selling my precious wares anywheres I come to, and not having no license?"

"We will look at it."

"So yer shall, and at anything I have to show yer, which is, I may say, all kinds of small goods which I pick up, from a needle to an anchor chain, which last is somewhat heavy, unless ye've got a tike to put it round his neck."

"Come, come—the license."

"Bless my blessed soul, where can I have put it; I had it not two hours ago, when I pulled it out with my watch. I must have left it inside that pretty purse I sold for three-and-six—not half its value—to that bright-eyed little gal. If yer honner will only wait I'll fetch it in a jiffey; stand out of the way, you ruffians, while I goes like a blessed flash of lightning."

The fact was Roving Rob had no license, he had merely rummaged in his pockets as a show, and would have shown the constables a clean pair of heels had they suffered him to go.

His departure was arrested by the magistrate.

"Another question, Mr. Robbing Rove, you will please to answer; where were you when you said you saw Master Ralph last night?"

This question, which had been suggested by the curate, seemed to turn the pedlar completely round; he looked a little flabergasted, and stammered in his reply.

"Well, yer see, I was walking for my health, when I seed a suspicious looking fox jump over the wall, and, thinks I, if he gets over there he'll kill ever so many chickens, and as I haven't had no dinner, and the flesh of chicken, if nicely roast or biled, ain't by no means despisable, I'll jest git over and drive him away, and as he's sure to kill ever so many a dozen or more, as I says before, thinks I, it will be no sin to rob him of his meal, and eat one myself, which, says I, will be a saving him ten or twenty fowls, at the very least."

"So you got in there and stole the squires chickens."

"Never a blessed one; for, as I was saying, I seed Mister Ralph come, and so, as I says before, I follers him, and didn't get no supper at all; and I shouldn't vonder if the fox, like a thief, carried off a dozen or more, all acos I didn't stay to see that he didn't do nothink of the kind."

"Indeed! Taking your own account of yourself, you are a pretty rascal. Have you found your license?"

"It's somewheres, but I don't know where."

"Then I shall commit you to prison, fellow, for six weeks, as a rogue and vagabond."

This announcement seemed to take the worthy Rob by surprise. He opened wide his mouth and stared foolishly at the Bench.

"You're joking now. You wouldn't send a honest dog like me, that doesn't do no harm, to prison?"

"Take him away."

"What! and don't believe what I told yer about that wretch there? Oh, lawks! and he's done the job! But never sweat, yer cunning-looking vermin! murder will come out, as they says, and yer may make yer blessed mind easy, for the rope's a-weaving that'll go round yer blessed neck; and I'll get totally drunk, like a blessed parson, when I sees yer dancing in the air. Oh, lawks! here's all my goods of the best description, and no one to look arter 'em; they've been a long time on hand, but they'll go off wery soon now, I'll warrant. Sort 'em, sort 'em out; them as likes 'em can buy 'em, and them as doesn't like 'em must buy 'em till they does."

Here the constables, seeing that the magistrate was boiling over with rage, dragged the pedlar away; but to the last his lugubrious tones could be heard, as he cried—

"Here's a blessed go! To think that I should have dropped in for it hot like this, and all cos I tried to teach the beaks what they ought to have found out for themselves, but didn't. I'm in a pretty pickle, like blessed mackerel what they sells four a shilling and six a shilling when fish is cheap and the sun is hot, and they won't keep. Here you are, all alive—take 'em at your own price. Try 'em and buy 'em—take 'em home and fry 'em."

His voice died away in the distance.

A silence now reigned: the prisoner shifted restlessly—the Bench conversed together in a low tone.

Then Dick was ordered back to prison to await his trial before a jury.

An affecting scene ensued when they dragged him away: Charles clung to his neck, and was only by main force dragged away.

"Cheer up," he cried, wringing his uncle's hand; "I'll look well after Ralph. I know thee won't come to harm; if thee does there is no God above."

He burst into tears, and was taken away.

And Dick was placed in gaol to take his trial for the wilful murder of a fellow creature.

CHAPTER VII.

THE VISIT TO THE GAOL.

AMIDST the shame and bitterness of being put on his trial for a crime of such a heinous nature, Dick's thoughts had wandered in deeper sadness to one whose absence in his hour of suffering he keenly felt.

He had looked round the court in the vain hope of seeing the face of his still loved Mary. He had yearned for the solace of that sympathy which a woman's love alone can give; and when thrust back in his solitary cell, he felt indeed bereaved and deserted.

He knew not the cause of her absence from the court.

The news of his arrest for the murder of one who was dear to her as a sister had proved a shock too voilent for her to withstand. Her heart reproached her as being in some indirect measure the cause of the terrible deed; she reasoned that, had she not slighted him, he might not have been driven to such desperate criminality.

Like the rest, she believed him guilty; how could she know otherwise, all the proofs were so overwhelming. On the first intelligence of the dreadful event she had fallen into a swoon, recovering from which she was still so much affected that she continued in a succession of fainting fits lasting several hours.

In the meantime, Dick, without reproaching her, yet in his mind believed she had deserted him; he regarded her love as given to another, and in bitterness he gave way to his jealous and sorrowful emotions.

While he was sitting joyless and desponding, his gruff gaoler entered to announce a visitor.

"It's not according to orders," he said, "to let the likes of you have anybody to see you; but as the young damsel wishes it, although it's more than you deserve, she shall see you."

Dick started to his feet. Could it be Mary? Had she come to sooth him with her sympathy, cheer him with hope, show her belief in his innocence.

In the brief period that elapsed before her entry, he had built up visions of the most cheering kind; but they were all cast down when she entered.

She came slowly and sadly in, and seemed as if afraid to trust herself too near.

Then the gaoler read her fears; he entered after her, and said—

"Dont 'ee be afeerd, miss; I'll stay with you."

It was gall to Dick, and in confused anguish he remained at a distance.

For a moment or two she stood in hesitation.

Then she advanced and laid her hand on his arm. The touch thrilled through him.

"Oh, Dick!" she cried, "what have you done?"

He looked at her in troubled amazement.

"Done, Mary? Nought that they accuse me of."

She burst into tears.

"It is so dreadful. That poor girl too; why did you not resign the things you stole rather than murder her?"

"What, Mary! thee don't think I did it?"

"Would to Heaven I could think otherwise for both our sakes!"

He shook her hand from his arm and staggered back.

This was a worse blow than all.

"I might have put up with what others thought, but I did not expect you too would condemn me. Oh, Mary, this is a bitter cup."

He sobbed like a child.

Twice she attempted to speak to him, and show him that she p tied even while she condemned, but he waved her away.

Proud in his innocence he would not have her near while she believed him guilty.

"I had thought when all the world was against me I should have had you on my side; it would have been so sweet to have known that one whom I loved acquitted me when circumstances were so black; but never mind, get thee gone to thy new love—Dick will meet his fall alone: if he have to die for other's crimes he will, if not—he will have none near him when his innocence is proved who thought him guilty."

She was too much moved to tenderness to leave him thus: though marvelling why he should deny a crime that was so black against him, her love drew her to his side; at that moment she could have died rather than the deed should have happened.

She crept closer to him.

"You will break my heart; it has been pain enough when you have been unkind, but now with—with—that. Oh, I cannot speak!"

"No, lass! troubles of mine will never break thy heart; it beat for me once, but that is long ago."

"It is my fault; if I had not left you, though I only did it because you were sulky, you would never have gone to the house, and then this would not have happened."

"No, Mary; but if thee thinks me guilty, thee art as hard as the rest. I swear to God I never did the deed, nor knew of it! It lies at the door of Ralph; his hand put these marks of blood on my jacket, and the knife in my pocket."

"You went there."

"I did; but not to thieve parson's silver or gold; thee know I never craved aught but what I could work for. If thee will listen an' promise to believe me I will tell thee all on't."

He briefly told her, while she stood gasping in agony at the recital.

If that were true, what terrible sufferings were in store for both; he to die for another man's crime—she to know and share his pangs.

Earnestly she looked at him.

"Dick, I have never loved any other; tell me as we hope to meet our Maker, is all you have told me the truth?"

"Solemnly, Mary."

"Then you shall not die as, I will wander over earth to save you."

He uttered an exclamation of joy.

"Then thee do believe me innocent!"

"I do! I cannot think you would tell me false at such a time."

She fell sobbing on his breast.

His manacled hands prevented him straining her to his heart, but he gazed joyfully into her face.

"Bless thee!" he said. "I could die more happy now; put thy arms about me, and let me hear your sweet words."

She did so; her soft arms held him to her breast, while she kissed him with maiden love.

In those few moments Dick was happy.

The harsh tones of the gaoler broke the sweet spell. They had forgotten his presence, and looked up as he spoke.

"Time's up, Miss Mary; you mustn't stay any longer."

"Dear Dick, what can be done?" asked the young damsel.

"I'll tell thee, Mary. There's something wrong, or parson would have brought his wife. Go to her; see if there be anything she knows. Ask her if she saw who it was that came."

"Sure an' I will; don't despair—I'll see her this very day."

She put up her pretty lips to his; he kissed them fervently. She was all affection then, and he cursed the iron bands that kept his arms from pressing her to his heart.

"Come, miss," cried the stern gaoler.

Mary kissed Dick once more; his manacled hands she raised to her lips, then, with a sighing blessing, was ushered out by the gaoler.

"Be kind to him," she said; "he is wrongfully accused."

"Eh?" his innocence will be proved: please do not treat him harshly."

She tripped away, and the gaoler, looking after her to make sure that she was in her right senses, slowly shut the gates.

"She's gone clean daft," he muttered. "Treat him kind, indeed! Yes, I will, when he brings that poor girl back to life again."

From his prison window Richard watched the retreating form of Mary. When almost out of sight, she turned and waved her hand. Then she was gone, and Dick sank back.

He seemed to feel that he had parted with her for ever: he knew not *what* gulf would rise to sunder them.

Mary met the Rev. Mr. Wordly coming out of his house; he spoke blandly to her, but gave her to understand that Mrs. Wordly was not well enough to be seen.

The fact was, the testimony of his wife would not exactly have agreed with the statements he had made in court, and he had just had a very long interview with her, in order to coerce or terrify her into silence as to her suspicions.

The better to guard against any slips of her tongue, he allowed no one but a trusty maid to see her.

After he had gone, Mary returned to the house; but, though she tried her utmost, the parson's orders were well obeyed, and Mrs. Wordly was not to be seen.

With a heavy heart Mary retired. Crossing the fields, she heard her name softly called.

The voice was familiar, and, with a fluttering heart, she turned a little way off. Henry Warner was seen hastening towards her; he was pale, and looked agitated, and Mary, wondering at the change in his appearance, waited for him to come up.

Ah, Mary! had you known all that would follow that simple act, you would not have loitered there.

CHAPTER VIII.

A BRACE OF VILLAINS.

PARSON WORDLEY encountered Ralph shortly after he had left Mary. He came upon him unexpectedly to the latter. The fact was, the reverend gentleman had been very desirous of speaking with Ralph, and, having seen him from the window, issued forth to overtake him.

Ralph avoided his glance as they greeted. There was something in the sleek manner of Mr. Wordley he did not like, and, with a brief interchange of words, he would have passed on, had not the parson held him quietly by the button-hole.

"My dear Ralph, I have been wanting to see you, in order that we might have a few minutes' chat together."

"I am quite willing," returned Ralph.

"Just so. You see, this very sad and heartrending affair has quite convulsed the peaceful relations of the village."

"It has, sir."

"But—heaven be praised!—now that the assassin is in custody, we are likely to have a speedy settlement of the matter."

"No doubt of it," was the hardened villain's response.

"There was something of surprise in it, don't you think, Ralph? This Dick has been rather the reverse of thief and murderer. There are many others in the neighbourhood whom I should have been more ready to suspect if the proof hadn't been so dead against him."

Ralph ventured to look the speaker in the face; he found the clergyman's eyes fixed on him with a gaze that sent his glance to the ground.

But he answered, without restraint—

"Proof like that will not fail to bring him to the gallows."

"No."

"Everything shows his guilt."

"*Everything*," said the parson, with emphasis. "But doesn't it strike you as rather odd—the other half of the business?"

"What half?"

"The robbery, Ralph."

The murderer looked uneasily at the speaker.

"Why—what?" he stammered.

"Yes," continued the parson; "besides the tracks of other feet beside his, there was something remarkable in the way my plate disappeared."

"He must have had accomplices."

"Very cunning fellows they must have been."

"You bear yourself calmly, sir."

"Why, you see, I am not without hope—very strong hope—of *recovering* that which was stolen from me."

Ralph started.

"You are surprised?"

"Yes—no—at least——"

"You don't think it likely. Now, I do. By the way, Ralph, a singular fancy has got into my wife's head."

"Indeed!"

"She fancies she recognised one of the miscreants when in her room."

Pale as death, Ralph turned. Still the keen eyes of the clergyman was fixed on his face.

The latter continued.

"Of course it would not do to attach much importance to a frightened woman's notions, but who do you think she suspects?"

The criminal found it hard to reply.

"I do not know," he stammered.

"Can you guess?"

"I can't say who."

"I don't suppose you can. It's rather queer, you know, but she thought she recognised in the wretch who bent over her—laid his accursed hands on her, doubtless with the intention, d——n him! of violating her—why, what's the matter?"

"I am not well; the sight of the body——"

He could scarcely speak, the sweat was pouring down his features, and his lips were colourless as ashes.

"Ah! well, she thinks it was *you*."

"I, sir?"

He staggered back white as a sheet.

A smile played about the lips of the clergyman.

"The very idea gives you a turn. *I don't wonder at it*. That was my principal reason, Ralph, for not letting her come to give evidence in court."

"But I could have proved I was not from my bed," returned Ralph, sullenly.

"Of course; besides, Ralph, it would not have been much matter: the fact was, when the rascal came in my chamber I knew him in an instant."

A spasm shot through Ralph's heart; he gasped, but could not speak.

The parson, grimly watching him, went on.

"His mask was very cleverly put on, but I knew him and his companion—the villains! But I lay quiet, and pretended to be asleep, by which, I rather think, I saved my throat from being slit. Ha, ha! don't you think so, eh?"

Ralph could have ground his teeth out; how bitterly he repented that he had not murdered the parson as he lay in bed.

There was a deadly look in his eye which the clergyman did not fail to notice; but though noticing, he did not much heed it.

The fact was, he knew Ralph had dispossessed him of his property, and he meant to get it—if he could.

"Yes, I baffled them; and I'll tell you how I mean to have back what they robbed me of. I shall convey a quiet hint to the gentleman that, if by this time to-morrow my money and plate are not returned to my house—why, Ralph, my boy, I will give the *real* murderer up to justice. A capital plan, eh?"

He slapped the quaking wretch on the shoulder.

With his hand clenched, Ralph stood regarding him. There were thoughts of the most devilish nature in his mind.

"Do you think," he said nervously, "that he will be fool enough to give up what he has gained at such a price?"

"To save his neck, I do. Oh, Ralph, hanging must be a dreadful death! The tightening cord, the bursting heart, the jerk that starts the eyes out of the head."

He paused, there was a look so dangerous in the orbs of the wretch he tortured.

"You have not told me," he said presently, "what you think of my plan."

"I think you may whistle for your property."

"Indeed!"

He looked him through and through, with that cunning face of his.

Then he quietly placed his hand on his shoulder.

"Plain speaking, Ralph, is best between friends—you understand. If the plate you and that easily-led friend of yours took from my cupboard, and the money you took from my chamber, be not returned, I will hang both of you."

Ralph was as if staggered for a moment; but he rallied, and said defiantly—

"It's no use trying the game—you've sworn yourself too far. Whatever you may think, I don't care a fig for you or your threats."

"Don't you? Now, look here, Ralph. I don't mind the murder of that girl, because she had a little too much influence with her mistress. But I do mind losing my property; and, mind me, I will have it."

Ralph, who had recovered his brazen defiance, uttered a scoffing laugh.

"Ah! you may laugh. There are some very keen-nosed detectives in London. I'll have you watched, Ralph. There's that friend of yours—he isn't quite so deep; I warrant they will work it out of him."

Ralph changed countenance again at this. There was every probability of the secret being extorted from Warner's fears.

After all his matchless craft, then, there was a fear of the halter going round his neck.

"I will prevent it," he muttered.

He glanced at the parson; that worthy was still steadily regarding him.

"Have you made up your mind?" he asked.

"Yes."

"And your answer——"

"Is this!" cried Ralph, springing upon him.

Unobserved, as he thought, he had drawn his knife. When he sprang forward he intended, at one plunge, to have driven it to the parson's heart.

His surprise was great when he received a heavy blow on the forehead—a blow which sent him reeling back, until finally he brought up against a tree.

"No games of that sort with *me*, my dear young man," said Mr. Wordly, handling significantly a loaded revolver.

He had been prepared for some such act on the part of Ralph, and with the butt-end had beaten him back.

Staggering from the effects of the blow, Ralph leaned against the tree, regarding, knife in hand, the unruffled clergyman.

After letting his cynical glance rest for a moment on his discomfited adversary, Mr. Wordly said—

"I have propounded my terms, Ralph; you know what you have to do, only make up your mind to the result. I go now, but be assured that I shall in future take *particular* care never to put myself in the power of a man who bears towards me such amiable feelings."

Keeping his revolver pointed at Ralph, he slowly retired. When, however, out of sight, Ralph, with gnashing teeth and wildly-gleaming eyes, rushed scowling forward.

He saw no sign of the sleek, but villainous churchman. He heard voices, however, near him; and looking down an avenue whence the sounds emanated, he saw the figures of his friend Warner and Mary Westland.

They were standing close together; Warner's arm had encircled her waist, and her face was raised to his.

Savagely Ralph smiled.

"I have a plan in store for them," he muttered. "She shall not be all his if I can prevail."

Stealthily he crept towards them.

Unhappy Mary! had she forgotten her love, her faith to that unfortunate, helpless prisoner fretting his heart out in the county jail?

CHAPTER IX.

THE HUT BY THE HILL.

NIGHT came on—the air changed—clouds gathered. A storm was evidently brewing.

By-and-bye the rain began to fall. Not at first in heavy drenching showers. A few drops pattered on the leaves and on the ground. Occasionally they rattled against the panes of the barred window of Richard's cell.

And the wind swept moaning by, and whistled past the village houses, through the trees, and amongst the tombstones of the dead whitening in the village churchyard.

And it sighed over the new-made grave of the murdered girl.

Not a week had passed since she had walked through that very churchyard.

Not a week—and now she lay in the damp earth for worms to feast upon.

The signs of the coming storm kept most people in their homes; to some it was a welcome advent.

To Ralph and his friend Warner it gave hope of being able, unobserved, to finish the business which had already gone through its stages of blood, tears, and duplicity. At twelve o'clock they were together crossing the fields, on their way to the hovel under the hill, where, on their escape from the parson's house, they had stowed the booty.

They were each provided with long cloaks, as much for the purpose of concealment as for shelter against the weather.

Creeping along by the side of hedges, and keeping a vigilant look out, they made their way for some time in silence.

Ralph was the first to speak:—

"You've managed it all right, then, with Mary?"

"Not quite."

"What! is she still obstinate? I should have thought your eloquence and allurements would have overcome her long ago."

"They ought to have done so, but they have not. However, I think I have induced her at last; she has promised to meet me at ten o'clock to-morrow evening by the copse of firs yonder."

"When you mean to take her to your arms, willingly or not."

"I intend to get her away then. I shall have a chaise ready; once inside, she may bid adieu to the village and her associates."

"And her virtue?"

"You are severe."

"Bah! I know you pretty well. At ten, said you?"

"Precisely."

Ralph's visage glowed.

There was a purpose in his mind which would not have disposed Warner to confidence if he had known it.

"By that time," continued Warner, "our melting business will be finished and the booty shared."

"Do that to-night, I hope?"

"Hush!" cried Warner, starting and turning pale. "There is some one following."

"Eh!"

Ralph drew his dreadful-bladed knife; it was one similar to that with which the murder had been committed.

"If there's anyone on our track," he muttered, "they'll never find their way back."

He glared savagely round and listened.

"I don't hear or see anyone," he exclaimed. "Are you sure it was not the rain?"

"No. There! Do you see yonder?"

A shadowy form was seen for a moment gliding past the trees.

Ralph muttered deep curses and agilely sprang forward. Whoever it might have been was not visible. He searched and swore, but as no result attended either of those operations, he again continued his way, holding his knife in his hand, and looking at times as if he felt ready to plunge it into Warner's heart as he walked beside him.

"It must have been your cursed fancy," he muttered. "You're always full of fear. Curse me if ever I saw such a fellow."

"I hope it was fancy. I have sharp ears; I will listen."

Another silence ensued; but the rain fell faster and the wind sighed with a hoarser sound.

"I don't think there's much fear of anyone following us to-night," said Ralph, abruptly; "its too dark and stormy. Do you hear that?"

A deep boom of thunder rolled along the sky, and the rain followed in heavy showers.

"No; if it keeps like this we shall not be disturbed."

"You remember what I told you about the parson?"

Warner shivered.

"I haven't had any sleep since, and shall not till I get far away from here."

"A pretty chum to slip away and leave me to face it out."

"You will not stay, will you?"

"Somebody must; it won't do for us both to run away at once."

"Then you will start soon after me?"

"Oh, yes."

"If we get this job done all right, I shall certainly make my way to town as soon as possible. I mean to take Mary to my chambers, and live with her on the quiet, jolly enough."

"I wish you joy."

"They won't hear much of me after I get there."

"I don't think they will."

"What?"

"I don't suppose you will let them."

"No."

"And I'll take care I don't," thought the villanous Ralph. "If you get away with the tin and that girl I shall be out of my reckoning: I haven't done the business for you to share."

Had Warner noted the face of his friend, he would have seen there some expression of the thoughts that were impelling him to such diabolical intentions; but the night was dark, and, full of his own thoughts, he paid but little attention to the demeanour of his companion.

"We are going a long way round," Ralph said, presently; "let us go across the churchyard."

"I would rather not, Ralph."

"What! are you afraid?"

"I am not afraid; but I cannot pass the grave of that poor girl."

"Stuff! you didn't do the job. If you had had your hands deep in her blood as I had you might be shirky. Come on!"

But Warner showed no inclination to go that way.

"Are you frightened of meeting her ghost? What rubbish! Keep behind me; I'll go first, if you like. I am not afraid: across there I mean to go."

In a moment more he had vanished over the low wall of the churchyard, and was pursuing his way amongst the graves.

Warner followed, but with unmistakable trepidation; indeed, he shook like a leaf, and glanced quakingly round at every sound.

Ralph walked steadily on. To his hardened mind the dead were so much clay: he did not care if none of the living besides themselves were there.

Warner speedily joined him. His terrors were less when walking by the side of his unscrupulous ally.

The rain now showed signs of temporary cessation, but the wind was still high. They were near the extremity of the churchyard; Ralph proceeding in moody silence, and Warner almost crouching by his side.

At this spot Ralph felt his cloak gripped.

He turned savagely, and saw Warner, white as a sheet of paper, and trembling bodily.

"Why, what the devil's the matter now?" he cried.

"There—there!" Warner gasped, pointing with his finger amongst the tombs.

Though far removed from the fear that held possession of his confederate, Ralph, hardened as he was, felt a sudden terror creep through him at what he saw.

A little to the right, and almost in the path they would have to traverse, was a strange, gaunt figure, the aspect of which was, in the murky darkness of the night, most appallingly supernatural.

It was motionless, tall, enveloped in dim-looking garments, and with an arm outstretched towards them. It was, perhaps, no inapt representation of death on the pale horse.

Recovering a little from the first alarm, Ralph took a pace forward, but Warner, gripping him firmly, held him back.

"Look!" he cried, "it moves."

Such was the case.

A gleam of lightning showed the figure seated above a tombstone. The lightning vanished, and through the white, misty haze the apparition was seen gliding.

Almost in the instant after Warner's speech it had cast itself in their path.

With a coarse laugh at his companion's cowardice, Ralph started forward.

"It's old Mother Wykeman, the graveyard witch," he said.

Warner's terror was not diminished. Now that he had become aware of the nature of their unexpected and unearthly-looking visitant, he was in as much trepidation till the object of her crossing their path could be ascertained.

The witch placed herself directly before Ralph. Her lank arms were outstretched towards him, and with her fingers she pointed first at him, then at the terrified Warner.

Shrivelled and hideous in feature, her impression was enough to scare a trooper, and her hoarse, screeching words were horrifying in the extreme.

"Ha, ha!" she cried; "here they come—the murderer and his tool. Witch Wykeman has been by the grave of their victims; it is there where the white mists drive. Ha, ha! The mist will be chill enough when the rope that is now being wove is put round the neck of Ralph Merton, the murderer!"

She uttered a wild screech that sent the blood of Warner curdling in his veins, but Ralph, hardened and exasperated, drew a pistol.

"Get out of my path," he exclaimed, "before I spoil your witcheries for ever!"

But the old witch only raised her skinny finger, and thrust it derisively in his face.

"The graveyard witch warns you," she said; "when the rope is coiled she will come again."

Maddened almost by her words and actions, Ralph presented his pistol and fired. Warner uttered a cry of horror, but the witch, with a shrill laugh, bounded away, and was lost among the tombstones.

Warner tottered forward.

"Let us haste. I have had enough of this," he exclaimed.

Ralph bestowed a savage, scornful look upon him and, hurrying his pace, half dragged him from the place of the dead.

Two minutes after they had passed out, another figure bounded over the churchyard wall.

It was the boy, Charles.

Day and night he had tracked the pair in all their movements, and now he followed, knowing that on such a night they would not have stolen from their beds unless some dark enterprise were on foot.

He kept in their wake till, by the side of a hill, they disappeared.

Patiently toiling on through the storm, Charley found himself in the hollow of the hill; but here he looked in vain for any sign of the pair.

The faint glimmer of a light shining through the darkness shewed him what in the gloom he had not seen. By the end of the excavation was a peculiar formed hut; a mere cave, roofed in here and there where there was wet layers of clay. An opening at the side served as a window, and through that came the light that he had seen.

It was only in a certain position that the hovel could be seen; it was planned with such cleverness of arrangement that, but for the fact of his having scrambled to his present position, he would not have been able to see the light.

Satisfied now that he had housed them in some work that would tend to his uncle's innocence, he clambered up the soft clay, and, by firmly planting his knees, succeeded in gaining a view into the interior.

What he saw in no great measure surprised him, though it made his heart bound mightily.

Rude in the inside as it was on the exterior, the hovel was as bare of any article of use or ornament as the sides of the hill. A fire had been kindled on the ground, and on this was placed a crucible.

Beside the fire were Warner and Ralph, digging up from the earth, where they had buried them, the stolen property belonging to the parson.

The boy's feelings were bitter at that moment.

Justice and law had put forth their power to take atonement for the deed of murder. For that crime his youthful uncle lay ignominiously in gaol, while here were the very wretches melting into convertible spoil the booty for which they had perpetrated so great a crime.

Perched in his somewhat precarious position, Charley was in some hesitation as to the best mode of proceeding.

His first impulse was to descend, and, having entered, pounce on the two villains and attack them in the best manner he could.

But this prudence counselled him to abandon, not from any fear of the pair.

The boy was brave as a lion, and would have dauntlessly cast himself in amongst a score of armed desperadoes, but he remembered Ralph's position.

If he showed himself before them, charging them with their crime, they were desperate enough to devise any means for their own safety.

Of what avail would his unsupported assertion be, even if they did not, as seemed likely they would, murder him to screen their guilt.

Debating these matters quietly, the boy slid down.

He had made up his mind to proceed to the nearest house and bring those to see the pair in their labours whose testimony would be credible.

Never staying to cast a glance behind him, Charley, having once stole safely out of hearing made the best of his way towards the houses of the village.

The churchyard lay between him and the houses; and to reach the residence of one of the magistrates he crossed that, and plunged into a wood.

He had got thus far without hearing any other noise than the fury of the storm; but now another sound recalled his thoughts from where they had been wildly wandering.

It was a human voice.

He looked up, and found himself confronted by several gipsies.

They were mostly young men, and were known to the boy. Still, on the errand on which he was bent, he had no wish to encounter them, and stood chafing, when he was thus stopped and addressed—

"Hilloa, my young bird! where the d—— are you rolling to in such a storm?"

"I am going home," said the boy.

No. 4.

"This is a queer way to come, isn't it?"

"Pray do not stop me; I am in haste."

"I dare say, my young kidney. But what's the haste? Where are you running from?"

"I have been over by the hills. The storm overtook me——"

"Come, come! no spinners, younker. We saw you going on arter them two gen'lmen from squire's—Ralph and t'other. Where did you leave them? and what are they up to?"

"Nothing that concerns you," said Charley, attempting to pass.

"Stop there! You don't go till you've told us, so you might as well speak up."

The boy hesitated. If he could trust those men, they would be most valuable aids.

Not that the word of a gipsy would have been worth anything.

But the presence of Ralph and Warner, if caught and brought in with the stolen property, would be an irresistible proof of something wrong.

He looked from one to the other. If they really would befriend him, now was his time. There would be some delay in getting any men out, during which period the pair might make off.

Still he hesitated.

"Come, younker," said the one who had all along spoken, "no use considering. You might as well make a clean confession."

"Will you serve me?" asked the boy.

"In coorse we will."

"Honestly?"

"Whoever found the gipsy anything else?"

The gipsies laughed.

"If you will come, then, I will tell you what I should like to do."

"Lead the way, then, young cheroot."

The boy took them quickly on the way back.

"And now, what's up?"

"You know of the murder?"

"Heard of it."

"My uncle Dick is in on the charge."

"Bad job!"

"But he didn't do it."

"Oh, it's all the same."

"It will not be if you will help me to bring to justice the real criminals."

"An' who may they be?"

"Mister Ralph and London friend."

The gipsy whistled.

"Who told 'ee that?"

"There was a robbery."

"There wor," returned the gipsy, with glistening eyes, while his companions looked eager at the mere mention of anything relating to booty.

"Don't you think that the one that did the robbery was the murderer?"

"Well, it seems like enough."

"I have found them at the hovel by that hill over yon; they are melting down the gold and silver."

"Eh?"

"The plate-takers."

"Melting down?"

"Melting it down?" echoed the rest.

"Yes, that they may sell it. It is easier to sell thus."

"Much easier," said the gipsy, significantly.

And his companions looked as if they rather believed so too.

"They have a great quantity, the villians. Gold and silver ornaments, candlesticks, dishes——"

"Gold and silver, eh?"

"Yes."

"Real?"

"Every bit of it."

The gipsy looked at his companions; his companions looked at him.

There was a good deal in those looks.

When the boy suddenly glanced at them they gazed at the trees or the sky in perfect innocence.

You would not have thought that an idea of the precious metals was in their head.

"So," said the gipsy, "the villains have got all this working to themselves?"

"They had just began when I came away."

"We'll interrupt them, I take it."

"I would not have stayed if I had had one with me to make sure of both."

"Very glad you hadn't."

"Eh?"

"I mean it's a lucky go."

The boy looked earnestly at him.

"You do not intend any treachery?"

"Betrayed? no."

"If they are taken, and the property recovered, no doubt Mr. Wordly will reward you."

"No doubt; parson allers were fond of rewarding a body."

"Yes, with the gaol and a sermon," muttered one.

Charles, still dubious, suddenly stopped.

"I will not go, unless you promise——"

"Oh, that's all right enough," interrupted the gipsy. "We don't want to finger swag, do we?"

The gipsies looked as if they did not.

"If I thought you did, I would not go any farther."

"Clear on, young kidney; we know the spot well enough to find our way there by ourselves—so you may as well come."

This request bore such truth on it's surface, that Charles, although not altogether reassured, hurried on at the front, and no more was said till they got within a few yards of the hovel by the hill.

CHAPTER X.

THE EXPLOIT OF THE GIPSIES.

THE storm still continued; the rain fell with a determined sound, and the wind roared as if angry that anything could resist its fury.

The gipsies, as well as Charles, were wet through; but they bore the inclemency of the weather with wonderful mildness.

They evidently regarded their journey through the storm as a very satisfactory one.

Inside, the precious pair were still at work. Having finished the gold, they next proceeded with the silver articles, and had already formed a tolerably good-sized nugget of either metal.

To them the storm outside was a perfect godsend: the fall of the rain was something heavenly.

It drowned any noise they might make, and threatened to drown anyone who ventured from home in it.

So they thought themselves safe.

Indeed, so safe did they consider themselves, that Ralph thought a favourable time was come for putting into execution a project he had long since had brooding in his mind.

This was nothing less than the murder of his unsuspecting friend.

He had gleaned from him all the intelligence he needed respecting Mary; and the work of smelting was so far advanced that it could be pursued without much trouble to the end.

He had at first thought of getting rid of Warner in the woods, after the treasure had been removed.

There was a pool in an unfrequented place that would leave no traces of his deed.

But ultimate reflection led him to the belief that a more fitting occassion than this could not be found.

In that lonely place his body might lie for months, and, even when discovered, it would appear the work of gipsies.

And there was no fear of anyone interrupting him while at the job.

He could finish him off at his leisure, which was what he intended to do.

All the time that they had been working at, or drinking over their task, these thoughts had been uppermost in his mind.

Henry Warner never knew, when he gazed into the stolid visage of the man he called his friend, that his own murder was the subject of his thoughts.

So Mr. Ralph, having decided upon the deed, now deliberated on the best method of putting it in practice.

A favourable opportunity was now offered. Warner was bending over the cooling mass of silver, his mind apparently engaged in sweet anticipation of its value.

Ralph took out his pistol, and, grasping the barrel, prepared to deal a blow that would leave his friend stunned and at his mercy.

He stood now right behind the unsuspecting Warner.

The pistol was raised. In another moment the skull of his victim would have been crushed in.

But at that instant the door suddenly burst open, and Charley, attended by the gipsies, entered.

Warner had turned in time to see the menacing attitude and malignant features of his accomplice, and, glancing from his scowling face to the pistol, he seemed to guess at his villanous intentions.

But the abrupt entry of the gipsies, while saving his life, at the same time prevented him from giving utterance to his suspicions.

Darker grew Ralph's visage.

It was gall and wormwood to be thwarted of his murderous purpose, but to be discovered in the act of melting the booty was even worse.

One glance at the jeering faces of the gipsies was enough to convince him that even if they did not assist the boy to bring him to justice, they would dispossess him of his spoil.

But Warner, skulking by the melting-pot, avoided the gaze of the brave Charley, and began to quake in his shoes.

He thought he saw the officers behind the boy.

At that moment the gallows rose dark and grim before him.

The first act of Charley was to force the door close; he then turned to the gipsies.

"See," he said; "it is as I told you. They have done the murder, and are here with the plunder; oh, let us take them at once before the magistrate, and my poor uncle will be set free."

"Softly, softly," said the young gipsy; "let us first make sure of what they're melting: we can then give 'em a grip."

"Yes, that'll be the game," chimed in his companions.

As they advanced to the precious crucible, Ralph Merton stepped before them. The pistol which he had drawn to use against his friend he now turned towards them.

In his left hand he held another pistol.

Both weapons were pointed at the nearest two gipsies.

"Look here, friends," he said; "I don't know what you want, but I know what I will give some of you if you don't go."

"Do you? That's kind. Well, we'll tell you what we want: we're just going to help ourselves to that bit o' swag."

"Indeed!"

"And then we're going to drag you afore the beak; there's time for you to swing."

"Fool!" said Ralph, sternly; "step back, or I fire!"

The gipsy laughed.

"There's too many of us," he said.

"I'll scatter the brains of some of your number."

"There'll be plenty left. Come, put down that gimcrack."

For answer Ralph levelled the pistol at his head.

"Take out your pistol," he cried to Warner, who was shivering like a leaf, "and don't be skulking there like that. Now, fellows, are you going to leave?"

"Ha, ha! that's a good 'un. Leave! Why, it's our own crib. Turn us out of our blessed caboose! Look out, lads—give him a lift there."

Here Warner stepped forward.

"Pals," he said, "there's no occasion for us to set to about the swag. Say nothing, and we will share it."

"Hold your tongue for a fool," interrupted Ralph.

"Look's as if that was the best thing you could do," exclaimed the gipsy.

Charley interrupted him.

"You will not have dealings with such wretches. Bring them to justice; they shall not escape. I will drag them there myself, rather."

"So I should say; but keep yourself cool, my little man. Now, Ral, are you going to come in?"

Had not the scoundrelly assassin been blinded by passion, he must have seen that his best chance was to share with them; but he was too greedy to consent to giving away half, even to save the other. Besides, he trusted to his pistols.

The gipsies had only sticks and knives, and he did not think they would venture to attack him.

He was mistaken. No sooner had he replied to the young leader's words by a defiant oath, than the gipsies sprang upon him.

"Use your pistol!" he shouted to Warner.

Then he discharged the one his right hand held.

The sharp report rang through the hovel.

One of the gipsies fell, a bullet in his breast.

Bang! went the second pistol.

But the ball was diverted of its aim.

The gipsy leader had knocked his arm up with a stick, and the bullet lodged in the roof.

Surrounded and grasped by the excited gipsies, he yet found opportunity to draw his knife.

Before he could use it, Charley seized him round the legs and pulled him backwards. As he fell, several heavy sticks descended on his head.

Stunned, bleeding, and mortified, he sank to the ground, and would have been there and then despatched—for the injury to their comrade had roused the gipsies' blood—had not Charley interposed.

"Do not kill him; let him hang for the murder. I will take him to the magistrate."

At first the gipsies paid no heed to him, and continued beating Ralph about the head; but ultimately their young chief bid them desist, and Ralph was left to lie bleeding in the dust.

Warner had made no resistance. Pale as death, he had stood by when his accomplice was being, as he thought, murdered; and when they had finished with him, they turned to attack the other.

It was a terrible moment for Henry Warner.

His confederate in villany lay crushed and bleeding by the side of the fallen gipsy, and he himself was threatened by the same implements, that were all bloody with beating the squire's evil son.

Retreating step by step, and cowering whenever any of the gipsies made a blow at him, he got at length by the small window.

Here, looking up for the chance of escape, he received a knock with one of the sticks that brought him to his knees.

Struggling up again, he put out his hands to ward off the attacks of those threatening men, whose looks spoke murder.

"Finish him off, Jem!" said one of the gipsies who was in the rear.

"All right—here goes!"

The murderous-looking fellow drew an immense knife.

Warner shuddered at the sight; it reminded him of the murder of the parson's maid.

He had by this time reached the door. Here an occurrence unexpected by him opened the portal of liberty, and gave him hope of escape.

Charley had seized Ralph by the collar, and having opened the door, was dragging him out.

He knew that he was the greater villain, and that once in custody, the other could be easily taken.

Just as he had got him half-way out, Warner, backing for his life, reached the door.

The rush of fresh air told him that it was open. He glanced round, and prepared to take a spring.

One of the gipsies, seeing his intention, aimed a terrific blow at his head with a ponderous bludgeon. The one who had drawn the knife at the same time gripped him by the collar.

The faint-hearted wretch thought it was all up with him then; but with a visionary hope of escape, he wrenched away from the one who held him, and, bounding backwards, escaped the blow aimed at him with the cudgel.

But in his leap he fell, and lay on top of Ralph Merton.

"After him!" cried the gipsy. "Slit his d——d weasand!"

The fellow darted out.

Warner lay a moment prostrate. As the gipsy seized him by the arm, he leaped to his feet, and in the desperation of the moment, struck him a blow that hurled him back again.

Then, swift as his fear-strained limbs would support him, he fled.

Fled—leaving his associate in guilt to the mercy of those men—leaving behind the booty for which deeds so foul had been done.

Fled—but uncertain whither to flee; the brand of murder streaking his path, the gibbet rising before his sight, and the voice of conscience pursuing him with cries for vengeance.

In the meantime the rest of the gipsies had been hastily packing the spoil. The silver and gold which had cooled they concealed about them, and such articles as were not melted they broke up into fragments and stowed away, displaying remarkable skill and celerity in the process.

Charley—whom excitement at the chance which now appeared of rescuing Dick and making the real criminal suffer had rendered almost delirious—dragged Ralph a little way; when, seeing that he lay either insensible or dead, he left him on the ground and re-entered the hut.

"Are you ready?" he said.

"Werry nigh," returned the gipsy.

"Help me to carry him away."

"Presently, my lad."

"One has gone; but it does not matter now."

"No odds at all, my pippin."

"He will not be long before he is taken."

"Der say."

Every fraction of the plunder being now distributed, they prepared to depart.

But Charley, whose suspicions had been aroused by their answers and conduct, stood in the way.

"The plate," he said; "the evidence of their guilt—you have broken the last of it up."

"Easier to carry. Come on, lads."

"Stay! You do not mean treachery."

"All right, young cheesecutter."

"You are playing me false."

"Shut up, and get out of the road; we want to be off."

"Not with that plate. Oh, fool that I was to trust you!"

"Well, it was rather green; but now, as it's done and can't be helped, why you'd better go home and make the best of it."

"Then do not serve me so. Think of poor Dick. You will be rewarded, I know you will."

"We'll reward ourselves while we've got the chance. You can fetch the kiddies here when we've gone, and take that gen'lman to the pig. Good bye; we're off."

Charley's face became pale with agitation.

"I brought you here," he cried, "that you might aid me to unmask those villains and save my innocent uncle, and now you play me false for the sake of the spoil. By heavens, I will not be done! I will risk my own life to save his, and not one of you shall pass out without you consent to do what is right—unless you murder me."

The bold boy looked quite a hero as he stood in the doorway, his pale face stern in its resolve, and his dauntless heart swelling with brave energy.

At first the gipsies were touched by that spectacle of self-sacrificing heroism, and, pausing, silently regarded him.

Then one, more coarse than the rest, broke out into a derisive laugh.

"Great cry and small wool," he said. "Come, youngster, hook it before we chuck you over."

"I will not move," returned the boy. "I want the evidence to save my uncle."

"Save be d——d. Off with you, or we shall hurt you."

The gipsies, laden with their spoil, advanced to the door. When within a pace of it Charley saw the pistol which Henry Warner had dropped lying near his feet.

He snatched it up and presented it at the foremost.

"I don't want to fire," he said, "but for his sake I will shoot you, unless you accompany me to the magistrates."

"Pshaw! lad, thee be'st brave," one of the gipsies remarked; "but we be going now."

He raised a large cudgel and stepped forward.

"I have warned you," said Charley, and he pulled the trigger.

A taunting laugh saluted him: the pistol was unloaded. Wild at being thus foiled, the boy, with a cry of disappointed rage, leaped back, pulling the door to after him.

Planting his feet against the earthen sides, he held the door, his boyish strength availing to resist the efforts of those whom he had imprisoned within, while he loudly cried for help.

Had assistance been at hand, this *ruse* would have been successful. The gipsies inside battered away with their sticks, and occasionally the blade of a knife was thrust through a crevice.

But the boy nobly held on.

It was still very dark, and a wind was abroad that carried away Charley's voice as he shouted for aid. There were tears in his eyes as he thought of his uncle lying in prison for a crime the penalty of which he would suffer if he were not successful in bringing evidence to fix the guilt on the real criminal.

Though they often pulled the door an inch or so open, they never succeeded in dislodging his feet, and they might have been kept there till aid arrived but for a manoeuvre on their part.

One of them crawled out through the small window, and, shaded by the darkness, crept behind Charley.

"Will nobody come?" cried the boy, in vexation, as he was pulled nearly double in his attempts to resist those inside.

"Here's somebody," the gipsy said, springing upon him and pinioning his arms.

Charley, torn from his hold, grappled instantly with his assailant.

Then the door opened, and the others came forth.

There were scowling, angry faces turned upon him as the gipsies passed out, and many a cudgel was raised threateningly, but the young leader interfered.

"Let him go, Dove," he said to the one who held him; "and come on."

"D——d if I can," returned that worthy; "he's got me so precious tight."

The gipsies laughed.

"Rap his knuckles," said one.

"I don't want to hurt 'ee," the gipsy said, softly, addressing Charley; "but if 'ee don't let go I shall."

"I wont let go," screamed Charley.

"Then I must make 'ee."

"I'll bring the police after you," cried Charley,

kicking and fighting his assailant; "I know where to find you, I do."

Just then, getting his arm free, he struck the gipsy a violent blow in the face.

"G— d— thy knuckles," cried that worthy, "so 'ee knows where to bring 'em, do 'ee? Well for that we'll just shut 'ee up in here, and so keep thy tongue quiet: there's one inside to keep 'ee company, and may be some one will find 'ee out afore 'ee be starved to death."

To thrust the boy in was easier said than accomplished; he resisted furiously, beating his antagonist in the face, and kicking at all who approached.

The most valorous of the party grasped his foot, but was instantly visited with such a kick under the jaw, that he looked round to see if his head had fallen off.

The next got a paster between the two eyes, which nearly flattened his sneezer.

All this time Charley was shouting vigorously for help, but ultimately they proved too much for him.

One of the gipsies put his arm round his neck and stopped his cries; two others seized each a foot.

Being held passive, he was thrust into the hovel.

He jumped up from the floor where they had hurled him and rushed to the door.

The top of a thick stick striking the brave boy in the face, sent him reeling back.

Then the gipsies fastened him in and went away, and Charley was left with the body of the gipsy whom Ralph had shot, while his uncle, for want of that evidence which he could have given, was to take his farewell of hope and die.

The thought was terrible to the noble boy; he clambered up to the window and tried to get out.

But they had too securely fastened it.

Then he shouted wildly, madly.

But his voice died away on the windy air.

He looked out for the atrocious perpetrators of the crime which lay at the door of Richard.

But Ralph was not there.

The gipsies had looked out for him, but he had vanished during the struggle with Charles.

CHAPTER XI.

HOW ROVING ROB LEARNT DICK HIS TRADE.

Sadly enough passed the time with Dick. Neither Mary nor Charles visited him, and the day drew near on which he was to be tried and sentenced.

To die by hanging for another's crime!

The felicity he had experienced from the visit of Mary, and the promise she had made to come to him again, had raised his spirits for a brief while.

But soon they fell again.

Bitter as were his thoughts at the defections of Mary, it was an increase to his misery when the days passed and his faithful nephew made no appearance.

He deemed himself, indeed, deserted, and lost all hope.

Death did not look half so grim, now, to his gloomy mind.

He knew not what occasioned the absence of the devoted Charley, or how, while he blamed him in his heart, the noble boy was fretting his spirits out in the place where he was imprisoned.

The cause of Mary's absence we will presently explain.

Dick had found the gaoler surly enough, despite the appeal of Mary.

He was closely watched, and having once been suspected of an attempt to escape, handcuffs were placed upon him.

The cell in which he was confined was one of the ordinary country gaol kind.

It was neither too strong to resist the skill of a Jack Sheppard, nor too weak to suggest the thought of an outbreak.

Had all who were inside its walls been simple lads like Dick, it would have been sufficient for every purpose of incarceration.

But there was one there who had but little respect for the walls of a London sessions-house, still less for a provincial prison.

This was Roving Rob the pedlar.

It was the boast of that gentleman that no prison was in existence that would keep him inside, if he had his few *leetle* implements.

And in truth he had borne out his assertions by many a substantial proof.

Scarcely a county had he been in in which he had not committed some offence, for which he was courteously ensconced within the walls of its gaol; and never one had held him for his full term yet.

The worthy magistrate had committed an error when he ordered him into prison.

Roving Rob had made up his mind to escape.

And he had also resolved upon setting Dick free.

To accomplish both purposes his skill and ingenuity were already in request. Though he had been thoroughly searched, the sharp-sighted officers had failed to discover his petted instruments, and every night Roving Rob was busily at work in a direction none would have suspected.

His cell was the next one to Dick's.

Of this fact he had carefully assured himself as he went to work.

When the gaoler looked in upon him for the last time that night, he was sulkily crouched in a corner of his narrow cell, his food untasted and hurled over by his side.

"Getting a spell of it," thought the man, as he shut the door and locked it.

A low grunt or growl came indistinctly from within, and the gaoler walked away.

For about ten minutes the solitary occupant of that place was silent.

Then he slightly roused himself, and with a shrug of the shoulders disposed himself as if for a doze.

But directly after his cunning eyes took a survey of his cell, and his ears literally expanded, though his hand was perfectly still.

Roving Rob was listening.

There was no indication of anyone being near. The place was almost suspiciously quiet, and Rob, after sundry grimaces, stretched his long legs out and rose to his feet.

"A helegant apartment this is," he muttered, glancing at the confining walls—"a helegant place, and so werry comfortable; but stigger me, if I haven't had enough of it! Rob, it's time you was out and looking about you!"

He stole to the door, and, bending his long back, again listened.

"It's all serene, and, as I said before, it's time I was out; and so here goes. There's that bloke in the next chamber, I'll make summut of him when I've got him out."

The gaoler ought to have peeped in at that instant. But he didn't.

And so Rob had it all to himself, which was just what that gentleman wanted.

Creeping about so softly, that he would not have crushed an egg had he have stepped on one, he stole to the end of the cell, and put his hand behind the crevice of the wooden bench that formed his bed, chair, and sofa.

First, he drew forth a little instrument something like a long, thin chisel, but with an edge all down the blade, as well as a point; next a sharp, thin file; and finally, a small, sharp knife.

The worthy Rob chuckled as he took each article out.

"There's the gimcracks," he soliloquised—"stigger me if they aint—they aint the best a cove can have; but this angel knows how to use 'em, and blow my buttons if I don't get out with 'em."

Softly Rob; there are many warders in the gaol, and getting out is not so easy as getting in.

But Roving Rob did not stop to philosophise.

He went straight to work.

That is to say, he first placed his large red ear once more in the immediate vicinity of the door; then he took a long survey of it.

And everyone near enough might have heard him mutter—

"That's a good-looking door, but it aint the sort of door I fancy. No, there's summut about it I don't like; so here goes to get it out of the way."

It was of unusual thickness for the door of a county gaol, and was secured by a powerful lock and two heavy bolts.

The attention of Rob was not bestowed on them; he did not seem to mind them in the least.

Strange to say, the hinges gave him more concern; he appeared to have a great curiosity regarding their construction, for he went to work with his slender implements in a manner that showed his determination to get at them.

For about half an hour the little bladed chisel was softly working in and out, first at the top, then at the bottom of the door. And in each case when Rob heard the welcome click, as it grated against iron, a grin passed over his otherwise stolid face.

"Them's allers the weakest places," he said; "and that's the style to get at them."

He placed the first implement in his breast, and now took up the saw-like file.

As he was about to apply it he heard the warder's step.

Like lightning he ran his horny hand over the mutilated parts of the door, so as to rub them smooth and close.

He had worked in such a manner that this was easy to accomplish.

Then he crept back and lay on his bench.

The door opened. Roving Rob was glad he had not yet commenced to file the hinges.

The face of the warder appeared.

"Have you ate your grub?" he asked.

"Go to the devil!" was the reply vouchsafed.

"Do you hear what I ask you?"

"I ain't here to answer your kvestions," growled Rob.

"The governor sent me, I tell you."

"Let him come himself, and be d——d."

"You're a surly cuss. Old Splint will give you a dose to-morrow if you've lost your appetite."

"Get out," growled Rob, "or I'll shie a boot at your nob."

The warder muttered a curse and withdrew. His eyes had, as usual, looked suspiciously round the cell, but had never been raised to the crevice of the door.

"Like my luck," murmured Rob; "they're allers popping in on a cove when he doesn't want 'em."

When the warder had been gone about ten minutes he again slid off the bench, and inserting the thin file in the crevice, worked quietly and gently.

He did not forget to swear when, in spite of his care, a slight scratching noise was made.

"What a cussed fool I was!" he said, suddenly. "In course there's a drop of it left."

Taking off his jacket, he felt along the collar till his fingers touched a slender object concealed inside. It was a thin tube of leather, so sewn in that it bent with the collar, and would have passed for a seam.

Rob worked it out, and found there was just enough oil to lubricate the cutting file.

He made more progress now, and without creating the least distinguishable sound; still it was a tedious work of time, as he was obliged to draw the file so softly along the iron.

But by dint of cutting, prising, and filing, he succeeded in getting the door from one hinge; a repetition of the process had the same effect with the other.

Then Rob put aside his file, and after a few moments' listening, inserted the chisel in the crevice, and began to prise the door.

Very slowly it moved from its place; it was a work of labour now, and Rob's face perspired freely before he had lodged it out the tenth of an inch.

By the time he had got it out to the last fraction the sweat rolled off his features.

He could now take hold of it. Putting away his chisel, he grasped the door, and by a diligent application of skill actually succeeded in drawing it out from locks and bolts.

Roving Rob paused to wipe his face.

"That job's done," he said, and slid the door apart.

In another moment he was outside.

So far the way was cleared, and he now proceeded to hide the proofs of his escape, by re-placing the door in its original position.

This was not accomplished without the exercise of a good deal of anxiety and patience. The door had to be balanced by sheer strength, and it was then necessary to slide it into its place.

It was at length effected, and Roving Rob took a long breath. He would much rather have taken a long draught; but for that comfort he had to wait.

It might have been thought that, having made his way out, he would have no ambition to re-enter a cell; but, strange to say, his first act after he had adjusted the door was to attempt to make his way into the one where Dick was confined.

This was a less difficult task than the getting out of his own. In a very few minutes the lock yielded to the potent magic of his appliances. He drew the bolts back, and opening the cumbrous door, stepped inside.

Dick was sleeping on his hard bench; his arms were folded across his breast, and his manly face was placid, though touched by grief.

Roving Rob was about to close the door of the cell and softly arouse him, when he became conscious of an approaching footstep.

"It's that d——d gaoler," he muttered; "so it is. Now, Rob, you're in a blessed quandary."

The footsteps came nearer. It was quite clear that, whoever it was, was coming that way.

Roving Rob hesitated how to act. If he stepped out, he would be almost certain to be seen; while, if he remained there, discovery was about as imminent, either from the warder discovering the bolts withdrawn, or entering either cell.

It was, indeed, a regular fix; he did not know what to do. The steps came nearer, and he made up his mind.

Drawing his knife, he gently shut the door, and inside the cell, his body elongated against the panels, he remained, awaiting the coming of the gaoler.

The warder's tread resounded along the corridor; he came to the door — paused — and Roving Rob prepared for the struggle of death!

CHAPTER XII.

THE DARK DEED IN THE PARK.

LET us stay a moment, and lift aside the veil of London deeds.

Great cities are notorious for great vices. The great wen — as the metropolis has been called — stands pre-eminent for the multitude and magnitude of its dark crimes.

And for their non-detection.

It is a known fact, that in the dim purlieus and reeking haunts where vice nestles and is bred, deeds of darkness are continually perpetrated—yet are undiscovered.

How many a home deplores its missing member whose fate is shrouded in mystery for ever!

It is a noted fact that thousands of the London population live only by plundering their fellow creatures.

It is a noted fact, that traps are daily laid for

ensnaring guileless young girls, and honest boys, who are sold or educated to the vilest careers.

It is a noted fact, that within a stone's throw of more than one police-station an infamous brothel—the abode of prostitution, secret murder, and every infamy—rears its head.

It is a noted fact, that in the guilt-gardens of our metropolis, where daily and nightly the policeman stalks or lounges on his beat, a young population of both sexes is being trained to the most nefarious enterprises.

Yet, with all this acknowledged, the law is idle.

The blue-coated member of the force yawns againts the lamp-post, cracking nuts or gossiping with questionable characters of the localtty, while deeds awful to contemplate are actually being consummated.

Active interference is repressed, and so our highways and byeways swarm with criminals, and our gaols are fed, and the gallows rears for its victims.

The traveller journeying to the metropolis is pounced upon directly he steps out of the train, if he has been fortunate enough to escape sharps on the way, stylishly-dressed rogues gain upon his confidence, and by artful dodges inveigle him to their haunts, where of course he is speedily made their victim, and is even lucky if he escapes with his life.

A lady—perhaps maiden, perhaps wife—unaccustomed to the streets of London, by some accident finds herself abroad late at night; confused and timid, she hurries along, her fears increased by the absence of any night guardian, and the presence of so many dissolute women and prowling men.

Boys trained to their work tumble up against her from the gutter, and plunder her with dexterous speed—fashionably-dressed pickpockets offer her protection and lighten her of all the young thieves have left; well-dressed villains follow her with their infamous proposals, and if no one is near outrage her with impunity; painted and bedizened girls, shorn of every virtue, jeer at and insult her, and the sleek-toned procuress, ever on the alert for fresh victims, pours her insidious flatteries into her ear, and indeavours by every art to lure her to a life of infamy.

Little children stolen from the nurse, or as they go forth on an errand, are taken to bye alleys and there stripped of their clothes—if girls, basely assaulted by some miscreant in human form—perhaps stifled, and their poor little babies burned in lime to quickly destroy all traces of the crime, or else are taken to the rearing kens, there to be let out by the day to street imposters, or sold to a worse than slavery—happy are those parents who recover their lost children.

Such, faintly touched upon, is London, the pride of cities, in 1863.

Of these crimes and infamies I shall, from the evidence I have collected, give a passing view, unfolding to the reader's gaze some of the scenes of terror which hourly occur at his very elbow.

Eleven o'clock had chimed from Big Ben of Westminster; the night was fine, and though the lights were being rapidly put out and the shops shut up, the streets were far from dark.

As the hour turned, a tall, elderly gentleman descended the steps of one of the fashionable hells not many yards from Jermyn-street.

Pausing a moment when on the last step, he raised his glance to the sky, and then, with a satisfied expression on his face, turned quickly to the right, and made his way towards Pall Mall.

No sooner had he gone than a second individual—a singularly handsome, military-looking man—issued forth and followed him.

At the Guards' Memorial—the spot where Mr. Pilkington, M.P., was garotted—the first gentleman again paused, and seemed to be hesitating whether or not to call a cab.

Ultimately he decided not to do so, and, crossing Pall Mall, walked leisurely towards the Duke of York's Monument.

When just past the Athenæum Club-house, a woman, who was squatting on the kerbstone, put out her lean arm, and, in a plaintive voice, begged some assistance.

At first the gentleman did not heed her, but on her repeating her querulous request and rising before him, he sharply bade her begone.

The sound of his voice threw the wretched creature into a state of excitement. Starting after him, as she passed she uttered a faint exclamation, and, placing herself before him, looked hard in his face.

"My God!" she cried, hoarsely; "like this we meet. Oh, Henry, this is a terrible thing!"

There was a strange, wild pathos in her words: her eyes, sunken in her attenuated features, shone with a feverish glare, and she followed him up when he recoiled from her outstretched arms.

No wonder he recoiled. She was one mass of huddled tatters, her looks were starved, her frame lean—a hollow-eyed spectre, indeed, to come suddenly in the path of the honourable gentleman.

The military-looking personage who had dogged him now paused to await the issue of this strange rencontre.

At first staggered, the tall individual now found his speech.

"I know you not, woman," he said. "If you beg charity, here is a shilling for you."

Strange to record, the famished woman, who had clamoured savagely for alms, now refused the proffered coin.

"Henry," she said, "would you deny me after all you have done. Look at the thing you have made me, and ask your conscience whether you are treating me right."

The soldier on duty at the top of the steps paused to look at that energetic woman, in her squalor, placing herself on equality with a gentleman, but continued his tread when he spoke.

"Woman, you are deranged! Take this, and get out of my path."

He flung the shilling at her feet.

Then was seen a change in that starved, poverty-stricken creature. Her eyes flashed wildly, and, with her gaunt arm raised from its rags, she cried—

"Wretch that I am, you have made me so and now deny me. Had you given me but a kind word it would have been enough. Curse you! You have spurned me, but mark my words, I will be as great a curse to you as you have been to me. Wherever you go I will follow, and the world shall know who I am."

Her impetuosity intimidated him. He seemed to know her threats were not idle, for his eyes shone with a murderous light, and his muttered words were ground between his teeth.

His position was growing more unpleasant. Her words had attracted one or two passers-by, and there was every prospect of a crowd gathering.

Gathering strength from the increasing number, the woman, uplifting her finger, was about to commence another harangue, when the gentleman grasped her by the arm, and took her a little aside.

"All I can do for you I will," he said sternly; "but let us have no scene here."

"Cab, sir?" said a voice, ere the woman could reply.

A cab had drawn up to the spot.

"In," said the gentleman. "I will go with you."

She hurried into the vehicle, and the gentleman stepped in after her. The cab drove off, and the gaping wonder-mongers were left to gossip on the singular event.

Two minutes after a second cab drove away.

The military-looking gentleman was inside.

The first vehicle, with its singularly unmatched occupants, was driven at a moderate rate along towards Charing Cross.

For the first few moments neither of them uttered

a word. The gentleman, with a peculiarly spiteful look, sat gnashing his teeth and malevolently regarding the woman, whose gaze was fixed on the floor of the cab.

She ventured, after a time, to look up.

"You are angry," she said.

"Oh, no."

He showed his teeth as he spoke.

"Forgive me," muttered the wretched woman. "I have been driven mad. Oh, Henry, you know not what I have suffered!"

Nor did he wish to.

"But my trials are now over."

"They are."

"You must feel disgust, loathing, at looking on me in my wretchedness; but you shall soon see me different."

"I will."

"It was kind of you to take me in here with you."

"Come here."

His tones were harsh, but gladly she bent towards him.

The murderous look in his eye grew stronger.

"Bend your head down; we must speak low."

She lowered her head, that he might whisper. They were seated opposite to each other; her head was brought forward, her hand rested on his knee.

"How cold you must have been with only this scanty shawl!" he said.

"I was cold," she murmured.

"I will buy you another," he resumed, beginning to unfasten it.

The wretched woman thanked him.

"Let me secure it," he exclaimed, taking the ends.

One end he held in each hand. The miserable creature raised her head a little.

"I knew you would prove kind."

"I will."

"I have but few wants."

"You shall have less."

His hands, still holding each an end of the tattered shawl, were drawn crosswise. She was looking him in the face, when, with a sudden wrench, he twisted the shawl round her neck.

Gasping and terrified, yet not believing the truth, she put up her hands and clutched at the tightening shawl. But he pulled it tighter and tighter, till the unhappy woman fell off her seat.

Then he arose, that he might use more power. She knew he was in earnest then, and began to struggle for life. All the while her eyes were turned upon him with a sad, piteous look, and her thin fingers were tearing at the scarf as it strangled her.

On, on, along the Strand, past houses where there were gay revellers indulging their mirth and their appetites—on, past vigilant policemen and straggling wayfarers—on, on, with the street-lamps shining in upon them, went the cab, while silently that deed was being enacted.

The cabman heard no noise. Muffled up, and intent upon his coming fare, he paid no heed to what might be occurring within.

And so, without interference, the well-clothed miscreant completed his hellish work, pausing only when the eyes had ceased to start, the fingers had ceased to clutch, and the small, ill-shod feet to kick amongst the straw at the bottom of the vehicle.

He relinquished then his hold, and still and staring his victim lay at his feet.

As he stood exultant in his triumph, a cab rolled swiftly by; it had a single occupant, who leaning out of the window, looked into the first vehicle. The assassin did not see this, but in a few moments he stopped the vehicle and stepped out.

"Don't get down," he said, as the driver was about to alight: "here is your fare, drive the lady to Old Ford, Bow, she will tell you where."

The driver touched his hat.

A sovereign had been dropped into his palm.

The assassin hurried away.

"How queer he do look to be sure," soliloquised cabby, as he drove on, "but then it aint no wonder not every gent could stand sich a scene as he was mixed up in."

Not, indeed; but the driver little knew what that scene was.

He whipped his jaded horse to a trot, and out of sight he went with his throttled fare.

Back came the second cab; the military-looking gentleman got out, paid the driver, and walked after the first gentleman.

"There's something in the wind," said the cabman, turning the half-sovereign which he had received over in his palm; "it does'nt always shower gold, even in this haristocratic place."

And driving to the Red Lion, he got off his box and turned in for a glass.

The cowardly assassin walked briskly towards the spot where he had first encountered the unfortunate woman. He was deadly pale, and staggered when he saw the glance of the policeman turned towards him.

The soldier was standing by his sentry-box; it gave him a turn, when, as he was passing, the man stepped suddenly out.

He reeled down the steps, very fortunately without stumbling to the ground.

Keeping quietly on his track, came the handsome, military-looking gentleman.

By the time the other had descended the steps, and proceeded a little way across St. James's Park, he recovered his spirits. The dastardly deed wore off in its impression, and his step became lighter as he sallied along.

He did not keep in the frequented path, but crossing the grass, kept towards the palace. He was passing a clump of trees which our readers may have noticed, about forty yards from the Mall, when he heard a quick step behind him.

The memory of his recent deed, with its concomitant punishment, came again upon him. The pale face of his unhappy victim haunted his view. He could only imagine that, if he were followed, it was for that, and the cold perspiration began to ooze down his features.

He had not the moral courage to look back. On he kept, and was only arrested when a cloaked figure stood by his side.

It was the moustached, military-looking gentleman.

"A strange direction you are journeying," he remarked, with a cold, dry laugh that made the other shudder—"a dull path. What, if I may ask, brings the elegant Fitzhume here in the dews of night?"

Ghastly pale the assassin turned; he appeared to have an instinctive horror of that careless-looking gentleman—a horror inspired by other things besides the fear of his having seen and followed him after the silent deed of murder.

In point of fact, he dreaded his companionship.

"Why so fast?" the military-looking gentleman asked. "Stay, my friend; let us have a little conversation before we proceed farther."

"Not here. Another place."

"Nay, this will suit us as well. Ah, Fitzhume, you won largely to-night."

"A trifle towards getting back my own," returned he, hurrying on.

"By Jove! you cleared the room. I tell you what: we have made up our minds to have revenge on you for winning so immensely."

"You mistake; I have not won much."

"Ah! old fellow, you seem to have had a loss. By the way, what the deuce did that miserable wretch of a woman want of you?"

"I know not. I—I——"

"You took her off; but where the devil did you stow her?"

Fitzhume trembled in every limb.

His friend suddenly let his hand fall on his shoulder.

"Look here, my friend: you did the thing slap up."

"Did what?"

"Why, the business—choked her off—squared accounts."

"I do—a—not know what you mean."

"Why, the cab job."

"The cab?"

"The cab. Don't look so vacant."

"Vacant?"

"Yes, my boy. I saw you."

Fitzhume reeled and supported himself against a tree. Every trace of colour had left his features.

His very animation seemed frozen. The other, with a mocking smile on his lips, a cruel look in his fine dark eye, coldly regarded him.

"What—mean—you?" gasped the murderer.

"Oh, stuff. Fifty! What's the use of trying the angel; it's of no avail, I assure you. I saw the job: you managed it well, I can tell you."

"Lost! lost!" muttered the guilty wretch.

No. 5.

"No such a thing; the gagged cat was nothing to me. It was your business, not mine; only that, for old acquaintance' sake, I will take the liberty of borrowing just half of that snug little lot of cash you have about you."

"Let us leave this place; elsewhere we may converse."

"Oh no, this will do. Come, tip."

"I cannot; you ask outrageously. I have not much about me."

"Pshaw! You won about eight thousand to-night, all of which, in notes and gold, you have about you. Now, four thousand cool will hush up this little affair; otherwise, dearly as I prize you, I shall have to testify to that disagreeable deed which will bring you to the gallows."

Fitzhume grew paler, if possible.

"Come," said the other, "let us settle the bargain."

"Is it on condition that what you have hinted at is never spoken of?"

"Of course."

"I will lend you a thousand—not more."

"Four."

"I cannot."

"Indeed!"

"I will not."

"Oh! Well, now, as you have refused my offer, I will not make it again. But Fitzhume, you know, I am a man of my word; allow me to tell you that, unless the *whole* of the money you won from Kans is handed up, I will give you to the charge of a gentleman who will know how to take care of you."

The wretched delinquent gasped and looked round in alarm. He knew he was in the power of that elegant reprobate; yet, with the infatuation of a wrecked man, he could not bring himself to yield what he had so lately won.

"It would ruin me," he muttered; "there are debts which I must meet to-morrow. I dare not show myself unprepared."

"And for that reason you cheated everbody you played with to-night, myself included."

"Ah!"

"Never mind; are you willing to accede to the terms?"

"I have before said I cannot."

"Very well."

The military gentleman drew a pistol.

"Now, listen, friend. I was willing to make conditions; you have refused. I have long had a score or two to settle with you; I shall now do it."

"You would not do murder!"

"Why, seeing that you are not so very particular, there is no reason why I should be. I have just taken a lesson out of your book."

He calmly placed the pistol on full cock. Instinctively the other started back.

"You cannot mean this," he said, in a hoarse whisper.

"My dear fellow, I am just about to send a bullet through your skull; when that is done, I shall take your money and leave you here."

"But you dare not. The report of the pistol would bring aid."

"Oh! I will take care of that."

He raised the pistol, and laid the barrel against the ear of the other.

"Help! Major, you are mad! Come, we will share."

"Too late."

"I will give all—all. Do not put so rash an intent into practice."

"On second thought, my good fellow, I have changed my mind."

"You will agree to terms?"

"Oh, no. I mean I will not give you to the police."

"You mean it?"

"Yes. You see, I should not then get any of the hard cash for which alone I should sell you."

"True, true."

"And so, you see, distressing as it is to my feelings, and must, I have no doubt, be to yours, I am compelled to avenge that wretched woman by shooting you through the skull."

Fitzhume stood rooted to the spot. He could neither speak nor move, and only gazed with stupid, staring eyes into the face of the man who menaced him with death.

But when he saw his finger upon the trigger he raised his arms, and trying to push him off, supplicated mercy.

Even as the half-gasping, imploring appeal came from his lips, the military man pressed the trigger.

Fitzhume had put up his hands: the ball going clean through the right palm, entered his forehead; he fell without a cry, and the deliberate assassin calmly bending over him, proceeded to rifle his pockets.

There peeped out at that moment from behind the trees a human face, which was visible for a few moments, and then vanished. The assassin was expert in his work: almost before the sharp report of the pistol had died away, he had plundered his victim of all his property, and stepped hastily away.

But first he had placed the pistol in such a manner that it would seem that the unhappy man had committed suicide.

As he was crossing the wall he encountered a policeman, whom the noise of firearms had attracted.

"Have you seen anything unusual, sir?" he asked, respectfully.

"Nothing. You allude to the shot?"

"Yes, sir."

"Oh, it's nothing; the keeper often uses his gun at night."

This was a fact, and the policeman saluting him, went on his way.

Up the steps went the assassin; the sentry looked rather hard at him, and two or three people came hurrying to the spot.

None of these heeded the fashionable murderer, who in less than ten minutes after was in his club, the plunder in his pocket, which he had taken from that assassinated man, whom he had left lying upon the dewy grass, with a bullet in his skull.

We have seen one phase of night life. There will now be shown one more transcendent in its infamy and merciless wrong.

And one, unfortunately, not unknown at the present time.

CHAPTER XIII.

THE ICE-SHOP AND CAFE.

"£100 REWARD.

"On the 8th instant, near the hour of twelve p.m., a young married lady alighted from a Waterloo omnibus, at Regent-circus, and has since been MISSING. She was fashionably dressed, and had a gold watch and a sum of money about her. It is supposed that she was inveigled away for some improper purpose. The above reward will be given to any person who will render information that may lead to her recovery, or the elucidation of her fate."

In the second column of the *Times*, this advertisement shone conspicuous for about three weeks. Always the same, it seemed the daily, hopeless repetition of a heart's wish.

What we now relate will give some solution to the mystery.

Ye who have lost sisters or daughters, bethink you if their fate may not have been similar.

Twelve o'clock struck, and the Waterloo omnibus stopped at Regent-circus to put down and take up passengers.

"Five minutes before time," said the conductor, as he nodded to the policeman, and, leaping on his perch, gave a knock with his strap on the back of the omnibus, as a signal that it might proceed on its way.

Amongst those who got out was a lady, neatly and fashionably dressed, and somewhat closely veiled.

She paid her fare, and hurrying to the pavement, looked eagerly round with the air of a person who expected somebody to meet her at that place.

After looking anxiously in every direction, she crossed over to the other corner, where Regent-street commences.

Here, as before, she looked quickly about her.

Though her features were veiled, it was easy to see that she was young and ladylike. Her movements were light and graceful; and, when her gaze wandered up and down the street, two dark eyes flashed from inside the veil.

At this spot—the nucleus of fashionable vice, where the showily-attired and jewelled wanton awaits the chance of selling herself for gold to the first bidder, and where congregate the *roué*, the gambler, the pickpocket, the denizens and *habitués* of the Haymarket, St. James's, and Leicester-square, and their environs—a youthful and unprotected lady was certain not to escape observation.

Her anxious movements were perceived, and their cause guessed; and, regarding her as one against whom their villany might be directed, several "swells" crossed over to where she stood.

The first who reached her side was the very being who had done that dark deed in the silent park. He softly addressed her. Turning quickly — perhaps thinking it was the one for whom she waited—she moved abruptly away when she saw by whom she was accosted.

Not deterred by a manner to which he was accustomed, the professional profligate followed, still breathing into her ear his persuasive speeches.

Two others, who saw the way in which she avoided him, thought there was a capital opportunity for acting the gallant, and, stepping swiftly past, they presently turned and confronted her and her persecutor.

Each taking a different side, both bowed at the same moment, and offered an arm.

"You are being intruded upon by this fellow," said one.

"Suffer me to escort you safely, madam," the other exclaimed.

Bewildered by the strangeness of her situation, and experiencing all sorts of fears, the lady, declining the offer of each, kept on her way, and made no reply.

This emboldened them, and they again spoke.

This time she answered.

"If you are gentlemen, you will not insult me further."

Though the voice was low and tremulous, there was a dignity in the tones that made the debauched gallants feel some confusion. But as they still continued their addresses, the lady, seeing a policeman at the opposite corner, re-crossed, and took up her position near him.

The three ruffs then left her, though they still kept her in sight.

The lady began to grow vexed as the time passed and the expected one made no appearance. The lateness of the hour was in itself a source of anxiety, rendered more disturbing from the scenes she was witness to, and the conversations she heard around her.

Gaudy women, excited by drink, were quarrelling and using horrible language, in the midst of which a band of Ethiopians struck up, the two attractions collecting a crowd, in which the pickpockets found a fructive field.

Then an *emeute* occurred, caused by two roughs hustling a gentleman. The lady began to have enough of such scenes of depravity, and after one more searching glance round, she walked towards Coventry-street.

In a few moments she perceived that she was followed by two of her former persecutors, one of whom was the individual whose hand had so recently been raised against the life of a fellow creature.

Hoping to avoid them, and again make her way to the Circus, she turned down the first turning, and, hurrying her pace, made, as she thought, her way out towards her former place of watching.

Though she seemed to have given her unwished-for followers the slip, she was not unexposed to the temptations and insults she had before been subjected to. More than once she was encountered by a half-intoxicated rake, whose unblushing proposals made her cheeks blanch, as she shuddered and hastened by.

Once a "gentleman" caught her suddenly in his arms, and would have outraged her in the most shameful manner, had she not broken away from him.

There were not only men whom she met; young, beautiful girls, some of them mere children, with their golden tresses falling down their backs, their breasts exposed in a manner that was shocking to the virtuous mind, passed with some heedless, care-defying jest.

"Oh, God!" murmured the lady, "are these the scenes of London life? Can it be possible that men can be found so infamous as to take advantage of the frailty of these children?"

If she had entertained any greater doubt, it would soon have been set at rest. She saw these young girls, with their lewd smiles and indelicate language, accosted and led away by those whose sensuality was pandered to by this trafic in the virtue of fair children.

The lady hurried on; her heart ached to see such depravity. She had passed up many streets, and crossed in various directions, but each time she seemed to be led farther from the place whither she wished to go. In some trepidation, she darted down a short turning, and experienced great relief when she saw a blaze of light at the end.

Arrived there, she was surprised to find herself in a wide street with one or two *cafés* yet open, but which was not, as she could perceive, near the Circus.

The lamps of a large public were still alight; the shutters were up, but the door was open.

A glimpse could be obtained of the brilliant bar, at which, although it was closing time, a number of people of both sexes were drinking. The drunken hubbub that came from inside, the vulgar language of women, and maudlin debating bickerings of men, saluted the ears of the lonely lady.

She breathed a sigh, and passed on.

Now she stopped to look up and down the street, and ascertain if possible where she was and how she could emerge from a locality that appeared given to the glaring saturnalia of vice. There was no one to whom she could with confidence apply to direct her on her way; whichever way she looked, none met her gaze but those whom she shuddered to speak to.

The lights flashed from the crystal fronts of the *cafés* and divans—the haunts of wicked abandonment, which, like Dead Sea apples, had so fair an exterior, yet were so foul within. A pieman, with his can of savoury pies, stood at the corner of an alley, and glanced at the lady as she turned wearily this way and that.

A grizzly-faced old beggar, soliciting a penny, thrust his filthy hand before her.

She dropped the silver coin she held in her hand, and turned loathingly away.

Three ill-looking fellows, who had been holding a low conversation with the pieman, came stumbling towards her, their looks sinister, their aspect murderous.

The young wife—for such she was—found her strength and presence of mind leaving her. She knew not how to get out of their way, and felt that their intention was to assail and plunder her.

Her alarm increased as they came nearer. There was no one to whom she could appeal for protection—no house where she might seek shelter and direction.

The three men had got within a few yards of her, and she was hesitating whether to cross the road or turn back, when, on looking across, she saw a young girl standing at the door of an ice-shop and *café*, and after beckoning to her, trip lightly across to where she was.

With palpitating heart, the lost lady waited for her to come.

She was a sprucely-dressed, smart-looking young girl, not more than sixteen or seventeen. Her face was ingenuous and pleasing: the only thing fast or gay about her was her hair, which was thrown back off her forehead, and fell over her shoulders in unconfined ringlets; and a large brooch, with a photographic likeness of a dissipated-looking swell, was stuck at her breast—the latter, perhaps, a little too much exposed by the open frill of her dress.

Pausing when she reached the kerbstone, she

looked innocently in the face of the lady, and in girlish tones addressed her.

"If you please, ma'am, there is a lady in our house who wishes particularly to see you."

"A lady?"

"Yes, she was insulted just now by some low fellow, and came into the shop for protection; she fainted away as soon as she got inside, and was just coming to when she saw you, and asked me to run over and ask you to come in."

"Did she tell you her name?"

"I never thought of asking. She said, 'there's a lady I know,' when you came by, so I thought you might know who it was."

This was said so ingenuously, that the young wife could have no suspicion of anything wrong; she wondered who it could be that knew her, and glanced at the *cafe* as if to satisfy herself of the nature of the place before she trusted herself within it.

This hesitation was observed by the girl, who readily guessing the cause, said—

"If you do not like to come till I have asked her name, I will run across while you stay here."

The lady looked around: the three men had stopped when the girl first addressed her, and were now eyeing her with anything but assuring looks. From them she looked into the face of the girl; there could be nothing she thought wrong in going over, it would protect her from the men, and she might fall in with some dear friend.

The three brutal-looking fellows now came swaggering forward.

"I will come with you," the lady said in alarm.

The girl stepped into the road, and the young wife followed her across to the shop of French ices.

CHAPTER XIV.

A DEED OF MYSTERY.

The *cafe* was one blaze of light as far as the window was concerned. Plate-glasses were let in at the sides, and these threw back the glittering lustre that shone from the crystal fittings and ornaments.

Inside the shop there were narrow mirrors, let in from the ceiling to the panels; the paper was white and gold, and in the centre of each piece embellished with a pictorial representation of some slightly indelicate subject—being chiefly copies of the best works of old painters.

A marble counter ran nearly the whole length of the place, terminating in a bend that made a side counter, on which were fruits and confectionery.

At the extremity was a little parlour, screened by a thin partition, but the interior of which could be seen.

Behind the marble counter, with his back to the shelves, on which were placed ices, sherries, and aerated drinks, was a man, whose appearance was likely to attract attention.

He was a foreigner, and seemed to be about five and forty years of age; his hair, of jet black, was was closely cropped, and polished down with pomade or cosmetique; his chin was shaved, but a thick, scrubby moustache was on his upper lip; his face was round, full, and flabby, and entirely colourless: it might have been simply unprepossessing but for his nose, one side of which was jammed up, or eaten away by some corrosive agent.

There were three small scars on his right cheek, and one in the centre of his forehead.

Before him were the cups and glasses, in which he dispensed coffee, chocolate, and ices; and when the lady entered he was stirring round a large vessel of iced cream.

On the right-hand side a man of insignificant aspect was seated on a form beside a little girl, whom he was treating to an ice. The child's face was pale, and she looked excited; and when the waiting-maid conducted the lady in the man was seen in a flurried manner, to withdraw his hands from the child's frock, while the individual behind the counter looked on with a coarse grin.

Regarding the lady-like traveller with a supercilious glance, he bestowed a meaning look on her conductress; the young wife, too agitated to take note of circumstances, turned to her guide when she failed to see the lady spoken of.

"In the parlour, please," said the waiting-maid, in answer to her unspoken inquiry.

Scarcely assured, yet hardly knowing how to act, she followed her into the parlour. It was a small place, only dimly lighted, and the lady paused at the threshold.

"She's gone inside there, ma'am," the girl said, pointing to a green baize-door on the right. "It's more quiet and private, which this room is not."

Irresolutely the fair traveller stepped forward. The girl's manner and movements were so natural, that she was disarmed of all suspicion. Inwardly resolving to go no farther if the lady were not in that room, she followed the waiting-maid, who, pushing open the green baize-door, said—

"There is the lady, ma'am."

She could catch a partial glimpse of a well-dressed woman sitting inside. She entered, and the waiting-maid, with a meek curtsey, shut the door, retiring to the shop.

The person who had been sitting inside now rose, and, with a bland smile, addressed the young lady.

She was a middle-aged person with flushed heavy features and big teeth, which she displayed whenever she spoke; a few dark ringlets hung stiff on each side of her face, and her bosom, of enormous breadth and fullness, was revealed by her low-necked dress of satin brocade.

Heavy rings were on her short, dumpty fingers, heavy golden ear-rings depended from her thick ears, and a cumbrous gold neck-chain reached from her neck to her waist.

Resting her gloved hand on the velvet-backed chair, the fair stranger regarded this elegant person with a clear glance, and spoke.

"I fear there is some mistake. The maid told me a lady wished to see me. There is an error: I will go."

More blandly smiling, the woman answered her—

"It is all right, my dear; sit down. It was I who wished to see you."

"But I have not the pleasure of knowing you."

"You soon shall have, my dear. Take off your bonnet and mantle. The maid will bring in some refreshment. You must be dreadfully fatigued. I will help you to disrobe."

"Madam," said the young wife, repelling her, "I perceive I am not the person; and I therefore beg of you to show me the way out."

"So I will, my dear, but not yet."

"At once I must desire to be let hence."

"Certainly, love; but there is no occasion for haste."

"There is occasion. I did wrong to enter; my husband will be waiting for me."

"Oh, your husband; he will be glad to see you, no doubt. Let me know where he is likely to be found, and I will send to fetch him here."

"My husband," the wife replied, with dignity, "would not enter such a place; nor would I have him see me here."

"Perhaps you had better not, my dear; so now let us sit down: I want to have a little conversation with you——"

"I insist upon departing instantly."

The young wife moved to the door. A smile passed over the coarse features of the woman.

"Oh, you insist, do you? Well, my dear, I suppose you must go if you will, but I am only sorry for you. Your face is very beautiful, and you have a form that would be valuable in——"

"Madam, you insult me. I am not used to such

language; if I am detained here long, my screams shall bring assistance."

Boldly as she spoke, her heart gave no echo to her words; she was in deadly fear, and her face was blanched, as the thought of evil crept over her.

The woman's manner, the nature of the locality, the partial glimpse she had obtained into the character of the house, all tended to increase her alarm.

She knew not for what vile purpose she might have been brought there.

The woman smiled again when she placed her hand on the handle of the lock and tried to open the door. A thrill of fear coursed through her when she found it fast.

"Be pleased to open the door," she said; "I desire to go."

"So you shall, my dear, but not that way; this is the door to go by."

She indicated, by a jerk of her thumb, a painted door at the other end of the room.

"I will go this way, if you please; it is the way I came."

"Yes, my dear: but you would not wish to go through the shop; at this hour it is sure to be full of low characters. Here, Joseph—Spider—show this lady out."

She pressed her hand on a small bell. Immediately after, the door opened, and two men entered.

At the first sight of their faces the young wife shrank back. There was something so repulsive, so brutal in their looks, that it was impossible not to feel a terror at their presence; besides which, the entrapped wife recognised in them two of the men whose approach had terrified her in the street.

The woman, grinning vaguely, appeared to enjoy her terror. She laughed outright when the young lady, pulling at the door, screamed for help.

"Show the dear lady out," she said.

"All right, mum; we'll do it in a jiffey. Come along, young doman—this is the way."

"I will not go," cried the lady. "Help! help!"

"You've come to the right place for that sort of thing—ain't she, Ben?"

"She are."

The two wretches unceremoniously laid their hands on the unfortunate lady. Deprived of speech by the very terror of their contact, she could only look gasping up in their faces, and cling to the door.

But they wrenched her hands away, and dragged her across the room.

"O, God!" she murmured, "must I be the victim of these wretches? Help! help!"

"Come along, come along. He's waiting, and its all ready."

"I beseech you, let me go."

"Pull her along, Ben. Here, old woman, lend us a hand; she's as obstinate as a pig."

The woman joined her efforts to theirs. In the struggle the lady's veil was torn off, revealing a face youthful and beautiful, though now pale and agonised.

"Strike me dead," exclaimed one of the ruffians, "if she ain't the right sort!"

Conscious now that some terrible villany was meditated, the young wife, resisting with all her strength, rent the air with her screams; but the only answer to her cries were the brutal laughs of the wretches as they pulled her across the floor.

Great as was their strength, it was no easy matter for them to drag her away: her hold was tenacious when she could seize anything, and her resistance was exerted to the utmost.

The remorseless manner in which they used her tore her clothing into tatters; her face, still deadly pale, was now set to firm resolution, and her dark, flashing eyes shone with sparkling lustre. Even in her distress she looked supremely beautiful.

They had now got her as far as the door; it had been pulled-to when the men entered, and one of them kicked it open with his foot.

Its partial opening enabled the kidnapped victim to see within.

A woman takes in a whole view at a glance. It was so with the unhappy lady; in the momentary look that she cast into the room she was enabled to see almost all over it.

It was well illumined, and her eyes beheld something that caused her the acutest agony and the deadliest terror; for no sooner had she taken that glance than she closed her eyes shudderingly, and loudly shrieking, cried—

"Not there! Oh, heavens! let me die. Do not take me there!"

"Drag her in, Spider."

An exertion of their strength lifted her off her feet, and thust her half in; but still she clung to the doorway, shrieking for mercy, and closing her eyes as fast as they opened and looked into the dreadful secrets of that room.

Mercilessly they tore her hands away, and, with coarse violence, forced her into the room. The stout woman entered after her, and the door was closed.

The door was fastened, but it did not shut out all sounds—the screams and cries of that hapless lady came ringing through the chamber, and the barbarous responses of the wretches who made her their victim came coarsely on the air.

Silence now: not a sound—not even the feeblest muttering. Have they accomplished their infernal purpose? or has she swooned?

Hark! Heavenly Father, what a shriek! It echoes through and through the place, ascending to the roof, and seeming to make the very walls, strong as they are, vibrate.

It dies away: then come murmured appeals and heart-broken sobs.

Another shriek of unearthly wildness: shrill and agonising it rings through the place. Have those wretches nothing of human nature left in them, that they can hear and still continue in their infamy?

Quiet again; then the pleading voice of the young wife.

"Oh, mercy, mercy! Take my watch and rings, my money—take my life; but not that—not that!"

The coarse tones of the men, the bland accents of that woman-fiend, and the sound of a refined masculine voice came in reply.

There could then be heard the sounds of violent struggling, during which the unfortunate kidnapped being's cries grew fainter and fainter. The struggling ceased, and the shrieks of anguish almost died away.

But they rose suddenly, more shrill and violent—rising at regular intervals and sinking to a feeble gasp; and in accompaniment came a horrid switching sound, as if soft human flesh was being hacked and frightfully macerated.

There was no noise of scuffling now—no brutal responses of coarse men, or scoffing laughs; the only sounds that came were the still violent screams of that helpless victim, and that awful grinding, crushing hiss, falling at regular intervals.

The cries of the young wife ceased—her sobs were hushed; but that appalling and mysterious macerating still continued.

In time that, too, subsided, and an ominous silence reigned.

And all this time the husband, who had arrived an instant after his young wife had departed, was standing at the corner of the Circus, a prey to the most harrowing emotions as the time passed and the expected one made no appearance.

But who were those miscreants who inveigled her into their power?

What frightful deed had they perpetrated in that shut-up room?

And what scenes were imprisoned there, the sight of which had thrown the young wife into such wild deliriums of agony?

CHAPTER XV.

ROVING ROB AND THE WARDER.

FOR awhile we will go back again to the prison where we left Roving Rob and Dick — the former gentleman inside Dick's cell awaiting the coming of the warder. He was leaning against the wall, his slouching wideawake stuck knowingly on the side of his head, and his dark eye, to use his own expression, retreating round the corner.

Dick was lying on the bench in a troubled sleep, his face downwards, and his arms folded on his breast.

The warder's steps echoed along the stone passage, and finally paused, as Rob supposed, at the door of the cell he had just quitted.

"He's been an' gone an' done it," muttered Roving Rob. "O lauks! if anyone could honly see his blessed face, when he puts his ugly mug inside the door and finds out what I've been doing, it would be a hintyresting treat never before seen, as they says of the dancing halligator and the tumbling elephant. There—there he goes, like the unfortynite gemman what puts his head out of a blessed barloon and comes a-tumbling down arter it all through the hair. There he ar', he ar' inside now; blessed if I don't step out, as the young chicken said to the shell, and see what he ar' up to all this while in that unhinhabited cell of mine, which is as empty as the chicken's shell afore alluded to."

The peregrinating intentions of Roving Rob were, however, put a stop to, by the warder's footsteps again echoing in the passage.

"He's a-coming slow-like a precious lokymotive, steam up, and the whistle on. Lauks! only fancy when he pokes his nob in here—won't he see a sight, like the boy that fell through a winder, they'll let his heart slib up in his mouth, and put his nut where it didn't ought to be. Hush! here he comes. How sound that 'ere young man do sleep. Hark at him, all a-blowing and a-growing like flowers what they sells four pots a shilling when they haven't got any roots, and is seen at the winder at night and the werry next morning is as withered as a dried-up cabbage, what's been on a stall in Oxford-street—wish I was there now—and got shrivelled up with the sun and the smoke."

The soliloquy of Rob was put an end to by the the warder, evidently in a nervous manner, fumbling at the door of the cell. Rob, however, found time to say—

"Blessed if it ain't all up now, as the hostler says when he gives Dobbin a fig. Here goes to tumble on his unsuspecting nob when he comes a-grinning like a cat with her whiskers singed or a dog with his tail chopped off."

The warder opened the door suddenly and hastily stepped in.

He was astounded to see Dick lying on the bench asleep.

He was astounded to see the devil-may-care face of Roving Rob turned knowingly towards him.

In fact, this conglomeration of unexpected incidents so took him aback, that he stood half-way in the cell and half-way out, unable in any way to act or speak.

It is impossible to conjecture how long he might have stood gaping at the pedlar had not that worthy accelerated his movements by hitting the half which was in the cell, and which happened to be the head, a terrific spanker, which sent him up against the wall of the cell.

Here, aghast, he leaned for a moment, when Roving Rob took him by the collar, and, dragging him out of the way, shut the door.

"Oh, you needn't speak," he began, in his singsong chaunt; "I knows what you was a-going to say as well as if you'd been jawing for the last half-hour. You're in a precious fix, like the kid as tumbled atween the steamer and the pier, an' got jammed till nothing of him was taken out but his boots, acos the rest of him was made a pancake. Now, only stand still, as the old doman said to the train, when she cotched hold of the buffer, an' tried to get inside—an' I'll sing you a little story as you haven't heard since in this blessed place you've been."

While delivering himself of this, he had pinned the warder up against the wall, and, having jerked his knuckles into his throat till he was almost strangled, quietly proceeded to gag and pinion him.

"There you are now, all trussed an' ready for the biling, like a tender chicken. You've made a bite this time, as the urchin said to the cove what was a-fishing on a bough, with a long rod in his hand which broke and chucked him into the water, where a little, curly-tongued dog, with long whiskers and a short tail, fixes his teeth into a part of his person which allers goes under the name of tender."

The warder found it impossible to make any resistance.

Roving Rob had a method of dealing which effectually put to flight all ideas of delivering himself, and he was quickly at the mercy of his captor, who thrust him coolly in the corner of the cell, and, giving him a placing kick, advanced to Dick.

All this time the young fellow had slept—not soundly, but in a fitful, drowsy slumber.

Roving Rob seemed as much astounded at the fact of his sleeping while such proceedings were going on in the cell as the warder was at the treatment he had been the recipient of.

"What a deal of halteration I shall have to make in him," he soliloquised. "To think of all this rub-a-dub being kicked up in his cell, and he to sleep as coolly as if he was a blessed hinfant in his mother's arms. Wake up—wake up! as the bosen says to the sailor-boy, when he tries gentle means of getting him out of his roost—which gentle means consists of wiping him over the mug with a rope's end, and a-shoving a tar-brush in his mouth."

Dick opened his eyes.

"I have been sleeping," he said, confusedly.

"Well, you 'ave a-been doing summut of the sort."

"But—but—where the d——"

"That's just what the oyster said, when he tumbled out of his shell and fell into Mr. Muggins's mouth."

"But be this prison, and you here?"

"Well, if yer don't believe yer blessed hies, jest go an' knock yer precious nob agin them bars over the way; and when you've done that, go an' ax that gemman what's a-sitting up in the corner like a Chinese poodle, and a-looking as if he'd swallowed a fish and found the hook in his belly."

By this time Dick had fully aroused himself, and now gazed alternately at the warder and Rob.

"You have escaped?" he said, inquiringly.

"Not a blessed bit of it, or I wouldn't be here for you to look at, like the mouse what met the cat when he was taking his walk through the grub cupboard."

"You were a prisoner, like myself?"

"Why, so I wor; but that ain't neither here nor there. I ar' walked out of my shell, like the tortoise that went to look for his tail, which, unbeknown to him, a monkey had sawed off with a cheese-cutter. And here I ar', a-waiting to take you out of this blessed hole."

"To take me?"

"Lawks! yes. And—bless us alive!—you needn't stick your mug out like that, as the cove at the soup-kitchen said to the kid when he wanted a second dose. But come along, for the door of your blessed crib ar' slap-bang open; and them doors as isn't, why here am a chee-ild that ar' used to that sort of thing, he ar', and will open 'em like the sun do mussels on a hot day, when they sticks 'em all on a heap to sell ha'porths at a time, and fardenworths at no time."

Dick leaped wildly from his seat. The hope of freedom made his eyes flash, and his first impulse was to rush towards the door. But on the next instant a new thought struck him, and he sat himself down again, and leaned his head upon his hands.

"Well," exclaimed Rob, who, in mute surprise, had watched both movements, "if that ain't as rummy a way to act when the door's open and nobody's got the key, may I be blowed! Which was yer going to do—run yer blessed nob agin the door, or see if yer'd got use in yer feet, when yer tried that precious run, and jumped back agin as if you'd run your hie agin a red-hot poker?"

"I be mad," cried Dick. "Yet why should I try to get out? There be no one to care for I now Mary be gone. She promised to come again, but I know I shall not see her."

Roving Rob spun round several times on his heel.

"Well, if you ain't the rummiest cove I ever comed a-long of! Allers a-thinking of that gal, as if there worn't nobody else in the blessed world—not even yerself, that's a precious sight better nor such as she."

"She promised," began Dick.

"An' what are promises, 'cept, as they says, like egg-shells and heads, to be broke whenever there's a hopportunity. Come along, as the bluebottle said to the apple-woman. We'll be out of here in a jiffey."

"Thank'ee, noa. I won't run away: I'll stay here and die."

"What? Oh, my hies, what a blessed flat you must be! Stay here in this place of small dimen—shi—ons when there's a big place like London, where you may walk about as if yer was on Tom Tiddler's ground, a-picking up gold and silver! Only mind the peelers don't spy yer little game. Come here, I are all a-going, like a thimble that's took a walk out of a gemman's pocket into the mawleys of a prig; an' all I wants of you ar' just to step out along of me."

"If I run away *she* will think I am guilty. No; I'll stay."

"What! Oh, bless my grandmother's sister's aunt's cat's eyes! Stay here and be scragged up by the blessed neck, and left a-dangling in the air like clothes what they hangs out to dry from a pole at a back-garret winder!"

"Ay, if it maun be so."

"And leave yer pretty Mary for them 'nobs' to nob on to, and no one to nobble on to their nobs. When they gets her, they will do as they likes with her, an' send her back agin in a peculiar sittivation, when you'll be singing like the potboy what left his gal, an' found her in a peculiar way, an' goes about a-singing—

"'Cries he, vy did I stray,
For to leave my pots and tray,
Ven my Sally—so they say—
Is got in a most pe—cu—ly—ar vay,
Ven I listed vid a corperul
Werry much agin my my—ind:
Then, vot made me for to come to go
To leave my Sal behind.'

"Which is what yer'll go about singing. But what ar' I up to. I shall be a-fetching all the knowing blokes here if they hears my musical voice. Come on, if yer a-coming, an' don't keep a gemman waiting, as Bill the garotter sez, when he waits behind the stalker to put the hug on."

"I will come," cried Dick, suddenly—"I will, an' thank'ee. I will be sure of Mister Ralph, if they pull me to pieces after."

"That's the style. Oh, sort 'em out—sort 'em out at your own price this time! Here we are—here we are! Now, once more round. Everybody wins—no, the old man's chance this time, which is the way they chisels little boys—little hinnercent chucks what's got a holiday and a penny to spend. Walk up—walk up! Just in time to see the live hellifant swallow his keeper an' go through his hevilooshuns arter. Come on—come on; it's getting time we must mizzle, or we shall have all the kiddies of the place drawn up to do us honour when we steps out, and a-grinning like a lot of dried monkeys when they sees our little game ar' stopped."

Muttering this with great volubility, he, in a most wonderful manner, as it seemed to the astonished Dick, opened his hand-cuffs and set free his hands.

"That be a blessing," said Dick, straining his wrists to give circulation to the blood; "and if once I get my fingers in Ralph's throat—G——d——him! but I will make he suffer for it."

"So you shall, my tulip," cried Roving Rob; and taking Dick by the hand, he pulled him to the door, which he opened and passed out, giving the warder a parting kick ere he closed the door upon him.

Outside the cell Roving Rob displayed more caution and less celerity: he advanced on tiptoe, making Dick keep behind him, but never relinquishing his hand till he had conducted him down the steps and into the warders' lobby.

"It ar' my opinion, it ar'," he muttered to Dick, "that there is a gemman or two muzzing themselves with summut stronger than shandy guff over there; keep close arter me while I investigates."

The result of Rob's investigation was that he retreated quickly, dragging Dick after him into a room which fortunately was without an occupant.

"It is as I thought," he said; "four on 'em is a doing a sweat over a dose of swill that would do your throat good to get only the perfoom of."

"What can be done?" asked Dick.

"I ar' just reasoning that kvestion. Oh, there um the wery identical things. Come along arter me, an' when I steps forrard just don't you lag behind."

There were two beds in the room, evidently the sleeping apartment of the warders. Rob, who never seemed lost for devices, turned his wideawake up till the crown assumed an awful peak; he then put his hand up the chimney, and having rubbed the soot into the hollow of his face till it looked at a distance like a skull, he stuck his hair out at each side of his ears, and took two sheets and a pillow-case off the bed.

The two sheets he folded toga-like about his form.

The pillow-case he formed into a conical cap, and stuck above the peak of his wideawake.

As if Fortune were ever at hand to favour his practices, an unfortunate Tom-cat stalked into the room at that moment, and was returning with a melancholy mew on seeing the spectral figure of Rob, when that worthy with a pounce seized him by the neck and tied him in front of his body.

Having arranged the sheets so that only the black head of puss, with the glaring eyes, was visible, while the paws were at liberty to scramble underneath, Roving Rob, who by this time was as grave as a sexton, sallied forth, Dick following.

The appearance of Roving Rob was literally appalling—even Dick was startled a little; but the pedlar seemed to think there was nothing out of the way, as, with his grimmest look, he prepared to face the warders.

These gentlemen were cosily discussing the affairs of State over strong gin-and-water when the frightful apparition of Roving Rob came stalking in their sight.

Valorous and resolute when ordinary dangers threatened, the warders — four men with hearts of iron and sinews of a bear: men to whom the throat of a prisoner was so much stuff, to be squeezed in their strong clutch if he proved refractory — lost their courage as the silent spectre made its sudden appearance.

The glasses that were being raised to their lips were placed down untasted, and in dumb terror they stared at the ghostly intruder.

It must be borne in mind that the era of ghosts produced at will had not then arrived: to ordinary mortals, a spectre was a thing of dread, who walked abroad with horrible intent.

Professor Pepper had not assailed the prevailing idea, nor had Dircke looked daggers at the moving spectre from behind the scenes.

So it must not be taken as signs of cowardice if the warders, who were equal to any flesh-and-blood encounter, were dismayed at the startling apparition which came, grim and awful, to drag them to their doom.

Roving Rob, behind whom stealthily came Dick, paused when within about six yards of the warders. Raising his ghostly shroud in the approved fashion, till both arms reared above his white-peaked head, he gave vent to a dismal cry.

The black cat, struggling to get free, gave to the white folds of his drapery the most alarming motions —at the same time that his two yellow eyes glared wildly forth, and he howled as only a frenzied Tom-cat can howl.

The warders, who had rose to their feet, retreated slowly, with bending knees and hair stuck on end.

When a few paces off, the bravest one, who was farthest from the spectre, stopped.

"Wha—what is it?" he said, with chattering teeth; "let us not run—a—aw—away."

"No," said another; "it's no use being frightened."

Here Roving Rob waved his arm, and the Tom-cat howled frightfully.

They might have withstood the sheeted figure and its hollow moans, but the two fierce eyes staring from its waist, and the awful cries of Tom, were too much to endure; and Roving Rob had just begun an oration in his most ghostly tone, when the whole body of warders precipitately fled.

"Oh, lawks! Oh lawks!" cried Roving Rob, when they had all vanished. "Did you ever see such a sight in all your blessed days? I think we've scared every mother's son of them, and now we'll be off and mizzle by that ar' winder afore they comes to an' stops our little game."

The window being fastened from the inside, was not very difficult to unfasten. Roving Rob helped Dick through, and himself prepared to follow.

At this juncture, the most stout-hearted of the warders, returning to take a courageous peep, saw the hind-quarters of the ghost disappearing through the window.

While he was shaking all over, and marvelling on the circumstance, Roving Rob, having released the Tom-cat, put him through into the lobby.

Poor puss, terrified out of his life, made a dreadful scramble along the stones, and the warder, seeing something black and shadowy leaping towards him, flew back with such haste as to throw the rest of the warders into a cellar at the top of which they were standing.

While they were sprawling over one another, each imagining he was collared by the ghost, an outcry was heard from above that brought them all to their senses.

It was the cry of the warder with whom Roving Rob had so unceremoniously dealt, and who, having got his mouth freed from the gag, was yelling out the fact of the escape.

The pedlar and Dick heard the noise, and made the best of their way from so dangerous a vicinity.

But ere they had proceeded far, the alarm-bell rang, and unmistakeable sounds of pursuit came from their rear.

"Slope!" cried Rob, urging Dick forward, and stuffing the sheets and pillow-case inside his jacket. "There's a pretty kettle of fish a-biling. We'd better make ourselves invisible."

CHAPTER XVI.

WHAT BEFEL MARY.

It is time we saw what became of Mary after her meeting with Warner, which had resulted in her not again visiting Dick in prison.

By his specious arguments, he had so led her to believe in her sweetheart's guilt that she had been readily imposed upon to meet him on the following night, there to hear what he had to say before he left for London, whither he said important business called him.

The night following that one on which they had been disturbed during the process of melting the parson's plate was the one appointed for their interview. This, as we have seen, he had communicated to Ralph, whose dark mind had been laden with a plan of the basest wickedness.

His intention was to kill Warner, and possess himself of Mary.

In the former attempt he had been thwarted by the opportune arrival of the gipsies, but the idea had not been abandoned after the disastrous incidents of that night.

Each, after hurrying from the hut by the side of the hill, had fled home. Neither met on the following day. Warner cared not for stirring abroad, and Ralph was busy with his own dark schemes.

By nightfall these were prepared.

He knew the hour and place appointed for the meeting with Mary, and was aware that Warner would have a chaise prepared to carry her off.

Accordingly he resolved to waylay Mary before she reached the trysting place, and carry her off.

After getting her into a place of security, he intended, either with or without her consent, accomplishing his designs upon her virtue.

It was twelve o'clock, and Mary, whose conscience more than once reproached her for her broken faith to Dick, crept from her home, and hastened towards the place of assignation.

She had not entirely lost her love for Dick, but the evidence and the asseverations of Warner had caused her to look with suspicion on his protestations of innocence.

Then, too, there was a contrast between the homely manners of Dick and the flattering air of the well-dressed, fashionable swell who had supplanted him.

Mary was but a woman, and with a woman's faults.

The belief in Dick's innocence once dispelled, the rest was tolerably easy: it remained only for Warner to protest his undying love for her to accomplish what he had so well begun.

Tripping sadly across the fields, she found the tears starting to her eyes as she thought of Dick's probable doom.

She had loved him once, and could not bear to think of him dying on the scaffold.

While she was again reproaching herself for the part she had played, the moon threw the dark shadow of a tall, gaunt figure before her path.

She started, and, looking up, saw the spectre of woman's fears — Witch Wykeman, the grave-haunter.

Scared at the uncomely apparition, Mary shrank back; but the witch, stepping across her path, fixed her weird gaze upon her, silently regarding her for a few moments.

Then she uttered her unearthly shrill laugh, and pointing her skinny finger at the trembling girl, cried, scoffingly—

"Ho, ho! There she walks to her ruin; fair she was, but now is false and soon shall be foul, yet go: witch Wykeman crosses only the path of the *doomed*."

She laughed again her peculiar shrill laugh, and striding from the path, disappeared in the gloom.

But even after she had become lost to Mary's view did she hear her taunting, hollow laugh.

So alarmed was Mary by her words and manner, that she remained petrified in the position where the graveyard-witch had first beheld her.

"I have been guilty," she murmured, when at length she started from her rigid posture, "but I will sin no more; I will return at once."

The words were hardly uttered, when a soft step came behind her, and then Warner appeared.

He looked as scared as she, and doubtless from the

same cause, but his first act was to take her hand and respectfully raise it to his lips.

Poor Mary, she was half subdued by that delicate act.

"I am indeed happy at this meeting," he said, "though I doubted not your promise, still I feared something might intervene to foil my joy."

"Hush! release me, I dare not stay! Oh, but Warner, I have had a dreadful warning, I dare not stay here, I cannot listen as I said I would. I must return and atone for what heedless sins I have already commited."

"Return and leave me! Ah, Mary, if you knew how deeply I loved you, you would not speak like that; do not madden me by talking of returning when I have looked forward to this night with delirious joy as the one that should give me the dear possession of yourself."

The same old tale, told so often amidst enticing blandishments by lying lips, and received by too-trusting ears.

It came to Mary as the freshness of truth; she thought not of the wiles of deceit; and scarcely resisted when he drew her to his breast and pressed his lips to hers.

"Dear Mary, my own," he murmured, "all is prepared for our flight to London; by morning we shall be there, when holy bonds shall bind us together for evermore."

"I cannot—dare not come! My heart reproaches me when I think of poor Richard.

"A murderer!" said Warner, though the word came strangely, and he trembled when he spoke. "Would you leave me for him? Come, Mary dearest, I will be all to you if you will love me."

Poor trusting heart and misled mind! She was won over by his words, and suffered him to press her closer and closer in an embrace which her maiden modesty told her was too fervent to be permitted.

They were in this loving clasp—his lips against her burning cheek, his arm round her supple waist, his breast strained to hers—when two figures stole

No. 6.

towards them, but paused when that vision met their gaze.

One of the twain became terribly excited. It was only the strong control of his companion that kept him back, and finally drew him aside to where they could watch without being perceived.

While they crouched there, a third figure came creeping on, stealing towards the pair who stood in their close embrace by the screening trees.

As this figure came gliding by, his face was seen. It was Ralph.

He was creeping towards his unsuspecting prey. Warner and Mary now moved slowly on; he still held his arm round her waist, and was pouring his insidious flatteries in her ear as he led her towards the spot where his chaise was waiting.

And after them crawled Ralph Merton.

He had a loaded pistol in his hand, which he raised once or twice, but without discharging it.

He was afraid of the noise of the report bringing people to the scene.

So he continued his snake-like progress till he had got behind Warner, when he raised the pistol to strike him on the head with the butt.

But he was doomed for a second time to be foiled. Ere his arm fell, the two who had before hid out of the way were upon him; each seized an arm and held him back, while he was instantly dispossessed of his weapon.

Turning sharply round, he found himself held by Roving Rob and Dick.

CHAPTER XVII.

AN UNEXPECTED MEETING.

"Thumps following thumps, and blows succeeding blows,
 Swell the black eye and crush the bleeding nose;
Beneath the ponderous strokes the jawbone cracks,
 And the cheeks ring with the redoubled thwacks."

So silently had all this occurred that the pair in front were totally unconscious of the proximity or intentions of the villanous Ralph.

They passed out of sight and hearing, while Dick and the pedlar coolly drew him back without speaking a word.

Ralph had turned ghastly; he thought when he was first clutched that he was being arrested for the murder, and his dismay was not much lessened when he saw in whose hold he was.

There was something peculiarly unpleasant in the look of Dick's eye.

"I've got 'ee," Dick said, dragging him from Roving Rob — "I've got 'ee, Mister Ralph. They shut I up int' stone place yon, but I have got out to find 'ee."

"Be good enough to take your infernal clodhopping hand off me," said Ralph, a little recovering his assurance, though still deadly pale.

At the same time he tried to break away.

"Oh, no, Mister Ralph; I ha' got thee, and, darm thee soul, I wunn let 'ee go till we've squared up accounts. Thee got me into parson's house with thy lying tongue, and got me shut up to die like a dog after thee had done the murder; but I ha' got out; I ha' got out; and I ha' gotten thee."

The vengeful manner in which he thrust his knuckles into the jugular of the squire's son was a convincer to that gentleman that he was not to be trifled with. Still he tried to play off his best.

"End this farce," he said, savagely. "I am not in the humour to waste time with you. Take my advice, and make off before you are lodged again in gaol."

"Oh, no; I don't fear gaol now, nor hanging. I will have my pitch out of you. I care not then how soon they take me. There go two more, Mister Ralph, that you've undone. What he's come to be your doing; and then you'd try to kill him in the dark, though he be your friend. Oh, but thee be a bad-'un. I tell 'ee my fingers itch to drag thy liver out. I'll have—"

"Fool, let go; I will summon aid. Away, while you can."

"A Brummagem toy, dickey outside and a duffer in. Why, tain't worth the carrying, as the man said of the helifant."

Such were Roving Rob's observations as he turned over Ralph's watch, of which he had quietly possessed himself.

"A more goniwyer article this ar', sound and serviceable." This was to Ralph's pistol, which he had picked up. "There's a stone inside his gullett, too. One, two, three, and a pop."

He thrust the weapon against the temple of Ralph.

"Now, my pippin," he said, "this gemman's just going to have a quiet set-to along of yer; and I am going to see that he pays you well; an' if you squeal or show any tantrums, like the donkey that smelt the pepper out of the jar, why bang goes this in a jiffey through your nob."

"I would deal wi' him only one way," said Dick. "He swore away my life; I would take his. Give me the pistol. If he has another, we will see who is to leave alive."

"What! Now none of that game, as the squire said to the poacher. It won't wash. Give him a pistol, if you like, but no popping. He'el hang soon enough, like one in a blessed bunch of ingeuns, an' they'd only swear you murdered him. Come gemman, time's up. Walk round and show your muscle. Go it Dick—at it Sam. One for the peeper this time; slap on the canister—rattle his ivory-box. Here we are! here we are! going at it like six drunken washerwomen on a Saturday night. Walk up. Here you will see the moon made of green cheese, and the halygator what weighed fifty stone in his scales, and when they told him to wait laughed till his blessed criminy tail fell off."

"Mister Ralph," said Dick, "it be a right thing what I be going to do. Thee have brought it on."

"You would not murder me."

Ralph broke out in a cold sweat.

"No, I'll not murder thee; but I'll make 'ee so as thy bones shall ache for a month, and nobody shall know thee when they look at thy face."

And with that he stepped back to take aim at his face.

Ralph would have shirked the combat, but Roving Rob stood suspiciously near with his loaded pistol. He, therefore, put himself in an attitude, and calling his best science to his aid, met the attack of the young countryman.

Though not blessed with the skill of an accomplished pugilist, Dick knew how to deliver a straight-handed blow, and he went at his work with a steadfast vigour that put Ralph nowhere.

That is to say he might often have been seen going to grass as if struck by lightning.

At each of these well-dealt floorers, Roving Rob leapt round and round, flourishing the pistol over his head and performing the strangest of antics; and then, after about ten minutes of hard fighting, during which the mazzard of Ralph received blow upon blow till it became one puffed, discoloured mass, he saw Dick, by a straight one from the shoulder, send Ralph at least four yards, and stretch him on the turf; he crowed like a cock, and came and patted his man vigorously on the shoulder.

"Stunning!" he cried. "I'll train you for the champion's belt. Come on; you've given him enough, as the old sow said to the man that was pouring the wash into the little pig's tub; he'll pick himself up afore morning."

As much by force as persuasion, he guided the young countryman away, and Ralph Merton, justly punished, lay groaning on the earth.

While this was going on, Warner had taken Mary out into the road where his chaise stood.

More than once the young girl paused and hung back, her conscience reproaching her and impelling her to retire while she was safe; but each time the persuasions of Warner succeeded, and it ended only in a fervid caress.

By a turn in the hedge the chaise was waiting; it was a one-horse affair, the very model of smartness and speed.

The sight of the vehicle waiting to convey her away renewed an influence on Mary the reverse of what Warner had intended: she became suddenly faint and giddy, and fell back.

Warner's arms tightened around her.

"Come, dearest one," he said; "a few more moments and we shall be speeding to London and happiness."

"I cannot go—oh, heaven, I cannot!"

"Oh, Mary, you do not love me!"

"Not love you? Have I not proved different?"

"You have; yet now, when only this is wanting, you falter and turn from me."

"No, indeed; but I fear I don't know what."

How often on the brink of wrong have those words been said.

Little did Warner care for her feelings, so that he accomplished what he heartlessly sought—the ruin of the pretty-faced young girl.

They were in this position—he passionately kissing her lips, she nestling timidly yet closely to his breast—when Dick and his friend again caught sight of them.

Roving Rob surveyed the pair with that cool, business eye of his, but Dick started violently, and appeared about to leap upon them and slay them as they stood together.

All unconscious of their nearness, Warner continued his addresses.

"Why should you fear?" he said. "You do not mistrust me?"

"No, no," replied Mary, looking confidingly up in his face.

"Then why have doubts? Be kind as ever, Mary: let me take you hence; say you will be mine for ever—my wife, never more to love another!"

"I will be yours," cried Mary; "you cannot mean deceit—my fears are foolish."

"Then you are mine?"

"For ever!"

"Aye, for ever fallen!" said a voice well known to each of them; "for ever ruined, poor, foolish Mary!"

They looked up, Warner with a start, Mary with a scream.

Dick was standing before them.

CHAPTER XV.

THE LAST APPEAL.

THERE was sadness mingled with anger on the face of Dick. Roving Rob seated himself on the milestone, and placidly regarded them.

Warner shook, and became white as death, while Mary, trembling like the aspen, clung to his arm.

"Ah, poor lost one!" said Dick, "thee wor happy enough before thee mind wor turned, but now thou art like my sister, too easily won by flattery and falsehood."

Here Warner, recovering a little of his hardihood, ventured to look the young fellow in the face.

But his eye sank before Dick's steady gaze.

"These are strong expressions, sir," Warner said, "especially for one who has made his way by force out of gaol."

"I want nought to say to you," interposed Dick, "until I have spoken to Mary here. I ha' more than words for you unless she bid me go."

He turned to Mary.

"Mary, lass, there was a time when Dick didn't want to ask you to leave another and come to him; you've played a wide game of fast and loose, but I haven't come to reproach you for it, though you did leave me up there to gnaw the walls."

Mary hung her head, and said nothing.

"You think I did the murder, eh? That be wrong, indeed. I know who did the deed, and so does that scamp that be holding thee so close to his loathed breast. Oh, Mary, once had Dick seen ye like that he would have killed you and himself! But now he's cast you off he'll have nought to do with you unless you could prove you'd never done amiss, and would leave that bad man that only means you harm, never again to speak to him."

"Indeed!" said Mary, coldly, though she yet trembled. "I never yet stooped to give account of my actions."

"No, lass, but thee will stoop to worse nor that unless honest Dick helps you out of it. Look at me, Mary; do I look like the thing you thought me? do I look like a murderer?"

"Innocent men," said Warner, "don't generally break out of gaol."

"Ah, Dick," interposed Mary, "would I could think you never did that deed; for our past affection I should rejoice, though my word is given to another."

"Given," cried Dick, hoarsely; "it was not yours to give—'twas mine unless I gave it back to you. You have stole away the troth you vowed to me and given it to him, but mind you, Mary, it will be a bitter gift—he, with his fine cloth and jewels——"

"All Brummagem, mock, and not worth a tanner," interrupted Rob, after a casual glance at the articles.

"He, as I told thee, means you harm. I did love thee once; Mary, if it be not too late, turn back. I don't ask thee for myself—innocent though I be, I may yet be hanged; but come away from that black villain."

"Do not heed him, Mary," said Warner; "this is but the bravado of an escaped felon; you may judge of him when I tell you that yonder with him is one of the greatest rogues in London."

"Why, that's personal," cried Roving Rob, getting down from his perch. "Why, you half-made, ill-looking, wall-eyed scaramouch! Hold him back some of you while I jump on him. Say that again only just, and see if I don't make tea-leaves of you."

He flourished his fists before Warner's face in a manner that made him wince and retreat.

Even as he sidled back, Mary kept with him; Dick saw this, and it nettled him to the quick.

"I be going now, Mary," he said, "but first I will make this last appeal. I know thee art young, and was once true-hearted; let me tell you that he that you're clinging to is more the murderer than I. Remember it, for if you turn from me now, you will find its truth when it be too late. There'll be a day, lass, when it will all come out. Will you leave him or me? Take your choice, lass; Dick, as thee knows, is too proud to take thee against thy will, only he wants to save you, he leaves you to choose —take him or me, but, oh, Mary, think that ruin may be before you if you go with a stranger!"

For a moment Mary made a movement as if she would have flown to Dick's breast; but Warner held her hand, and she lingered yet.

Dick spoke again.

"These be open arms, Mary, if thee will come. Time be up; take your choice now."

"Yes, that's the cheese," cried Rob, coming forward. "Allers make your choice when you've got a chance—them's my maxims. Take 'em home and dry 'em, stick yer fork in and try 'em; here you are, yer can't go by 'em, but every blessed man Jack of a mother's son of yer can come and buy 'em. All hot! all hot!—smoking hot! Here you are, sir. Another pinch of salt, yer young scaramouch, for the gemman with the pepper-box for a nose; and make the butter-knife warm there, so that it won't take up too much butter."

Warner looked superciliously at the odd-speaking pedlar, while Mary glanced sadly at him, and sighed to think that Dick should have such disreputable company.

As she saw his gaze turned towards her, as if imploring a reply, and found that her tongue would not give utterance to her words, she drew yet closer to the hypocritical Warner.

That was her answer, and Dick read it.

"Go thy ways, Mary," he said. "Thee has chosen to enter the wrong path. Dick will have done with you; he'll never plead again. No—his heart may break, but he will remember your choice."

He turned to Warner.

"You who have beguiled her from her troth, beware. I have threatened you before. Be sure Dick will keep his word if you play the villain to the poor, misled lass."

"I will answer you, fellow, when you have answered for that crime for which you were sent to trial."

"And you shall answer me. Never fear, Lunnon mister, but the day will come when the rope will go round the right neck."

"Tum, tum, tum—fee, fo, fum—round it spins! Take your turns at the wheel, my lads. Everyone's sure to win when they doesn't lose. Make way, you scamps, for that young gemman with the silliver threepenny-bit in his pocket, that he's going to win with out of the wheel of fortin. Look here, yer spectacle-nosed, straight-haired, tallow-faced whelp, and be d——d to yer! Roving Rob will set his mark upon yer; and if ever he stalks across yer little game, why, slap-dab and thimble-scales, but he'll swop yer, so he will."

Roving Rob finished with a flourish, and jerked his face before that of Warner. The latter drew Mary back.

The next moment a joyful cry was heard, and the boy Charley bounded over the hedge.

He was by Dick's side in an instant, kissing his hand and pressing his face to his arm.

"I have found you, Dick," he cried. "Glad enough am I to see you out of that dreadful hole."

"I thought there was one left who hadn't deserted me."

"Deserted you? No, Dick. They shut me up by the hill because I tried to get the evidence of Mister Ralph's guilt. I saw them, Dick, melting his plate, but the gipsies that I brought to help me shut me inside; but I tore away the woodwork with my teeth till I got my way out."

"Faithful Charley."

"But you must not stay here. I heard them coming after you from prison; they will drag you back, and all for a deed Ralph and the other did."

At this moment catching sight of Warner, he sprang towards him, as having lifted Mary into the chaise, he was about to follow.

"That be one," he exclaimed; "he and squire's son did the deed; stop him till the constables come."

Dick bounded forward, but Warner was already in the vehicle. Snatching up the reins he applied the whip to the horse, and dashed off as Dick laid his hand on the hind part of the conveyance.

The sudden jerk took it from Dick's hold, and directly after the horse and chaise were careering down the lane.

Roving Rob's voice was now heard.

"Stand out of the way all you little wretches what harn't got no mammies and no ha'pence, while I takes a pop with this ar' hinstrument. Here you are, pull away, pull away, the bull's-eye every time —every time you doesn't miss it; pop bang, now for the church-steeple."

Bang went his pistol which he had pointed at Warner.

Mary screamed, and fell forward.

The horse stopped a moment, then plunged madly on.

Warner, white as a sheet, was seen bending over Mary as the vehicle dashed out of sight.

Dick would have started after them, but Rob held him back.

"'Taint no sort of use walking arter them; they'll be seven miles on the road afore yer get breath. So you must make yourself easy, as the nettles said to the skinned cat. Hallo, lilli—fol—long—tong! look at that; blessed if there ain't the old precious biling on 'em come from the house!"

"What house?" asked Dick.

"That caboose as we just left without paying the landlady," returned Rob gravely. "Sheer off my nipper, or you'll get it warm. Look out there; I'm coming in amongst you, as the cannon-ball said just as it left the gun."

"No, stop there; murder, reward, catch them!"

Such were the breathless shouts of a whole bevy of faint constables as they came blundering over the hedge.

"Dick," said Rob, "we've been here long enough, as the mice said when they found their way into church."

"I shall not attempt to escape," returned Dick, moodily.

"Oh, you won't—won't you? Well, then, shiver me! I'll just show you how I'll serve you."

Without more ado, he suddenly seized Dick, and giving him what is called a "cross-buttock," gently trotted away with him, Charles keeping by his side.

The constables, catching sight of the party, now separated, to take them by different routes.

This was what tacticians would call a division of strength, and as such did not escape the knowing eye of Rob.

He prepared to take advantage of it.

"Let me down," said Dick, when they had got a little way.

"Ready to oblige you, as the bailiff said to the tenant, when he turned him out. Only promise that you won't let them blokes set their clappers on yer, and I lets you off like the horse did its rider."

"I promise," Dick said.

Roving Rob quietly, and without the least exertion, deposited him under a hedge.

"Now, then," he said, "this is the way; the end hasn't come yet. Just sneak along by that hedge, and keep arter me."

By one leap Rob was across the hedge, and making towards the three advancing constables.

Rushing at full speed into their midst, he brought up against one, whom he swept off his feet after the manner in which a skittler takes off a pin.

They rolled to the ground, and instantly collared one another.

"I've got you," cried the officer, holding on by his collar.

"That's just what the fish said when it swallowed the worm with a hook in its belly," said Rob, rising and dragging his man with him. "Oh, would you ride rusty, eh, in kicking, you brute! I'll hold you till they comes."

"Hold *me!*" exclaimed the astonished officer.

"The very son of a gun! Haven't I had all this run after you, you sweep, ever since them constables called out to me to stop you?"

"It's a mistake," said the constable, to whom the person of the pedlar was unknown. "We're after an escaped prisoner."

"Two escaped prisoners."

"Then, by the cow's iron tail, ye'll have them, for there's one given me the slip, and the other's skulking over there by the big tree."

Off darted the constables in their search; and Roving Rob, giving a peculiar knowing chuckle, continued his way.

He was soon joined by Dick and Charley, whom he led at a brisk pace over the fields.

"Keep under here," he said, when they had reached a spot where an excavation was being made. "If yer lie quiet, I'll put every man Jack of yer in a rig afore we start that no one will find yer out in, and that yer won't know yerselves in till you gets to London."

Dick and Charley threw themselves down; but at that moment a distant shout told them that they had been again seen by the constables, and were being closely pursued.

CHAPTER XIX.

THE BOOZING KEN.

WE will take the reader to London over the border, that portion of the metropolis where vice, crime, and destitution engender and flourish.

It was growing towards dusk; the alleys, courts, and dens of the straggling districts of Spitalfields and Whitechapel were pouring forth their straggling denizens whose evening's work was yet to come.

The itinerant musician, the gaudy or tattered unfortunate, the thief, the beggar, the burglar jostled the passers-by of the broad thoroughfare of Shoreditch and Bishopsgate as they emerged from the narrow gaps that led to the labyrinth of smoke-dried, reeking habitations, where foul women, amidst dirt and stench, stand with pinched-faced, colourless babes at their breast — babes to be reared in the garden of guilt, and trained step by step to the full-blown criminal.

Unheeding the motley crowd, let us single out one individual whom the reader has seen before — the low, ruffianly-looking fellow who had aided in the outrage committed on that unhappy lady whom they had inveigled to that terrible unknown doom.

Passing along Leman-street, this man emerged into the Whitechapel-road, and pausing a moment to exchange a coarse greeting with another of about his own stamp, crossed the roadway, and directed his steps towards Brick-lane.

At the corner he encountered a woman, showily clad, and highly powdered and painted. She wore a fashionable skirt, with a crinoline beneath sufficiently ample and elevated to disclose at every step a pair of well-moulded ankles, and half-way up to the knee of a very pretty leg.

A turban hat with sweeping feather was set daintily above a profusion of glossy ringlets.

At the first glance she seemed the fascinating, attractive, lively girl, whose charms would have allured strict morality from its sternness; a second glance, however, showed that the cheeks to which the *rouge* lent such bloom and roundness were sunken and wasted, and the brilliancy of the dark eyes was the momentary result of immodest excitement.

On coming suddenly in front of the brutal-looking ruffian, she stopped and accosted him.

"What, Jem!"

"Holloa! Ratcliffe Sal, what's your game?"

"I've just left Undertaker Joe he's queer."

"That last job turned him up."

Ratcliffe Sal laughed.

"It was almost too much for him, and he ain't got a very delicate stomach."

"Not werry," returned the ruffian, with a grin. "Ah, that bloke never thought what was up when he poked his beak in there. It was a go though, I can tell you."

Even through her paint and powder the young girl became pale.

"There's been a 'nose' down in Tiger Bay," * she said.

"Smelt anything out?"

"Not likely; but I'm afraid it's getting warm."

"Oh! it's all right; are you going up to Mother Rawlings's?"

"Not I; I had enough last time. I shan't go there in a hurry."

A close observer might have seen that she shuddered.

"Haymarket?" asked Jem, after a pause.

"Yes."

"You'll see me about twelve; if you get any nob in tow I'll have a cab ready."

---

* A notorious locality near Ratcliffe Highway.

"Very well."

"Got the stuff serene?"

"Yes."

"The hankercher?"

"Everything's right."

"That's the hammer; it was d——d awkward the other night. Well, I'm off; tol-lol."

"Tol-lol," returned the young girl, and they separated, she to continue her course westward, while he made his way leisurely up Brick-lane.

Turning down a narrow street, Crusher Jem, as he was called, whistling a common tune, passed through several small, dim alleys, till he reached one, where a little way up stood a dingy, tottering house, begrimed from roof to basement, and having its windows curtained by thick festoons of dirt.

By the basement there was an iron grating, beneath which could be seen a window dirty as the rest, but guarded by stout iron bars, and having a discoloured Holland blind on the inside.

There was something peculiar about this blind, though the material was frayed and torn here and there in rents, nothing could be seen within, and even at night, when the room might be supposed to be lighted up, no glimmer came from the crevices.

Besides this, it hung with a certain amount of stiffness, not enough to excite notice, but which once observed would have been sufficient to excite suspicion.

The ruffian walked across the grating, tapping his foot lightly on the middle of the centre bar; he then leaned up against the doorway, and looked up and down the dim aperture.

In a few moments the door was opened, though no one appeared.

Crusher Jem put his hand inside and made some mysterious movement of the lock, which accomplished, he stepped into the passage.

No one was there, and he shut the door, and having bolted it, descended a flight of dark, rickety stairs.

At the bottom a boy appeared, to whom he spoke a few words in a gruff tone, and passing along the passage, entered a room, the door of which was slightly ajar.

Before he reached it he was aware by the sound of voices that came forth that it was tenanted; a blaze of light, too, shone from the opening.

The room was well lighted up by means of gas; it had something of the aspect of a low coffee-room in a squalid neighbourhood.

Each side there were compartments with tables and forms. At the end was a kind of bar, behind which a blotchy-faced woman was standing to serve out the refreshments, called for in that den of infamy.

It was a thieves' kitchen.

Those hardened, crime-branded wretches seated together, discoursing in low whispers of slang, and looking suspiciously around, or tossing off draughts of strong liquor, bore the unmistakeable traces of ruffianism.

That jaded creature, with her lean arms on the table, her haggard face on her hands, as she is bowed in thought—whilst opposite to her sits a thin, shabby-genteel man, not unlike a lawyer's clerk—what is her mission there, but sorrow and sin?

The entrance of Crusher Jem was marked by a chorus of shouts. He was evidently a well-known guest, and, when he took his perch in one of the compartments, many of the inmates came crowding round him.

But Crusher Jem was in a sulky mood: he deigned his admirers but little notice, and, having gruffly ordered for himself something to drink, was soon immersed in the pleasures of the pewter-pot.

He had not been seated more than ten minutes, when the sound of a light tap, twice repeated, and seemingly produced by the vibration of iron, was heard in the kitchen.

Crusher Jem glanced towards the farther end of

the room, where the window should have been. The secret of the blind could be here explained: it hung on a sheet of thick iron.

Night and day that abode of hunted criminals was illumined only by the light from within.

Never was that shutter removed, or the glare of day admitted.

The same boy who had waited on the "Crusher" ascended some steps on the right side of the room, by means of a ladder, to a place of espionage, and reported that all was right, and by the same means as had been employed before unfastened the door.

Five minutes elapsed, and then the face of Roving Rob poked in at the doorway.

A greater shout than had greeted the arrival of Jem announced how welcome a visitor was the roving pedlar; but that meek individual, overpowered by the fervour of the ovation, modestly waved his hand, and ushered into the kitchen Dick and the boy Charles.

There was a reckless look on the countenance of Dick, but Charley took no pains to express the repugnance he felt. He held his uncle by the hand, and tried to urge him not to enter.

"Here we are again," cried Roving Rob, dashing his hat down on a table, "smoked up and piping, and a-looking out for grub like hungry lions in Womel's 'nagerie. Come along, you little obstinate cur. Walk in, my pippin, an' see how you like your crib, as the undertaker said to the stiff 'un."

This was addressed to Charley and Dick, the latter of whom entered the compartment after Rob, dragging Charley with him.

"Oh, let us come away," said the boy, when Rob's attention was engrossed by his old friends; "we shall do no good here."

"And no evil, lad. Make theeself easy; I han't going to do anything wrong."

"But you don't know. Look at these men, how evil they look."

"Hold thee tongue. I tell thee Roving Rob would not take us into bad company."

"Bad company!" said the boy, bitterly; "I am sure we be in the midst of them."

This assertion startled Dick, and he looked round. Certainly the faces that met his view did not tend to dispel the suspicion evoked by Charley's words.

He touched Rob on the arm, as that worthy was tossing off a glass of rum.

"Hello! who's that? as the d—l said when the monkey stirred up the fire with his tail."

"Rob," exclaimed Dick, "what be this place?"

"What be it? Why as snug a ken as you ever clapped your blessed peepers on."

"But these people?"

"Oh, they're right as ninepence."

"I don't like the looks of them."

"Well," Rob returned, surveying them attentively, "they ain't particular handsome no ways notsoever; but if your in a go, they're the kiddies for you."

"Let us come away," whispered Charley.

"What does the infant with the luggy—gubrious mug, that looks as if it was cut out for a chaney tea-pot, say?"

"He says we'd better go elsewhere."

"That's his gratitude, is it? Why, where could you be so snug as in this caboose? If you want to go anywhere else, over the vay or round the corner, as the bull said when he tossed the penny-a-liner, now's your time; only see how soon you'll be taken up, you will."

"Who'll take me?"

"Why, the blues, to be sure."

"The blues?"

"Yes; the crushers."

"Crushers?"

"Bobbies—peelers."

"And who be they?"

"Why, you hinnercent chick," exclaimed Rob, regarding him with unmitigated pity, "you most hinnercentest of chicks—which is what they allers used to call me afore I cut my teeth—them's the gemmens what wears a splendiferous youniform, with bright buttons—which little kids, when they tumble arter 'bus-wheels, long for—and shiney hats——"

"Policemen?"

"Well, that's the name some gives 'em."

"They would not know me here."

"That's a whopper, like the hegg that Boney Meg chucked into the beak's hie. Why, you precious duck, they've got your helegant description long afore you got into this de—light—ful 'cality; and if they claps their blinkers on you, off you goes in a jiffey, to be scragged for the old job."

Dick fell to musing, and Rob continued—

"So, you see, you can't do better nor stay in this 'ere crib, which am what the shark said when he swallowed the nigger-boy whole. Well there, you mother gimlet-hie, turn that helegant beak of yours this way, and let's have a quartern and a half of the best turps and a toothful of strong water for these chickabiddies."

The liquor was brought, and Rob, draining his glass, bade Dick do likewise.

"Toss it down—it'll be a warmer, like a hot poker in your belly—and make your miserable life happy, while I tells you a few of the little hintyresting okkipations of these gemmens."

CHAPTER XX.

ROVING ROB EXPLAINS THINGS TO DICK.

CRUSHER JEM approached the pedlar, and nudged him on the elbow.

The worthy Rob instantly rose, and took his seat with him at another table.

"What's the game?" asked the Crusher, indicating by a jerk of the head Dick and the boy.

"Only a couple of kiddies what doesn't know their way about."

"Put 'em to the dodge?"

"That's a kvestion difficult to answer."

"There's some stamina in that cove," said the Crusher, again jerking towards Dick.

"Just my opinion."

"Wants putting up to a move or two."

"As green as grass," rejoined Rob, with just the lowest shade of pity crossing his features.

"Won't do for a swell-mobsman?"

"Make no sort of hand at all."

"Cadger?"

"No," smiled Rob, disdainfully.

"What's the lay, then?"

"See by-and-bye."

"Tell you what, Rob—he'd do for a small go at a crib."

"Might."

"I'll undertake to break his hand in."

"When?"

"To-morrow night."

"Job on, then?"

"Out-an'-out crib, all ready for cracking."

Roving Rob mused.

"I'll think it over."

"And t'other—the young kiddy?"

"Well, I think I must train him myself to some honest profession."

After a little more conversation of a like nature, the pedlar returned to the compartment where Dick and Charley were seated.

"Now you've come to London," began Rob, "what do you mean to do?"

"Get work," replied Dick.

"Which kind of razor would you like, my little dear—the one that shaved the man in the moon, or the one that cut itself out of its own handle?"

Dick stared at him.

"I mean," continued Rob, "what hinteresting 'vocation would you like to begin with?"

"Anything that's honest."

"Stone-breaking?"

"I don't care if it be to carry stones."

"Of course you can give a character?"

"A what?"

"A character."

"They will not take me for a thief."

"Nor they won't take you for a blessed vorkman, will you show a blessed good ticket?"

"I will tell them I am honest."

Roving Rob burst out into loud laughter.

"What a precious toffy you must be; look here, if you haven't got any letters, reckemendations, nor that, don't wear your boots out looking for work, acose you won't get it."

"What had I to do then?"

"You'll have to set up business on your own accord."

"How can I do that?"

"Oh! that's easy enough; blessed if you won't stretch your jaws off if you open your good-looking tater-trap like that."

Dick's mouth closed.

"Fill up and swipe," said Rob; "and now afore you goes to doss I'll put you up to a wrinkle or two that may be useful to you in this ere big splendiferous city."

The boy, Charley, leaned his head on the table; the foul, stifling odour of the pent-up place, rendered more impure by the fumes of tobacco, and the essence of vile spirituous compounds overpowered him.

Dick was about to rouse him, but Roving Rob stayed his hand.

"Let him alone, he'll come all right after a nap."

Charley, however, was not asleep. Had they raised his head they would have seen that his face was bathed in tears.

"How do you like this crib?" Roving Rob asked.

"Not much," Dick answered, glancing with distaste at the bare walls and the ruffianly faces around him.

"The company are *rayther* select," Rob observed, as he remarked the look Dick gave, "some of all sorts, like fish in a net, gemmen of all trades."

"What may be their trade?" asked Dick, innocently.

Roving Rob took a hard stare at him.

"Lord bless you, they're fly to all sorts of moves, that is trades—(what a precious muff he are!)—a sprinkle of every profession. There's that gemman there, with the patched eye, and the hat like the Brigand wears at the 'Vic.,' he goes about selling chickweed and groun'sel for the little birds, and never objects when a hodd humberella or anything of that sort comes in his way."

Dick did not feel much prepossessed in favour of the individual.

"Then there's that cove with the little bits of tape and the lots of pins stuck in the breast of his coat—which it wouldn't hurt if it had new cloth all over—he goes about picking up the pins out of the gutters when they sweeps 'em out of the shops first thing in the morning."

"Picking up pins? What for?"

"It's a 'obby he's got. Once he picked up a pin that came out of a gemman's scarf, and was wery near being blued for it. There's that lot of downy-looking coves over there, what looks as if they had been shot out of a dusthole—can you guess what they does for a living?"

"I could not. They don't look too honest."

"Well, it ain't a harticle of their stock in trade—leastways, not often. Them's the blokes what does the 'lays.'"

"Lays?"

"Yes; them's the dodgers. That one's the wooden-legged sailor what lost his limb at Sebastopol; he has it screwed on afore he goes out, and sits by the kerb with his own leg stowed away under him. Him there, with the fat head, does the stalking dodge; he takes four little kids out by the hand, and he gives the palaver to his 'Christian friends,' and a nice penny he turns in with it."

"But the children?"

"They gets 'em so much a nob. Then there is the dreadful sufferers by the last explosion, which took away their arms."

"But they have their arms now."

"In course they has; they only has the stumps fixed up when they goes out. They allers goes in threes, singing and sticking their stumps into people's eyes as they pass."

"What roguery!" ejaculated Dick.

"It are a dodge. There's the cove what shows himself with his foot. That there old blowen what's sweating off the gin is the 'diskonsolate widder,' with four kids, all like steps in a ladder, and of a sanctifectious mug. She sings hymns, and drags the kids through the snow and rain. They gets more when they looks more wretched. The kids they gets at sixpence a day each, and they wollops and starves 'em a good 'un if they don't turn in much sugar."

"And this is London!"

"Lord deliver your precious soul! only one little hole of it. Ah! there he comes. That's the shivering cove. He's allers shivering like the man as couldn't get warm—leastways, when he's in the street. He ain't got no paralysing now. Him up in the corner is the dauber as draws mack'rel, eggs, bits of bacon, and legs of mutton on the pavement. A cadger pays him so much, and does the lay by it as long as he can. Some of the kids does it for themselves, but they ain't so clever. You'll twig 'em: them's the downies as chalks 'I am starving' on the ground, or does it with pebbles. They're jolly enough now."

"Can they make money at such practices?" Dick asked.

"What a flat you must be! D'ye think they'd come it twice if it didn't pay 'em? Not they. Some on 'em does all sorts of tricks to get the coppers. They straps their leg up till it ain't no bigger nor a broomstick, and fries their faces, arter they've done 'em over with compo', till they looks like a lot of Lazaruses in a wery bad state. Then there's the kiddies as puts pennies on sores in their legs, and sticks 'em out on the pavement; and the blind blinkers what shows only the whites till they've done their day's work."

"Be it possible that folks can give to them day after day?"

"Bless your hinfant hinnocence eyes, there's many on 'em makes so much tin they stows enough away to make some people's fortunes."

"Don't the people find 'em out as cheats?"

"They changes their spots too often, like the wonderful leopard; they allers takes advantage of the hoppertunity if there's a war—you see lots of wounded soldiers and salts; when there's a blow-up of a powder crib you sees 'em with limbs blown off: a haccident in a coal-mine lays the same blokes out as injured colliers 'what's lost their limbs in the bowels of the earth;' a haccident on the underground railway, and you find 'em by its arches, then they fakes the froze-out gardener and 'got no work to do' job. Then they turns their skins ag'in when the blokes were starving in Lancashire; they comes out in gangs then, and sets up bands, all on 'em togged up to do the Lancashire cotton-spinners' fakement. Ah! there's some rum goes about London."

"It makes me wish I didn't come."

"You'll be all serene; there's the swell what sells the flash rings an' Brummagem chains in a chaise: he does the gold ring fake sometimes."

"What's that?"

"He drops a paper when he sees some softy coming, and makes a scramble and picks it up when they're looking; then he agrees to give 'em half, an' unrols it: he pretends to stare when he twigs a gold ring in it. 'Well,' says he, 'this ain't no use to me—here, it's worth so much, give me a crown for my share, an' you shall have it.' Which they does if they ain't wide awake: especially if it ar' a young girl what's thinking of getting spliced."

"And the gold ring?"

"Ain't worth a farden."

"Robbery!" ejaculated Dick.

"Hush! there ain't no such word; lifting, they call it—or finding, or smelling warm—never robbery. Ah! there ain't every cove is up to the 'lays' as I am, though I never do it on my own account."

Dick was glad to hear this; he had been entertaining some misgivings on the subject.

"You've heard a good deal of London shops and thieves?"

"I have."

"Some on 'em comes here sometimes."

"Here!"

"In this crib they're well togged, some on 'em; the swell-mobsmen pertikler — they rigs your thimble or waters your wipe when you're axing your way of the peeler; but they ain't half up to the cracksmen."

"What is that?"

"He breaks into cribs."

"Burglary!"

"That's the newspaper word for the crib; oh! and a splendiferous one it ar'—nothing like it: there's the skeleton keys yer carries in your pocket to open people's doors as if they was your own; then the jemmy and the crowbar, and such like—it's a fine lay to walk into a genuine crib, and with your dark lantern and bludgeon to stalk after the swag, and then to come out and live like a blessed nob."

All the while he was speaking he had been attentively regarding Dick's face.

"That was a bad move of yours, the way you nobbed on to that blessed crib at the parson's. We shall teach you how to walk without being had through a dozen doors or winders, if you stay with us."

"I will learn nought of the kind. I will work honestly for a living, and if I can't get my bread by the sweat of my brow, I'll starve."

Charley, whom they imagined asleep, started up.

"God bless you Dick for that!" he murmured, fervidly; "that's how you used to talk. We need never be afraid while you act up to it."

Roving Rob appeared to take no heed of the interruption. He filled his glass, and, with an indifferent air, tossed off the burning liquid.

Then he rose to see about their lodging for the night.

CHAPTER XXI.

THE GALLANT TOM.

The fearful dens of vice, infamy, and destitution known as thieves' lodging-houses abound in those parts—more especially the east of London — where the old and rising generation of criminals—male and female—congregate.

Squalid dens of wretchedness as they are, they bring in an enormous profit to the proprietor—frequently one of their own clique, who, by rapacious extortion and bilking, has risen to his present position.

Usually the houses are situated in the densest and most fœtid quarters. The habitations themselves are old, and, in appearance, unlikely to last beyond the next gust of wind. As a general rule, they contain from three to four separate rooms.

These rooms sometimes contain closely-placed mattresses, and others only bedded by a shake-down of straw cast over the floor.

Threepence per person is charged for the night's lodging—the use of the kitchen being accorded.

This charge is always paid in advance. There is no departure from this rule, the landlord being inexorable on this point; no money no bed, is the principle, and he never departs from it. He knows neither charity nor pity: he keeps the house for his own profit, and not for the privilege of exercising these Christian virtues. It is his business to consult his own interests, and disregard the interests of others.

Woe be to the penniless wretch whose rent is not ready!

Out he goes into the dark and stormy night, as cruel and pitiless to his shelterless head as the landlord, and not one whit more so! And the companions of that destitute being look on, and consent to and help in his expulsion. No considerations of friendship influence them; selfishness is the monarch of the place.

For nothing but the certainty of an enormous return would induce anyone to carry on this traffic. To destroy, then, the security of the landlord by making his gain uncertain would drive him away from the locality.

London Bridge is a cold place of a cold night, damp, and bad for the rheumatism, redolent of fever and ague: it is much better to be in the filthy kitchen, with its roaring fire than sleeping under one of those terrible arches. So the thieves respect the interests of the landlord for their own sake.

The male portion of this community consists of criminals of every degree, and vagabonds of all denominations. Thieves, coiners, murderers, and malefactors of ever kind live here together, with beggars and itinerant venders of boot laces, meat skewers, groundsel for birds, and other small wares.

The females are, of course (for none others would be found in this locality), lost and degraded women, living with these thieves, and being supported by them.

Marriage is totally ignored.

Utterly separated from every remnant of morality or respectability, with an impassable barrier between them and the better portion of mankind, their hand against every man, and every man's hand against them, they ring the changes of their discordant lives on crime and concealment, drowning all better thoughts, should such glimmer through the darkness of their lives, in drink and debauchery.

Male and female, twenty or thirty, will occupy one sleeping-room, all notions of propriety being disregarded. Take them as an average, that seventy persons occupy these rooms every night. Seventy threepences give 17s. 6d. per night, or £6 2s. 6d. per week; thus showing a total income of £318 10s. per annum!

All this made out of the poverty, misery, and sin of the degraded denizens, whose crimes render their concealment in some such place necessary.

By the intervention of Roving Rob, Dick and Charley had a better sleeping apartment found for them; even then the boy would have induced his uncle to leave the place, but Dick remembered the pedlar's word.

He had come to London not so much for the purpose of getting a living, as of meeting Mary, and her seducer.

To be taken by the police, hurried back to gaol, and tried for the murder of Parson Wordley's servant, were things he most especially wished to avoid.

After they had been attended to, Roving Rob and the Crusher sat down to renew the matter they had before touched upon.

Their plans were devised towards getting Dick into their confederacy.

He was one who, well trained, would be a desirable aid to their ranks.

In the first place, he had strength and stamina.

They could read that he was too true-hearted to betray anyone he might be linked with, and, therefore, in any desperate "lay," he might be safely made the scapegoat.

Again, his simple appearance would be invaluable in decoying moneyed flats into the power of sharps.

He only wanted a little training, and that they felt capable of giving him.

In his present mood, he seemed easy to work upon.

As to Charley, his intelligence and energy made him a valuable prize.

There were many purposes he might be used for.

As the quiet boy, to give secret warning to those engaged in some nefarious work.

Or he could be made the instrument, in the hands of forgers and counterfeit-money coiners, to pass their fabricated spoil.

True, he was a more stubborn conquest than simple-minded Dick.

But then, boys as virtuous had been subdued to their fraternity, and they doubted not that Charley would be their own.

The night passed strangely with Dick and Charley. In the morning they were unrefreshed; and after a wash—which the good offices of Rob made comfortable for them—they breakfasted, rather sumptuously, it must be confessed.

Roving Rob "standing Sam" for the expenses.

But for this, they would have gone breakfastless, as neither Dick nor Charley had a penny in their pocket.

All that day they hung about the place, making but little association with the frequenters and denizens of the locality, to all of whom Rob was familiar, and who either slunk in from the perpetration of some crime, or were hiding from the penalties of some late one.

In the evening, Rob took advantage of a time when Charley was out of the way, to draw Dick away. The faithful boy had been near his uncle all day. He had heard the conversation between him and Rob on the previous evening, and apprehensive that some means might be taken to lead Dick to the perpetration of some deed of wrong, he had kept near him all day.

When he returned, and discovered Dick's absence, he at once conjectured that he had been led away to

No. 7.

assist in some nefarious project, or to be inured to the infatuation of criminality; and with a heavy heart—for he loved his uncle dearly—he started out after him.

The first breath of fresh air was, to the young boy, like breathing new life. He had been so long pent up in that stifling kitchen, where fresh air and daylight were things not admitted, and the foulness of which had sickened him.

It was cheering, too, to be away from the companionship of the low characters by whom he had been so long surrounded; and though he found himself in the midst of squalor and filth, he did not mind so long as he had his liberty—freedom from those evil men—and the chance of watching over Dick.

He wandered along the close, dingy streets, wearily trying to find his way out. When at length he emerged into Whitechapel—a locality he was happily ignorant of—he knew not which way to turn to seek for Dick.

Bitterly reproaching himself for once leaving him, the true-hearted boy passed up and down the streets, looking into every face in the hope of seeing Dick, and crossing over when he caught sight of a form that seemed to bear resemblance to his lost uncle.

As the time wore on, and the almost hopelessness of finding Dick grew upon him, his fears of the purpose for which he had been wiled away became stronger.

"They knew I would not suffer him to do wrong," he murmured, "and have taken him, so that I shall not see him again till he has lost what he has most prized—his honesty."

He walked down an alley, where he thought he saw him.

"What will they lead him to?" he continued, the tears coming to his eyes. "Perhaps make of him a thief—lead him to some deed where he may be taken as the real criminal. I wish I could see that big fellow. I would hit him, big as he is, for taking Dick away."

Lights were appearing in the shop windows.

People with stalls along the High-street were displaying the illumination of lamps and candles.

Dick recoiled from the reeking odour of people who passed him by, and who seemed to be just let out from some lazar-house of pestilence.

Nor was there anything prepossessing in the faces of the throng.

Those who had articles to sell, and stood on the kerb-stone or had stalls in the road, seemed many of them more accustomed to rob, outrage, and murder, than to get their living by honesty.

Few people took any notice of the excited boy, as he made his way in any direction that seemed likely to be the one whither Dick had been led.

Eight o'clock chimed. Still the boy had been wandering up and down—no signs of his uncle. He had more than once thought of returning to the thieves' lodging-house; but, independent of his aversion to the spot, he knew not how to find his way to it, or what place to enquire for.

And his terror increased with every moment.

"Poor Dick!" he cried. "He may be taken, put again in a prison, or led to burglary—perhaps be concerned in another murder, for which he will be made to suffer. I wish we had never, never come away. Oh, Dick! when shall I see you again?"

At this juncture he caught sight of a figure somewhat similar to Crusher Jem.

Calling loudly on him to stop, Charley ran up the street.

The man took no heed of him if he heard; and when Charley got to the top, he was not to be seen.

But, confident that it was Crusher Jem, he commenced threading the various alleys, in the hope of yet meeting him.

He was guided down an avenue by hearing the voice of a little child pleading in agony, and imploring, as it appeared, to some hard heart.

Charley quickened his pace, and arrived at the end of the turning as a child's scream broke on his ear.

In a moment he had turned the corner.

What he saw at once aroused his boyish rage and pluck.

Crusher Jem had taken hold of a little girl. She was a pretty, interesting-looking child, and was dressed in a plain manner. She had neither bonnet nor shawl, and her sweet, pale face was upturned to the ruffian, who held her brutally by the wrists.

"Oh! please, don't," Charley heard her say. "Please let me alone!"

"Let you alone?" cried Crusher Jem; "not if I knows it. I wants you—leastways, somebody else do. So don't make a fuss, but come on."

The child resisted, and screamed when the bully dragged her away.

By that time Charley had arrived.

He was a boy of good pluck.

Then he hated the Crusher.

And he was always ready to help anyone, especially a little girl.

So when he saw the child so roughly handled by the Crusher, and heard her scream for help, he rushed to where she was struggling, and, without a moment's hesitation, struck the bully with all his force in the wind.

So heartily was the blow given that Crusher Jem, who had not seen Charley approach, was for the nonce completely knocked out of time.

He let go the hand of the child, and fell back.

Charley instantly took the little girl's hand.

"Don't be afeard," he said. "He is a brute; but he shan't hurt you."

The little girl looked at him with thankful gratitude.

"I am so glad you came to help me," she said.

Charley saw that the tears were in her eyes, and that she shrank from the Crusher.

The boy's heart was melted.

He looked resolutely at the ruffian, who, having now recovered his breath, bestowed a significant leer on the noble interferer.

"What's up, you cursed kid?" he said. "Have they let you out, then? Sheer off, my nipper, or I'll smash you."

"I'm not afraid of you," said Charley; "and I won't leave this little girl for you to hurt."

"Oh, you won't—won't you? And what's the little kiddy to you?"

"She's got no one to protect her; and I won't leave her."

"Well, I don't want to hurt her, nor you either. But she must come along of me."

"She shan't," Charley said, resolutely.

"Well, then, I'll show you how she will."

He stepped up to the boy and took his arm, holding it in his grip till it was almost useless; but this did not make Charley let go.

He still kept his arm round the little girl.

Exasperated by his resistance, the bully pulled him with such fury as to drag both him and the child from the kerb.

At the same time he took hold of the girl's arm.

The force of the tug excited the boy's dander. As Crusher again prepared to tug him away, he doubled his fist and struck the bully such a spank in the eye that it sounded all up the street.

Galled at this nob-light invitation, Crusher Jem viciously took Charley's collar, and commenced in the most brutal manner to kick and beat him.

The child screamed, and Charley, rendered uncontrollable, returned the bully's attack by a furious kick on his shins.

So deadly was the ruffian's rage at this treatment, that he rushed at Charley with the intention of dashing his brains out.

"You whelp!" he cried, with a foul oath. "I'll smash your skull to a paste!"

"Not just yet, my bloomer," cried a manly voice. "Hob off, you hulk! A pretty game, isn't it?"

What answer Crusher Jem might have returned it is impossible to say, for no sooner had he recognised the new comer than he received from him a clapper on the mug that floored him like a shot.

"That's more of your measure," said the new comer, who was no other than the "Gallant Tom." "Get up, and I'll put another in the same spot."

But Crusher had received quite enough from the first visitation.

He got up, and, with a very spiteful look, crawled away, his eye bunged up already from the blow.

The gallant Tom had put in the "auctioneer."

While the children were wonderingly and gratefully regarding him, he looked after the retreating Jem, and muttering something about a settler, turned to speak to Charley.

"Well, my young Bendigo," he said, "what was that gentleman's game with you?"

"He wanted to take her away."

"And who's she? your sister?"

"No; I haven't got one. He was hurting her; I heard her scream, and came up."

The gallant Tom uttered an oath, subdued, but still emphatic.

"I'd have given him a bigger dose," he said, "if I had known that. What did he want with you?"

"He tried to drag me away; I don't know what for. There was a woman with him once. She wanted me to go with her; she promised to find me nice clothes and money; but I wouldn't go."

"And mind you don't ever," said Tom. "They don't mean any good to little girls. You'd better go home to your mother, and tell her not to let you out so late at night by yourself."

"I haven't got any mother," the little girl said, sadly, while a tear glistened to her eye.

"No mother! Who looks after you, then?"

"Mrs. Manigan. She keeps a mangle in the court; she sends me home with the things."

"Is she kind?" Charley asked.

"She beats me sometimes."

Sometimes! She was all wails and bruises under her clothes.

"I wish I had a house," Charley said; "you should come there and live like a little fairy."

The child's eyes sparkled.

"You were so kind to protect me. He would have taken me away if you hadn't come."

"Well," said the gallant Tom, "tell you what, my little 'un; come along with me, and I will put you with an old granny that'll make you happy."

"I dare not," said the little girl.

"Dare not—why?"

"She would find me. I lost my way once, and she hid me in a cellar with dreadful rats."

"Don't go back; she can't hurt you then."

"She'll find me," the child said, with a shudder. "I ran away when she beat me, but she got me again."

"Well," said Tom, "and you——"

"I am looking for my uncle."

Very briefly he explained the circumstance.

"Well, my little man, I'll see what I can do for you."

He took each of them by the hand, and led them again into the open street. There a chaise was waiting, with a tall powerful prize-fighter* seated in it. He challenged Tom gruffly when he saw him with his *protégés*, but the brave fellow only laughed good-humouredly.

"Now, my little fellow," he said, "if you'll just scramble up here, I'll lift the little girl in."

"Oh! I must not," the child cried; "that is the way to my court."

The child was too terrified to be induced to enter the chaise; and as Charley insisted upon accompanying her before he resumed his expedition, the gallant Tom, finding he could be of no further use at that moment, gave Charley a list of the fighting

---

* Ben Caunt, since dead.

houses where he might be always heard of, and having seen them safe across the road, drove away.

"What is your name?" Charley asked, as they turned down the street opposite.

"Lucy; but they don't call me that. They call me Tott."

"Your own is a prettier one," Charley was saying, when from the top of an alley a tall, raw-boned Irishwoman was seen striding at full speed.

A short, scanty cotton dress, revealing her clumsy ankles and bare arms, seemed almost the only article of dress this personage had on, if we except the thick boots and stockings visible beneath. Her hair was frizzled up and stuck wildly about. She came at a quicker pace when she caught sight of Charley and his charge.

The little girl clung timidly to him.

"It's mammy!" she whispered.

Mrs. Manigan's first act was to strike Charley a smart box on the ear, at the same time jerking Lucy away.

Charley's cheek reddened.

"What did you do that for?" he asked.

"Do you——" Mrs. Manigan cried, using an epithet of the foulest. "I'll learn yer to be warking about with that hell-cat. Where's the money that I sent yer for, yer little cant?"

"It's here," said Lucy, shrinking from the woman's noisome breath.

"Give it me, then; and to the devil wid yer."

"Don't hurt her," Charley said.

"Hurt her, yer whelp of a mother's son!" cried the coarse woman, pinching the child's arm till it became almost lifeless. "Be off, and be cursed to yer, or it'll be worse for the pair on yer, I can swear."

Charley would have made some further reply, but little Lucy cried, tearfully—

"Please go—mammy will get so cross."

"Good-bye," Charley said; but as he spoke the drunken Irishwoman raised her brawny arm in a menacing manner, and dragging Lucy away, shook her fist after the boy.

Charley noted in his memory the situation and name of the court down which she dragged his little friend, and determining to return there at the first opportunity, turned away to re-commence his search after Dick.

CHAPTER XXII.

WHAT WAS CUT OUT FOR DICK.

CHARLEY was quite right in his conjecture of the reason of Dick being spirited away while he was absent.

Roving Rob had made up his mind to initiate Dick into the art of getting a living in a manner according with the talents he had no doubt the young countryman possessed.

As Roving Rob's principles were slightly different to the generally-received notions of society, a little explanation of them may be advisable.

From the hour of his birth, so to speak, he had commenced his roving life. It was never his boast that he had been brought up at an academy, and reduced by "unfortunate" circumstances to his present forlorn condition.

His father was a rearer of ponies: he used to bring up little "pups," as Rob used to call them, when they were as little, as active, and more shaggy than goats; which ponies, after a year or two "out at grass," he used to travel with, selling them at a very advanced rate upon the original price.

Besides rearing ponies, he took to rearing Rob: that worthy's first name was "Davy," so called after his father.

But the early propensity displayed by Rob for attaching his fingers to other people's property caused him to be christened by his present name.

Numerous were his early proofs of precocity in

the abstracting art. Orchards were too small for his ambition—the squire's preserves suffered all along the road of march.

Often when his father had lost him for an hour, he would find him luxuriating in a wood, devouring the tender portions of some entrapped game.

It was not the crime his father cared to reprove him for, but the gluttony of devouring all to himself.

Rob's greatest hit in this way, was when he stole the knife out of the shepherd's pocket (having made friends with the dog), killed a sheep with it, and having dexterously trimmed it, dragged it away, inviting the shepherd to share the feast, which he, suspecting nothing, accepted.

When the discovery was, however, made, Rob would have paid dearly if he had not attacked the shepherd with the warm sheepskin, and so "bunged up his eye" that he was unable to follow him.

A keeper came to complain to Rob's father, and Rob stole his snuff-box, actually selling him the snuff half an hour afterwards.

Another time he was stopped with a hare up his back: he got a whipping for that from his father, who did not mind so long as he was not taken.

But when taken his own honour was called into question.

The farmer, who saw the boy wanted a licking, lent the father his riding-whip to beat the boy with.

After his castigation Rob was sent back with the whip, which he sold on the road for a shilling, helping himself to the silk handkerchief which he saw sticking out of the buyer's pocket.

Committed to prison for stealing the minister's walking-cane as he walked out of the church, he filched the watch from the constable's pocket as he was carried kicking away; and, on his cell-door being opened, he butted the chaplain in the stomach as he was about to exhort him to repentance, and whipping his coat-sleeve in the eye of the astonished gaoler, made his way out.

But all these pranks might have been forgiven had he not interfered with his father's trade. He had been let off for winding a sheet round one of the little ponies and putting him on the church roof to the extreme terror of all who passed at night, and whom he (disguised in a black sack, and with a pair of red horns on his young head) knocked down with a bag of soot, and robbed when they were reeling past the terrible object on the church roof—he had been forgiven that.

But having, while his respected parent was asleep in a tavern, walked off with the whole of his ponies and sold them on the road, Davy, senior, came to the conclusion that Rob was incorrigible, and when, soon after, he heard of Rob being captured as he was roasting the hind quarters of a bullock, which he killed and was about to feast off, like Jack in the forest, he breathed a sigh over his fate, and passed on his way.

Rob was locked up, but he managed to wriggle up the chimney and get out, when he had to depend on his own resources for a living.

His first act was to make for London: the metropolis had been his ambition. He got there safely, after a series of adventures that would have filled a book.

As he looked rather out of his element in the big city, he was soon taken in tow by some leary blades.

One of these, seeing he had some shiners about him, took him to his lodgings, and, as soon as he was asleep, emptied his pockets.

In the morning he took him out, and purposely lost him; stalking into a tavern to regale himself on the plunder, he found not only that the money was gone, but his own in the bargain.

Rob had helped himself to both.

While he was cursing the mishap, the precocious infant himself swaggered in.

The leary gentleman instantly pounced upon him, and demanded the tin; but Rob's innocent look, and his pathetic appeal, got sympathy on his side. He was protected, and the leary cove was bundled out of the house.

A second dodger instructed him how to help himself from other people's pockets. After the first lesson, the instructor found he had lost seven half-crowns, which he had stolen shortly before.

Rob had proved himself an apt pupil.

When these little eccentricities became known, Rob was given up as knowing enough, and left to pursue the even tenor of his way.

Now, Roving Rob was not dishonest; he would have scorned the imputation of being a thief.

Once intimate with a friend, that friend's possessions were safe.

But no one else was safe.

It was an instinct—a mania—a something uncontrollable—indefinable: not even the sacred majesty of the law could keep his hands from picking and—finding.

He was never conscious of the act; but his fingers were always sticking to people's property.

He had been known to wake up from a fit of dreary abstraction and find somebody's watch ticking in his pocket.

As for handkerchiefs, purses, and pocket-books, they used to fly into his pocket.

But, with all this *penchant* for finding, he was sometimes ashamed as a—well, in this honest world, more honest since Diogenes went to another world to find another lantern—it is hard to find out any class of men honest enough to compare Rob to when he was not in a "finding" mood.

Rob's "roving" propensity was as great, so great that, while it always led him out of any prison where he might be placed, it very often led him into some gentleman's house, whither he walked for the mere purpose of observation.

Some people used to call this burglary, but Rob didn't.

When we have made this statement, we have confessed to Rob's greatest peccadilloes. Much as he might find in the course of the year, he was always poor, for Rob's was not a purse kept tightened when his mates wanted "sugar."

He once broke into an old miser's house for the mere purpose of distributing his hoarded gold to a number of poor tenants, whose goods the moneyed usurer had taken for rent.

No tramp ever passed Rob on the road without receiving a substantial "lift."

Then, again, his courage in the cause of the unprotected was as great as his prowess was exquisite.

He once got locked up for knocking down, and soundly thrashing, a ruffianly lawyer who had insulted a young lady in the street, but whose word was of more value than Rob's.

With this we have done with his past history and character. His future deeds, as they will prove numerous and remarkable, must speak for themselves.

To return to him and Dick.

His intention in training Dick to the career which he had found so pleasing in his own respect, was founded on the following reasons:—

He was well aware that Dick was always liable to be seized for the murder of the parson's servant, no matter what position he might be in.

And he was sufficiently conversant with life and Christian philanthropy to know that, without a recommendation, and with the ban of the past clinging to him, Dick would starve before he obtained employment.

Give a dog a bad name, you know, is enough in Christian England.

"And so," reasoned Rob, "if I leaves him to look out for himself, he'll be like the crocodile which had his shell stole when he had walked out of it to take a bath, and found it wasn't nowhere when he com'd back. Some bloke will be sure to nail him to some lag that won't be good for him; whereas, if I trains him to this one course, vy, in sartin, he'll be safe from any other."

So Roving Rob had taken Dick forth that he might be that night present at an actual case of crib-cracking—not that he was wanted to do any part of the performance, but simply that he might see how such things were done.

Dick walked with him very moodily. His thoughts were with Mary. He was thinking, spite of his resolution, how he would like to see her again.

Unfortunately, he was always thinking the same. As for Warner, he ground his teeth when he thought of meeting him.

"Tell yer what," said Rob, suddenly, "if yer practises that game of tearing your hair, you'll be worth your money to a walking caravan, with a haligator inside. 'Here you are,' the bloke can say, 'nim-kem-spivey, here yer are; he's just turned his jaw round to look for the little boy what he swallowed yesterday. Hark at him grinding his dreful *teeth*. Gr-r-r-gr. He'll champ you up in a minute. He ate the top of the monument yesterday, and—'"

"What be thee talking about?" Dick asked.

"That's what the boy said to the cow when she nibbled his ear off."

"Pals, thee beant able to talk to I like Mary was."

"No, I aint up to that; but come in here; you're going to the bad like a hat that's lost its brim. Come in here: I'll make a man of you."

He led Dick unresistingly into a public-house. They went into the tap. It was untenanted.

Dick, as soon as he had sat down, laid his arms out on the table and laid his head upon them.

Roving Rob raised the pot of cooper to his lips, but leered at Dick over the brim. He saw Dick writhing till he drew his head to the edge of the table, when he heard him groan and tear away the splinters with his teeth.

He touched him on the shoulder.

"Come, Dick, up with your pecker; 'taint hanging day yet."

"Ah! Rob, Rob, you don't know what I be thinking about."

"That's one for you, as the usher says when he begins with the cane. It's that gal of you'rn."

"Eh! Rob, she was dear to me."

Rob looked at him pitifully.

"She's dear to *him* now, Dick. Turn your lips up. There's more than one Mary in the world. What? mope after a frowning wench that left you to rot in jail while she went along of a fine-looking chap? She aint worth a snap—"

"Thee be right," cried Dick, standing up; "She be not worth a thought. Let me have some drink—strong drink, stronger nor that. I'll make fire burn here."

He struck his breast with his clenched fist.

Roving Rob ordered in some spirits and drained the pewter pot.

Dick tossed off his brandy with a gulph. Rob let his fall down his throat like milk; then the two hurriedly left the house.

CHAPTER XXIII.

CRACKING THE CRIB.

ENGROSSED in his own gloomy thoughts, Dick took little notice of where Roving Rob was leading him; nor did the latter strive to interfere with the current of his reflections.

He knew what he was thinking of, and that, in spite of all that Mary had done, Dick's heart still clung to her.

And it was so. He remembered their early peaceful days when they had spent their evenings together, wandering amidst fields made fragrant by the new-mown hay or the fresh-reaped corn, and he thought of the many visions they had cherished of future happy days, when, joyful in each other's love, they would see their children grow up in innocence.

But all this was dispelled through the first temptation to which the pure-minded, but too easily flattered, girl had yielded.

Dick thought of her, as at that moment she might be in the arms of her seducer, who he felt had but one object in weaning her from his love, and that was that he might make of her a ruined wreck, and then abandon her to her misery.

As the fancy of his Mary lying in the embrace of his rival crossed his mind, his teeth again grated harshly together.

He longed to have Warner there, that he might have throttled him.

The fumes of the brandy rose to his brain, filling it with fire, and impelling him to reckless deeds.

He was in that mood when the Tempter might mould him to his purpose.

He was in that mood when he might be led easily in the path of crime, and he knew it.

With the knowledge grew a fevered, frenzied feeling.

Why should he care, whom none in the world regarded? What mattered it what were his acts? There was no wife, no sweetheart, no mother to woo him to the right way.

No; he felt the blood bubbling in his veins, and almost longed for some opportunity of doing fierce outrage against society.

Had he not suffered enough from the world? His sister ruined — *murdered* — himself arrested, and branded as an assassin and thief through the depravity of his fellow-creatures.

Why should he care?

Voices seemed to whisper it in his ears as he passed along. He was excited, maddened. A feeling crept over him that it would be but vengeance on the world if he linked in some desperate deed—it was a glory—he would face it.

There came other visions before him. He saw himself arrested for a deed he had not committed.

Condemned unjustly, he fought against strong men, and made his escape.

Then he saw two who were never from his thoughts.

Mary and her destroyer!

In fancy he leaped at the throat of the latter, and held him in his grip till the eyes started from the sockets and the seducer fell a lifeless form at his feet.

Though the street was full of people he saw them not—he forgot Roving Rob, who walked calmly by his side.

Another was beside him.

It was the prison chaplain.

The rumble of vehicles as they rolled by was deadened in the sound of the solemn bell that tolled the hour of execution.

The hubbub that he heard around him was the cries of the mob swaying and bending forward to see him die.

And, in what seemed his last moment, his mother stood by his side.

And ruined, forsaken Mary stood sadly before him.

To this, whispered a voice, would he come if he took the first step in crime.

The vision startled him — he woke up as from a walking dream, and clutched Roving Rob by the arm.

"Where be going?" he said. "I'll not go with thee; you would lead me to crime."

Startled by his energetic manner, Rob merely looked at him in silence; but when Dick stopped and declared he would go no further, he put his arm in his and led him on.

"Hold your head up, Dick," he said. "You want to have that bloke by the throat what's walked off with your Mary? I'll show you how to. Keep along of me, as the whale said to Jonah, and I'll put you so as you'll be able to meet him like a gemman, and not let him have it all his own way."

"Why, look here," he continued, seeing that Dick was silent, " there isn't a blessed place you can poke your nose in with safety, acos of that job for which you're all alive. Keep along o' me: you'll meet him and her, too, but don't let it be afore the beak."

They had passed from the frequented streets: the neighbourhood of shops and stalls they had left far in the rear, and were now amidst tall, silent houses, with here and there a lamp burning in the hall, to indicate that the inmates were not yet in bed.

Five o'clock pealed from the Westminster bell. Dick had no conception that it was so late. Where they were walking he could see was in a wealthy locality, and he began to have some glimmering of the object of Rob's visit, when Crusher Jem made his appearance.

He was, of course, expected by Rob, who, however, made a great pretence of being surprised at the meeting.

After a few words, Rob inquired in slang whether the job was right, to which Crusher Jem replied in the affirmative, and the three continued their way.

The lights of the houses were now fewer, the street-lamps wider apart, the place more silent. They passed the solitary policeman, who regarded them suspiciously, but as they went off his beat, did not trouble himself any further about them.

The conversation that was kept up being mainly in slang, Dick could gain no idea of its purport, though he had some belief that it bore reference to himself.

The trio stopped before a house that stood by itself at the corner of what seemed a suburban square.

Roving Rob leaned against the lamp-post, while Crusher Jem, with remarkable agility, slipped round the corner, to reconnoitre each way.

He returned to report the coast clear, and Rob moved from his post of observation.

There was a low garden-wall running round the side of the house, with a small postern at the end next the square.

Dick was surprised to see the Crusher apply a small implement to a crevice, and force it open at a dash.

He entered, and Roving Rob took Dick by the hand.

"Come along," he whispered.

But Dick shrank back.

"No, I will not go in there."

"Don't be a sawney. It's all for your good. Walk in; one penny will admit you."

"I tell 'ee I wont go."

"Won't you? Dick, he lives here."

"London mister?"

"The very identical."

"Thee don't say it!"

"Well, that's a whopper!"

"Be he there?"

"Come in—you'll see."

He dragged Dick through the gateway.

The Crusher was already at work at the shutters of the back-parlour window; an application of the jemmy brought them open, and he gave a signal to Roving Rob, who instantly slipped through.

Crusher Jem handed him the silent matches, a pair of list slippers, a jemmy, and a bunch of skeleton keys.

Rob beckoned to Dick to follow, and disappeared.

"Now then," said the Crusher, turning his lantern on the inside of the room, " bustle in after him."

On the threshold of that crime Dick paused. The fumes of the brandy with which, at his wish, Rob had plied him, did not prevent him from seeing that what he was about to commit was a great crime.

But then he thought of Mary. If she should be in that house, and with her betrayer!

That thought was enough.

He grated his teeth, and was about to leap in at the window, when a well-known cry was heard behind him, and the voice of Charley exclaimed wildly—

"Dick! O Dick!"

The next moment the faithful boy had seized his hand.

"Oh, Dick!" he cried, "I have followed him," he pointed to the Crusher, " and am faint with running; but I have come in time. Don't 'ee go in there; be honest, Dick. If we starve, it is better than being thieves."

Dick turned his head away; he could say nothing.

"Now then," said Crusher Jem, gruffly; " don't keep us standing all night. The glim will bring the peeler here. Jump in."

"No, no, Dick," exclaimed Charley; "don't let let them take you in there. They mean you harm. Oh! think of the other time, when bad Ralph got you to break in."

"Look here, you whelp," cried Crusher Jem, remembering the pasting he had got from the gallant Tom; "I've got one agin your carcase, and if you don't hold your cursed piping, I'll settle your business for you."

"No you won't," said Dick; "let him bide. Go home, Charley. I be going in to see him; thee knows who. Stay thee here till I come out again."

But Charley clung to his uncle.

"I knew they would lead you to bad," he said. "Oh! Dick, come away."

"They won't lead me to anything. Don't fear they'll make me a thief. No; I be going in, but not to steal."

"Dick, dear Dick, don't go. I know you wouldn't be a rogue; but if you should be caught."

"Caught, be d—d," cried the Crusher. "Look here, my pippin, if you don't take your carcase out of the way, I'll make a hash of you."

"I won't go and leave him here."

"Oh, you won't, won't you? Well, I'll show you how we'll deal with you."

He drew a tremendous clasp-knife, the blade of which he slowly opened with his teeth.

Charley, facing him boldly, clung to his uncle.

"I'll stop your piping," the Crusher said, taking Charley by the collar.

Then Dick spoke.

"Don't he attempt to harm a hair of his head," he said, in a tone that made the Crusher understand what he meant.

Now, the Crusher had taken a good estimate of Dick. He knew that he had good courage, and would not be forced to anything.

He therefore tried a different tack.

"If you're afeard," he said, with a laugh, "you'd better go. We don't want the white feather to show here. The bloke can make hisself all serene with your gal—"

"I beant afeard," Dick said; "I'll go. Bide thee here, Charley."

"I won't. Come away; they'll make you a thief."

"Hist!" cried the Crusher; " here's the cursed copper. Hook it inside, or they'll nab you in a jiffy."

The steps of a policeman were heard as he came slowly on his beat. Dick on the instant sprang into the room. Crusher Jem had taken the precaution to turn out his lantern, and put his arm before Charley's mouth; the latter was but in time, as the boy would have called out for the police to come and help his uncle, in which case the Crusher would have made no scruple of cutting his throat in an instant.

As it was, he had him effectually muffled. Silently and deftly he lifted him into the room, pulling the shutters to after him.

"Make a noise now," he said, "and you'll get Dick sent over the herring-pond."

He closed the shutters, and Charley and Dick were shut inside the house they had burglariously entered.

CHAPTER XXIV.

WHAT CRUSHER JEM FOUND AFTER HE HAD GAGGED CHARLEY.

THE policeman, suspecting nothing, continued his round. Dick, whose senses were in a measure stupified by excitement, found himself held in the brotherly grip of Roving Rob. Crusher Jem had careful hold of Charley.

Within the house all was silent enough. No one seemed to be aware that there were desperate characters there, who had nefariously entered the dwelling with intent to clear the place of every valuable.

The first movement made was by the Crusher, who turned the light of his lantern half-full, and let it gleam on the face of Dick.

From him he turned it to the resolute face of the boy. The look of Charley's eye was sufficient for him to see what the bold young fellow would do if he had his limbs and tongue free. Crusher Jem felt very much like strangling him, and would perhaps have done so but for the presence of Roving Rob.

"It's all square," said that worthy; "mind what you're up to with the glim."

"'Taint the glim," the Crusher growled; "it's this whelp I'm sticking at."

"Ah!" soliloquised Rob, "it ar' necessary to look arter his health; he's a little bit wild, like a mountain boar, and is in the habit of showing his tusks, like the pink elephant."

Very quickly did Rob take off his necktie and fasten it round Charley's face. The boy kicked and resisted stoutly, creating a din with his heels that made the Crusher feel again for his clasp-knife.

"It's all for his own good," muttered Rob, seeing that Dick was becoming angered; "if he'd only keep quiet like a young hoss, we'd let him go, but there's no holding him still, there ain't."

And so saying, he effectually bound Charley to a table.

"Open your ears, my little creature, do," he said. "We is going to take a walk through this crib; if you want Dick took, you can't do better nor try and make a noise, 'cos if somebody gets in arter us he's sure to be nailed, in coorse he ar'."

He turned to Dick.

"Now, Dick, we'll just leave him here, we will, while we steps through the caboose to see if there are any light articles whatsoever laying about that we can find a use for."

"I'll do no robbing," said Dick.

"Robbing! there ain't no such thing. In course, if we does come across anything as we thinks the gemman here can very well spare, why, we shall take care of it for him; but if you want to clap your peepers on *him*, you'd better come on and say nothing."

"I be ready," Dick said, clenching his hand.

"Don't speak so werry loud, as the deaf bloke says to the cannon-ball when it takes off his nob. Come along, it's werry likely, it ar', that he ar' making his blessed self all serene with the just young gal of your affections."

"Which be the room?"

"We'll take you to it all in course of time."

"If there's any business to be done," grunted Crusher, "let's look alive."

A little tampering of the locks was necessary before the door could be induced to open; but this was finally managed by Rob, and then he and the Crusher guided Dick out of the room.

But in the passage all was dark and still; the Crusher, advancing on tip-toe, led the way, shading the light with his hand, and peering into every corner.

Behind him came Roving Rob with Dick, whose boots they had taken the precaution to remove.

Skilled in their profession, these worthies did not make the least noise, and even Dick, rendered cautious from a desire of not being detected by that man in whose house he believed he was, trod with a care that elicited silent approbation from the pedlar himself.

Once or twice Dick would have spoken, but the jerk of Rob's finger kept him silent.

They passed along the passage, and into a room, the locality of which had evidently been found beforehand by the Crusher, as he easily effected an entrance by means of a skeleton key.

"There's lots of swag here," he said, in a low murmur. "Hold the glim while I open the bag?"

He took from his pocket a simple-looking instrument, consisting of a nob of iron attached by a swivel to a handle of ironwood.

This he raised menacingly before Dick.

"No shrinking now," he said, "no drawing out, or I'll beat your skull in with this at a blow."

"Look here, mister," answered Dick; "I don't fear thee nor thee murderous looks not a bit. I be come to get at *him*, not to steal what be in the house where he stays."

"And we've come for the swag; so, now you're in for it, make the best of it."

Dick said nothing: he would rather not have remained there, but as he did not know his way about the house, or in what part of it Warner might be sleeping, he sat down on a dusty chair to wait till they were ready.

The room presented the appearance of not being often used. An ink-spotted desk, a high stool, two broken chairs, some shelves, and two large iron safes were all the furniture it comprised.

The Crusher would not have cared if it had contained nothing but the two latter—he knew there was enough in them to pay for the journey.

Roving Rob, who had a dexterity for that sort of thing, was already fitting keys to the locks of the safe; but this was a work of time and difficulty, and at each fresh key that was applied: the impatience of Crusher Jem became more manifest.

"Can't you get it open?" he asked.

"It ain't as easy as a crocodile's jaws."

"Here, let me try."

Here Dick started up.

"Some one be coming!" he said.

"Dowse the glim," whispered the Crusher.

Roving Rob instantly turned the lantern out.

The hollow sound of a foot bearing heavily on the stair came to their ears.

Then all was still.

Roving Rob crept to the door and peered out.

Nothing was to be heard or seen.

He listened a little while, and then crept forth, the Crusher and Dick staying behind.

The pedlar went very cautiously forth: his head was stretched right and left.

Satisfying himself that no one was near, he proceeded to the banisters and looked over them.

It would have been an easy matter for anyone to push him over at that moment.

But no one was there to do it, and he softly ascended the stairs.

He made no sound—the list slippers deadened the fall of his feet, and he trod too tenderly for any creaking to arise.

When Roving Rob got to the top of the flight of stairs above the drawing-room, he was considerably surprised to see a light shining through the crevice between the bottom of a bed-room door and the floor.

The pedlar felt for his stick—a never-failing friend —and then peeped through the keyhole.

No human being was to be seen—no sound issued forth. He descended as softly as he had gone up.

"Be alive," he said; "there's some bloke not in his doss yet."

He had, before going out of the room, fitted a key into the safe; it now only remained to open the door. This was effected, and the sight of the booty ensconsced within was a sweetener.

There were gold and silver ornaments and plate, bags of gold, and heaps of equally valuable papers.

Rob's eyes sparkled as he saw the treasures.

"Look, Dick!" he whispered; "there'll be enough to let you live like a gentleman."

Crusher made no remark; he went to work in quite a dexterous manner, stowing in careful places the plunder of the safe, the door of which they closed again.

"That's a queer-looking door," Rob whispered, pointing to one carved to imitate the old panels; "I should like to know what's inside."

"More swag," the Crusher exclaimed.

"We'll see."

"We must tumble to it quick, then, or they'll lag us."

"All serene," Rob said, as he wrenched open the door.

A stifling and most foul stench saluted him.

"The glim, Jem!" he cried, in a faint whisper.

Crusher Jem turned the light of his dark lantern —which a silent match had enabled them to re-light —upon the interior of the cupboard.

Even he seemed a little taken aback by what he then saw.

The cupboard had neither shelves nor iron chests. There were one or two pegs in the wall at the back.

On one of these pegs was the ghostly form of a woman. Her hair was twined round one of the pegs, her hands, wasted and black, were by her side, and her face, discoloured and wasted, seemed falling to shreds.

There was no vestige of recognisable features, and what remained of the garments was difficult to judge by.

"That's some of the bloke's work what owns this crib," Rob said; "he never was over particlar. Lawk! what would she fetch now for a hexibition mummy? Well, it ar' a spectacle, it ar'."

"Hist! some one is creeping here."

Roving Rob shut the cupboard-door, and spun round.

"Where? where?" he whispered.

"On the stairs. I can hear 'em. Look arter the swag—it's time to hook it."

Rob again listened attentively. There was no mistaking the patter of occasional stealthy steps; it seemed more than one, and the Crusher and Rob looked at each other in uncertainty.

An instant after, a crash was heard below; then hasty footsteps sounded through the house, and a voice cried—

"Wake up, people; you are being robbed!"

"It's your whelp of a boy," the Crusher answered, as Charley was heard crying through the house.

"It is him; he has got loose. It will be all a chance if we get out of here again."

"There's some one else. Look!"

There was a simultaneous banging open of doors; heavy treads resounded from various parts, then a man's voice was heard saying, in an authoritative tone—

"Take care, my men, that the villains don't get away. It's a clear planned robbery. Look after them."

"We're sold," Crusher Jem cried, as, with an oath, he hid away the booty, and stepped to the door.

There was a momentary gleaming of a light; it vanished; then all became silent and dark.

But those men knew that the hour of danger had come, and that only their desperate courage would save them.

CHAPTER XXV.

HOW CHARLES GOT LEFT BEHIND.

ROVING ROB had deceived Dick in telling him that Warner was in the house they had broken into.

That had been a *ruse*, on which he congratulated himself for having thus got Dick, of his own free will, inside.

The house belonged to, and was inhabited by, a certain philanthropist and Christian reformer of the name of Wilblow — a gentleman noted for his examplary piety and unmeasured benevolence.

So great had been his zeal in furthering the cause of his less fortunate human brethren, that he had been appointed president of one or two well-meaning societies, and was treasurer of the funds of various benevolent associations.

Mr. Wilblow had also been director of a bank, which, unfortunately, had broken—and manager of a mining speculation, in which, through unforeseen causes, the shareholders had all lost their money.

Had anyone else but the eminent philanthropist been concerned in such questionable matters, he would have been pronounced a rogue and swindler, and have been prosecuted accordingly.

But Mr. Wilblow was the pink of perfection. Three times regularly every Sunday was he to be seen in his pew at the fashionable church, where his fervent responses were to be heard above all others.

Prayer-book in hand, his white choker stiff as Beau Brummell's cravat, his hair brushed up, so as to reveal his well-washed bald pate, which shone like pink ivory, he was the noted one amongst a whole congregation of the virtuous.

Morning and evening he had prayers in his house; and so rigid was his piety, that he had discharged, without a character, his housemaid, who, worn out with work, had fallen asleep while he was reading the morning prayer.

Though he professed to have been a great loser by the transactions above mentioned, and had lessened his account at the bank in consequence, he was in possession of a goodly stock of gold and notes, all of which were locked up in that iron safe which Roving Rob and Crusher Jem had opened.

The fact was, Mr. Wilblow was one of those saintly hypocrites who make religion a cloak for their peculations and sins.

His piety was cant, his principle rotten, and the money which he kept snug in his safe was what he had defrauded from those who had put faith and funds in his banking or mining concerns.

Roving Rob was well aware of his character, having seen him in a different guise, at various haunts of sin, and hence, in a great measure, excused himself the act of appropriating another man's goods.

Like all hypocritical evil-doers, Mr. Wilblow took the surest precautions against being robbed of his treasured plunder, for, like all who have money secreted, he was in continual apprehension lest it should be stolen.

But the efficacy of his bolts and bars had been as nought to the professional burglar.

Now, it happened that Mr. Wilblow was lying by the side of his wife, whom he had been abusing till she had sobbed herself to sleep; and his vicious nature keeping him awake, he was revolving in his mind whether some method could not be devised to free himself of a wife of whom he had long since grown tired.

She was his second. The first had dropped down dead while descending the stairs: a blue bruise was on her left breast, but the fall was stated to have caused this.

But Mr. Wilblow knew different. It was where his clenched fist had basely struck her, giving her the blow of which she died.

His second wife was not so young as the first

MURDER OF THE POLICEMAN.

She was about eight and twenty, and had brought him a fortune of £2,000.

Since the first month, he had made her the recipient of every kind of ill-usage, and yet she lived.

As he looked at her sadly sleeping, his fingers itched to quietly strangle her.

More than once he thought of his razor; but the certainty of discovery deterred him from cutting her throat. If he could have made it appear that she had done the deed herself, he would have had no hesitation.

But that was difficult.

Now, while his fiendish mind was debating on this murderous intent, the eminent philanthropist thought he heard a sound that should not have occurred in the house at that hour of the night.

And, by patient listening, he became convinced that there was somebody who had no business there.

Mr. Wilblow could scarcely be called a coward: he was too deliberate and cunning in his mode of dealing with people.

No. 8.

Of course he would not have liked a knock on the head, nor would he have fancied having his throat cut by a desperate burglar.

But there was another way of meeting the difficulty: having listened till he had assured himself that his cherished treasure was the object of that night visit he softly opened his window and looked out.

In about ten minutes a policeman came slowly in sight. But Wilblow had before established a system of signals with the night guardians, whom he feed to look after his house; when, therefore, the peeler saw him waving his chamber-towel, he knew that assistance was wanted, and springing his rattle very gently he brought to the spot two other constables, who came to the door for Mr. Wilblow to let them in.

Arming himself with a loaded pistol and a heavy club, both of which he always kept at hand, he, as gently as if he had served his apprenticeship to housebreaking, descended the stairs.

The policemen made no noise when he admitted them—he gave one the pistol he had, and taking his club in both hands, led them up the stairs.

It was at this very time that Charley got his hands free, and having removed the gag from his lips and unfastened the thong that bound him to the table, he rushed from the room, calling as loudly as he could to alarm the household.

At once the members of the force sprang up the stairs, while Mr. Wilblow, shouting to them not to let any of the burglars escape, crept, club in hand, after them.

Charley, unacquainted with the situation of the room, made his way into the back drawing-room, overturning several articles in the dark, as he tried to find his way out again."

"Dick! Dick!" he cried. "Oh, he'll be taken!"

At this very moment Mr. Wilblow entered the front drawing-room.

"A young hand at the business," he soliloquised, raising his club.

It was very dark; still one accustomed to the room could make his way without creating a noise.

Guided to Charley by the noise he made, he stole softly towards him.

He had reasoned to himself that from the fact of Charley calling out in warning, he must be alone; and he exulted in the idea of making a Christian example of one of the burglars.

So, as I before said, when he saw the dim form of Charley in the dark he raised his heavy club.

And he was in the act of taking steady aim when Charley, unaware of the vicinity of anyone, overturned a chair, and darting forward, cried—

"Dick! Oh, my poor uncle! They'll take him —they will."

Anyone but the hardened philanthropist might have guessed, from the pathetic tones of Charley, that he was not an obdurate criminal; but Mr. Wilblow suffered no such thought to sway his pious mind.

His house had been nocturnally entered by thieves, whose mission was to carry off his money—money wrung from the widow and orphan, but not the less his.

Moreover, his night's rest had been intruded upon. One of the burglars was in his presence—within his aim. What glory it would be for the papers to state how courageously he had dealt with the villains.

He had taken deliberate aim, and as the boy sprang away, he cried—

"Taken? Of course he will be; and so will you, my young chicken. Where are you running to? Ha! I thought that would stop your gambol."

The club fell with a heavy crash on the poor boy's head.

Stunned and bleeding, he uttered a loud cry and fell to the ground.

But here the instinct of his love for Dick was all prevalent, and he feebly cried out for his uncle to escape.

But Wilblow threw himself upon him.

"Ha, ha! I've got you, my boy. Come along; we'll see what you'll say to this when the rest are taken."

Bang came the report of a pistol. Loud oaths and cries, with the sounds of a fierce struggle, next rang through the house; and its owner knew that the constables were engaged with the burglars.

At the first alarm Crusher Jem and Roving Rob had with cool precision put the booty about their clothes. The dark lantern was extinguished, and Crusher Jem put his hand on Dick's shoulder.

"If you don't want to take a stalk across the herring-pond," he said, gruffly, "keep close along of us; and mind, if there's any peaching or any game of that sort, I'll knock your d——d brains out."

"Here they comes as large as life, and ten times as natural!" ejaculated Rob; "lawks, don't I hear 'em a spinning up the stairs and a trying to walk as if their boots was made of gingerbread. Now's your time if you don't want it hot and strong, like the boy as eat the pepper pie. We'll have to give 'em a dose, or we shall have their mawleys on our chumps."

"I beant going," said Dick, "till I've seen *him*."

"Why, bless your hinnercentest gumptions, there ain't no such a kiddy in the crib. It war a yarn, it war, and blow my stumps if it ain't time to step it.

"You have played me a trick; I'll go no more with you."

"That's what the gudgeon said when he swallowed the hook. Will you come!"

"No; I'll stay here."

"You ain't such a flat, quite. In course, you see when they comes blundering in, they takes all they can find, just as we does, and if they collar you into limbo you'll walk, and p'raps take a trip at the expense of govermint, which, as I says, when there's a move on the board——"

"Come on, will you," muttered the Crusher, "don't you hear the peelers."

Charley's voice was at that instant heard.

"When I get hold of that cursed kid, I'll wring his neck," remarked the Crusher, as Dick, excited by the voice of his faithful nephew, accompanied them from the room.

They began descending the stairs.

Very quietly and very slowly.

Each knew that there were police in the house, waiting to lag them as they came forth.

Each knew that if taken they would have no mercy from the law.

Roving Rob was leading Dick, and the Crusher followed.

They had just got to the bottom of the stairs.

On the landing it was as dark as pitch. Rob had to peer through the gloom for the expected "coppers."

"Look out," he muttered.

He had scarcely spoken when the three policemen leapt from their hiding-place; a light shone upon the scene, and Rob found himself seized.

"We've got you. You may as well give in quietly."

"Not if I knows it," said Rob, as he ducked under the legs of one, throwing him over. The fist of the Crusher sent the third flying on his back, as he had presented his pistol at the retreating Rob.

The weapon exploded, the ball going unpleasantly near Dick's ear.

"Come on," Rob cried; and with the Crusher he leapt away.

So momentary was all this, that Dick found himself alone; and before he had time to realise the whole affair, he was seized by the two discomfited policemen.

Now the love of liberty was strong in the breast of Dick; he had experienced enough during his sojourn in the county gaol.

He wished for no further test of its torments.

The cry of Charley had reached him; and impelled to sudden action, he flung the policeman in his might against the wall.

Perceiving that they had got a novice, they held him firmly, thrusting their knuckles into his throat. But Dick's strength was immense. He hurled them from him on each side, and as they closed again dashed his fists in their faces, and sped along the passage.

The policemen sprang their rattles.

Dick saw a dark form before him. He was preparing to strike, when he recognised the voice of Roving Rob.

"All right; come along."

Dick allowed himself to be led into the room where they had first effected an entry.

The Crusher had already opened the shutters and window.

"Charley?" said Dick. "Where is he?"

"All right; look alive."

"I'm not going without him."

"He's right, I tell you. Come on, or I'll stick this into you."

The Crusher displayed his knife.

Roving Rob took hold of Dick's arm.

"He's gone off long ago," he said.

"I don't believe it."

"I tell you he did. Wasn't the winder open?"

This last argument might not have succeeded with Dick, but at that juncture there rang through the house the most piercing shrieks, followed by a scuffling sound, to which wild din the policemen's rattles added a furious accompaniment.

Then there came a loud knocking at the door, and voices were heard below.

The Crusher swore a deep oath.

"It's all up. We shall be lagged," he muttered.

"That's another," remarked Roving Rob.

Dick thought of the deed done at the parson's: a stupifying horror seized him, and he made no further resistance to the efforts of Rob to get him from the house.

The Crusher was the first to alight on the ground; hardly had his foot touched the pavement, when he felt himself collared.

"Game's up," said his captor.

He saw the number on the collar.

"428," he said; "it's a gooser with you."

The policeman had driven his knuckles into his neck, and was gripping him firmly. The right hand of the Crusher was free.

First of all forcing his captor against the garden-wall, he shook himself like a monstrous mastiff, but did not dislodge the policeman's hold.

The looks of the Crusher were deadly enough at that instant. The policeman seemed to read their murderous import, for he turned pale, and sprang his rattle.

Crusher Jem gave another jerk; that brought him at arm's length from the "blue."

There was a whizzing noise in the air as his sling-shot cut round. The leaden bullet fell with a thud on the constable's head, sinking into the skull as if it were no thicker than an egg-shell, and lodging in the brain of the unfortunate man.

A single groan came from his lips; he reeled, his grasp still clenched on the Crusher.

Jem wrenched himself away as the policeman fell, and Roving Rob and Dick stood beside him.

Petrified with horror at the sight, Dick yet had power enough to resist the efforts of Rob.

"That be a foul deed," he said, looking at the prostrate policeman. "Poor Charley, too—if he be yet inside!"

Crusher Jem raised his terrible sling-shot again.

"We've had enough of you," he cried, with an oath; but Roving Rob put up his hand.

"Help him away. Don't you see he's scared?" he cried, himself pale at the spectacle of violence.

The Crusher vengefully took one of Dick's arms, Roving Rob locked his in the other, and quitting the garden by the gate, they turned down the street.

Policemen were running from all parts the spot; people shaking in fear were thrusting their heads out of window; the stragglers who at night may be found in our streets made speed to reach the scene of the catastrophe.

Inside, the screams of women and the whir of the policemen's rattles still kept up their discord, the "blues" making their way to the front of the house, to admit those who were knocking there, and assist in capturing the burglars, while others rushed to the place where the murdered policeman lay stretched out by the garden-wall.

CHAPTER XXVI.

DICK MAKES AN ASSAULT ON ROVING ROB.

THE pace at which the Crusher and Rob proceeded took Dick almost off his feet. The spectacle of the murdered policeman was yet before his eyes.

He was sick at heart and in a sort of benumbed despair.

This mode of proceeding was, of course, contrary to the usual order of things. The rule is, when there is an alarm, for the pals to separate, each to take his own way, and re-unite at one of their boozing-kens.

But Roving Rob knew that if once they left Dick to himself he would go back to look after Charley and be caught. As for the Crusher, he still swung the terrible instrument with which he had beaten in the skull of one "copper," and was ready to beat in that of any other.

They encountered many people as they hurried along the road, and at one corner a policeman fell into the arms of Rob.

Had he been on the Crusher's side, the sling-shot would have dealt with him, but Rob's mind was not quite so bloodthirsty. He, however, considering the precarious nature of things, went so far as to give the "blue" the *hug* and deposit him gently on the kerb.

There were plenty of evidences that they were being pursued; but Rob was on the alert, and presently espying a brougham proceeding at a leisurely pace, he left Dick with the Crusher, and walked up to the driver.

"You're a pretty-looking hobject, you are, to drive a broom!" he exclaimed, having at a glance taken the measure of his man and seen that the vehicle was empty. "Why, I've seen a better man made out of cabbage-leaves. Why don't you drive properly that *hanimal* that looks as if his bones was a-walking out of his skin to look after the flesh that's mizzled. Here, jump down, and get inside the horse, and put the reins in his mouth; he'll take you home all right."

This double attack both on himself and horse was what no jarvey could stand; he therefore, in very soft tones, told Rob to go to h— and warm himself, which remark excited Rob's laughter only.

"Is all the frame there?" he asked, pointing to the horse.

"Ax my foot!" was the coachman's elegant reply.

"Foot?" said Rob, scoffingly; "why, it's like a blessed parish pick-axe—your stump's in the middle of it."

"I'll put it where you won't like it."

"You?" said Rob; "why, I've licked a better thing than you afore breakfast, lad! There, knocker."

"Leave the horse alone, will you, before I knock your head off?"

"What?" cried Rob; "here, somebody hold my coat. He ain't got none to hold; lost his last time he went to buy his shilling vestket in the lane."

And he commenced squaring up to the coachman.

The street was tolerably silent, and the lamps were as dull as usual. The coachman, who was rather good at a "set to," jumped off his box, and aimed a spanker at Rob's head.

The pedlar danced him round till he got him opposite the door, when he suddenly ducked his head, missing a terrific swinger from coachy, and butting him in the stomach with his hand.

"I'll show you now," said Rob, "a new trick."

He got the coachy's arms behind him, and holding him in that position, scuffed a "king's man" in his mouth. The Crusher, who had smelt the business, opened the door of the brougham, and Rob, by main force, lifted his struggling opponent in.

The coachy found himself gagged effectually in almost no time.

"It's all serene," Rob observed, seeing his astounded gaze; "we ain't going to hurt you, but we wants a hinteresting ride—so I'll take your togs——"

The coachman kicked, but Rob very expeditiously stripped him of his coat, which he put on; the gold-trimmed hat had fallen into the road; he picked this up, and putting it on his head, the rig was complete.

"Oh, lawks!" he muttered, as he got up in the box, "here is I in a new character, like the bloke what plays Mazeppa in the play, and the cat in the pantomime. Here we go, up again. Bless me! what wicissitudes fortin *do* bring. Ah! here comes them gemmens in blue, knocking the breath out of their blessed bodies, and making *puspurashons* by the quart. Hope that unfortinit cove what knocked his head agin Jem's bit of iron ain't got a settler nowaye, notsoever, nevertheless, as the Bible says, which I ain't looked into since the time when I found the flimsy fiver which nobody never comed to own. Ha! here they comes, a-tearing like Joey's buffaloes."

The appearance of four constables drew forth these philosophical remarks. Crusher Jem had been expostulating with Dick, and in a significant manner fingering his bullet-sling. The sight of the policemen was more potent. He knew what would result from being taken, and he suffered Jem to hand him into the vehicle.

The door was closed, the blinds put up, and the brougham moved away.

The policemen were coming at a rattling pace; behind them four men were carrying on a stretcher their dead comrade.

He who had been affectionately hugged by Rob had recovered, and joined in the chase, giving intimation of the direction taken by the burglars.

There was no other vehicle in the street; every door was closed. The "blues," looking suspiciously about them, approached the brougham.

Crusher Jem set his foot on the prostrate jarvey; Dick pressed his lips firmly together.

Roving Rob put on his most innocent look.

The foremost policeman came in front of the horse. The pedlar flicked the whip in the ear of the horse, causing it to give a start, which made the "peeler" step back.

"Stop!" he cried.

"What do you want?" asked Rob, surlily.

"Have you seen anyone running down this street?"

"Only you and the other bobbies," replied Rob.

"I mean three men running away."

"No, I ain't seen no three men."

"You needn't be uncivil. There's been a burglary at Mr. Wilblow's—house robbed and one of our mates killed."

"His there thou?" murmured Rob. "Lawks! what a thing it ar' that chaps won't let other people's property alone; it's a pity too almost when parties as did ought to know better keeps a lot of swa—— money in their cir—— house; one on your mates dead—killed is he?"

"Outright; his skull is smashed in."

"Is he though? Ah! what a thing it ar'—what despirate parties one *do* meet to be sure!"

All this time the horse was walking; the constables had some of them stayed, the others still springing their rattles, and anxious to distinguish themselves by the capture of the burglars.

Dick was deliberating whether he should let down the blind and reveal himself. It was not the fear of the Crusher's presence that deterred him but the dread of prison.

"Three on 'em did you say?" asked Rob in the simplest tones.

"Yes; but they've been spotted; they're sure of being nabbed, and then, perhaps, they won't all hang."

"Perhaps they won't," thought Rob.

"Anybody inside?" asked the policeman, abruptly.

Rob felt as if a piece of ice had slipped down his back.

"No; don't you see the blinds is up?"

"Yes; I was just thinking whether I should drive up to the station in your vehicle, and get more constables."

Crusher Jem ground his teeth together, while Rob looked blank for a moment.

"Ours ain't a public conweyance," said the pedlar, with an assumption of dignity.

"We'll press it into the service. I think I'd better go the station; you lads can keep on the look-out."

He took hold of the door-handle.

The fingers of the Crusher tightened on his weapon of death—his left hand felt for his knife. Dick folded his arms, and moodily awaited the result.

Rob felt, for the moment, slightly staggered.

"Here's a precious go," he thought. "He'll make a mess of it presently, like they does of the sogers' dinners. Oh, lawks! there he goes."

The policeman fixed his glance on his face.

"You saw no one running by?" he asked.

"D——l a one. I only twigged three codgers rolling home arm in arm; precious muzzey they was too, for they says to me, 'Jemmy,' says they——"

"D——n you for a fool, that was the very three, hurry off mates; I'll get in here, drive me to the station."

"Better jump up, you might twig 'em on the road."

The policeman's hand turned the handle; an inch or so the door had opened when Rob spoke, he seemed to be struck with the idea, for he paused in the act of opening the door.

That pause saved his life, for the Crusher had raised his sling-shot; it saved them from being then taken, for even had the blow despatched the constable, there were others who would have been sufficient to seize the three.

The policeman shut the door, Crusher Jem looked a little more human, Roving Rob inwardly chuckled, and the "blue" took his place beside him.

He never thought how near he had been to the actual criminal.

"Now, is there any speed in that horse?" he asked.

This was what Rob did not know, but he answered boldly—

"Yes."

"Le's see a little of it."

"So you shall, as the big sea-serpent says when they axes to look at his tail."

He lashed the horse, and the brougham whirled towards the station.

"Blessed if this ain't a go!" thought Rob. "Only to twig 'em, driving the very blokes they wants to the jug, and then have to smell nothing of the job. Lawks! it'll make 'em run when they opens their bunged-up *hies* and diskiver how we've give 'em the double. O Lord! suppose there should be any bloke as wants to get inside! or suppose—lawks!— that, as a feeler, this gemman's only got me to drive there acos he knows the hinnercent pups he's after are stowed inside, like kittens in a hamper! That ar' a choker, that ar'."

Such was the strain of Rob's reflections as the horse trotted along.

He thought the policeman looked more cunning when they had got to the station; but this might have been fancy.

Rob was as cool a card as ever figured in a lay; but it was not without a slight sensation of uncomfortable doubt that he saw the policeman alight, and, after telling him to wait, enter the station.

Crusher Jem tugged at the check-string.

"Why don't you drive off?" he whispered hoarsely.

"Stop a bit," thought Rob. "If I takes my vehicle off it might make some of them suspicious gemmens sniff something; and then agin, if I stay, it's likely as not some bloke may want to get inside, which would be wery orkard, and we should have to cut our lucky sticks or be scragged. Hilloa! it's all up, as they says when they kill the king with the hot irons, in somebody's castle. Here they comes thick as thieves, and all in a hurry, like young inguns."

About ten policemen issued from the station. The one whom Rob had brought there, and whom he now saw was a sergeant, stepped forward and put his foot on the wheel.

"That's a awkward place to put it," thought Rob, as he tightened the reins.

It seemed to him that the eyes of all the members of the force were regarding him and his vehicle suspiciously.

"They mean it now," thought Rob.

But, to his surprise, the sergeant took out a half-a-crown.

"Here, coachy," he said, "that's for your trouble. We've sent out notice everywhere. There's no doubt we shall soon find the ruffians."

Rob took the half-crown.

"I won't refuse," he said, "'cos why? half-dollars, like half-quids, is scarce. Here's off home to get a wink of sleep. I shall dream of them ruffians. Good night. Here's to the hope that you'll catch 'em."

Never in his whole life did Rob more joyfully bring the whip down on the flank of the horse. Still there was not the least hurry in the act: Rob's was too cool a head. His motion was to all appearance the most mechanical, and he looked all the "jarvey" when he leaned back, and, with whip across the reins, brought his gaze to the centre-spot between the horse's ears, where he kept it fixed.

The brougham rolled away. It had been an awkward predicament, as Rob afterwards muttered.

"It warn't the most comfortablest thing to be waiting outside the police-station with the very blokes as was wanted—one on 'em on top of the box, tother two inside the brougham."

In which opinion, we think, the reader will coincide.

The station was soon left behind. Rob drove the brougham far from the vicinity of that neighbourhood, and drew up at the corner of a mews.

"We've come far enough with this," he said, when he had descended and opened the door. "Let's change togs again, and get this bloke all right; then we can draw the horse down the mews, and leave him to come to."

This was done. The coachman was permitted to re-appear in his fitting habiliments; but lest he should recognise any of those who were concerned in the business, he was blindfolded, and left in the bottom of the brougham.

"There'll be some peeler come to make him move on when it's light and he's been here long enough," said Rob; and the trio moved away.

Silence continued amongst them. The Crusher was sulky and savage, Dick was downcast and sad, and Rob had enough to do to think upon the feat he had so cleverly played without disturbing his thoughts by speech.

They made hurried progress. Rob knew it was dangerous for them to be out now the morning was near; the coachman, too, might be released, and tell his tale.

Ere the light of dawn showed their haggard faces he had led them into a night-house, where they were sure of a place of refuge for so long as they might require it.

"Well," said Rob, when the three were seated at a table *underground*, in a room where their presence would never be suspected by the ordinary *habitués* of the house, "here we ar', like three mackerel strung to a reed and chucked into a hole. Here we ar', I say, come safe and sound, arter a night of adventures worse nor tiger-fighting and cock-hunting."

He meant tiger-hunting and cock-fighting.

"Yes, it's werry well," muttered the Crusher. "Your cussed sqeamishness with that white-haired bloke was near getting us scragged."

"Didn't I bring you safe out arter taking you to the station? Ah, Jem, you'll be lucky when you rides away from there and can come and sit snug in a caboose like this. 'Tain't allers it can be done; they generally shoves you somewhere else."

The Crusher muttered an oath.

"That piping kid," he growled, "couldn't keep his jaw shut."

"Well, he ar' not so nobby that way as we must make him."

Here Dick spoke.

"I see what it be, Mister Roving Rob. You have brought I into this to make us both rogues; but you shan't do it. Noa, I've been led wrong, but I haven't done any dishonest act yet; and I'll bear all rather than lose my character."

Roving Rob took a drain at the pewter. He expected these outbursts from Dick, and took no notice of them.

"More nor that," Dick cried, "you've been and let poor Charley get into trouble. I know it, or he would have been there when we come out."

"Well, it ar' likely that they've popped their clappers."

Dick rose from his seat.

"It be your doing," he cried; "it be all your doing. If it hadn't been for you, we should never have been there, and then this wouldn't have happened. But I tell 'ee what, Mister Rob, Charley bean't going to bear all the punishment now. If wrong be done, the right ones shall suffer for it. I'll bear my part, and so shall everyone else."

Crusher Jem brought his fist heavily on the table.

"Blind me!" he said; "would you peach?"

"Take him quietly, never mind the risk," cried Rob. "He's tender on one point, like the cat that fell on to a bayonet. Why, you gratituded gemman, if it hadn't been for me you would have been yet in that genteel place I helped you to come out of. But we won't go over old scores, as the sot says to the jolly old landlord. The truth, and the whole truth, is that Charley ar' taken, he ar'; I heard 'em knock him over. He's safe."

"Safe? And you brought me away?"

"In coorse. If you'd stayed they'd have nabbed you too."

"Oh, Rob, but thee be a villain!"

"Which it ar' kind of you to say so."

"That poor boy, he is my sister's child, and he in prison! If I had minded him at first I should never have been led by bad Ralph. But he shall come out; he shall not stay a day in prison. I'll give myself up for him; he shall never bear sorrow for my folly."

"That ar' the way to put it."

"For you, who have helped to do it, you shall suffer. Darm thee! if aught harms him, I'll wring thy neck."

Dick was dreadfully excited; his honest face was flushed and his eyes gleamed. To the astonishment of Roving Rob he hurled the pewter pot out of that worthy's hand, just as he was in the act of drinking, and took hold of him by the collar.

Rob looked as amazed as "honest Iago" might have done when incontinently collared by the angered Othello. His dismay was on the increase when Dick commenced violently shaking him.

Now, Dick was very strong; he had immense power in that arm of his; and as he shook Rob to and fro, that worthy jerked out his words in this wise—

"Wh-y, Di-ick, wha-what's the g-game? as the t-tom-c-cat—oh!—said—d when—oh!—the red-hot poke-poker f-fell on his nose, and singed his wh-whis—oh!—whiskers."

"I'll tell thee, I will!"

"Here—d-draw it—oh!—mild—puff—as the—puff —vinegar-faced l-landlady says to the—oh!—chap as pai-painted her port-rait."

Still Dick kept vigorously shaking. Rob's face got very red, and there was a look in his eyes like that of an easy-natured mastiff getting too much teasing.

Dick evidently meant mischief; once or twice his clenched fist was thrust in the puffing face of the patient Rob.

Crusher Jem got up with a growl.

"We don't want none of that sort of game here," he said. "If there's to be any dust kicked up, here's a settler."

He stepped behind Dick, intending to stick his knife in his back.

Roving Rob saw the intent, and finding that, like Charles Lamb when he was to be dipped, the business would be finished before he could give his directions, he slung round so as to drag Dick out of aim of the murderous weapon; then, with a wrench, he freed himself, and stood between Dick and the Crusher.

"That ar' one way to treat a friend, as the stork said when the lion gave her a dish she couldn't get her beak in; put that cheesetoaster away, Jem; we don't want any ruling here. Well, if I were not warranted sound and taut, I shouldn't be whole now. I should say you served your time to the shaking business; but don't do it again: 'cos why — I might be angry, as the crocodile said when the plover picked a hole in his jaw when he was a nibbling the insects out of his precious mouth."

"I want no more to do with you; I will go and see after Charley."

The Crusher put himself in his way as he advanced to the door.

"No peaching here," he said, "you're in, and we don't mean you to go out till this job is blowed over."

"Will you prevent me?"

"Take your blessed davy I will."

Here Rob, ever the pacificator, interfered.

"You're out of temper, Dick, which ar' nat'ral, but arn't perlite. The blessed kiddy ar' took, but they can't do much to him."

"Much! they should do nought."

"Well, p'raps they'll do that, though it ain't often they deals in that article; but, howsomdever, he ar' in, and, in course, they'll keep him to see what they can get out of him."

"He'll split on us," the Crusher said, using his favourite oath.

"Noa, he be too firm to say anything," Dick cried.

"Which ar' the fact; he ain't a gal of that sort, not nohow."

"And he shall not be in gaol. I'll see who'll stop me."

"Now, now, Dick, take a friend's advice, which ain't neither pisen nor physic; if you go to the beaks, what will they do but clap you in quod? and if your clapped in quod, why, who knows but what it'll be——"

He drew his fingers round his throat in a significant manner.

"If I thought you'd peach when they took you," muttered the Crusher, "I'd stick you like a cursed pig."

"You seem mighty fond of using that knife of your'n," said Dick. "Maybe we'll try who's best man."

"Now, no quarrelling among friends. Ain't I brought you here for you to make your lives happy?"

"Happy? What, with that black deed of murder done that I saw?"

The look the Crusher gave him testified to that gentleman's feelings.

"That ar' the pint: it's a hunlucky go, it ar', but the job's done, and a hundred words won't fill a bushel; you was there when it happened, and you was one in the crib, which ar' quite enough to convict you any time you let's the blues clap their blessed mawleys on you."

"Ah! but it be a cursed trick."

"It will be a trick if they lays hold of you; they'd think very little of swinging you out to dry from the Old Bailey some fine morning. Ah! it's a cold job that. Don't run your neck into the rope, Dick — keep it as long as you can without being stretched."

Dick covered his face with his hands and groaned. He could realise how true were Rob's words. He had been one to enter the house; he was escaping when the policeman met his death. In the eyes of the law he was guilty of being an accessory to the murder, and as such would assuredly swing, as Rob had stated.

"This be all come of doing wrong," he cried. "Poor Charley! it be hard for thee. I will swing for you, but what you shall get off."

"Don't flurry your bile, Dick. The kiddy ar' took, but he ain't going to be let stay there. Roving Rob never yet was the skunk to leave a pal in limbo while there was a ha'porth of a chance of getting him out."

This was an unintentional rub for the Crusher, who had been known to leave a pal to be hanged rather than run any risk himself.

Dick's face brightened.

"I have done thee wrong, perhaps," he exclaimed "But help to get Charley out, and I don't care what becomes of me."

CHAPTER XXVII.

WHAT USE THEY TRIED TO PUT CHARLEY TO.

BURGLARY WITH VIOLENCE!
TERRIFIC STRUGGLE!
A POLICEMAN KILLED!
SIX OTHERS ASSAULTED!
CAPTURE OF ONE OF THE GANG!

Such were the leading lines that drew attention to the burglary at Mr. Wilblow's house, the following account of which appeared in the daily papers: —

"Last night, at a late hour, the dwelling of Mr. Wilblow was burglariously entered by a gang of villains, who, having forced their way from the back of the house, proceeded to possess themselves of a quantity of plate (principally heirlooms and family souvenirs) which was kept, with a sum of money, in a safe, the situation of which must have been known to the burglars, as they proceeded to the room where it was kept without disturbing any of the household.

"It appears that Mr. Wilblow — a gentleman whose services in the cause of philanthropy and for the benefit of humanity are well known — was the first to hear the burglars, as they were engaged in their nefarious spoliation.

"With a presence of mind which cannot be too greatly commended, he opened his window, and having signalled a policeman, went down the stairs, passed the room where the ruffians were assembled, and noiselessly admitted the policeman and two others, who had meanwhile arrived. Some warning of their coming was given by a boy, evidently stationed on the watch, who cried out to his confederates to escape.

"The constables, accompanied by Mr. Wilblow, rushed up the stairs, and encountering the gang on the landing, a frightful struggle took place.

"The warning of the accomplice having put them on their guard, they attacked the constables (whom they far outnumbered), beating them with every kind of weapon, and at last forcing their way by — some leaping over the banisters, some out of the staircase-window, but none escaping without receiving a severe visitation from the courageous constables.

"The constables pursued them; and Mr. Wilblow hearing a suspicious sound in his drawing-room, fearlessly entered, though it was enveloped in a darkness that might have concealed half a dozen murderous housebreakers.

"He was scarcely inside before he was attacked

with the most tiger-like fury by some one who sprang upon him from the gloom. He stoutly struggled with his assailant, and at length succeeded, by a happy blow of a weapon with which, in the excitement, he had armed himself, in overcoming his desperate antagonist, who was subsequently discovered to be the boy who had given the alarm.

"The worst remains to be told. Escaping from the house pell-mell, the villains were stopped by a constable of the name of Roberts, who had no sooner captured one of them than he was attacked in the most shameful manner, his skull actually being *beaten in* with some terrible instrument carried by the assassins.

"It is lamentable to add that the ruffians succeeded in making off, after brutally trampling what little remained of life out of their unfortunate victim.

"Of course, such a tragedy occurring in the midst of a highly select neighbourhood, could not fail to create an immense amount of interest, and in less than half an hour after the actual occurrence groups of eager faces might have been seen clustered together, as the neighbours, aroused from their beds, came forth to learn the exact particulars, and gathered round the fatal spot.

"It is with regret we have to state that, notwithstanding the most vigorous and untiring pursuit, the band of villains have as yet eluded capture. From this fact and others, it is possible that the whole affair was a well-organized plan, and that the assassins had confederates posted in the neighbourhood to give assistance to cover their retreat when they came forth with their ill-gotten booty.

"Too much commendation cannot be bestowed upon Mr. Wilblow, both for the presence of mind he displayed and the courageous manner in which he faced the burglars; and it is only necessary to add that the constables fought with a desperation worthy of being crowned with success."

"LATEST PARTICULARS.

"As yet no tidings have been gleaned of the perpetrators of this atrocious crime. The whole neighbourhood is up in arms, and call aloud for justice on the wretches who can commit, and for alterations in a system which can allow, such doings in its midst.

"The body of the unfortunate constable, who so nobly gave his life in the execution of his duty, was conveyed by a party of his brother officers to his home, there to await interment.

"In losing him the force is deprived of an active and zealous *employé*, whose assiduous services are likely to be missed in that department, in the furtherance of which he lost his life.

"We understand that Mr. Wilblow no sooner heard that the constable so brutally murdered had a wife and family than, with his usual liberality and humanity, he assisted them in their hour of need.

"We must not close this brief announcement of a deed so desperate without bestowing a mead of unqualified praise on Sergeant Bullam, who no sooner heard of the murder than he rode off in a brougham to the station to give notice of the occurrence, and send out a bevy of active officers.

"The accomplice who was taken, though quite a boy, looks the fit and trained associate of the gang with which he is connected. Since his incarceration at the Westminster Police-court, where he has been placed to undergo his examination, he has maintained a sullen and obdurate demeanour, the most assiduous endeavours failing to extract a word from him relative to his confederates.

"Those who anticipated, from his youth, that he might be made an instrument in the hands of justice are deeply mistaken. He is evidently well trained and tutored, and no one looking on his hardened features can fail to see the peril Mr. Wilblow must have faced when exposed to the sudden attack of one so determined and zealous in crime."

Dick, who had been reading this account in the paper which had been brought down to them, moaned aloud.

"What a lot of whoppers!" cried Rob; and looking at the paper as if it were a slimy serpent, likely to sting him, he looked askance and wise.

"Poor Charley!" Dick cried; "to make him out like that! It would break his heart if he heard of it."

"He's a brick," muttered the Crusher; "no peach about him."

"He ar' true to the backbone," Rob said, "and we'll get him out yet. Stay here, my pals; I'll go and have a peep at the court."

A second edition, published two hours later, gave the subjoined intelligence.

"STARTLING NEWS!

"THE ASSASSINS AT THE POLICE STATION !!

"Since our first going to press a singular piece of intelligence, illustrating the worse than inefficiency of the police, has been certified.

"It appears that about half-past six a brougham, which had been observed by a policeman on duty remaining for some time in a spot where it would be dangerous for it to be when the business of the day commenced, was discovered to have its driver inside, gagged, blindfolded, and bound.

"The poor fellow was nearly dead when taken out, but as soon as he could speak he made a statement which shows how little the exertions of our police are to be relied upon where the life and property which they were specially organised to protect are concerned.

"He states that shortly before dawn, while driving slowly to his stables, he was attacked by a gang of six men, four of whom suddenly leaped upon him, and dragged him half stunned from the box, while one held the rein, and a sixth opened the door of the vehicle, into which he was thrust.

"At this time the pursuit was hot after the assassins and housebreakers: there is no doubt, then, that these were a portion, if not all, of that criminal gang; but the most astounding piece of information is that not only by means of this device the ruffians escaped, but that this was the very conveyance which took police-sergeant Bullam to the station, the murderous wretches being at the time actually *inside the vehicle* with the gagged coachman, one of their number being on the box, disguised in the dress of the driver.

"In ordinary cases justice may not be supposed to be too keen-sighted; but what are we to say to this, when an acute officer suffers himself to be driven to the station by one of the very gang for which he is searching—the remainder of the desperate wretches all the while inside?

"It is lamentable to think that the carriage containing them remained outside the police-station, with its criminal freight, for at least *ten minutes*, and was eventually permitted to go away with its exulting burthen—the clumsy obtuseness of a qualified officer not enabling him to scent the trick, or judge of the difference between a thorough coachman and a disguised ruffian.

"Some consolation exists in the fact that—though *not* through the exertions of the police—a clue is in the hands of the right parties, and will doubtless lead to the apprehension of the stealthy vagabonds, whose murderous night-marauding has plunged an usually quiet neighbourhood into an excitement and a fear unprecedented."

From these accounts it will be seen that everybody was fogged by the trick so adroitly carried out by Roving Rob, and thus lashed out their censure right and left indiscriminately.

Let us now return to Charley himself, who, as the real capture that had been made, was the hero of that night's adventure—no enviable notoriety, for the rumour of his deeds, as related by the philanthropical Mr. Wilblow, and heightened by the glowing imagination of the reporters, had inspired everyone in the vicinity to behold the hardened boy who had at so early an age proved a proficient in the art of housebreaking.

Poor Charley! it cut him sorely to find himself the theme of such comment. He had but one solace, and that was that Dick had escaped.

He cared not what he suffered, so long as his uncle remained out of danger.

The blow which the courageous philanthropist had dealt him had swollen his face and fractured his skull.

When first seized after his capture by the owner of the house, his appearance as he was dragged along—the policeman's knuckles jammed in his throat—his face discoloured, swollen, and covered with blood—his eye blackened—was almost enough to confirm the statement of the penny-a-liner.

It had been a cruel, merciless blow—one that might have felled an ox, and it was only by a miracle that the devoted boy had escaped having his skull smashed in.

A buz went round the court when two policemen dragged him in, and stood one on each side of him, holding him, half-throttled, as if there was danger that he would make an outrageous attack upon them in that sacred hall of justice.

Mr. Garnaud, the magistrate, regarded him as if he were some escaped beast. He listened with greedy attention to the story related by Mr. Wilblow, who came into court with a sad and downcast look, arising, people said, from his goodness of heart, which would not allow him to give evidence even in the cause of justice, against a fellow-being.

They were juggled. The honest Christian's grief was for his gold, which had been successfully abstracted.

The tale he recounted was similar in substance to the account given in the papers. He spoke with a wavering, broken voice; and occasionally, when he glanced at the obdurate prisoner, a Pickswiffian tear was seen to glisten in his eye.

Mr. Garnaud, having made his notes, and decided the case in his own mind, turned his glance on the prisoner, when, after a cold stare, which everyone knew meant commitment, he asked what he had to say to it.

Charley declined to answer.

"You have heard what this gentleman has recounted. Do you deny any portion of it?"

Charley felt his emotion swelling his breast, as he said—

"A good deal of it is not true."

"No doubt," said the magistrate, drily, picking his teeth with a small, ivory tooth-pick—his favourite custom when he had made up his mind on a case.

"I never attacked him. I did not know he was in the room till he struck me with his heavy club, and knocked me down."

"A club?" Mr. Garnaud asked, turning to the eminent philanthropist, in evident expectation of a denial.

"A sort of club."

"Ah, yes, something adapted to keep away burglars."

"Just so, sir; we do not expect to drive them from our premises with a feather."

"Of course not."

He turned his frowning glance on the undaunted boy.

There were many in court who thought that for a person who had been so severely attacked, the philanthropist looked in remarkably good cue, while the bruised face of Charley bore testimony to the awful visitation he had received.

But they knew that in that court an expression of their sympathy, even for the unjustly accused, would draw upon them the indignation of an arbitrary magistrate, who had been twice unbenched.

"You confess, then, that you *were* in the room?" Mr. Garnaud said.

"Yes, I was there."

"But you never assaulted Mr. Wilblow, nor assisted in the outrageous work that was being carried on?"

"I never spoke, except to give the alarm, and to prevent Dick being led into crime."

"Oh. And who is Dick?"

Charley remained silent.

The magistrate repeated his question.

The policeman gave the hardened prisoner a jerk.

The usher looked as only the usher of a police-court can look when the supreme majesty of the law, in the shape of a slim magistrate, is set at defiance by a collared criminal.

Everybody in court turned their gaze on Charley.

"He be my uncle," the boy answered.

"Ah! your uncle. We shall get at it presently. Where does Dick, your uncle, reside?"

"He has nowhere to live."

"Well, where is he likely to be found?"

"If I could tell you I wouldn't."

"Eh?"

Everybody looked surprised.

"No. Thee would only have him dragged to prison, and that's all I tried to prevent. You wouldn't believe him if he spoke the truth."

"We might. What may be the truth?—that he was not there?"

"Yes, he was there; but he ought not to have been."

"Oh! we know he ought not to have been."

The magistrate's answer was intended to be very cutting.

"No; but you don't know what I do."

"That's precisely what we want to learn."

"He was led there by bad men; he has never done anything wrong, but has always been honest and good; but he has been wronged and hunted down for what he never did. When I lost him, I was afraid what they would lead him to, and I only found them out when they had got him here."

"A most likely tale. But who were 'they' you speak of?"

"Two bad men."

"Their names?"

"I will not tell."

"Well, where are they to be found?"

"I can't tell."

"Remember where you stand," said the magistrate, sternly, "and think not to evade justice. Who are your accomplices?"

"I have told you truth, God help me! I was no accomplice; I would have done all to keep Dick out of trouble—I don't care what you do to me if he be safe."

"Well, if your story is so true, let us hear a little information about 'Dick' what is his name. Where is his home?—who are they that will speak for him?"

Gladly would he have answered, but he knew that to refer them to his village home would be to further jeopardise him for a crime of which he was the innocent victim.

So he resolutely remained silent.

All the arguments, the menaces of the court, the jerks of the constables, and the looks of the officials failed to move him from his determination.

The spectators—the very class among whom such reticence would be appreciated and admired—already began to make a true hero of him, and inwardly hoped that he would continue firm.

There was no need of fear in that respect: Charley would have suffered himself to be torn limb from limb ere his speech should have placed Dick in further peril.

"Prisoner," exclaimed the magistrate, losing all patience, "a crime of unequalled enormity has been perpetrated; the house of a gentleman, to whose worthiness and humanity I can testify, has been broken into, his property abstracted, his person assailed, and a constable, who nobly performed his duty against unequal odds, murdered under circumstances of the greatest brutality; you, whose head

MARY, THE BELLE OF THE VILLAGE.

is not much above the dock where you stand, are by complicity arraigned on the charge of aiding the murder of a fellow being; it is in your power to further the ends of justice by disclosing the whereabouts of those who have so well tutored you in a course that, if followed, must lead you to the gallows. Much as it may err in the principles of even-handed justice, I am permitted to inform you that your evidence will exonerate you from all share in the consequences of this crime; you need, therefore, have no fear of speaking the truth."

"I have no more to say," was all the answer Charley gave.

The magistrate's face flushed purple.

"In the whole course of my magisterial experience," he exclaimed, "I have never witnessed juvenile hardihood and depravity to equal this. It has been long known that the young are too cleverly trained to these enterprises, but never have I known a more successful instance of their tuition."

At this moment a gentleman of quiet and distinguished aspect stepped forward. The magistrate, supposing he had something to communicate regarding the prisoner's antecedents, gave him the most courteous attention.

"I have listened to this boy's story," he said, in a quiet calm tone, "and cannot help being struck by a certain air of probability about which he alleges."

As this was going directly opposite to the magistrate's expressed opinion, that dignitary bestowed on him only a questioning stare.

In the same mild tone of voice the gentleman continued—

"We often hear instances of people, till then honest, being beguiled into crime and it does appear that there are occasions where a timely interference might save those who are trembling on the brink of crime. Now, I take it for granted that the object of the law is more the suppression and prevention of wrong than its punishment: it may be that there are circumstances in this case which would repay some trouble in their investigation."

Mr. Garnand looked vacantly before him, and recommenced picking his teeth.

"I have, therefore, to offer on behalf of this friendless and already severely-punished lad, to take him under my charge. I do not doubt that by careful management the plain facts may come to light. In this we are all interested; if, therefore, you will liberate him on bail, I will be bond in heavy amount for his re-appearance to answer the inquiry."

Tears rushed to Charley's eyes: he did not look for sympathy in that stern place, and this kindness of the stranger touched him to the quick.

"Really," Mr. Garnand said; "I do not know how any one could offer bail under the expectations that it would be accepted, where the case stands so serious."

"I presume," remarked the gentleman, "my position is satisfactory?"

"In every way, Mr. Elsden; but you must see, in a matter of such vital importance, it would be against all precedent to set a prisoner at liberty."

"I ask it in the name of justice as well as humanity. I presume this gentleman would not oppose any measure that might result in elucidation of this sad business?"

"My pleasure would be only too great to assist in such a cause," Mr. Wilblow rejoined. "I candidly state that it has been a source of extreme pain to me to have to appear here this day in the character of prosecutor against a fellow creature, and that a youth, being connected with wickeder beings, should draw our sympathy: but a dreadful crime has been committed; a fellow being—a father of little children—husband of a devoted wife—has been by violence burned before his Maker; and till that deed is affixed on the guilty party, I don't think it would be justice, even to the prisoner, to give him a chance of evading this inquiry. With every confidence in your motives, I am aware that circumstances will occur which render it imperative that the law should be the custodian of its prisoner."

So quietly he spoke, glancing pitifully at the youthful criminal, and controlling his visible grief the while, that the spectators were deceived and drawn on his side.

He seemed such a gentle, amiable, Christian being, one whose heart was plucked by each word that brought penalty to another.

"The sentiments of Mr. Wilblow do honour to his nature," remarked the magistrate; "I fully concur in the observations that have fallen from him relative to the custody of the prisoner; therefore, Mr. Elsden, I regret to say I must decline your proffered bail."

"Oh, no regret, my dear sir; I spoke in behalf of the lad's welfare. I am convinced what evil an acquaintance with the interior of a prison may work on a youthful mind."

"I do not think you have ground for compunction on that score. I would venture to assert it will not be the first one he has seen the inside of."

"I never was in a prison before," Charley cried, fiercely.

"I find it easy to believe him," Mr. Elsden remarked, "and shall at once engage adequate counsel to defend the boy and fathom the case."

"I am afraid," said the magistrate, "you will have to employ clever counsel to remove the case from the prisoner."

Mr. Elsden looked pained.

"Really, sir, as a magistrate, these remarks scarcely seem just. I hope the case will not be pre-judged."

Mr. Garrand became of a bilious hue.

"The prisoner is remanded till Thursday," he said. "Take him away."

They led Charley back to his cell.

Then the gentleman who had interested himself in his behalf left the court.

But not before a murmured (though unheard) word of approbation had been bestowed upon him by a rough-looking, straight, shaggy-whiskered individual, evidently, by his odoriferous garments, a vendor of fish, and who soon after took his departure.

That individual was Roving Rob.

CHAPTER XXVIII.

WARNER'S PLANS TO MAKE SURE OF MARY.

WARNER'S arms were encircling Mary when the chaise drove off, she was leaning trembling on his breast when the pistol was fired by Roving Rob. The report and the fear that somebody was hit had caused her sudden scream, and Warner, who believed she was struck by the bullet, let fall the reins and supported her with both his arms.

"Mary, my Mary," he exclaimed, "are you hit? look up dearest."

"I am safe," she replied faintly; "but you?"

"I, too, am unhurt."

"And Dick?"

"It was he who fired the weapon: fired at you Mary, out of revenge; he would have added this to his other crimes, but thank God he has failed."

Mary sobbed afresh; it was not difficult for her to believe that Warner was stating the truth, and her tears flowed freely at the thought of her former lover striving to take her life.

She forgot at that moment that even if he had done so she had given him sufficient provocation to justify the act.

Need we say how she had wronged Dick's nature; his vengeance was directed against her betrayer, not against herself, for her he had only pity and sorrow.

The clouds were drifting before the moon—dark heavy clouds that threatened a coming storm; the wheels of the light vehicle rattled along the road and whirled up the dust.

When Warner had dropped the reins, Mary's scream, and the report of the pistol, had startled the horses, and they dashed off at a rapid canter.

On the first moments of his excitement Warner scarcely heeded this fact, it had been too serious a matter to have to see to the safety of Mary.

His conviction had of course been that she was hit, and it would have placed him in no very enviable position had he found himself riding with a corpse.

It would have surely led to startling consequences, and might have got him into serious trouble.

But satisfied of her safety his attention was called to the horses.

They were whirling the chaise along at a terrific rate.

And the reins were dangling out of his reach.

Fortunately, hitherto the bend of the road had been but slight, and as another vehicle came in the way the path, even at the pace they were travelling, was tolerably safe.

But the speed of the horses was increasing every moment, and at any moment something might come in their way, in which case a smash would be the result.

Recovering from her faintness Mary was not long in perceiving the real state of affairs; unaccustomed to horses the speed at which they were proceeding was enough to alarm her, but the fact that her companion possessed no control over the horses was absolutely terrifying.

Warner, who saw the dismay depicted on her features, spoke cheeringly to her, and persuading her to sit still leaned forward and attempted to regain the reins.

But they were out of his reach, and Mary, fearful that in his eagerness he would fall, held him back.

The horses seemed to know they had it all their own way.

They shook their heads and tossed their manes snorting as they rattled along.

The moon became entirely hidden, the path before them became partly obscured.

With the darkness came fresh dangers.

And the pace of the horses was increasing.

Warner could not conceal his fears; at the best he cannot ever brave, and the probability that he would be dashed to pieces was extremely repugnant to his feelings.

He had anticipated getting Mary quietly away and stopping with her at some quiet house where he could by the exercise of his specious arts, make her his own.

In place of this it now seemed hazardous how long he would succeed in keeping himself safe from broken limbs.

In proportion as his fears increased that of Mary's subsided.

She looked her danger calmly in the face and awaited its coming.

All at once a vivid flash gleamed before the horses' heads.

Then came a wild crash that made Mary almost leap from her seat.

Two or three drops of rain fell with a dull heavy patter.

The storm was commencing.

Mary shrank back trembling.

Warner turned deadly pale.

The horses whom that clap of thunder further scared flew madly on.

Again the lightning flashed its sheeted fire.

Again the thunder pealed wildly.

The chaise rattled along the road, its wheels scarcely touching the ground, so rapid were their evolutions.

And now Mary's terrors returned in all their force.

It seemed to her that the storm and danger were but a visitation for her conduct in deserting Dick.

She trembled violently at every clap of thunder, and shuddered as the lightning played before her eyes.

A greater peril now appeared, hitherto unopposed, and, without deviating the horses, had continued their course.

But now came the part of the road where it wound round slightly to the left.

In front was a hedge-row with a gate belonging to a field that was skirted by the road.

Towards this gate the horses were tearing.

Everyone knows that when a horse takes fright it will dash straight forward, and that even when an obstacle appears it will seldom deviate.

These two horses, each steaming from their exertions, were excited to the velocity of madness, and even with the reins in his hand Warner would have found it difficult to turn them.

As it was they were making straight for the obstacle.

The hedges on either side flew by; the rumbling of the wheels grew confused; still on, on, dashed the horses.

Mary closed her eyes and sat shivering.

Warner pale as death, bewildered whether or not to let himself out as they reached the barrier.

The frightful rate at which they were travelling convincing him that it would be no worse to be pitched out than to throw himself out alone deterred him.

They were near the gate now, the horses snorting as they saw the obstacle.

Warner's teeth chattered.

He looked at Mary and almost cursed her at that moment, since but for her he would not have been there.

Still with a last remainder of decency he put one arm round her and with the other held on to the side of the chaise.

A moment now and they would be dashed against the barrier; the horses were within a bound; he closed his eyes and prayed for mercy.

Literally spinning the chaise along, the horses met the gate.

Then came a crash.

The vehicle vibrated with the concussion, and Mary was nearly jerked out of Warner's arms.

Not an instant did the horses halt; the force with which they swept against the gate carried it away, and almost without a check they were on their way again.

Safe!

Warner ventured to look round.

They were whirling over a field of grass.

The lightning had for a while ceased.

The few drops of rain were ended.

The thunder no longer rolled.

But the clouds, yet hung heavy and threatening.

He tried to look across the field; there was a dim low line, doubtless the hedge that fringed the road.

If there was another gate there, they could scarcely hope to be as fortunate as they had just been.

Most gates opened inwards, and to that simple fact had it been owing that they were saved.

If the gate had opened outwards, the resistance would have dashed them to pieces.

Yet that was precisely the danger which they were likely to encounter.

He looked at Mary.

She was gazing timidly, fearingly around her.

If he could throw her out and spring after her.

The ground was soft, the grass tolerably high; he hesitated a moment, and then looked before him.

They were approaching not the gate, but the quickset hedge.

It gave him some hope to see that the bushes were low and had several gaps in them.

He whispered to Mary to take heart, and awaited the shock.

They were not travelling so fast now—the ground was not so good for the horses' feet as the hard road.

The wheels, too, sank into the turf, and were impeded by the grass.

These causes combined to slacken their pace.

Still only a tolerable amount of speed would take them clear of the quickset barrier; if they slackened too much, they would have a greater chance of sticking in the middle.

That is to say, the chaise and the horses would.

Both Mary and Warner would speedily find themselves landed on the other side.

It is not every one who can look forward with hope to the chance of flying through a hedge.

But Warner knew that it was their only chance.

The obstacle, too, might give the horses a check, and enable him to recover the reins.

So he waited with bated breath and palpitating heart.

But the shock came before he expected it. When within a dozen yards of the hedge, one of the horses stumbled and fell.

It made an attempt to rise, but the shaft impeded its movements, and, to the joy of Warner, it again fell.

The other horse went forward a pace or two, dragging the fallen one after it; but the weight of the struggling animal soon brought it to a standstill.

Then Warner alighted, and lifted Mary out.

She had clung to Warner; Warner had clung to the chaise, and so they had escaped being hurled to grass.

Very pale and with a sinking heart, she stood trembling a little way off, while Warner got the fallen horse to his feet.

The animal was not much hurt—a little scratched with the shafts and harness, but not disabled.

Warner blessed the happy accident which had saved their lives, and, again lifting Mary into the vehicle, gave her the reins to hold, while he led the horses to the gate.

Having unfastened this, he led them out into the road, and once more took his place by Mary's side.

They went this time at a moderate trot. Warner had had enough of galloping, and the horses were none the better for their flight.

Before they had gone six miles along the road, the thunder again began to herald the storm.

Mary drew her cloak around her.

"It will rain heavily," she said.

"Yes; we shall have a storm of no ordinary magnitude. I do not know what we can do, unless we meet with some inn."

"I am afraid we shall not," sighed Mary.

"If we do, I will soon knock the people up."

The truth was, Warner knew there was an inn not three miles farther on; more than that, it was one where he had often before put up, and, being on intimate terms with the landlord, could do almost as he liked.

He concealed this from Mary, because he had framed his plans against her innocence.

The storm was more his friend than his enemy, if it drove them to seek shelter.

His intention was to alight at the inn, engage a chamber where Mary could be shown, he himself following after.

To this arrangement he thought he could soon talk her over, after it was made; or, if his specious flatteries and protestations failed, he thought she would not make any outcry in a strange inn.

These thoughts were passing through his mind, while, with one arm around the waist of the unsuspecting girl, he was drawing her unrestrainedly to his breast.

Of course, to a great extent, Mary had placed herself in his power.

She had forsaken Dick, and consented to accompany him unmarried, and unaware almost of his nature or intents.

But she had been beguiled by his insidious arts, and now, as he pressed her to him, it was she thought only the pleasing attentions of a lover, and it came as a cheerful contrast to her late peril.

In a very short time the brisk trot of the horses brought them in sight of a Gothic building, at the corner of a cross road.

"An inn, I do believe," cried Warner, as the rain came pattering down; "how fortunate; we shall escape the storm, and in the morning we can continue our journey to London."

"Oh, I hope we shall be able to make them hear," Mary said, as they drove up to the gateway.

CHAPTER XXIX.

THE CHAMBER AT THE INN.

THE inn was dark outwardly and internally.

A silence reigned, proclaiming that all the inmates were in bed. Warner leapt out of the chaise, and pulled the bell at the gate.

The barking of a dog replied from the yard; then the rain, now falling sharply, drowned every sound, and began to drench everything.

Warner pulled the bell again.

A minute more passed.

Then a night-capped head appeared at the gable window.

"Hulloa," cried the owner in a sleepy tone; "what d'ye want?"

"Shelter for the night."

"Eh."

"Bed for ourselves; lodging for our horses."

"Oh!"

"Come, make haste; the lady will get wet."

Mary blushed. Warner's words caused a strange feeling of shame.

"Eh," said Boniface again.

"It's raining; the lady will get wet."

"Oh! a lady!"

"Yes; don't you see there is—my wife; come, make haste."

"Warner!" said Mary reprovingly, when the head was withdrawn.

"Don't mind, Mary; it was only to bring him down; he would not have come down if I hadn't said that."

The rain came pelting harder.

The wind rose high.

Sheet lightning lit up the whole scene.

But inside the house all was silent.

Mary, who had entertained some thoughts of not entering the house, grew anxious to get inside, as the storm grew more furious, and no sound came from within testifying that some one was coming down to admit them.

"Confound the fellow," said Warner; "how slow he is; you will take cold, dear Mary."

"No," answered the young girl artlessly.

"If my love could shelter you," continued Warner, "not a drop of rain should come near you."

Mary looked at him gratefully.

Directly afterwards the landlord was heard unfastening the door.

Before he had opened it the ostler undid the gate, and came to the horses' heads.

Warner handed Mary out.

"Take the horses in and look over them carefully," he said to the ostler; "we had a downfall on the road."

"I'll attend to 'em, sir," said the sleepy ostler, as he took them into the yard.

Inside the hostel the landlord stood, with a candle in his hand; he greeted Warner respectfully, and looked somewhat curiously on the lady.

He had hastily assumed a more fitting guise than what he appeared in when his head was thrust out of the window, and, when he had shut the door, he said respectfully—

"I have ordered the room to be got ready; the maid will be here directly. I suppose, sir, you will step into my parlour and have a glass of something hot, while the lady retires?"

Mary, with crimsoning cheeks, looked at Warner. Villain as he was in heart, he could not meet unabashed her steady gaze.

"My dear Mary," he exclaimed, "let the maid show you to your room. I will order you some refreshment: you must, I am sure, stand in need of it."

The maid at that moment made her appearance; she was a spruce looking girl, not too refined in looks, nor too demure in manners.

She curtseyed to Mary, and the young girl, bashful at her position, and reassured by Warner's speech, followed the maid upstairs.

Then a significant look passed between the landlord and his guest.

The apartment into which Mary was ushered was one of those old-fashioned chambers to be met with in many country inns, in which the furniture, not of the most elegant pretensions, has that substantial air of comfort about it which is so cheering to the tired traveller.

The chamber-maid was not very loquacious; she asked Mary whether she would like to sit up till her refreshment was brought up, and, receiving an answer in the negative, offered her services in assisting her to undress.

This was a process which Mary had always been instructed to do for herself; she felt strange at being attended by any one else, and in a very little time signified to the officious maid that she would prefer attending to herself, and that she could bring her up whatever was prepared.

"Bashful modesty," thought the girl, who easily scented out matters. "Ah! it's plain enough; she's a young hand, or she would have put a ring on her finger."

Mary was almost undressed when she returned

with a tray bearing some sherry and some light comestibles. The young girl would have preferred a cup of tea, but, as that would have involved the trouble of ordering and preparing, she sipped a little sherry, and made a frail attack on the viands.

"Have you come far, ma'am?" the maid asked, as she busied herself in putting the chamber straight.

"Yes; many miles."

"What a storm you have escaped."

"I am afraid it will be violent. I was so glad when I saw your inn; I had begun to think we should have had to endure it all night."

"Why, ma'am, you didn't mean to travel all night?"

"Oh, yes; if it had not been for the storm, we should not have stopped here at all."

"She's what they would call in my country rather innocent," mused the girl.

"There, ma'am," she said aloud, "I think that will do; the chamber looks nice and tidy."

"You have given yourself needless trouble."

"Well, ma'am, we always like to have it put straight before the gentleman comes."

"The gentleman!"

"Yes, ma'am: some don't mind how they find a room; but I daresay your husband is not like that."

"My husband!" cried Mary, turning pale.

"I think that's him coming."

"To my room?"

"Susan!" cried a shrill voice on the stairs.

"Yes, ma'am: it's missis: good night, ma'am; I'll come early in the morning—if you want me for anything in the night there's a bell behind your bed that rings in my room."

She withdrew quickly, and left Mary pondering upon the significance of her manner and words.

There was much for Mary to ponder upon; she had trusted herself to Warner's care as a child would have done.

With her maidenly instinct telling her she was not doing right, she had put faith in his honour when led by his wiles to accompany him from her home.

But there was much to alarm her fears; in a strange house, where it seemed that she was introduced as his wife; one chamber prepared for them! she felt herself almost entirely at his mercy.

As these thoughts crept over her, she determined upon resuming her attire, and demanding to be let from the house; but love teaching her confidence, cancelled the intention.

At all events she resolved to avail herself of the bell indicated by the maid if Warner should refuse to leave her chamber: she had just assured herself of its position when Warner's step was heard ascending the stairs.

Her first impulse was to rush to the door in order to fasten it; but there was no bolt, and the key was on the outside.

She hurriedly placed a chair against it and hastened into bed.

Warner came and gently pushed at the door; the chair did not offer any impediment, and he entered softly.

There was a look of conscious shame in his eyes; it humbled him to be there — prowling into the chamber of that maiden who had trusted him, his purpose worse than that with which the wolf seeks the lamb.

Mary sighed sadly when she saw him close the door and advance to her bedside.

"You have come to wish me good night?" she said, "I had forgotten; but pray do not linger here."

"Linger, dearest!" exclaimed Warner, as he came nearer.

"Ah, Mary! who could banish himself from such an Elysium?"

"Henry! what am I to understand from this conduct?"

"That I love you so devotedly, so fervently, that I cannot keep out of your presence."

Flattering as were his words to the single-minded girl, her womanhood was sufficiently firm in its dignity to repel his advances.

"Henry," she exclaimed, "I have trusted myself to your love, do not let me think that you could take advantage of my confidence to make me regret that I had trusted you."

"Never shall you! by this kiss I swear it!"

"Not now, it is not right," she exclaimed, pushing him gently away with her hands, "oh, Henry! must I weep already?"

He was a little puzzled by her manner.

"Believe me, I seek only your happiness; what would you have me do? speak, and I will do it!"

"Leave me, then, please; in the morning we can meet."

"Where, then, shall I go?"

"To your own room—leave me, I entreat!"

"My dear Mary, I have no room; there is no room to spare but this."

"No room?"

"You see they took us for husband and wife, and so got this chamber for our use."

"Oh, Henry! you have deceived me! I will not stay—I will go forth, rude as the night is!"

He sat down by the bedside and calmly spoke to her.

"Mary, dearest one, do not lose your trust in me; we have been near death together, and before heaven I swear I would not do you harm—rather would I lose you for ever!"

He knew how he was lying, but she did not.

"Yet you have done this," she said.

"It was a necessity: there were no other terms under which we could have presented ourselves; they would have not admitted us if they had guessed the truth."

"Alas!"

"You know, Mary, pure as our love may be in the eye of heaven, it would not look so to the world; people would think it strange to see two of opposite sex travelling together by night."

"How wrongly I have acted! oh, Dick! was it for this I left you?"

"No, no; be composed; it is but a necessary deception, one that saved a hundred inquiries and suspicions—true, we are not yet united by the ceremony of the priest, but our hearts are joined; no bond can link them closer; why, then should we stand falsely to ourselves because of the world?"

"Ah me! I fear it is not right."

"To the world, no; but to us—to heaven—it is."

How often is heaven mocked by such blaspheming wretches!

"Henry, be kind; leave me till the morning."

"If you so ruthlessly desire it."

"I crave it as a boon."

"Then I will go; yet where I know not; yes I will lie on the mat outside your door; in the morning when you will permit me I will enter; we shall soon depart, and none of the gossips here will have anything to talk about."

The young girl paused in bidding him to go; not that she was willing he should be there, but like most maidens who love their sweethearts she did not wish him to lie on a hard mat while she slept in a cozy bed.

It is to this tender and unselfish feeling of true woman which, basely taken advantage of by those whom her devotion should conquer, leads to the seduction of so many virtuous girls.

"I should not like you to go there," she observed, "yet I know what can be done; I will ring for the maid and share her bed, then you can remain here."

"My dear Mary," said Warner, bending over her and taking her hand, "I will do whatever you wish, but think what will be thought of so strange a proceeding."

"Our hearts will tell us we do right."

"So they will now; we are here as husband and

wife, and I am in your chamber; have I done you harm by remaining so long? it is nearly morning, an hour or two will soon pass away; now that I am here is it not better for me to remain till the first thing in the morning when I can go out without exciting remark."

Mary was silent.

"I will not come near your couch; an hour's sleep in that chair in my clothes will be sufficient, then I can go out and order breakfast while you rise."

There was a slight trace of fervour in his tones; to the young girl it seemed emotion, and she remained silent.

"You will permit this."

"If you will promise," sighed Mary.

"Firmly I do; and now, dear Mary, let me persuade you to sleep, morn will soon be here, to-morrow night I hope to have the right to stay beside you.

She allowed him to kiss her soft lips and cheek.

Dick should have been there at that moment.

Assured of the necessity for consummate acting, Warner left her bedside, and throwing himself into a chair (having taken the pillow which she insisted upon his having), made his head comfortable and soon appeared to be fast asleep.

But he was not so.

The foe creeping to his prey was not more wary,—the wolf creeping to the fold not more wide awake.

He was watching his victim, as although believing him to be asleep she lay endeavouring to keep her eyelids from closing.

The heart of Warner was elate.

He felt as sure of his victim as the tiger with its prey between its jaws.

He had basely mixed a drug in her wine before it was brought up, and though she had drunk but a small quantity, not half a glassful, he knew she had drunk enough to answer his purpose.

Besides the greatest point was effected—that of remaining in the room.

By this he had saved a world of unpleasantness.

So he waited and watched, while Mary, poor deluded girl, paying now the consequences of allowing herself to be led away from Dick, struggled against the drowsy influence which was momentarily overcoming her.

The house was silent enough, as far as any interference was concerned, he might as well have been with his victim in a house untenanted by others.

It was that thought; the conviction that the young girl lying defenceless within his enamoured gaze was all his own that gave the elation to his evil breast.

He listened for a long time after her heavy breathing had assured him that his basely administered drug had taken effect.

Then he rose on tiptoe and advanced to the bedside

The wax-lights were still burning; they enabled him to look upon the pretty face of the innocent girl; closer he crept, feasting his eyes on that sweet vision and exulting over his successful villiany.

Then he commenced to prepare himself for bed.

The unhappy betrayed being lay all unconscious of his polluting gaze—his treacherous intentions.

But when he stooped over her and kissed her face she aroused herself and dreamily struggling with her lethargy murmured for him to protect her.

"It is I dearest,' exclaimed, maddened with passion.

The drugged girl unclosed her eyes.

"You will protect me," she said drowsily.

"I will be your slave for ever," he cried, imprinting burning kisses on her lips.

She was too unconscious of his villiany to make much resistance to his villiany; when she murmured her defencelessness he placed his arms around her and assured her of his everlasting love.

All too successful was his infamy; powerless—not conscious—no protector nigh, she was his prey.

He knew no scruples for the dastardy of his act, nor cared for its criminality.

He only thought that he was there alone with that young creature, whom he had beguiled from her village home, for the actual purpose of bringing to ruin.

He had no remorse—no compunction for the years of misery he would cause her; his passions were bad, and there were none to help her.

It had been well for her if she had remained true to honest Dick, and never allowed herself to be beguiled by the soft phrases and flatteries of one who counted her as one only amongst his victims.

She had taken the first step to wrong, as many others of her sex have done, by a mere coquettish flirtation, and now, like them, she fell.

The night went down on her virtuous and proud; the morning found her dishonoured and degraded, and at the mercy of her betrayer.

What that mercy was we will show anon.

CHAPTER XXX.

THE PREACHER THAT CAME TO CHARLEY IN HIS CELL.

Poor Charley suffered acutely from his incarceration; he dreaded what might now occur to Dick.

He was, of course, certain that he had no hand in the murder of the unfortunate policeman, nor could he believe that he had taken any part in plundering the house.

He could see that he had been deluded into accompanying them in on their burglarious expedition, but he feared that the same impulses might give them a hold upon his nature to work him as they liked.

Besides, the fact of the deed having occurred had, he was sure, implicated him in his own eyes, and therefore given them a greater power over him.

A power that they might, perhaps, use to make' of his uncle a convict.

Cheerfully would the faithful boy have died to save Dick. He would have given much to have seen him, if only for a few moments; but the course would have been attended with risk.

Had Dick come, he would have been sure to be followed and taken. On the other hand, he knew that Dick was kept away, or he would have been there before.

This, as the reader will remember, was the case; and so, all things considered, Charley was glad his uncle had kept away.

There was another on whom his thoughts were sadly fixed—the little girl whom he had rescued from the crusher.

Charley had been much affected by her simple ways, and had been enabled to read at a glance what a life she led under the treatment of Mrs. Morgan.

He was convinced the poor child's existence was one series of beatings and brutal usage from the ill-favoured drunken woman who made her her slave.

Charley had been building many castles in the air of how he would take little Lucy away from the bad woman, when he had got Dick from the thieves.

How he would place her in a nice room, and go out to hold horses or clean boots, or anything, till he could get a situation, and have lots of money to make her happy with.

And many other sweet visions the brave young boy had indulged in, but they were all scattered by this sudden stroke.

It weighed his spirit down. He knew not that it was but one of a series he would have to meet; he never dreamed of the vicissitudes that would attend his young life—how he would incur dangers on Dick's behalf—how little trained thieves would try to get him into their gang—how he would be thrown amongst the outcast boys of London, the boys, in rags, that tumble after omnibuses—the boys that, jaded and famished, but still striving to be honest, go round to doors with heavy bags of hearthstones, selling it in exchange for rags or bones, which they sold to dealers—the boys that sold newspapers or fruit in the streets—the mud-larks who dived in the river's mud for halfpence—the shoe-blacks, the rag pickers, the boys who swept crossings, and all that class of young, ill-fed, ragged urchins, who, reared in crime or poverty of the lowest, have to fight their way honestly or dishonestly through life, beginning, some of them, with pilfering fruit or vegetables from the stalls of the markets, and ending with picking oakum in the convict prison, or wearing shackles at Botany Bay; beginning, some of them, with selling boxes of fusees, and ending by sending their sons to college, through the fruits of persevering industry.

With all this class of life and others, too, was Charley to meet; and so shall our readers, if they will patiently follow our guidance.

Charley was not, of course, left alone by the subordinates of the law; officious policemen tormented him with an authorised examination, and sleek detectives tried to wheedle him into a confession of the haunts of those they termed his accomplices.

But to all the boy was firm in his answer.

Failing in that, the chaplain's son, a sporting street minister, was permitted to visit him, and try the power of his persuasion, which he had found efficacious in the case of other prisoners.

If he did not succeed, there were brothers in the land who were ready to undertake any amount of the like dirty work; and scripture-reading ladies, who, with the cant of God's grace and forgiveness on their lips, would try to worm out disclosures that would drag, perhaps, repentant men from their wives and children, and drive them to a jail.

So this young sprig of sanctity, the chaplain's son, was shown into Charley's cell.

He looked in a very deprecating manner at Charley, whom he seemed to hold in more than usual abhorrence.

He was a very young man, perhaps not more than one and twenty; his figure was slim, his countenance pale and rigidly pious; his hair was cut short, his chin was smooth, and his stiff dog collar stuck up in a religious sort of style that was quite effective.

Our readers may have often seen him holding forth in the streets or the parks. He always looks very much agitated, and bellows out in a strained voice the most eternal damnation and fire everlasting to unbelieving sinners.

When he had taken a good look at Charley through his eyeglass, he took out a dainty white handkerchief, and dusted his nose, as if the air of the cell and the presence of the young prisoner quite overcame him.

"Sinful brother," he began, in a snuffling tone; "you are very young; why will you turn away from Jesus?"

Charley looked as much as to say he hadn't seen him to turn away from; and Stiffneck continued—

"Know you not that there is flaming hell for such as you; brother, I grieve to say you are going the road to damnation."

"I know I am not good," said Charley; "but I didn't do anything in this."

"My boy, don't let Satan have such hold upon you; he is at your elbow now, whispering in your ear."

Charley looked round, but without seeing the individual.

"God is merciful," resumed Stiffneck; "but he will not for ever call the wicked; therefore I say repent, or be damned."

Charles thought this was very much like swearing, but he said nothing.

"I tell you you will be accursed. He will say unto you, 'lo, I stood at the door, and you would not hear me; therefore is your portion fire and brimstone, darkness and flames, silence and gnashing of teeth.'"

"What have you come for?" Charley asked.

"I have come to reclaim you—to snatch a brand from the burning—to see if there is yet hope of saving the lost sheep."

"Will you make me good?"

"The Lord will, if you will turn in sackcloth and ashes, and pray, saying, 'I am a sinner.'"

"I know I am wicked, but I always pray."

"You pray?"

"I never sleep without. I pray for Dick, and I pray for all the world."

"Oh, my boy, don't let the devil have such sway; remember, the hypocrite shall be seen."

"But I'm not a hypocrite."

"Hush! it is Satan speaking; you are young in years, but old in sin; you have stolen, and become criminal."

"I never took anything that was not my own."

"And verily you are the accomplice of thieves; you have erred, but there is a way of redemption even to such a wretch; the gates of mercy are always open, wherefore repent, and say where live these wicked men, who have broken God's commandments, and entered like a thief in the night into the house of the goodly and God-fearing Mr. Wilblow."

"You want to know where Dick is, but I won't tell you."

"Let us pray," exclaimed Stiffneck, flopping down on his knees, having first spread his handkerchief on the ground, so that he should not soil his trousers.

"Oh, Lord! deliver this sinner from the power of Satan; let his heart not be hardened. Brother, pray with me wrestle with the tempter; say, 'get thee behind me, Satan, and oh, ye devils, be cast out.'"

He rose snuffling.

"Has the Lord opened your heart? Verily, he sent me to deal with you."

"He didn't send you to come here and get Dick into trouble; no, although he didn't do any wrong, I know he'd be punished if he was taken."

"Only for his offences he shall be chastened; better is it for man to deal with him than for him to burn in hell hereafter."

"I won't speak to you; you're a sneak! God would'nt punish him, He knows how innocent poor Dick be."

The very shirt collar of Stiffneck shook to be called a sneak, and, by the hardened boy he was trying to convert, it was too much.

He took from his pocket a Bible, and, with a preliminary snuffle, opened its pages and began to read.

After reading for nearly an hour he ventured to look at Charley.

The young boy was sitting against the wall, his arms were folded, and his head was drooping on his breast.

And there were tears running down his cheeks.

But they were not called there by the cant of the preacher; he was thinking of the time, not so far back, when he had read those passages to Dick.

"Praise ye the Lord!" quoth Stiffneck, "the sinner is humble; yea, there is victory in the Word of the Lord! there is forgiveness for the penitent; let it be known where the guilty may be found, and there is pardon here for you; yea, the prison doors shall open, and ye shall be free!"

"I won't let you find Dick; I'll kick you if you try to get him in prison," Charley cried, jumping off the bench.

So determined was his aspect that Stiffneck, in very great fear for his personal safety, retreated to the door, and, casting his eyes up to heaven, shook his head sorrowfully, and, with many dolorous exclamations at the perversity of the young incorrigible, left the cell.

An hour passed, and Charley, in moody sorrow, sat on the hard bench.

He was not shedding tears now; but as he gazed round the narrow walls, a heaviness was at his heart.

He seemed already in a tomb.

He saw how it was with the world! though free

from sin, and honest all his life, he was set down as an obstinate and hardened criminal, old in wickedness, and trained to stubbornness.

His very devotions in screening Dick was taken as a proof of his incorrigible infamy.

Very naturally he reasoned that if they refused to credit his assertion who was so young, they would not hesitate in pronouncing Dick guilty of the murder.

Poor Charley had suffered enough from the tender visitation of the criminal philanthropist; his face was swollen, and his eyes were still blackened.

Charley was getting into a very mournful state when the door of his cell was again opened, and he heard the voice of his jailor saying—

"Well sir, you'll see; if you don't find him the most 'ardened hincorrigible you ever set your eyes on, I'll heat my 'ead off."

"*Peccavi, peccavi, misericordia*; we have all sinned, we have all transgressed; but the body of Christ yet remaineth to be partaken of, oh, holy Virgin, *beatificus!* What saith the Word? — *non nobis Domine.*"

These learned phrases ushered in an individual who, with scrupulous black cloth, starched collar, and shaven chin, was the exact impersonation of one of the members of the Brompton Oratory.

Piously raising his hands when he saw the prisoner, he turned to the jailor, and with a fervent benediction, waved him away.

"Be instant in season and out of season," he began; "for to the service of the Lord there shall be no delay; there is joy in the house over one sinner that repenteth, *benedicite, cursidicite, demidicite*; turn your eyes to heaven, you young irreligious whelp, which, our dear Christian friends, if it were not for circumstances over which I have no control, you would not see me in this guise; but I appeal to your benevolence, which am not for myself, but for my poor sick wife, laid up with the small pox and scarlet fever, and seven small children—all blessed babbies, like steps above each other's precious chumps. Why you lumpy-faced scaramouch, did you never set eyes on me afore? because if not I am the 'Downey Cove or the Knowing Codger,' and glad I is to see you heer alive."

It may be imagined that Charley looked up in great surprise at the delivery of this harangue; the make-up of his visitor was so perfect that he would not have suspected him to be different from what he seemed; but he was skilful in remembering faces, and now that he spoke in that manner remembered him, as the seedy-looking gentleman in the thieves' kitchen whom Roving Rob had pointed out to him as the fat-headed gentleman who was up to every move, and who did the stalking dodge with the little children.

Charley joyfully sprang forward.

"Dick," he cried, "is he safe?"

"Safe enough, my young cowcumber, I seed him this morning, looking as down in the mouth as if he had been lagged instead of taking his time comfortably out of the way."

"Poor dear Dick! how I wish he was safe away from this place."

"Now don't kick up such a shindy, alluss seem to speakin a tone of woice not above your breath, so that nobody shan't hear you—and now, how are you my precious one? you've been a brick, and no mistake! but there's been blokes looking arter you, and your wirtues shall have their reward."

"Did Dick send you? I did not expect any one to come."

"Ah, my tender bloke! we never leaves a pal in distress; when one of our mates is nosed out and laid up by the heels, we takes as much interest in his doings as if he was a child of our own."

Charley sighed to think that he should need the aid of such as those.

"And so you see we haven't forgot you—not at all likely to when a kiddy shows he got such stuff in him; so keep your pecker up; you don't like this crib, but you needn't stay in it much longer."

"I shall never get my liberty again."

"Tell your grandmother; you'll be out in a jiffey. I tell you your friend Rob was in court when you was up afore the beak, and he heard what the gemman said he'd do for you."

"Yes; a gentleman spoke kindly for me when everyone was against me; but I don't think they will let him help me."

"Your pals aint a going to let you wait for that."

"How?"

"Don't open your tater-trap so wide; you're to be had up agin afore the beak to-morrow."

Charley sighed again.

"Now while you're waiting you must be took awful bad."

Charley stared at him.

"You must look like a corpse just stood upright—awful; here's a bit of powder, if you can rub it over your face do, only look out that you put it on clean, its what I rubs over the kiddies' mugs when they looks too bright, and precious ghosts it do make 'em look."

"Pretend to be ill."

"Haven't I been laying the law down to you this ten minutes; now don't look as if you'd got black-beetles stuck into your eyes. I wants you to look werry queer, and then says you, when you've done a gasp or two, and staggered a bit, says you, I do feel bad."

"Does you, they'll say, here, that'll do, none of your games here my young kiddy."

"Which when you hears you grows white and does a shiver."

"I feels awful, you'll say, after which we'll make 'em look at you."

"Perhaps they'll say you'll feel worse when you goes over the herring pond, or summut of that sort, but you never mind that, keep to your dodge."

"Then when you looks as if you was going to croak, you'll say—"

"I thinks if I was to go to the beak I should be hill."

"Which when you've said two on 'em 'ell dig their bunch of fingers in you throat, and the sergeant will order 'em to take you there, while your pals will manage the rest."

"I know you mean well," said Charley, "and thank you; but I wouldn't like to do it; I'll stand my chance."

"Which means, my blessed hinfant, that you'll go across the herring pond and not never come back no more."

"I must put up with my fate."

"All stuff and humbug; get out of the stone jug as soon as you can, it's bad enough to be in trouble for what you've done let alone what you hain't."

"I don't care what they do to me; I have done nothing wrong."

"Which you soon will if you lets 'em pack you off; now be a wide-awake kiddy and leave 'em in the lurch, there's Dick gnawing his knuckles off; now you're here he wants to come."

"Did he tell you to ask me?"

"In course he did, says he try what you can do with him, and if he won't do it tell him I'll come and give myself up."

"Did he say that?"

"He did just, which it ain't likely we should be the blokes to let him; but he might get out unbeknown to us."

The Downy Cove could not have hit upon a better "lay" for getting Charley to accede to the plan he proposed; the very thought of his uncle delivering himself up for him was enough to make the devoted boy agree to anything, and he exclaimed sadly—

"Then I will try, though I did not think Dick would have asked me to play the hypocrite."

"Don't be a duffer; he wants to see you safe out

CONFESSIONS OF A TICKET-OF-LEAVE-MAN. 73

CHARLEY SECRETING HIMSELF IN THE CHIMNEY.

of here, which it ain't pleasant for him to see you in."

"It will make it worse if I should be taken after attempting to escape."

"Don't fret afore the time comes; you're a brick of a kiddy; take it easy, and you'll do. We shall make you the king of the kids, if you're sharp."

"Tell me," asked Charley, unheeding the observation, "has Dick been dragged to—to commit—"

"Has he been up to any other lay — no — not exactly."

"It wouldn't do to show him just yet, not no ways; no, he keeps dark enough, and so will you have to for some time arter we gets you out, which, stiff-necked and unconvertible sinner, great were the subtleties of Satan—he setteth his mark upon his own; but verily I say, though your sins had been scarlet, they should have been white as wool; but, for your hardness of heart, there shall be judgment, unless you repent."

This sudden alteration in the manner of the Downy Cove was caused by the appearance of the jailor, who came to say that the gentleman who had interested himself on Charley's behalf had sent a solicitor, who was waiting to come in.

The false priest waved his hand in an apostolic manner for the jailor to retire, and, continuing his exhortations, mumbled a number of Latin sentences, which, although they were dubious of meaning, and were strung together as his memory enabled him to remember them, had their effect upon the jailor, though they did not upon the prisoner."

"Son of sin, angels weep for your shortcomings; I depart now ; but Satan shall yet be quelled; 'turn not away,' saith the Lord. Vale unhappy boy! remember—REMEMBER!"

No. 10.

Uttering this impressive word twice in a manner that would have done justice to Bishop Juxton himself, the Downy Cove placed his hands above Charley's head, and, silently breathing a blessing, shed a tear and departed.

"The Holy Spirit will work within him yet," he said to the jailor, looking solemnly in his face, "We are weak vessels; but, by His grace, redemption shall be perfect."

He let his hand fall to his breast, and his eyes to the ground; his hands unconsciously formed themselves in an attitude of prayer; his lips moved.

There was no doubt the holy man, much moved, was praying inwardly.

Straight on he marched; never once did he turn to the right or left, and only awoke from his pious reverie when far away from the vicinity of the prison he raised his foot to kick into the gutter an urchin who had thrust a box of fuzees under his sacred nose.

CHAPTER XXXI.

HOW THEY TRIED TO SET CHARLEY FREE.

THE solicitor whom Mr. Elsden had instructed to defend Charley was well versed in the proceedings of the courts of criminal jurisprudence.

From what he had heard from Mr. Elsden he came prepared for the sort of client he had to defend, and a very few moments opened to his clear-sighted view the true circumstances of the case.

He talked very quietly to Charley, telling him that the charge upon which he was taken up was a very serious one, that even if he had not, as he believed, been concerned in it, the evidence was very hard against him.

He pointed out what he thought his duty in such a matter.

"There was many cases," he said, "of boys who were taken to be trained up to all manner of crimes, and it behoved him who had at the first outset, through his connection with bad men fallen into trouble, to make such a statement as would lead to the full facts coming to light.

The quiet method and gentleness of the lawyer did more with Dick than all the bullying of the detective, or the cant of the preacher.

Convinced that he would not betray his confidence, he told him frankly all that had befallen him from the time his uncle had been inveigled into the parson's house, to the night of the robbery at Mr. Wilblow's.

Of course he concealed Dick's name, and the name of the place where the occurrence had taken place, and kept secret the locality, as far as he knew of it, where he believed Dick was hidden.

The former reticance was totally unnecessary, seeing that the lawyer had studied the whole case of the murder of the parson's servant ever since he had read the account in the papers.

He had had his suspicions about the affair—suspicions to which Charley's statement gave colouring.

Having very kindly bidden Charley hope for the best, and promised that everything should be done that was possible, he took his leave, and Charley was once more left alone, but this time in a more hopeful mood than he had been for some time past.

He was aroused early next morning, and, after a wretched attempt at breakfast, was conducted before the magistrate.

All that the lawyer had said to him, while it gave him comfort to find he was at least believed to be innocent, had strengthened the words of the Downy Cove.

True, he would not, had he consulted his own inclination, have entertained for a moment the idea of attempting to escape, and by such base artifices; but as it was Dick's wish (as he supposed), he looked upon it in the light of a mandate, and prepared to obey it.

But it must be confessed it was with a very backward heart.

Charley was not one of those who admired the daring practices of skillful thieves, nor applauded their escape from justice.

The history of Jack Sheppard had no charmes to his mind.

His guiding policy was honesty, and he would have submitted to be punished wrongfully rather than have attempted to make his way by violence out of prison.

Yet he was not a coward.

Many a youthful delinquent who could have shifted the bars of his cell, crawled up the chimney, or cut out a panel of the door, would have trembled at dangers that Charley with a bold heart would have faced.

The brave boy had but one wish, and that was to toil for his living till, by his industry and honest worth, he should attain an eminence of respectability.

It is easy, then, to conceive how it had cut him to the heart to be already adjudged a felon.

The policemen who came stamping into his cell, and with a coarse "now, then, young shaver," bade him accompany them, treated him, he could see, as though he were worthless and abandoned.

Yet it was not from any repugnance to the name of crime!

To a policeman a crime is simply a "charge."

The policeman who is months on his beat without a "case" is looked upon as a noodle.

On the other hand, he who can bring up most offenders achieves the greatest credit.

Thus it is that the policeman feels in his element when there is a case of coining, smashing, assault, burglary, or even murder, in which he can display his talents.

Thus it is that at so slight an occasion he is ready to drive his knuckles into "somebody," and march him to the station.

It matters not who that "somebody" is, or whether innocent or guilty, so that the charge can be brought against him, and the charge once made, even when circumstances or knowledge convince them that it is unjust, they spare no effort to ensure a conviction.

For to bring a charge and fail in proving it, is looked upon as worse than bringing no charge at all.

But as the members of the force know the advantage of sticking together, they never fail to swear hard and fast for one another.

This may seem like an exaggeration, but it is true.

After all it is only human nature.

If any of our readers doubt it, let them take a prominent part in *witnessing* any disturbance, and they will see how long they can keep the policeman's knuckles out of their collar.

And here let us give a word of warning.

When "collared," if ever so innocent, never resist or speak.

It only gives them the opportunity they desire of swearing you furiously assaulted them, and, as you cannot get away, they shake you till the breath is nearly out of your body—tear your clothes to tatters, knock you over the head with their staves, squeeze your throat as if it were a lemon, kick your ankles, and in the end, having dragged you (followed by an admiring crowd) to the station, thrust you headlong into a cell, where, being dragged forth in the morning, you find, in addition to the first charge—of which you were entirely innocent—a charge of assault of the greatest magnitude, in which constables who were not near the spot swear so hard against you that you begin to think you must have been attacked with a fit of madness, and think yourself lucky when justice, with severest frown, sentences you to a monstrous fine or a lengthy imprisonment.

The policemen having joked with one another

about Charley's likely "get," jerked him into the van—that long black coach, a little more lively than the black case on wheels in which the bodies of the dead are jolted to the cemetery.

Shut up in his dark solitary compartment, Charley, remembering the coarse observations of the policemen, gave way to his sorrowful reflections, and was buried in thought when the police van stopped in front of the court of—we had almost said justice.

They handed him out, not very tenderly, but with fingers gripped on his arm. There was a crowd of idlers gathered before the door to satiate their morbid yearning of gazing on the prisoners' faces, and wondering what they would "collar,' — that is, receive as an equivalent for the charge.

Charley was not the first to get out. The inside of a police van (let us hope our readers may never find themselves there) is composed of compartments, in which the prisoners are locked solitarily in.

From there they came forth one at a time.

Hence, an exhibition, entertaining and select, is offered to the curious.

First came an old man, with a few rough gray hairs on his head; he stooped and tottered—people wondered what was his offence.

But they began to hiss when they heard that he was charged with an assault upon a poor little defenceless girl, whom he had ruined for ever.

Then came a slim venerable-faced man; he was stared at in silence, for he was a clergyman, arraigned for petty theft.

A dashing military-looking man, handcuffed, next stepped jauntily out.

He was the son of a gentleman of position, charged with forgery.

He seemed to think little of his position, and less of the mob, as he glanced scornfully around him.

Then they helped out a woman — a wan-faced hopeless-looking woman, weary and worn.

She was a poor betrayed girl, who, in misery and indigence, had leapt with her child into the river, preferring death for both to lingering starvation and sin.

Her child had perished; but she had been rescued, and now stood for the crime of child murder.

Poor feeble creature! it looked as if the hand of the law would have to be swift ere death cheated its harshness.

Gazing on her sad pinched face, one could scarcely refrain from thinking that it had been almost as merciful to have let the waters complete their work.

A few more prisoners — some dejected and unused to their position; others to whom it was a continued place of life, and whose only speculation was what to be at when they got out again.

Charley came out last; most people had heard of him, and great was the curiosity to get a glimpse of him; many, too, were the remarks he heard passed upon his appearance.

Knowing what he did of his own innocence, Charley was surprised as well as pained at the harsh things that were said with such confidence.

If he had been ever so dejected, these observations would have put him on his mettle: his cheeks flushed, and his eyes grew brighter.

And at that moment when he looked amongst them, his glance rested on the face of a broad-shouldered coalheaver, in whom he recognised the illustrious Roving Rob.

That personage thought he had sufficiently disguised himself to be out of the ken of Charley, and was immensely mortified at the result. He looked his most vacant stare, and, had Charley spoken, would have stared still more.

But Charley was too true to betray one who was there to befriend him; it was only the momentary fixing of his eye on Rob's that told that worthy he had been recognised.

His features were schooled, and without a gesture of recognition or surprise he passed on.

And the crowd pressed into the court-house.

"I wonder, I do," mused Rob, "what there ar' in my personal appearance for that young bloomer to twig me by? I'll be precious more wide awake next time; he ar' a wide awake beauty, too! a regular trump! 'taint every kiddy as could have seed me and kept their mug as he did; he's an out-an'-out stunner, and Roving Rob won't leave him in the lurch."

While thus mentally soliloquising, he had shouldered his way into court, and was apparently a listless spectator like the rest.

Charley's counsel was already seated in court conversing in a low tone with his brother lawyers: he looked very grave, and had rather a voluminous mass of writings before him.

Mr. Garnand had not yet arrived. It was that gentleman's practice to remain an hour or two over his newspaper occasionally, when he should have been in court disposing of cases.

His absence caused, of course, great inconvenience; but then there was nothing to get him there except his conscience, and that was not a very severe monitor.

Charley kept in the room apportioned to persons before they were summoned to face the bench, was pondering whether he should obey what he believed to be Dick's wish.

His agitation and emotion at that moment made him pale enough without the application of the chalk which the Downy Cove had offered him, but which he had refused.

The policemen saw him turn pale, and attributing it to fear hinted at its cause.

"The youngster's showing the white feather," said one.

"Hullo!" cried another; "what's the go?"

Strange as it may seem, at that juncture Charley was attacked by an actual fit of dizziness, doubtless brought on by the state of his mind.

"Hold up," cried the one who had just spoken.

"I am not well," Charley said faintly.

It did not need his statement to assure them of that, his looks were enough.

"What's the matter; want to go before the doctor?"

"No," Charley answered.

"Feel sick?"

"Yes, very sick."

Which was the truth.

"Hold up, don't be frightened, you'll be better presently."

"I'm not frightened, but I think—"

"What?"

"If I were to go to the back for a little while, as I am so sick, I should be all right."

This was the deception. It cost Charley a hard struggle to say it; but he schooled himself as to a task, and uttered the deceptive speech.

The serjeant looked hard at him.

"You may go," he said, "but no tricks, remember. Here, Jenkins and Watts take him off, and look well after him."

"All right," said the policemen, as they led him away.

The Downy Cove had seen the greater part of this, and inwardly applauded Charley for, as he thought, so skilfully playing his part.

"He'll make a rare hand yet," he thought, as he got himself ready for his part of the morning's performance.

The two policemen who went with Charley knew that there was no chance of Charley escaping, unless he passed them; and as he was really very sick they left him to himself, and leaning against the wall chatted cozily.

About ten minutes passed, and as they were not particularly wanted, and Charley seemed far from well, and as besides they were having a comfortable skulk they did not hurry their prisoner, but continued their gossip.

Charley himself felt very much better; he had, assisted by an unexpected attack, performed the part assigned him, and though with much repugnance to himself, still it was done.

But nothing had come of it.

There had been no rescue, no attempt at communicating with him.

Perhaps in his heart he was not sorry at this.

The policemen now thought it time to bring Charley back, but just as they were intimating this fact a third policeman, whose whiskers at once proclaimed him one of their late recruits, whose bleak growth had already been the object of much curious adversion.

Stepping authoritively up to them he said hastily, "Jenkins and Watts you are wanted at once for the Cremorne case: there's a fellow swearing hard against Rackett, and you'll have to mind what you say; look sharp, I'll bring the prisoner."

It was quite enough for Jenkins and Watts to know that they had the chance of crushing a fellow who was outswearing one of their own kidney, and off they started.

Then the whiskered policeman seized Charley by the wrist.

"Come," he said, and Charley recognised the Downy Cove.

CHAPTER XXXII.

WHAT ATTENDED THE AUDACIOUS ACT OF THE DOWNY COVE.

CHARLEY uttered no word; the Downy Cove seemed to know he could rely upon him.

Merely telling him to walk boldly, he led him along the passage.

At the end he relinquished his arm.

Two policemen were lounging here; they listlessly looked at the boy and the officer who had him in charge.

Then the Downy Cove took him towards the court.

Entering one of the rooms in which several witnesses were waiting, he walked out again, leading Charley by the hand.

The boy was astonished at the cool manner in which the disguised thief acted.

But cool as were his proceedings, he had been very speedy in them.

As he emerged from the room a dirty coalheaver came knocking up against him.

It was Roving Rob.

Giving Charley a friendly but apparently rude kick with his knee, he swaggered on in the rear.

In a moment more Charley was outside the court, the Downy Cove still leading him by the hand.

There were, as usual, several policemen standing at the entrance.

They stared at the boy whom they had seen arraigned for such a crime.

Not unquestioned would he have passed but for the custody he seemed in.

It fortunately happened that the whiskered recruit was but slightly known, and thus the Downy Cove was not subjected to any impertinent observations.

But one of the policemen said—

"What's up?"

"Going to put him in the way of peaching," said the disguised cadger.

And he passed on.

Roving Rob, whose knees threatened to knock together, following him.

"Who is that?" asked one policeman of another.

"Oh, that's Benson."

"What, the new fellow?"

"Yes, I think so."

"Didn't look like him."

"Hark!" cried the other.

There came from the interior of the police court a sudden outcry.

Then a dozen policemen rushed over one another to the door.

"He's off."

"Who?"

"The boy."

"When, where?"

"Somebody's led him out."

"When—how—what?"

"Somebody rigged as one of us."

"Where's he gone?"

The policemen looked at each other; it was a question not easily answered, and after staring dubiously at one another's collars, and stupidly in each other's faces, they darted off in various directions.

CHAPTER XXXIII.

THE PURSUIT AFTER ROVING ROB, AND WHAT HE DID TO SAVE CHARLEY.

THE commotion inside the court upon the discovery of Charley's flight may be conceived.

Mr. Garnand had seated himself at the bench, with the express determination of committing Charley for trial. Mr. Wilblow was there, looking eminently benevolent. Mr. Elsden, too, was in the court, near the counsel whom he had instructed to defend the boy burglar, as Charley was called.

The policemen whom Rob had so cunningly outwitted had pushed their way to the dock, where the accused whom they were to swear against stood, and were only stopped in their zeal by the inspector, who pompously inquired their business.

"We've come to be evidence," said the bobbies, looking nervous.

"Evidence! where's your prisoner?"

"We've left him with the other constable."

"What constable?"

"Him as you sent."

"Sent, fools!"

Here the policemen, seeing the cold glance of the magistrate turned upon them, looked very foolish.

"I've sent no one," said the inspector.

The policemen stammered, and turned pale and red.

"You'd better see after your prisoner," said Mr. Garnand, who began to scent something wrong.

Hereupon the constables bundling over one another blundered out of court, but soon returned with faces aghast and looks confused.

Of course they had not found the prisoner.

Then arose the tumult, during which the unlucky constables, having the dread of suspension, dismissal, or imprisonment before them, betook to flight after Charley.

The magistrate put on his most cynical look, and turned to Mr. Elsden.

"Your protegé does not appear confident of his innocence being proved."

Mr. Elsden was silent. Charley's flight produced a bad impression on his mind; he reasoned that if Charley had not been the pupil of that gang, they would not have been so ready to get him off, nor he to accompany them.

So without cause Charley was set down as a hardened criminal, a thief, a burgler; deceitful and murderous.

And the law was directed against him, that he might be sent to jail or the hulks whenever found.

This was very unfair.

The bold boy was quite willing to bear his punishment.

If it had not been for Dick, he would have refused to accompany Rob in the present instance.

That worthy being silently and very expeditiously led him along.

When he had got into one of those alleys in rear of Rochester Row, he took him in to a low beerhouse.

The landlord, a short-cropped low-browed individual, turned very pale when he saw the shining hat and the number on Rob's collar.

"Back room empty?" asked Rob.

"Yes—who—what's up?"

There were only two out-of-work bricklayer-looking men before the bar; they were staring at Rob and his charge.

The landlord gave them a meaning look as he said to Rob—

"Find the room quite empty, sir."

"That will do; come with me."

The landlord seemed more fidgetty: a frowsy old woman, very dirty and very corpulent, came from the inner room, and looked from one to the other.

Rob, who was getting in a hurry, led Charley in, and the landlord followed, not without many misgivings.

The fact was this honest boniface had been in daily expectation of the visit of the police, owing to a little matter which had occurred a few nights before, when those identical seeming bricklayers had brought into the house a young gentleman, whom they had induced to come in and play a game at skittles.

This same young gentleman had a sum of money about him, which the skittlers lightened him of by means of drugging his beer, and robbing him of all he had when he was in a half-stupified state.

They had then got him out, and, after giving him a knock or two to keep him quiet for a time, had left him in the gutter.

As the landlord was a sharer in the benefits, he had begun to tremble, lest he should also have to pay the penalty, and he was very much put out at the visit of the supposed policeman.

The first thing Roving Rob did was to pull off his false whiskers and wig.

Then he began unbuttoning his coat.

The landlord looked more cheerful.

"A lay?" he said.

"Yes," returned Rob; "and now, old flick, I want a change of togs."

"What, Rob?"

"Yes; it's that hidentical gemman; but don't stand there gaping like a whale; there's the blues arter me and this kiddy, who they've took a precious fancy to, and we must bilk 'em."

"All right."

"I'll stand a gin or two, if you're quick."

"Well, I ain't got much of a box of togs, but I'll find you some, I daresay."

The landlord sidled out of the room.

He found the two labouring-looking men waiting for him outside in the passage.

"Anything up?" asked one.

"Only a do."

"Is it all serene?"

"Yes; he wants some togs."

The two men went back to the bar.

The landlord went upstairs.

In a few moments he was down again.

He had got some queer-looking garments.

A corduroy jacket with one sleeve, very much torn, a velveteen waistcoat, and a pair of worn-out military trousers.

All the articles looked damp and tumbled, as if they had been washed and put hastily out of the way.

In places the mildew was thick upon them, and on the right breast and torn sleeve of the jacket there was a large dark stain.

In addition to these garments, he had a rough cap under his arm.

"They ain't much," he remarked, when he entered the room where Rob was waiting; "but maybe they'll do."

"They're the sort," Rob replied, as he took them from him, and quickly commenced arranging himself.

He shrugged his shoulders as the damp struck to him, and looked hard for a moment at the dark stain on the jacket.

Then he looked hard at the landlord, who reddened and looked uneasily at his feet.

"Got another jacket?" he asked.

"Ain't nothing else but that."

Rob silently put it on.

He neither looked nor felt comfortable in the clothes.

They had an odour like what one might attribute to dead men's garments.

They seemed rank, too, with crime.

If Rob had taken them from the corpse of an executed criminal, he could not have experienced a greater sensation of unpleasantness.

But he said nothing, knowing that there was no time for picking and choosing.

He gave the landlord a sovereign.

"Street clear?" he asked.

"I'll go and see."

He was saved that trouble.

As he stepped out of the room, a policeman put his head inside the door; then another.

Finally these stepped in.

More were waiting outside.

The landlord stepped quickly back.

"It's all up," he said.

"Oh, it ar', eh; how many?"

"Three more waiting."

"Anywhere's we can get?"

"They'll look in every crib."

"Jemmy, I don't want to be took; stow us away."

There was a meaning look accompanying Rob's tone that not only made the landlord feel suspicious, but caused him to give the proposition of Rob every consideration.

"There's the back, but they're sure to be there."

"We'll try that," muttered Rob. "Come, Charley, lad; Dick will be anxious if we don't get there soon."

This roused the boy: for Dick's sake he was willing to fly like a hunted criminal from the pursuit of justice.

Poor boy! many a bitter vow had he registered that, if once he got with his uncle again, he would not leave him till he had got him away from those bad men.

It had not been with a vague idea of escape that Rob had led Charley into that house. At the last moment it had been decided upon by the Downy Cove as the place where he could meet them with a cab.

He himself was to be the driver.

As he had not arrived, Roving Rob began to fear that some accident had kept him away; but the Downy Cove was at that moment outside with the cab, having arrived at the moment that the policemen had.

He was sitting on the box, looking as "cabbyfied" as possible, and wondering how the pedlar would manage to get out.

After speaking to Charley, Roving Rob hurriedly addressed the landlord.

"Look here, Jemmy; I think I can do the bobbies, as I—or can't you stow this youngster somewhere?"

Jemmy looked thoughtful.

"Come, be sharp."

"Well, there's only one crib as I know of."

"Which is it?"

"In the alley."

"That's a likely spot."

"It's the best."

"First crib they'll spot."

"Yes; but they doesn't know that there's a chimbley."

"Ah!" muttered Rob, thoughtfully.

"If as the young gemman wouldn't mind being up there a little while."

"Up a chimney!" Charley cried.

"Tell you what, old woman," exclaimed a voice outside; "they were seen to come here, and so, in case they ain't gone yet, we'll take a peep over the house."

"You shan't make a disturbance in my house, if you are the police," squeaked a shrill female voice. "Where's your warrant?—where's your right to go about people's houses?"

"They is coming, they are," Rob said; "now, Charley, be a brick. If they take you, they'll lag you, and the beak will soon do your hash."

"Come along, if you're coming, or I'm off," the landlord said.

"I don't care if I am taken," exclaimed Charley.

"Well, there's gratitude agin; he took and let me be scragged, all a'cos I wanted to get you out of a scrape."

Roving Rob looked the picture of virtuous and injured innocence. Charley lost his doggedness in a moment.

However, he might blame Rob as the cause of his troubles; he could not overlook that he had jeopardised his liberty for the purpose of setting him free.

The boy was not ungrateful.

"I will go," he said, "if the chimney be on fire."

Rob whipped up the policeman's disguise.

"I knowed you was a brick; off; take these togs; stow 'em up; here they are coming like bears with their tails greased. I'll stick here. Set the pins up, Jemmy."

The landlord made his exit by the back door, followed by Charley, who carried the policeman's suit.

Roving Rob sat himself cosily in a chair, and waited for the door leading from the bar to be opened.

Jemmy Stag led Charley out into the yard, and across to the skittle alley.

This skittle alley was in fact a shed and wash-house amalgamated into one.

As our readers may, perhaps, be aware, there is not much open space at the back of houses in the heart of Westminster.

This yard was backed in by dingy tenements—houses where the lowest of the lower classes congregated from floor to floor, each room occupied by whole families.

There were many windows overlooking the place—windows dusty and dim—with broken panes and sheets of paper pasted where glass was not; but they only overlooked the top of the skittle alley, from the fact that it was roofed in almost from the door of the house to the opposite wall.

Consequently nobody could look in, as the windows by which light was admitted into the alley were painted inside.

Jemmy Stag was not so expeditious in his movements as he would have been had Rob been there.

On entering the alley he closed the door after him.

At the end a padded sacking ran along the wall; this Jemmy, after a little exertion, pulled forward.

A rusty fireplace was behind.

It was evidently long disused; the dust had crept in and lay thick above the rust of the hobs.

Jemmy took the policeman's coat from Charley, and, kneeling down, spread it carefully out.

His next exploit was to put his hand up the chimney, and pull down a quantity of shavings covered with soot.

Much of this soot as he expected fell on the open coat, which, with the bundle of shavings, he put on the ground.

"Up you get," he growled to Charley.

The place was not inviting. Charley saw that to be effectually concealed the sacking would have to be replaced.

If the chimney was stopped at the top, as some are when not used, he would be suffocated before he had been there five minutes.

However, it being his only chance, he stepped forward, and put his head up the chimney.

A faint streak of light came down the soot-begrimed tube; it enabled Charley to see the soot corrugated thickly upon the inside.

The odour, too, was very disagreeable.

Charley for a moment hesitated.

In the company into which he had fallen, he might expect to be led into strange escapades.

Every step that he was taking was rendering his actions in a worse light.

But it was only left him to fight against his destiny, and that was not to be done by giving himself into the merciless clutches of the law.

So he took a long sniff of fresh air, and, as the landlord warned him to make haste, commenced climbing up the chimney.

The soot came down in handfuls. Jemmy muttered a few curses, and as soon as Charley's heels had disappeared, stuffed the policeman's coat up for him to take.

Then he took the shavings, and carefully placed them with the soot uppermost, and strewed some sawdust over the soot that had fallen.

The sacking went back into its place, and poor Charley was shut up in the chimney, trying to keep his perch on the sooty projection, and looking up to the top where the faint ray of daylight rendered the interior more ghastly.

All this had been accomplished in a very short time.

Jemmy heard the policemen coming just as he had finished.

So far he had managed it very nicely.

But his hands were rather black.

That he knew would betray him.

He stooped down and rubbed them in the wet sawdust, till all traces of the soot were removed.

Having accomplished this to his satisfaction, he began leisurely placing the pins, first throwing the ball against the sacking.

Roving Rob had comfortably settled himself in a chair by the table.

Taking from his pocket a sixpence and several halfpence, he began computing in the most Babbage-like manner.

When he had got his face to the most serious cast, the door was kicked open, and in came the three policemen.

Behind them, looking innocent enough, were the two men in white jackets before alluded to.

"Let me see," muttered Rob, "one game, two games: I can spring a couple; they doesn't look like coves used to floorers. I think I can diddle 'em. Hullo! why here's an invasion of the blues."

He scrambled up the money, and put it hastily into his pocket.

The policemen, who had paused, looked at him from head to toe.

Roving Rob with more coolness returned the survey.

"What's up, guv'ner?" he asked.

"Nothing much," said the first policeman.

"Oh! that's it; well, 'taint much you want here. Ready for the game, Jack?"

This was addressed to one of the "bricklayers."

"We're ready if you are."

"Come on then; Jemmy's there, I daresay."

The two men elbowed their way in. Roving Rob rose.

"There's summut wrong," one of the sharpers exclaimed, in an affected low tone; "these gen'l'men wants somebody."

"Does they? well, as long as they doesn't want me, I don't care."

"We may want you," the policemen said.

"I hope you won't."

"It's very likely we may want all who are here."

"You don't say so. Here, Jack, we'll play our game to-morrow: I'll cut."

Roving Rob made a movement towards the door. The policemen sharply got in front of him.

"What, mayn't I go?"

"Not yet."

"What's the row?"

"Stigger me! I ain't that article, ar' I?"

"It's not only him. There was somebody who got him away."

"Oh!"

"And we believe them both to be here."

"You'd better look till you find 'em."

"We intend to; and first, we'll look at you."

Roving Rob put himself into an attitude as if he was standing to have his portrait professionally taken.

Not satisfied with a casual look at him, the policeman took off his cap and stared in his face.

"I call that cursed impertinence!" muttered Rob.

"We want some more—them that were at the window," the policeman remarked, as he gave back the cap.

Rob quietly put it on his head: his hand being before his face enabled him to conceal the change that passed over it.

It seemed likely enough that they knew him.

But they did not. The police are not generally active in discovering crimes—as the Waterloo tragedy, the tragedy at Mr. Kent's, the murder in Seven Dials, that of Elizabeth Hunter, and many others, prove.

Very likely they had been often enough as near the criminal as they were to Roving Rob, but yet had not judgment enough to prevent themselves being outwitted.

The shortest of the policemen, a chubby-faced bunch-whiskered man, now spoke.

"It's my opinion they're both hiding in: they never came out, and our other chaps have gone to the back."

"Who's in the front?"

"I told that cabman, that stopped when he saw us come in, to call if anyone came out."

Roving Rob had to school his features or he would have smiled.

He had no doubt who the cabman was.

"Sure to be here," the other policeman said. "Let's go through the house."

"We'll have our game out," Rob exclaimed; and the two sharpers followed him to the ground.

The policemen separated here: one went upstairs, while the other two accompanied Rob.

They evidently had their suspicions of that alley.

The inimitable Jemmy, when they opened the door, was just preparing for a smash among the pins. He had taken careful aim, and, as the policeman entered, he threw the heavy ball.

Jemmy had intended a floorer.

He got one.

One that he didn't seem to expect.

Just as the ball went spinning out of his hand, the policemen zealously rushed in; the foremost, unfortunately, stumbling at the first step, came right in the way of the ball, and got a spank that made him grunt like a pavior, and, doubling him up, sent him amongst the pins.

"Spoilt my nine," shouted Jemmy.

The other policeman, suspicious as policemen always are, drew his staff, and went to help his comrade up.

The fallen man was very pale and groaned audibly; the ball had caught him in the waist, and knocked all the wind out of him.

Jemmy stepped forward, and, with every appearance of commiseration, helped him out of the pins.

"Werry sorry; hope you isn't hurt."

The bobby looked at him; he was too ill to speak.

"That all comes of practising," remarked Rob. "Was you getting your hand in, Jemmy?"

"Just having a shie."

"'Twasn't fair; as soon as that gemman's out of the way, we'll begin."

"Just pitch up the cheese," cried Jemmy.

"Wait!" exclaimed the policeman; "we're going to look over this place before there's any playing."

Here Jemmy, with every appearance of surprise, opened wide his eyes.

"Why, what does you want?" he asked.

"Never mind what we want; we'll see if we can find it."

"Oh, werry well, only let us know when we may play."

Jemmy sat on the long bench at the side. Roving Rob picked up the ball, and began to balance it; the two sharps commenced setting up the pins.

The unlucky policeman, who had been knocked over, had partially recovered, and they began the search.

The walls did not seem to offer any place of concealment, but they nevertheless tapped them with their staves.

Then they went carefully over the floor, raising the piece of matting, and stamping on the boards to ascertain if they were hollow.

Twice they went to the end where the sacking hung; once when they seemed about to begin pulling at it, the landlord spoke.

"What are the gen'l'men looking for?"

"It's a kiddy they wants, and a bloke what took the kid."

"What, and brought him here?"

"So they thinks."

"What stuff; here stand out of the way; let's have our game out; you can have yours as long as you like."

"Yes; that's the cheese," remarked Rob.

"'Cos, look here," continued the landlord, "if as how you thinks there's any one in my crib, why, in course, I'm willing to let you look about; but me and these gemmen's got a match on, and we'd like to play it off."

"And you've looked everywhere here," said Rob.

"We don't know that," the policeman replied.

"Well," said Rob, "I'd advise you to have a good look while you're about it."

"We mean to."

"Have you looked under the ball?" asked Rob, innocently.

"Or inside the pins?" said Jemmy.

"That isn't him behind you?" observed Rob.

The policeman turned round.

"Or outside the windy?"

Again the active members of the force sprang round. They looked exceedingly nettled when they saw that they were being hoaxed.

They did not like being laughed at.

"There's a heap of sawdust up in the corner," cried Rob; "have you looked under it?"

"We'll look under you," retorted one of the blues angrily.

Whereupon Rob put himself in an attitude whereby they were enabled to accomplish that feat.

"There's one of them tiles loose," Jemmy chimed in; "they haven't got through there, have they?"

"There's enough of that," exclaimed the policeman; "we don't want any more."

"That's what the pups said, when the mangle fell on their backs."

The blues began to look perplexed.

The laugh was decidedly against them.

"I don't think they're here," remarked one in an under tone.

"Nor I; but Judkins always thinks he's smelt out something."

"Let's go and see what the others are doing."

The door of the skittle ground was at that moment opened, and two more policemen entered.

They looked very suspiciously at Rob and the others, and glanced at their mates.

"Well, gen'l'men," said Jemmy, "have you found what yer was looking for?"

"Look out that you don't find more than you're looking for."

"I wish I might."

The policeman turned to the others.

"Have you looked all over here?"

"Everywhere."

"Well, it's my opinion, and I'm not often wrong, that they're here, and, as sure as my name's Judkins, we'll find them, if they are."

"I don't know where you'll look then," retorted the other policemen, who, like most of the force, were envious of the rising talents of their fellow constables.

"Well, we'll look."

"I suppose we can have our game now?" exclaimed Rob.

Judkins looked attentively at the speaker.

Rob, with skittle ball in hand, returned the stare.

Then Judkins walked quietly up to him.

"Should think you'll know me when you see me again," remarked Rob.

"I think I know you since I saw you last."

"Law! does you?"

"I do."

"What *lies* you must have."

"Good enough to see you with. What's your name?"

"Jehoshamekowaggleyfinikinsbangerangerwrangerwobelly."

"I ask you your name."

"I know you does."

"And I want to know it."

"Lawks! well now, if I didn't think as how you knowed it."

"I caution you to mind what you're at."

"Werry kind you is."

The constable began to feel rather warm, he did not fancy being retorted upon in this manner before his brother blues.

"That's a pretty suit of clothes you've got on," he said.

"It ar', fit as if it wash made for me. S'help mine Got, as goodsh ash new. Phat phill you give? let us have your monish. Splendid shuit!"

"Shut up that nonsense; where did you buy it?"

"You'd better find out; you're paid for that."

Judkins looked red.

"I'll have my eye on you."

"And a good-looking one it ar'; leastways, it would be if it belonged to a badger instead of a *hossifer*."

"Silence!" said Judkins.

"Hats off!" cried Rob, "don't you hear a gemman speak?"

"I'll have you up for interfering with me in the execution of my duty."

"Your dooty ain't to ax me impertinent koestions, ar' it?"

The irascible Judkins took Rob by the collar.

"I believe you're the man I want."

"Is that your *hexpress* belief?"

"It's enough for me to take you up."

"Will you take me with a bit of sugar or a bit of salt?"

"Here, look after this man; I'll make him give an account of himself; catch hold of him some of you."

Although not much relishing being ordered about by one of themselves, two of the policemen took Rob by the collar.

"Take him to the station."

"What charge, Judkins?"

"Eh!"

"What charge?"

"Yes, that ar' the koestion; it ar' what ar' the charge? as the seedy bloke says when he takes his gal to Greenwich to have a gorge of tea and shrimps."

"Being suspected."

"Suspected of what?"

Judkins looked angrily at his brother crushers.

"You saw what he did."

Now, as they had not seen him do anything, they were rather at a loss, so, too, was Judkins, who, after for a moment glancing alternately at them and Rob, shouted—

"Never mind; let him go; we'll have him presently."

Roving Rob shook himself; he had been rather afraid that the peeler had recognised him; in fact, Judkins had an indistinct remembrance of him, but he did not know where he had seen him, and the imperturbable coolness of Rob quite took him off the scent.

So, with increased wrath, he commenced a search for the missing pair.

"I'll take my throw," said Rob, again picking up the ball.

The pins were standing, and, while the bobbies were hunting about the ground, Rob hurled the "cheese."

There was a shout. Rob had floored the lot.

Charley, inside the chimney, heard the ball rattle against the sacking pad; he was nearly suffocated with the soot, and was longing for release.

The pins were being stuck up for Jemmy to throw at, when Judkins, after taking a hungry look round the alley, let his eye fall on the sacking.

"He ar' smelt it out," thought Rob, as he saw him step forward.

Judkins walked up to the end, and took hold of the sacking frame.

"Anything behind here?"

"A mouse or two, I daresay," Jemmy responded.

"Perhaps there's something else."

"P'raps there is."

"I'll soon see!"

"So you shall."

As Jemmy saw that Judkins was bent on examining behind that; and, as he further knew that the sacking frame, being but slightly secured, it would soon give way, he thought the best plan would be to make a virtue of a necessity, and remove it for the search, trusting to fortune for the result.

To him it was not so much a matter of moment whether Charley was discovered.

He knew they would be too glad to get the prisoners to take any steps against him for their concealment.

But, for the credit of his house, he hoped such an event would not take place.

When we say the credit of his house, it is not meant what the neighbours might think of him.

Jemmy knew there was little profit likely to accrue from their good opinion.

But his little caboose had been, occasionally, made the resort of thieves and convicts; and he knew what a good effect it would have with the gang if he aided Rob in baffling the blues.

Thieves' pay was better than the pay of honest men.

So, having revolved all these things in his mind, and without taking very long to do it, he said, with every appearance of unconcern—

"You can look if you wants to. There ain't nothing there but a chimbley."

"Oh, only a chinney?"

"That's all!"

Rob looked at Jemmy. Was he betraying him?

It could scarcely be; for he knew that Jemmy was aware of what would be the penalty for peaching.

"A chimney, oh!" said Judkins; "well, we'll take a look at it."

"All right! Let me have my throw first!"

As he spoke, Jemmy threw the ball. The zealous Judkins was in the act of directing him to wait, and had already got his hand on the frame, for the purpose of tearing it away, when Jemmy threw.

Of course he had no time to get out of the way, nor had Jemmy time to stop the ball.

The policeman did that, not as his unfortunate brother did, for, in this instance, the ball hit the pins first, and having scattered them out of the way,

THE ENERGETIC POLICEMAN.

came with a bounce against Judkin's shins—falling thence on his foot, where he had a tremedous bunion.

The kick on the shin and thump on the foot caused him to tumble backwards; and he sat amongst the pins, looking forlorn in the extreme, and rubbing his foot and leg.

"I am unlucky to-day," cried Jemmy; "blowed if it ain't the second time the ball has served me that trick."

The peeler who had received the first tap in the waist thought it was a trick Jemmy had screwed the ball to, but he said nothing.

But Judkins, with water in his eyes, jumped up.

"You damned vagabond, you did that on purpose."

"It was a haccident; there, gemmen, there wasn't no time to stop myself."

"You'd no business to throw."

"Couldn't move the least without upsetting the pins; so I thought might as well have a shie."

"Shie! I wish you'd broke your thick neck."

"That's Christian," remarked Jemmy, as he stepped up to him. "Now, if you wants to look up the chimney, here you am; 'tain't very difficult to get to; precious dusty it is; I make no doubt but you won't mind that?"

"Oh, no," said the smarting official; "we won't mind that."

Jemmy went to work, and in a short time had the padding pulled away.

Roving Rob, who had come forward, inwardly commended Jemmy for the dexterous manner in which he had obliterated all traces of that ascent of Charley.

The dust had been so thrown that, when the back was pulled away, it did not seem to have been disturbed for years.

No. 11.

Jemmy had taken good care, too, to create as much dust as possible, the consequence of which was that the peelers were almost choked when they came crowding to the grate.

Jemmy's only hope was that, after a glimpse at the place, Judkins would be satisfied. Rob, who did not know how high Charley was, had awaited the opening with much anxiety.

He was not at ease now, for any moment might reveal to the badger-eyed official some indication of Charley's presence.

"You see there ain't much room," Jemmy said, "for any bloke to get."

"Not much."

"It would be a tight fit for any one blessed with an ounce of flesh."

"Still, some one might get up there."

"They might."

"Not if they was as fat as you," remarked Rob to Judkins.

Now, as Judkins was of the earwig species of slummers, and had, in fact, for some time been the butt of his brother constables, this observation of Rob riled him exceedingly.

But, as he had found it was playing with edged tools to have much to do with him, he merely gave him a muttered caution to mind what he was about, and poked his hand a little way up the chimney.

"What's it stuffed with?" he asked.

"That's more than I know; it's never been used since I came."

"Pull it down, whatever it is."

"No," returned Jemmy, "do your dirty work yourself."

"Hope he won't have that pulled down," thought Rob; "if he do, it's a gooser with Charley."

Neither Judkins nor the other policemen relished that job of pulling down a lot of sooty shavings and stuff; but, as the zeal of the former officer would admit of no obstacle, and none of his brother peelers would do a task he had imposed upon himself, he was compelled to pull down the mess, or let it rest where it was.

"Better leave it where it is," remarked Rob; "it looks as if there would be a precious mess if it was pulled out."

"We'll see," said Judkins, as he put his hand up the chimney.

CHAPTER XXXIV.

HOW CHARLEY CAME DOWN THE CHIMNEY.

The two bricklayer-looking individuals, suspecting that something was up, came closer to the peelers, suspiciously so, as one of them thought, for he quietly put them back.

To Roving Rob the moment was one of intense uncertainty.

That Charley would be discovered appeared almost inevitable; and the question that occurred to him was how he might be rescued from their hands.

As they at present stood, they were four to four, but then there was no doubt that more policemen were outside, who would come in at the first sound of a "scrimmage."

As for Jemmy, he was keeping himself as cool as a cucumber.

This time he had one of the pins comfortably within his reach, and that his eye was on.

Judkins, keeping his face as far as possible from the opening, pulled down the shavings.

A cloud of soot rose that set them all sneezing.

Judkins threw the sooty mess down.

"Here, hullo!" cried Rob; "have you looked inside the shavings?"

The laugh that this occasioned rather nettled the zealous crusher.

"Who's going up the chimney?" now asked Rob.

"Better get a boy," said Jemmy.

"Can't do that," Rob replied; "the *hact's* agin sending a boy up."

Disregarding these and many other remarks, Judkins stooped, and poked his head in a little way above the bars.

"Now for it," thought Rob.

Judkins looked very steadfastly up the chimney. Jemmy, whose eye longingly rested on the pins before mentioned, was very much inclined to give him a poke with it that would send him entirely up.

But he refrained.

"Can you see the chimney-pot?" asked Rob.

"I can see something."

"It ain't a cat, is it?"

"We'll soon see what it is; here, one of you lend me a stick."

"Ah!" thought Rob; "poor Charley, he have stood it like a brick, he have; but it be a go now."

A piece of broken plank was handed to Judkins, who, with an air of great sagacity, commenced poking about the chimney, dislodging great quantities of soot, but nothing else.

"You're making a nice mess," remarked Jemmy.

"Never mind that," retorted the officer, who was getting hot and dirty; "here, Joe, look up here, see if that ain't something."

Joe, a whiskered peeler of dignified look, came forward, and reluctantly let his head go a little way up the chimney.

He withdrew it quickly.

Judkins, who imagined he had seen somebody, snatched the piece of wood from his hand.

"Where—what?" he asked.

"There's nothing there—only a brick."

"A brick?"

"That's all."

"He ar' right," thought Rob; "it ar' a brick that's up there, but not one of the chimley 'uns.'"

Judkins was far from satisfied with Joe's decision he again commenced operations.

"I can see something," he muttered, "just there: I'll have it—and I've got it."

He had; the bit of plank went with a jerk along the chimney, and down came such a heap of soot: there had been a hard mass resting in one corner, and he had succeeded in dislodging it.

As his face was upturned, and his eyes and mouth were wide open, and the quantity of soot fell directly on it, it may be imagined that he received the full benefit.

It came with a spank, bunging up his eyes, plugging up his nose, and cramming his mouth.

Down his neck, too, it went, and all over his uniform.

There was a general shout of laughter when he pulled his head quickly back, and tried to shake off the sooty load.

"How—boo—some water; I'm choked," he cried.

"Ha, ha!" laughed Rob; what a figure he do cut. If they only was to see him in court now, or down that *airey* where he sneaks of nights."

"You'd better carry him out," quoth Jemmy; "there's a tap at the butt."

"I'll help him off with it," said Rob.

But Judkins had no desire for such assistance; clearing his eyes as well as he could, he staggered out of the alley, two of the policemen going with him, the third remaining.

Rob breathed more freely. All the time of the search he had been expecting to see Charley pulled down by the legs; but this happy *contretemps* had, he thought, put Judkins off the scent.

Only he wondered where Charley had stowed himself.

Our young hero would have been discovered the instant that Judkins pulled down the shavings, had he remained where Jemmy had left him.

But he had heard the remark made by the peeler.

and, before Jemmy took that throw at the pins, had scrambled higher up amongst the soot till he had got to a part where the chimney made a bend to meet the flue of another fireplace.

Here he perched himself, and though most unpleasantly situated, owing to the hot draft that came from the other fireplace, where a fire was burning, he maintained his perilous position, and was so far out of the reach of discovery.

The only question was how long he would continue there.

In a few minutes Judkins came back; he was flushed and out of sorts, and bore palpable traces of the visitation his zeal had occasioned.

As Rob had expected that one dose had been enough for him he avoided the chimney as if it had been a furnace, and bestowing many indignant glances on Rob, went away with the others.

Jemmy and the two skittlers followed them, the landlord declaring that if they had been civil he would have stood a quart for them to wash their throats down, but as it was they shouldn't have a drop without paying for it.

And Judkins was resolved that Jemmy should have no money of his; the whole party, after a further search in the house, withdrew to continue their quest elsewhere, or watch the house of which they yet had some suspicion.

Any one not accustomed to the ways of policemen might have supposed that the road was clear, but both Jemmy and Rob knew different.

They were pretty confident that one at least of the blues was lying in wait.

So they were obliged to keep Charley in his confinement a little longer.

And the better to keep up appearances they commenced a game of skittles.

Events proved that they acted wisely.

In about half an hour Judkins unexpectedly poked his head inside the door, but seeing that the sacking was replaced and the suspected individuals were hard at play he withdrew believing that he had not been seen.

But he had.

Both Rob and Jemmy had twigged him.

They finished several games and then went to the bar to have some lush.

Still Charley was kept in his uncomfortable position.

The brave boy was becoming more and more weary of his stifling imprisonment.

Placed as he was he could not distinctly tell who was in the alley, but when the knocking down of the skittles had ceased and all was silent for some time, he began to ponder upon the probability of a partial descent.

He had just moved one foot from the ledge on which he rested when the sacking and frame was pulled away, immediately afterwards he saw the opening by the grate suddenly darkened by a head.

It was a thick chubby head with short shaggy locks; the scanty light that came in at the bottom enabled Charley to see that beneath the head under some thick whiskers was a white number.

Charley at once knew that it was a policeman.

He had remained motionless for a little while; then the face was upturned, and Charley could see a great red straining face with eyes almost starting from their sockets.

These eyes took a calm survey of the whole flue, first in one direction, they rested then in another. The foot of Charley had as yet remained pendant against the side, but now he could not resist the opportunity of gently putting it forth so as to dislodge a large quantity of soot.

This soot fell quite unexpectedly in the face of the looker-up; back went his head, and Charley heard him phew and splutter underneath.

This energetic individual was a policeman, who had for a long time been waiting for a chance of gaining renown in his calling.

More than once he had taken up harmless people whom he had found crouched on doorsteps, and had charged with attempted robbery; and his crusades against the keepers of the stalls in the Broadway and Strutton Ground had gained him the good wishes of that itinerant tradespeople.

But all these had failed in satisfying his inordinate ambition.

In the search after Charley he thought he saw all that he wished; and so when even the astute Judkins was put off the scent, he, taking advantage of the ground being empty, had got in through the window and was now on the search on his own account.

He was not aware that his burglarious entrance had been witnessed by a little urchin whom he had once taken up for turning head over heels before an omnibus, and got sentenced to a day's imprisonment, and who had at once hastened round the front to inform Jemmy of what had taken place in the rear of his establishment.

The fact of the officer having got in that way convinced Rob and Jemmy that he was working on his own hook, and assured them that they could without difficulty deal with him.

So having resolved upon giving him a wholesome lesson, they crept very quietly to the skittle-alley.

It would have been quite a treat to have seen Roving Rob's face when he got to the alley, and took a peep at the officer, whose hind-quarters were visible protruding from the flue.

"What a spectacle he do cut!" thought the pedler. "What a picter he do make, and what a picter he'll make presently!"

After making several grimaces of the most convulsive nature, Rob led the way quietly in.

The fact of the policeman having his head up the chimney prevented him hearing their entrance, and he would have been seized before he had become aware of their presence, had not an unforseen calamity suddenly occurred.

Charley perched, as he thought, in security, and having so successfully sooted the crusher, thought he would try the effects of a second dose; accordingly, when the peeler, having cleared a little of the first lot off, had again got his head well up the chimney, and was wriggling his body up as far as he could, in order to have a good chance of survey, he again put out his foot, and scraped down a quantity more of soot, which, like the former, fell on the executive's face.

But the act had revealed Charley's foot as it went out after more soot.

"Ha, ha!" cried the peeler, smarting with soot, and eager with joy; "whew—I've got you—pish—come down; I'll cage you."

His sudden outcry caused Charley to make a precipitate movement to get nearer the other flue; but in his haste, and being very insecure where he was perched, his foot slipped, and he felt himself falling.

He made a frantic clutch at the bricks, but the soot gave way from his hands, and down he came, covered with the black powder, and tumbling heavily on the policeman's head and shoulders.

The shock caused the peeler to utter a howl of pain, and then sent him flying out of the chimney with a jerk, that made him feel as if his neck was broken.

Charley, too, unable to stay his descent, came tumbling out feet foremost, and, after having scraped his backbone against the bars of the grate, fell again on top of the sprawling constable.

Neither one nor the other looked very interesting as they lay together, begrimed in soot and kicking helplessly; for each, by a natural instinct, had grasped the other. The cloud of soot that at first rose, almost blinded the lookers-on, who stood for a moment or so gazing at the ludicrous spectacle.

Charley was from head to foot as black as a

chummy; the peeler was not much better, only that the black specks on the blue coat gave him a sort of firebald appearance.

Roving Rob, who had been silently enjoying the scene, took Charley daintily by the collar, and drew him from the grasp of that individual.

"Ha, ha! I've got you safe; whew spluttered the peeler: I'll lag you—pish—damn the soot—don't run away, my poppet, I want you."

He sprang up, and clutched at him. Half blinded with the sooty particles he could not very well see, and did not find out his mistake, when he collared Rob instead, until that worthy spoke.

"Take it mild, take it mild; don't flurry your nerves: it hurts the digestion. Got me, have you? ah! and I've got *you*."

Which he had most unmistakeably.

The peeler opened his eyes; he had thought himself alone with Charley, and was more than astounded to find himself confronted by four determined-looking men.

He looked round in alarm.

He had heard of cases where policemen had, in the execution of their duty, been basely murdered by those whom they had endeavoured to take, but who had preferred adding that to their crime rather than be taken.

What if that were his fate.

He began to shake, whereupon Rob gave him a jerk, that made his teeth chatter.

Jemmy came forward with a big skittle.

"What do you want here?" he asked.

Now there was something about Jemmy that admitted of no mistake when he spoke; what with his short-cropped hair, his low forehead, and repulsive mouth, he looked the very man who would do what the policeman had most feared.

So that worthy thought when he looked at him, as he came armed with the heavy pin.

And with the thought he got rather more frightened.

The thought of his wife and family came to his mind: what if those wretches should murder him, and leave him to be discovered years hence—his features disfigured by blows, and one mass of blood and soot.

People who did such crimes had out-of-the-way places where they could stow away his body.

It was truly awful to think of.

When Jemmy, in a tone no less ferocious than meaning, repeated his query, his knees began to shake, and he cried—

"Murder! don't kill me!—oh!—oh!—mercy!"

"Murder," growled Jemmy; "we'll show you what murder is."

He raised the big pin.

At this Charley came forward.

"Don't do him any injury," he said.

"You're a pretty looking hangel," muttered Rob, with a laugh.

"Please don't do any harm to him."

"Well, we shan't, my little chummy; unless he makes a noise, when, in course, we shall be obliged to quiet him.

As the peeler knew what they meant by "quieting," he remained stock still.

Jemmy, however, had not quite done with him; he brandished the skittle in a manner that made the peeler howl, under the expectations of being maimed every time it was raised.

"Stop that howling, cuss you," cried Rob; "we ain't going to hurt you. We'll jest put you up the chimbley; you'll come down again like a smoked *haddick*, three a penny, all whoppers. Now, Jemmy, put down that pin, and help us to put up the peeler."

To this Jemmy replied with a grunt; he seemed more inclined to put the blue in an unconscious state before he poked him up the chimney. But Rob was master of the ceremonies, and having given the peeler a hint to the effect that if he did not remain quiet his head and the skittle should have a battle to see which was the hardest, they lifted him bodily, and commenced cramming him up the flue.

The aperture was rather narrow, so that the planting of the peeler was a work of some difficulty, during which they had all the toil, and he all the jamming.

But, as in the case of a wedge being driven into anything, either one or the other must give way, so with the policeman; and, as the flue was of the most unyielding nature, the unlucky copper had to be squeezed and jammed till he was got up the flue, and left with his head amongst the soot, and his feet on the bar, feeling very much like a convict standing on the drop, and waiting for the bolt to be withdrawn.

His captors, having ensconced him thus, snugly arranged the padding in its place, and left him to the comforts of his position, while means were taken to place Charley in a more natural guise.

CHAPTER XXXV.

THE POLICEMAN'S TREACHERY.

AFTER Charley had thoroughly washed the soot from his face, and a suit of clothes, rustic, worn out, and humble, had been procured for him, he was taken upstairs to the landlady's bed-room, there to remain for the remainder of the day.

Let not the reader enter into suppositions respecting Charley's morality; the landlady was not there, nor likely to be.

Jemmy Stag was not one of those who would have trusted his wife in the company even of a boy, under circumstances which might prove so dangerous.

Frowsy, vulgar, and coarse as she was, he preferred her for himself.

And Charley was better satisfied to be by himself. Roving Rob, as soon as his toilette had been completed, took him up a jug of steaming egg-hot, and, as Charley was really faint from his prison incarceration and his cruise up the chimney, he drank with less scruples than he would at first have entertained.

Roving Rob said little to him: he had thoroughly read the boy's character, and knew that it would be better to make no comments relative to the recent incidents.

He left the jug of liquor on the table, and descended to the lower room.

Here the Downy Cove, having given up the cab to its proper owner, who, not having seen them at the place appointed, had come after it; he was a wary cad, and laughed heartily at the affair of the police hunt.

The Downy Cove and Roving Rob, with Jemmy Stag, sat talking, drinking, or singing together till evening, when the Downy gentleman rose, and prepared to take his departure.

He had to prepare his six small children for their night's work, which consisted of standing in a busy thoroughfare—himself with an apron on and almost cadaverous face—the children, with faces touched up to the most ghastly and woe-begone expression, to bear each a placard, "we are starving."

"Must you go?" asked Jemmy Stag.

"Must do the lay," replied the Downy, "lost all day as it is: more than seven and tuppence out of my fob."

"Right," said Rob, "you've done your part with us; the younker's safe, and well you've managed it."

"If so be as you wants me any more to fake the dodge or do the lay—"

"We're right now," rejoined Rob, "tell the kiddies we'll be there to night; can't say when."

The Downy Cove shook hands with each and departed.

About an hour after this Rob and the landlord kept up their carouse, broken only when Jemmy was called to the skittle-ground to attend to the wants of the players, who were by this time dropping in "plentiful as blackberries," as Roving Rob said.

When Charley was left to himself he drew the rush-bottomed chair (only one the chamber boasted of) up to the rickety-legged dressing-table, turned by Jemmy into general use, and leaned his elbow upon it while his head rested upon his hands.

He had been enjoined if he heard a slight whistle in the room, produced by an appliance in the passage below, to clamber up the pole of the four-post bedstead and take refuge in the old hangings that formed the canopy to the loves of Jemmy and his spouse.

All thoughts of this, however, passed from his mind, as he sat there brooding over the past and revolving upon the future.

Few of our boy readers, we hope, have ever been in a position similar to Charley's.

Strictly honest and persevering, as well as clever, he had, by circumstances over which he could have no control, found himself in the company of thieves and impostors, and, in spite of his struggles to escape, was growing day by day more enmeshed.

His affection for Dick alone had kept him in the trammels; it was only that he might get Dick away that he now consented to remain in such repugnant company.

It was very hard to be barred from all chance of honest living by being suspected of infamous complicity in deeds he would have suffered his hand to have been cut off rather than to have joined in. But Charley knew that by the world appearances were taken as proofs, and that destiny so far had been against him.

"If I once get poor Dick away," he exclaimed, "they shall never see him again; we'll starve first."

"Poor Dick," he murmured, "he was always upright and used to listen to me; I don't think they'll get him to mix again in their bad acts; and yet that Rob he has great power with him, he don't tell him the truth about poor Mary; I'm sure he don't, but he leads him with it like a child."

Poor Mary—Dick's misled betrayed love; there was the shoal on which he feared Dick's integrity would be wrecked.

To gain revenge on the betrayer of Mary, what would not he suffer himself to be led into!

Neither Charley nor Dick could guess how the latter would meet hapless ruined Mary, nor what that meeting would result in.

It was a long day to Charley. Once or twice Roving Rob came up, and, after telling him to wait patiently till night, went down again.

The last time he came up he brought Charley some coffee and toast; for Rob was solicitous of the boy's welfare, and did all he could to make him comfortable under the circumstances.

It was a long day to wait; but the waiting was not so dreary as it had been up the chimney, or in the close cell of the police station.

Charley thought of the peeler stuffed up the chimney. He had not troubled Rob with any questions as to whether he was released; he was acquainted with the rules of safety adopted by prigs and beggars, and knew that they would not set the policeman free while there was any chance of danger to themselves.

This was also a fact patent to the unfortunate Robert, who had made himself hoarse with bellowing up the chimney with no greater effect than bringing to the top a wandering tom cat, who wondered what thing it was that produced the indistinct howling sound.

Night came at last, and Roving Rob thought a venture might be made. So he ascended the stairs, and acquainted Charley of the fact.

Charley was most willing to get away from the house, and he readily rose to leave.

They had dressed him in a suit not so neat as that he had been in the habit of wearing, and one that Rob did not intend that he should long retain. It suited him no more than a white waistcoat would have suited Rob.

It was a worn out tattered suit of corduroy, made for a boy much taller than Charley: a boy evidently possessed of sharp knees and sharp elbows, judging by the gaps in these portions of the attire.

Very few buttons were remaining, and the pockets were worn to threads.

Charley felt as little at home in the disguise as Rob did in the graveyard-like suit which Jemmy Stag had procured for him, and which, with its musty dampness, and dead man's odour, was sticking about him like a mildewed shroud.

But necessity admitted of no choice, and after a few words of caution to Charley, he led him down the stairs.

Before they left the house, Charley stopped.

"The policeman!" he said.

"Where? young tulip," asked Rob.

"Him up the chimney."

"Oh! him?"

"Yes; you will not leave him here."

"Won't I?"

"It is no harm now to let him out."

"Isn't it? guess I'm not quite such a happlicant for Bedlam."

"Don't keep him up there," said Charley, who had a vivid remembrance of the unpleasantness of the place.

Roving Rob put on a curious face.

"What do you think, you innocent child, would happen if I were to let him out?"

"He would not betray us."

"Walker."

"I'm sure he'd be too glad to escape."

"Werry true that; but we'll let him stay where he is a little while longer."

"If you don't want to be nabbed," growled Jemmy, "you won't trouble about him: I'll look arter his health."

Charley did not like the look or tone of Jemmy Stag, so he said firmly—

"I won't go till he's let out."

"What?" growled Jemmy.

"I will not go."

"Eh," said Rob.

"No; let him out: I know he will promise to say nothing about us."

Roving Rob pulled another queer face.

"No doubt whatever of his promising to behave himself; but it ain't so certain as he'll do what he promises."

"Ain't wery likely;" chimed in Jemmy, "let him be where he is: he shouldn't be so sharp looking arter people."

This policeman was particularly obnoxious to Jemmy, and he wished to leave him there, in order that he might prevent him, by a peculiar method of his own, from again interfering in his domestic affairs.

A suspicion of this struck Rob, and he stared hard in the face of the landlord.

"I think, Jemmy," he said, after a hard look which had satisfied him that Jemmy's intentions were not strictly merciful, "we'll just hear what he's got to say."

"Your daft if you do."

"No; we ain't nothing of the sort."

"You won't let him out."

"Pr'aps."

"Well, if you're took it will be your own doing."

"I don't think as how we shall be took."

"I'm sure we shall not," Charley said.

"I didn't think you were so green," muttered Jemmy, as he proceeded, followed by Rob, to the skittle-ground.

There were two players there, two disreputable characters of roughs—who by day go about vending stinking fish or other worthless articles—not the genuine costermongers who buys good if he buys cheap, and though not over polished in his demeanour, is honest and hardworking.

"Gentlemen," said Jemmy, "when you've finished your game we'll shut up the ground."

"Why; what's up?"

"There's a few crushers coming to have a look about; they want's somebody, and I shouldn't like 'em to find any one here."

The mention of the intended visit was enough for the two roughs; their looks expressed a large amount of alarm, and one of them leisurely said—

"We've done, Jemmy; we'll go."

"All right."

"But, I say."

"What?"

"There's been a row somewhere at the back here."

"A row?"

"Yes; when me and my pal comed in we heard somebody a hollowing as if they was half choked; but they have left off it now."

Jemmy looked hard at the speaker to see if he had any meaning in his words, but there was nothing to show that he was acquainted with the secret of the chimney.

The two men having put on their jackets paid their score, and were soon out of the house.

"I didn't think the bloke could be heard when the matting was up," growled Jemmy, as, having shut the door, he pulled away the pad. "Now there, if you're going to speak to him, look sharp, but take my advice and don't let him go, leastways, not just yet."

"How long would you like to keep him here, Jemmy?"

"Till it was all square."

"He'd be smoked like a dead herring before then."

"A good job too: here, you up there."

Jemmy jerked his voice up the chimney.

They had of course expected the policeman to jump down at the first opening of the trap, but to their surprise he remained where he was.

"Come down," Jemmy said, "we want you."

"Yes, walk down, as the cat said when the mouse got up the gas pipe; we jest want's you."

But there came no reply from up the chimney.

Rob pulled the board out of the way and looked up.

The policeman's feet were visible resting on the top, but his legs were quite stiff and motionless.

Roving Rob experienced a slight shock; even the callous Jemmy had a turn. It was so startling to see those still limbs when they had expected a lissom living man to come bounding down the flue.

Was he dead?

This was the thought which at once passed through their minds, and which became a conviction with Charley.

"He is dead,' he cried, "you have smothered him."

"You stood it," growled Jemmy, "why shouldn't he?

"If he hadn't why he ought to," Rob observed.

"But he don't speak or move."

"Dead or no he won't stay up there; down he comes."

"Hi!" Rob yelled up the chimney; "yo-ho—yellow hoy; come down—hoy—hi—yo-ho! we want you."

And by way of lending force to his appeal, he grasped one of the peeler's legs, and gave it a pull.

The next moment he received a kick in the mouth from the heavy toe of the policeman's boot.

A policeman's boot is always a thick clumsy affair. If you see only the leather-cased foot coming round the corner, with a heavy thump upon the pavement, you may know that it belongs to one of the force.

Policemen all rejoice in flat heavy boots and big feet.

At least they appear so.

When this identical boot was jerked spitefully out, it caught Rob's teeth with a snap, and made them quite rattle.

Surprised at this unexpected treatment, the pedlar, keeping tenaciously his hold of the leg, pulled the owner down the chimney.

A sight he presented when he showed himself! He had bawled and halloed up the flue till the soot had lined his throat almost as thickly as it did the chimney, and so smothered his cries, but not before the tom cat before mentioned had, in an enterprising attempt to discover who it was that lodged there, come tumbling headlong down.

The crusher, apprised of the coming of something by the shower of soot which suddenly fell, blinding him, received a violent blow in the face, and before he had well recovered from that, the cat's claws were fixed in his neck.

Poor puss, alarmed by his unexpected descent, and not knowing where it might end, clung to the first object that presented itself: and as that object was the policeman, he found himself dreadfully wounded in consequence.

No one likes to be pulled and torn less than a peeler: our friend was no exception. Nettled at his long durance and unavailing yells, he became absolutely vicious when he had recovered from the alarm this sudden attack caused.

Smarting with the pain, he grasped grimalkin by the body, intending to execute summary vengeance on him.

Puss, terrified at the unlooked-for encounter, and, no doubt, wondering what animal it was that had its residence up that flue, bristled up for hostilities, and a regular fight was the result.

It ended in poor Tom beating a precipitate retreat by scrambling up the chimney, after he had severely punished his opponent, and had himself had the whole of his nine lives nearly beaten or squeezed out of him by his exasperated assailant.

His howls were dreadful as he went, and the soot which his paws sent down choked up the gaps made by his long sharp talons.

After this battle, the peeler, finding that he was likely to be left there for the night, and being of a philosophical turn of mind, leaned his tall back against the sooty bricks, and was soon fast asleep.

In this situation he was when Rob took hold of him; and being awakened by hearing a violent yelling, and discovering himself held by the leg, he, believing that his infernal enemy the tom cat was again clinging to him, shot out his leg, with the result before mentioned.

He was the picture of confusion when the peeper that was not closed enabled him to see by whom he was confronted. The cat's tail had so whisked in his eyes that his vision was not of the clearest, and he was unaware at first whether those before him numbered two or six.

"What a specimen he ar'," Rob observed, "with his hies bunged up, like mine was when I tumbled into the dike; and his face, all soot and scratches. Why, what have you been up to? you look as if you'd been a-fighting a crocodile."

"Been a-tearing your own skin?" Jemmy asked.

The policeman rubbed his eyes, and stared at them.

"It was the cat," he exclaimed.

"Ah, that's the gemman what breaks all the chaney, and gorges all the pork and mutton pie; but how did you like your stay up the flue?"

"You will suffer for putting me there."

"Don't talk too fast," said Jemmy, with a meaning look.

The policeman understood the quarter he was in, and looked abashed.

"You needn't be frightened," Rob observed; "d'ye want to go up there again?"

The policeman looked as if it was not the exact place he would prefer if he had his choice.

"You don't like it; well, what do you say if we let's you out?"

"He'll nab the kid," Jemmy exclaimed.

"Will you split on us?"

The policeman hesitated; he did not like to look afraid of them, and it was clearly his duty to take them into custody at once, and without further preamble.

If he had yet possessed his rattle, he might have been plucky enough to have sprung it, but Rob had taken care to lighten him of that and his staff before he was thrust up the flue.

"Look here," Rob said, "we can stuff you up there and leave you up if we like; you know there's no one could help you, and it ain't so jolly comfortable up there, especially when you've been up there a week or so; but we don't want to go to extreme measures with you, as the sword-fish said when he sawed off the tail from a *h*alligator, 'acos you've only done what you're taught is your duty, which, though it ar' not right to stuff this kiddy into quod for what he never did, nor couldn't help, is what you're paid for; but howsomedever, if you ain't a mean peaching skunk, we'll make a bargain to let you go, when you've brushed your clothes, if you'll swear not to take any kind of notice of us."

"And if I won't?"

"You go up the chimbley again."

"It ain't for that," said the peeler, trying to look big, "but I know sometimes a youngster is led into a sort of thing that he isn't bred to, and this one don't look up to any fugling." Here he took a good look at Charley. "I'm quite ready to let him cut, if you'll give me up my staff, and make off before I get out."

"That's fair: here's your staff: I'm going to keep your rattle; you must buy another; won't cost you much, and might make you break your word, knowing who had it, and then be after getting your own nob knocked in."

Having given utterance to these significant words, Rob called Charley to accompany him, and the pair were soon outside the house.

Jemmy would have liked to have administered a settlement on his own account to the crusher; but he was not courageous enough to act boldly against him, and the peeler, evidently suspicious of him, kept a watchful look out while he hastily brushed his clothes.

"Remember," cried Jemmy, as he was going, "no peaching."

"All right," said the policeman.

Jemmy gave him a meaning scowl, and showed him the door.

The policeman glanced casually up each way of the close narrow street.

He saw two figures turning the corner.

"I shall overtake them," he thought, as he turned in the contrary way; but once out of sight of the bobby, Jemmy Stag hurried through a court that brought him out almost as soon as Rob and Charley came the other way.

Leaning his tall form against a lamppost, he coolly watched which way they went, and then treacherously followed them.

CHAPTER XXXVI.

WHAT ROVING ROB DID TO SAVE CHARLEY.

It was scarcely to be expected that the policeman would keep his word: Roving Rob must have had an unusual fit of confidence to have supposed that he would.

There is not much of a code of honour amongst the members of the force.

Quite the contrary.

It matters not to them by what means they manage to bring a fellow being to justice, so that they accomplish it.

In the zeal of their office they must, at times, almost forget that they are human.

This one was an example of the class: he watched Rob, as he wended his way from the spot, and, keeping carefully out of sight (for Rob did not go far without looking behind him), he waited till he could meet one of his brother constables to help him in capturing the prisoner.

Westminster, with its murky gloom, its dull lights, wandering population, and street sellers, was all life—such life as occurs in the close haunts of poverty and sin, amidst which these, fittingly, was the suggestive police court.

The Christian crusade had not then been made against the keepers of the stalls: they were yet permitted to earn an honest livelihood by disposing of their commodities to the needy poor.

It had yet to come, that officious policemen, bribed by mercenary men, should drive them to theft and deeds of violence, or send them to prison for persuing their market trade.

But it was not in the thronged thoro'fares that Rob proceeded: he kept in the darker purlieus, those close alleys, where, perhaps, a single gas, yet flaring from an open cellar, indicates the only mart of business in the street, except where, at the corner, indispensable concommitant, the gin palace, with its frowsy frequenters, towered above the stunted dwellings around it.

Guided by one of these yellow flames, Roving Rob took Charley into a dim court, and led him into the establishment which this one light illumined.

This establishment was a dirty looking cellar, along each side of which left-off boots, patched up and soled, were ranged; inside the cellar thousands of pairs were hanging in bunches—long Wellingtons, half ditto, Clarences, Bluchers, spring boots, shoes, some light, but the greater proportion made heavy, with stout hob-nails driven in, to suit the requirements of that vicinity.

Descending four wooden steps, each one more perilous than the rotten plank at the top, Rob, followed by Charley, stood in the mart of boots.

The proprietress, a stout full-faced woman, dressed rather dowdily, but sporting a profusion of heavy false jewellery, and wearing on her fingers six or seven genuine rings, of varying value, nodded to him familiarly, and, after a strange glance at Charley, whom she surveyed in an instant, first at the feet and then at the head, said, in a brisk hearty tone—

"Ah! Mr. Pedlar; haven't seen you for long. What can I do for *you* to-night; I've all sorts, you see."

"So you have, Mrs. Grampus; there's enough to choose out of. Just cast your hie, Charley boy, round these clusters of 'translated;' twig them Wellingtons, big enough for Gog and Magog, even if they poked their feet in both on 'em at a time; then there's them antigrophiloes, what they coves puts on afore they goes down them traps you sees in the street into the sewers. Look agin, an' you see Wellingtons an' Bluchers, enough for a harmy of both; there's some as has been worn by sojers in the war, an' some as has been made for 'em and never was worn; not a bit of good in 'em, except the hob-nails, which is drove in to prevent the soles coming off, which they'll do the first wet day; them genteel looking blokes, with the thin soles and shiny fronts, is for the seedy coves as can't spring a new pair, and comes here to buy a pair as will look as if they had been bought new once; these clumped 'uns, with the big nails, is for the navvies and labourers, what takes their penn'orth out of a pair afore they've had 'em a week—but they wouldn't suit you; there's the boys, them with the light heels, tight round the ankles, and sharp at the toes; them's what the prigs fancies, 'cos they can run lighter in 'em than in any others."

"Well, I never," said Mrs. Grampus; "if you ain't telling off my stock in trade; never mind."

"I allers does; it's a way of mine: you won't mind it; and now, as I've cried up your wares, which, no matter of what I've been saying, is good wares, why I'll come to the point, as the crusher did when he sat on a spike, which, all unbeknown to him, one of his boys had fixed in his coat tails."

"I never; if you ain't *such* a funny man. I declare I often says to my sister Bet as comes here sometimes, says I, 'you're fond enough of going to the pantermime, but if you only just was to hear Roving Rob run on as he do sometimes, it would be the best pantermime you ever heard, and bangs harlyqueen, clown, panterloon, and the whole biling of them.'"

"Which readerly ar' my hexcuse that I doesn't take off my hat," said Rob, in reply. "And now, old doman, if you've just got a tidy suit of togs as will fit this youngster, and another that will fit me—for blessed if I like these ones I've got—I don't mind standing a half quid or so."

The woman took a momentary survey of Charley, and said—

"I'll fit him as well as Moses, and shan't charge you a half nor a quarter as much; but I don't know what I can do for you, unless you has the togs which poor Grampus left behind him, which—"

"What! is *he* kicked over?"

"Yes; he is gone."

"Well, I'm blessed."

"Ah! poor soul; he's been gone a long time."

"And he won't never come back again; and so you're a widder—my eye! well I never."

"La! Mr. Rob, how you do go on; one would think you—"

Here the disconsolate "widder" paused, but made amends for her shortness of words by the look she bestowed upon him.

"I've often thought," soliloquised Rob, as the facinating proprietress of the second-hand (second-foot it must be) boot shop occupied herself in pulling from a heap of old garments the ones designed for Charley; "I've often thought that, if ever I was to give up single blessedness, it would be along of some such a doman as Mrs. Grampus, and she's a widder. Well I'm blessed."

Rob became lost in the reverie this astounding fact caused.

"I'm blessed," again began Rob, when he was interrupted by a voice from the street.

"Mother Grampus."

"Yes; that's me," said the majestic lady, coming forward with five pairs of trousers in her hands and over her arms.

A meagre-looking figure, dressed in costermonger's garb, stood at the top.

"Goodness gracious, Paul, how you do look!"

"Mother Grampus, if there's anybody here that's wanted—"

"Hullo," cried Rob, "tongs and crocodiles—"

"Wanted," echoed the stout-faced widow.

"That's it."

"Who—what—"

"'Cos if there is they'd better not come out this way, as there's a score of blues waiting to nab 'em."

"La!" cried Mrs. Grampus, casting down the five pair of trousers, and letting her plump arms fall to her side; "what a turn you *did* give me. Who can be wanted here?"

"This identical indiwiddel, ma'am, and that sprig over there."

"Goodness gracious—deary me—why never; you don't say so?"

"I'll take that pair of boots now," said the "costy."

"Yes, yes, here you are; back with you—him with you," cried Mrs. Grampus, in her excitement, handi'   --- the first pair of boots that came to hand,

which proved to be a pair big enough for him to have put his body inside as well as his foot.

At the same time she pushed Rob back to the rear part of the shop.

The "costy" took the boots.

"If they ain't as he likes 'em, I'll bring 'em back."

"Very well," said Mrs. G., hardly knowing what she said or did.

A policeman came by with heavy tread; he cast a sidelong glance down the cellar as he passed. Roving Rob had pulled Charley out of sight. The costermonger stood at the entrance with the immense boots in his hand.

As soon as the policeman had gone by he moved off.

"Lord, Lord!" exclaimed Mrs. G., suddenly catching sight of the ponderous boots; "to think what I've been and gone and given him. They'll know, if they're waiting, it's a do; them boots was never made for him. What did he say? here you, tumble out there; you'll be in for it, I know. Oh! Rob, what *have* you done?"

"Not wery much—they wants this kiddy, and I does't want 'em to have him."

"Lawks, no—I should say not, poor dear boy; here Mr. Rob; the ladder; get up the trap there. I'll stand before you."

Rob cast his eyes upwards; the trap referred to was in the roof, and led from the cellar to the room immediately above; from there, of course, there were modes of egress, and Rob, thanking her for her prompt suggestions, thrust the ladder under the opening while Mrs. Grampus cast her portly person between him and the opening at the street.

This procedure was not more than necessary, as a policeman was over the way trying to see what was going on inside.

He was unable to do this in consequence of the narrowness of the opening and the width of Betsy, who, that her attitude might not look suspicious, pretended to be selecting some pairs of boots from the side of the cellar.

At the same time she was giving under-breath instructions to those behind.

"Mount up quick; get out of the back window; make haste; shut the trap after you; hark! I hear them."

"Charley," Rob said, "if you are taken, I will be. Shall they lock us up in prison?"

"They shall not take us."

"I'll trust in you; jump up after me."

Rob was up in an instant; Charley, agile and active, was through the trap immediately afterwards. Mrs. G. stepped back, and pulled the ladder from its place. The trap was closed but only in time.

A policeman came at the entrance.

The other still stood over the way.

Two more were in front of the house.

The policeman whom Rob had cheated had met with the others, and had led them to the shop.

That was his gratitude for being let out.

The first policeman thrust his head inside, and then descended to the shop.

"How do you do?" asked Mrs. G., with all the gravity imaginable, though feeling most inclined to hit him about the head with the hob-nailed boots her hand held.

"How do you do?" returned the policeman.

This customary greeting ended, the pair had a good stare at each other.

"I've come," began the policeman.

"I see you have," interrupted Mrs. G., "'tain't often any of you gentlemen comes to my humble shop; nevertheless, I'm always ready to serve any comer, be they who they may, as I've said over and over again to Mr. G. What can I show you, Wellingtons, Bluchers, Balmorals?"

"I don't want any boots," returned the policeman. getting further in.

"Not want any? why?"

THE QUARREL IN THE THIEVES' KITCHEN.

"Not from you; there's no need of any nonsense with us; we're looking for some one."

"Are *we*," thought Mrs. G.; "I hope *we* may find them."

"An atrocious deed has been committed, and, from information received, we have come here for the criminal."

"Come here?" began she.

"Come on down, you; our birds was here; we'll get them too."

The first half was addressed to the other policemen, who came cautiously down, walking as if they were dubious of breaking their shins from below, or having their heads broken from above.

"We've come, as I've been telling her, to take them as we wants."

"Yes, that's it," exclaimed the bobby who had been up the flue.

"We don't want to hurt anybody."

"Of course not."

"But we must have 'em."

"So we must."

"Well, I'm sure," cried Mrs. G.; "a pretty way to come bouncing into a honest woman's house. Do you suspect me, sir, of harbouring thieves?"

"We know they came in here."

"Do you?"

"Yes; and we'll search them out."

Without further ado the constables commenced looking about for the flown birds; they were not long before they discovered the ladder and trap-door.

"That's were they're gone," said one, "two of you stay out there to nab them if they show face; the rest of us will go up."

This was effected: two of the police remained in front, the other three ascending by the trap-door, while Mrs. G. stood in high dudgeon—the very picture of outraged innocence.

Roving Rob lost no time when, with Charley, he found himself in the room above: hastening to the window he soon had it open, and was about to help Charley forth, when an idea occurred to him.

"Strikes me," he soliloquised, "that if we gets out of there they'll have such a hue and cry that we are like to be took; while if we ain't there, but they thinks we are, why they'll have a chase all to themselves, and we can be snug upstairs."

Rob decided the instant this thought manifested itself.

"Come along of me, Charley," he said; and Charley, who implicitly followed his instructions in the system of escape, obeyed him silently.

"We'll go upstairs, Charley, and they'll have a hunt without us being afore 'em."

Upstairs they went; Rob, not contenting himself with the second-floor, went to the next, which was the top of the house.

Then they got into the back attic, which was untenanted, being disused by Mrs. G., except for lumber, since the remains of the regretted Mr. G. lay there in solemn state.

"Let's sit down and make our wretched lives happy," Rob said, as he closed the door.

Charley sat down by the window; Rob seated himself placidly before the door.

"We're doing them," he remarked, after he had applied his ear to the keyhole.

The police found the window slightly open.

"They've got out here," one said, and all three bundled into the street.

But it happened that the upstairs progress of Rob and his *protegé* had been seen by one of Mrs. G.'s lodgers, a lady not very friendly at that moment with her landlady; she having cautiously stepped upstairs and listened at the outside of the keyhole— at the outside of which Rob's auricular organ was glued—came to the conclusion that it would be an inspiring event for herself, and a means of wreaking her spite out against Mrs. G., if she descended to the officers below to acquaint them with the truth, and admit them silently.

Being a notorious tattlemonger, her curiosity had been, in the first instance, excited by the policemen over the way, and when she saw more enter, she left her room to see if she could come at the reason of the visit.

Her ears positively glowed at the thought of the scandal she could retail on the morrow.

She stepped as softly as a cat till she reached the street-door, which she opened as quietly as if it had been oiled for the purpose.

The police, attracted by her beckoning finger, stole quietly into the house, and followed her up the stairs.

This busymonger thought she had reached a pitch of greatness, to lead the police on the track of hiding miscreants, and to be the means of exposing the malpractices of Mrs. G.

What was such a triumph worth?

Her head grew giddy at the thought, which, perhaps, accounted for the mad adventure that occurred to her.

Turning round to motion them to pause for a moment while she ascended to the room, she, in the act of leaning over the banisters, overreached herself, and her foot slipping, she lost her balance, and fell down a few stairs.

She would have fallen down them all had she not in her wildness clutched the first leg she came to, and as the policeman whose leg she grasped snatched at the fellow next to him, all three came down together on the middle stair.

The frightened shriek of this lady—the noise she made in her precipitate descent—satisfied Rob that what he had feared when first the creaking of the stairs reached him was true, they were followed— betrayed.

Without pausing to study how they were betrayed, Rob glanced round to ascertain the readiest mode of escape.

There were two ways: one the window, the other the door.

The former was a break-back height from the ground.

Outside the latter the officers would be the next instant; Rob's eyes fortunately lighted on a coil of old rope.

Hastily he piled a few boxes against the door, and, picking up the rope, stepped to the window.

As he opened it the police came battering outside.

Rob took in the whole chances of the affair with a practised eye.

There was just one minute—not more—that he might hope to keep the police out of the room.

When they came in they would take whoever they found there.

If those they sought had escaped, they would follow by the same means.

The rope would occupy half of that minute in securely fastening to the window. A pane of glass would have to be broken first, and would, by the noise, acquaint them with what was going forward.

There was just time for one to slide down the rope, if the other held it.

He had no doubt that if he asked Charley to hold it for him to so descend, the bold boy would perform the part.

But then there would be no time for Charley to follow, even if he could secure the rope.

He looked out in the street; it was very dark, but he could see that there was no one below.

He beckoned to Charley, and dropped one end of the rope out of window.

Rob had determined to give Charley the first chance of escape, and himself trust to what turned up.

"Slide down quickly," he said.

Charley, accustomed to his decisive method, swung himself out of window, and clung to the rope, which Rob held firm by ledging against the window sill.

"Get out of sight directly you're down," Rob whispered, as Charley began to descend.

"And you?"

"I'll look after myself."

"Dick?"

"Never mind Dick; don't you hear 'em hammering at the blowed door?"

"Open here," cried the police.

"We ain't oysters," muttered Rob, who in moments of danger could not break himself of his phraseology.

Charley, expert at pole-climbing, was down the rope in no time. On the ground he paused a moment to look up to Rob.

He wanted to see him safe before he took to flight.

A gesture of Rob's hand motioned him away, and he hurried up the alley.

"Now then," thought Rob, "shall I go down? if I do, they'll know how we've got out; if I don't, I shall be nabbed."

His deliberations were ended abruptly: with a burst the door was dashed in, and the police entered pell mell.

Rob, at the instant unperceived, hurled the coil of rope on to the roof of the opposite house.

Then he turned coolly round.

"Hullo!" said the policeman who had been up the chimney, "we want you."

"A pretty sort you ar'. You ar' a Bristol stone china mug not worth a farden; why, afore I'd be such a thing as you, I'd hang myself with my own hair."

"What were you doing there?" asked one of the police, rushing to the window.

"Looking out; what do you think?"

"Perhaps you were trying to get out."

"P'raps I was."

"It's my opinion you *were* trying to get out."

"Well, I was thinking about it."

"Where's the younker?"

"Who?"

"The boy."

"Boy?"

"Yes; the boy you took out of court."

"Boy I took out of court! What a blessed fake!"

"Well, the boy you brought in here."

"Oh!"

"Where is he? you may as well tell."

"P'raps he's gone out of winder."

"He may have done so."

"So he may," remarked Rob, thoughtfully.

"Come, come—no nonsense; where is he?"

"Gone out of winder; didn't I say so afore."

The police, who had before been under the impression that Charley had escaped by the window, were put off that scent, when Rob declared that it was so.

Looking from the height of the window to the ground, and seeing no way by which the pavement could be reached, they thought Rob was merely striving to put them off the quest, and accordingly, while one held Rob, the others began to search the little attic.

Every part of the house was afterwards searched anew, but without the discovery of Charley, and the baffled police were fain to quit the place.

They took with them, however, the one prisoner whom fortune had thrown in their way, greatly to the consternation of Mrs. Grampus, who was all lamentation, when she discovered Rob handcuffed and collared by the wrathful police.

Roving Rob, however, suffered his arrest to give him little concern. There was only one thing he cared for; he might be detected as one who had been present at the murder of the policeman before Mr. Wilblow's house: charging matter, if it were proved against him.

But even this he hoped to avoid by a plan of escape, which was then forming in his nob.

CHAPTER XXXVII.

CHARLEY WANDERS ALONE IN THE STREETS OF LONDON.

OBEYING the injunctions of Roving Rob, Charley no sooner found himself safe on *terra firma*, than he walked at a brisk pace up the narrow street.

Arrived at the top, he was surprised to discover that the pedlar was not in sight; he waited a few moments, and then a thought struck, which induced him to recontinue his flight.

He was free.

Neither police nor Roving Rob were there to control his actions.

He could make use of his liberty to do as he liked.

It was likely that Rob might keep him wandering about for days and nights longer, or even prevent his meeting Dick at all, lest his influence should lead him out of their power.

He resolved to make the best of his way alone to the locality where he and Dick had first been led.

Once there, he thought it would be easy to find out the thieves' kitchen, where he did not doubt Dick yet was.

It never occurred to him to make use of a subterfuge, and, by pretending that Roving Rob wanted Dick, get him away from that place.

This, however, would not have been practicable.

There were certain methods of explaining their wishes to one another in vogue among the frequenters of the kitchen, and, as Charley was unacquainted with them, his mission would not have been successful.

But under the impression that he would conquer, he hurried out of the purlieus of Westminster.

Ere he had gone very far, another thought brought him to a standstill.

What if Rob were taken.

He had risked much to give Charley his liberty, and it was like cowardice on his part to leave him there: he might be looking about after him till he was seen by the police, if not already taken.

Charley was too plucky a boy to let a thought of baseness take hold of his mind.

"He's helped me out," he said; "and though I don't like his ways, I'll see where he is."

And he quickly retraced his steps.

When he got to the dark alley at the back of the house, it was still as the grave.

Not a sound came from any of the houses—not a light showed from any window.

Charley had some difficulty in discovering the house, and, when he had succeeded, there was nothing by which he could determine the fate of Rob.

Up above he could see the window—it was closed; all was dark within.

The fact of the window being closed gave him an uneasy feeling.

If Rob had escaped, he could not have shut the window after him.

"I hope he is not took," thought Charley. "I was cowardly not to wait till he'd come down."

He waited for some time in the street—now silently watching the house, then moodily walking up and down.

But there was no good to be obtained by this.

An idea struck him.

He could go round to the front of the house.

There might be policemen there, but he could ascertain that before he went far down.

The cellar belonging to Mrs. Grampus was closed; the front of the house was as dark as the back. With palpitating heart Charley raised the knocker, and gave a single thump.

A minute elapsed: then the door opened a little way, and the face of Mrs. Grampus appeared.

The portly dame uttered a sound that was between a shriek and a groan on seeing Charley.

She opened the door a little wider, and said—

"Well!"

The tone was not inviting; the "widder" was affected at the capture of Rob, and looking upon Charley as, in some manner, the cause of it, was not disposed to regard him favourably.

"I've come," Charley said, "to see if Rob be gone."

"Gone!" echoed Mrs. G., looking more flustered.

"Yes; he stayed behind."

"Stayed behind! of course he did; and what for I should like to know—to let you get off; and a pretty sort of grateful body you are."

"He told me—"

"Told you! he didn't tell you to run away while he was being took; and then, when I could see by his eye he wanted me to tell you something, you wasn't to be found. I've no patience with such ways: there, be off with you, it ain't worth while to be kept out of my bed for the likes of you."

She slammed the door in Charley's face.

Though the door was closed, he could hear her sobbing aside.

"Poor dear Mr. Pedlar, to be took like this; I declare he makes me think of Mr. G., he do—and such a funny man too."

Charley stood for a moment before the house. His feelings were hurt at the manner of the proprietress of the boot-store; he scarcely thought he deserved such reproof.

This thought came to that lady herself a moment after she had slammed the door.

"I'm sure," she thought, "I don't know how to find it in my heart to be hard agin him. He is a nice lad, that he is, and how cross I have spoken to him; well, it's all on account of Mr. Rob being took. Well, poor boy, it may be wasn't his fault after all;

and now, I recollect there was a look in Mr. Pedlar's eyes that *did* say, as plain as plain could be, look arter the lad if he comes back, and give him some decent things to put on. I'll open the door, I will, and see if he's in the street, so as I may call him back."

With this benevolent intention she opened the door.

Charley, with the most doleful of faces, was just turning away when Mrs. G. appeared; he expected another outburst, and was agreeably surprised at the mild tones which greeted him.

"Where are you going to? There, don't look like that; I've been cross, I know, but I didn't mean it. Come in, and you shall stay as long as you like, and I'll rig you out like a real nobleman's son."

"Will you?" said an uncouth voice, "don't trouble yourself, we'll find him a suit of clothes and board, and lodge him in the bargain."

These gruff-sounding tones caused Mrs. Grampus to utter an exclamation of dismay, which had not subsided before the cause, a lanky-looking great-coated peeler, "hove in sight."

He had been standing in an adjacent doorway, and now put out his hand to take Charley by the collar.

"Come along, my fine lad; we've had some trouble, but here you are."

Mrs. G. ran hastily down the steps, and, without a word, took the crusher by the collar, and gave him a sudden shake.

Then she spoke at the same time, putting her fist in his face.

"You shan't take him, you shan't; he's not the sort to be locked up in a station-house. Don't you attempt to take him, or it will be worse for you."

"None of that," returned the policeman; "take your claws out of the way, or it will be worse for you."

"Let him go."

"When I've got him to the station."

"You brute," cried Mrs. G., "to think of taking a child like that; let him go. I'll shake the life out of you, I will."

The portly vender of boots was so excited, that she actually wrested Charley from the policeman's grip.

"Run," she cried; be off quick. I'll hold him; he shan't have you. I'll serve him out, I will; be off quick."

Charley stayed a moment; the policeman was feeling for his rattle. Still, he would have remained in preference to getting Mrs. Grampus into trouble, but that energetic lady, yet holding the peeler with one hand, with the other gave him a push in the nape of the neck, and bundled him off.

Reminded by this gentle hint Charley put speed to his heels, and ran rapidly out of the street.

"You'll pay for this," exclaimed the excited "copper." "Let go—huff—I'll have him—huff—let—huff—go."

He made a spring backwards to free himself from her grasp.

It happened that, at that moment, Mrs. G. relinquished her hold. The peeler, hurled back by his own impetus, tripped on the uneven stones, on one of which his head came with a bump, that made the old houses of the alley look more hazy and toppling.

He sprang to his feet as Mrs. G. banged too the door, and bolted it.

Charley was already out of sight. Muttering imprecations and threats, the peeler sprang his rattle, and in a very brief space of time four more were with him in the chase after Charley.

An unsuccessful one it proved.

Charley, with wonderful good fortune, threaded the mazy windings of that part of Westminster, and got safely out into Victoria Street.

Casting a glance on the magnificent structure—the Victoria Hotel—Charley, with a thought of the fortunate ones who partook of its luxuries, continued his flight.

When he came into the more lighted spots he slackened his pace that he might avoid suspicion.

Presently he heard the noise of the policemen's rattles.

A cab was passing.

He ran behind it, and catching hold of the rail, let it conduct him whither it pleased.

This was an excellent device on his part. With so many coppers after him, each moment was dangerous that he was in the neighbourhood.

If seen running he was liable to be pounced upon by any officious peeler he passed.

Numbers of boys were in the habit of running behind cabs, and thus, while it averted suspicion, it enabled him to make great haste.

Once, when near Buckingham Palace, some ill-natured boys cried out to the cabman to "put the whip behind."

Cabby lashed out his whip, but as Charley preferred to be cut to relinquishing which might prove his safety, the cabby thought he had been gulled, and laid the whip across the back of the next boy who came running up with the accustomed cry.

The vehicle stopped at the foot of the new Westminster Bridge. Charley reached the pavement, and made his way to it.

There were few people on the bridge, and with its low parapets, spectral lights, and the moon shining on the dull waters, it had a strange influence on the mind of Charley.

He thought how easy it would be to fling himself over, and drown.

Lonely as he was in the world, and unfortunate as his life had hitherto been, he was more than tempted to cast himself over.

A policeman came up unobserved.

Charley stood stock still when he saw him.

"Come, my boy," said he, "it's getting time you were home."

"I'm going," Charley replied, moved by the unexpected words of the man whom he had expected was there to take him up.

He left the bridge, and found his way to the New Cut: thence over London Bridge, and so on to Whitechapel.

Here he wandered for more than two hours, but without finding any traces of the locality where the kitchen was situated.

Tired, weak, forlorn—hunted by policemen, who drove him away with oaths when he sought rest in the shelter of a doorstep, the poor, lonely, friendless boy—stifling his bitter feelings, and restraining the grief that nigh choked him—wandered again from the purlieus of thieves, entered again the bounds of the city—silent at its confines as when three hundred years back the drowsy watchman nodded at the corner of its streets, or muttered his sleepy cry of "hang out your lights."

Through the city, past the Old Bailey — grim solemn spot—where so many of his fellow creatures had been led out to die, through the broader viaducts and channels leading to the market, then beginning in the gas-lit dusk to prepare for its early morning business, past quaint St. Sepulchres, where he stayed a while to take a draught of ungrudged water from the drinking fountain in its wall—Charley wended his way, while sleepy cabmen dozed on their boxes or inside their cabs, and brawny butchers and market-men came blustering from the coffee-shops were they had been taking their early breakfast.

Unheeded, unnoticed, save when some frowsy jaded girl of the streets made to him her repulsed proposals, Charley, deep in a gloomy reverie, struggled on till at length, hardly knowing how, he found himself in the Strand.

This narrow avenue of the City and West End was, as usual, more lively than any place he had yet passed; gay women were promenading with swells who came rollicking from the Coal Hole, Cider Cellars, or the night-houses of either side.

Charley, sickened of the sight he saw, and attracted by the lamps, entered on Waterloo Bridge.

A few drops of rain were pelting on the pavement, the friendless boy looked up and saw the misty clouds gathered dense overhead.

At the turnstile he was stopped by the tollman for the due of one halfpenny.

The rain was coming faster.

When the tollman made his demand, Charley was brought to a stand; he thought the bridges in London, of which he had heard so much, were built for people to walk over when they pleased.

Tolls were things new to him.

And as he had not a halfpenny in his possession, he merely looked blankly in the man's face.

Perhaps the look of sorrow that was on his features touched the heart of the toll-keeper.

Perhaps he had boys of his own, and contrasted their condition with that of the delicate-featured tattered boy before him.

At all events he spoke kindly.

"Haven't you any money?"

"No, sir," was Charley's sorrowful answer.

"And where are you going?"

Charley looked sadly along the surface of the river which the rain was beating up in plashes.

"I don't know," he answered.

The toll-keeper saw that the rain was descending fast, and that the boy before him was ill clad and weakly.

"Do you want to go across?"

"I wish I could."

"Well, run along then; don't go through the stile; there, run across the road, and make haste over, for the rain's coming on pretty stiff."

Charley knew that, so he thanked the toll-keeper for his kindness, and crossed by the carriage-way.

The reason why the tollman wished him to go that way was because when a passenger passes through the stile it registers one; and if Charley had passed through the man would have had to pay his fare of one halfpenny.

So Charley crossed the broad road, which was already becoming sloppy from the falling rain.

He saw one or two human beings in rags and wretchedness crouched on the stone seats of the alcoves on the bridge; they did not seem to mind the rain, and Charley, with a thought that their lot was even worse than his, passed out at the other end.

No check is given in passing this bridge, and so he was unquestioned when he reached there.

A few people only were to be seen in the Waterloo Road; those were fast hurrying away, with the exception of the unfortunates who stood in doorways, or at the entrances of the still open coffee-shops.

Charley, wet now to the skin, continued his way unmolested by anyone, and scarcely troubled when the shiny-caped policeman turned his bull's-eye and suspicious look upon him.

The rain having thoroughly wetted everybody, and made the roads quagmires of mud, began to abate, and Charley, whose hands were blue with cold, and whose body, exhausted by weariness and hunger, asked himself what he should do or whither he should wander.

If he kept on that way, it seemed that he might drag his exhausted limbs on from day to day, and fall at last from sheer starvation, before any one noticed him.

This was not what he expected from the great and opulent city, but he was beginning to find out that it was true.

He stopped: hunger and fatigue both induced him to seek some hole or corner where he could hide his head, and gain the nourishment of sleep.

Where was he?

By one of the brick arches of the railway.

A dark miserable place, where the dampness steamed from the bricks, and the water converted the ground into miry clay.

In these dark arches there could surely be found some spot where he could crouch unseen.

He turned out of the road, and made his way through the sloshy quagmire.

A good deal of *debris* was heaped about: houses had been pulled down to make way for the railway, and towers of brick-bats, old wood, and rubbish reared on either side.

He walked over the ankle-spraining mess, and got to one of the arches that seemed screened from passers by.

It was almost dark here; he could feel that the ground was less sloshy too: the arch above gave more shelter from the rain.

It was for all that a most uninviting place.

But Charley sought it not for comfort.

He sought it because of his soul-weariness, and because he wished to slink, like a perial dog, to some out-of-the-way spot, where, if need be, he could lie down and die.

Shivering with cold and wretchedness, he crouched down to the ledge of the brick ward, and, folding his arms, gathered his drenched arms more tightly over his breast, and closed his weary eyes.

CHAPTER XXXVIII.

THE NEW FRIEND THAT CHARLEY FOUND, AND THE STRANGE HABITATION INTO WHICH HE INTRODUCED HIM.

THE rain fell fast again.

It pattered against the lighted windows of shops, within which trade, infamous, or tending thereto, prospered.

It beat sluggishly on the swollen river—that river dull and gurgling—looked upon by how many frenzied eyes as a cradle of rest.

It spattered in road puddles, and hurled against the panes of cab windows as the wheels rolled through the shining slosh, while within the vehicles sat muffled travellers, journeying to catch the early train, or bedaubed hollow-eyed women creatures, without heart or vitality, hurrying with rapid strides down the pitfall of appalling destruction, but yet plying their horrible trading of their bodies with rakish and diseased night ramblers.

Charley heard not the patter of the rain, nor wallowing glide of wheels: the hollow laughter of painted loathsomeness or despairing cry of suicidal wreck reached him not in his weary slumber.

He heard not the coarse oaths of New Cut bullies, nor the beating of the rain or moaning of the wind.

Not, at least, for such time as his unrefreshing slumber lasted.

He awoke drearily.

Cold, cramped, icy, he knew not where he was.

Something had touched him.

Something human beside himself in that desolate miry place.

Something rude and ungentle, not pitiful.

There were no angels near but fallen ones.

A light flashed in his eyes as he unclosed them.

A dazzling, dimming, sheeted light, that stole the power of vision from his aching orbs.

He shrugged his benumbed shoulders, and pressed his clasped hands tighter on his strained knees.

And his eyes would have closed again.

Something heavy touched him again on the shoulder.

A voice—surly, gruff, coarse—challenged him.

He looked up this time, to realise fully where he was.

A policeman stood before him.

He had found the boy there crouched up out of the rain, with his back to the miry walls—his feet in the clayey slough.

He had found him, and judged by his wretchedness, his tattered garments, his forlorn aspect, that he was one of the uncared for, unhelped, unregarded, outcasts.

His flaring lantern had played on his eyes, but this not awakening him, his heavy boot had been used.

"Come," Charley heard him say, "take yourself off out of this."

"Yes, yes," moaned Charley.

"Come, move off don't I tell you?"

Charley heard the rain: he shivered, and was silent.

A third time the policeman used his boot.

"Be off, will you, you d—d young rascal: what are you doing here at all, I should like to know?"

"I was resting," answered the boy, sadly.

"Resting be d—d, you young lurcher; none of your tricks. Where do you live?"

"I have no home."

"No parents, I s'pose, either?"

Charley's eyes filled with tears.

"None."

"I thought not; well, take yourself off, or you'll soon find your mistake out."

"Must I go?"

The boy asked pleadingly.

"Of course you must; haven't I ordered you off?"

"I have nowhere to go to; may I not rest here till morning?"

"No, get off at once."

"I am doing no harm in this desolate place, surely?"

"You won't stay here, whether or not; these are just the sort of places the likes of you gets to to play the rogue."

"I am honest," Charley said, proudly.

"I don't want to know what you are; be off. How am I to know what you are here for? anyone might be robbed as easy as anything."

"Surely," thought the boy, "none but the most wretched would come to such a place as this."

"Well, are you going to get up before I lock you up?"

Lock him up! it would be better than such a place. A cell, though close, was dry; he would, at least, know the comfort of a breakfast.

He staggered slowly to his feet.

"Take me there if you like," he said.

"Yes; that's the way with you d—d young nippers. You're always ready enough to get into prison, get off. It's all our work to look after you."

"I'm not fond of prison, but if sleeping in the street is a crime, and I have nowhere to go to, I might as well be there."

"You'll be there soon enough, no doubt, you young thief."

"I'm not a thief," Charley said.

"I tell you you are; hold your tongue, will you? Here, come out, I've wasted time enough on you; I'll take you off to the station, and see what they'll do with you there."

Very much exasperated the policeman took Charley by the collar. That moment two greedy-looking eyes were fixed upon him; they belonged to a youngster, whose head protruded from *inside* the actual brickwork, for leaning against which poor Charley was taken into custody.

The head was totally unobservable in the darkness, and was pulled in when the policeman dragged Charley out.

Roughly using him, he pulled him over the rubbish, and brought him to the Waterloo Road; here, a quiet-looking young girl, an unfortunate, was standing in the rain.

She saw the white face of Charley, and moved by pity, common enough in her much-abused class, accosted the policeman.

"What's up?"

"Oh, a d—d young skulk that I couldn't get out from the arches."

"What are you going to do with him?"

"Lock him up."

"Don't do that, he seems frightened at the thought."

"Frightened, no doubt; good cause I daresay."

"Oh, he doesn't look such a bad 'un; let him go; come on, we'll have that drop I promised you, we can get it over the way."

The mercenary policeman, to whom this bribe was one of many, exacted by fear—for he was a tyrant in his way—gave Charley a good shaking.

"Don't let me catch you there again," he said, and let him go.

"I wasn't doing any harm," cried Charley, nettled at the treatment.

"What?" shouted the policeman, feeling for his truncheon.

"There, go away," said the young girl, "don't mind him there's a good soul. Run away my boy: go home."

Home!

Where?

It was a home; the best he knew how to find that the policeman had dragged him from. He turned away sorrowfully, while the young girl went before the policeman to smuggle the two pen'orth his sordid mind was not above receiving from such as her.

Charley had not gone many steps when a light step sounded behind him and someone trod on his heel.

Looking round he saw a boy about his own height, but by his looks much older—both in years and experience.

There was a look of premature wiseness and sharpness about the boy's face; he gave a knowing wink with the left eye as Charley looked at him inquiringly, and making a pantomimic gesture over his shoulder with his thumb, placed his three fingers over his mouth, and emitted the faintest of whistles.

It was the same boy that had peeped out from inside the brickwork of the railway arch.

"I say," he said, lengthening his face to a most knowing expression, "what's the lay?"

"Lay," repeated Charley, vaguely.

"What's up? what did he shove you out for? doing a mouch?"

"I wasn't doing anything," Charley said.

"Didn't he know you then?"

"I never saw him before."

"Well, I'm blessed, I thought when he twigged you as you'd been and done something."

"I have not done anything but what is honest."

"My eye!" cried the boy, "but, I say, what made you come to the arches?"

"I had nowhere else to go."

"Nowhere else; crikey! ain't it jolly!"

"Jolly?"

"A regular flare-up; you haven't got no home I know, and you ain't up to the fake; but I've got a crib—a stunner—least it ain't p'raps the sort of cheese you've been used to, for I can twig them togs doesn't suit you nohow, but if you like, and will come, we can go smuggins."

"Come," asked Charley, "where?"

"To my crib, tain't far, you've been werry nigh it; but I'll put you up to a move or two, you want's getting your hand in; come along; I've been wanting a quiet bloke for a chum; them others is such nippers, and cracks a cove up in no time, we will be so jolly together; come on?"

The boy took Charley by the hand, and led him back again out of the Waterloo Road, and amongst the moist arches. He took, however, a direction that kept them clear of the slosh.

"My eyes," he cried suddenly; "won't it be stunning: and I've got such a blow out."

"But you are taking me under the arch again."

"All serene."

"But you—"

"Nobby Ned's my name."

"Where do you want me to go to?"

"I'll show you, only come along; we'll make ourselves jolly where no one won't twig us."

Charley listlessly followed his new conductor. There was something in the boy's face which warranted an opinion Charley had at first framed—that his course of living was not so honest as it might be; but, as there was also a kindliness of look, and he was his only friend, he had less compunction in accompanying him.

The boy, having given many a knowing glance behind, winked at Charley, and stopped by one of the inner arches. It was the one that he had been hunted from by the policeman.

"They won't let you stay here," Charley said; "the policeman made me come away."

"Yes; but he won't come where we're going."

"There's no place here."

"Ain't there? only just wait; here you are, follow the leader. Let's look out first that no crusher's coming."

He stooped down to the very ground, and, greatly to Charley's surprise, put his head out of sight, as it seemed, in the solid brickwork.

It was too dark to see how this process was effected, but he heard Nobby Ned say—

"Come on; stoop down. Poke your head in first."

The body and heels of Nobby disappeared: then his hand was put out.

Charley stooped down, and saw that there was a small hole in the brickwork—a very small hole it was—scarcely large enough to admit a good-sized tom-cat comfortably.

"I can never get in here," Charley exclaimed, after a glance at the narrow aperture.

"Oh, yes, you can; it's a slap-up crib when you get inside, and I've got a nice fire and some supper."

Fire and supper! forgotten luxuries. Charley had no doubt that Nobby Ned was indulging in a little romance.

He, however, suffered himself to be persuaded to enter, and, after a good deal of wriggling on his part, and some assistance from his young friend, he managed to get inside.

To his surprise, when once within, there was plenty of room. A hollow had been made, descending to the foundation of the brickwork, and forming a cavern large enough for several boys to bestow themselves.

Providing they could get in, there was every chance of their being comfortable.

The floor of earth and bricks had been jammed down, till it was hard and level. A heap of bricks was piled up near the middle, where was burning a fire of old plastered sticks, a supply of which were stowed away in one corner.

"Fine crib, ain't it?" said Nobby, looking round the place as proudly as if it had been a mansion he had erected. "I dug it all out myself, and got these things in. I doss here every night; ain't it jolly?"

"It is more comfortable than being outside."

"Eh! I should think it was and all; sit down there, that's the chair, you know: this is the table. I'll make it all serene, if you'll sit quiet."

The chair pointed out was a single brick near the heap.

Charley mechanically sat down, while his kind-hearted young friend scooped up from a hole in the ground a half-quartern loaf and a penny saveloy, both of which articles of diet he regarded with the air of a gourmand.

"Allers keeps 'em there," he said, as he put them on the table of bricks before Charley; "somebody might come in, you know, and they'd eat it all up. I don't get much sometimes, but I never minds sharing what I has, if coves won't try to steal all. I used to have a chum here, but he used to eat up my share when I was out—said the rats ate it, but I was too wide for that. They doesn't come here yet; besides, they never ate his'n—allers mine—so I made him hook it."

"You looks froze," he continued, as Charley shivered; "jolly hungry too."

Charley's eyes were fixed on the eatibles.

"Ah! I knows what that is; get closer to the fire: you'll soon dry, and we can have supper, and tell tales, so jolly. Why, what's that on your face; you ain't crying, is you?"

Charley was! The kindness of that boy affected him; he contrasted it with the conduct of the Christian Mr. Wilblow, and thought how much better of the two was that unlettered and, perhaps, dishonest boy—the good Samaritan to a friendless one like himself.

"Don't cry," said Nobby, fumbling in his pocket; "here, here's a hankercher."

The article which, after a good deal of rummaging, he pulled out of a very tattered pocket, was as little like a handkerchief as possible; it was a dirty bunch of rags. At one time, perhaps, it was a cotton kerchief; but colour and shape had long since gone.

"Take it," he said, "and wipe your eyes on it."

"Thank you," Charley replied; "I am not going to cry."

"Ain't you? that's jolly. Now then, let's have a go in."

Knives and forks were superfluities in that chamber. He pulled the loaf in two, and gave Charley half; the saveloy he broke also in half, but the part that he gave Charley was the biggest.

"Munch away; there's no one to pay."

Charley cheerfully partook of the food given him by his new friend; and it seemed to afford Nobby more satisfaction to see him eat than he even derived from himself devouring the long-hoarded viands.

He had given Charley more than half his store; it might be days before he got any more; yet he ungrudgingly gave, and that without the least hope of return, for he could see Charley was penniless.

It was then a noble act; yet that boy was one whom the minions of the law would have run down to jail—whom philanthropists would have voted to the penitentiary; in short, he was a thief.

He had just taken the first mouthful of his saveloy, when a face was poked in at the opening.

Nobby had his eye fixed on the intruder in an instant.

"Who is it?" Charley asked.

"It's only Tony Nip. I let's him come in because he ain't a bad sort, and don't mind what he does for a cove."

"You may come in, Tony," he cried, as the new-comer rolled the whites of his eyes towards Charley; "it's only my chum."

The face went down; a shock head of hair was seen for a moment; a bundle seemed to be poked in, and Tony Nip was before them.

This individual was very different to Nobby Ned; he had not that astute sharp look; on the contrary, his features were round, flat, and heavy, and he had a great good-humoured eye, which, in the present instance, had a vague terrified expression.

He was tall and thin; boy he could not be called: he seemed rather more as if boneless, so lithe was his frame. His face was dirty, his hair wild, his garments tattered, and caked in mud.

Making a grimace at Charley, he put his finger along the side of his nose, and sat down.

"What's up?" Tony asked Nobby Ned.

"I'm hungry, and can't get no one to give me a halfpenny."

"Ain't you had no supper?"

"Ain't had no tea."

"Nor dinner?"

"No, nor breakfast, nor nothing."

"There," said Nobby, giving him his half of saveloy, and breaking his bread in two; "you must be starved."

CHAPTER XXXIX.

DICK AND HIS COMPANY.

LEAVING Charley for the present in the good society into which he has fallen, we will return to Dick, who, honest, yet was emmeshed in a career that would take him, step by step, even against his actions, to the position of a ticket-of-leave man.

In accordance with the practice amongst criminals, which will not suffer one of their gang, unless under very peculiar circumstances, to stir abroad till the crime for which they may be arrested has blown over, Dick was kept day after day in the house where Roving Rob and the crusher had brought him.

He was not stinted in food nor in company: nearly every evening a choice assemblage of thieves and prostitutes was admitted below, and a concert was usually knocked up.

In Dick this was more than distasteful; he had no fancy for such company, and his confinement was irksome in the highest degree.

Roving Rob had been gone some days; the crusher went to and fro, looking each time more dissatisfied than ever, and scowling at Dick as if he were the cause of whatever unpleasantness he suffered.

It was growing hot for the crusher outside: a description of him had by some means or other got abroad, and his active co-operation in fresh burglaries was somewhat checked in consequence.

And he knew that, if taken for the slightest offence, the murder would be brought up against him.

One evening he came in, looking as sulky as usual, and, in a surly tone, ordered some liquor. Having seated himself at the table near Dick, he drank one or two glasses in silence, and then spoke.

"A pretty cursed mess we're in, through that d—d boy of yours," he growled. "It's as much as I can do to stir out without being nabbed."

"It's no fault of Charley's; he didn't take you there."

"No, but he was very near getting us lagged afore we left; d—m him; I'll give him what for, if ever I come across him."

"No you won't."

The crusher looked fiercely at Dick.

"Look here," he said; "I don't want any row with you; there's something else to be done. Are you ready to take your chance?"

"I be ready to get out of here, but to get with you in any more crimes is what I won't do.

"Don't be a cursed fool; there's a job on now. I'm going it on my own hook. Will you share?"

"I'll have nought to do with it."

"Oh! you've no occasion to be afraid; there won't be no lagging this time."

"I tell you I'll have nought to do with you. I know you're a murderer; there's blood on your hands, and you'll come to the gallows yet."

The crusher swore a fearful oath.

"You shall come," he cried, "or the gang shall crack you off."

Dick rose from his seat.

"Tell you what it is, I've been in your gang long enough; I'll go now. If I be took, I shall be; but I won't stay here any longer."

"Oh! you'll peach, will you?"

"No; there'll be a time when you'll have to answer, as I told you, on the gallows, for the murder of that policeman."

"And so will you," cried the crusher, springing up. "Damn, if it hadn't been for that bastard brat, I shouldn't have had to do it at all."

"You know it be different to that; you needn't have killed him. Ah! man; it ain't the first time blood has been on your hands."

The crusher grew white with passion.

"Tell me that again, and I'll dash your brains out."

"Like you did his; no man. I be going now; I don't be seen again in such company."

"You'll go, will you! so help me G—d you don't. Here Nipper, Ben, Dousy; look out—here's a peach."

Those few low characters that were in the room, drinking or planning in corners, started forward, and got before Dick.

Many a vindictive blood-thirsty look was fixed on the man who had been denounced by the crusher as an intended peach.

"He wants to sell us," the crusher said. "He'll have us all lagged; he says he will go."

"Will he, though," half a dozen voices echoed, while the thieves got closer to Dick.

"I'm not going to be stived up here with thieves and murderers," Dick said; "don't any of you attempt to stop me."

"I'll stop you," cried Crusher Jem, "if no one else don't. Do you think we'd let you out to lag us?"

"No, no! He shan't go! Stick the ———! Let him have it!"

Such were the exclamations that greeted Dick.

The commotion below brought from other parts of the building a number of flash women and low prigs, who all helped to block Dick's passage, the women even more threatening than the men.

"Does he know what's the hump for any cove as peaches?" asked a cunning-looking thief—a youth scarcely eighteen, but who had been in prison nearly as many times as he had lived months.

"Croak him!" squeaked a jaded-looking woman, one of the victims of disease, brought on by her terrible course of existence.

The tumult was at its height, when a quick light step was heard coming down the stairs; the door opened suddenly, and the girl we have before mentioned as Ratcliff Sal made her appearance.

She was pale with excitement, and, eagerly closing the door, looked round on the priggish crew.

Many a fearful glance was cast behind her by those who imagined the police were coming after her.

"What's up, Sal?" several voices asked in a breath.

"Up!" echoed the girl; "it's all up with Rob."

"With Rob?" was the general shout.

"While you've been stowed away here they've took him; he's lagged, and in quod for murder."

Crusher swore a deep oath.

"It's through that infernal brat," he said.

"It is," returned Sal; "he never need have gone if it hadn't been for him; and he might have got away, only he let him go first."

"The kiddy's gone, then?"

"Like a cur: walked it as soon as the copper showed."

This intelligence increased the ill-feeling against Dick. Roving Rob was a general favourite; and the report that Charley had left him in the lurch further influenced their minds against him.

"I thought that's what it would come to," the crusher said. "He's a cursed white feather; and this hulk ain't no better. The kid's gone off like a skunk, and now he wants to sell us."

"Humane and benevolent creatures—kind Christian friends—you see before you an unfortunate fellow being, driven by the force of circumstances to appear before you, and appeal humbly to your humanity and Christianity; six small babes, as you see, each of an height, and all equally hungry—their poor little insides never once filled since the whole seven of us ate the last mouldy crust, which a benevolent Christian gave us yesterday; unfortunate is our lot. Chums, it is a sacred fact, Roving Rob, our beloved and earnest compatriot—our zealous and cautiously and unremittingly-help-himself-to-other-people's-property pal—has, by a succession of circumstances over which he could exercise no kind of control whatsoever, been and gone and found himself the respected and much-taken-care-of inmate of one of Her Majesty's jails."

THE BURGLARY

Piously delivering his orations, with eyes upturned, face lengthened, hands crossed, the Downy Cove walked with slow steps into the kitchen.

"It's all through that d—d kid," cried Crusher Jem, "he'll lag us all yet, you'll see."

"It is unhappily his misfortune," said the Downy, "that the persuasions of a loving community are thrown away on his infernal obstinacy."

"You are a set of curs," said one of the women, "to stand still and let the kid get us all nabbed."

"There's his uncle," exclaimed Ratcliff Sal, "and he's no better, nor so good; you, I mean, you awkward, cowardly, country clodhopper."

Dick looked at her scornfully; excited, furious as she was, he could see, in spite of her dissipated aspect, that she had once been pretty and virtuous—and so had Mary been. His heart bled at the thought that she might become another such a wreck.

Ratcliff Sal, who mistook his calmness for a tame want of pluck, came up to him.

"I've a good mind to scratch your ill-looking mazzard, you hulk," she said, "it would do me good to do it."

"Give it him, Sal," yelled another woman; while the rest of the gang joined in the uproar, which now became terrible, everyone shouting out such imprecations as their bitiated mind goaded them to.

Amidst all this storm Dick stood perfectly unmoved.

Then the crusher uttered his usual oaths, and pushed up to where he was standing.

"You cuss!" he exclaimed, "we'll see that you don't get any of us nabbed."

Dick looked at him steadily and said—

"I can see what you all mean; but I don't care for you. Charley be free, and I be glad of it. I be

No. 13.

sorry that Rob is took for the murder, because he didn't do it; but he shan't swing for it. If it comes to that I'll go up and say who it was that did it."

"Do you hear the ———" the crusher shouted; "he'd see us all took as long as he got off."

"He don't go," said a precocious young thief.

"No, by God, he don't!" Ratcliff Sal cried, "if there was nobody else I'd stop him."

"So you could, Sal."

"Lynch him!"

"Give him a croaker!"

"Let him cop a dose!"

"Give him the laws of the gang!"

Such, uttered in slang and with frightful oaths, were a few of the exclamations against Dick..

"Send someone to look after the brat," yelled one.

"Perhaps you'd like us not to find him?" said Ratcliff Sal to Dick.

"I do hope he'll never fall into your hands," Dick answered, "poor lad; it is for misery that I brought him up to Lunnun; but he be better than the whole tribe of you; he kept with me, and didn't mind what he did if I wor safe."

"Poor lubberhead," said Sal, scornfully.

"He run away from Rob," one of the thieves exclaimed.

"I don't believe it."

"Give him a dig with this," cried one, holding a sharp knife.

"Yes, knife him! knife the ———!"

"You'd better mind," began Dick, but he was interrupted by cries of derision.

Dick could see that his danger was growing deadly: more than one pocket knife was being opened, and there were several formidable life-preservers suspiciously raised.

At that juncture a young girl made her way through the gang: she could not have been more than eighteen, and, notwithstanding the life she led, the traces of juvenility and the bloom of prettiness were not totally drunk under

Her cheeks were yet plump; her eyes full and bright, her lips rosy; she was tall and even graceful.

Judging from her neck—too wantonly exposed—and her limbs, she would have been a magnificent woman had she not fallen into the wearing destroying paths of vice.

Dick had seen her several times, and had been more than shocked; of all those boisterous dram-drinking, swearing women, she was the noisiest and the hardest drinker.

Glasses of gin or brandy she would toss off, one after the other, without the least effect being perceptible, she had horrified Dick when he first saw her drink, and heard her conversation.

She had never entered without speaking to him; and her manners were so engaging and ingeneous at first sight, that he had supposed her one but slightly turned from the paths of virtue.

Indeed, she would have deceived even a *roué*, with her bright eyes and girlish looks.

She was showily but tastefully attired, and as she came forward, looked like a princess amongst the fallen. It was evident that amongst that lawless set some respect was felt for her from the manner in which they made way for her.

Truth to say the male thieves were all more or less smitten with her charms, while the women were in mortal fear of her, for she was a greater termagant amongst them, child as she seemed, than Ratcliff Sal, whose nails had been down more than one of the faces there congregated.

"You're all of you set against Dick," she said, "I should like to know what for; is'nt he as good as any of you?"

"Hullo! What does Tiger Loo want?"

"She wants to see right done," said the young girl, turning fiercely on the one who spoke, a low-looking thief, who shrunk away.

"Very well, Loo," Ratcliff Sal said, "you shall have right done."

"By God, I will."

"By God, you shall."

"But it shan't be by hurting him."

"Oh, oh! Loo's got her fancy man at last."

"No, she has'nt; he's too good for me or you, or any of us; and it's a shame for him to be here."

"Well, he don't go."

"He will though."

The two women looked cat-like at each other. At first sight, appearances were in favour of Ratcliff Sal, in the event of any set-to between them occurring; not so tall as Tiger Loo, sunk in frame, her limbs were spare, but firm; her fingers were long and thin; Tiger Loo, on the contrary, had a soft plump hand, yet white as the driven snow.

Those who knew Loo's temper were aware that if a battle took place—a not unlikely thing—Ratcliff Sal would have to look out that she did not get the worst of it.

After they had looked at each other for a few seconds, Dick spoke—

"Don't interfere for me, lass; I don't mind if there be a hundred here."

"I'm not interfering for you," returned Tiger Loo, sharply, "I interfere, because I don't think right is being done, and I like fair play, always."

"Look here, my nabs," exclaimed the crusher, "if we let this white-livered bloke out, we shall all be copped."

"We don't mean to let him out," cried Ratcliff Sal.

"You won't prevent him," shouted Tiger Loo, with an expression that made Dick shudder.

Ratcliff Sal laughed, derisively.

"Hark at her, what a fuss she makes about her fancy man; Loo never could get one to her likings before, so you musn't interfere now she's got him."

Whether it was the sentence, or the manner in which it was uttered, that excited Loo's passion, certain it is that her temper was up in an instant. She swore a dreadful oath, and struck Ratcliff Sal in the face.

"Take that, you ———," she cried.

The smack was a vigorous one; it sounded over the room, and made Sal's eyes flash again.

Not a moment had passed, however, before she had returned the compliment by dealing Tiger Loo a stinger on the cheek.

While every one was anticipating a terrible battle between the pair, and there was every sign that it would soon take place, the Downy Cove, always in favour of pacific measures, came between the two.

"Let us have no quarrelling among pals," he said, parting them gently.

Loo stepped up to Dick.

"If you don't want to stay, now's your time: go. and, if you want your boy nephew, keep him clear of thieves' dens for the future."

"He don't go," shrieked Ratcliff Sal; "Crusher, will you let him?"

"No!" swore the crusher; "he'll cop the laws first. Now, Loo, get out of the way, you ain't missus here, if you are in Tiger Loo."

"You're not my master."

"We'll see if I ain't."

"Fingers off! I'm not afraid of you."

By this time the confusion was at its height: oaths, cries, and imprecations mingled; women shrieked, and the thieves uttered the most horrible slang.

The two female champions had each their partisans; but the greater portion sided with Ratcliff Sal and the crusher, of whose spiteful and savage temper they had before had wholesome samples.

In the midst of such an uproar, the voice of the Downy Cove, attempting to still the tumult, was totally drowned. Knowing that Dick was Rob's *protegé*, he did not want to see him knocked about.

The crusher had taken hold of Tiger Loo's arm. With expressions the most fearful, the young fallen girl was daring him to act, when he with a furious oath dragged her aside with such force that she almost fell.

Rushing forward, she took the crusher by the necktie with one hand, and tore the other down his face.

Stung by the pain, and feeling the blood start down his cheek, Crusher Jem raised his powerful fist, and dealt the young fury a vicious blow on the forehead.

She fell to the floor, and, after making a momentary struggle to rise, fell back again.

Dick's blood boiled with passion, while the crusher was preparing to give her a second blow if she should rise; he dashed his clenched fist in his face, giving to the blow the whole strength of his frame.

The crusher, staggered by the unexpected visitation, had not time to return before Dick made a second investment on the same place; this time actually flooring his big-framed antagonist.

The crusher and Tiger Loo rose together: the young girl exhibited a large blue bump on her forehead; the crusher had a black mark under his right peeper, and the blood was oozing down his cheek.

Before he was well on his feet, the excited girl, rendered almost insensible by his blow, again attacked him.

A perfect Babel of tumult would have been little to the confusion that now reigned; the animosity of those who were in favour of Ratcliff Sal was of course directed against him: women pressed forward to scratch and strike him, while the evil faces of young prigs bespoke their evident intentions of mawling him.

Dick's whole attention was, however, bestowed upon the crusher, who, having again whirled Tiger Loo out of the way, rushed upon Dick.

The young countryman put himself in an attitude of defence, and, as his opponent came in, struck him a third "good'un" under the jaw. Boxing, however, was not the crusher's intention, he had felt how hard Dick could hit; and whilst all his teeth were made to rattle by the last blow, he had taken out his huge clasp knife, and with that determined to be revenged on his enemy.

Catching Dick round the neck so as to hold his head in chancery, he got him across his knee and opened the knife with his teeth.

In this position, Dick had his feet and arms at liberty, and he did not forget to use them, for he saw the murderous look of the crusher's eye, and knew there was little help for him there if once he succumbed.

So he beat the crusher about the shins with his heels, and struck at his mouth with his hands.

The powerful bully did not stop to ward off Dick's attack, but deliberately opened the clasp knife.

"Now, you ——," he cried, with his usual oath, "I'll give you a settler."

By the exercise of his whole power, he brought Dick over his leg in such a position that he had him bent backwards, his chest alone advanced.

His first intention had been to slit him across the throat, but now he was bent upon sticking the knife again and again in his chest.

Long before this Tiger Loo would have interfered, but Ratcliff Sal had got hold of her to keep her back: the crusher had Dick at his mercy, and when he raised the huge knife, every one in that kitchen waited to hear the gash, and see Dick's blood spurting out amongst them.

Before the fatal stroke was dealt, the Downy Cove seized the crusher's wrist with both his hands.

"Now then," cried the bully.

"Don't, Jem; stash it; don't let him cop."

"Why, what's he to you?"

"Rob won't like him to be made a lamb of."

"Rob be d——d; let go, I tell you."

To the powerful-formed crusher the strength of the Downy Cove would have been of little import in preventing him carrying out his purpose; by a little exercise of sinew he could have freed his arm, but there was another not so easily dealt with, though of slighter strength.

Tiger Loo wrested herself from the clutch of Ratcliff Sal.

Not at first did she spring at the crusher; she looked swiftly round, and snatched from a prig's hand a small bludgeon, which he had been holding ready for use.

As the crusher wrested his hand from the Downy Cove, she struck his fingers with the bludgeon, and dashed the knife from his hand.

Ratcliff Sal and a number of her pals rushed to pick up the knife; they found themselves confronted by the lithe form and flashing eyes of Tiger Loo.

The knife was in the hand of the latter in an instant.

"Now, let's see who'll interfere," she cried, whirling the bludgeon round; "I'm a woman, but curse me if I'm not able for you all."

She turned round on Crusher Jem; foiled in his aim, and aware that, in her fury, the young girl would not mind driving the knife between his shoulders, he let Dick stand on his feet, and, still keeping him hugged round the throat, faced his new assailant.

But the first use Dick made of this partial liberty, was to hit his opponent a forcible blow in the side; while the crusher was getting his breath, he ducked his head out of chancery, and repeated the dose.

Then he found himself beside Tiger Loo.

The face of the girl was brightly flushed; her form was erect; her eyes gleamed vividly. Before any of the gang that menacingly surrounded them could find pluck to begin the attack they meditated, she had put the bludgeon in Dick's hand.

"Go through them," she cried; "hit right and left. If you can't fight your way out, you're not worth being helped."

"I won't go to leave you," said Dick, who feared the result of her interference.

"Don't be afraid; they dare not touch Tiger Loo; let them try it on, if they like. Off; run a muck; they'll get out of your way."

"Come with me; I should be a coward to leave you."

"If you don't go I'll stick the knife in you," exclaimed the furious girl.

By this time the crusher had brought to with his terrible sling-iron, swinging which, he advanced to Dick. There was quite a circle round the three; a circle which was widened when the heavy instrument was seen.

The crusher was not particular whose head he hit, when he was in one of his savage moods.

The foregoing scene had not been enacted without some of the loose women giving utterance to screams of horror, and finally threatening for fits of hysterics. There would, no doubt, have been active interference on Dick's behalf by many, who, though so far debased as to prostitute themselves for money, or join in deeds of thefts, were not so hardened as to behold murder with indifference.

But these were overawed, and kept in check by the rest. The screeching, oaths, and cries were such that, had not Dick been firm of nerve, he would have been bewildered by the many shouts, and the terrible uproar.

He turned like a hero to meet the attack of Crusher Jem, while Tiger Loo with her knife dared any to come on.

No one cared to encounter the "Tigress of the East," as she had been christened by the sailors; and the conflict was looked for between the crusher and Dick.

The former made straight towards him, whirling the swivel sling round, he made a cut at Dick's head, that would have battered his brains out, had it reached him.

He would not withal have been able to save himself, but Tiger Loo pushed forward one of the low-looking thieves, a foremost one in inciting the rest to the death of Dick.

Unable to check himself, the crusher, when the young prig came in his way, brought down the sling-iron on the top of his head.

The thief dropped instantly to the floor, his head beaten in as if it had been an egg-shell!

A terrible instrument was that wielded by the crusher.

This catastrophe saved Dick's life; at the moment of the blow falling, he had, in self-preservation, struck out with the bludgeon, and succeeded in reaching the crusher at the same moment that the prig fell.

Crusher Jem had a thick skull, but the bludgeon was hard and solid; he guarded off the first force of the knock, but it struck him with sufficient momemtum to send him back as if he had been kicked by a horse.

Dick heard the shrill shrieks and curses round him, saw himself encompassed by a legion of murderous men and raving women; knives, sticks, and implements of menace flitted before him, he heard the voice of Ratcliff Sal crying out that he had killed the crusher, the voice of Tiger Loo bidding him run a muck; then something heavy struck him in the face; something warm dashed down it, and trickled in his mouth, a delirous madness seized him; he glanced towards the door and dashed amongst his baying assailants, striking right and left, amid the group of faces.

Ratcliff Sal screeching till it seemed that she would burst a blood-vessel; Tiger Loo shouting in triumph and shrill laughter; groaning men's curses, opposing foes' imprecations—these all sounded discordantly behind him when he reached the door.

A face was here that seemed familiar to him; but in his fury, all who stood before him were opposing obstacles; he whirled round his bludgeon, and the Downy Cove who had sneaked to the door to open it for him, dropped to his knees in time to escape a blow that would have put him like so many whose skulls Dick's bludgeon had in his brief flight made acquaintance with.

There was a low flight of stairs, narrow and dark, Dick bolted up them.

A man stood at the top, evidently on guard, while the turmoil below went on.

He cowered down as he found himself grasped by that angry madman.

Dick had him by the throat; by one grip he squeezed almost the life out of him, and then sent him headlong down the stairs.

Above was a rough trap, it was secured at the top; a thrust of his shoulders moved it, though it almost dislocated his neck; the next moment he was through it, and found himself in a passage, having a window at the end.

This was fastened; Dick dashed the sash open and leapt to the street.

The window was only a few feet from the pavement; Dick bounding past the house, dashed by two or three men standing at the door of the house.

They made a dart after him to stay his flight. A swing of the bludgeon brought the foremost to the ground, and the others stopped behind to pick him up.

Straight on, like a frightened horse, Dick fled; at the end of two or three streets he swept round the corner, and fell against a guardian of the night.

The peeler had seen his coming; had seen the weapons he held; and had stepped back so as to pounce upon him at the rightful moment.

This he did so skilfully that Dick was immediately collared.

The peeler on seeing the bleeding face of Dick, his bludgeon coated with blood, his eyes strained to madness, freed one hand to spring his rattle for help to secure the supposed murderer.

CHAPTER XL.

THE PUNISHMENT OF TIGER LOO.

No one had dared to follow Dick: his course had already been too marked with havoc; five besides the crusher lay bleeding and battered, and one of them was a woman.

In rear of all, Tiger Loo, with the knife flashing in her hand, looked an impersonation of a Gorgon, one of those furies whose hair was snakes, whose hands grasped whips of scorpions.

She expected an attack, and was ready to defend herself. Ratcliff Sal was kneeling by the crusher, whom she had herself raised from the ground; while the Downy Cove set in the corner where he had fallen when Dick aimed at his head, and whence he now looked dolefully on the scene around him.

"Has he gone?" screamed Ratcliff Sal; "have you let him go, all of you?"

No one cared to take upon himself the onus of reply.

"Cowards!" she continued, "skunks, you're not worth a curse, to see Jem get knocked about and not interfere."

Considering the many battered heads that had resulted from the interference of the members of the thieves' kitchen, this was rather strong.

The Downy Cove got up and came to Tiger Loo.

"You'd better mizzle," he whispered significantly.

"Not if I know it," was the girl's reply. "I'm not afraid."

"No; but——"

"If they come, I'm ready; I've got this for the first."

She raised the knife meaningly, and the Downy Cove raised his eyes pathetically to heaven, for he could see by the looks of the lot that Tiger Loo was threatened.

The crusher was now raised to his feet, and supported so that he could gaze around.

His murderous glance sought out the face of Tiger Loo.

"It's all through her," he muttered.

"Yes! and she shall pay for it;" Ratcliff Sal said.

A closely-cropped thief here stepped forward.

"Pals!" he said, "tain't usual for our set to get into trouble through one of their lot; but when they does, you know the rules."

"They mean it now," muttered the Downy Cove.

"Tiger Loo!" continued the others, "has helped the peach to get away, and got a good deal of damage done. Is she to go scot free?"

"No, no!" was the universal cry.

"What ought she be done to?"

"Try her."

"Yes! that's what we'll do; form a circle, pals."

Amid much tumult a circle was formed; the Downy Cove kept near to Loo, who stood undauntedly, fingering her dagger.

"Gentlemen!" exclaimed the Downy; "for what Loo's done, she's werry sorry."

"No, I'm not!"

"Yes, you are, I tell you. She's werry sorry, pals; and so let us be merciful, as good Christians ought to be."

"Try her!" shouted twenty voices.

"Oh! I'm ready;" cried Loo.

The thief who had before spoken was now by acclamations elected as president of the tribunal thus hastily formed for the judgment of one of their gang. The preliminaries were very brief. These ended, the first point to be got over was to bring the criminal before the bar.

This was a matter requiring some exertion, as the look of Tiger Loo showed that she did not intend to cry *peccavi* just yet.

A little youth, however, a precocious pickpocket,

with a waist like a woman's, and hands purely white, crept behind Loo, and when the Downy Cove's attention was directed elsewhere for the moment, slid his arms round her.

This was the signal of a general attack. Those who had been before afraid to come near fell upon her. She was dispossessed of the crusher's knife, and brought to the centre of the circle.

Her attempts now were powerless; the intercessions of the Downy Cove were fruitless—the passions of those criminal beings were roused—and amidst a terrible uproar, the sentence of the gang was pronounced against her.

That sentence was a horrible one; one that had before been carried out on refractory members.

There was a deep well-like hole under the flags of that kitchen; it was just wide enough to admit two people bound closely together.

When they were lowered there, they were in their tomb.

A worse than tomb, for they would be living.

Only for a time.

In darkness and in suffocation they would perish; while above them was the carnival of life.

When Loo heard her sentence, she ejaculated the most terrible curses on all, and fought like a panther to get away.

But they bound her arms, and, to stifle her cries, slipped a gag over her mouth.

The sentence was not that she should be put there to die.

There was still a chance of life.

She was to be kept there till Dick either gave himself up, or was taken.

When that occurred she would be taken out.

If still surviving, she would be liberated.

If so great a period had elapsed that she was suffocated, she would be let down again.

A flag was raised in the middle of the kitchen, almost at the very spot were Loo stood. A rope was brought, and fastened round her body.

Two of the gang meanwhile holding back the Downy Cove, who was getting rather nervous on Loo's account.

A frightful stench came up from the gloomy aperture.

It was the odour of decomposing human bodies.

There were many mouldering relics at the bottom; relics ghastly, and which Loo would soon be if left in that dismal region.

Still she was as defiant as ever; her face was flushed, and when they took the gag from her mouth, as they were lowering her down, she screamed out the most demoniac curses.

Her feet went out of sight; then her body; lastly, her excited face.

The stone was closed over her.

CHAPTER XLI.

HOW THE CRUSHER WENT OUT ON BUSINESS—SEVERAL DAYS PASSED AWAY.

It was strange that after that fearful scene, the Downy Cove should have remained a friend of the crusher's.

But so it was.

Several enterprises they had in hand were arranged for stated nights.

As yet Dick had not shown himself.

No one had interfered regarding Loo.

There was, occasionally, a sleepy look in the Downy's eyes when the crusher mentioned her with one of his accustomed brutal oaths.

He seemed to know something.

Something he kept to himself.

Crusher Jem was a great admirer of the Downy Cove.

His tact in matters of danger was so valuable; his cleverness in scenting out a "lay" so great.

The Downy had discovered that there was a house in Grosvenor Square where a quantity of plate and valuables were kept.

The people were out of town, and servants had charge of it.

It is not often that this quarter is selected by burglars, on account of the vigilance of the police, who, being specially fed by the masters of these mansions, were pretty often about there; other and less profitable "beats" being left to themselves.

The house in question had long been "spotted" by the gang, from the reported wealth of the owner; but, as yet, none of them had ventured to attempt an entry.

It was not until the Downy Cove, by his superior intelligence, made himself master of the favourable chance of a break in, that one was resolved upon.

The servants, who were left in charge, were three.

The cook, the housemaid, and the footman.

Each of these three had their failings.

The footman loved company; when he could he had friends there, whom he regailed with his master's wine and cigars; when he could not have friends there, he went out secretly.

The cook's affections had been bestowed upon a ripe specimen of a butcher's boy—a lad about nineteen years old.

Her chief happiness was in walking out with him, or inviting him there to sit with her.

The housemaid, following in the steps of the other, had been captivated by the shiney hat and white buttons of a policeman.

Often had she, with bounding heart, watched his elegant figure as he stood near the corner lamp-post, his back picturesquely turned towards her, his eye fixed on some passing butcher's tray.

Of all these facts the Downy Cove had made himself informed.

More than this, he discovered that the cook and housemaid, having come to an understanding, had resolved upon giving a supper to their respective beaux, a certain night being chosen when Jeames would be out of the way, a fact of which they had assured themselves by surreptitiously opening and reading a letter which the young lady—who yielded her charms to him—sent, stating when they might meet.

This night was fixed upon by the crusher and his mate.

A stratagem was to admit them.

The Downy Cove was to waylay the bobby as he sneaked to the house, and assume his garb; thus disguised he was to enter and subsequently admit the crusher.

When the night chosen arrived, the crusher's head was so far healed that he was able to sally forth with his pal.

The Downy took up his post, and watched the trusty Jeames leave the house to seek his amorous sweetheart.

He had been left in charge of his master's property, but this made no difference.

There was Betty, the cook, and Sarah, the housemaid, each capable of screaming if attacked.

So he strutted forth, looking as important as a new Lord Mayor.

The policeman, who had charge of the beat that night, was attracted elsewhere by the charms of a light-of-love damsel whose father kept a public-house not many yards from the square.

Every night when he was on his beat she was in the habit of meeting him, bringing a small pitcher of rum inside her muff, and listening to his love-speeches when he had half-emptied it.

The bobby who was invited to the house in Grosvenor Square watched his brother officer away, and then stole up to the spot.

When about three doors off, and indulging in

pleasing anticipations of the coming supper, &c., he was astonished to find himself gripped round the throat.

He thought of the garotters, and tried to get his staff, but the hug was put on too well; his sweet visions of his supper and the rest banished, and he became insensible.

Then the crusher, who had done the deed, lifted him in his arms, and carried him across to the railings, inside which he, with the assistance of the Downy Cove, dropped him.

The Downy Cove was soon attired in the victim's suit; a pair of whiskers were put on to match, and, leaving the crusher behind to gag the bobby, he stepped briskly up to the door of the appointed house.

Sarah was on the tiptoe of expectation.

Long ago the blubber-faced butcher-boy had put in an appearance, and was at the present moment sitting by cookey's side, their greasy faces pressed together, and love-making of the most desperate kind going forward.

When the Downy Cove, as per arrangement, tapped at the gate, she came quickly to the door below.

Then the Downy stepped gently down.

At the door, Sarah, who was redolent of perfume so lavishly bestowed about her that the Downy Cove was almost suffocated, put her arms round his neck, and let his whiskers frisk lightly about her face.

The Downy Cove who had before noticed that she was far from being a plain girl, took advantage of the opportunity to visit her lips with a regular "smacker," one that she seemed to like, for she squeezed him prettily, and let him do it again.

It was at the moment of drawing back from that warm embrace that she discovered some trifling difference between the caressed individual and the bobby on whom her affections were placed.

So she took a hard look at the Downy Cove, and discovering her mistake, gave a start, and would have screamed if the Downy had not clapped his hand on her lips, and whispered a warning hush.

"Oh, lor!" cried the frightened housemaid, "it ain't Joe."

"No, my dove, it isn't; but it's one just as good."

"Monster! Where's Joe? my Joe."

"Hush!" said the Downy, softly making his way in, and closing the door. "I'm his friend!"

"You bad fellow, I don't want any friend; I want Joe."

"Why, you delicious creature! I do wonder what you could see in Joe; more especially as the scoundrel has gone off with Maggy over the way."

"What!" almost screamed Sarah.

"Yes, he's been and deceived, like a villain, that he is, he always does; oh, young woman, never put your trust in his words or his whiskers, they are both of them equally false."

"The wretch."

"Yes, he is all that; but my kiddlewinks, just listen."

"What, go away! What made you come?"

"Why," my duckey diamond! When I heard him say that he was going out with Maggy, an idle slut; I said to him, 'What a villain you must be to her, you've promised to see Sarah;' 'cos you see he told me what a nice young woman you was, and how he could come when he liked, and when he didn't he could stay away; it was all the same he said, 'you loved him so.'"

"Did he? I'll learn him to know different."

"That's just what I thought; and so when he said you'll be looking out for him, and couldn't find him, 'acos why, he's gone off with Maggy; why, says I, blessed if I don't go and tell that young woman, which he has so grossly misled, what a villain he is."

"He's a brute," Sarah cried, hysterically.

"Never mind, my dear; I've come, and I'll stay with you."

"I won't have you; you're all deceivers, you men; policemen, especially," sobbed the betrayed innocent.

"Ah, don't be cruel; we are not all like Joe; which all in the force says he's a scoundrel, and breaks the heart of every girl what puts trust in him."

"He won't break mine, I'll let him know."

"That's right; I like to hear you say so. There don't be vexed; one kiss—and—"

The fair one struggled, but the Downy Cove gained his way; at first Sarah was fractious and refused to listen to what he had to say, but ultimately she softened down, and allowed herself to be persuaded.

Whether it was that his manner was too winning and fascinating to be resisted, or that she did not like to look foolish before the cook, by the defections of her expected lover (as the Downy Cove artfully took care to explain to her), cannot here be explained; certain it is that in a short time her tears were dried, and after a final soothing caress from her new beau, she led him into the kitchen, to introduce him to the pair already there.

It was very easy to deceive them, as the cook had only seen him once or twice, when it was too dark to make out his features, while the butcher-boy had only heard of the fame of Sarah's lover, and had never seen him at all.

When, therefore, the Downy Cove made his politest bow, and Sarah, with filling voice, introduced him as "Joe," the cook arose, and made her best curtsey, while the red-faced butcher-boy bobbed up, and stammering out some inaudible words, bobbed down again.

Sarah, with the officiousness of love, placed a chair for her beau; and without further ceremony, flopped herself into his lap.

This he thought rather strong; but as he was not aware how far the exuberance of love had led her and the rightful Joe, he bore it meekly.

Sarah took his hat which he was yet fingering, and Betty at that moment offered to put it on the dresser; Sarah, however, could not permit such sacrilege as that, and having carefully hung it up, returned to her seat on the Downy Cove's lap, and began caressing his whiskers.

This was all very well, especially when it led her to put her rosy lips against his; but he was in momentary fear lest she should pull off his whiskers —a catastrophe awful to contemplate.

"Ah! you dear man," said Sarah, "I'm sure I shouldn't love you half so much if you had not got such beautiful whiskers."

The butcher-boy, whose face was as destitute of hair as a bladder of lard, got very purple, and looked uncomfortable; but the cook hastened to heal the wound by flopping her great red arms round his neck and kissing him.

"I wonder when this slobbering is to be over," thought the Downy, whose knees were getting stiff.

Half-an-hour longer he had to walk in the voluptiousness of love, when Sarah relieved him of her weight, and rose to help Betty prepare the supper.

A howl from the cook, who had gone into the larder, gave the butcher-boy and the Downy equal pangs of alarm.

They feared that the good things of the larder had vanished.

"What's the matter?" asked Sarah.

"Shameful! I declare if that brute of a Jeames hasn't been and gone and drank nearly all the beer I had fetched in for supper."

"Scandalous," echoed Sarah.

After mutual expressions of disgust, it was decided that Sarah had better go and fetch some more.

Sarah accordingly went, after lavishing another

slobbering kiss on the Downy's face, and informing him that she would not be long.

When she returned, she manifested great symptoms of alarm.

"Oh! Betty," she said, "there's a great rough man walking about when I came from the public-house looking at our house."

"At *our* house?"

"Yes, and such a *h*evil-looking man, he looked like as if he wouldn't mind murdering any one in their beds."

"The crusher," thought the Downy Cove.

"I'm so glad you're here," Sarah said, addressing him; "you can protect us, if it should be a burglar."

"With my life," said the Downy, nobly. "Don't be frightened; I won't go from you all night."

Cookey blushed, and Sarah looked interestingly modest.

The supper was placed on the table—a boiled leg of mutton with capers (policeman's savoury dish), a pair of boiled fowls, some steaming sausages.

The Downy Cove looked the hypocrite when cookey, with bared arms, commenced to carve.

Neither of the lovers were neglected by their respective partners. The Downy Cove (who seemed to have taken a policeman's appetite with a policeman's disguise) made a truculent attack on the mutton; the butcher-boy consumed prodigious-sized sausages; whilst the fair entertainers supped alternately of love and chicken.

Supper ended, at length, and whiskey and water having been indulged in to a great amount, the Downy Cove, having lured the butcher-boy to drink till he was almost helplessly inebriated, a faint proposal was made by Sarah that the lovers should depart.

This was, of course, stoutly resisted by the Downy Cove.

"What! leave you; and a burglar looking at the house; no—my duty is to stay *here*. I must be secreted where robbers would never think of finding me, that I may pounce on the villains when they come into your room."

His speech, the meaning of which was well understood, was echoed in a stupid sort of way by the fat butcher-boy, and shortly after, with sadness best composed, the frail maidens suffered their lovers to accompany them from the kitchen.

CHAPTER XLII.

THE WORK OF PLUNDER.

TIME, under varying circumstances, passes strangely quick or slow with different individuals.

To the crusher it seemed an intolerable time before the appearance of his confederate.

He paced about the streets, or leaned against the railings, after the last public had closed, and swore repeatedly at the Downy Cove for not making a move in the right direction.

"He's cramming his cursed maw," he muttered, "or else fooling with them gals."

To the Downy Cove it did not seem by any means a long time: the supper passed off pleasantly, and afterwards, when he had assured Sarah of his readiness to befriend her by becoming a sharer of her couch, no time actually seemed to have passed.

But as the Downy Cove, though gifted with a leaning towards the softer sex, was not forgetful of his duty, he tore himself from the charms of his entertainer, and, leaving her placidly sleeping, slipped down the stairs, and admitted the crusher.

"A jolly nice time you've been, curse you," he muttered out loudly.

"All right; slip in."

"Is it all serene?"

"As right as ninepence."

The crusher glided in, and the door was softly fastened.

"You look cold," muttered the Downy Cove.

"Cold be ——; cursed. If you'd been sticking there, you'd be cold. What have you been doing all this time?"

This question the Downy customer did not think fit to answer, but meekly said—

"Couldn't do it before, Jem."

"Well, it's square now, I suppose?"

"Come on; I'll show you."

The crusher was eager for the plunder: no sooner did his pal show him to the rooms than he commenced with adroit expedition. The Downy Cove was not idle; and a considerable quantity of booty, comprising various classes of valuables, was packed up.

"Take this," exclaimed the crusher, pointing to a chandelier of solid silver.

"Too big, ain't it?"

"It ain't too big to sell, is it?"

"No."

"Collar, then."

The Downy "collared."

"Hush!" he said, as he was in the act of breaking up the branches.

"What's up," growled the crusher.

"Somebody's a-letting hisself in."

The crusher swore sullenly.

"It's the footman," remarked the Downy, after listening.

"If he comes here," said the crusher, "I'll give him pepper."

The crusher had scarcely spoken, when the door of the room where they were at work was opened, and Sarah, the housemaid, entered.

She was in her night-dress, and, on seeing the pair at their occupation, uttered a shriek, and let the candle fall from her hand.

"Stifle your blab," muttered the crusher, squeezing her mouth with his hands.

"Murder! thieves!" screeched the girl, in a horrified whisper.

Crusher Jem put the girl's arms behind her, and holding them with one hand, closed the other on her throat.

White with terror, the poor girl implored mercy; but the crusher would have wrung her neck with a little compunction as he would have wrung a kitten's if the Downy Cove had not interfered.

"It's all right, Jem; let her alone."

"What!"

"She won't say anything."

"Not if you let me go," said the terrified domestic. "Oh! Mr. Policeman, do save me: he'll kill me, he will."

"Kill you! I'll squeeze the life out of you, if you speak."

Sarah slipped down on her knees.

The crusher paused.

The Downy Cove listened.

Footsteps were heard on the stairs.

"Look out," muttered the crusher, "if we're lagged, it's all up."

The door opened, and the face of Jeames appeared.

He was very much inebriated, but had an inquisitive look, that speedily vanished when he saw the crusher and the policeman with the housemaid in her night-dress.

His head, that had been poked inside, was quickly withdrawn. He had caught sight of the plundered booty, and was about to retreat to summon aid, when the fist of the crusher reached him.

He was as quiet as a lamb when that worthy brought him in.

"What shall we do with 'em?" whispered the Downy Cove.

"Tie 'em up; stick 'em in bed together, so that they can't howl."

This advice was at once acted upon. The pair were at once gagged, and, half dead with terror, were carried into the bedroom; the crusher taking Jeames—the Downy Cove bearing in his arms the light-clothed servant.

"Don't be frightened," he whispered to her; "you'll only have to stay quietly in bed along with Jeames."

Whether this gave her no pleasure, or she was too terrified at the idea of her master's house being robbed, she seemed but little pleased at the suggestion, and was very near fainting when the crusher tied her and Jeames together, and, by the Downy Cove's help, fastened them in bed.

They then left them to the pleasures of their position.

While all this was taking place, Betty and her butcher-boy were snugly passing the night together, and lay unsuspiciously asleep when the desperate burglars, having rummaged the house, evaporated with the booty.

Leaving the domestics to be found as they were by the master of the house, then on his way to the square, and leaving the Downy Cove and Crusher Jem to make the best of their way to the kitchen with their booty, we will resume the history of Mary, whom we last saw the victim of the unscrupulous Hal Warner.

CHAPTER XLIII.

WARNER DISCLOSES HIMSELF.

Mary slept not that fatal night that saw her a prey to the wiles of her betrayer; before morning came she begged him with tears in her eyes to leave her awhile to herself.

Despoiled of the brightest ornament of her life, the young village girl alternately despising and blaming herself, shed many tears.

Not all the specious arguments of Warner could reconcile her to what had occurred, or persuade her to look calmly upon the future.

Her self-esteem was gone for ever.

After the first outburst she became strangely calm.

She had thought of Dick — of the honourable manner in which had wooed her, never offending her by a look or word indelicate, and she had been with him in positions of temptation that would have proved him had he intended aught that was against the teaching of virtue.

But Dick's respect had been too great for her honour.

What then was Warner's? who at the first opportunity had taken advantage of her position to seduce her.

The voice of reason told her that he was a villain; but love, still all powerful, pleaded in his favour, and when he returned, and with many affectations of solicitude kissed her and cheeringly consoled her, she blamed herself for doubting him.

They reached London that day: then came the first damp to her trust.

Another excuse kept him from his promise.

After many persuasions and entreaties he induced her again to let him stay with her.

The next day was one of tears and pleadings on her part, promises and vows on his.

But night came, and still she was dishonoured; this farce of pretence could not long continue, he would not throw off the mask, for as yet he liked her too well, but her entreaties to be made a wife were hard to meet.

A week passed; they lived in elegant apartments. She had but to express a wish, and it was gratified.

Servants waited upon her; presents unlimited were given her.

She did not know that for all these he was running deep into debt.

One day, when she was more than usually earnest in her reproaches, Warner went away promising to return with the license.

He did not come back that night, nor the next.

For three days he stayed away, Mary all the time in the greatest fear on his account.

On the fourth evening he returned to be clasped in the arms of the girl who loved him too well.

As the villain had expected, the separation had made him more dear to her; she lavished her caresses upon him, and that night nothing was said about marriage.

She was only to happy to have him with her. In this manner he continued playing with her fears or affections for him, until a month had passed, and he began to grow tired of the deceived young creature, whose only request was that she might be made a wife.

At the end of this time, having recovered his hardihood, he had the audacity to cooly propose to her that they should live together as man and wife; and when Mary refused to consent to a fruitless union unsanctioned by heaven, he told her that it was impossible she could ever be united to him.

Aware then of her shame, poor Mary bewailing her weakness and his sins, bitterly reproached him for deceiving her, and became so agitated that the base libertine, fearing serious consequences, was obliged to retract his words, and swear, at any hazard, they should be united.

This, in some measure, pacified the weeping girl. But Warner did not intend any such reparation.

On the contrary, his only study now was, how he might rid himself of his victim, whose reproaches were becoming unpleasant.

Though yielding to him, the nature of Mary was in the highest degree virtuous, but notwithstanding this fact, the vitiated mind of Warner suggested that as she had yielded to him, so she might be induced to give way to others, if exposed to the power of temptations, in which case he would no longer want an excuse for turning her away.

Leaving her with many hypocritical expressions of affection, Warner quitted the house, promising to return again before evening.

On the way as he went along, his brain was full of base schemes for the destruction of the girl he had, in the first instance, ruined.

While in this frame of mind he encountered the very man, of all others, who was most likely to serve him in his designs, Major Harkall, late of Her Majesty's cavalry, from which he had been cashiered for felonious conduct.

Major Harkall was a handsome and distinguished-looking man; he had the air of a west-end swell, and from top to toe was the very pink of elegance.

He appeared to dress in the most fashionable style, his moustache was curled to the most dandyfied turn, his hands well-gloved, his feet in the glossiest of patent boots.

Over head in ears in debt, he yet pursued a career of dissipation and extravagance, caring little whom he brought to ruin, so that he pursued his headlong career.

In addition to the qualifications here alluded to, he was a most confirmed *roué*, a gambler, a duellist (when occasion would permit), and a turf-hunter.

As our readers may recognise the portrait, we may as well mention him as the military-looking individual who had perpetrated the murder in St. James's Park.

It will be seen, then, that he was not the one to stand for trifles.

Warner did not know of the extent of his peccadilloes; he knew him to be a rake and a gambler, but did not think he would have stained his hands in blood.

And so when he encountered him at the very time when he was looking out for some such a man, he experienced a secret satisfaction.

MAJOR HARKALL ATTEMPTING THE SEDUCTION OF MARY.

"Ah!" said the major, gaily; "how do? By Jove, thought we had lost you for ever."

"No; I have been much occupied, as you are aware."

"With Hebe or Adriadne, may be; a sweet little bird that you keep so snugly hidden. Really, I think I must trespass on your friendship for an introduction to the bower of love."

"You shall have it; and that freely."

"Ha! what's in the wind; freely, eh? By Jove! those who know my reputation with the fair sex are not so ready to give me the *carte blanche* with their amorousas."

"Aha! Juanie as ever, I see; but I have no fear. I think I have found at last one to whom the gallantries even of yourself would be aimless."

"Oh, oh! found at last; the peerless pearl—the chaste Diana. Upon my word, I must crave admittance; and Warner, old boy, look well that I do not put your paragon to the test."

"You may do so with safety, major."

"Enough!" returned the major, who at a glance read the meaning of the libertine. "I read; charms grow flat—entreaties weary. Warner, my boy, you want to be clear of this exquisite beauty."

Despite his baseness, Warner had not the hardihood to look the speaker in the face.

"I see it is so. Well; I'm not in the habit of doing dirty work for my friends, but as I have seen the *belle*, and am somewhat tempted by her charms, I will enter the lists. Within a week, I warrant you she shall be in my lodgings."

"I will leave you to her virtue," Warner replied; "if she resists you——"

"You will be deucedly troubled who next to try. Pshaw! man; never fear. I have a way which

No. 14.

will make her yielding if she were of snow. Well, good bye! Stay! the introduction—when shall it be?"

"To-night, if you are agreeable."

"Perfectly; at your service and the lady's."

The elegant major raised his hat to a passing carriage, a smile was on his face; the occupants of that equipage would never have dreamed that he was then planning such villany.

After a little more conversation on the same subject, it was arranged that the major should be introduced as an intimate friend; that after the introduction Warner should stay away a great deal, the major to take advantage of his absence by visiting Mary.

They parted; each satisfied.

The next evening Warner introduced the major; dangerously fascinating, that individual took care to treat the unsophisticated girl to the most delicate attentions; his bearing was courteous in the extreme, and at parting he pressed her hand in the most gentlemanly manner.

In no degree could Mary find fault with his manner or observations.

Warner carried out his part of the diabolical plan; though it galled him at times to see the insinuating major getting gradually, by the more studied ease and polite friendship, into the good graces of Mary; and though he felt many a jealous pang at the thought of her yielding herself to the accomplished gallant, yet the certainty that she would cling to him, with her entreaties for marriage caused him to persist in his design; and as he was much absent, the major had ample time to prosecute his part.

A keen observer it did not escape him that Mary's affections were firmly given to Warner; nor could he hide from himself that, although she treated him with the most unsuspicious friendship, she was neither attracted by his personal appearance, nor led by his artful and fascinating manner.

But with the major to know this was not to despair; and as the absence of Warner became more frequent and prolonged, and he took occasion to present himself often at her apartments on the plea of having appointments with Warner, he thought he could not fail in making sure of her.

At such times as these he, while taking care to praise the character of Warner, yet continued to let fall observations most likely to unsettle a woman's mind, and to appear most vexed at his absence.

"Really," he said, one night, when he had waited till rather a late hour, "I am almost angry with the derelict; in truth, if it were not that his absence affords me the enviable pleasure of a *tête-à-tête* with your charming self, I should be inclined to upbraid him severely."

To this Mary made no reply, and the gay libertine was fain to turn the conversation to another channel.

Twelve o'clock came.

The major daintily pulled out his watch.

"Midnight," he said; "upon my word this is too bad; and to leave you the task of entertaining so great a bore as myself; really he must have confidence in his pretty bird."

"He has confidence in me as I have in him."

"Still it is dangerous; we are but frail; and—well, well, really ill-natured people *might* say that we were not innocently together."

"Why should they say anything else, sir?" asked Mary, quietly.

"Because, dear lady," said the gallant rake, taking her hand, "they know the temptations a mortal must suffer in such presence. Ah! dear madam, who could hold that hand and not feel a flutter at his heart? Who gaze upon the veiled charms of one so fair and not feel a stirring devil in his blood, making him almost ready to lose his friend's esteem to gain his mistress."

"If such were your sentiments," returned Mary, with dignity, "I should deem myself debased by your mere company."

The major saw that he had said enough, and with the pretense that he feared he had unintentionally offended her, took his departure.

He knew that Warner would not be there for another hour, and believed that Mary would find the house more lonely waiting by herself than in his company.

He was mistaken; she preferred rather to sit still and listen for Warner's coming than to hear the glib tones of his insinuating friend.

"You must give me a clear field to-night," said the major next day to Warner; "that inamorate of yours is as unimpassioned as marble."

"It shall be all to yourself," the base villain replied; "did I not tell you it would task your Juanic powers?"

"It shall not, by Jove! I'll bet you fifty guineas to-morrow night shall witness my conquest."

"I will take your bet; but, remember, no violence."

The major smiled, and they went their different ways.

"If Major Harkall comes this evening," Warner observed to Mary, "entertain him till I return; it is a matter of importance that I wish to see him upon; and you will do us both a service if you will treat him with a little attention."

"I will do so Hal; but could you not appoint some other place of meeting?"

"Why? you are not afraid of the handsome major."

"Not afraid; but I am mistrustful; he is so different to you, dear Hal; amidst all his gallantry and politeness there is something dangerously deceitful."

"Do not think so; he is a steadfast friend, and may do me a service—besides, this is his own appointment."

And with these words on his lips Warner went forth, promising to be there almost as soon as the major.

The major came at about ten o'clock. He was exquisitely dressed, and had his blandest smile on his lips when he was shown into the room with Mary.

His greeting was frank, his manner genial, yet Mary could not but feel her suspicions confirmed as she met his glance.

There was something in his bold leering eye that made her mistrust him.

The major seated himself, and daintily pulled off his pinkish gloves.

He conversed in an easy manner about the opera, the park, the parliament, changing his theme with a versatility peculiar to him.

Lastly he approached tenderer subjects.

Touching even on the softer topic of love.

From this he passed on to Warner.

Assuming the frankest manner with, at the same time, the most tender pain, he disclosed to Mary what he conceived to be the cause of Warner's absences—his alliance with another.

Mary heard him, pale as death, but started back in horror when he threw himself at her feet, and, with a volubility and eloquence worthy of something nobler than the seduction of an inexperienced woman, confessed himself her admirer, besought her forgiveness for his presumption, and ended by offering to be her protector.

"I will lead you," he said, "far from such ignoble destiny: flowers shall spring around you; birds warble over your couch; elegancies shall be at your command; and amid all, I, your earnest admirer, will be your slave."

Mary drew away the hand that he held, and struggled to her feet.

"If he is base, and I could almost deem him so to have such a friend, I at least will not be worthless; I have sinned enough in listening to his fatal suit; but to be this that you would make me—a cast-off from one—the second-hand mistress of another! Go, sir! I have at least the feelings of a woman, if my position has degraded me from their virtues."

Major Harkall still persisted in his suit.

"I swear to you," he cried, "that the man you love has basely deceived you; he has brought you here as his mistress, and intends to cast you off."

Mary's lips grew colourless as she listened.

"He has deceived me," she exclaimed, "in saying you were his friend. Leave me, sir; I will summon help."

"No, my beautiful, I will not leave you; I am the slave of powerful passions; and if you are cruel, I must bear the consequences of my temerity."

He grasped her in his arms.

"Sir," cried the tearful girl, "if you are a gentleman—a man, release me. I am not what you take me for, though I have done wrong."

"You are an angel, and I can but love you," exclaimed the major, pressing his lips to hers.

"Release me, sir! Help! oh, help!—Warner!—mercy!—help!"

"I am too mad to heed you. I must have your love, if I die afterwards."

The libertine gambler held her in his powerful arms; though she struggled with him she was fast becoming faint, and her screams were almost stifled.

She gave herself up for lost, when the door opened, and the housekeeper came in.

Major Harkall instantly let Mary stand on her feet.

"A violent fit of hysterics," he said, addressing the housekeeper, "delirium, too, brought on, I fear, by the absence of her husband."

"Her husband!" exclaimed the housekeeper, sneeringly, for Warner was excessively in her debt, "he's no more her husband than you are."

"Ah, poor thing! how she did cling to me and upbraid him; now I understand it all; see! she flutters now; give her every care; I will go and seek this scoundrel."

He slipped a sovereign into the housekeeper's hand when he had laid the fainting girl on a couch, and left the house full of bitter chagrin at the non-success of his purpose.

Before he reached his apartments he met Warner.

All villain as he was, the latter was glad to see the major there.

It showed that he had not yet consummated their diabolical plannings.

"Ha, major! you here?—She has—"

"Curse her! and you for a fool!"

"You are excited."

"Excited be d——d! Why do you have a lot of meddling people about the place."

"Ah! you tried violence."

"I tried to succeed."

"That was against our terms, and you have lost fifty guineas."

"Lost. Well is it not enough to do your dirty work without paying for it?"

"Pardon me, a fair bet."

"Well, claim it," cried the major, fiercely.

"You are heated," returned Warner, moderating his tone; let us adjourn to a bottle, but you need not have minded the housekeeper if no one else was there."

"Pshaw! do you think I would have all the world know how I spend my time; you must remove her if you want this managed."

"I will remove her," Warner said when he had drank largely of wine, "I know a snug rural box where she can be got to; I'm tired of the piping thing, I will manage to smuggle you into her chamber, where you can be found together."

"Do that," exclaimed the major, "and you shall hear no more complaints of her chastity."

When Warner reached home, he found poor Mary in a state of tremor and agitation.

Pretending to hear the story for the first time, he was loud in his denunciations of the major's perfidy.

"I will look him out," he exclaimed, "and demand compensation for this outrage."

But the thought of his exposing himself to the mercy of such a man terrified Mary, and believing the miscreant to be innocent, she besought him to abstain from getting into danger on her account.

Only she besought him not to let the major have entry there.

"I will make doubly sure," said the villain, "we will leave these apartments; in a more sequestered retreat we can dwell happily and undisturbed together."

Next day he took her to the place where he knew he came to leave her to be the victim of the heartless major.

CHAPTER XLIV.

CHARLEY CATCHES A FEVER.

Tony Nip was a great glutton; just before he had entered the hole in the arch he had swallowed the last crumb of a roll, the penny for which he had begged by his tears and tale of hunger from a benevolent-hearted cabby.

He now gormandised the half loaf and saveloy which Nobby Ned had given him, and the latter would have gone entirely without if Charley, on seeing what he had done, had not insisted upon sharing what remained of his.

That sumptuous supper ended, and Charley's clothes being nearly dry—he himself was shivering though sitting by the fire—Tony Nip and Nobby Ned began to converse upon the subject of their respective callings.

Tony Nip's life was a vulgar and dangerous one. He was one of those boys who turn summersaults by the sides of omnibuses, receiving from the "outsides" halfpence, and from the policemen kicks, as his reward.

On Sunday he was to be seen with about fifty others at the River Thames, diving in the mud for coppers thrown by the spectators.

His was a dirty occupation; but he was rather proud of it, and offered to initiate Charley into the secret.

But Charley did not seem as if that or any other living trade would find a votary in him. He was cold, sick, and weary; and when he lay down with the other boys he thought that he would never open his eyes again.

But he did, to frighten his companions by his wild looks and heated face.

Both the boys tried to rouse him, but he could not heed them—he was in a raging fever!

This was a calamity to all three. Tony Nip was abashed, Nobby Ned was aghast. What were they to do with him?"

"We're in for it," Tony said.

"Why?—what!"

"He's been and cotched the fever!"

"Oh crikey!" said Nobby Ned.

In a little while Charley, who had been lying still with the fever sweats thick on his face, began to rave in such a manner that the two boys were almost too terrified to speak.

"It's all up," Tony said.

"What's up? Get away—Charley!—hi!—come old fellar."

Charley's only reply was a subdued raving.

"We'd better get a doctor," said Nobby Ned.

"Yes; but how? They won't come w't money."

"And then they couldn't get in here."

"No more they couldn't!"

The boys looked puzzled.

"I know," cried Tony.

"What?"

"I'll go out and do a tumbling for some coppers."

"Yes."

"And then we can get him some brandy; p'raps he'll be all right then."

"Brandy ain't good for fevers, is it?"

"Yes."

"How d'ye know?"

"It's what my gaffer used to send out for when he had had the fever and used to bellow out like him."

"Who do you call bellowing out?" exclaimed Nobby Ned, "I'll hit you if you say that agin."

Tony Nip threw himself into an attitude of the most prostrate meekness, and finally wedged himself out of the hole, not a little glad to escape from the presence of Charley, whose ravings terrified him excessively.

As soon as he had crept out he began to cry, for, glutton and lubber as he was, he had taken a fancy to Charley, who was so different to the rest of the boys.

He could not bear to see him ill, and so his face was very sorrowful when he got to the bridge, and began following the "bus" by rolling head over heels by the wheels.

The streets were very muddy, and Tony's garments were of a most ragged description. His appearance, then, with his long lubberly figure and uncombed hair (almost hiding his face), was not very taking.

He managed, however, to get a good many coppers thrown to him from people riding on the top of the "bus."

But when his occupation was getting lucrative a policeman spied him, and, to put a stop to his capers, slipped quietly after him.

Tony was just turning from one of his gyrations, and as the policeman put out his hand to catch him by the collar, he received the muddy soles of Tony's feet clean in the face.

A shout of laughter from the passers by increased the chagrin of the peeler, and poor Tony only became conscious of what crime he had committed by finding himself in the awful clutches of a crusher.

"So you young vagabone, I've got you."

"I ain't a vagabone."

"Come on with me; I'll soon let you see what you are."

He dragged Tony away.

"Oh, if you please," began Tony.

"Well?—what?"

"Please don't take me."

"I daresay."

"Oh please don't."

"What for?"

"Please I was only doing it to get a few coppers."

"Get something better to do."

"I will, sir; please let me go."

"Where do you want to be off to?—buy your mother some gin?"

"Oh no, sir, I—I"—

Tony stopped, for he thought it would not do to reveal the hiding place under the arch, and Charley's position could not be mentioned without.

"I see," said the crusher; "want to gammon me?"

"No, I don't; I've got my poor granny waiting for her breakfast, and there's Aunt Jemima and my five brothers and seven sisters, they won't none on 'em have any breakfast if you takes me."

"Let the boy go," cried a passer-by.

"Yes, you villain, let him go."

The peeler found himself exposed to the remarks of a number of indignant people, and, after a great deal of fluster, he let Tony go, having first extorted from him a promise that he would sin no more by turning up his heels after the omnibus.

As Tony was wending his way towards the public to get Charley's brandy, he saw a carriage and two horses coming down from the bridge.

This was too much for him to resist, especially as he had only taken fivepence as yet; so he once more went wallowing in the mud, and floundered over head and heels towards it.

The occupants of the carriage threw him sixpence to get rid of him.

Elated at his good fortune, Tony made a walk towards the coin.

But at that instant he heard the dreaded voice of the policeman, crying,

"At your tricks again, you young rascal; wait till I get hold of you."

This, of course, was what Tony did not wish to happen; so he made a scramble, and clutching the sixpence just in time to escape being collared by the peeler, went rolling over before the carriage to get to the other side out of the way of the bobby.

Poor Tony, he miscalculated his distance; the horses were too close upon him, and, as he made his summersault, the hoofs of one struck him, and hurled him over.

There was a cry from the occupants of the carriage; the policeman stepped back; the passers-by raised a dreadful outcry.

Tony made a most desperate attempt to get away even after the kick, but he was too late; the horses seemed literally to double him up, the carriage passed over his body, and when the people rushed to his rescue, they found him a crushed and bleeding heap, the fatal sixpence yet clutched in his hand.

Of course there was a great commotion; a crowd collected, and the occupants of the carriage and the officious peeler were alternately abused; but, as Tony continued insensible, and was considered by many to be dead, he was carried off at once to the hospital.

Thus Charley was deprived of one of his new found friends, and we will now see what occurred to deprive him of the other.

Nobby Ned waited till his patience was more than exhausted, still Tony Nip put in no appearance.

The reader knows why, but Nobby Ned did not; and he began to accuse Tony of all sorts of things.

Meanwhile, Charley got rapidly worse.

Nobby Ned thought of numbers of plans, each of which was however discarded as futile.

Once he thought of getting Charley out of the hole, and carrying him to the nearest doctor's.

But then he thought it would be likely enough that they would walk him off to the workhouse.

"And that's," mused Nobby Ned, "where I've been myself, and shouldn't like him to go to. No, I'll let him doss here; Tony will be back soon, and I'll get him something jolly."

But Tony did not come back, and Charley's condition was the reverse of jolly.

So, after a long while, Nobby Ned made up a fire with the last sticks, and placing the straw for Charley to lie upon, moved him out of the reach of the fire, and crept out to look for Tony.

"I'll be back in a minute," were his parting words; words unheard by the delirious patient.

Nobby Ned was not long out before he heard what had befallen Tony, and how unjust were his reproaches. This was quite a calamity to Nobby Ned, as he was eager to go and see poor Tony in his misfortune, and yet could not stay away from Charley.

Besides, it now devolved upon him to forego the brandy and nice things for the poor destitute invalid.

Nobby Ned walked sorrowfully along, looking in at the shop windows, and wishing some one would let him take what he liked for Charley.

Not bred to the strictest respect for the rights of property, he might not have resisted the temptation to help himself to what he thought best, but for the fear that he might be taken.

"And then," he mused, "who'd look after Charley?"

It happened just then that his glance rested upon

the end of a silk handkerchief hanging out of the pocket of a quiet looking gentleman, who was walking leisurely along, and whom Nobby Ned at once recognised as Mr. Corrie, the well-known magistrate of Bow Street Police Court.

Why he recognised him was because he had once before walked off with his handkerchief, without being discovered.

It was this remembrance, and the consciousness that he could at once get money on the article, which caused him to creep up to the worthy magistrate, and, by getting close to him as he passed two or three people, to slily jerk the "wipe" out of his pocket.

In an instant it was out of sight.

Mr. Corrie felt the jerk, slight as it was, and, by the force of instinct, clapped his hand to his pocket, and found out his loss.

Upon which he quietly looked round.

He saw one or two people near him, but the one that most particularly attracted his attention was a quiet-faced innocent-looking boy, who, at a very steady pace, was slouching off.

Now there was nothing remarkable about this boy, except his very quiet look, and the sleek manner in which he was stealing away; and at any other time the magistrate would have thought what a heavenly boy he was near, and how innocent, in spite of his humble garb.

But he happened to remember that the last time he lost his handkerchief that same quiet-looking boy was behind him, wearing the same angelic look and irreproachable aspect.

So he fixed his magisterial eye upon him, and, the moment the young urchin was gliding away at an intended run, seized him by the ear, and brought him back.

Nobby Ned looked the picture of a youthful saint, when the magistrate thus checked his start; but his face fell when Mr. Corrie beckoned to a policeman— the same one that had caused the catastrophe to Tony Nip—and gave him in charge.

"I ain't done nothing," said Nobby, with the greatest simplicity and *sang froid*.

"You've stolen my handkerchief."

"Handkercher; why I never uses such a thing."

"What's this?" cried the policeman, producing the identical handkerchief from the inside of the back of Nobby's jacket.

"Oh lor! it's all up. What will become of poor Charley?"

Such were the thoughts that flushed to Nobby's mind, as the policeman led him to the station.

The oddity of the case created, as might have been expected, considerable amusement.

Mr. Corrie, of course, could not try a case in which he himself was prosecutor; but, no other magistrate being in attendance, it was absolutely necessary that the prisoner should be charged before Mr. Corrie, as he could not be detained in custody over that day and Sunday without being placed at the bar. He was accordingly brought up and charged, in order to be remanded to a day when another magistrate would sit.

Police constable, P 406, deposed—"I was on duty near Bow Street this morning, when the prisoner was given in custody by you, sir, on the charge of picking your worship's pocket. (A laugh.) And I have to apply for a remand, to secure the attendance of the prosecutor." (Laughter, at once suppressed by the ushers.)

Mr. Corrie (who could not himself refrain from a smile)—"And I presume you have reason to believe that, if I remand the prisoner, you will be able to obtain further evidence." (A laugh.)

The officer—" Yes, sir."

Shore, of the F division, said he should be able to show that the prisoner had been repeatedly in custody.

Nobby was remanded; and, as he was only bidden to hold his tongue when he attempted to mention about Charley, that unfortunate boy was left in his lonely abiding place, with no one to tend him, while the fever that was raging in his veins was gathering poison from the damp around him.

CHAPTER XLV.

THE PURPOSE FOR WHICH THEY TRIED TO GET MARY.

THE policeman who pounced upon Dick, after his escape from the house where Tiger Loo was thrust under ground, thought he had made a discovery when he first saw him.

He thought he had made a capture, when he sprang his rattle to summon his brother constables to help him.

Other constables came, but Dick was not in the mood to be held; he found himself firmly secured for a little while, but when they were off their guard he suddenly commenced the most violent struggles, and so took them by surprise that he hurled them right and left almost in an instant.

He then sped swiftly up the street: they after him raising a great hue and cry.

Avoiding one or two policemen, and knocking over a butcher who tried to fling him down, Dick, after traversing several streets, found himself in an alley that had no outlet at the bottom.

Literally run to earth, he was almost in the clutches of his pursuers, when he saw a long ladder standing against the corner house.

He was up this with alacrity.

The policemen and the mob, raising a wild halloo, reached the bottom of the ladder as Dick reached the top.

One of the peelers had already set his foot upon it, when Dick leaped to the tiles.

He made this movement in time to prevent them dragging the ladder from under him.

He stood on the top of the roof a moment, looking round for a way of escape.

Then he seized the ladder, and, bending forward, flung it to the ground.

Its fall created a general dispersion, as nobody wished to get a broken head or neck; and when the confusion had subsided, Dick had vanished.

The baffled policemen got quickly to the roof, but after a patient quest were obliged to give him up as lost.

Nobby Ned had hardly been removed from the dock, when there was placed at it a woman who has had mention already in this work, and whose atrocious deeds, enacted amid the vigilance of our police, exceeded the infamies of Mother Brownrigg.

The name of this precious lady was Mother Rawlings; she has been presented to the reader incidentally, but she will now, in her enormities, occupy a prominent part in a few chapters.

She was brought up before Mr. Corrie on a charge of inveigling into her house, for an unlawful purpose, an elderly female, whom she afterwards violently assaulted.

The dwellers in the metropolis will not need to be told that there are haunts where infamous women live, termed procuresses, whose sole calling is that of getting young girls into their establishments: first to be sold as maidens to some sensual nobleman, and afterwards to be sent out to a life of prostitution.

Many hundreds of virtuous young girls are thus entrapped, and, after being violently used, are forced to acquiesce in that life of infamy.

Let a titled vagabond set his eyes on a young girl, whom his lustful dispositions hanker for as prey, and he has only to give the name and address to the procuress, who will find sure means of getting the young girl into her power and his.

Many are the devices resorted to; sometimes force

is used; sometimes the unsuspecting victims are deceived by offers of high situations in France, and leave their friends only to find themselves barbarously outraged and ruined.

In this case it was not the virtue of a young and innocent girl that had been trafficked in.

The complainant was an elderly female, well qualified, as it seemed, to take care of herself.

But what she revealed in open court evinced a large amount of silly credulity on her part, and something much worse on the part of Mother Rawlings.

The injured spinster, Miss Harriet Skimmer, created a profound sensation when she entered the witness box.

She was extremely far from youthful or prepossessing; her features were wrinkled up, her complexion was sallow, and her eyes were of the class called goggles.

But what was wanting in personal charms she made up in decorations: her hair was dressed in smooth ringlets, and though the weather was rather cold, she wore a muslin dress with flounces, a high white bonnet with flowers and feather: she had on light boots, and a shawl, like Joseph's coat, of many colours, and, like the virtue of Potiphar's wife, very flimsey in substance.

After an indignantly virtuous glance at the frowsy face of Mother Rawlings (who wore satin and jewels), she commenced in a very high key to relate what befel her.

She saw, she said, in a local journal, an advertisement headed "Home (comfortable)." The advertisement went on to say that "a lady" gave a furnished bed and sitting-room, with attendance and every comfort, for a very low price. In consequence of that she called on Mother Rawlings, and after an interview with her engaged to lodge with her. On the day appointed she went to the house with her luggage, and then it was that she found out that it was a house of ill-fame, for she had not been there long before improper words were made use of to her, and she was told that she could not sleep in the room she had engaged except with a companion. She locked herself in in the first-floor front, and then Mother Rawlings broke the room door open, assaulted her, and said that that room was required for a gentleman.

There was a slight titter in the court at the horror she evinced at the idea of sleeping in a room with a gentleman: whereupon the virtuous Miss Skimmer swept her indignant glance round the court, and, declaring she would not stop to be made a laughing-stock of, was about to sail out of the court when the usher led her back to her place.

The following strange proceedings then were revealed.

Miss Skimmer, in a whining tone, begged that the public might be sent out of court, as what she had to say was too dreadful to speak before them.

"I cannot do that," replied the magistrate; "let us hear, first, its nature."

"Why," murmured Miss Harriet Skimmer, "not only was it a wicked house, but that abominable woman made a most infamous proposal and attempt upon me."

"Describe it," said the magistrate.

"I can't, sir; indeed it's too shocking."

"We can't go on unless you do—"

"Well then, sir, she actually—oh! dear!—asked me to allow myself to be flogged, sir."

"Flogged?" ejaculated the magistrate in surprise.

"Flogged, Sir," reiterated the modest spinster hysterically.

"For what purpose?"

"Abominable, sir."

"What, she wanted to flog you."

"Worse than that."

"What then?"

"I can't tell, indeed I can't," Miss Skimmer ejaculated; presenting every appearance of going off in a faint.

"Come, come, who was to do it, Mrs. Rawlings?"

"Oh no, sir."

"Who, then?"

"A gentleman, sir," shrieked the maiden dame in a hoarse whisper.

"A gentleman?"

"Yes, sir; and worse, she wanted me to be flogged without—oh!—"

The court and spectators listened anxiously.

"Without—"

"Without what?"

"Without MY CLOTHES, sir, oh!"

Here the maiden lady was so agitated that a glass of water had to be given her.

A buzz of sensation went round the court, and the magistrate exclaimed in surprise—

"Your statement is very strange. Why should a gentleman wish to flog you in the manner you describe?"

"For their wicked passions," returned Miss Skimmer, "for their base lusts, sir, I assure you they tried to do it, they got me in a room, and tried to tie me up to a machine, the—flogging machine—but I got away; I ran out of the house, but that wicked woman kept my things; I was so flurried, I didn't know what to do, and its one of the wickedest houses in the place."

The magistrate consulted with the chief clerk.

"What goods did she detain of yours?"

"There are two pair of kid gloves, worth 2s.; a silk scarf, 1s.; two sprays of French flowers, 1s. 6d.; a cap front, 6¾d.; and ribbon, velvet, and black lace, 1s. Why, sir, you would hardly believe it, but the very flowers that she (the infamous being) is wearing in the front of her bonnet are the very ones that she took away from me."

Here the coarse-featured Mother Rawlings, clasping her hands and looking up to the ceiling, exclaimed in a theatrical tone of voice; "Oh, you wicked old creature! how can you stand there and say such false and malicious things of me? You ought to be choked for doing so. As for my house, it is the only respectable one in the neighbourhood, but the houses near me are gay. I am disturbed all night and all day by persons—some of them captains and real gentleman—coming into my house and asking for Kate, and other ladies. All my lodgers are highly respectable, and there is not one woman that would speak to any man but her husband; and as for me doing so, I am done speaking to any man, for I have a supreme contempt for them. As for what she says about flogging, it's like the rest of her lies, but I'm sure I don't know who'd like to look at her like she says."

Three police constables were called and stated that the house kept by Mother Rawlings, as well as two other houses next her, were known and had the repute of being brothels.

Mother Rawlings again denied that her house was "gay," or that she kept "lady" lodgers. She also denied striking Miss Skimmer, and said that when she first came to the house she was drunk, and she had not been there long before she wanted her (Mother Rawlings) to go with her to a fortune-teller's, in Bath Street, City Road. She said—the shameful creature that she was a single woman, and had been living with a married man; and he left her to go back to his wife, because she was near her confinement. He gave her some flowers, and as she knew the language of flowers she could tell that her lover's wife would have a son, that she would die in her confinement, that the child would die, and that her lover would be very disconsolate for a time and then return to her, all would be forgiven and forgotten, and that she should then be married, and all would then go on happily and comfortable, and that's what she hoped, the infamous old hussy.

At this attack the maiden spinster became so

agitated that the usher was obliged to interfere, but not before the clack of the two women's tongues had almost deafened the magistrate.

Ultimately, as neither would allow the other to speak without violently contradicting, and as witnesses came on both sides, who swore most steadfastly against each other, the magistrate, bewildered by the confusion, dismissed the case, and ordered the two women out of court.

This was a triumph for Mother Rawlings, and she went away well satisfied, but the unfortunate maiden lady, Miss Harriet Skimmer, was forced to depart without the satisfaction of getting back her goods, or having reparation for her wounded virtue.

Although Mother Rawlings had succeeded in denying the accusation of Harriet Skimmer, it was not the less true—horribly so—it was this woman who had entrapped the unfortunate lady into the ice-shop near the Haymarket, and for that purpose most abominable in its nature, that of being flogged to pander to the beastly sensuality of beings in masculine garb! wretches, who poured down gold that they might have the satisfaction of whipping the flesh of some fair woman, preparatory to their lustful gratification.

In a city of Europe it would seem impossible that such abominations should be practised, but the papers not long ago contained *some* disclosures of the horrible practice, but nothing compared with the revelations now to be given to the reader.

That unhappy lady, yet sought after by her husband, was still in the power of these miscreants; still to be brought out, whipped, outraged, and barbarously used, without the hope of getting from the terrible den of crime.

And now they had another victim in view.

Mother Rawlings had not got far when she encountered Crusher Jem; the bully ruffian having skulked long enough out of sight, thought he might venture out now with impunity.

Mother Rawlings beckoned the crusher to come to her, and called a cab, into which they both entered.

"I want you to get that girl to-night," she asked.

"All right."

"Lord M——'s coming and I've promised that he should have a fresh one."

"He's werry fond of flogging fresh 'uns," muttered Crusher Jem. "What's to be done with that donna we got in there?"

He referred to the young wife.

"She's making a great row about being birched; we shall have to quiet her."

The crusher grinned.

"Won't do to let her get out and blab."

"I'd cut her up in mincemeat first," said the vicious woman.

"Wouldn't be the first one you'd tried your hand on that way," remarked Crusher Jem.

"Nor you either, for the matter of that; but never mind about that now; let us have that girl there to-night."

"I'll bring her."

"Don't be late; get out here."

The crusher alighted and went on his way; the task that was required of him was one to which his brutality lent a charm.

He was used to such outrages, and prepared for the night's job with some satisfaction.

The young girl against whom this indignity was designed was no other than the pretty Mary, Dick's lost sweetheart.

CHAPTER XLVI.

THE OUTRAGE ON MARY AND WHO CAME TO THE RESCUE.

LET it not be thought that Warner had given Mary to this vile use.

Bad as he was he would have shrunk from such a deed.

He had sold her to the major, and had at that moment made his plans for ensuring her further downfall; but this was a thing beyond even his infamy.

It had chanced that a certain nobleman (so called) had once or twice seen Mary at the window as he passed: lying in wait he saw her occasionally go out, and every time attempted to get into conversation with her.

But the village girl repulsed him with dignity, and when he made a baser offer to her, threatened to give him into the custody of the law.

Repelled by Mary, he had only the resource left of appealing to the exertions of Mother Rawlings, who promised that Mary should be kidnapped from the house and made his prey.

The crusher was thus selected for the abduction, and when night came he made his way to the Terrace where Mary resided.

Lord M—— came there in a cab. He had learnt the nature of Mary's connection with Warner, and having sent a boy with a note to the house, waited inside his cab for Mary to come.

The crusher stood in a doorway ready to deal with his intended victim as soon as she appeared.

The letter purported to come from a friend of Warner, stating that he was dangerously ill and had sent a cab for her.

Mary, unsuspicious of anything wrong, hastily put on her bonnet and mantle.

"Where is the cab?" she inquired of the boy.

"At the top of the street, ma'am."

Mary hurried on; despite Warner's faithless excuses, she yet loved and clung to him. She was somewhat agitated, and scarcely noticed which way the boy took her.

When she turned the corner the crusher came behind her, and threw a muffler across her mouth; it was here quite dark and lonely. Mary had not time to utter a sound, before she was forced into the cab by the crusher.

"Excellently done," said Lord M——; "now, jump up and drive to Mother Rawlings."

Crusher Jem got on the box, and the cab drove away.

Lord M—— had taken Mary in his arms, and forced her to a seat; he now held her so that her arms were powerless, and commenced pouring into her ear the most enticing proposals.

The young girl recognised him; gagged, terrified, and trembling, she could only gaze in an agonized manner in his sensual countenance.

But as the cab rolled, and his words convinced her of the purpose for which she had been abducted, she struggled with him, and getting her hands free removed the gag from her mouth, and shrieked for help.

In vain Lord M—— attempted to silence her; she thrust him back, and, though he held her arms, succeeded in getting her head out of the cab window.

"Help—help!" she cried.

"Keep her quiet," shouted the crusher.

But there came an answering voice; the nobleman had, at length, succeeded in forcing Mary back to the seat, and stifling her cries, but not in time to prevent their being heard, and by one who, of all men, would least have suffered her to cry for aid.

Dick, whom she had rejected—Dick, whom she had wronged, heard her voice, and recognised it: he tore along the street, and seeing the cab driving furiously away leapt at the window.

Crusher Jem, who recognised Dick, dealt him a blow with the handle of the whip, and lashed the horse; but Dick made good his footing on the vehicle, and, clinging to the window, forced open the door.

His first act was to deal Lord M—— a violent blow in the throat, his next to seize Mary: almost in the same minute he had made a bound, and, with her in his arms, sprang to the ground.

The motion of the cab had not had time to affect him; he was, besides, a good leaper, and when his feet reached the road, he merely staggered with the weight of his burthen.

In a moment he had steadied himself, and stood enragedly awaiting the attack of the abductors.

Crusher Jem was taken all aback by Dick's actions, but he pulled up the horse, and jumped from the seat.

He had taken out his life preserver, and, with many muttered curses, was advancing to Dick, when Lord M—— cried out—

"Jump up, and drive off."

Carriage wheels were heard approaching.

Crusher Jem swore a deadly oath, but, obedient to his instructions, got on the box.

Then his lordship put his head out of the window.

"Don't be too secure, my pretty one; I'll yet have you in my power."

"Try it," Dick cried; "you'll find that she's got one to take care of her."

The cab drove away.

Hitherto Mary, whom the rapid succession of incidents had cast into almost a swooning state, had lain trembling on Dick's breast, unconscious by whom she had been rescued.

But, at the sound of his voice, she looked up.

Their eyes met.

What a history was in that glance. Mary shrieked, and, hiding her face from him, shrank away.

Dick looked at her earnestly.

"Mary," he said, "do you shrink from me now? would you rather that those villains yet had you?"

"Oh, no! but to meet like this."

"Ay, ay," murmured Dick; "this be a sorrowful meeting. Oh! Mary; if you had kept to Dick he would not have left you to be used like this. Speak to me, Mary. Where is he that brought you away, you said, to be his wife? Has he married you?"

"Oh, Dick!"

"Did he marry you?"

"Alas! I am not yet married."

"Not yet? then you never will be by him. Ah! Mary, this be what I told you; he has deceived you, and yet you love him."

"He will marry me; he says so."

"He says a lie," cried Dick. "I would I had him here. Where is he? tell me, and I will tear his heart out."

"Oh, Dick! do not be violent. I have done wrong, I know; don't go to him."

Dick put her back a little way, and looked sadly into her face.

"It is not my Mary that speaks," he said; "she was too pure; she would not have been made a thief, and yet have preferred the villain that ruined her; for that is what he has done. He has ruined you, Mary, and will do worse, if you stay with him."

He paused, for the tears were coming down Mary's cheeks.

Dick was moved by her signs of grief; he drew her closer to him, and spoke more kindly.

"You are not happy, Mary; your cheeks are pale; they used to be rosy once. Do not go to him again; come with me, Mary. I will protect you as a sister. I could never make you more than that; but he should not destroy you. Mary, you don't know all that has come to me. I was honest—I was innocent of the murder; but since I have come to London I have been among those that I would not for all the world have been seen with. I have done no crime, and yet am hunted as if I were a wild beast. Poor Charley, too; I have lost him, and have no one to care whether I be hanged to-morrow."

"Poor Dick," Mary said, "I have been the cause of this; I wish I had died before I broke my word to you."

"Ah, Mary; then you can yet be a sister to me.

Leave that man. We will not be parted again; I will work to keep a home for you, and if *he* comes I will wrestle with the villain and strangle him."

Moved by the words of the man she had once loved truly, and half-fearing that she had been deceived and betrayed by Warner, the young girl—grateful, too, for her rescue—was on the point of suffering him to lead her away, when the noise of wheels was again heard, and a voice called out—

"There, he's standing there with her; seize him, men."

Mary turned pale as death, Dick felt a tremor course through her frame.

It was Warner's voice.

"It be he," Dick whispered, hoarsely, "stand out of the way, Mary, let me have at him."

"No, no," Mary cried, "let us go away; they will take you."

She tried to lead him away.

They were already seen by the new comers: these were Warner and Major Harkall in a carriage and two policeman on foot.

Leaping from the carriage Warner rushed towards Dick, he did not recognise him till he was within about two yards of where he stood; but on seeing the man he had so injured he stopped short, and gazed from him to Mary.

"Look again, London mister," said Dick, "it be I; look at her, brute Warner, and touch her if you dare!"

By this time the police had come up, and Warner, recovering his presence of mind, ordered them to seize Dick.

"Take him up for abduction; he forced her out of the house—take him in charge; I'll prosecute."

"Stop!" Mary cried, "it was not he; he rescued me from the cab."

"A pretty tale, it is bad enough to see *you* with him—*a murderer*. Take him, constables; he's an escaped prisoner, escaped from the charge of murder."

Mary screamed, and clung close to Dick. The policeman, at the mention of the word murder, drew their truncheons, and prepared to take their prisoner.

But before a hand was laid on him, he had sprang at Warner's throat.

"Scoundrel!" he cried, "you say I did that; I will pay you for all now."

The force of his bound caused Warner to falter on the pavement; here the grip of Dick was so tight, that he would have been choked had not the police dragged Dick off.

Major Harkall descended from the carriage, and came to Mary, who, however, refused his proffered aid, and attempted to get to Dick.

The policemen had him now securely held, and were waiting for orders what to do with him, when Crusher Jem, with two more policemen, made his appearance.

"That's him," he said; "I'll turn evidence. He did the job."

"Richard Parker," said the foremost policeman, "I arrest you for the burglary and murder at Mr. Wilblow's."

What a scream came from Mary's lips! she strove to reach Dick, but Major Harkall and Warner forced her into the carriage.

The crusher scoffingly treated Dick; and with a brutal look at Mary, took to his heels.

"Stop him," Mary cried; "he forced me into the cab."

But the crusher was already out of sight; and as Mary sank fainting in the carriage, Dick was carried off to the station.

His struggles to get away were of the most desperate nature, but the constables held him fast; and after a scene of violence seldom witnessed, he was ironed and thrust into a cell.

———

THE FLOGGING MACHINE.

CHAPTER XLVII.

THE FLOGGING MACHINE.

REVELATIONS made some time ago opened the magistrate's eyes to the existence of a system so barbarous, and disclosing such frightful depravity, that nothing but its truth induces us to allude to it in these pages.

A case was brought before Mr. Selfe, at the Westminster Police Court, when, from evidence, it was gathered that there exist a number of houses in the metropolis, where poor girls are inveigled, or being fallen already from virtue's high estate, have been submitted to the horrible process of being flogged naked by individuals of the upper classes.

The establishment of Mother Rawlings was, as we have before hinted, making one in catering for this abominable passion.

Lord M——, the tall, fair gentleman, about thirty years of age, referred to in evidence, after his failure with regard to Mary, repaired to Mother Rawlings to see if any other victim was there.

Mother Rawlings was in the drawing-room, into which his lordship was shown; a strangely furnished drawing-room it was.

The walls were padded with stuffed leather; the floor was covered with the same; the sofas, chairs, and lounges, were all of the most luxurious but at the same time of the most indecent description.

Where there was space subjects of the most disgusting nature were painted on the woodwork, and the legs and arms of chairs, sofas, &c., were carved into the most indecent devices.

The whole of the ceiling was taken up by a cartoon

of the most seductive subjects; pictures of a similar description, and voluptuously-tinted photographs hung on the padded walls.

There were stereoscopes which, had any one looked into them, would have been found to contain the most revolting slides.

On one of the sofas lay some straps, and several rods of birch and furze; and at one part of the room was a singular machine, consisting of two upright poles covered with padded leather and having sockets of covered iron.

This was the flogging machine; the sockets were to receive the limbs of the victim, the straps to secure her there.

Lord M. surveyed all the preparations with vexatious disappointment.

"Have you no one here?" he asked.

"No one, my lord, except that woman you had brought in that night, when she was opposite the ice shop; perhaps you'd like her to be put up again?"

The face of the brutal woman, as she put this suggestion, was hideously revolting.

His lordship considered a few moments, and then decided upon having the unhappy lady brought out.

Crusher Jem, who was below, was directed to bring her in.

She looked different, indeed, to what she was when we first saw her alight from the omnibus at Regent Circus.

The length of her imprisonment there, the barbarity to which she had been subjected, had exercised their effect upon her.

She had no longer the fresh bloom on her cheeks; the brightness of her eye was gone, and her frame was reduced to a mere skeleton of its former self.

Had her husband, who was then seeking her everywhere, seen her, it is almost doubtful whether he would have recognised her, so great a wreck had she become.

There was a wildness about her looks as she glanced first at her brutal captors, then at her lordly persecutor; when her gaze rested on the diabolical machine a shudder thrilled through her, and Crusher Jem had to hold her to prevent her falling.

Without a trace of pity or feeling, the so-called nobleman regarded his unfortunate victim, while the vile procuress urged the crusher to drag the lady to the machine.

Recollect, reader, this was a deed enacted in London —Great London—the city of the world. A lady, young, beautiful; a wife, virtuous, loving; is suddenly lured from the open streets, dragged into a house of ill-fame; her body vilely scourged.

She shrank now from the dreaded ordeal so that the crusher's exertions were not enough to get her into the room, and Mother Rawlings had to come and assist.

Yet she had before been similarly treated.

Forced to the ground, she raised her imploring glance to the moneyed villain.

Her agony might have moved him when she cried,

"Sir, be merciful; don't let me be outraged again, let me depart, that I may die."

But the nobleman regarded her pleadings with indifference, and while her screams went thrilling through the room she was dragged to the machine.

She writhed and strained to release herself from the bonds, that too securely held her limbs and body fixed.

Then Crusher Jem, being no longer required, was sent from the room.

Lord M—— and the procuress were left with their victim.

Can language depict what followed?

The lordly villain lashed and goaded the woman's quivering flesh with whips and straps and rods of prickly furze till in her delirium at the indignity, the outrage, the blood started from her lips.

Then only was she taken down, and the miscreant, lifting her bodily from the machine, carried her to a couch.

Agony and pain had unstrung her brain. She was raving mad, foaming at the lips, and defying him to come near by the fear of being torn piecemeal.

And for that fate was Mary to have been inveigled into that house had he been successful in the abduction.

Poor Mary, whose troubles were but a tithe shown yet, who had to pass through a hell of sin before the horrible tragedy of the Bloody Hand should take place.

CHAPTER XLVIII.

WHAT BEFEL MARY.

WARNER did not fail to take advantage of the fact of Mary having been found with Dick.

After she had regained her consciousness he assailed her with the most scandalous assertions, telling her that she had arranged with Dick to be taken away, and that she had been unfaithful to him.

Mary defended herself indignantly from the accusation, but Warner, who saw in this an easy means of gaining his object, pretended not to believe her.

In fact, had it not been for his arrangement with Harkall, he would have made this an excuse for infamously casting her forth.

But the major had been nettled at the failure of his plans against the victimised girl, and for a price he had bought her of his friend.

So, after having uttered the most cruel accusations, Warner left angrily.

Poor Mary had listened to him with pain and remorse; his words had increased the heartbreaking she had begun to feel. Her meeting with Dick, his arrest, and the charge that was made against him had cut her to the soul, and after her seducer had left the house she laid her head on the table and wept bitterly.

Of Dick she knew not what to think; it was hard to believe him guilty after what he had said; and yet there seemed too much truth in the charge made by the officers.

And Warner the beguiled girl yet loved; she had, in a greater degree than she knew, transferred her affections from Dick to him, and in spite of the deceit he had practised towards her she loved him sincerely.

The heartless fellow knew that, and when he left her in the semblance of anger, it was only that her overwrought feelings might make her a more easy prey for the unscrupulous major.

The hours of night passed slowly away, while Mary sat hoping Warner would return and make reconcilement between them; but twelve o'clock— one—came, and he did not appear.

She reproached herself as the cause of this, and after spending another hour in the greatest wretchedness sorrowfully undressed and went to bed.

Weariness and grief had exhausted her, and after lying for a little while, steeping the pillow with her tears, she sank into a troubled slumber.

She woke suddenly from a fearful dream; she had seen Dick in her slumbers; she had been at his trial, where, as an outcast—a guilt-branded pariah— he had been tried for the murder of his fellow creature.

More: she had seen him at his execution.

There had been an immense crowd, foremost of whom they had placed herself, stifling her shrieks with violent hands.

She saw the terrible scene when the rope was secured round his neck, and he stood beneath the fatal beam to die.

He had turned his face on her, and though they

had instantly covered his features with the white cap, it did not hide from her his reproachful glance.

Then the drop fell.

She saw him struggling and writhing in the air; she could hear his frightful gasps as he tried to get breath—the rattle in his throat as the rope was strangling him. She tried to get to him, but the mob held her back.

Then, while she looked in agony and terror, the cap came from his face.

It was an awful sight.

Black, swollen, convulsive; the muscles like thick cords; the eye and tongue protruding; foam about his lips. Horror held her, as it seemed, speechless for the moment: then she saw his arms break loose from their bonds, and in his last death agony he stretched them out before her.

In the anguish of that instant, when she was yet struggling with the mob that she might get to him, she woke with a scream, not half assured that all she had seen in her sleep was not reality.

An arm was holding her, though not violently. She was delighted at finding that the dreadful scene had been all a dream: that pleasure was enhanced at the thought that it was Warner who was with her.

"Dear Warner."

But the voice that answered her was *not* Warner's. In horror she recognised the tones of the libertine major; she screamed for help, and struggled to get away from him.

Poor girl! it never entered her head that she had been basely bartered by the man who should have protected her, even if she had fallen with him. She thought it was a treachery on the part of the major alone, and frantically tried to get free from her destroyer.

He strove his utmost to pacify her.

"Be calm, dearest! I swear I will love you for ever! Do not fear Warner; I will take you where he shall never molest you."

How hollow his promises sounded after his base villany! his words only increased her agony of mind, and she had just succeeded in forcing herself from his hold when Warner burst into the room.

All was as prearranged.

The young girl was taken in the snare.

Warner had a candle in his hand: opening the door with a burst, the locks having been previously unscrewed for the purpose, he pretended to be petrified by the scene before him.

Poor Mary knew not how to speak: ignorant of their dastardly intentions, her fear was that he would adjudge her guilty without hearing.

This was indeed the case. Rushing to the centre of the room, he commented in the wildest manner accusing Mary and his friend.

We will draw a veil over the scene that followed: the cool effrontery of the major who charged Mary with having admitted him, the simulated rage of Warner, the tears of his victim.

Poor girl, she was indeed lost when those two scoundrels had her in their power.

That night saw her go forth in agony and tears; an outcast;.a thing without a name. She went forth, but only to hide her head in shame, or bury her infamy in the veil of self-destruction.

And the night that Dick lay heavily ironed in his cell, saw those two miscreants exulting together at the success of their infamy.

CHAPTER XLIX.

THE TRIAL OF DICK FOR MURDER.

Dick had been ironed and thrust into a cell; caged like a wild beast, and with a terrible doom hanging over his head; it required only a few days of his confinement to render him nearly mad.

His jailor scarcely dared approach his cell.

His food was brought to him and placed just inside.

Dick did not taste it.

Once when a policeman entered to expostulate with him, he kicked the tin of water into his face, and drove him out quaking.

When he was brought up before the magistrate, he maintained a stubborn demeanour, that made him appear as determined as the charge sheet had represented him to be.

And there was something so threatening in his stolid look, that four or five policemen were at his side, for fear of an outbreak.

When taken again to his cell, he was as moody and obstinate as before.

The magistrate thought him a hardened brutal ruffian; the newspaper reporters described his convict appearance.

Everybody had something to say against him.

Dick was altered to himself.

In his cell he muttered gloomily, and grated his teeth till it benumbed his jaws.

Often in the darkness he thought he saw Warner's exultant face: at such times, had his hands been free, he could have throttled himself out of sheer passion.

That interview with Mary had exercised a terrible influence upon him.

The day of his trial came at length: witnesses were in readiness to swear away his life, if necessary: the police were in attendance who had been at the house when their comrade was killed by the crusher.

And Mr. Wilblow, having had ample time for forgiveness, came sanctified and canting to get Dick punished.

Placed in the criminal dock, Dick looked vacantly about him; he could not help thinking of the time when he stood in a similar situation at his native village.

He remembered how nearly he had been condemned for a crime not of his doing, and for which he would assuredly have suffered, if Roving Rob had not got him out of prison.

But Roving Rob was not here this time, and if he had been, the prisons of London were better guarded and more secure than county jails.

It was strange that during all the time he had been in the hands of the police he had never once thought of escape. He appeared to have lost all energy and strength, and gave himself up to his fate, whatever it might be.

When the charge was read against him, and the scrutinising looks of the jurymen were turned upon him, as if he had been some guarded brute, he suffered his head to droop on his breast in apathetic indifference.

Even when the astounding nature of the evidence was made apparent, he manifested no anxiety.

The reporters set down in their note books his hardened and brutalised appearance.

Yet the mass of accusation against him was most serious, and enough to make his life not worth an hour's purchase.

The policemen deposed to stopping him on the stairs of Mr. Wilblow's house, and were particularly careful to impress the court with the fact of his unparalleled violence in escaping.

Mr. Wilblow said sorrowfully that he saw him in the house, and perceived he had in his hand an instrument like the one with which the policeman's skull was believed to have been beaten in.

Other evidence the police had carefully prepared went to prove that it was his hand that did the murder.

More than all, an able lawyer had put the case in its strongest points against him.

Still Dick said nothing.

He refused even to answer when called upon to

plead guilty or not guilty, and made no attempt at explanation or defence.

There was a dead silence in the court, when the judge began his summing up: he, of course, spoke in glowing terms of the enormity of the offence, and hinted at the sullen character of the prisoner; he painted in pathetic colours the noble heroism of the policeman—his brutal murder; and was carefully putting the evidence strong against Dick, when a slight hubbub arose in rear of the court.

The judge looked round, in surprise; several police rushed stealthily outside.

They came back instantly, followed by what had occasioned the stir.

Two policemen came into court, bearing on their shoulders a stretcher, on which lay a being on whom all eyes were turned.

A huddled-up mass of ragged clothes it first seemed. Then was made out a head, a sickly sweated face, a hand like a corpse's.

The policemen lowered the stretcher, and assisted the burthen out.

Charley!

It caused Dick a hard stare, ere he recognised in that wasted form and pale white face, with the deep burning eyes sunken in their sockets, his noble-hearted nephew.

People in court stretched their necks to see what was the matter.

The judge inquired the reason of their coming.

The policemen led the poor weakly boy towards the bench.

He could not walk unaided; he was emaciated to a mere skeleton, and had such a look of pain and weakness on his features, that every glance was turned upon him in sympathy while the policemen told their story.

It appeared that one of them, searching after a young thief who had sought refuge under the railway arches, heard a groan, which for a long time puzzled him as to where it came from.

After a great deal of diligence, he found out that it proceeded from the inside of the brickwork; he discovered where after a long search, but then was at a loss how to get inside.

But the boy whom he had followed came up, and offered to go in and fetch Charley out (whom he said he had seen inside there fearfully ill), if he would let him off for what he had done.

The policeman consented, and Charley was brought out.

A crowd soon gathered there; the policeman sent for a stretcher; and while they were waiting some of them, after talking of other things, mentioned Dick Parker and his trial.

"At this," said the policeman, "the boy made a dreadful outcry, said he could tell about it, and screamed to be brought here, and I have brought him to your worship."

Charley was led to the witness box; he had not yet seen Dick, his eyes were fixed on the judge's face.

When interrogated, he spoke in a very faint voice, and gave a truthful account of the manner in which the burglary had been effected, including the share he had taken in it; his attempts to get Dick away; the blow he received from Mr. Wilblow, after arousing the house; his ultimate escape; and all that had befallen him since.

His recital was listened to with apparent interest. When he alluded to the blow he had received, Mr. Wilblow put on his most saintly look. He drew tears from the eyes of several of the women in the court, when in a hoarse whisper (his voice was almost lost), he described his search for Dick; the misery he had endured since; how the good-natured boy, Nobby Ned had led him into that place, and given him half his supper, when he was starving and perishing with cold.

And lastly, he spoke of the days and nights that had passed since Nobby Ned had left him, and he had been alone in his sickness and suffering.

It was at this moment that a groan from Dick attracted his attention to him.

Instantly a change came over him.

"Dick, dear Dick," he moaned, hoarsely, and strove to get to him.

But he was to weak to stand, and when, in the energy of his first movement, he had broken from the policeman, he sank to the ground.

At this moment, says the evidence, a scene took place which, we believe, has never been witnessed in a court of justice.

When the prisoner first came to the bar he looked a very harmless young man, but during the evidence of Charley he became restless, and moved as if in pain.

Immediately after Charley had fallen to the ground he threw one leg and arm over the front of the dock, and very nearly succeeded in getting over.

Two warders, who were in the dock, rushed at him and seized him, and other warders at once jumped into the dock, and an almost deadly struggle then took place, Dick kicking, fighting, and roaring more like a wild tiger than a human being, and it required nearly ten strong men to hold him. Several had hold of his legs and arms, and some were holding him by the hair of his head. This continued for some minutes, and when it ceased it was only because he was held fast.

A few moments of calm now ensued, during which Charley was lifted up by the police; he was like a corpse, and could not speak.

The sight of the poor faithful boy again excited Dick almost to madness; he had promised to cherish that boy, and now to see him in that terrible weakly condition—the last threads of his life almost sundered, whilst he himself was held like a savage beast, and unable to get to or speak with him—drove him half mad, and for the space of half an hour a scene of violence was renewed, that put fear into the hearts of all in the court.

"My poor Charley," Dick cried, foaming at the teeth, "let me get to you; they have made us like this; let me get to him, or I shall go mad."

His tones were roared out like a lion's. The spectators made for the door, while the counsel fairly shook in their wigs; as for the police, they were puffing and sweating vigorously.

Dick's paroxysms continuing so terrible, the fear that he had gone mad became prevalent, and it was suggested to the judge that, as well for the safety of Dick as for others, it would be better to put irons on him.

The judge said he did not like to do this; but the violence continuing, his lordship gave way, and consented to the irons being put on.

Dick, before Charley's eyes, was then heavily ironed and strapped — certainly as much as any maniac could be; but it was some time before this could be managed, on account of his extreme violence.

As may be conceived the greatest consternation reigned, it seemed impossible for the trial to go on.

After half an hour's delay, the judge went out to consult Mr. Justice Byles, and their lordships remained in consultation for a considerable length of time, during which Dick appeared to be completely exhausted, and appeared, as it were, asleep.

A surgeon was sent for, and Mr. Serjeant Shee returned into court, and ordered him to be taken into a private room, and examined by the surgeon.

With some difficulty he was carried out of court.

Charley, who had crept up to him, being again held by the police.

When they brought Dick back he was quieter; his features bore evidence of the effect his paroxysms had upon his mind. His face was haggard; his eyes were red and bloodshot; his lips swollen, and coated with foam.

Poor little Charley, permitted by the judge to go Dick, in the hope it would keep him quiet, tottered up to him, and, taking his manacled hand, laid his thin white face on it, and sobbed bitterly.

There were few in the court that were not affected at the scene.

But one who was not was the eminent philanthropist, Mr. Wilblow.

He had not forgiven Charley, though he had used him so cruelly, and was certainly unsparing in severity against Dick.

The trial proceeded.

Charley's statement had not been without its influence on the judge; he believed the boy's truthful earnest face, and thought it probable that Dick might have been led on in the manner described.

The manner in which he finished the summing up, which he had begun so dead against Dick, led every one to believe that he intended him to receive the benefit of the doubt, and be acquitted.

Still many had a vague feeling of fear when the jury retired.

An unnecessary one it would have proved, if it had not been that two of the jurymen were tradesmen who supplied Mr. Wilblow with things for his house; they had been previously honoured by a conversation with him, in which he had so impressed his belief in the necessity of the conviction of the prisoner, that, fearing to lose his custom if they dissented, they made up their minds for a verdict of guilty.

The jurymen, it is a well-known fact, are often, even in cases involving human life, most easily led to a verdict.

Frequently, ignorant of the law and practised upon by the specious phraseology of some cunning lawyer, they are soon persuaded to follow the lead of any of their number who express their convictions whether for guilt or innocence.

In this present case they were soon worked upon to agree to a verdict of guilty.

True one had stuck out for the prisoner's acquittal.

But one of the leaders, in a glowing speech (he remembered that Mr. Wilblow had only the day previous paid his bill), so persuaded him of the duty he owed to society, and of the peril that would result from letting murderers go loose, that he grew frightened, and gave in with the rest.

The buzz of the court subsided when the jury came back.

Those who were in favour of Dick's acquittal felt their hearts sink at the sight of the grave faces of the arbiters of his destiny.

The usual questions as to their finding was put to them.

In the silence of that moment you might have heard the breathing of the prisoner.

Charley had his glance fixed on the jury.

Dick gazed impressively round.

The foreman spoke.

"We find a verdict of guilty, my lord."

The judge looked surprised. Charley uttered a faint cry, and started forward. Dick glanced wildly before him.

"You say you find guilty?" said the judge.

"We do, my lord."

"Unanimously?"

"Unanimously, my lord."

The judge looked as though he did not believe them; but such being their verdict, nothing was left for him to do but to put on the black cap and sentence the prisoner.

In tones marked by emotion he said—

"Prisoner, you are found guilty of the frightful crime of murder: the sentence is that you be taken from this place to the jail, and from thence, on the appointed day, to the place of execution, there to be hung by the neck till you are dead! dead! dead!"

A faint hoarse cry came from Charley.

"No, no," he exclaimed, "he is innocent: this is murder! Dick, dear Dick, look up; they dare not kill you."

Then with a furious glance Dick glared round.

"I did not expect justice here," he cried, "I have seen enough of the poor man's doom: but I've been hunted from place to place, driven almost into crime for no sin of my doing, you have found me guilty of murder. I don't fear to die. I have not much to live for but Charley here, and he be the only faithful one I've known; but I'll never be took out and hanged like a dog when God knows I be as innocent of this charge as those who have tried me. I'll not be hung up like a choked beast! I'll be torn in pieces first!"

With this he turned again in fury on those who held him. The scene of before was re-enacted, but in greater terrors: women shrieked; men cried "shame;" the judge looked palsied.

It was fearful to see that strong man doomed to be led hence to die.

Above all poor Charley's cries could be shrilly heard.

Had Dick not been so heavily manacled not all the exertions of the police would have kept him there; but with their help they were enabled to overpower him at last.

They held him and he stood in their grasp, his great chest throbbing, and his eyes rolling wildly.

"Oh Dick! Dick!" Charley exclaimed, "don't be afraid that they can kill you—they can't; don't be down; I am ill now, but I'll soon be well. They've had you run down for other men's crimes, but I will hunt them down, and bring them here to answer for their wicked deeds."

"Prisoner," the judge remarked speaking in great agitation, "although not embodied in the verdict of the jury, I will see that a full statement of the case, with a recommendation to mercy, shall go to the proper quarter."

"I want no mercy," Dick answered, "I only want justice, if there be justice for the poor man I shall have it."

"You shall, Dick," Charley murmured faintly.

"Bear up, my brave boy," said a gentleman in the court, whom the police recognised as Mr. Elsden, "Dick is not deserted yet."

The boy did not hear him.

He had fallen into a fit at the first sound of his voice.

Dick's violence broke forth anew when he again saw Charley fall; it took ten police to get him out of the dock and into the cell, where they thrust him, palpitating and exhausted.

The condemned cell.

Where he was to lie till the hour come when he should be dragged out, all innocent as he was, to die before a gaping brutal throng; to have the strong life throttled out of him by the hangman's hands.

CHAPTER L.

CHARLEY RESOLVES TO KEEP HIS WORD AND BRING THE CRUSHER TO JUSTICE.

Mr. Elsden, as soon as Dick was taken away, had Charley put in a cab and conducted to his house, where the best treatment was bestowed upon him. When Charley came to, he bestowed a pitiful vacant glance on the kind countenance of his protector, and murmured his feeble thanks.

Then he attempted to leave the bed.

This Mr. Elsden prevented.

"In a day or so, my poor boy," he said, "you will be better, and can then rise."

"But, poor Dick," Charley said, " he is in prison."

Mr. Elsden calmed him; he told him that exertions would be made to save Dick from execution.

"I will use my influence," he observed.

"And will Dick be set free?"

"I cannot promise that; he will at any rate have a chance of proving his innocence."

"But they kill innocent men sometimes. Oh, sir, let me go to him; he will think I have ran away from him."

"As soon as you are well enough I will take you to him; but now you are so weak, you can do nothing. Get your strength up; and, in the meantime, you can be telling me about these men who have tried to lead you into sin."

His words were so kind and soothing, that Charley was affected by them, and induced to think that what his benefactor said was best.

But he did not like the idea of Dick being shut up in the condemned cell while he was lying there in luxury.

Mr. Elsden had taken a great interest in the friendless boy; this interest had been extended to Dick, when he had seen him during the trial, and he at once consulted with the lawyer who had before had charge of Charley's case, for the purpose of taking measures for the discovery of Crusher Jem.

But Charley was more active in his measures than the slow process of the law; he lay in his bed till the thought of Dick's position so excited him, that, on the first occasion of his benefactor's absence, he got out of bed, dressed himself, and hurried from the house.

His weakness was at first so great that he could scarcely stand; but, by degrees, the cool air revived him. Mr. Elsden had provided him a decent suit and taken away his old rags, little thinking that he would so soon attire himself in them.

Charley's appearance was thus respectable, though somewhat startling; and when he presented himself at Newgate, the known circumstances of the case enabled him to procure the necessary order for seeing his uncle in the condemned cell.

A warder was with Dick; he was apprised of Charley's coming.

As soon as the faithful boy entered, he ran to his uncle, and clasped his hand.

"I knew I should not be left," Dick exclaimed; while Charley wept bitterly. "Eh, Charley, boy! all has come as you said; if I had listened to you, and kept away from all, I should not have come to this."

"Dick, dear Dick, you will be released; they cannot keep you here."

"So they said, Charley, boy, but they have kept me here, and they tell me I am never going out again. My poor boy, you don't know what I have felt since I have been here; you don't know how horrible it be to lie here and know that the day be fixed for me to be took out, and strangled like a dog."

"Poor, poor Dick."

The warder, anticipating that Dick's feelings would lead to a new ebullition of his violence, walked to the cell door; but Dick remained passive, gazing on his boy-nephew's face.

"How ill you seem," he said; "they have made you suffer, curse them."

"Hush, Dick; be calm; the lawyers are trying what they can do for you."

"The lawyers!" Dick answered, sadly; "it be they that do all the mischief; they never care if an honest man hangs, so that they get their case made out. That was a lawyer, too, that took Mary—poor Mary; if I could be out only for a day to get at him."

In his agitation at the remembrance of Mary's betrayal, Dick's veins swelled, and his face became marked by a paroxysm of anger. Charley kissed his hand, and tried to calm him.

"I have come out, though the kind gentleman told me to keep in bed; I could not rest. Good-bye, Dick; I am going to get that bad man taken for the murder of the policeman."

"If you can do that," Dick cried, wildly; "but no, they be too much for you; they be too cunning—too bad."

"I don't think they will be so; I will give night and day to the search. I shall know him, Dick, when I see him, and when I see him I will not let him get away; I'll cling to his legs, and he may beat me to death, but I won't let go till he is taken."

"God help you, my poor boy; if this villain could be taken, I should be satisfied. He got me here—he sold me for his own crime; they dragged me away just when I had found Mary."

"Found Mary!"

"Ay, lad! but she be gone again."

"She will come—"

"No, she will never come to see Dick, till he is taken out to die."

"They shall never do this," Charley cried; "good-bye, Dick; I will go where I shall find this bad man."

"Take care of thyself, Charley," Dick murmured; and the faithful boy, after an affectionate parting, left the condemned cell.

While Charley is on his way to the low localities where Crusher Jem was most likely to be found, let us take the reader to one whose fate we left in some obscurity—the young girl, Tiger Loo.

Her passion had not deserted her when they let her down in that well of horrors, where the darkness and the stench were insufferable, and where only air enough came to enable her to breath with difficulty.

Up to a late hour of the night the kitchen had been tenanted, and when the last of the criminals had left, or lay on one of the benches asleep, it was near the break of day.

The rules which the thieves have amongst themselves are, it is well known, binding; and though some of them may have felt a desire to see Tiger Loo relieved from her dreadful position, none would dare to interfere now that her doom was passed.

Except one.

The Downy Cove.

This gentleman, besides his zeal in the cause of humanity, had too great a partiality for the young girl to look with calmness on her death.

So when every one was out of the way or asleep, the Downy Cove crept into the kitchen, and made his cautious way to the trap down which Loo was thrust.

He had a coil of rope under his arm.

Removing the flag without creating the least disturbance, he whispered softly—

"Loo!"

A scratching sound answered him; it was her nails ferreting against the sides of her loathsome prison.

"Loo!" again whispered the Downy Cove; "here's a rope."

He heard her grate her teeth and make a snatch at the end of the rope, when he had dropped it down.

Then she began dragging it with her weight.

This rope was for the purpose of enabling her to walk up.

One end was fastened round the Downy's back; he had his legs stretched apart, so as to give him purchase to bear the strain.

Nevertheless, when Tiger Loo commenced tugging at the rope, he found it hard to keep himself from being tugged over; at the same time he felt as if he were being torn in two.

But he bore it with fortitude.

"Climb," he whispered down the hole.

And Loo did climb.

With the agility of a civet cat, she was up the rope.

Her face appeared at the mouth of the pit. The Downy Cove was half frightened at the sight.

She had altered so terribly in the long hours that had passed since her incarceration there.

The Downy Cove helped her out, and she stood erect.

"Thanks," she said, in a tone of deep passion. "I will repay this. I will repay the others, too."

"Never mind that now," returned the Downy. "We isn't out of the wood yet; which, take a pull of this brandy, while I put back the trap."

Tiger Loo grated her teeth harshly, and, before helping herself to the drain, helped to put back the flag.

It gave her a spiteful satisfaction to be able to close it on the empty pit, when the rest supposed she was there.

"Now," said the Downy, when Tiger Loo had stamped fiercely on it after the fastenings had been secured, "let some of them come."

"Not by no means," rejoined the crusher, pacifically; "let all on us go."

"I would settle with them first," said the impetuous young girl.

"Don't do nothing of the kind; come out; you'll be waking them kiddies over there; and you know what I should nab for letting you out."

This recalled the hot-tempered girl: she pressed the Downy's hand in silence, and in a few moments they were out of the house, Tiger Loo well disguised and guided forth under the watchfulness of her rescuer.

And where, in all these changes, was the wonderful Roving Rob?

CHAPTER LI.

WHAT HAPPENED WHEN CHARLEY SAW THE CRUSHER.

"Why bless my infant eyes if that ain't the werry identical young kiddy."

Such was the exclamation of the Downy when he and Tiger Loo were walking down a street in Spitalfields.

It was the first night that Tiger Loo had been abroad since her deliverance; the Downy had insisted upon taking her to his lodgings—to keep her out of harm's way, he said; though there is too much reason to fear that the weak part of the Downy's nature was at fault, and that he had taken the young girl there in order that she might be to him for a while as wife and sweetheart: a proceeding to which she, from gratitude perhaps, agreed without opposition.

This present exclamation was caused by their seeing, a little way in front of them, a slim pale-faced boy, who was looking attentively at the houses on each side of the way as he passed.

"Kiddy; which one?" asked Loo.

"Why the youngster as kicked up such a shine in the crib where the crusher did his little business."

"Dick's boy."

"His nevey, or something—"

As the Downy was speaking Charley caught sight of him, and instantly ran up to him.

"Well my young sugar-stick," said the Downy, "so you have come this way again."

"Yes," Charley cried, "I have come to find you and the others; Dick be took through you, but I know who did the murder, and if you don't tell me where to find him I'll bring the police here to take you."

"My boy," observed the Downy, "it ain't usual for us to split against one another, and don't make a noise, because round about here there are more theives than coppers, a precious sight."

"I don't care," Charley exclaimed; "Dick shan't be hanged for another's crime."

"Oh, he's took," said Loo; "you didn't tell me that."

"Didn't want to make you uneasy," replied the Downy.

"Is he tried?"

"Well, it's about a nubbing with him."

Loo's brilliant eyes flashed fire.

"And you sold him?"

"Well, no."

"Was it the crusher?"

"I guess I must say, yes."

"Another score," cried Loo; "come with me, my boy: if your uncle is to be hung for *his* murder, I will see that the crusher don't get off."

"Loo," observed the Downy Cove, "there mustn't be no peaching."

"I don't belong to your set now, and will do as I like."

"You know the consequences."

"I am not afraid of meeting them."

"Well."

"Don't trouble yourself, Downy, you can go where you like; I am going with the boy."

Thus peremptorily dismissed, the Downy stayed not to add further arguments to his cause, but slipped off; Loo, with Charley, being already on their way.

Truth to tell, the Downy was of a very philosophical turn of mind; and thought that, if any one must hang, it might as well be the one that committed the offence; and therefore if the crusher got taken, he might stand his chance like another man.

So he went on his way.

Charley would not so readily have left him, if Loo's words and manners had not convinced him she was in earnest.

He, of course, did not know the character she bore; and as her features, owing to the Downy Cove's care of her, had recovered their engaging and youthful look, he thought what a kind sisterly girl she was and wondered why she consorted with such ruffians.

At times, it is true, she surprised and startled him, by her fierce looks and excited exclamations, when he narrated what had occurred to Dick.

Tiger Loo knew generally where to find the crusher; so she took Charley by the hand, telling him that, if he followed her advice, he would succeed in lagging the crusher; but, if he did otherwise, he would most likely fail in his object, and fall a victim to the violence of the bully.

By the time she had given him instructions in the rules of the thieves' gang, she had arrived at a dimly lighted house, of too suspicious an appearance for the lonely traveller to choose for a house of refreshment.

"Now's the time," said Loo, "the crusher's inside. Stay here; I'll go round to the back, there's another way there; if he comes out, follow him till you see a blue; but mind, don't attempt to interfere with him yourself."

"I will follow him," Charley answered resolutely; and the young girl leaving him there, went round to the back.

She had scarcely gone out of Charley's sight, and he himself had only just slunk into a hiding-place, when Crusher Jem came out.

He had evidently been drinking deeply, and came swaggering out as if he intended knocking down the first person he met.

Charley regarded him, loathingly; the impulse to leap upon his was strong, but he remembered Loo's counsel, and restrained himself.

The crusher, after looking round without seeing Charley, went down the street; and Charley, gliding from his hiding-place, followed him.

He was quite aware that Tiger Loo had not had time to enter the house before the crusher came forth, and he was in doubt whether he had not better wait and see her; but the fear of losing sight of Crusher Jem was too great. He found his impatience to get the bully taken increasing now that he saw him, and giving a last look at the house in the hope of seeing Tiger Loo, he kept in the crusher's wake.

He was not acquainted with the modes of communication adopted by thieves, or he might have made a mark that would have been well understood.

As it was, reflection told him that Loo would be sure to know who had gone after the crusher when she found them both gone.

They walked some distance, the crusher taking his way through passages that Charley would never have found—mere slits, as it were, in the wall.

Charley kept a good look out in every direction, but no sight of a policeman could he see.

As is usually the case with these gentlemen, they were not to be found at the time they were most wanted.

They were getting near the high road now; Charley knew that by the width and illuminations of the streets they were traversing, yet no policeman!

He looked round.

There was no sign of Tiger Loo.

In a few moments more the crusher might get in amongst a crowd and be lost sight of.

He had made up his mind not to go much farther without an attempt to stay the crusher.

"The people will help me," he thought.

So he resolved, big as the crusher was, to attack him before he got into the high road.

But a movement of the crusher interfered with this plan.

He turned, by a short cut, into a wide street, where many persons and vehicles were passing, and stopping at a public-house, was about to enter.

Charley thought that if he once got in there, he should have no chance of taking him.

So, without further thought of the consequence, he stepped suddenly in his way.

Crusher Jem looked ferociously at him.

He knew him in an instant.

The boy's agitated face told him that something was in the wind—a something he determined to prevent.

Giving him a jerk in the chest with the knee, he took him by the collar.

"Ha! my young nipper," he cried, with an oath; "it is you, is it?"

"It is," Charley said; "I have been looking for you, and now that I have found you, I do not go till I have you taken up for the murder."

"What?" growled the crusher.

"For the murder that they've tried Dick for, but for which you shall hang; I saw you there, and know you did it."

"Get out of the way," cried Crusher Jem, spitefully shaking him.

But Charley flew at his throat, and, holding him by the necktie, hung so that his knees were in his chest.

"Help me," he cried to the passers by; "he's a murderer—help—police!"

"I'll choke you," the crusher muttered, with a new oath.

"You may, but I won't leave you."

"Let go."

"I wont. Help! police!"

Several of the passers-by stopped and gathered round; they could see that the crusher was almost choking the poor boy, but it was no business of theirs; so they did not interfere.

And Charley might have been throttled then had not a policeman been seen walking leasurely to the spot, as policemen always do when they see a mob.

To be sure, one or two women made an outcry against the ill-usage of the boy, but a kick from the crusher, which one of them received, prevented any one taking upon themselves to take Charley's part, and face the bully.

Although pinched till he could hardly breathe, Charley, still clinging to the ruffian, found voice to cry out for the police to help him.

Thinking that there might possibly be something the matter the policeman quickened his steps, but no sooner did he catch sight of the face of Crusher Jem, whom he knew they wanted for past crimes, than he vigorously sprang his rattle, but without, however, making too great haste to seize the ruffian who had hold of Charley.

The springing of the rattle brought a bigger mob; the crusher saw two or three peelers coming to the rescue, and could detect several threatening faces amongst the crowd, so he thought the time had come to get rid of Charley at any risk.

"You whelp," he cried, "I don't want to hurt you, but go."

"I won't let you go; take him, people, he's done murder."

"Get off, you whelp."

"You shall kill me first."

"Let him go," shouted several.

"You brute to illtreat the poor boy."

"Make way; here comes the police."

The crusher saw that this was the case: using his heavy boot, he cleared the way to the kerb, the crowd getting out of his way like a pack of curs.

When he reached the kerb, he pressed Charley's throat till the strength of the poor boy gave way, and his grip slackened from the crusher's neck-tie.

He had held him till then with a grip that defied removal.

But now the crusher had him at his will; he lifted him with a wrench, and hurled him off the kerb.

There was a cab passing at the time rather swiftly.

Charley reeled a moment in the road.

People cried to the cabman to pull up.

Some started forward to seize the reins.

But all too late.

Charley fell back right under the horse as it came.

A cry of horror came from the mob.

Charley fell under the horse's feet.

The cab passed over him.

While half the mob rushed to pick him up, and abuse the cabman, who stopped at once, the others made way for the police to get at the crusher.

But he was already making off.

"It was his own fault," he growled.

The mob began to hoot.

The threatening look of the crusher kept them back.

He was clear of them, when a policeman took him by the collar.

"We want you," he said.

Others were coming on.

Another moment, and there would be enough to do to take him.

The crusher was a man of action.

He cared not a straw for human life—save his own.

That he was careful of.

He knew that if he was taken the rope would end his existence.

So he drew out his life-preserver, and as the policeman's grip closed on his collar, he raised it to strike the blow.

The policeman dodged, but not in time.

The heavy instrument struck him in the face, and he fell bleeding and senseless to the ground.

The crusher stayed a moment only to deliberately jump on the prostrate policeman.

The poor man gave a groan, turned over on his side and lay still.

The other policemen came up.

The mob raised fresh cries.

They called on the police to do their duty and take the ruffian.

But before the police could see him the crusher flew over the road, rushed down an alley, and was out of sight.

MARY'S ATTEMPT TO DROWN HERSELF.

He had escaped!

They picked up the prostrate groaning policeman.

They raised Charley, and carried him to the pavement, and the mob and police rushed after Crusher Jem.

CHAPTER LII.

THE CAPTURE OF THE CRUSHER.

When they picked Charley up, they found him bleeding from the nose and mouth; he was insensible, and it was thought that he was dead.

People gathered round in pity for the poor boy, whom they might have helped before, if their cowardice had not been so great.

While they were preparing to carry him to the hospital, Tiger Loo, out of breath with her pursuit after Charley, came up, and forced her way to the inanimate boy.

"Cowards!" she cried, when she had heard what had happened; "if you had not been a set of curs, the poor boy would not have been hurt, and he wouldn't have got away."

Charley here opened his eyes, and, seeing the young girl, spoke.

"I shall be able to walk in a minute."

Tiger Loo bent over him.

"Where are you hurt?" she asked.

"Nowhere except by the fall. I am better now."

They put him to the ground. It was as he said. The horse had not touched him, nor had the wheels, after he was thrown down.

The force with which Crusher Jem had pitched

him into the road had stunned and shaken him; but the bleeding at the nose helped to bring him to, and, after being steadied for a little while, he found himself able to stand.

Tiger Loo sent for a drop of brandy. Charley drank it as if it were the elixir of life.

Then he looked round in the crowd.

"You saw him try to kill me, and let him go; but I will get him taken yet."

"You shall," Tiger Loo answered. "Come away from these curs: we'll have him right enough."

They got into a cab which Loo called, and drove from the scene of the accident; but, before they had gone far, a weakness overcame Charley, and he fell into a fainting fit.

The generous-hearted but fallen girl directed the cabman to stop and get more brandy, by which she brought Charley round; but he was evidently so weak that to have kept him out longer would have been cruel.

So Tiger Loo had the cab driven to a better-class lodging-house, where she knew Charley would be taken care of so long as she had money to pay for him.

Having seen him attended to, she left the house to gain intelligence of Crusher Jem.

Charley had promised to wait till she came back.

She had directed him to sleep, but this the anxious boy found it impossible to do.

Half the night had waned and Tiger Loo came not, Charley, who was in a fever lest the brutal ruffian should escape, stood at the window looking out into the dark street in the hope that he might see her return.

Poor Charley, he was agitated by the position of Dick, and would have been ready to tear his own heart out if Crusher Jem got off; his excitement then may be conceived when he perceived the burly form of the ruffian coming up the street.

Crusher Jem looked fagged and desperate; he had been hotly chased by the police and mob, and had narrowly escaped capture; he was in his most savage mood, and glared about him like a famished tiger.

In front of the house he paused and looked up at the window; Charley thought he was seen; he would have been if it had not happened that he had no light in his room, and so was able to look into the street without being seen.

Under the impression, however, that the crusher had detected him and would either enter the house or make off, he hurried out of the room, and gliding down the stairs rushed into the street.

The brutal bully was almost out of sight—he was making moderate haste.

"The coward," thought Charley, "he runs away from me."

And he pursued him.

He was mistaken, had the crusher known he was behind him his first act would have been to stop and squeeze the life out of the faithful boy.

But, unconscious of the pursuit, and fancying himself now secure, he never even turned to see if anyone was following him.

The fact was Crusher Jem was now merely looking out for a crib where he might hide himself.

He was getting wanted for so many plants that out of doors was becoming too hot for him.

And so he determined to lie by till Dick was hanged and the other matters in which he had been concerned forgotten.

He might have succeeded in this, for the police were not too vigilant; but he had an inveterate pursuer in the boy, whose uncle was doomed to die for his guilt.

Charley had not the most remote idea where he was being led to; but, remembering what had resulted from his incautious actions previously, he kept out of sight till he saw the crusher stop at a flash gin shop, which he entered after a crafty look round to see if any one was near.

It struck Charley at once that he had gone in there to remain; and he noted well the position of the house that he might not miss it when he came back.

Returning to look for a policeman, he saw a piece of coal lying in the gutter: he picked it up, and making a mark at the corner of every street, began his search for one of those gentry who are never to be found when wanted—the peelers.

He passed one sooner than he expected; it was in a dirty street where a number of low devils were swearing and wrangling: the "bobby," accustomed to such scenes, was thoughtfully cracking nuts.

Charley, seizing him by the arm, caused him to turn sharply. The boy's white anxious face did not disturb him; on the contrary, he looked inclined to grin, as he said.

"Now then, what's up; dad wollopping your ma for popping the flat iron?"

"I want you to take a man that's done murder," Charley said.

"Oh!"

The policeman was all impatient instantly; he felt for his staff, and, in a dignified tone, said—

"Where?"

"I'll tell you," Charley said, "if you come along; if we stay, he may be gone."

So Charley got him out of the street, and told him all about the crusher.

"What," said the peeler; "a large house, with a potato crib next door?"

"Yes."

"Then," said the policeman, grandly, "'taint my beat."

Charley looked at him in dismay.

"You'll come and take him?"

"Can't."

"He'll get away."

"Can't help it; 'taint my beat."

Now the idea of the policeman refusing because it happened to be the next street off his beat, was to Charley singularly preposterous; so he very excitedly told the peeler that he believed he wouldn't come because he was afraid.

This riled the "blue," and he would have cuffed Charley, if a second policeman had not then been in sight.

Charley ran to him, crying,—

"If you won't come, he will, perhaps."

"It's his beat," rejoined the peeler, philosophically, putting another nut in his mouth.

From the calm discussion of this he was soon called by the other "blue," who, having heard Charley's story, decided that two heads were better than one to receive the cracks which would most likely be showered about by Crusher Jem's companions; and policeman No. 1 was obliged to walk off with policeman No. 2.

All this had been very tantalising to the eager boy, who feared that by the time they got there the bird would have flown; the bobbies, however, coolly replied to his express fear by saying,

"Don't be afraid of that; they don't go there when they're run down, only when they wants to hide for a month."

"Then we may take him?"

"We'll try to."

"Don't let him get away."

"Not if we can help it."

"He'll try to; he's so desperate."

"Yes, sure to try; but we mustn't let him."

They soon got to the house, the description Charley gave of it enabling the policemen to proceed thither without going the roundabout way he had marked, to say nothing of the fact that a keen eyed covey who had found out the first mark was assiduously following the track and softly rubbing out all the marks he could find.

The policemen took their measures with as much coolness as if they had been merely intending to walk in and surprise a friend in place of being about to enter into a den where more than one constable had received blows that had sent him to his grave.

They went upon a plan which was well understood by the police themselves.

The police force has done much to mitigate the ruffianism and exclusiveness of the old thieves.

Better organised, composed of younger and stronger men, they have proved themselves more than a match for any combination, even of the most determined and desperate characters.

But they did not gain the mastery without fearful and deadly struggles. The public knew little or nothing of the numbers that have been kicked and beaten to death in the public streets and thieves' resorts, or mutilated horribly for life.

A frightful history might be written of the brutalities committed on them, in Irish districts particularly; but desperate thieves and Irish ruffians did not always escape punishment.

The constable were selected for duty in particular localities, on account of their pluck, strength, and determination, and the result has proved that roughs of all kinds have found their masters; and localities that no stranger, even in broad daylight, dared venture into, may now be traversed at all hours of the night with the same security that one may walk down Regent Street at noonday.

But it was not only by downright brute force that the police gained the upper hand; it required a good deal of address, and not a little humouring of the rules tacitly established among the thieves themselves.

For instance, at a recognised house of resort for thieves, a constable would have little difficulty in taking into custody a culprit "on suspicion," provided he did not venture into their penetralia or show his staff.

Woe to the policeman who should be so incautious, or so foolhardy as to disregard this latter condition.

The reader may ask how it happened that public houses, known as the resort of thieves, were not reported to the licensing magistrates, and proceedings taken against the landlords, with a view of getting their licences suspended. The reason simply is—that it was found best to wink at such houses, because, in case of need, the police knew where to go in order to apprehend their man. If the known houses were suppressed, the thieves would resort to unknown houses, and the difficulties of the police would only be multiplied without the list of thieves' houses being either diminished or suppressed.

Sometimes the eagerness of young constables has resulted in fearful harm to themselves. A little while ago, a policeman went into one of these boozing kens, and, fearlessly walking in among the thieves, produced his staff, and claimed his man.

The upshot of that was, the whole body set upon him, and he was kicked to death.

The two who were with Charley were too experienced in the business to do that, unless all other measures failed. The one whom Charley had first addressed agreed to remain below while the other went up to demand his man.

Charley was directed to stay behind, but the boy was too impetuous: he rushed in, and kept at the constable's heels.

A number of ill-looking roughs were idling about; they glanced askance at the well-known "blue," but continued their drinking when he passed them unnoticed.

"Who's he come to nab now?" asked one.

"Don't know; unless it's Crusher Jem."

"Who's that kiddy?"

"A sneak he looks like."

Unheeding these remarks, the policeman walked up stairs and along a dim passage, at the end of which was a closed door.

Before they reached it, a sharp whistle was heard to sound through the house.

"That's the signal," said the peeler; "you'd better go back."

"I will never turn back till he is taken," Charley replied, his eye flashing.

The policeman said no more, but tapped at the door.

The gentleman who opened it was a powerful young ruffian, with a deep chest and short bull neck. As he stood with the door a little way open, he looked very much as if he would have liked to have given the peeler a dig in the body with a knife, and so got rid of him.

"What's the row?" he asked.

"The crusher is wanted," said the policeman, coolly.

"He ain't here."

"Go and look; you'll find him, I think."

"Tell you he ain't here."

"Come, come; go and look, my man."

The young ruffian glared murderously at the peeler. "He ain't here; you can't have him, can you, if he's somewhere's else?"

"Just go inside and ask for him."

"Who's that whelp?"

"That's my boy."

"Better send him away."

"I shall if necessary."

The emphasis laid on the word made the young bully understand what was meant.

"Jem ain't inside," he said, sullenly, as he shut the door.

"He'll escape," Charley said.

"No he won't; 45 is on the look out."

"But he's shut the door."

"They'll open it again, presently."

Charley was forced to remain content with this, though uneasy about it.

In a few moments the young fellow again appeared to tell the policeman what he had before said, that the crusher was not inside.

"Oh! he ain't there."

"No; and if he was, I should think him a precious softy to come out."

"Should you? look here, my man, the crusher is wanted; if he likes to come, all well and good; he'll stand his chance like many a good man before him. If he don't choose to come, I shall step in and take him."

"You'll what?"

"Come in and take him."

The policeman said this in a firm decisive tone.

"You know the rules, if you come inside you'll be malletted; and you won't get him without I can tell you."

"Very well: I've one or two waiting down stairs. I shall walk in if he don't walk out in one minute from this; in one minute after that if those outside don't hear me coming out there'll be enough here to take the lot of you."

"You may go to ———," said the ruffian, with a curse, as he slammed the door.

Charley looked up in the policeman's face to see how he would take this.

To his surprise he quietly leaned his back against the wall, and taking out a silver watch counted the seconds.

The minute passed.

The door remained closed.

He tapped against it with his knuckles.

No answer came.

He turned the handle.

The door was fastened by a bolt: a thrust of his foot forced it open with a crash.

Coolly putting back his watch the policeman entered the room followed by the brave boy, who was there to see the crusher captured.

A dozen voices cried out in terrible oaths; a score of bully ruffians came forward threatning.

The policeman looked calmly round till his glance fell on Crusher Jem.

That ruffian was surrounded by a number of admirers, who gave the policemen who came in looks that warned him of what he might expect.

He was about to speak when the crusher, glaring at Charley, cried—

"Pals, there's the whelp that blabbed before! look after the copper while I get hold of him."

Never did boy look so like a hero as Charley did.

The oaths of the ruffians who crept menacingly to the intruders, where as ferocious as coarse, some cried out "strangle the lives out of the pair;" others suggested choking, and many seemed inclined to carry out their own intent of beating them to death.

Amidst all this outcry the policeman stood quite unmoved. Only as Crusher Jem made a leap at Charley with his murderous bludgeon in his hand, he stepped in the way and took the ruffian by the collar.

"Game's up, Jem," he said quietly, "I don't want to call any more up, nor to take your pals."

Crusher Jem looked him savagely in the face; he even raised his bludgeon, but the calm determined glance of the "copper" disconcerted him.

Ruffian as he was he felt disconcerted by that steady look.

"Jem," continued the officer, "there's a jolly lot against you! don't make it worse by kicking up a dust; you must be lagged, and may as well take it like a lamb."

"If I do may I be cursed! Let go, or I'll smash in your skull!"

"No you won't, Jem; I havn't come here for that. Come along—wish your pals good bye."

The crusher's answer was a violent attempt to wrench himself away.

"I'll batter your nob to a jelly!" he cried, savagely.

"No, Jem, I'm not here alone: you'll only make the job worse if you kick."

"Curse you for a set of curs! Will you let him lag your mate?"

"No, no! mallet him!"

"Douse the glim, and let him have it."

As these cries rang through the room the crusher made a violent attempt to get loose, and tried to strike the policeman on the head, but here he found his match; the peeler had taken out his cudgel, and after parrying the ruffian's blow he gave him an admonitory tap on the head—a tap administered in the right place, and which, for the moment, almost knocked the bully silly.

The instant after he made so desperate an attempt at escape that Charley, who thought he had succeeded, sprang at him and clung to his arms.

"Dowse the glim," the crusher cried.

"Go down stairs, Charley," said the policeman, "and tell the others they're wanted."

This quiet speech had its effect in cowing the ruffians, who knew that if a number of police came there, they would all stand a chance of being marched off; but the crusher, getting one of his arms free, hurled his cap at the lamp, extinguishing the light.

He then gave the policeman such a terrible kick in the stomach, that he fell to the ground, relinquishing his hold of the crusher, who instantly seized Charley by the throat, and tried what he had before attempted—to strangle him.

The policeman rising with pain found himself attacked by a number of ruffians, who commenced beating him about the head and body in the most brutal manner. The crusher, meanwhile, was wreaking his revenge on poor Charley, and the pair would have been murdered there and then, if a whistle from below had not warned them of some one coming.

Scarcely had the whistle sounded when the door, which one of the thieves had fastened, was battered in: a light appeared, and Tiger Loo rushed into the room, followed by the policeman who had been below, and four others.

No sooner did the light, which emanated from a policeman's lantern, appear than the crusher giving poor Charley a finishing spiteful squeeze, pitched him to the floor, where the poor boy lay palpitating and almost lifeless.

The policeman who had been so brutally attacked was in no better condition; when the light came in amongst them, it showed him in the midst of six or seven powerful criminals, who were battering him about in the most sickening manner.

They now desisted from their brutality, and looked round for means of flight, while Crusher Jem sprang to the window.

Knocking down one of his own pals, who tried to get there before him, he was in the act of wrenching it open, when the voice of Tiger Loo arrested him.

She had flown to Charley whom she had raised and now supported with one arm; her eyes were flashing like stars, and her whole aspect was like that of an inspired fiend.

"Move, if you dare, Crusher Jem," she cried, "and I will shoot you if you do."

Her voice thrilled through the ruffian; he turned in fear, and beheld the vindictive girl he had deemed at the bottom of the well glancing passionately upon him, while her hand held a pistol which was pointed at his head.

"Ah! Jem; you did not expect me—if you move I'll shoot you like a cat."

Crusher Jem gnashed his teeth in fury, and, muttering a frightful oath, hurled his bludgeon at her and leapt to the window.

The instant after Tiger Loo's wild laugh rang through the room, followed by the report of the pistol; the crusher yelled a spiteful curse, placed his hand to his back, and fell to the floor.

By this time the police had been taking their measures; one stood at the door, while the others raised their illused comrade.

Bruised and battered as he was he was able to point out four of those who had astacked him; these were, after a little difficulty, collared and handcuffed, their pals standing in too much awe to attempt a rescue, and only too much gratified to find they were not taken.

These worthies being secured, and one of those who came crowding outside the room having been despatched for shutters, attention was bestowed on Crusher Jem, who, hitherto remaining groaning on the floor, was supposed to be safe enough.

Tiger Loo, after her wild tiger-like cry of vengeance, turned to the bruised and bleeding boy, whose head she supported.

He was in that state of stupor that he could not speak, but he glanced gratefully at the young girl, and seemed to speak his satisfaction when he saw the crusher fall.

Poor boy, he was severely hurt: and Tiger Loo, with flushed face and burning eye glared yet upon the crusher as if she would have liked to have lodged another bullet in his body.

In her tenderness for the brave innocent boy she kissed his cheeks and wiped the blood with her handkerchief from his beaten forehead.

The shutters was now brought, and Charley was laid upon one of them, the policeman on another; the crusher was strapped, the wound that had dropped him having been found to be not severe, but for the present quite disabling.

A great concourse of people were assembled outside, they gazed in morbid eagerness on the burdens carried on men's shoulders; first came the policeman lying on his back with his eyes closed, and his face smeared with blood, and looking as if he had already ceased to breathe.

Then came the slight form of Charley, whose gaze was turned piteously on men's faces,

Lastly, the crusher, whose teeth were heard to grind, and whose looks as he passed were those of an absolute savage.

People' could understand what it took to take him if he had pals on his side.

The police came after guarding their prisoner, who looked considerably chopfallen, and down in the mouth.

Tiger Loo walked with Charley, gaining the admiration of those who had heard of the part she had taken in the matter.

And in this manner they proceeded till they separated, for Charley and the policeman got to the hospital; the crusher was carried to prison to be attended by the medical officer, and then thrust into a cell.

And Tiger Loo followed to see Charley safe at the hospital, and hear the nature of his wounds.

She had cause for exultation: by the capture of the crusher the punishment that had been put upon herself was avenged, and she was elate.

But for Charley she was grieved.

The brave boy was not.

He had suffered severely from the vindictive fury of the crusher, but that ruffian was taken, and the boy believed his uncle would be safe.

CHAPTER LIII.

MARY TAKES A RASH STEP.

ON the cold night Mary was made the victim of her devilish wrongers, she was thrust out of the house of her betrayer, to bear against the inclemency of the weather, and the miseries of her destitute condition.

Destitute, indeed; for she was destitute of honor, virtue, of friends, and of means.

She was betrayed and abandoned.

They were bitter tears she wept for the first half hour, as she took her way wearily along; policemen eyeing her with suspicion, and the few loose characters, or dissolute men who were abroad at that hour, making her the subject of their coarse remarks.

It seemed at first all a dream, she could not realise what had befallen her, it was so stupendously wrong.

She loved Warner truly, and tenderly; he had exercised a spell over her, that had won her from Dick, from her home, from her love. In the deep faith of her simple mind, she had given up her truth and self-esteem to him, and this had been the end.

Whatever feelings she might have entertained for him, his arts and flatteries had cherished and increased them, and though she had been weak, she felt that it was due to him to be certain of her guilt before thrusting her forth.

There came at times swimming through her mind the dreadful thought that she had been made the victim of a fearful plot; the conviction of the truth, but which the single-hearted girl could not bring herself fully to credit, even after it had come upon her spirits with its frightful suspicions.

She could not think Warner already so base.

So she wandered on drawing her cloak round her weary form, and weeping and praying as she went.

Far, far from the house whence she had been cruelly ejected, many dreary miles and miles of road she passed, pausing with a sudden shock when she came in sight of the frowning walls of Newgate.

Dick had not been from her thoughts; but this brought his position in all its vividness to her mind. Within that prison, shut up in the condemned cell, was the lover of her early days; her promised husband—promised before Warner, with his glib tongue and foul heart, wiled her woman's truth away.

How quickly all the scenes of their youth came to her mind: she recalled each word of honest love he had spoken; how his honest tones thrilled upon her memory; they had never seemed fascinating, like the sleek accents of her seducer; but there was a frankness, a depth of truth about them, that she now contrasted painfully.

Never till then had she known how great a prize was his love—that love which she had cast aside, rejecting its simple worth for the false tinsel of the polished libertine.

And now was gone for ever all hope of being given the merest halo of his love—irretrievably, utterly, she was lost—an abandoned thing of shame—and her lover shut up within close stone walls, to eat his heart out in agony—the strong agony of a noble mind unjustly maligned—till the hour should come when they would bind him in every limb, and lead him out to yield his life by a violent death, before a gaping crowd.

Within those very walls he sat—those walls with their hard cold frown, that looked so dismally upon her. Outside those walls, so stern and grim, would he be led to suffer, and for a deed which she did not believe he had committed.

What a sting it had been to her, when, to make her misery more bitter, Warner, ere he hastened her from his house, had told her of Dick's fate, and bidden her go and perish like him.

And now she stood beneath the gloomy prison. It was too frightful to dwell upon, yet it lived vividly in her brain, with its maddening influence. Her heart seemed wrung from her breast, when, with that sad sob breaking from her lips, she tottered forward, and fell sinking on the stone by the gates of Newgate.

A few night wanderers, some houseless, like herself—some virtueless, as she was—some fallen, as it seemed she would be—passed her by. In the great Babel, who cares to pry into another's misery, save for selfish objects of their own?

Nobody stayed to notice her; or, if they caught a glimpse of her bowed form, turned their glance away, and went on—on—leaving her in her grief and her agony, and her loneliness.

St. Sepulchre's clock struck three. The anguished woman started, and clenched her hands together.

And she murmured—

"Oh, Dick! dearest Dick! would that we had never lost each other."

And then she sobbed and wept again. She could but think that, through her levity and her faithlessness, these miseries had fallen upon herself and Dick.

For she never knew how truly she loved him till now, when she knew how unworthy she was of him, and when, if worthy, the iron hand of destiny had snatched them apart for ever.

Poor sinful, simple girl! all the tears she could shed would not restore an atom of that self-esteem which had gone when she gave herself up to betrayal: all her moans and sighs would not open those stone walls, nor reach the ears of him who was held in bondage within.

She had wandered wilfully from the true path, and now all this evil had come upon her.

Think of this, ye whose ears are made glad with the libertine's soft language; think of this, ere ye forsake home lovers—virtue for the foul fancies of gilded deceit, casting yourselves on a rock that must shatter your peace for ever.

Think of what must come, when the first wrong step is taken, for there is no recalling the past; and the weary heart that is broken, when the tabernacle of chastity is ruined, may find no rest till the body ends its lingering death.

It seemed to Mary, in that hour of blighting sorrow, that her future was unfolded to her view. She saw herself alone and friendless—despised by the good—shunned by the pitying—and sinking deeper and deeper into the abyss of vice, till she became one of those wan, bedizened, ghastly things, whose lives are infamy and loathsomeness.

She saw herself in the last stage of disease, seeking oblivion from life as so many others have sought, in the dull waters, in whose depths were immersed the woe and awfulness of her ghastly wasted features.

She rose from the hard stone, the picture was so terrible.

"I will never be this," she cried. "If I am to die in my misery it shall be now. Dick, dear Dick, farewell! I would kiss these walls but that they are so hateful to hide you from my sight. Farewell! if I have brought you to this and cannot save you, I can die before you."

She was turning quickly away when a hand arrested her and a voice said—

"Stay, daughter. What meaneth this? Hath thy mind so little peace? Pause ere you rashly fly the face of your Maker."

It was an elderly saintly-looking man who addressed her. He was attired in black, and by his appearance as well as his words, seemed to be a minister.

Mary hid away her face and shed copious tears.

He who had interrupted her took her hand and gently strove to look into her face. It seemed that his hand pressed rather firmly on the soft, fair arm; but Mary in her agitation did not notice it; she only wondered who could be found to take pity or interest in such as her.

"Come," he said, tenderly, "dry those tears: look up: there is mercy for such as humbly kneel at His footstool."

"Ah, sir," Mary cried, "but I am very wretched."

"None are so wretched, but they may obtain comfort."

"Oh, no, no; I am too guilty: there is no peace for such as me."

"There is peace for all," her interrogator replied, raising his eyes to Heaven; "come, my daughter, let me lead you from these walls: we can converse as we go, and I will strive to lift your heart to Him who washes out the sins of the erring."

Mary, looking sadly through her tears, strove to calm herself and answer him.

It seemed that he had already overheard enough to make him understand the cause of her grief; for, as she was murmuring Dick's name, he said,

"I see, child; you have some one inside these walls whom you love."

"Nay, sir, in the condemned cell."

"Ah, dear me, that's shocking; and pray what is he there for?"

"It is murder, sir, they say; but it is not true."

"Sad, very sad."

"It is sad, and I am the cause."

"Do not weep, daughter; you may yet be comforted."

"How—while he is there?"

"You would wish to see him, perhaps?"

Mary clasped her hands together.

"Oh, sir, if I could.

"Well, well, come with me; I will see what is to be done. It is possible, that I may be able to procure you the liberty of seeing him."

"Oh, sir; if you could do that."

"Now be calm, mind I don't say I can for a certainty, but I think I can; I am the chaplain, and shall have every opportunity of getting you the interview."

"If I may see him," Mary said, "I shall die content."

"Tut! dont talk of dying, something may turn up yet that may set things to rights."

"He may not blame me," Mary continued, mournfully "but I can but know that I am the cause; it is through me that he has come to this; and, though I suffer in being what I am, I shall not be able to save him."

"Things have happened that have seemed improbable; accompany me, we will get into a cab, and ride to my residence, my wife's maid is sure to be up; she can conduct you to a chamber, where you can remain till morning: we will then see about visiting this unhappy man, when we can hear what he has to say in the matter of forgiveness."

Mary glanced at the face of the speaker; he was a hoary sanctified individual, but not exactly the sort of being one would have liked to trust implicitly with his wife or grown up daughter.

To Mary there was nothing suspicious in the fact of his offering to conduct her to his house: it was only an act of kindness for which she was grateful.

Had she known more of the world, she would have learnt less to trust the wolves in sheep's clothing that prowl about our streets.

Giving a last weary glance at the dim walls, she turned away with her conductor, who forthwith proceeded to hail a cab.

Mary suffered him to hand her into it: she was too sad and wretched to attend to his manner or listen to the address he gave the cabman, or see the halfcrown slipped into the cab's hand.

She sat far back in the seat, and kept her face hidden with her hands.

The good samaritan sat on the other seat; his grey fishy eyes were fixed on the face of the young girl, and a peculiar look at times beamed from them.

Mary did not take much heed of the time, but it appeared to her that they had been a long while on their way, and she was about to call his attention to the fact, when she found that he had pushed himself so much forward that his knees were against her dress.

She shifted back, and the good samaritan bent forward from his seat, and putting his arms swiftly round her waist, pulled her forward, attempting to kiss her.

This outrage aroused Mary's indignation; but the pseudo-chaplain was not in the least degree disconcerted; he got closer to her, and murmured proposals which made the young outraged girl turn cold to hear.

"Who and what are you," she cried, "to take advantage of a friendless girl? I have been bitterly enough used; God help me, I need no further sorrow."

"My dear girl, let not the flesh prevail, I will be your protector; you will find it much more comfortable living with me than wandering about the streets by yourself all night. Now, don't be cross."

"Sir—base man: let me get out at once."

"Now, don't be captious."

"You are vile, sir; you told me you were the chaplain of that prison, a minister."

"So I am, my daughter, a minister."

"Then you disgrace the sacred calling; the wolf in sheep's guise. What misfortune threw me in your way!"

She screamed for help.

The cab stopped.

Mary got to the window, and gazed out.

A dark lonely place it was she looked upon. A place for violence.

A place for *murder*.

Most women would have been alarmed at finding herself in such a position.

She was in an out-of-the-way spot with two men, each, as it seemed, unscrupulous villains.

Such spots as these were generally noted for crimes of the worst order.

All this came to Mary's mind as she met the look of the godless minister; but she was not the one to quail.

If she had been betrayed by one miscreant, it did not follow that she was to be any one's leman; and, as the sanctified villain took hold of her, she thrust him back, and opened the door of the cab.

They were in a lonely out-of-the-way place: a dull lane with nothing but barren wastes and ruined brickfields on either side.

Mary would have been the prey of her cowardly assailants if her screams had not been heard by one whom they least expected to find on the spot, and who came to the rescue as Mary was forced to the ground.

This individual was Roving Rob, who, escaped from the police who that day had him in charge, had been prowling about that suburban vicinity ever since—afraid to venture near his old haunts for fear of being seized.

"Hullo!" he cried, as he came in sight, "I should know that voice, as the kitten said to the bear. What, nobbing on to a lady? Here I is then, in among you like a monkey in a hay stack."

Mary found strength to wrest herself from the minister's grasp, and cry again for help.

Roving Rob did not need the summons.

Armed with a heavy knobbed stick he sprang amongst them, letting his cudgel fall first on the head of the minister, whom it sent on his back to the ground, and then on the nob of the cabby, who after one tap, staggered on to his box and whipped his horse away.

"Here I ar', I ar'," cried Rob; "only say which of your turns it is next, and I'm your man, as lively as a mouse in a corn bin; get up you white-chokered white-livered robber; get up and be off, or I'll make your head ache for a week with bruises."

The sacerdotal ruffian did not wait for further visitations; he slunk off limping and aching, and Mary stood looking on the bronzed face of her rescuer.

"Now, marm," said Rob, "whosoever you be, let's hear which way you wants to go, and if you are—why, stigger me—no—if it ain't—it can't be—what! Mary?"

She had not recognised him till then, but now she remembered his face.

Roving Rob made some very queer flourishes with his stick.

Then he danced nimbly round the village girl.

Finally he stopped and looked hard at her.

"Well now," he said at length, "I don't know whether I ought to be glad or sorry at meeting you here; I'm glad nevertheless, noways notwithstanding that I helped you from them gemmen; but tell me, for his sake, ar' it all square with you: have you comed up to find him, or—I'll tell you your answer afore I say any more."

"I cannot answer you," Mary rejoined, sadly; "I am more guilty than you can conceive; but Dick, poor Dick, he is shut up in prison, to die."

The manner of Rob changed.

"I thought, at first, you might have come to look arter him, seeing how true he was to you: but I don't know why I should have expected it. Harkee lass, Dick is lagged and is like to swing, and you may just thank yourself as the cause; if you hadn't been and gone along of that fellar, he never would have done what he did."

Mary, who had hung her head at the rebuke, hastily exclaimed—

"But he is not guilty of this crime."

"They've found him guilty, and they'll hang him just the same."

"Oh! no, no, no."

"But it's yes, yes, yes."

"Poor, poor Dick."

"Poor! I won't be harsh; but what do the likes of you care what becomes on him; not you. Go back, Mary, to the fellar you left Dick for; see how long he'll be to you what Dick would have been."

"Oh, help me; you know something of this; you can say he is not guilty."

"Well, I might, but they wouldn't believe me no more than if I was Balaam's ass."

"But you can try and make some effort to save him."

"There ain't the ghost of a chance."

"Oh, God! what shall I do? my heart will break."

Rob looked at her earnestly; he was far from feeling what he himself was saying: on the contrary, he had resolved to give himself up, and make a clean breast of it, taking the chances of being strung up, to seeing Dick die unjustly; but he would not tell Mary so, because he thought she deserved some punishment for deserting Dick.

But these heartbreaking words touched him, and he was on the point of relenting, when Mary suddenly exclaimed—

"Let me thank you for saving me from those men. I would not have been willingly their victim. You may see dear Dick again; tell him you saw me; that I begged forgiveness; that I die, because whether he lives or dies, I cannot but shun his path."

"Die, be blowed."

"Peace: I have lived too long; you need not seek to stay me—I am too resolved, and come what will shall consummate my purpose."

"If you do, may I be—"

The rest of Rob's speech was lost, for Mary, bounding from where she stood, dashed up the lane.

Rob did not hurry himself at first, as he had no doubt of being able to catch her; but when he reached a part where he was enabled to see a long way up the lane, he was surprised to find that she was out of sight.

"If that ain't as good as the ghost," muttered Rob, as he quickened his pace.

Turning the bend of a lane he came plump in the arms of a policeman.

"Hullo," cried Rob.

"Hold up," said the peeler.

"Seen a woman up this way?"

"No; but I've seen some one I want."

"That's me, is it?"

"You're the man, Roving Rob?"

"That's likely, but not this time, thank you. I'm off, as Joe the groom said, when he tried to ride the malicious horse, and got pitched through the sky-light."

And, so saying, he gave the peeler a tremendous "buster" on the top of the hat, and, knocking it down over his eyes, gave him a finishing punch in the belly, which enabled him to knock the breath out of his body, and made the best of his flight after Mary.

But she had somewhere disappeared, and, after hunting about till morning, Rob was compelled to give up the chase.

This was vexing to him: he was not earnest in the cruel words he had said to Mary. He read the young girl's character, and knew how she had been wiled away, and that her goodness of nature was her own punishment.

The remembrance of the state of excitement she was in made Rob very uncomfortable: he was too much afraid that she would keep her word.

It was, indeed, Mary's intention. After eluding Rob, she had hurried on, never caring which way her steps took her, and yearning for some vehicle to approach, that she might cast herself under its wheels, and end her existence.

Daylight came, and found her still wandering on in the same weary frame of mind. She found herself now in a more frequented neighbourhood; long dingy lanes, with old tottering houses on either side, appeared whichever way she turned. At one or two places there were coffee stalls, at which great lumbering fellows, with heavy boots and weather-beaten sou'westers, were standing. A few dirty little shops were open, and the same class of boatmen-looking people were issuing from or entering them.

From these and other signs Mary concluded that she was near the water's edge.

It was so; she was in one of those little frequented neighbourhoods at Blackwall, and every step she made was taking her nearer to the Thames.

There was a wild fluttering at her heart when she first caught sight of the murky river. A large vessel lay at some distance, and she could yet see its spars peeping, as it were, from behind the houses.

At that early hour she believed the deed she intended might be committed without interruption: she could cast herself into the water, and, unseen, unknown, go down to the bottom, and rest there for ever.

Now the river opened out more fully on her view: the damp cold air came from the bank; an incline of rough stones led to the side of the water; and the self-doomed girl rushed frenziedly down these natural steps, her gaze fixed on the welcome water.

Her only eagerness was that she might soon reach its depths. She had looked behind her to see that none came after her. A few steps more, and she would be on the brink. Now! she is down! she has not taken her glance off the river; and only a moment she stays poised on the rude pier of stone and planks, ere she takes the fatal leap.

But before she recovered again, a rough voice arrested her.

"There miss, this way; the boat's just about to start."

A shock coursed through Mary's frame: she stood still, shivering, and then looked round.

A rough, but honest looking waterman, was standing within a few paces of her; a little to his left was a boat, in which two persons, an old woman and a young girl, were seated.

In her wildness, Mary had not noticed them, and now she stood glancing frenziedly in the face of the boatman, who repeated his observations, and asked—

"Ferry you over, miss?"

Mary looked at him and the people who were in the boat, and whose glances were fixed wonderingly upon her. A moment's thought deterred her from taking the fatal step then; and, hardly knowing what she did, she suffered the boatmen to lead her down the steps.

She took her seat unconsciously in the boat, the passengers staring at her white jaded face, and marvelling at her agitation; the ferryman grasped the oars, and pulled away from the shore.

What maddening emotions still chased through the veins of Mary as she went further and further from the shore; it made her head swim as she gazed on the cold still waters, swelling and rising around her.

She half rose from her seat as a wilder thought possessed her, to drown herself while the boatman was busy with his oars.

She found the old fellow's glance fixed on her, and sat down again.

It was very tempting to look on the swelling waters, and feel herself gliding over them, when a plunge, a movement, would place her beneath; once or twice she had nerved herself for the leap, but each time the look of the old boatman restrained her.

But at length she had worked herself to such a pitch of nervous frenzy, that she could sit there no longer; jumping up, suddenly, she, before the old ferryman had time to lay down his oars, sprang to the side, and leaped with a splash into the river.

The water, dashed up by her plunge, splashed in the faces of those in the boat; the waterman stopped instantly, and laid his oars inside.

So quick had Mary's act been, that the screams of the passengers had hardly been given, when she rose again to the surface a little way off.

The boatman instantly threw off his jacket, and jumped in after her, having first thrown an oar to the spot.

But Mary's pale sad face as instantaneously disappeared.

The old boatman waited till she came up again, when he made a plunge towards her, and succeeded in catching her by the shawl before she sank again.

Mary had so unresistingly given herself to her fate, that, even when the boatman caught hold of her, she was nearly past all aid: the water was rushing in at her ears and down her throat; but, with the horrible sensation of drowning, she was willing to die.

The boatman's first care was to get Mary's head above water, his next was to grasp the oar with one hand; but, by this time the boat had been carried so far away with the tide, that, with his burthen, he found it impossible to reach it.

They had both then been drowned, the helpless woman, who sought death as relief from misery, and the gallant old fellow who had come to the rescue, if it had not been that the whole affair had been seen by a younger ferryman, who was hastily rowing to the spot.

It was a hard pull against the tide, but he got there in time to take the inanimate form of Mary and lay her in his boat, while her brave rescuer, almost exhausted, scrambled into his.

"I had my doubts of her, poor lass," he said, "when I saw her come down first and stand on the edge by the water; but I thought I'd keep my weather eye open." How is she?"

"Dead, I'm afraid."

"Never; let's hope not. Here, let's get her across; put your fares into my boat, and I'll have her across in a jiffey."

The passengers got into the other boat, but the young ferryman refused to let the old man take the labour of pulling swiftly ashore.

"You may take my fares," he said; "and can pull easily, while I scud across."

Mary lay quite inanimate at the bottom of the boat: on the other side of the water a number of people were already gathered, who had been drawn to the spot by the report of the intended suicide, and many a glance of pity, and more of curiosity, were turned on the pale form which was lifted ashore.

"Bear a hand, my hearties," cried the young fellow.

Half-a-dozen instantly came to his aid; they lifted Mary, whom they placed on a blanket, and carried ashore.

A medical man was quickly fetched; but, before he arrived, Mary had been carried into a house, and the usual methods adopted by anxious people to restore the drowned to life were being adopted.

Poor Mary, she lay so calm and deathly, without a throb or a trace of colour, that all their trouble seemed vain.

Had Dick seen her then, he would have forgiven her all: even Warner, villain that he was, must have felt some compunction.

Mary, however, was not to die yet; she had more to endure: a darker fate than she had conceived was in store for her.

But of that anon.

CHAPTER LIV.

TIGER LOO MAKES A PLAN FOR DICK'S ESCAPE FROM NEWGATE.

DICK was tried for murder and sentenced.

Sentenced to death.

The day on which he was to die was fixed.

There seemed no hope for him.

The judge who tried him had forwarded his recommendations to the Home Secretary, stating his opinion that Dick was deserving of mercy.

But the Home Secretary did not see any grounds for interference.

What was it to him if one man more were executed in the course of the year?

It was only one more in figures.

People must be hanged at times, or where would be the use of having the law?

Nobody had been hanged either of late.

DICK ESCAPING FROM NEWGATE.

It was quite time a treat was afforded for the people; a treat when they could, without paying anything, see a man strangled to death.

So the day was fixed, and all that class who attend executions began to speculate upon how Dick would die.

Some said he would die game.

Others that he would show the white feather at the last moment.

Some that he would prove too much for the executioner, and make his escape when the rope was being put round his neck.

Many again said that for fear of this an extra body of police were to be out that morning.

All these and similar matters did the gallows-attenders discuss.

Nobody stopped to inquire whether Dick was innocent or guilty.

Crusher Jem had been carefully attended by the doctor, in order that he might be brought up for trial.

But Crusher Jem didn't want to be tried just yet.

So, when the doctor reported Jem quite ready for trial, Jem got a penny-piece and, at night, had it bandaged over the wound.

The doctor didn't know what was the matter with that nearly-healed-up sore.

It was inflamed and humoury.

But he quietly dressed it again.

Then it began once more to heal.

The doctor made his second report.

Jem put on the penny a second time.

The doctor was a second time puzzled.

So the trial was delayed.

But the third time Jem tried the dodge the doctor had his eyes open to his customer; he popped back all of a sudden one night, just as Jem had got the penny comfortably on.

Jem was altogether taken aback by this, especially as, to pay him for his exertions in the cause of science, the doctor got him sentenced to receive ten lashes by way of a commencement.

But still Jem's purpose was secured.

The wound had got so poisoned that it now refused to heal: Jem almost lost his life over that.

But the doctor brought him round at last.

He had taken a great interest in Jem, he had.

Often had he looked at the crusher's neck, and pondered on the effect a rope, being drawn suddenly tight round it by Jem's being dropped through a trap in the gallows, would have.

And to satisfy his mind, which was curious on this point, he used his greatest care to get Jem nicely round in time for the next sessions.

But as all this had nothing to do with Dick's sentence, inasmuch as he had been proved guilty, he was quietly told he might prepare himself for the cold job on the Monday morning.

Dick's heart seemed turned black at the intimation.

He could have choked the man that brought him the news.

He had heard of the capture of the crusher, and of Charley's misfortune.

He did not expect to see the faithful boy again.

But Charley got round much quicker than the crusher, and came to see his uncle.

The meeting in the condemned cell was very affecting.

Poor Charley was reduced almost to a skeleton.

But Dick seemed to have grown stronger with his imprisonment.

He was a fine stalwart fellow, and looked more powerful with each day's growth.

A ripe subject for the hangman's hand.

The last one, Calcraft had been heard to say, was not worth the trouble of hanging.

There had not been an ounce of life in him.

He had been hanged because his wife was found dead, and somebody said he had killed her.

And that somebody got him hanged.

But Dick promised to be a fine subject.

He grasped Charley's hands fervently when the gaoler showed the boy in.

"I never expected to see you again," he said.

"You will see me out of this place," Charley cried.

"No, no, lad; I have had my run."

"I will not believe it; no, Dick, we shall get you free yet."

"I hope you may, Charley, but I am without hope."

"Dick," Charley said, "will see you any one besides me?"

"Who?"

"Some one you have been much with."

"Be it Roving Rob?"

"No, Dick, one you were more fond of."

"Only one besides you, lad. It be not her—not Mary?"

The drops of agony stood on Dick's brow now.

"Oh, Charley!" he cried, "I did not think I should be like this, ashamed to see her because I was made worse than she."

"But you will see her, will you not?"

"See her! be she here? no, no; she would not come."

"She is here."

"Here? let her come then, Charley, if I never see her again."

A low sob sounded from the door, it was opened, and a female form fluttered into the room.

Heavens! could that be Mary, that pale ghost-like creature, emaciated and wretched.

Dick could scarcely deem it possible that he looked on Mary.

He did not know what she had endured since he had last seen her, nor what she had suffered since her rescue from her attempted suicide.

They had brought her up to the police court for attempted suicide, and there Tiger Loo had seen her, and hearing her mention Dick's name, had no doubt from what she had before heard that she looked upon the wreck of the fair country girl who was his betrothed.

So Tiger Loo offered to take care of her, and nothing particular standing against Tiger Loo at the time, she was allowed that privilege.

And thus Tiger Loo, who herself loved Dick, got acquainted with Mary, and in that condition Charley saw her, and induced her to come to Dick.

Poor Dick, his heart bled as he looked on the corpse-like girl.

He forgot in a moment how she had wronged him, the memory of old touched him to tenderness, he opened his arms, and Mary, who had stood humbly aloof fell on to his breast.

Then was heard one heavy deep sob of grief, so heartrending and agonised, that the turnkey felt his eyes grow moist, while Dick let the tears gather in his eyes and roll down his cheeks.

"My poor poor one," Dick muttered, "like myself foully used by the world; would that I had one day of freedom, that I might rend the heart from the villian who has made you thus."

"Oh, Dick, Dick, do not look kindly on me, I am a thing that you should shun; too debased for you even to speak to, I have sought to die, but they would not let me; and I have come to see you before I end my wretchedness."

"I would that I could end it for thee, Mary, but not in the way you mean; I would end it by making you happy."

"You could not forgive me."

"I would forgive all but him who has made you this; for him I would not pause till my hands clutched his liver and dragged it from his vile chest."

The strong youth strode across the cell, while Mary hung her head in shame and sorrow.

"If I had him here," muttered Dick, grating his teeth and clenching his fingers, as he looked at Mary and thought of all that had occurred between her and her betrayer; "I would choke his black heart, though I were torn in pieces for it."

"Come, come, Parker," said the warder, "don't take on like this."

"You don't know what a villain he be," Dick answered, though recalled to himself by the man's words; "they don't know that he and Master Rolfe did a murder for which I was taken up; but for which, mark me, they will yet swing, if they don't for others as well."

As Dick spoke, Mary turned as cold as death; it seemed as if a winding sheet damp from the grave had been thrown over head.

She shuddered, and Dick, who saw her agitation but attributed it to doubt of his words, again spoke—

"You don't believe me, Mary; you wouldn't believe me before when I told you what a bad man he was, but the day will come when you will see it's true."

"I do believe you, Dick."

"No, thee don't, Mary; you think you do: but when you go from here, you'll forget what I've said. No matter, I'll not speak of the past; it has driven me to things I never thought I should come to: I've been put in prison like a felon, and now am to die like a convicted criminal; but I've one consolation, Mary, I have never done any dishonest act: I've stole no man's money, nor forgot that I was a man."

Dick looked noble then; Charley crept up to him, and took his hands.

"Noble, dear Dick, you have done right in spite of all temptations; and, when you are released, it will be with an honest name."

"It will be *when* he is released," thought the warder, who now informed them that they must take their departure, the time allowed for their visit having more than expired.

The scene that followed tried even the stolid nerves of the hardened warder; Mary clung, shrieking, to Dick; and, when she was borne away, it was only because she had fainted, and could no longer resist.

To Dick it seemed that he had looked upon Mary for the last time; it was now Friday, and Monday was the day fixed for his execution: the poignant anguish he had suffered during the interview with Mary, convinced him that she was not yet totally shut out from his heart, however he might try to banish her memory from her sinfulness with Warner.

The only manner in which this acted was to make him rage inwardly, because he could not retaliate on Warner before he died; he had looked with a tender eye on the charms of the pretty-faced village girl, and there was bitterness indeed in the thought, that the sweet flower he had longed to prize and cherish had been despoiled of its fragrance by the hand of a libertine.

So when Mary was gone, he set himself down on the hard bench, and, with his teeth harshly grating, hid his face in his clenched hands, and groaned frenziedly.

The warder, accustomed to worse demeanor, sat himself silently down, and, folding his arms, paid no further attention to the prisoner than a casual glance.

Not that the man was thoroughly bad at heart, but custom assimilates a man taking to every of human wretchedness, and Dick was merely a sentenced criminal awaiting execution for murder.

And, as we have before said, on Monday he was to die.

That is to say, if no means could be found of getting the sentence deferred.

Of that there was only one chance since the application of the judge had failed.

And that was Dick's escape from Newgate.

Which escape was already being planned, though Dick was not suffered at present to know anything about it till everything was ready, and the hour for action had come.

Tiger Loo's desperate brain was at work on this scheme, and she had an able aid in Charley, who cared not what befel himself so that Dick was got safely out of prison.

Besides Tiger Loo, there was the Downy Cove, who was ready to do his best for Dick.

The trio were discussing the matter the evening after the visit to Dick in Newgate.

Mary was not with them: firstly, because Tiger Loo thought it would be unwise to trust an inexperienced girl with so important a matter; and, secondly, because she was so ill that the good-natured fallen girl had insisted upon putting her to bed.

"Strikes me," said the Downy Cove, "that we shall have to use all our bumps if we get him out."

"It is a desperate essay: poor Dick," said Charley.

"Desperate or not, let us try, we can but fail," was Tiger Loo's impetuous answer.

"Which it ar', right it ar'; this is the way, my nobby young 'uns: the big bear is just about to swallow up a child like a toasted muffin; here I ar', I ar'. Who says? your own price, remember; and no blessed do about it."

These words, uttered in a very familiar tone, caused the Downy Cove to leap up, while Tiger Loo and Charley looked in astonishment at the intruding head which was that of a valiant and whiskered guardsman, and was thrust in at the door in a cool defiant sort of style.

"Blessed if I ain't glad to see so many birds of a feather stuck together. Downy, give us your fin, as the whale says to the porkypine; Loo, I'm your man; Charley, if it's yourself that shudder, I sees, as the man what fed on herrings' heads says, when he twigs hisself in the water, why, I ar' glad to see you, I ar'."

"Roving Rob," cried Charley, springing up.

"Which it's my name, ain't Norval, it ain't."

"Beloved brother," snuffled the Downy Cove, shaking Rob warmly by the hand; "have evil men prevailed against you?"

"I'm here with adventures enough to break the back of a blessed drummerderry."

"You have come in time," exclaimed Charley; "Dick is in prison, and we want to get him out."

"And Rob's in prison, and we want to get him out," said that worthy, drawing himself with difficulty out of the guardsman's jacket, and pulling off the false whiskers and moustache. "Aha! Downy, they've lagged me once or twice since that eventful day that I was collared all in a heap; they nabbed me, but they forgot to stop up the chimbley where they stuck me, and so I got out, I did. I should have been copped again as safe as a blessed mouse, if I hadn't pitched into a fellar as wore these togs and got 'em over my own; but draw it mild. Dick's goosed, leastways unless we get him out, which ar' I see by your hies what you are a trying at."

"We are," Charley exclaimed; "they won't let him go, though they've got the brute that deserves hanging twenty times."

"The crusher," remarked the Downy.

"I've heard all about it," said Rob; "and you'll be in a pretty mess, like the bloke as fell into the treacle tub, if you don't look out. What are you going to do to get Dick out—blow Newgate down?"

"We can manage another way," said Loo.

Rob shook his head.

"Oh, ar', no easy matter to get out of Newgate."

"He will never get out if we sit on our thumbs, and say we can't do anything."

"Nobody means to, but which way, young fiery girl, do you think of doing the business?"

"We must get in with an order to see him for the last time; somebody must manage the warder, and Dick must come out instead of somebody who goes in."

"I tumble; and a nice way too. Well, we'll see what can be done, as little Joe said, when he fried his mammy's gold fish on the gridiron. I think this child can make up for a warder."

"But who will take Dick's place?"

"That blessed sweet picter of innocence," answered Rob, pointing to the Downy.

"*Me?*" said that worthy.

"You'll do with a little jamming up; we must crop your hair and give you a wig, and make you look broader and not look a hingy rubber hook; and then you'll look summit like Dick: not much though, unless the bloke that makes you up gets you to turn out wonderfully."

"Indeed, what's the matter with me?" asked the Downy, meekly.

"Why, a more orkard hobject it ain't never been my lot to diskiver; turn him round, ladies and gentleman, look at his tail which he keeps covered by his coat; he walks with his knees rubbing each other out of the way, and his toes a kicking of——"

"The devil," interrupted the Downy Cove.

"Werry much like him."

"Is this attempt to be made?" asked Loo.

"In course."

"You will be the warder?"

"I will, as they says in church."

"The Downy's to be Dick."

"He ar'."

"What am I to do?" Charley inquired.

"Keep your blessed heels cool till Dick's got out."

"A word," observed the Downy; "am I to be heinously locked up?"

"You ar'."

"And am I to swing instead of Dick?"

"No: it will be quite enough when you swing for yourself."

The Downy Cove was fired at this insult, but the fist of Roving Rob being big and his boot thick, he thought proper to pocket the affront.

CHAPTER LV.

THE ATTEMPT AT ESCAPE.

Our readers may not have been inside Newgate, even as visitors; we trust they will never go there in any other capacity.

They may, perhaps, not have heard much about the condemned cell.

But we dare say most of them have seen the walls of Newgate.

Not, we trust, on a morning of execution.

It is a terrible thing for a fellow-creature to be throttled in cold blood by a man whom he has done no injury to.

It is terrible for that man who is paid for the work, and receives the dead culprit's clothes.

But it is shocking to see a heedless, mocking, jesting crowd gazing, swearing, robbing at the gallows foot, while a human being is being deprived of life.

The walls of Newgate, then, are known to be very strong: the cells are secure; there are gaolers and warders ever on the alert.

But chiefly secure and guarded in the condemned cell.

They are careful of his life when condemned to die; warders sit up with him, and all that bars, bolts, and thick walls can do is done to keep him safe within till the morning of execution.

Roving Rob knew all this when he agreed to Tiger Loo's plan for getting Dick out.

He did not think there was much chance of doing it, but for the sake of Dick and Charley he made up his mind to do his best.

An order was got for them on the following morning to see Dick for the last time.

"The last time in quod," Rob thought and hoped.

At an early hour he began to get the Downy Cove in trim. He jammed him up till he was as straight as Dick, padded out his shoulders, threw forward his chest, and finally divested him of his flowing locks.

The Downy bore all but the last in patient meekness, but his spirit nevertheless *did* rebel at the thought of being cropped, as he himself expressed it, "like a prig."

But Rob cut him short with a slip of the shears, and the Downy said no more.

A wig and whiskers of a sandy hue, now overcased the Downy's cropped head, and Rob pronounced him a do.

The pair of them then repaired to Newgate; a halfcrown from Rob dropped in the palm of the goaler, made that functionary very civil.

"Passed a dreadful night," he said, alluding to Dick, "been a grinding of his teeth to powder almost and tearing up splinters of the bench."

Dick evinced unmistakeable tokens of having suffered greatly in the four-and-twenty hours; his face was wildly haggard, and but little like his former self.

Charley went silently to him, and pressed his hand, "You've come again," he said, "I did'nt expect I should see you any more?"

"We would not leave you, Dick."

"Not till the last moment," snuffled the Downy.

"Not till the last moment," hysterically cried Loo.

"Not till the last moment," muttered Rob.

Dick glanced in surprise, from one to the other.

The Downy Cove had his handkerchief to his eyes.

Roving Rob was clenching his fist, grinding his heel on the stones, &c.

Tiger Loo was in paroxysm of tears.

They had their parts to play, and were playing them. Suddenly Loo fell forward on the breast of Dick.

"I can't part from you, dear Dick," she screamed, "I can't let them kill you, oh, Dick, Dick, Dick!"

She sank, sobbing, hysterically.

Dick was very much astounded at the exuberance of affection displayed by Tiger Loo, but he strove to assuage her grief.

The young girl, however, only became more violent.

"How she do take on," observed Rob, to the warder. "Poor thing, he's been werry good to her, and it's hard to part with her."

"It's hard, certainly."

"Oh, ar'."

"Pity he did it."

"Pity I can't wring your neck," thought Rob.

The warder was certainly moved by Tiger Loo's grief; he saw a young, pretty, and interesting looking girl overcome with wild emotion, and really believing the whole scene to be sincere, he turned away and looked towards the grating.

Rob slipped a crown piece in his hand.

"Thanks," he said, "their parting will be sad."

"Don't mention it," replied the warder, "grief should have no intruder."

He pocketed the crown.

Nothing could now be heard, but the sobs of Loo, and Dick's occasional smothered groan.

The warder kept his glance resolutely on the bars. Rob slipped the Downy's wig off, and put it on Dick's head.

Dick, in astonishment, would have spoken, but Tiger Loo, with a fresh burst of grief, placed her arms round his neck and stopped him.

The whiskers now went on.

He began to realize what was meant, and would have regretted the idea of escape, by placing another in jeopardy, but Tiger Loo's raving look, and the supplicating gaze of Charley, kept him silent.

"I cannot bid you farewell," cried Loo.

"Come, come," said Rob, "we must bear this separation; try and bear up, and say good bye."

He lugged the Downy's coat off.

"No, no," sobbed Loo, "I cannot leave those dear, dear lips I have kissed, never to kiss again."

"Remember, we shall meet in heaven," snuffled the Downy, who was being thrust into Dick's jacket.

The remainder of his attire had been prepared by the skilful Rob, in exact fac-simile of Dick's, and a finishing touch made the transformation complete.

Dick hardly comprehending the matter, stood the long-haired ginger whiskered visitor. The Downy hardly knew himself as the cropped convict.

A great fuss was now made of taking leave, and after an affecting scene, Rob tore Loo from the Downy's arms, and the Downy hiding his face in his hands, sunk to the hard bench, and appeared to give way to the most acute anguish.

The gaoler, unsuspicious of the change that had been made, turned and whispered to Rob.

"You'd better get her away, before he's violent."

"Right," said Rob, who was more anxious to get her away, than the warder thought.

Loo also was eager to be outside those hated walls, but it was necessary that she should make a little more display of acting.

She made a vigorous attempt to get back to the supposed prisoner, but Rob held her firmly, and with a great show of gentle force, got her to the door of the cell.

Dick and Charley, the former walking as if in advance, brought up the rear, and were given by the warder to the fellow who was to conduct them out.

One more scream from Loo, a miserable groan from the Downy; the first part of the play was over.

Dick was outside the cell, with the door closed upon him by the warder, who was placed there expressly to see that he did not get out.

The condemned cell opens upon a stone corridor, a ghastly horrible place where they lay the bodies of the culprits after they have been hanging the accustomed time.

It sounded hollow and well-like, as Dick walked over it; he who had been condemned to walk above it in life, before going out upon the scaffold to return carried in a shell to be placed beneath the flags that he had so short a time before trodden upon.

Others besides him had these feelings, but there was no time for interchange of thought; the gaoler hurried them away, and they on their part were eager to quit the gloomy precincts of the prison.

The gaoler once or twice looked very hard at Dick, and then at Roving Rob. Tiger Loo, who was watching every change that took place, knew it; and that his suspicions were excited, and she closely scrutinized his movements.

Roving Rob, too, saw the turnkey's glance, but he was too old a soldier to display any excitement.

But he, too, watched the janitor.

"You found him very obstinate," said that worthy.

"Werry frantic," Rob answered.

"He didn't like parting with *you*," said the gaoler, looking hard at Dick.

"No," Dick replied, starting at the man's words.

The gaoler looked at him searchingly.

"Haven't I seen you before?"

Dick thought it was very likely he had, but merely said—

"You may have seen me."

"I think I know your mug."

"You've seen it in the jug," exclaimed Rob, coming to Dick's rescue.

"Yes, and maybe I'll see it there again."

"Eh?"

"Just come in here, my fine fellow, and we'll have a good look at you."

"At ME?" asked Rob.

"All on you come on, 'strikes me there's some game on."

"And you likes to be cock of the walk."

Roving Rob's careless manner did not allay the suspicions of the turnkey; he had smelt something wrong, but not being sure of what he surmised, directed them to follow him into a room, where he intended to satisfy himself with regard to Dick.

The door of the room stood a little way open, Dick, who seemed to be reckless whether he was caught or not, stepped in.

"What do you take me for?" he asked.

"Why you look precious like him as is to be swung on Monday."

"Do you think I'm he?"

"Werry likely."

Now Rob knew that if the gaoler got them in, then not only would Dick be taken, but they themselves would be lodged for the attempted escape; but he was rather at a loss to know how to act.

If there was no one in that room they might manage to deal with the janitor, but that would place them in a perilous position, as they would infallibly be stopped before they could get out of the prison.

But while he was hesitating, Tiger Loo was preparing to act. She followed Dick hastily into the room.

The gaoler, with the air of a man whose authority was unquestionable, took Dick by the arm, and, looking into his face, said—

"Werry near a clear do; but you may take off them false hairy things, and we'll see if you ain't a somebody else."

"What do you think he is?" Loo asked, excitedly.

"Why, I think he's Parker, the gallows bird, and I'm going to keep him here till he's put back where he came from."

Charley gave vent to a groan; Roving Rob looked a little flushed; Dick alone stood calm; but Loo, whose aspect was a agitated as when she had shot Crusher Jem, exclaimed—

"Going to keep him here, are you?"

"Yes, my girl, and you too."

Before he had spoken the words, the supple arm of the young girl was thrown round his throat; her other hand brought his head back, and held him so that he could neither move nor speak.

"Before you should keep us here, I will kill you." she cried.

The gaoler struggled, but she held him so that he could not even utter a groan.

Her small round arm was rendering him insensible.

"Now," she exclaimed, turning to the others, "take him away."

At the first movement of the tigress-like being, Roving Rob skedaddled to the door to see that no one came.

The promptness of Loo spurred him to equal action, and had any one come they would have met with a similar hug.

But, as there was no one outside to be grappled, Rob contented himself with performing a light fandango on his heel and toe, while waiting for Dick to come out.

Conceiving Loo to be in jeopardy, Dick would not quit the room: but, with an imperative gesture, she bade Charley drag him away.

"I will be with you instantly," she cried.

"Come, dear Dick," said Charley, dragging him away.

"Stop them, help!" exclaimed the gaoler, getting his throat free for a moment.

Tiger Loo had it instantly jammed up with her arm.

The turnkey ought to have been grateful.

Her arm was very beautiful.

But the squeeze was not.

And it was continued now till, after a faint gurgle, the turnkey dropped to the floor of the room.

"Come, my lass," Dick exclaimed.

"Now, Dick," whispered Rob, "you're outside."

"Hence, quick!" cried Loo, kneeling on the chest of the fallen warder.

Dick, with a strange and moody perverseness, remained obstinate, whereat Rob, who was getting impatient, walked in and led him out by the ear.

The gurgling noise in the room continued; then came a sound as of the man's feet kicking against the stones.

The instant after Tiger Loo came out, flushed, but in a state of tremulous excitement, her eyes glistening with a strange wild.

"Halloa," said Rob, "what's wrong?"

"Nothing; quick, let's get out."

"That's what we're trying to do; but put off that sacred look, or blessed if the first one that sees us won't nab us."

"I cannot help it," whispered Loo, hoarsely, "we have no time to lose; we shall be taken. I—think—I have *strangled* him."

Rob changed colour, but no one else overheard the words.

CHAPTER LVI.

THE DISCOVERY

WHEN the gaoler in Dick's cell had allowed sufficient time for the prisoner's grief to evaporate, he thought he might as well try doing a little to console him.

The Downy still sat with his arms before his face, and his back hunched up; he was blubbering, extensively, and groaned, at intervals, in the most heartrending manner.

"Come, Parker," said the warder, "keep your preachings."

But the Downy only shrugged his shoulders, and tried the effect of grating his teeth, as he had heard Dick do, at times, but his teeth were weak, he grew frightened, lest he should grind them out of his mouth, and so he relinquished this part of his imitative process.

"It's no good giving way."

"Boo, boo," blubbered the Downy.

"Come, it ain't so bad, arter all."

"How, now," groaned the prisoner.

The gaoler thought he might as well make a show of sympathy, especially as the men had not got much time to live; so he came up, and laying his hand on his shoulder, tried to make him cheer up.

"Hold up your head, and be game," he said.

But the Downy preferred modestly hiding it.

"Come, Parker, you're not like the same man."

"I ain't the same man," thought the Downy Cove.

"Seeing your friends has changed you."

"Very much, indeed," thought the prisoner.

"Here, come, take it like a man."

The Downy groaned, solemnly.

"It'll only be a jerk, and it's done; I've heard Calcraft say that he's seen chaps die as hadn't known there was anything the matter, it's only before you walks up that it's bad, and then you know, you must fancy you're going up for a look at the populace."

The Downy howled, dismally.

The warder cheered him, and tried to lift his head.

The Downy, meekly, hid it with his arms.

The warder tried to get his hands away, gently.

The Downy Cove rolled to the floor, and hid his face on the stones.

So the warder thought it best to let him alone for a time.

"How do you feel," he asked, presently.

"Awful," groaned the Downy.

"Ah! you'll be better, presently."

"Oh, oh!"

"Don't take on, why, you're got a long time to live yet; it ain't till Monday."

The warder was not going to be hanged that day; he would have thought it a very short time.

"And you can have anything as you likes."

"I'll take a walk out after them," thought the Downy, as he tore his nails along the floor, in agony.

"I'm blowed," said the warder, "if you ain't worse nor any chap as I've seen yet; they takes it quiet, most of them; but you're kicking up a row afore the time comes; here, get up."

He took the Downy by the collar, and helped him to his feet.

Still the Downy hid his face in his hands.

Which was very sad, so the warder thought.

And somehow, as he looked at the prisoner, it seemed that he was altered; in fact it did not strike him that he was the man.

Of course, there could not be any mistakes there, and yet there was a difference which struck him as strange.

He seemed fallen away wonderfully, his legs too were slimmer, and his throat more meagre.

And the hands were whiter and less hardened.

Such changes were, indeed, marvellous; it was a phenomenon he could not comprehend, so, to make himself more acquainted with its features, he got the Downy's hands away from his face—and—

Stood openmouthed and staring.

Then he took a step back, and stood speechless.

The Downy Cove looked as meek as a lamb; there was, indeed, a change in the face of the prisoner.

The turnkey looked staggered, and as the Downy afterwards described it, "all of a blessed heap, like a bloke who was chucked out of window."

"What the devil's this?" he cried, when speech came to him.

"It's me," softly said the Downy.

"Me be—"

"Ah! don't say that."

"Say!" vociferated the warder, fiercely, "you've played a trick; Parker's got out—damme—"

"Don't take on so; ain't I good enough to hang?" asked the Downy Cove, in his mildest tones.

"Be cursed."

"There come, take it like man."

"I'll take you like something," the warder cried, rushing to the door. "Look out, there, Parker's escaped!"

"Well, I never;" observed the Downy, "if that ain't a rummy go."

The warder looked at him, as if he thought choking was too good for him.

"You don't mean to say it; got out of his cell; well, I'm blowed, most extraordinary."

"You'll find you've dropped in for something over this job," yelled the gaoler, rushing out upon the corridor.

"Sweet spirit 'ear me prayer," murmured the Downy Cove, piously, "and don't let 'em cop him."

Just before the warder's warning was heard in the prison, Dick and his party encountered another of the officials. By Rob's advice, they were proceeding leisurely along. Loo's face being hid in her handkerchief, as if she were shedding tears.

Rob, who took the lead, turned to look behind him.

"He might as well have shown us all the way," he said, "before he went."

"Have you been left to find your way here?" asked the official.

"No, he told us to wait."

"What made him go."

"Some bloke called him."

"You have been to see the prisoner, Parker."

"Hist!" whispered Rob, leaning towards Loo.

"Much affected?"

"Hysterics," Rob answered.

"Ah!"

"Expect her to faint, I wish that fellow would come."

"'Tain't my duty," remarked the man, "but I'll show you out."

Rob slipped a half-crown into the man's hand.

Charley, whose face was deathly pale, brightened up at this.

Dick walked moodily on.

They reached the door by which they were to get out.

A few moments would now decide their fate.

A few moments, and Dick might be free.

Rescued from the gallows!

A few moments might see him dragged anew to the condemned cell.

It was a critical time for all; but the acting of Loo was superb on the occasion; dropping the handkerchief from her tear-steeped face, she gave utterance to a violent sob, and fell on Dick's neck.

"Take me to him," she cried; "take me back; I will not be taken away from my poor Dick."

There was every prospect of a scene.

Policemen, who were standing about, looked curiously on.

The official who had conducted them so far made a gesture for them to make haste.

"Take her gently away," he whispered to Dick; "the court will be disturbed."

"Take her gently away," echoed Rob, feeling very much as if he would like to perform a jig in the stone passage.

"Good day, sir," Charley said.

"Good day, my man."

Dick went out, leading the half-fainting girl,

Charley followed, keeping close to his uncle.

Roving Rob brought up the rear.

They were outside.
Hurrah!
Safe!
Hark! what is that?
A tumult behind them.
All Newgate in alarm.
"Quick," whispered Roving Rob; "it's all up inside."

CHAPTER LVII.

FLIGHT AND PURSUIT.

"CAB, sir."
The cabman's vehicle was near.
"In," said Rob, hurriedly, though calmly.
Dick helped Loo in; they got in after her.
"Drive to Smithfield," said Rob.
The cab rolled away.
Tiger Loo had much to do to keep herself from shrieking—her feelings had been at such a strain during the time of escape.
As for Dick, he scarcely realised the fact that he was free. Charley, like the faithful boy he was, had taken his hand, and was shedding his tears of joy at his uncle's deliverance from yawning death.
But all knew that they had not yet got out of danger.
The alarm was given.
The number of the cab was known.
Their description would be soon circulated.
The telegraph could be put in motion.
Rob expected, whenever a vehicle came by, that it contained the police.
The cab drove them to the Barbican; they got out here, and, paying the cabman, crossed the road; but, as soon as he was out of sight, they recrossed, and went into Cloth Fair.
Thence emerging by a narrow court, they found themselves in Aldersgate Street.
An omnibus was just on the start.
"Jump in with me," said Rob, "and get out when I do."
They went a very little way, when a policeman mounted the step.
Tiger Loo turned white as death.
Charley suppressed a groan; but Roving Rob and Dick took no notice whatever.
It was a groundless alarm: the policeman was merely a passenger; but Rob thought fit to wait till he got down before he ventured out.
When they had paid their fares, they hastened down the first turning that led them out of the open thoroughfare.
"Thank God, we are safe," Charley cried. "Oh, Dick! to see you out of that dreadful place—"
"We ain't safe yet," muttered Rob. "Here's a cab coming; we'll get into that, and drive out of the sound of Big Ben."
"Ah! Rob," muttered Dick, when they were seated inside; "thee has a true heart, in spite of all. It is like a dream to me to be out of that cell; but I don't think it will be long before they have me in again."
"Keep out of it while you can."
"What will they do to him that's there in my place?"
"Well, that's a hard question; they won't hang him any way."
Dick passed his hand to his throat, and grew pale; while Charley shed fresh tears.
Avoiding going anywhere that might give the police a clue for tracking them, they reached an out-of-the-way public-house, where the cabman was dismissed.
They did not enter here, but proceeded to another, and more lonely house, a little way off, where they entered, and went into a room by themselves.

As soon as they were seated, Dick laid his head on the table, and gave way to his feelings.
Nobody attempted to check the outburst; they knew what they had themselves endured, and could feel for him.
Presently he raised his head, and took the hand of Loo and Rob.
"You've done me a service that I shall not forget," he exclaimed; "I'm out of that prison, and if it's only for a day, it will be long enough for what I want. I've longed for this, that I might get hold of *him*; but I never expected it to come. I thank you; would I could repay it."
"You'll repay it, Dick, by keeping dark here by yourself, till we can get you safe out of the way. If we keep together, we shall be taken; each must separate."
"I will not leave Dick," Charley said, firmly; "if he is taken, I will be taken too."
"He can stay," remarked Loo, "if they both keep out of sight. We had better go now; good-bye, Dick; if there's a God I hope he will bless you."
Dick rose, and took her hands again.
He was struggling with his feelings; twice it had happened that he had owed his life to one whom, beside Mary, he had considered as not worthy to be named in the same breath; yet she, the fallen dissolute girl, was his salvation; while Mary, whom he had loved and worshipped, had almost been his destruction.
The thought came hard as he held the little hand of the young girl—so young in years, but so old in sin—so fairly formed in feature—so vitiated in mind. He looked at her sadly, while her eyes were suffused with tears, and her fair cheeks grew a deeper scarlet, and then turned ghastly as death.
"Good-bye," he said; "God keep you, and keep you from that course which has proved your ruin."
Tiger Loo pressed his hand in silence; then with a sudden movement she clasped him round the neck, and kissed him twice on each cheek.
"I know I am not worthy to touch you," she muttered, "but you are too good to spurn me for this; come, Rob; I feel as if I had lived enough, and should like to drown myself."
Rob, who was adjusting his necktie, turned, and looked at her in the blankest dismay.
"Drown yourself!" he cried, aghast; "drown rats and mummies, as they coves says at the Vic. Drown! well, if that ain't as good as a halligator wanting to swallow up the fire, after he'd stirred it with his tail."
"I am in earnest, Rob."
"Blind kittens and pups! here, come out of this; there's the Downy Cove to get out of his mess, and mind, Dick ain't quite out of the rope yet, he ain't. Drown yourself! that's what the blokes that sells bad stuffs by the lot would call a horful sacrifice."

CHAPTER LVIII.

WHAT THE DOWNY COVE FOUND HIMSELF IN FOR.

NOTWITHSTANDING the instantaneous alarm that was made after the turnkey had made the discovery of the change of prisoners, Dick with his party was out of sight when pursuit was made, and the police, who were despatched on the quest, returned to communicate only a failure.
Of course such an event caused the greatest furore, and the Newgate officials might have been seen almost jumping down each other's throats, in their eagerness to do something, whereby they might distinguish themselves.
The warden who had been outwitted was as furious as could be, but he was a little mollified when he

learned that somebody besides himself had been imposed upon.

He learnt this by their finding the unfortunate wretch, whom Loo had dealt with, lying on the floor nearly throttled, and too much exhausted to do more than point to the handkerchief, which Loo had twisted round his throat, to keep him from giving the alarm.

From the police, who had seen them go out, every accurate description of all four was obtained, and enquiry being made, led to the discovery of the cab which had taken them to the Barbican.

But this did not lead them to the discovery of anything else.

In about an hour after the escape, the Governor of Newgate entered the cell where the Downy Cove sat meekly listening to the curses the outwitted gaoler bestowed upon him.

The governor entered haughtily. He had come to frighten the Downy.

"This is not the man who was tried?" he said.

"No sir," answered the jailor.

"Where is he?"

"They must have changed, sir, when his friends were here."

"Changed!—how? Did he take off his skin?"

"No sir."

"How could he change when you were in the room?"

"I was looking another way when they must have done it."

"A pretty story! You will be locked up for creating this confusion."

He turned to the passive Downy Cove,

"How did you come here?"

"'Specs I dropped from heaven," returned the Downy, piously.

"Indeed!—do you know what you dropped in for?"

"I confess this understanding is not enlightened."

"Well, then, I will tell you—this is the condemned cell!"

"No! you don't mean it!"

"The cell where they put prisoners when they have been sentenced to hanging."

"Poor and unfortunate fellow Christians!"

"From this cell they walk to the gallows: now this is what you have dropped in for."

"Eh!" cried the Downy, turning white.

"That's what you've dropped from heaven for."

"But—but I didn't do it."

"Prisoners always say that."

"But it isn't me."

"A new dodge—we know it is."

"But I ain't the man!"

"Never mind, you'll do as well."

"What for?—to be hung?"

"Precisely so: that's what you dropped from heaven for."

"Oh Lord! then, dear sir, I've dropped from the other place—but you don't mean it?"

"I do; if you have any confession to make that may ease your mind before you suffer for the dreadful deed, the chaplain will visit you before the fatal hour."

"Fatal hour?"

"Of execution."

"Execution!—me?"

"Yes."

"But I ain't him! him isn't me!—Oh, Lord, here's a go!"

"You've been tried for murder—"

"No, I havn't."

"And are sentenced to be hanged."

"Never!—here, let me go; it's all a lark—it's a accident that brought me here."

"But an accident won't take you out again."

"What! no! you're joking; here, you with the buttons, am I the bloke?"

"If he is not, you will be transported," said the governor,

"In course you are the bloke; who else could come here?"

"Oh, my!" cried the Downy; "why, I ain't Dick; I'm the Downy Cove; everybody knows me. I does the psalm fakement with the kids; there ain't a street in London but what somebody lives as has chucked me halfpence when I've took the kiddies out a singing psalms, and craving their assistance for an unfortynite reduced fellow Christian; oh, no! I ain't the bloke."

"You'll have to tell that to the hangman; nobody else will believe me."

"What, not believe that I'm the Downy Cove."

"Not likely."

"In course not," added the turnkey, who hoped that such might be the case, "you'll be scragged, and serve you right to."

"But, but," echoed the Downy, gliding about the cell like one possessed; "you can't hang a cove for what he never done."

"We don't hang people here for what they have done; we hang them because it's their sentence."

"But it wasn't me they tried."

The governor laughed.

"No."

"Who was it then?"

"Why Spanker Dick, as we calls him, not as he did the murder, 'cos he didn't; but he was the bloke that they tried, and not me; do I look a gemman of that sort?"

"Your looks would convict you if nothing else did; so prepare for Monday morning."

"I shan't do no such thing; I know you can't hang me for helping Dick out and taking his place, you can only give me a few months in quod for it, and that I can do on my nut."

"We couldn't if it were so; but you see a man has been tried for murder, and put into the condemned cell to await his execution. Now, on Monday, when the scaffold is up, and there's a great mob outside, and the newspaper reporters here waiting to see the execution, the hangman will come in and pinion the prisoner that he finds in the cell; and then they will lead him out; and, of course, when he's out, they must hang him; and that will be you, you see."

"But, I don't see."

"Why, they must take the man out of the cell."

"Well, let 'em take this bloke here with the buttons, or you be took; it's ever so much better than taking me; or you be took; you look like a cove as wants to be hung, you do. I won't stand in your way; you can go out there and make a speech to the people and die game, and they'll see what a game cock you are."

The Downy put on his most winning look, but neither the governor nor the warder paid any heed to his appeal.

"Oh, Lord," cried the Downy, "there's my seven wives and one small children, which is six of 'em, is here, and the rest is down with the scarlet fever, and havn't had a blessed morsel in their blessed little mouths since the middle of next week; at least—the last week, I mean,"

"I leave you now, the chaplain will visit you presently."

"No, no, don't go; stay, there's a good gemman."

"Have you anything to confess?"

"I ain't got nothing to confess, I'm too humerical."

"Perhaps the chaplain may move you."

And the governor, in spite of the Downy Cove's entreaties, walked out of the cell.

"I say," said the Downy to the warder, "he don't mean it."

"Oh yes, he does though."

"But they won't hang me?"

"Won't they? you'll see on Monday."

"But I don't want to see."

"Never mind, you'll feel."

THE DISCOVERY.

"I'd like to see you with what the devil shaved his grandmother with," muttered the Downy, as he went and sat down on the hard bench, and gave himself up to reflection on his position.

Truth to say that he had dropped in for something warm; he knew the English law was not too particular in its treatment of persons who came under its clutches, and that it would make very little difference to Jack Ketch whom he hung on Monday.

And all things considered, it seemed very probable that they would actually make him hang in place of Dick.

Now the Downy Cove was not a cur, nor did he wish to see Dick executed, but hanging was a process that was particularly disagreeable to him; of course, he thought the right man ought to hang, but, failing that, he preferred of the two that they should subject Dick to that proceeding rather than himself.

No. 18.

A little imprisonment he did not mind, knowing what a capital life the convict leads; but to be taken out and jerked through a trap with a rope round his neck and a white nightcap over his face, it was horrible.

"Here," he cried, jumping suddenly from the bench; "there's the crusher, a much bigger bloke than I am, and he's got better neck for breaking; it would look ever so much better with the rope round it than mine would, have him, he's in the jug."

The door of the cell opened, and the chaplain entered, not the hypocritical old villain who had tried to get Mary into his power: to him the Downy Cove repeated his assertions, not giving time even to open his mouth, to deliver the exhortations he had been framing.

But the chaplain only shook his head: he refused to believe a word of it.

The jailor, too, began to swear hard and fast that the Downy Cove was the man; and altogether that illustrious individual found himself in a pretty fix.

After the chaplain had exhorted him to repentance and confession, he gave him a hint that, if he wanted to escape hanging, he would have to tell a more explicit tale.

Whereupon that injured individual went down upon his knees, and implored the chaplain to rescue him.

"I ain't the bloke; indeed I ain't."

"Where, then, is he?"

"He's gone, sir."

"Gone where?"

"Off somewhere, where I wish I was."

"Prisoner," said the chaplain, solemnly, "unless you are willing to be executed, you must explain where the real criminal has disappeared to, if, as you say, it be true that you are not he."

"It's true, indeed."

"Well, you see, some one must suffer; and the jailor here, worthy man, says you are the prisoner. Unless you can produce him you say you changed places with, you will most assuredly suffer in his stead; that is to say, I mean that, if you are, indeed, not the man, the other must be brought here. I will leave you; there is not much time to be lost. If you can give the officers such information as will result in bringing before them this fellow, they may let you go; if not, they will believe you to be suffering under some hallucination, and you will be executed accordingly."

Finishing this with a short prayer, to the effect that the person's heart might be opened, he departed, leaving the Downy Cove in a mood by far the most unenviable that mortal could be left in.

And soon after the jailor was taken away, and locked up for his share in the transaction, and the Downy Cove now sat himself down in a state of stupor.

The case, as it stood, was pretty clear regarding him.

If he could bring Dick up by betraying his whereabouts, he might have a chance of getting out of the scrape, with a slight touch of Millbank Prison.

If not as sure as he sat there did it seem that he would suffer death by hanging in front of the Old Bailey, at eight o'clock on next Monday morning, before the eyes of a gaping crowd.

Not that the Downy minded the crowd—no—he didn't care a straw for that; it was the rope—the hangman—and the unpalatable fact that he was the individual who was to be throttled.

CHAPTER LIX.

THE HOUSE WHERE MARY WAS LEFT.

Recent doings have thrown the characters into some confusion.

Dick, by a chain of events unlooked for, found himself out of the condemned cell.

The Downy Cove found himself looking forward to what he had not anticipated, merely being executed in place of Dick.

Mary was left in the house where Tiger Loo lodged, the scheme of Dick's escape having been kept secret from her.

Roving Bob and Tiger Loo were on their way to study the probable change of events, and to prepare Mary for Dick's rescue.

The crusher was in prison and likely to pay dearly for his past deeds.

Nobby Ned was in confinement for stealing the magistrate's handkerchief.

Tony Nip was in hospital recovering from the effects of the crushing he had received under the wheels of the carriage.

But now other mutations were about to arise.

We return to Dick.

He remained in the little room where he had been left trying to realise the sweets of liberty, and dwelling upon the circumstances that had led to his being what he then was, a criminal hunted from society, and only by an artifice snatched from the gallows.

Charley, who left him only for a few minutes at a time, could see when he returned that Dick was struggling with the fury of passions that enraged him to desperate and unkindly deeds.

"Dick, dear Dick," the boy said "you are saved from that great danger; oh, be cautious now, let us not risk sweet liberty by any bad acts: remember what we have already suffered."

"Ay, Charley; I remember all that has passed. I remember that I was honest once, but now I am a gallows bird: that Mary was virtuous, but now she is what I am too much ashamed to name."

"I know, Dick, but it will be well yet.

"Well, Charley, thee don't know what a heart they have made me: it is full of burning wrongs: I am turned in all my strength against the world: if I go to ruin now in reputation as I have unjustly in prospects: if I become full of crime and desperate malice, they who have shut me out from all right because I was a poor man shall bear the blame."

"Dear Dick."

"They have torn my peace to shreds, but I will be tame no longer: I will seek him who has done wrong to both, and if I find him, it will be a black hour for him and me."

Charley vainly tried to calm his uncle.

"You don't know, Charley," he said, in his tone of deep agony, "how I have fretted in prison till my heart was changed to gall: when I have crouched within those walls, and thought of his triumph, while I, like a caged bear, could not get out to reach him, I swore that if I got out but for one hour I would wring his heart from his body, and now I am out and at any moment may be led back to linger there and die I will keep my oath."

"Dear Dick, if you would only think a little of me. I have no one if you are gone, indeed I am lonely, I shall be more miserable if I lose you but for a day again."

The boy's eyes were filled with tears, there was a touching tenderness in his words, they fell upon the ears of Dick with a softening influence that held him like magic, he grasped the hand of his faithful nephew, and suffered himself to be led like a child to the seat from which he had risen.

"Don't mind me, Charley," Dick said, calmer now, yet torn by his great emotions, "there was a film before my eyes and a bitterness in my heart, but I will strive not to think of that which has made me almost mad."

"That is like it was of old: you used to speak like that: oh, Dick, if we could only get back to our quiet home, and live as peaceful and honest as we used to live, away from these people, half so cruel, and half so criminal!"

"Never, never, we could not be as we were, we might hide ourselves like guilty fugitives, but though they leave us alone they could not restore our unblemished character, they could not give Mary her virtue, and a ban must hang over us, and any hour might see me dragged to be made a convict, a felon."

The boy's affection kept him calm again, for the intensity of his feelings had been working him up again; he sat for some time and they talked of their village home, of Charley's mother lying in an unhonoured grave, of the murder whose stigma had cast itself upon Dick, of Ralph and Warner.

And when the last name was mentioned, Dick's teeth grated so harshly, that Charley feared his passion would again prove uncontrollable.

Evening came, and neither Rob nor Loo came or sent any message; Dick, growing more restless as the the minutes went by, rose at last.

"It be no use, Charley, I must see her and then see him."

"Let us go to Mary, she will help me to persuade you: she had influence once."

"Ay, she had influence once, but then she had the virtue that made me her worshipper, she does not lead me now, she only goads me to avenge her. Come: let me see her: the risk I run from seeking her is less than which I bear by being restrained."

Charley said no more, and they left the house to make their way to the dwelling where Mary had been left by Tiger Loo.

CHAPTER LX.

THE BETRAYAL OF DICK.

DICK and Charley left the house where Rob had told them remain, and started to find Mary. Dick was but a stranger yet to the mazy windings of London, but Charley had been more about its intricacies, and he was able to lead Dick from their suburban retreat.

It was a long journey, as they walked the whole way, but they got at last to the street where Mary lodged.

They were both very much exhausted, and Charley was in a state of fear lest Dick should be seen and caught. Dick, however, displayed a bravado in venturing under the very nose of those who were on the look out for him.

When they got to the house, Dick stood for a few moments to control his emotion; he was about to meet Mary, but how?

As a hunted felon—a convicted criminal; while she was even more fallen.

He moaned a little as he raised the knocker, and gave a moderate summons.

The wretched-faced landlady opened the door, and said sharply—

"Well?"

"I want to see—" Dick began.

"No use, she ain't here."

Dick started back.

"Not here? not Mary? where is she?"

"How should I know, indeed? went out of her will; 'tain't my place to ask where, I suppose?"

Dick staggered.

"Gone!" he cried; "Oh! Mary, Mary."

"Where has she gone? when, how?" he cried, anguishedly.

"Went the usual way, of course; some one sent for her, and she went. There's been Tiger Loo and some one else after too; don't know what they all want, I'm sure."

"Oh, God!" Dick moaned; "my poor Mary."

"Why, it's no use worritting like that; if she's gone, she's gone, and there's an end of it."

"I don't believe she has gone," Dick exclaimed; "she's here; you want to hide her from me."

"Well, I'm sure," cried the lodging-house keeper.

"But I won't be put off like this; I'll hunt the house over to find her."

"Hoity, toity; fine talk."

"It be what I mean," Dick shouted, pushing past her, and rushing into the house.

Charley followed, but the landlady, recovering her breath, commenced shrieking in the wildest manner for a policeman.

Dick, unheeding her cries, hurried up to the room Charley indicated; he pushed the door open; the place was deserted—dark and silent; it did not seem to have been tenanted for years, and Dick groaning hurried down the stairs.

Charley, who was first down, pulled him back as he was about to issue forth.

"What be it, Charley?"

"The police; oh, Dick! she has brought them to take you."

"Don't fear, lad; I am too strong for them to take yet; I will find him that's made Mary thus, and then they may take me."

The landlady's cries had drawn to the spot one or two of the neighbours, and a couple of policemen; to these last she was telling her tale—a tale of treachery, for it was the betrayal of Dick.

As a matter of course the whole affair of his escape was known among the force, each member of which was most anxious to be the chief instrument in getting him captured; when, therefore, they heard from the senseless woman that he was inside, they drew their truncheons and stepped inside to take him.

They had made up their minds to take him without any ceremony; but as is very often the case, they had reckoned without their host.

Dick was a powerful man, and he was panting for the sweets of his newly-gained liberty.

He was panting to avenge poor Mary's wrong, for he did not doubt that Warner was in some way concerned in this.

It so happened that just as the police had come to the laudable conclusion that the best way of taking him would be for each to take a hold of his collar and drag him out, Dick and Charley confronted them.

Under any circumstances they would not have been likely to have paid much attention to Charley; their whole faculties were absorbed with Dick, and how to take him; and so, directly they caught sight of him, each made a pounce at his collar.

Each made a pounce forward; each simultaneously and instantaneously pounced back: not content with falling a little way back, they rolled against the passage wall.

The cause of their performing this curious feat was that by a peculiar coincidence his fists had come against each of their heads at the same moment, and, as the blow was given with pretty good force, they fell as aforesaid.

The first who got up fumbled for his rattle, which having got out, he attempted to spring; but a well-administered kick from Dick's heavy boot sent it flying out of his hand.

"What do you want with me?" Dick asked angrily.

"Oh come," said the officer, mildly, "don't make a fuss, Dick, we must take you, you know; you can't get off."

He laid hold of Dick by the ancle.

A strange thing then ensued—the toe of Dick's boot rose, the face of the peeler fell, so did his whole body. He lay ingloriously on his back.

The other had been wise enough not to attempt to rise; but at that moment the evil-faced landlady came forward, sneaking behind Dick with a large rolling-pin, with which she was just in the act of striking him when Charley pulled Dick out of the way, and, as a consequence, the spiteful old woman fell.

She had no sooner touched the ground than one of the policemen, who in the dark could not see very well what he was about, took her by the hair of the head, thinking it was Dick.

The old woman screeched lustily, and the copper let her go; but each had fancied he had Dick near him—each raised his truncheon, each struck a terrific blow, and each fell straightway on his back.

They had hit one another!

Policeman A had his crown nearly beaten in.

Policeman B had his nose flattened and half broke.

As each still entertained the idea that he was grappling with Dick, they began to pepper away soundly at each other; and while they were at this healthy and agreeable work, Dick and Charley hurried to the door.

One or two people were standing about, afraid to enter for fear of getting their heads broken, these made a general scatter, as Dick and Charley came out, and after getting sneakingly out of the way, commenced trotting after the pair raising the neighbourhood to the inspiriting cry of "Stop thief!"

This cry, at first feeble and indistinct, increased as it was freshly taken up, till the pursued pair heard it ringing on all sides,

Boys heard it, and made a great halloo; the few street passengers having nothing to do, and the idle roughs and thieves, seeing a chance of getting plunder, swelled the shout.

A policeman who heared it made an attempt at capture.

Waiting by a corner, he darted out at Dick as he passed.

"Stop a bit," he said "I've got you."

"Not yet," said Dick, as he took him by the arms, and spinning him round as if he had been a log, ended by hurling him into the road.

It had been raining, and the streets were sloppy: by the kerb there was gathered a great pool of soft mud.

The policeman went rolling into this, he did not content himself with falling on his face, but put out his arms so as to roll over on his side.

In the meantime Dick sped on.

The crowd was getting bigger and noisier; one would have thought he had done them all some great injury, so eager were they to see him run down and taken.

But so far from this they did not know why they were running after him.

The noise they now made, and the sound that came before him, convinced Dick that he could not be able to keep up his way long: in a cold state of excitement he turned the corner.

"I kill the first man that comes near me," he muttered, and stopped, for he found himself in the arms of a man.

"Wery kind that be, it ar'," said the assuring voice of Roving Rob, "what made you come out here, as the cook says to the eels, when they walks out of the oven, to look for their heads arter she had skinned 'em and put 'em in the pail?"

"I'm hunted, Rob," Dick cried breathlessly."

"In course you are, what else could you expect, no business to come out till I let you know, here take my wide-a-wake, and give me yours, look alive, and jump into my coat; there you are, now shout away stop thief, as loud as you can; I'll lead 'em a precious dance, I know."

Off started Rob, not staying to hear a word Dick had to say, and not waiting to answer his hurried query about Mary, left him him standing there.

Dick would have paid no attention to Rob's desire, but clearly seeing that he was a good way ahead, shouted out with all his might.

Round swept the mob.

Five policemen with them.

Five policemen, flustered, red, and full of sagacious resolutions.

They heard people still crying stop thief.

They looked at Dick, but saw no resemblance between him and the man they had chased.

So they turned him from where he stood, and carrying him along with them, flew after the suspected escaped one.

The foremost of the pursuing mob were two policeman, who had resolutely made up their minds to capture the daring criminal; the daring criminal having meanwhile made up his mind not to be captured.

Rob's only intention was to lead them off the track, so as to allow ample time for Dick to effect his escape.

Dick was still with the crowd, but he was on the alert for the first opportuny of getting away.

Of course the chase was getting very exciting as it went on; everybody wished to see the daring criminal caught, and everybody wondered how it was he managed to avoid the frequent attempts made to stop him.

But the fact was confirmed. Roving Rob was gifted with a very swift pair of heels, and by a dexterous use of them and a strong pair of arms he cleared all obstacles.

When the crowd had swelled to a somewhat extensive mob, a virtuous citizen passing homeward, heard the unwonted cries, and being of opinion that it was the duty of every honest man to arrest a rogue, he put himself in Rob's way as he came up.

"Friend," he said, "I think you have had a long run, I must therefore stay you till the worthy police come up."

To Rob's surprise, he laid hold of him by the collar.

"I ain't of your opinion, as the bull said when they told him he was fit for killing," Rob observed, and then in the quietest manner possible he dropped the worthy gentleman on the back of his head in the road.

This little act was done so swift and clean, that the the would-be capturer lay in the road wondering whether it was an earthquake that had brought him there; he had just got Rob by the collar, and was indeed surprised to find himself lying stunned by himself.

Having briefly accomplished this feat, Rob gathered himself for a breathe, and started away at a pace that would have speedily taken him out of sight.

Charley took Dick by the sleeve.

"Let's come away now," he said.

"Eh!" muttered an individual behind them, who was dressed in a large overcoat with big black buttons and a white number on the collar.

Neither Dick nor Charley heard him, and the latter dragged his uncle out of the way.

But the gentleman who had just then spoken muttered cunningly to himself, and then as quietly followed them.

All the rest went after Rob.

It occurred to our friend, that as they had given him a brisk run on their own account, he would give them a treat for his own gratification; so he made for a house that was well known to him—a little beerhouse, the landlord of which was a jolly old buffer, and cherishing a mortal hatred of the police.

He reached this house when sufficiently in advance of the crowd for them to see him at its entrance, he took good care to make as much noise as possible in summoning for admittance.

The pursuers, who saw and heard all this, were loud in their joyful cries.

"He'll be took now," ran from mouth to mouth.

The officers were elate: they made sure of their prisoner.

Old Peter, the landlord of the house, was one of those long-limbed, sturdy-looking individuals, very quiet and methodical in his doings, and dry in his remarks.

As we have before said, he had a hatred of the police.

They used to come at unseemly hours of the night, and interfere with his business: twice they had got him fined for serving beer to travellers after prohibited hours.

Once he narrowly escaped a similar blessing. A detective, made up to represent a traveller, knocked at Peter's house, and, being admitted, called for some beer.

But it so happened that Peter knew his customer, and, being a knowing old fellow, he dropped something in the detective's beer, which wasn't either sugar or hops, the consequence of which was that, as soon as the detective had drunk his beer (for he was very thirsty), and commenced laying down the law to Peter, the drug operated upon him, and made him to all appearance thoroughly drunk.

Whereupon old Peter had the police called in, gave him in charge for being drunk and kicking up a disturbance at his door, and, after seeing him locked up in a cell, went to bed chuckling.

The detective was ill for a week after that, but he had never been able to catch Peter since.

Now, when Peter heard an untimely knocking at the door, he thought it was somebody else come as a traveller, so he got out of bed, opened the window, and put out his head, and a jug of water, the last intended to pour over whoever was below.

Rob saw the mug and jug in time to escape a ducking, and very briskly intimated who he was, whereupon Peter pulled in his jug and put out his mug, in order to have a survey of the scene.

"The blues, is they?" he said. "What does they want, Rob?"

"They thinks they want me."

"Oh!"

"Don't hurry yourself, Peter, as the turtle said to the bloke as was cutting him open."

Peter made a grunt, and, shutting the window, put his long legs in motion, and came downstairs.

The mob raised a shout when they saw the door open.

"That's him," they cried; "don't let him in; stop thief;" and the rest of it.

"Oh, ah!" muttered Peter; "no doubt; a pretty lot of gentlemen. Come in, Rob; come in."

The pair went in, and the door was shut.

"What do they know you by?" asked Peter.

"This 'ere cap and jacket."

"Give 'em to me."

Rob took them off.

"Go in there," said Peter, opening the door of a room on the first floor; "and go to sleep like a lamb."

"I feels shleepish," muttered Rob, as he bundled in.

For the present we will leave him to the adventure that there befel him, and follow Peter, who, after making one or two arrangements, sneaked into his own bed, just as the police got up and began knocking at the door.

Peter was not a bachelor; he was blessed with a wife, "a perfect stunner," as he used to call her.

To some extent she might be said to lay claim to that title, for she must have weighed at the least twelve stone; she was a big strapping woman, gifted with a very short temper and a very long arm, and, as she was very prompt in action, she was not over nice in giving any one a cuff with her palm and knocking them down stairs.

When Peter noiselessly sneaked into bed, she woke, and, Caudle-like, commenced abusing him for getting out.

While she was uttering her lecture, the police began their knocking at their door.

"Peter," said Mrs. P. to her liege lord, who pretended to be dropping off to sleep.

Peter gave a snort, and lay still.

The police knocked again.

"Peter," cried the lady a second time.

Peter gave a second snort.

Whereupon his irate better half grasped him by the hair of the head, and bumped him against the bedstead, till he thought fit to wake.

"Bless me, my dear," he said, rubbing his eyes; "I think the cat's under my pillow."

"Cat! Mr. P., got up and listen. Don't you hear that rub-a-dub-dub at the door?"

Peter put himself in an attitude of easy listening, and at that moment the police made another summons.

"Bless me," Peter murmured; "what *can* it be."

"Get up and see, Mr. P.; a pretty thing, indeed. Where have you been, I should like to know? with Betty, I do believe. Get out, you wretch. If I thought you'd been with Betty, I'd scrunch you up, I would."

Now it was Peter's object to get his lady into a great passion in order that the police might meet the full fury of her wrath, so he pretended to be dropping off to sleep again.

But a tremenduous serenade at the door and a frightful pull at the nose from his wife, caused him to leap up and stalk to the window, which he raised, carefully putting his head out.

"My dear," he said, "the police is come."

"The police," shrieked Mrs P., "what do they want here, I should like to know?"

"They want to come in."

"In here? only let them; only let them come in, Mr. P."

"She's up now," soliloquised Peter; "she'll do."

He put his head again out of the window.

"Hullo!" he said.

"Come down, Peter," said policeman A.

"What for?"

"We want to come in."

"Want to come in, do you? want to get me to go agin the law? be off the whole mob of you."

"Peter, we must come in; if you don't open the door we'll break it in."

"And I'll break your back if you do," Peter said, as he drew in his head.

The police commenced hammering away again greatly to the annoyance of Mrs. P., who was getting into a very excitable state when Peter stepped into bed again.

"I'd like to know," she began, "why I'm to be disturbed like this, Mr. Peter? I didn't marry you for this. Speak to them, tell them to go away, or I WILL."

That was precisely what Peter wanted, so he replied, "They won't move for me; they think you ain't here, so they won't go away."

"Won't they? a pretty stick you are when a mob can come round your door in the middle of the night and make this disturbance; oh, you meek wretch! but I'll see if they're to do this; I'll see whether they are to have it all their own way."

Mrs. Peter got out of bed in great indignation; by two strides she had reached the water jug, it was full, but as the water was too clean she took the trouble of rubbing a lot of soap into it.

About two more strides took her to the window.

It happened that at this moment an interesting young fellow of the crowd was being helped up on the shoulders of two policemen, that he might make an entry by the window.

He was just looking up when Mrs. P. flung her head out of window.

"I'll teach you, you villains, to come here making this disturbance at an honest woman's house; take that, some of you, and see how you like it."

Out went the jug of soapsuds, it came full in the face of about a dozen who were gazing up at the window and half drowned them; but the worst part followed; the impetus with which Mrs. P. jerked the jug caused it to snap from the handle, out it flew, and coming against policeman A's head it floored him like a shot.

Mrs. P. shut the window with a bang and left them to their fate.

It very fortunately happened that the policeman who received the jug in his face was gifted with a very hard skull, and though he was pretty near stunned by the thwack, and thought he was killed, he did not sustain any fracture.

But the jug had broke and sadly scratched his face.

The groan that was made below frightened Mrs. P., who was afraid she had killed somebody, and when Peter wanted to get out and let the police in she held him in by the hair of his head and his whiskers.

But, ultimately, he prevailed, and after another discussion with those below he agreed to open the door and let in four police.

As for the crowd they kept aloof lest the washhand-basin and other articles should follow the jug.

The four policemen brought in the one who had been knocked down; they made a great deal of the occurrence, but Peter only grinned at their threats.

"I will let you in," he said, "but if there's any nonsense, I'll kick you out."

"All right, Peter; we want a man that's in here."

"Are you going to look for him?"

"We are."

"Come and tell us when you find him."

"You'd better come with us."

"Perhaps I had; you don't look too honest."

"What do you mean?"

"Mean! why you mayn't be policemen at all, for all I know; not that it makes any difference, because if you ain't you're rogues, and if you are you ain't no better."

So saying Peter turned on his heel, and the police followed him, with the exception of the one who had received the clout from the jug, and he was allowed to sit in the bar, a privilege he made use of by pulling away at the beer till he got quite drunk and fell under the counter.

The police looked full of importance as they crept upstairs; they had resolved to search every room, no matter who was inside.

Which Peter thought a great liberty.

"If there's any bloke you wants," he said, " knock at the door, and ax if he's inside."

But the police put their fingers to their nose in a knowing manner.

"Very well," said Peter; "if you gets popped on to, it ain't nothing to do to me; only look out, there's one of the lodgers keeps a big bloodhound under his bed, and the other allers has pistols under his pillow; he'll shoot any one as comes near in the night; I never durst go nigh him, nor nobody else, but you can if you likes."

The policemen did not like this intelligence, but they thought it best to keep up an appearance of bravery.

The first door they came to they tapped at.

Peter grinned to see the effect of his words.

No answer came from inside.

Peter grinned again.

"The door's locked," he said.

"Then we'll break it open."

"'Tain't no easy job to do that," Peter retorted.

The policeman raised his foot, and gave the door a kick; its being locked was all a huff; it was just caught inside, and as soon as the fat boot of the peeler went against it, it flew in with a bang.

And so did the policeman, who, being entirely off his balance, and unable to stop himself, tumbled headlong into a bath of cold water, which Peter had placed there in readiness.

Peter, pretending to help him out, took occasion to give him a quiet push; the policeman kicked and splashed till he got out, when he presented a pretty picture.

He was boiling with rage against Peter, but as going in there had been his own fault, he could do nothing, and so was obliged to follow the others in his wet clothes.

They went into the room, which, of course, was empty; but it was not until they had hunted in every out-of-the-way corner, that they became satisfied of that fact.

They then went to the next room; this, in like manner, Peter had prepared for them, though it had an occupant.

He had laid a large zinc pail of water on the top of the door, balancing it so that, on the opening of the door, it would fall on the head of the intruder.

As soon as the police saw the door a little way open, they made a rapid entry.

Old Peter stood with his usual grin on his face.

He heard the sudden splash, and saw them all jump back.

All except one who had caught the pail; it had fallen on his head, nearly cutting his shoulders open with its rim, and with the fall of water made him believe he was killed outright.

His cries were very amusing to Peter, who laughed outright when he saw his frightened face after they had lifted the pail off him.

"You old scoundrel," he said, "you did this on purpose."

"It's the lodger," said Peter, quietly; "he don't never like to be disturbed."

"We'll disturb him though," they cried, as they made their way in.

"Hullo!" cried the first.

"Hullo!" Peter answered.

"Look here; here they are; we've got him."

"Hold him tight," put in Peter.

"We mean to."

"Do you though?"

"Yes, you big-headed, long-legged thief," cried the policeman, nettled at Peter's *sangfroid*.

"What have you found, beauty?" asked Peter, quiet as ever.

"Look! the cap and jacket; let's take him off. Here, come out of that; no skulking; we're up to your dodge."

This was addressed to the individual in the bed, who had been awakened by their noisy entrance. He had a large night-cap on, and the bed-clothes were tucked tightly round his chin, which caused the police to make sure that it was their man.

"Come on," said one.

"What do you want?" asked a mild frightened voice.

"Want you."

"Me! what for? goodness gracious—"

"Here, come out."

Two police caught hold of him, and tried to pull him out.

Now, this was not Rob, but a very earnest old gentleman, who had put up for one night at the house, and being of a naturally nervous character, suspected that he was about to be robbed by the men who had come into his room.

He was the gentleman who kept the pistol under his pillow.

He had it there now, and when the police caught hold of him he took it out.

"Ah!" he said, "it's thieves!—murder!—I'll shoot!—fury!"

He pointed the pistol at them.

The way they jumped back was amusing. They were as much terrified by the presentation of the pistol as they were surprised to see an unmistakeably old gentleman in the place of Dick.

They got further back, and sneaked behind one another when the old fellow cried—

"Go away!—I'll shoot you!"

"Oh! oh!—don't fire."

"What do you want, villains?"

"Murder!—we're police; it's that scoundrel we want—a thief."

"Thief?" cried the old gentleman, angrily.

"Yes; but not you—pray don't—he's somewhere in the house—we thought he was here; here's his cap and jacket."

"Cap and jacket?"

"Yes."

"In my room?"

"There it is."

But there it wasn't, for Peter had gently removed both articles during the tumult.

The police looked very foolish; the old gentleman very angry and determined; Peter very cunning. The police saw they were outwitted, and, being still afraid of the pistol, they backed out, followed by Peter, his mocking grin yet upon his countenance, and his eyes twinkling gleefully.

There was a rod in pickle for them yet, and he was chuckling over it.

CHAPTER LXI.

HOW MRS. PETER MET THE OFFICERS.

So far the police had been unsuccessful; but they had an idea that their man was not far off. So they made the tour of the rooms, going into the servant's chamber and terrifying her nearly out of her life when she looked and found the policeman's bull's-eye turned upon her.

Old Peter chuckled when he saw how excited they were getting.

He chuckled, too, as he thought what a warm reception they would presently receive.

They passed Peter's chamber twice, but each time the cautions of Peter had the effect of keeping them out.

They were afraid of the termagant inside.

When the third time they came to the door they resolved to enter.

The prisoner might be hiding there, they said.

Whereat Peter grinned, and leaving them to their fate, softly slipped down stairs, merely saying first—

"Don't go in there if you don't want to get more than you like: it's my wife's bedroom."

"He wants to keep us out," said one.

"He's trying to frighten us," remarked another.

"Perhaps our man's there."

"Let's go in and see."

They knocked at the door.

Mrs. Peter had been lying in bed in a high state of excitement.

She had heard the officers rummaging about the house, and her feelings were worked upon in consequence.

Whenever they stopped near her door she seized the warming pan by the handle and sat up in bed.

When the knock came at the door she asked sharply who was there.

"We're the police," was the reply.

"And pray what do you want, Mr. Police?"

"We're looking for somebody."

"Well, don't come here to find him, that's all."

Now this speech caused the sagacious minions of the law to believe that their man was in there, so they opened the door and went in.

Mrs. Peter uttered a perfect yell; their impertinence in entering there touched her to the quick.

"Go out," she cried, "you filthy ill-looking wretches!—go out of a decent woman's bedroom."

"We don't want to look at you, ma'am; we're looking for a thief."

"Oh!"

Mrs. Peter always meant a good deal when she said "oh."

If at any time Peter offended her, and she gave vent to that single monosyllable, Peter always took care to get out of the way as quickly as possible.

But the police were not used to her moods.

So they came sneaking in, taking no notice of the warming pan which the brawny hand of Mrs. Peter yet clutched.

One of the policemen stepped to the bed, and, despite the screech of rage with which he was greeted, raised the hanging and looked under it.

Another walked to the chimney and poked his head up it to see that the man they wanted was not there.

It was at this moment that the pent-up ire of Mrs. Peter found vent: the immediate object of her attack was the fellow who was impudently searching under her bed.

Leaning over, so as to get a good swing, she whirled round the warming-pan with such fury that it fell like the shock of an engine on the posterior of the recumbent policeman, and sent him sprawling.

He was immediately above something into which his head dipped with a dowse that came far from pleasant, and caused a yell that rose high above the screech of rage which Mrs. P. emitted as she dealt him a second clout, knocking him out of the something aforesaid with considerable damage to himself.

These double blows had been given in an instant, in the next Mrs. P. had sprung from the bed.

"She's at it!" thought Peter, who was outside, engaged in the delightful practice of rubbing the edge of the stairs with a large lump of greasy soap, in order to accelerate their descent.

And she *was* at it: the policeman whose head was up the chimney had not time to withdraw it before, knocking the other one out of her path, she caught him in the same part as she had caught the first one, and sent him jamming up the chimney.

He scrambled down, yelling out that his back was broken; the soot was all over him, and he looked a very pretty object.

"I'll break your back!" screamed Mrs. P.; "I'll scrunch up every bone in your skins, you pitiful, mean, miserable wretches! I'll teach you to come like thieves into an honest woman's house. I'll teach you—"

Whack went the warming-pan on the skull of the fourth.

An exciting scene now ensued; the four policemen, drawing their staves, made a direct onslaught on the furious landlady, but as well might they have tried to stop an avalanche with a penny candle, as to have withstood the force of that exasperated creature.

She had jumped out of bed in her *déshabille*, and certainly looked very formidable, every movement that she made exposing some portion of her mighty limbs.

The police, however, were too much engaged in withstanding her attack to give their attention to anything else, and so the very interesting position of Mrs. P. was lost upon them.

Not so the cracks they received on their skulls or knuckles, each one raising a bump and creating a sound as if a box had been knocked in.

Old Peter, who heard the play from outside, was intensely gratified at the progress she was making. Whenever a pat sounded louder than usual, he rubbed his pate, and then set to work diligently anointing the stairs.

Blows, well directed, will accomplish wonders. It is not always the number that will decide the fray.

Mrs. P., armed with that warming-pan, would have been more than a match for double the number of police.

Had there been more, she would merely have had more heads to hit at.

And hit she did, with a vigour that was astonishing even for one of her brawny limbs and powerful frame: as the terrible warming-pan, wielded with such fury, fell on skull after skull, the policemen's heads might have been seen rolling about as if they did not know where to get to, which, in fact, was the case.

The puny attempts of the truncheons were of no more effect than feathers; the sweeping weapon came swinging round, hitting head and knuckles with a fury that nothing equalled.

Valour may endure a long time, but there are limits to it; and these came to the policemen's bravery.

They found they were getting all the cracks and giving nothing in return, and so, to prevent being actually beaten up into a mummy, they, finding they could not beat Mrs. P., beat a rapid retreat, and stumbled pell-mell out of the room, followed by the victorious Mrs. P., flushed with conquest and glowing with exertion.

The first one who came bundling out tripped over the long gaunt form of Peter, which lay at the door. Peter, instantly collaring him, gave him a lurch that helped him down the stairs.

The others halted a moment; but the heated face

and night-capped figure of Mrs. P. appearing at their backs, they dodged, and fled.

The first who reached the edge of the stairs went down so quick that he thought he had left one half of himself up stairs; the second slid down so smoothly that all the skin of his back was taken off; the last, to escape a terrific blow aimed by Mrs. P., made a bound, alighted on the fourth stair, and, slipping thence, fell on his prostrate comrades.

Old Peter rose, with his wonted grin upon his face, and was about to utter his chuckle of triumph, when the warming-pan, which had been aimed at the last policeman, unfortunately descended on his back, Mrs. P. not being able to stop it in time.

It caught him in the middle, almost cutting him in two, and completely beating all the breath out of his body.

He gave a woeful groan, and lay panting on the top, while the police lay puffing at the bottom, and Mrs. P. stood triumphant and glorious above them all, with the battered warming-pan, like a sceptre of power, yet grasped in her hand.

CHAPTER LXII.

THE MYSTERIOUS INMATE OF THE CHAMBER.

THE crowd were yet waiting expectant outside.

Roving Rob, who had led them such a dance, was safe inside. He had been intensely gratified by the sounds of the conflict that reached him, but his attention was principally engrossed by the secret of the apartment where Peter had pushed him in.

And to explain this we must go back to the time he first entered.

The room was then in darkness, and Roving Rob quietly closed the door.

Darkness had no fear for him; he did not anticipate meeting anybody there that he need be terrified at, so he made his way to the middle of the room, feeling about as he went for a table, bedstead, or chair.

This last was the first thing he came in contact with, and he at once sank down in it.

"Here I ar'," he muttered, "fresh and lively as a heel that's just been skinned; there's them gemmans 'ammering away at the door: I spose they'll have to come in, which it ar' time then that I was in my caboose, a-snoring like a starved helefant."

When his soliloquy was about ended, he heard Peter open the door and admit the police.

"Here they comes, all of a bunch," he muttered again, "and I'm not inside the sheets yet! lawks, if they was to pop in here now! though they wouldn't know me for one fix they might for another, which ar' just the reason I must keep quiet."

Rob got up and fumbled about for the bed.

His hand came in contact with something like drapery, and he heard a rustling sound.

"Hallo!" thought Rob, what's the go here?"

He took hold of the article.

"Stuffs what they makes domen's gounds of! wonder if there's a doman inside?"

There was nothing inside but the bed-post.

"That ain't much like one of the blessed creters," Rob thought, "never a blessed bit it ar'."

And relinquishing the garment, he groped his way up to the head of the bed.

"It's werry like," he soliloquised, "that the doman as that gound belongs to ain't werry far off: I hope she ain't here, anyways."

Was that hope sincere? we think not. The worthy Rob was not more immaculate than the Downy Cove, and of his innocent way the reader has had a sample.

"Leastways," continued Rob, "if it ar' so, and she ar' here, I musn't let my modesty come in the way of my safety."

There, however, was nobody within reach, and Rob, undressing, jumped into bed.

"Here I ar'," he resumed, under the blessed clothes, and as jolly as a mouse with a hot cinder in his tooth. How werry tight that gal of Peter's have tucked up these here clothes: whew—tug—come out. Why, dear take 'em: hillo! wha—wha—what's THIS?"

The immaculate Rob's hand had touched the hand of somebody else.

Of course he drew it away like lightning for fear of its being a woman; and then, to make himself sure, he put his hand up to the pillow, where, sure enough, lay the clustering tresses of a female.

Rob quietly drew his hand back.

"That Peter's a villain, he ar', to put me here with a feminine—it ain't the cheese, it ain't; blessed if I ain't almost afraid to move: now, if I wakes her she'll screech, and then—no, Rob, it ar' your destiny to 'lay heer along of a doman, but to keep your distance from the same."

Rob found his hand pleasantly wandering again to the pillow.

"I wonder if she wears whiskers? No, not a sign —lawks! if her cheeks ain't as cold as if she'd sat on a doorstep all night! Why, blessed if she ain't cold!—now—I say—excuse me—it's only Rob—but what makes you so cold?"

No answer came to his gentle inquiry.

He lay still again for a little while, and then, villain as he was, his hand wandered to his silent bed-fellow's arms

"She sleeps as sound as a deaf donkey—hullo— why—she ain't—no—that villain, Peter—blessed if —oh Lord."

The exclamations came quick after one another.

Rob had made a discovery.

His bed-fellow was not like to wake beneath his loving embraces.

She was dead!

Rob turned rather when he found that out; of course if he had lain very still he would not have made the discovery and might still have rested there in unconscious bliss.

But when he found himself lying beside a corpse he felt rather queer.

"A stiff un," he muttered: "Peter, Peter, wait till Rob gets hold of you."

Our worthy friend would, without doubt, have jumped out of bed and made his exit from the chamber if a feeling of prudence had not counselled him to remain.

So he lay quietly, getting as far away as he could from the body, and devoutly wishing the police might be buried an age for every hour they kept him there.

He only had one solace, and that was produced by the sound of the thwacks Mrs. P. was delivering upon the heads of the devoted police.

At times, when he heard a louder bang than usual it made his own head feel sore.

He heard them go rolling down stairs, and in spite of his proximity to the corpse he indulged in a low laugh; he also heard them kicking up a terrific row at the bottom, and firmly resolved upon having another search.

He could distinguish the shrill tones of Mrs. P. daring them to come on.

"That doman are a brick, she ar'," was his soliloquy.

The police had determined to enter that room; Peters had hitherto kept them out of it, by telling them it was the chamber of death; but, aching from their combat with Mrs. P., they were resolved to take their prisoner.

So they came up, and entered the room.

Now, Rob was puzzled how to act; he did not like to be found lying beside the dead woman, and if he got out he would be taken, to a certainty, on suspicion, if on no other grounds.

But Peter's words, as he came in, gave him the cue.

"Go in, if you like; you will find two dead ones there. He died and she died, and I left them both together till their friend comes to bury them."

"I ar' to be a stiff un' then," thought Rob.

He accordingly stretched himself out full length, and, half closing his eyes, bended the blanket against his finger-nails, till the effect on his nerves made him quite pale. He set his features to an admirable corpse-like rigidity.

The bedstead stood in the centre, and was approached from either side. Peter, who took in at a glance Rob's position, let the police to the other side where the woman was.

"There they lays," he said, eloquently, "like the poor little babbies in the wood. Look at her and look at him, poor fellow—he do look sad now he's gone."

Rob felt inclined to groan dismally, but as this was not in exact keeping with his character, he refrained and lay as still as his lifeless companion.

The police turned their lanterns on the pair. It was very hard for Rob to lie there with the lurid light playing on his face, but he managed it, though he wondered why the deuce they quizzed his and his bedfellow's features so.

He thought it was because they had their doubts of his being dead and he had serious ideas of intimating that fact—his decease.

But he was mistaken.

Their suspicions went another way.

"Peter," said one, sharply.

Rob's heart gave a leap.

He thought they had smelt out the truth.

Peter merely jerked his head round.

"Hullo!" he cried.

"How came these people to die?"

"Couldn't get their breath, I fancy," Peter answered, grimly.

"Couldn't they?"

"No."

"Well, Peter, p'raps you'll tell what they died of?"

No. 19.

"Better ask 'em. I aint a doctor, and I aint died."

"We'll find out another way," observed Policeman B. "We'll have a coroner's inquest on 'em."

"All right."

"And to see that there's no tricks, some one shall stay here."

"They're quite welcome."

"No they aint," thought Rob.

"Jeffries, will you stay?"

The official thus addressed took a furtive look at the still ones.

He didn't think it very jolly to be left there with them.

But as he would have been laughed at if he had raised any objection, he bravely said he would stay.

Whereat Peter grinned wisely.

And Rob inwardly swore.

"Is he going to sit with them?" Peter asked.

"He'll stay in the room."

"He may get in bed if he likes," Peter observed.

"If he does, I'll kick him out," thought Rob.

He did not give utterance to the idea by which he was possessed, but for all that a rather uncomfortable feeling crept over him.

Rob was not a stickler at trifles; the reader who has followed him in his interesting career will readily believe that.

But lying beside a corpse was not the most pleasant thing in the world,

"I'll frighten him if he does stay," was Rob's mental resolve.

The police, having now taken a survey of the apartment, turned to depart, all excepting the one who was to remain.

He got a chair, and drawing it to the table, sat down.

"Bring me a light," he said to Peter.

"Don't sell 'em," was the answer.

The peeler uncovered his lantern.

"Let's have some beer then," he growled.

"Past the time and you aint allowed," growled Peter in return, a knowing grin playing about his features.

The policeman swore a deep oath, which did not have the effect of in the least disturbing old Peter's equanimity; he seemed in fact quite amazed at Rob's predicament.

Perhaps he knew that there was a treat in store for him when Rob got tired of his situation.

"Well," said the peeler, "if I can't have something to drink I must sit without, but I'll see that you play no tricks."

"Shall you be long?" he asked of the others.

"Not long; we will just have a peep after the fellow we want, and then we'll have a doctor here."

The policeman stretched out his legs, and Peter followed the others out of the room.

It is needless to add that the remainder of their search proving unavailing, they started off to get instructions how to deal with Peter for having two dead people in his house.

In the meanwhile the officer whom they had left was trying to be as heroic as possible under the circumstances.

He had placed his lantern at first so that its light fell on the faces of those in bed, but finding the sight of the two ghastly forms not altogether cheering, he turned the light so that it illumined the door.

But after having his back towards the bed, he began to feel many a qualm and fear lest the inmates should rise and creep behind him.

So he shifted again, growing every moment more and more uncomfortable, and wishing his brother officers had not been so officious in leaving him there.

Presently he stole another look at the bed. The pair lay as quiet as might have been expected, so he stretched his legs out again.

"How still the house is," he muttered.

If he had looked round at that moment, he would have seen the figure of Roving Rob sitting up in the bed; but very fortunately for himself he did not, as the fright would certainly have killed him.

"I'll pitch the pillow at his nob," soliloquised Rob to himself, "if he don't go soon."

The policeman thought he heard a movement in the bed.

It was Rob getting down again between the sheets.

He turned as soon as fear would allow him to do so.

Both of his charges lay as still as before.

He looked again.

The eye of one of the corpses seemed to wink.

He stared harder.

Was that a shake of the bed-clothes?

He began to grow very nervous.

All seemed quiet, however.

"I wish somebody would come," he muttered.

"I wonder what they died of?"

"Hush," whispered Rob.

The policeman leapt up and gave a frightened glance towards the bed.

"How—when—" he stammered.

Nobody answered him.

His fears departed.

"What a fool I am!" he said, "I thought some one spoke?"

He gave a sudden start.

The bed-clothes moved.

He stared hard and found his knees shaking.

But again he persuaded himself it was fancy.

"I wish they would come back. I shall stop it directly. I don't care much about this job—O—oh—ho!—ho-w—O Lord!"

He had turned again.

Horror of horrors.

One of the corpses was sitting up in bed.

There was the white head with the white sheet round it; two dull eyes staring at him.

No wonder he shook and found himself unable to speak.

The corpse moved.

He raised his finger.

The peeler sank to his knees.

"Mercy!" he gasped.

"How—ow—ow!" groaned Rob in the most sepulchral tone.

"Mur—mercy—oh—I didn't do—anything!"

The corpse slid from the bed.

The peeler would have shrieked, but his tongue was fixed.

"Fee—fa—fol—fum!" groaned Rob.

The policeman saw and heard no more; he fell prone on his face, the cold drops of sweat oozing to his brow, and every limb quivering.

His heart almost gave over its beating when a long deadly sheet was thrown over him, and a hand cold and stiff glided down his neck.

He scarcely retained consciousness when the same horrible fingers clutched his throat, another ghastly hand seized him in another part, and he was lifted up, and—horror of horrors! carried towards the bed where the other body lay.

The sweat rolled off his face, so it did off Rob's, for the peeler was heavy, but he lifted him up and dropped him on the bed.

"Ou—ou!" he groaned again, putting his mouth to the policeman's ear and sending cold shivers through that worthy's frame.

The peeler gave one groan and fell into a fit.

Roving Rob did not stay to see this culmination of the man's terror.

He was already bolting from the room.

Old Peter was in the passage.

"How did you get out?"

"Showed him how dead men could walk."

Peter grinned.

"I'm off!" Rob said.

"Take a drink first?"

He handed a tray of ale and gin.

Rob took a pull and felt refreshed.

"How did that dooman come there?" he asked.

"Don't try to learn too much," Peter replied.

"A nice trick to put me there?"

"If you'd kept away from her," Peter remarked drily, "you wouldn't have found out whether she was alive or dead."

Which being true, Rob could say nothing to it, but soon after shaking Peter by the hand, bade him good night, and made his way out.

"That's a sweet pet," soliloquised Peter; "a sweet pet! they'll be clever gentry that get the blind side of him."

CHAPTER LXIII.

WHAT WAS IN THE ROOM WHITHER ROB TOOK THE POLICEMAN.

It will be remembered that when Dick and Charley separated from the crowd, an enterprising member of the police force thought proper to follow them, his suspicions having been excited by the boys' eagerness to get away.

He kept very close on their heels for some time, for, said he to himself, "If this should turn out to be the fellow they're looking after, how clever I should be in taking him."

Which he would have been, because, in his present mood, Dick would have defied the efforts of a brace of such constables to capture him.

But, unfortunately, having let them get a little ahead, in the hope that they might think themselves safe, and enter some place where he might safely house them, he managed to miss them, and was looking everywhere over his misfortune, when he again stumbled across them. This was more than an hour afterwards, and his unexpected good luck caused him to mutter his gratification.

This muttering was overheard by no less an individual than Roving Rob, who having got so far on his way, saw Dick in front, and was about to hail him, when the sight of the policeman caused him to draw back and await the chance of events.

There were two courses opened to Rob when he became aware of Dick's danger.

One was to give the policeman the leg, the other to pick his pocket, and then run off so as to get him away.

He would have effected the latter if he had not been directed from his object by the sudden disappearance of Dick and Charley.

Where they had both vanished to was a great puzzler to him, as it was to the keen-scented policeman, who looked in every direction for the missing pair.

When Rob had stalked up, he found that he was in front of the house where the robbery had been committed, in which Dick had been inveigled—the house of Mr. Wilblow, the good Samaritan and philanthropist.

A rapid thought flashed to Rob's brain.

He stepped up to the policeman and said:

"You're looking for a bloke and a boy?"

"I am."

"I seed 'em smuggle into that house."

He pointed to Mr. Wilblow's.

"I thought that was where they went."

"What have they done?"

"Escaped from Newgate, one of them"

"Let's have then out then!"

"I mean to."

The policeman rang the bell.

It was some time before any attention was paid to his summons. A servant's head came out of the window, the owner thereof being considerably surprised at seeing the "Blue."

"What is it, please?" he asked.

"Come down!" said executive, sternly.

The domestic shivered into his trousers and came down trembling.

"Is the house on fire!" he asked.

"No it isn't."

"What then, thieves?"

"No stammering. There's somebody in here that I want."

"In here!"

"Yes."

The policeman put too the door.

"If you don't want to be taken off too, tell us where you've stowed them."

The domestic stared at him open mouthed.

"Stowed—who?"

"That will do. I see I must look for myself."

"There's nobody here unless they've broke in!"

"Broke in or not we must have them."

The servant began to get frightened, from the fear that somebody had entered the house to rob it; and as his agitation was set down by the policeman as proof of his guilt, he was a confirmation of Rob's assertions.

"You'll help me look through the house."

"I'm your man!" was Rob's answer.

The servant looked from one to the other.

"If there's anyone in, please don't tell master; he's in the country, and I should be discharged if he thought I had not looked better after his house."

The policeman thought this only a dodge to put him off, more especially as Rob knowingly shook his head the better to gull the peeler, and thereby give Dick time to make off.

An interesting contretemps ensued on the stairs. The housemaid, alarmed by the unwonted noise, and being of a courageous turn of mind, sallied forth from the bedroom *en deshabillé*, and had just reached the bottom flight of steps when the head of the policeman appeared.

She had presence of mind to jerk out the candlestick she held in her hand into his face, and having accomplished this feat, she gave a terrific screech and fell down stairs.

Rob picked her up and carried her to the first room, where he left her, and returned to the executive, looking very much as if he had done something that he ought to be ashamed of.

The domestic was too frightened to go into the rooms with them; he stood at the doorway shivering with fear, and anticipating every moment to see some desperate burglar run out and knock him over.

"What's in this room?" asked the policeman, when he came to one that was fast.

"Don't know; master always keeps it locked."

"Does he?"

"Better have it open," Rob remarked.

"I should say so."

The policeman's boots did the business.

A rush of close air came forth when the door was forced in. Rob and the policeman entered, and the domestic stayed outside.

It was certainly very bold on the part of the audacious Rob to walk so boldly about the house where he had actually been engaged in a burglary, but it was in keeping with his character, and the reader will not be surprised when we inform them that he had already possessed himself of five spoons, three silver ornaments, seven silk handkerchiefs, the policeman's rattle and truncheon.

"There's a cupboard there," he remarked, "I wonder what's inside?"

"Very likely them as we want."

A few moments sufficed to wrench it open.

A sickly odour came forth that almost suffocated them.

The policeman stepped back and raised his lantern, the rays fell upon a ghastly object.

A woman's form, stark, stiff, and horrible.

Dead!

Ah, and corroding.

She had evidently meet with foul usage.

Her hair was secured to a peg at the back of the cupboard; a tight scarf was round her neck.

Her teeth were showing from her lips.

She had been throttled,

A nice discovery in the house of the eminent philanthropist.

What a pity his admirers could not see within that cupboard and read its mystery!

While Rob and the policeman were gaping at the figure of the poor wan woman, a furious knocking was heard at the street door.

"Its Mr. Wilblow," the domestic said.

"He'd better come up," remarked Rob, "there's something here we'd like him to look at."

Mr. Wilblow came rushing up the stairs; drops of sweat were on his face, and his lips were white.

His bones trembled as he entered the room.

"What do you here?" he cried. "What means this?"

Here his eye fell upon the ghastly figure.

His features underwent a terrible transformation. His jaw fell, and his eyes seemed bolting from their sockets.

Of course he was shocked to see that body there.

"Mr. Wilblow," said the policeman, "can you explain this?"

"I—I—know nothing about it," answered the trembling wretch,

But he told a lie.

He knew who it was, and how she came there. It was a poor, young, trusting girl, whom he had betrayed, and whom he had thrust in there when she came pleading for aid for herself and her unborn child.

He had lured her to that room, and in the silence of the night, when no one was there to help her, he had stolen there, and thrust a scarf round her throat, strangling her as she asked for mercy.

Then he had tied her by her hair to the peg and left her.

He had the room shut up, and did not think he should ever again look upon her.

Judge, then, why he was agitated when he found himself looking his mouldering victim in the face.

"Looks like as if you knew a good deal about her!" remarked Rob, ironically. "Poor thing, if she could only tell a tale, what a frightful one it would be!"

Rob's voice aroused Mr. Wilblow; he recollected the face, and trying to hide his excitement, cried:—

"I know nothing of this; but you I know to be one of those who stole into my house the night that policeman was murdered—take him in charge, constable—I will prosecute."

"Don't trouble yourself. I think he will be like to take you in tow till you can give a good account of this job."

Mr Wilblow's cheek grew ashey.

"That's what I shall have to do, sir," observed the policeman.

The eminent philanthropist tried the effect of bounce.

"Get out of my house, fellow! I'll prosecute you for being in it."

"Never mind about prosecuting; I'll take you up for this; there's been a murder committed, and I shall do my duty in taking you."

The polished scoundrel drew a pistol; checkmated in his villany, he thought the best way to free himself, would be by fresh crime.

"Touch me, and I will send a bullet through you!" he exclaimed.

"That's very kind of you," remarked Rob, "which it ain't allers one meets with such a gemman, but for all that, Brumagem game cock, you'll go to quad."

Rob was dexterous in his actions when emergency arose. Mr. Wilblow thought he had them both at bay.

But the truncheon Rob had taken from the policeman suddenly came in contact with his hand, and knocked the pistol to the floor.

Then the policeman collared him.

"Hold him!" cried Rob. "I'll go and bring one or two more police; hold the varmint tight!"

He vanished, taking with him the policeman's watch and Mr. Wilblow's pocket-book, both of which he had evidently abstracted in that brief struggle.

Of course he did not mean to return.

He had served his purpose.

And his pockets were filled.

So he left the policeman and the philanthropist glaring at each other, and the servant staring at them both.

CHAPTER LXIV.

AN OLD ACQUAINTANCE AND HIS NEW VILLANY.

For a very long time we have lost sight of Ralph Merton, the heartless son of the honest old squire, whom he had so cunningly deceived.

The last we saw of him was when he lay on the green sward, where he had been stretched by the lusty arm of Dick, whose brawny fist had bestowed upon him a small portion of well-deserved punishment.

After he had crawled away and recovered from the effects of his bruises, he discovered, with very malignant feelings, that not only Mary and Hall Warner had departed, but that Dick was safely away.

He swore many a bitter oath, and had he then come across his quondam friend Warner, he would not have hesitated in drawing a knife across his throat.

Ralph Merton, as we have seen, was one of those brutal men whom a trivial cause converts into a blood-thirsty enemy, eager to shed the blood of their victims.

Such men it is that murder their sweethearts upon a slight provocation, or mercilessly kill their wives and children.

Ralph Merton vowed, as I have said, many a bitter oath against Hal Warner.

He wanted Mary, and was chagrined at losing her. He was vexed, too, at having been despoiled by the gipsies of the booty he had taken from Parson Wordly's house.

He was more angry, because, whenever he met the worldly-minded parson, his sneering look and cold hints told him that he held his life on a slight tenure so long as the minister had power to say a word against him.

"I shall not wait much longer," the parson more than once said; "I have sent my wife to a private asylum, but I hear she is fast regaining her senses; and I find she is perfectly certain whom it was that cut my servant's throat, and so, my dear Ralph, if that gold and those valuables the assassin took from my house are not forthcoming, why I must let her tell what she knows, and then, Ralph somebody will be *hanged*.

These words rankled in Ralph's evil mind; and one evening, when his passions were blackest, he saw the parson walking leisurely through his orchard.

A purpose terrible and cruel had for some time

been forming in his mind; and now, when he saw the minister—the man who so often told him he could hang him by one word—the vile feelings of his devil-disposition urged him to a deed of crime.

He crept upon the godless minister, and while he was chuckling to himself, threw a scarf round his neck, and pulled him to one of the branches of a favourite apple-tree.

And when his struggles were over, he let him down, and flung him into a little pond, where the parson had been wont to rear shoals of gold fish.

When the water had closed over this dark deed he hurried from the district, and came to London to hide himself from danger of detection, and to seek out some of those whom he longed to serve as he had served Parson Wordly.

Supplied with money by his fond old father, whom he still managed to deceive in the most consummate manner, he set up in style in the metropolis, commencing by taking as his mistress a gay lady from the Row, and making his companions of the worst class of professional swindlers, blacklegs, forgers, and gamblers.

Four weeks he was in London before he discovered Warner's retreat; and then he learned that Mary was not there.

But one evening, when prowling, as usual, in company with one of his worthless associates, he saw Mary and Tiger Loo together.

He watched the poor betrayed girl to the house, and then went away to concoct a plan for getting possession of her.

So at night, while Mary sat lonely and sad in her room, waiting for her now only friends to come back, he drove up to the door in a cab, and knocking loudly, brought the landlady forth.

She came, all smirks and smiles, and smoothing her apron awaited his pleasure.

"You have a young person lodging here—a country girl."

"Yes, sir, and she's up-stairs now. She isn't one of our regulars; but between you and me and the bed-post, she isn't quite such a hinnercent chick as she would have one believe; none are so quiet but what they know enough, or else why does they want to hide theirselves?"

This was a most unjust speech. Mary had no idea of the nature of the house when she accepted Loo's invitation; and if she now suspected it, what could she do?

Friendless and destitute, there lay only the choice between that and the streets, or self-destruction.

Ralph Merton slipped a half sovereign into the woman's hand.

"I want to see her," he observed.

"Oh, certainly, sir. Up this way, sir; you'll find her up, I daresay; if not, may be it won't make much difference to her, and you won't mind."

"I shall very likely take her out for a little while," Ralph said, as he ascended the stairs.

The landlady merely curtseyed; and pointing out the door, went to her room.

Mary was sitting by the bedside, her face on the bed-clothes. Tiger Loo had desired her to go to bed and sleep, but she had merely lain down, and now sat in hopeless weariness, thinking of her village-home and her lost Dick.

Ralph opened the door so noiselessly, that she did not hear him; and, with a self-satisfied smile on his lips, he crept to the bed, and slid his arm round her waist.

She started up with a scream, and stood looking him wildly in the face.

"Mary," he began, "I have come to see you; don't you remember me?"

"Aye, I remember you," she answered, drawing away.

"Do not be angry at my entrance, I come as a friend."

"A friend!"

She repeated the words mechanically.

"Yes, Mary, as your friend. You are ill—in want—tell me what has happened to you since you left the village."

"All—all that I might have expected, since I sold myself to him who was your friend."

Ralph put on the most practised look of just anger.

"Has he deserted you? By heaven, Mary, if he has proved such a villain, I myself will make him suffer for it!"

Mary looked steadily into his evil face. She was getting more accustomed to the deceit and vileness of man.

"There are more villains than he," she replied sadly; "there are none on earth whom you may trust. Trust you!" Mary cried; "are you not a great a villain?"

"Mary!"

"Do not simulate indignation; are you not bad! Did you not play the villain with poor Dick!"

"I, Mary; never!"

"They say you did the murder that he was taken up for," she said, still looking him hard in the face.

"They told a lie!" he cried, his lips blanching. "Mary, I would befriend you. You may not know it, but you are in a house of sin. I will take you away. I have a cab at the door."

"No; do not try, sir, to tempt me. I am with sinful people, I know, but they have proved more kind than those who call themselves Christians."

"Ah! but you will come."

"I will not."

"Can you not trust me?"

"I trust none!"

"Not I?"

"I have read too deeply of the world's infamy."

"Mary," said the crafty villain, "you are not used to this wretchedness; let me take you where you will be happy."

"That would not be with you; these offers have been made to me before; I know their worthlessness. Go, bad man, I will not listen to your wickedness.

Ralph Merton had not expected to find Mary so firm; but he had come there with only one purpose, and that he was determined to effect.

So stepping closer to her, he seized her arm, and said: "I have come to take you away, and, by fair means or foul, I will take you. I will watch your daily wants. I know he has cut you off, but yo will be good to me."

Mary drew back. His manner had changed. She saw the infamy of his looks.

"If you do not go," she exclaimed, "I will call people to take you to prison."

"I don't think you'll find any one here to help you," said the villain; "and so you may as well come quietly."

She turned to get away from him, but he had got firm hold of her; and to prevent her screams he threw his cloak over her.

Confounded by the weight of this muffling garment, and to a certain extend gagged by it, as well as held by his strong arms, the poor girl began to struggle desperately with her determined assailant yet with a fear that he would prevail.

She did not think Tiger Low would have deserted her if she had been there, but she had noticed, that when she was away, the vulgar-looking landlady was more rude to her; and for all she knew, might have betrayed her to the infamous man who held her.

But Ralph only laughed at her struggles, and twisting the cloak tight over her mouth, lifted her in his arms and made his way out of the room.

Only the strength of passion enabled him to get her down the stairs, in the passage he met the landlady, who put on a peculiar look at this unexpected scene.

"Hasty toils," she exclaimed; "what now I wonder! pretty goings on I must say!"

"Pish!" said Ralph, thrusting a sovereign into her greedy palm; "take that and hold your noise: another when she is in the cab."

The golden ointment had a magical effect: her mean changed instantly.

"You can't take her out like that: perhaps she wont come so quiet, let me get her bonnet; but don't take off that cloak till I come."

She returned with Mary's bonnet as Ralph took off the cloak, the poor girl uttered a faint scream, and made an ineffectual attempt to get away; but the brutal woman thrust a bottle to her nostrils.

The effect of this was to half stupify Mary. She was at once in the power of the violater.

The woman who kept that house was well versed in such trials: she knew how to place an innocent girl at the mercy of any who might bribe her so to do.

Under the influence of this essence she had inhaled, Mary, though not rendered insensible, was so far stupified as to be unable to speak or offer any resistance to Merton.

She was more, in fact, an assistance to him, since her powerless position made her yield herself to his dictates.

This was a mixture the landlady kept for unwilling victims: it made them respond willingly to the aggressions they had before resisted.

"You'll find her just to your liking to do with," the landlady said, giving Ralph a significant look; "only get her in doors as soon as you can."

She opened the street door.

Mary heard the woman's words, but the spell was too strong upon her, and when Ralph, who pretended to be leading her forth tenderly, emerged she seemed leaning on his arm for support.

At this moment she was led to the cab and helped inside: the cabman shut the door, and jumped on to the box.

"You'll let me see her again soon," said the landlady in a whining tone: "poor dear, she's quite overcome."

"All right," Ralph said.

The landlady put her head inside.

"Now then," she exclaimed, "the quid!"

"The what?"

"The sov you promised."

"Sov be d—d," muttered Ralph, "drive on cabby;" he pushed his head out as he shouted the last words.

Of course, it was very natural for him to put out his head, as by that means he could more easily communicate with the cabman; but there was no reason why his forehead should come in contact with the woman's face and knock her skull, which it did.

But the fact was now that the job was so far done, Ralph did not intend to pay any more money to the woman, who had assisted him so far.

This was very poor policy, inasmuch as it converted the amiable landlady, who had before been his ready aid, into a bitter enemy.

She was not only mortified with the manner in which she had been done, but the blow Ralph had given her had brought tears (not of repentance) into her eyes; and she was ready to do anything in her spite.

But she did not know exactly how to set about stopping him.

She had a great mind to call out and tell the cabman what had been done to Mary, but as that would have been betraying herself as well, she hesitated, and while she hesitated the cab drove off.

But she was not the one to be outwitted like that. She made a spring and got to the door; "I'll be one with you for that," she cried, putting her excited face in at the window, look out! "I'll drop on you when you don't expect."

"Go to the devil!" said Ralph, putting his fist in her face and thrusting her away.

While she was struggling in the road, the cab went on.

"What's up?" some familiar voice asked.

She turned, and saw a boy-thief, who was well known to her.

"Jem, I want you: run after that cab; don't let them twig you, tell me where he takes the girl he's got inside."

Jem winked knowingly and was off.

He kept in sight of the cab, although it was a long way off, and saw the house where Ralph stopped. He saw him lead Mary out and go inside, and when the door was closed and the cabman had gone, he marked the doorstep with a piece of chalk, and went back.

But as he did not return just then, the landlady was not able to tell either Tiger Loo or Dick where Mary had gone; she merely said that she had gone with a gentleman.

Dick believed that she had allowed herself to be again taken away by Warner, but Tiger Loo thought different.

CHAPTER LXV.
THEY LEARN WHERE MARY IS KEPT.

TIGER Loo did not suspect that Mrs. Gordan had been connected in getting Mary out of the house, because she had always liberally repaid that woman for anything she had required: she went out to see what she could glean, but the course of her inquiries led her to a different conclusion.

Dick, whom nothing could now keep from Mary, came back after a vain rambling: Charley was with him, and they met Roving Rob on the way.

The latter scratched his head when he was told the tale.

"Mother Gordan aint the gal to let a bloke take anyone out of her house without knowing all about where they're going to: come back."

"Do you think she has betrayed poor Mary?"

"I don't like it."

"Oh! Rob I thought she had gone again to that —him as brought her to London."

"I didn't," Rob muttered drily, "them German's dont allers come about taking back a gal whom they're once—hem—leastway, I don't think as how she's there."

"Who could she have gone to?" Dick asked in agony.

"Why it's more like, then, not as the saying is that, old mother Gordan's been and sold her."

"Sold her, Rob!"

"Yes, they do them things in London; they sells 'em. Many a likely gal gets lost that way in London, and nobody ever hears of 'em again till they're found in some of these bad houses, not worth a dump by that time. Oh, you needn't stare like that, as the Whale said to Jonah before he swallowed him, it's all gospel."

"Sell them!" Dick cried hoarsely, "to make of them what?"

"Why, to make prostitutes of 'em."

Dick's teeth grated together.

"They would not do that to Mary."

"Might be not, but they do it to a great many that thinks themselves a precious sight more certain: they kidnaps a gal and shuts her up till she gets as lonely as a lost bullfinch, and then they puts books and pictures in her way, what are calculated to make her think about things as she didn't ought to; and when that's done they send a gemman into her room: in course she holds out at first, but they gets over 'em a little way at a time or else forces 'em; and thus it comes after a time natural enough, and they can let them out."

"Infamous!" Dick cried.

"They don't think so: many of them what you'll see at the Haymarket and thereabouts has been real ladies' kidnapped like that, and kept a long time indoors before they let them out: they're always well looked arter to."

"Oh Rob! what a terrible place London be."

"Well, it aint the shiniest of cribs."

"But they shall not make Mary this! she have come to bad, but not to that; and shan't while I can interfere."

"We must look sharp, then!" Rob said, pulling him along.

Before they reached the house they met Tiger Loo; she was looking about in a very dissatisfied and spiteful manner; but as soon as she had saw Rob and Dick, she rushed forward and shook hands with them.

Then she looked in Dick's face as if willing to speak to Mary, but unable to communicate the sad intelligence.

But Dick read her looks.

"I know all about her," he said. "Rob here thinks that woman has sold my Mary. If she has——"

"If she has," Tiger Loo cried, "I'll tear her life out. Come back at once. I'll find out the truth."

Mrs. Gordan turned rather a queer colour when they showed themselves at the door. Tiger Loo pushed her back into the little parlour and entered quickly with her.

"You hamdan!" he cried with a terrible oath, "You've sold Mary!"

"Me!" muttered the old woman

"Don't *me* me! Tell me where she's gone, or I'll tear your tongue out of your throat!"

"How—how can I tell where she's gone?"

Tiger Loo uttered a frightful curse, and took hold of her by the hair of her head.

"If you don't tell me!" she exclaimed, "I'll beat your brains out against the wall!"

Mother Gordan had seen something of Tiger Loo's temper, and had heard more; she fancied the long lithe fingers looked remarkably eager to enter her thorax, and meddle about her lungs, and so she thought proper to gag.

"Let me go, and I will tell you."

Tiger Loo let her go, with a jerk that sent her to another end of the room.

"Now tell me before I lay hold of you again."

"A man came here, a gentleman," cried the terrified woman.

"Yes, yes!"

"He went to Mary's room."

"What did you let him for?"

"Keep off. I won't tell you if you come near."

The look Tiger Loo gave her frightened her out of her wits.

"Go on," she said, working her fingers eagerly.

"She went away with him."

"Where to?"

"I can't tell you."

"You wont!"

"I don't know."

Tiger Loo springing towards her,

"Will you tell!"

"I sent Jim to see where the cab went."

"Well."

"He hasn't come back yet."

Tiger Loo looked very much as if she was going to pull the old wretch's tongue out. She would certainly have laid violent hands on her if Dick had not spoke.

"What was he like?"

Mrs. Gordan was good at faces; she described Ralph so well that Dick at once knew him.

"It was the other of them," he said; "poor Mary, she has fell into bad hands."

"And you let her go with him, you old thief," cried Tiger Loo, again catching her by the hair of her head and lifting her up. "If Jim don't come back soon and tell us where to find her, I'll wring your neck."

"Take her off!" screeched the old woman, "take her off; she's like a tigress."

"You'll find me one," was Tiger Loo's reply.

Knock came at the door.

The old woman uttered a joyful cry.

"There's Jim!—he'll tell you."

"It's lucky for you he's come," Tiger Loo answered.

Jim came in and explained the position of the house.

Dick hurried out of the room. Rob and Charley followed, and Tiger Loo, giving a vicious look to Mrs. Gordan, went after them.

"If I get him by the throat," Dick muttered, "oh! but I'll worry him."

CHAPTER LXVI.

HOW DICK MET RALPH MERTON.

POOR Mary was in that semi-unconscious state when Ralph got her into his room. The lady of the town whom he had been living with had a day or too previously decamped, and there was no one to consult on what he was going to do.

He looked with a fiendish thought on the helpless girl whom his villany had been so successful against. She was indeed in the power of a miscreant when she was shut up with him.

He let her sink to a couch, when she fell back in a deadly stupor; her face white as ashes; her form cold as the dead.

The heartless fellow was a little alarmed, and he hurried away to get some brandy to revive her.

He got some of this down her throat, but it was a long time before she came round; but then she had recovered full possession of her strength and energies; and when she found herself supported by his arm, her first act was to spring from his embrace.

He followed her not, fawning as one who supplicated her favour, but exultant as her master.

Mary was too brave a girl to let him overcome her, and as for yielding willingly, she would sooner have suffered him to dive to her heart the knife he menacingly displayed.

In proportion as her resistance to his efforts withstood his villany, so did Ralph become more deadly in his passion.

"I have brought you here," he said, "and I'll take care that you do not escape me. "If I have to lay you weltering in your blood, I will accomplish my design!"

Poor Mary, looking the villain in the face, saw how desperate his wickedness was; but even the contest of that knife, when he pressed it to her breast, did not subdue her; she forced him back and rushed to the window, shrieking.

She had raised the window, and in that moment of excitement would have flung herself out if Ralph had not rushed to her, and thrown a band round her face which drew he back, at the same time gagging and blinding her.

But in that living moment her face had been scanned, her voice heard, by one who remembered both, and as Ralph forced her to the couch there came a furious knocking at the door.

Ralph glared savagely round.

"If they come here," he muttered, "I will slit your throat!"

The unfortunate girl heard him shiveringly; she was already half-insensible from the brutal manner in which he was using her.

A half-smothered cry for help she uttered, and then lay palpitating and still beneath the knife he pressed against her breast.

But there was a sudden crush at the outer door; it gave; footsteps sounded through the house; the door of the room flew open, and Dick stood before Ralph.

Dick—not the simple country man Ralph had left him, but a strong, hard-faced, desperate man.

There was something terrible in the glance he cast upon Ralph ere he leapt upon him. Ralph instinctively drew back, and Mary sank on her knees to the ground.

The villain had raised the knife to meet Dick's attack; so used to deeds of blood he would not have hesitated at plunging it into Dick's heart, and might have done so in the rashness of Dick's attack.

He would only have been too glad to have disposed of him in this manner had there been none there, but even as his knife was raised for the murderous act, Roving Rob, Charley, and Tiger Low came into the room.

The two bullies lifted Mary and spoke soothingly to her; but she raised her glance to Dick, and with a wild shriek murmured his name and tottered forward.

Ralph heard the recognising cry, so did Dick; they had got each other tight now in the grip of Will.

Even with the others in the room Ralph would have used that knife, but Dick, who was the stronger of the two, got it away and held it to his breast.

"I could now slay thee," he cried, "and should be doing right; but I will not shed blood of your's here."

He lifted him in his arms like a child.

"You'll go out!" he exclaimed, "and find a resting place on the stones. Out! out of window! I will treat you like a dog."

He got him to the window. There was an instant's fearful struggle. Roving Rob caught sight of the white deadly face of Ralph, and the inflamed countenance of Dick, and stepped forward to stop what he looked upon as a very dangerous proceeding.

But he only got to the window in time to see the face of Ralph disappear, and hear a crash as he went headlong below.

A cry! a groan! several wild shouts as of people alarmed, came from beneath.

"Dick, my lad, make yourself scarce," said Rob. "If you aint broke his neck, you've broke his back, and there's a mob of the blues coming up."

"I care not," Dick cried, "I have done what was right. He would have done as much to poor Mary there?"

Poor Mary, she came trembling to Dick. The lovers of old stood facing each other for a moment. But how changed from what they were in their village home.

A moment they stood looking at each other, and then fell into each other's arms.

Those sobs that come from Mary's breast seemed rending her life; she wept and laughed and clung to Dick.

She had believed he was yet in that terrible prison, and now to see him free, and at such a moment, was almost maddening in its excitement.

He gazed upon the poor suffering face. Had there then been left the opportunity, how willingly would he have gone with her away from that Babel of misery, that united to each other they might have forgiven the past and atoned for the sins that each had committed. But that was not permitted. The voice of Charley and that of Rob warned Dick to fly.

"The police, dear Dick! they will take you. Escape if you love us!"

Dick looked sadly on the boy.

"They must take me sooner or later," he said.

"God bless thee, boy; but I cannot, will not flee, as if I were as guilty as they would believe me. For what I have done to him let them make me suffer if I have done wrong."

He drew Mary closer to his breast.

Then the voice of Tiger Loo was heard.

"Make them part, Rob! get him away! if he is taken he will hang on Monday morning!"

These words brought a sense of the results to Mary's mind. She looked up in Dick's face, and with a shriek said:—

"Oh Dick, don't stay! I shall die if you are taken there again! leave me! hasten away! we shall meet again! but do not linger now!"

"Yes, that's it! off you step it!" put in Rob. "Come on! Mizzle! dear, hear the blues coming up."

Dick unfolded his arms from about Mary.

"I will leave you," he said regretfully. "Not because I fear them, but because you ask, I flee from them like a coward."

"Not this time, my man," a harsh voice said.

They looked round as the door opened, and a sergeant of police entered, followed by two constables.

Dick glanced to the window.

There was yet a chance.

He drew Mary to his breast, and imprinting a kiss on her forehead, the first he had given her since he fell, whispered:—

"I will leap from the window; good-bye."

She drew from him sobbing.

The police had stepped forward to seize him.

He cleared his path by a blow of his muscular arm.

Next moment he was at the window.

Tiger Loo uttered a cry of delight as she saw the act, and stepped between him and the police.

"Off!" she cried; "they shrink from me till you have gone."

"He may save himself the jump," said the sergeant; "we've got enough down there to take him!"

But Dick had not stayed to hear. In the moment that he had leaped to the window-sill he took the spring.

Roving Rob and the others turned to the window. They heard his heavy fall. Then the hubbub of a number of voices.

Charley, with a low cry, flew out of the room and down the stairs.

Mary shrieked and fainted.

Tiger Loo, white with passion, looked as if she could have killed the officer.

Charley was soon below.

They were raising Dick from the ground. He had bruised and battered himself beyond hope of movement, and the police held him securely.

Charley shed tears as he took his uncle's hand. All that they had risked and done was in vain.

The doom he had escaped would now be his.

He was taken disabled.

Then a second time through his love for Mary.

Charley glanced tearfully round and saw Ralph Merton's spiteful triumphant face as he lay helpless on a stretcher.

CHAPTER LXVIII.

THE CRUSHER'S SENTENCE.

The injuries Ralph Merton had received were severe enough to keep him under the doctor's hands for a number of weeks. Dick had fared but little better; he was sadly bruised and shaken.

They carried him to Newgate, where he was put under the attention of the official medical attendant: neither Charley, nor anyone else being admitted to see him.

On the capture of Dick, Mary had fallen into a swoon, in which state she was taken away, waking to consciousness to know that only for her was Dick again taken.

The hurts he had received, and which he so much deplored, were, indeed, his safety, since, had it not been for that, he would assuredly have been hanged on the ensuing Monday; but that day arrived, and found him lying on a bed of sickness, and in such a state that even the officials of English law did not think it advisable to have him out to execution.

The news of his capture had been spread about, and public feeling was high to see him on the fatal morning; but the Sunday papers contained a statement to the effect that, in consequence of his dangerous state, he would not be put to death until he became better.

Many people laughed at the idea of bringing a man to perfect health for the mere purpose of squeezing the life out of him on the gallows; but the fact was it was not always that the law had been so merciful.

There had been some who recommended that he should be brought out, ill as he was, and seated in a chair which he might be hanged in.

But this had been over-ruled.

And so Dick for the present was saved.

And this safety kept him from the gallows; for in the interim the police gained intelligence which induced them to add a little to the Crusher's case, and as soon as that worthy could be got round, he was tried on the same charge for which Dick was to have suffered,

Crusher Jem looked very blue when he was put into the dock; he had been brought down by his prison confinement, and the many hints he had received, of what was likely to be his lot, had not put him in the best of temper.

And so when they tried him for burglary and murder he became very excited.

Charley came to the court the day of trial; he was called as a witness, and gave his evidence against the Crusher in a manner for which that worthy thanked him; he defended himself in a savage style, and was not sparing of his threats to the witnesses.

After a long trial it was found that there was a flaw in the evidence, and he was acquitted of the charge of murder.

But for the crime of burglary and violent assault upon officers, he was found guilty.

The judge, who had made up his mind to pass sentence of death, was exceedingly disappointed at the failure of justice.

He told Jem so.

"You are one of those brutal beings," he said, "whose existence is a danger and a terror to society. No law has restraint for you; your life is one career of violence and crime. I feel it my duty to sentence you to the highest term I can inflict, and that is penal servitude for life!"

Now the Crusher had been glorifying himself upon the fact of having got off the capital charge, the other he thought a mere bagatelle.

Twelve months was the most he expected. But penal servitude for life!

That was a dose he did'nt expect to have. As soon as the judge had finished sentencing him, he gave utterance to a most savage oath, and seizing an inkstand, which unfortunately lay near, hurled it at the learned gentleman's head.

It did not hurt him, but passed so close as to make the judge believe he was knocked over. Of course there was a great commotion in the court; the Crusher was pulled down by half a dozen policemen and dragged away.

This act of the prisoner rather enraged the judge. He would have given him a little more punishment if he could have done so, but as there was no term longer than life, he could not imprison him beyond it.

But he called him back as they were taking him out of court.

"I gave my opinion of you just now," he said, "and you have verified it. There is no longer term than the one I have sentenced you to, but I shall take care that a statement of your conduct shall be sent to the prison authorities, who besides looking after you, will see that indulgence of a Ticket of Leave is not extended to you. The remainder of your life you may look forward to spending in a prison, and without the indulgences accorded to your fellow-prisoners. I will take care that you do not have any to spare, and such things as puddings shall not be allowed you."

Do not smile, good reader, at the inclusion of such things in the fare of prisoners. They have many such luxuries, and the restrictions the judge made in the Chrusher's case was one that Jem felt in the highest degree.

"Thank you," he said, "I will try and make it shorter if I can."

He turned his scowling glance on those who had given evidence.

"And if I do get out, I won't forget some on you, particularly you, you young whelp," he cried turning savagely to Charley.

The boy looked disdainfully at him, but made no reply. He had done his best to bring about his conviction, but did not fear him even if he should make good his word and escape from prison.

As they were leading him from the dock, he again cried to Charley, giving expression to a fearful curse at the same time.

"I shall get out soon my young nipper, and then if I don't wring your neck may I die."

The policeman hurried him away, but to the last his savage tones could be heard as he cursed right and left of him.

When they had taken him to the van, Charley returned to Tiger Loo, who had been staying with Mary. They were concocting a plan with Roving Rob for coming to the rescue of the Downy Cove, who having been taken from the condemned cell, was put in another, to answer the charge of attempting to get Dick off.

But nothing could be done, and the Downy was accordingly left to take his chance, his friends merely getting on his side one of those able lawyers always to be found in readiness for any Old Bailey trials.

The part which Tiger Loo and the Downy Cove had taken in getting the Crusher lagged, had made them outcasts from the fraternity of thieves and scamps, and had it not been for the protection the presence of Rob gave, Tiger Loo would have been the object of some secret revenge; for these gentry and sisterhood have a way among themselves of settling such matters, and the one who "peaches" usually comes in for something very strong.

Strange to relate, at the trial of the Downy Cove, the rascally lawyer who had charge of the case made such an able use of the circumstances, that the officials were puzzled in what form to proceed against the Downy, and he was ultimately let go.

This unexpected termination to his misfortunes quite overcame the Downy Cove. He thanked the magistrate with tears in his eyes, and offered up his prayers in the most pious manner as he went from court.

Mr. Gloden, who had before interested himself about Charley, happened to hear all about Dick, and he made a very able case out for the consideration of the Home Secretary; the result of this was, that Dick was respited from hanging, and sentenced to transportation.

Poor Charley! he was affected, indeed, when the dreadful doom that had so long overhung Dick was announced; and Dick, with a sullen discontent, heard the reprieve which, for an unjust charge, sentenced him to be sent as a felon from his own country.

Mary came to see him often. Charley usually accompanied her; and many an affecting scene took place in the little room where they were allowed to meet. Mary was more light-hearted now that Dick was given his life, and because that Gloden had promised to use his influence to get the whole of his sentence remitted, and then take him in hand to make of him an honest member of society.

"I have never lost my honesty, though I have lost my character," Dick had said, when they were telling him of this; "and if I get clear now, I will not again fall into such snares as I have been thrust in. We will go far away, dear Mary, and forget what has happened."

And then Mary would kneel down by him, and weep upon his hands, and say she was unworthy of being with him; but Dick, though it had cost him a hard struggle to forego her avengement on Hal Warner, had said he would not look again on the past.

Mr. Gloden's promises so raised their hopes, that they looked upon Dick's acquittal as certain.

They did not know how difficult it is, even for an innocent man, backed by strong recommendations, to get out of the clutches of the law when once they have laid hold of him.

And so it turned out, that, in spite of Mr. Gloden's influence, the sentence of Dick was not annulled; he was to leave the country, and then it would depend upon his conduct there whether he was permitted to return upon a ticket of leave.

This intelligence came like a thunderbolt to those who had learned to look upon his release as sure. Dick himself was much cast down. He clenched his hands, and stared hard into the kind-hearted gentleman's face.

"A ticket-of-leave man!" he cried. "Oh! sir, I did not think I should be made this. I could bear suffering and hardship, but to be branded as a felon, to be sent away to work in chains with a felon gang, and then to come back and find my character gone, and everyone sneering me, as if I were a leper, oh! Mr. Gloden, it be hard indeed!"

"It is sad," Mr. Gloden said.

"But I am afraid there is no hope now till some little time, at least, of your sentence has been carried out; but I will not forget you, I will use all my power to bring you back as soon as possible. I have some influence with the chaplain, and do not doubt that you will soon be set at liberty."

"It is kind of you," Dick said, "but if I am there only for a day it will cling to me for life; poor Mary, too, and Charley,"

"I will take care of them," Mr. Gloden answered kindly, "they shall not be alone while I am here."

Dick felt the tears gushing to his eyes, he grasped the hand of the good-hearted gentleman in his own, and cried.

"Oh, sir, if there were more like you, there would not be so much wrong, so much suffering in the world; I have been ungrateful, for you have given me my life; I will bear my punishment, and though it his hard to be looked upon as a convict, I will not give way; they shall not lead me to do anything that will give them cause to keep me there."

"That's right, Richard; I am glad to hear you talk like this; we have all our troubles more or less, and yours have come heavily; but do not despair, the same hand that has saved you from one unjust doom, may set all things to rights yet."

"It will," Dick exclaimed, "don't 'ee fear, Mary, I will come back again, and we shall see the bright days we used to dream of."

"Dick," Mary said, "I will not stay here if they send you away; I will go to, that's if you will let me."

"It will not rest with me," said Dick, sadly, "I shall be sent away as some wild brute; I might as well be dead, as far as that goes; still I think you had better stay here; here is one good friend, and I don't know where you will find one if you come with me."

"She had better stay here," Mr. Gloden, observed, "you will be allowed to write to each other, and she will be free from many trials which would fall to her if she were there?"

Mary, however, still insisted that she would go, and Mr. Gloden did not seek further to dissuade her.

But Charley did.

"Let her stay here," he said, "till we see if you are coming back, and then we will both come if you are not."

"I think that is the best course," Mr. Gloden remarked.

"It will," Dick replied; "think of it Mary. Mr. Gloden will see that you are not left in the power of those villains that have had their malice against me; in a few months I may come back."

Mary tearfully assented, and it was decided that both she and Charley should remain at Mr. Gloden's house till Dick's case was settled.

A few days after this saw Dick manacled and in chains, on board a vessel *en route* to a penal settlement. The parting with Mary and Charley had been a sad one, and had nearly drove him mad, and now, as the days and nights passed wearily on, he almost wished that the law, in the first instance, had taken its course, and put him out of his misery.

We will leave him now on his way to a land where the felon toils amid ignominy and shame, and return to the Crusher, whom we left being led to his cell, from which he had promised to make his escape.

CHAPTER LXIX.

HOW THE CRUSHER GOT OUT OF JAIL.

They put Crusher Jem in the prison at Pentonville, and stuck him in, what is called, the penal class, where he had the worst usage of the body, his character having been so well placarded by the judge in his commitment paper.

Crusher Jem bore the extra drill and work to which he was subjected, with the stoppage of those indulgencies accorded to other persons—he bore all this with a sullen sort of determination, holding little conversation with those who came to him to see how he got on with his labours, and indeed never speaking except to indulge in some muttered curse.

As his character, in this respect, remained, day after day, the same, he became looked upon as one of those desperate men who required extra looking after, for fear of their savage passions leading them to such little eccentricities as the choking or stabbing of warders.

Crusher Jem would not have stood nice about doing either if he had been given the chance, but the warders were pretty active and vigilant; they never allowed him any opportunity of wreaking his vengeance on them.

So after a while Jem thought he had been there long enough. He got up very early one morning, and having previously loosened the bricks that supported the bars of his window, he got out and thought he would take a morning walk.

But some of the warders were up as early as he, and before he had gone far he met two of them, who, fearing that he might be ill if he went out without his breakfast, walked him back, after a great display on his part, which was only quieted by the application of some stout thwacks on the head with a heavy stick.

The next time was when Jem was let out for his regulation exercise, when he tried a little in the gymnastic way and got to the roof of the prison, but just as he was taking a leap he found himself pulled back by one of the never-failing warders.

He was looked after so well from this, that it was three months before he got another chance of getting so high up in the world, and then he made a jump from a much higher spot.

But as ill luck would have it, one of the spikes caught his jacket, and he hung head downwards till about an hour afterwards, when, being missed, he was sought for and found in that interesting position.

The repetition of a number of these attempts induced the authorities to think that the air of Pentonville was too bracing for him, so he was sent to Millbank penitentiary, and made to work there like a horse.

Whenever he went out for his official exercise, he was well searched by a warder, to prevent any unhappy *contretemps*. Crusher Jem used to growl savagely at the way they pulled him about, but he had made up his mind to a most desperate plan for escape, and was resolved to get out or be taken not alive.

One day when Jem was at work one of the supervisors, a young hand incautiously laid down a knife by his stool; it only rested there a moment. Jem, who was hard at work making mats, let some of the rough stuff fall and picked up the knife with it; it went instantly up his waistcoat, and then was wriggled round till it lay, flat and unobservable, against his back bone.

The young fellow, who had laid down the knife, having been hurriedly called away, came back looking about for the article; he could not exactly tell where he had left it, and as Jem was working away with the dogged apathy of the convicts when employed at any trade in the prison, there was nothing in his manner to indicate that he had seen the weapon.

So after a vain look about, the young fellow walked away.

How that savage heart of Jem's exalted when he saw him go! He held a weapon at last, and if it did not help him to liberty, would at least allow him an opportunity of having his revenge.

How he would have like to have been shut up in the cell with Dick or Charley, that he might have thrust that long knife into their hearts.

But he worked away till it was time to leave off.

None would have known that the black passions of his breast were singeing and revelling in the contemplation of murder.

Ay, murder!

The Crusher had taken a particular dislike to one of the warders: the man had come with him from Pentonville; he was always near him, and had been the means of some extra punishment being imposed upon Jem.

Jem did hate this man, if ever one hated another.

And this warder had got a habit of coming to Jem's cell at untimely hours, to see what he was up to.

In going to and from his work or exercise, this warder—Marks was his name—was very officious in having Jem searched.

He had, what was popularly termed, his knife in Jem, and Jem wished for the chance of having his knife in him, only literally instead of figuratively.

Now the plan which had suggested itself to Jem's mind was this:

Marks' anxious regard for Jem's welfare, was so well known, that it was enough to say "Marks had searched him," or "Marks had been to his cell; they knew they could trust then to his being safe.

So Jem thought that, if he could get to his cell with the knife, he could lie quietly in wait till Marks came, and then as soon as he was well inside, he could give him just one lunge with the knife, taking care to drive it well home.

Jem did not want to make a long job of it, nor had he any particular desire for the melodramatic revenge of standing over his victim, and revelling in his agony; he wanted to do the job swift and sure. It would be satisfaction enough to feel the knife going into the warder's breast, and to see his look of agony when he drew the reeking weapon out. He often thought and planned while his fingers went on as usual with their work, neither faster nor slower, but just at a dogged, sullen, steady pace.

After he had disposed of the warder—so his thoughts ran—his chance of escape would present very favourable appearance, from the fact, beforementioned, of their leaving him as looked after when Marks took the matter under his care. He could creep out of his cell, and still armed with the red and formidable weapon, fight his way out.

Crusher Jem was not anything of a romancer; he had enjoyed hard experience of prisons, and knew that getting out of them was even to the most desperate of men a very trying and hazardous operation.

But Jem had used his eyes and his wits, and had mastered one or two difficulties in getting out.

He brooded over his plans until he in imagination thought himself out of that prison, and already wreaking his revenge on poor little Charley.

In the midst of these agreeable reflections he felt the touch of a hand on his shoulder; he knew whose voice it was that spoke.

"No. 49—want you!"

The Crusher sullenly put down his work and rose.

Marks was standing by him.

He was tempted then to risk all upon the hazards, and plunge his knife into the other's body; but the steady eye of the warder was fixed upon him; he seemed to be reading his thoughts and preparing for his action.

"What d'ye want?" Jem asked, sullenly.

"Come with me."

Two other warders came up; the trio conducted Jem to his cell.

The Crusher knew what was the matter.

They were going to search him.

No chance then of his little scheme of vengeance having effect. The keen eyes of Marks would detect his secret.

It was very galling to be disappointed in the first flash of his plans, and the Crusher grew white with rage when Marks said—

"No 49, we want that knife."

Jem muttered a deep curse: thoughts passed through his brain like lightning. A deep frown clouded his mind, and he resolved at that instant to make the most of his chance, and even if he were hanged for it, satiate his spite.

Quick as lightning he had the knife out, and make a swift lunge at the warder's breast, a thrust that had been his enemy indeed, for it must have gone right through his body, had he not been as sharp as Jem.

At the first moment he stepped aside, and seized Jem's arm.

The next instant the Crusher found himself disarmed and held by the two warders.

"I thought you had the tool," Marks said, as he held up the long dangerous weapon, when I heard Ansell say he'd lost it. "I'm very glad, too, that you've shown us what you wanted it for, because now there will be no difficulty in putting a few stripes on your back."

The Crusher ground his teeth; he saw that he had fallen into a trap; he muttered many a deep curse, as they put the irons on him previous to locking him up.

It was not right of the warder, even supposing the man to be ever so bad, to bind him down in the way he did; he would have done the same to a better man had he taken a dislike to him, and this persecution, which is too often practised towards the prisoners, is the cause of many a warder being stabbed by the convicts.

The object of punishment should be to give the man a hope of amendment, and not be made a means of worrying him on to fresh crimes.

Sullen and savage as the Crusher was, no treatment would have subdued his murderous nature, but he might have remained quiet if Marks had not been ever about him.

Next morning came, and Jem was brought up. The charge of secreting a knife and attempting the life of the warder, was read over to him, and as a summary means of dealing with him, he was sentenced to receive thirty lashes at once.

And he did, Marks standing by while they were administered.

It is a horrible sight to see a man flogged; horrible to hear the strong swinging hiss of the lash as it sweeps through the air and tears along the culprits back, leaving its red track of blood and agony.

Crusher Jem stood it with the savage obstinacy characteristic of him. He never winced, but ground his teeth together, and muttered his savage curses, while the blood oozed from the gashes, and his back became one raw, lacerated mass.

When they took him down, they were startled a little at the expression of his features.

Only Marks regarded it with absolute indifference.

It was some time before Jem's back healed. There was little difference in his manner; only at times, when he caught the eye of Marks, a murderous look gleamed from his own.

He had sworn, come what might, he would have that man's life.

But he had learned one lesson, and that was, to wait.

He had learned a subtler cunning than he had before possessed.

If it were not possible to reach him otherwise, he would strangle him, and suffer death.

But if it were possible, he would get out of that prison, and make it his business to lie in wait for his man, weeks, months—it mattered not how long—so that he reached him at last.

Oh, yes! Crusher Jem had learnt the value of being able to wait.

Very secretly Jem went to work now. He wanted to make a certain escape out of Millbank Prison.

His nearest way was out of the window, that was about forty feet from the ground; so that if he got out, it would not do to jump it.

No, he must have a rope to descend by. That was the first difficulty, and Jem went to work to overcome it.

He never sat at his work that some portion of the fibrous material he used did not find its way up his sleeve, or inside his trousers—a few shreds at a time, never more.

He never went to the chapel on Sunday that he did not contrive to tear up a few shreds of the cocoa-nut matting.

All these he carried away, and secreted in his cell.

Very cunning must Jem have been to secrete this where it could not be found; but Jem did.

And how?

Let us see.

Jem, one day, in a fit of spite, broke up his drinking mug. The handle he chewed in a dozen pieces.

Jem had strong teeth.

But he had put that handle to a use before it was taken away.

There were some bricks forming the wall at one end of the cell.

Jem worked with the handle of this mug till he had got away the outside mortar in large pieces, which he carefully put by.

Then he worked away till he cleared out all the mortar from between the sides.

And lastly, he got the brick out.

How Jem chuckled when he had managed that.

This was where he concealed the stuff he got to make his rope of. When it was lodged behind, he could fit the brick in, and lay the pieces of mortar in their place. It took a delicate touch to do this, but Jem was very careful.

Of course, when he had got the brick back, there was some powdered mortar that would not go back. There was no way of getting rid of that by throwing it out of window, because there was a skylight immediately underneath, and it might have been heard to fall.

So Jem gathered it up in his hands, and swallowed it.

He even licked up what remained on the ground.

Day after day did Jem perform his toil of oakum and mattting, and night after night he sat in his cell weaving a tough, strong rope.

It was slow work, but he accomplished it. He managed to conceal it all behind the brick, only that, as the rope became longer, and took up more room, he had to swallow more of the mortar.

Jem would have gnawed away the whole brick to have got out.

Jem had got a good way on his venture when he had made the rope long enough to reach the roof below.

He didn't mind the punishment he got for breaking up the mug; it all went down to the one score.

The rope was finished, and he was really for getting out. The concealment of the material had taught him a way of escape he had not before dwelt upon; and that was, to make a hole in the wall large enough to get out by.

No easy task; but what will not perseverance effect!

The day came upon which he had resolved upon his escape.

There was no change in his conduct, nothing different in his looks or manner; and yet Marks, who was still on the alert, had an idea that Jem was up to something.

By the same instinct, the Crusher had an idea that he would meet Marks before he had got much further in his attempt.

When they brought him his last meal, Jem amused himself by neatly taking off the wire rim of his tin mug, and occupied himself in forming it into a sort of hook.

He twisted and bound it up very closely before he was satisfied, and then he let them take away his mug.

The absence of the rim was not observed.

Evening came, and Jem was locked in by Marks. They caught the glance of each other's eyes just before the door was shut, and each had his former suspicions strengthened.

Two hours Jem allowed to pass, and then he went to work briskly. He first pulled the brick out of the wall, then he powdered up the mortar and sand that he pulled out, and, making a bag of his handkerchief, put it therein.

He had judged well in all his measures. He sat himself down then beside the hole, and worked away, till he got another brick out.

When he had removed half-a-dozen of the first layer, he tried his hand on the second.

This was venturesome and slow work. There was no purchase for his fingers; and he had nothing else to work with, except the small hook of wire, and with this and his fingers he tore away at the mortar till he loosened it all round this, and got out the brick.

Then another and another.

One by one he arranged them along the floor of the cell.

It was frightful work, his nails were torns and split, and his fingers were bleeding to the quick.

Still he persevered.

And at last he came to the outer row: the first brick was got out and the moonlight, with the fresh air, came in.

Crusher Jem had worked himself into a cold sweat; thick drops were on his low ruffian brow and sallow cheeks.

And at this moment, when his energies were at a fearful strain, he heard a sound which he well knew.

There was a panel in the prison door with an iron grating through which the warders could look in upon their prisoners.

This was being opened.

It fortunately did not command a view of the corner in which he was working, which was at the side (he had taken care of this before he began), but the end he was supposed to sleep on was almost opposite, and of course it could be seen that it was unoccupied.

So Jem was not the least surprised when he heard the door heavily opened, nor did he fail to guess whom it was that came to honour him by so late a visit.

He rose to his feet and got behind the door as it opened, and Marks stepped into the cell.

He had scarcely entered before the Crusher raised his fist and struck him a terrible blow on the temple. Marks uttered a faint cry and grappled the Crusher violently, but the powerful blow had taken effect, and he fell back stunned.

Crusher Jem bore him quickly to the floor of his cell and knelt upon him. That moment he had wished for had come.

His bitter persecutor was in his power.

How he wished he had a knife then; he felt in the warder's pockets for one, but he had not such an article about him, nor had he his official sword with him.

The Crusher tried first the piece of wire and then the sharp edge of a broken brick, but with all his power neither were sufficiently pointed to cut the warder's throat open.

So the Crusher took his throad in his deadly grasp, and squeezed it till the last convulsive struggle of the warder had ceased.

Then he savagely jumped on his face and breast.

If he had possessed the time he would have stayed to batter his brains out, but as delay was dangerous he contented himself with thus disposing of him, and returned to complete his escape.

Having one brick out of the wall it was not difficult to tear away others, and he soon had an opening wide enough to squeeze his body through.

He took up his rope and the hook and bag of sand and crawled out of the aperture. Having fastened the rope to the side, he let himself down on the roof of a building called the general ward, it being about twelve feet down. The roof of this building is partially of glass, the building itself being used as a Roman Catholic chapel, and capable of holding from 280 to 320 prisoners. Having got into this ward through one of the skylights, the Crusher possessed himself of a piece of board about six feet long by nine inches wide, forming one of the tables, and also took all the sash lines of the windows.

The object of getting to this place was to possess himself of the lines from the windows to lengthen his rope, as he did not think it advisable to attempt egress by means of the chapel.

It was therefore necessary to re-ascend to his cell, and to do this he secured the piece of board so as to form a kind of platform, its support being so frail that the least movement threatened to precipate him below.

Whilst in this precarious position, and whilst trying to get up to the skylight, he fancied he heard a sound beneath him.

This sudden movement caused the board to swing, and for a moment Jem being between life and eternity, it was a crisis of peril; he thrust out his hands and touched the wall with the tips of his fingers in time to save his frail platform from over-balancing and hurling him below.

Whatever sound it was that had so startled him, he did not hear it again, and he now made a most desperate effort to regain the roof.

He balanced himself on the board so that it stood perfectly evenly poised, and was just preparing for a spring, when he felt the board sliding from under his feet.

To fall would be to be shattered in pieces on the stones of the chapel floor, to rest there or catch at anything, impossible; he could not have time to support himself again by the wall ere the plank gave way, or if he did there was nothing to hold on by, and the sliding of the plank would hurl him down.

He thought for a moment of the man whom his fingers had choaked, and who lay up above in the cell, and then made one desperate and tremendous spring.

All this was in an instant, and as his foot left the plank it fell below; if then he missed his hold or failed to clutch it firm enough to hang on by it, it would be all over with him; every nerve in his system was strained; his fingers were apart, they grasped at the line of the skylight above, clenched on the wood and tightened there, the small panels of the broken glass cutting into his hand.

For a few seconds he hung there powerless. He had reached the frame; but another spring was required to get through; and the glass was so cutting his hand that to hold on much longer would be impossible.

Crusher Jem grew cold all over; he let his grasp relax a little, then gathered himself up. All his body seemed thrown into a coal, and up he rose, his elbows resting on the frame; slipped, he felt himself falling; a second plunge, his arm lay bleeding along the jagged glass, but he gained a purchase there that he held, despite the agony, until he got his whole body through, and stood upon the roof.

He sat down overcome; he tore strips from his shirt, and wiped the sweet from his face and the blood from his hands.

Then he tried to get the bits of glass out of his fingers.

Having done this as far as possible, he bound up his wounded arm and prepared for the ascent.

The cord rope hung for him, he wound the rest about his body, and ascended.

Half way up a thought occurred to him that made him pause.

If anyone should have come to the cell, they had the advantage to seize him as soon as he made his appearance.

After doing so much he did not like the thoughts of being taken.

Certain death it was for what he had done to the warder.

He paused, climbed a little way, then listened, and finally recommenced his ascent.

Not a sound came from the cell.

He sprang up and peered in.

The warder still lay where he had left him.

He was quiet enough.

No one else was there.

The Crusher re-entered the cell.

He went to the door and satisfied himself that no one was near.

Anyone else might have thought that the best way of getting out; but the Crusher knew he should not go far before he was stopped.

He was proceeding upon a plan which he had formed and mastered, after making the most of the observations allowed him in his exercise at work and in the chapel.

All being still, he gave the prostrate form of Marks a kick, and again crept out of the hole in his cell.

Up above along the roof of the prison ran a gutter for the conveyance of the rain.

The Crusher, throwing up his rope, having fastened the bag of sand and mortar to the hook, got it to catch on the edge of the pipe; he then fastened the rope of sash lines to it, and easily climbed up.

The gutter bent and shook with his weight, and the frail hook threatened to slip off; it was indeed an insecure hold, and his neck was not worth a moment's purchase as he hung to the rope.

A little more bending of the gutter, or the least shift of the hook, and he would have been precipitated to the roof of the chapel.

He got to the top at last in time to see that the hook had been drawn by his weight nearly straight, and caught by the merest purchase in the world.

He grasped the rim of the gutter, and by a leap gained the roof.

Looking down he saw the perils that had threatened him; it was, indeed, a wonder that he had not fallen to the bottom.

He was now on the roof of the principal building, and he walked across till he came to the edge that looked over the garden.

It was dizzy to look down. The Crusher had to act cautiously, and fixed the rope round one of the chimneys.

He then let the end fall, and found that it reached within a foot or two of the ground.

He slid down it safe, but the wounds in his hand were torn open again, and the agony made him groan.

Yet he had accomplished the most perilous part of the most desperate escape of modern days.

Jack Shepherd himself never made one so hazardous.

He now stood in the garden, shut in by the boundary wall, which is about 25 feet high, too high for the most astute climber; but the Crusher was prepared; he had let the hook end of the rope fall to the ground, and giving the rope a jerk, broke it about the required length.

The hook required only a little more bending; he threw it up with the sand bag still attached, and made a lodgment on the wall.

This accomplished, he stayed only to throw off his jacket, and hastily climbed up.

He had just reached the wall when the first sound that had broke the silence of the night came from the prison.

It was his cell!

The cry of escape!

They had discovered his flight. The desperate man, Crusher Jem, hurled the rope back into the garden; there was only a piece of open ground with some iron railings to keep him in.

He was across the ground, over the railings, and making away, before the outcry within the prison had awakened the officials to the search.

Half an hour afterwards he might have been seen cleansing the blood and dust from his body in the waters of the Thames, near Lambeth.

The whole prison was on the alert. The alarm had been caused by Marks, who, only half strangled by the Crusher, was, in a measure, brought round by the parting kick the ruffian gave him.

Crawling to the door, his faint calls summoned the warders, and the way of Jem's flight being speedily discovered, the most vigilant efforts were at once made for pursuit.

But though the police were immediately made acquainted with the escape, morning came, and no tidings came of the Crusher, except the report that a waterman had been knocked down, and robbed of a part of his attire by a powerful-looking man who had suddenly rushed against him.

Beyond that, inquiry was fruitless, and the officials of Millbank Prison had to record one of the most remarkable escapes ever known in the annals of prison intelligence.

Of course, the authorities were astounded at the escape; it seemed so impossible that, with their system of vigilance, a man should escape from the strongest of our modern prisons.

Only a few of the facts were allowed, at first, to leek out; and the report published of the event will show how much they were mystified at the daring outbreak.

"It appears," says a daily paper, in chronicling the affair—and we give the words, that the reader may see we do not draw upon fiction: "it appears that after his conviction he was removed to Pentonville, where he made certainly one, if not more, attempts to escape, but was frustrated in his endeavours, and removed from thence to the Penitentiary at Millbank for more safe custody. With a knowledge of his antecedents, he was there placed in what is called the penal class, being the worst class of prisoners, and during the time he has been at Millbank he has made nearly a dozen attempts to escape.

"On one occasion, indeed, he had nearly accomplished his purpose, having got out of his cell unperceived, and reached the roof of the prison, when he was detected, and for some time after kept heavily ironed.

"On that occasion he had in his possession a large knife; and it remains a mystery to the present day how he became possessed of such a formidable weapon, as it was not one of the knives in use in the prison.

"Moreover, the convict had at that time been in the prison for some months, and according to the regulations had been regularly searched and stripped twice in each week, the cell examined twice every day, and a search also made when he went out for exercise in the care of a warder, also when he came in; each prisoner, as it appears, going out separately with a warder in charge.

"It would seem from this almost impossible for any one of the prisoners to obtain possession of such a weapon as the knife referred to, or to keep possession of it if obtained, unless with the connivance of some one inside the prison. The escape just made seems to have been effected in this manner, and certainly immense ingenuity and fearlessness must have been exercised in the attempt which proved so successful.

"This daring escape was from E ward, in the fifth sexagon, the one that faces towards Ponsonby-place, and for coolness of execution and determination has hardly been surpassed. It is almost needless to say, that the utmost vigilance is being shown to effect the re-capture of the convict, but as the time goes on, of course the difficulty becomes increased."

It will be seen, then, that the officials did not explain everything that took place, especially about the knife; the true account of the manner in which it came into the possession of Crusher Jem we have given.

CHAPTER LXX.

THE CRUSHER BEGINS HIS WORK ANEW.

WHILE Dick, an innocent man, was being sent across the seas, to suffer in a penal settlement for other men's crimes, those who should, instead, have met the punishment, were abroad, doing fresh truckling.

There was bad Ralph, watching and plotting now that Dick was out of the way. And there was Crusher Jem, longing for revenge on Tiger Loo for causing him to be taken; and on Charley, for bearing evidence against him.

Poor little Charley! he was, indeed, inconsolable for his uncle's loss; but he remembered that he had a solemn charge committed to him—that Dick would look to him to watch over Mary, and keep her from the meshes of those who were planning against her welfare.

Mr. Gloden was very kind to both Charley and Mary. He did his utmost to cheer their spirits, and was unremitting in his endeavours to get Dick liberated.

He was a true Christian, without the ostentation of one. His were no noisy acts of cold charity. He worked in secret, doing good where it would most be felt.

He felt a great interest in Charley, and often took him out where he went.

One of these occasions was unfortunate to Charley as tending rather to suspicions that afterwards by Chrusner's malice fell on him.

A dirty ragged boy, with a worn-to-the-stump birchbroom in his hand, ran suddenly from the crossing where he had been sweeping the mud, and begged a "copper" of Mr. Gloden.

But all at once, just as Mr. Gloden was taking a "brown" out of his pocket, the stumpy broom fell to the mud, and the ragged urchin putting out a very dirty paw, caught Charley by the sleeve, and exclaimed in the tones which a London boy only can assume—

"Haloo! well, s' help me never! oh criminy! kiddle-a-wink! if it aint! What, don't you know me?"

Mr. Gloden stepped back. There was such a contrast between Charley, well clothed and clean, and the dirty, tattered boy who claimed acquaintance with him.

But Charley remembered his youthful interrogator.

It was Tony Nip. The boy whom we last saw carried to a hospital, after being rode over by the carriage beside which he had been turning head and heels.

So Charley, though he did not altogether like being stopped in that sudden manner by so wretched an object, was of too sterling a nature to disclaim an acquaintance whom he had known under such different circumstances.

Mr. Gloden, however, took Charley away. For the time he had forgotten his associations with strange characters, and he looked pained at this meeting.

"Do you know this boy?" he asked, with, as Charley thought, some trace of severity in his tone.

Charley briefly explained the circumstances under which he had known him.

Now it was Mr. Gloden's object to get Charley entirely out of the circle of those characters, and so he said sharply to Tony Nip—

"What is your name, boy?"

"Tony Nip, your 'onner."

"Where do you live?"

Tony grinned.

"I aint got no home," he said.

"How do you live?"

"How—why I fakes the tumble and does the sweep."

"If," Mr. Gloden remarked—this answer being totally incomprehensible to him—"if there's any chance of bringing you to an honest livelihood I will help you. At six o'clock this evening, I will send my servant to you, and we will see what can be done?"

He was on the eve of giving the boy a five-shilling piece, but a look at his knowing face and delapidated attire, induced him to believe that he would be doing him no service by giving him so large a coin, and he dropped a sixpence into his hand, and bidding him be there by six o'clock, crossed the road with Charley.

There is something very incomprehensible about the London street boy: his impudence; his cool defiance; knowingness, are things in which no boy in any country can approach him.

Johnny Crapeau, the nick-name for a French *garcon*, would be terrified out of his wits by the pluck of the true British boy.

Put out your hand to claim the attention of the London street boy, and his first movement is to dodge away from an antagonistic blow, which from conscience or the remembrance of unatoned delinquences, he seems always haunted by the fear of.

His next act is to bring his head up as rapidly as it went down, and with a look of the coolest defiance on his young-old face, square up to combat his assailant.

The London street boy delights in seeing a horse fall down, a house tumble in, or any such catastrophe. A chimney-pot flying suddenly on somebody's head, extorts from him a yell of pleasure, and when the plug is up in the street, he may be seen gazing in rapt admiration on the bubbling water, or splashing wildly through the flood into which it is his great joy to force weaker boys than himself, and the more innocent their look the greater his satisfaction at the trick he has played them.

At a fire his lugubrious voice may be heard terrifying old ladies and alarming timid old gentlemen. Drunken women and wild-brain creatures he marks as his especial prey, and may be often seen and heard following them with a body of his mates.

He loves to be always yelling the last popular song, of which "In the Strand" is his favourite. Generally his mouth is wide open as he utters the refrain or penned up as he whistles the symphony. He enjoys the trepidation of an old woman running after an omnibuss with a bundle in her arms, and should the said omnibuss make a lurch just as she gets one foot inside, and throw her on her back in the road, or forward into somebody's face, his delight knows no bounds.

Another great feet of his is to drop squibs and crackers amongst quiet people, invoking screams of fright from them, when he runs off in high glee; but his greatest enjoyment is when he can villify and dare an overgrown one of his one class—not yet a man—but too great to be considered a boy.

Unbounded is his glee in teazing this victim—for he knows that he can do so with impunity. If the goaded wretch did succeed in overcoming his many dodges and hitting him, he would not fail of being well abused by the passers-by for hitting the "poor little fellow."

In point of fact, the London street boy had better be left alone, as he invariably comes off best in all his tricks. A troop of them yelling and deriding some excited youth, whose collar, hat, boots, or respectability have excited their notice, are more sympathise with than their persecuted victim.

No respect has he for gracefulness or height, as he applies the epithets "lankey," "long'un," "shadder," "rasher," and "yard of pump water" indiscriminately to those whose tallness call forth these remarks, and is not awed in the least by the haughty stare with which he is tried to be put down.

If he can call out "whip behind" in time to see the cabman's lash curl round the shoulders of some one of his class who is running behind the vehicle, or, when no one is there, can excite the cabby to lash vigorously the back of the cab, his paroxysms of delight are frantic, and usually find vent in a Calmuc kind of yell.

He may be seen under all phases and circumstances, slouching along with his hands glued to his sides, or playing at "one-hole" with big stones. As a doctor's boy, he sallies forth with a basket on one arm, but as this occupation usually brings upon him the ignominy he exposes others to, and lays him under the bane of being called "squirt," buttons," and other opprobrious terms, he never essays this except as a last resource. As a butcher-boy, with a tray on one shoulder, the sharp handle of which it is his delight to so level as to come in contact with somebody's eye, when, with the most innocent look, he slouches off, leaving the victim smarting with pain.

As a newsboy, he saunters along with a bundle of papers under his arm, and pulls at the door-bell, where he has to deliver them, with a fury that sets them ringing for ten minutes afterwards, and brings hot looks of wrath from Jeames or Sarah.

During the day, he may be seen staggering under heavy loads, often dragging, at arm's length, a perfect pyramid of kettles and saucepans, or other articles. But when so laden, he is usually exposed to the reproaches of idle ones, for the London street boy has a great pride of his class, and thinks his dignity outraged if he is compelled to work. At night he may be seen staggering under heavy shutters, which, if he has a spite against his master, he thinks nothing of letting fall accidentally through the plate-glass window—the master's pride and boast.

We are led to give these details by the antics which Tony Nip indulged in as soon as Charley's benefactor had departed, leaving the sixpence in his palm.

By a very simple process, the coin was spat upon and carried to some unrummageable recess called a pocket. A grimace of the broadest kind then spread itself over his lubberly features, and his dirty thumb rested against his puggy nose, the fingers working curiously in the direction of Mr. Gloden's back.

But on seeing that gentleman turn suddenly, the jaw fell, the hand went down, the broom was picked up, and the stump end went to work, scattering the mud in all directions.

Mr. Gloden had, however, no sooner gone out of sight, than Tony flung his broom into the gutter, and took out the silver coin, which he again spat on, and turned over and over in his palm.

"A tanner!" he cried; "and ain't took a brown afore. Here's for a blow out, and the Vic. Wants me to stay here till six, as if I couldn't see as all he wanted was to shirk me off. Won't I tell Nobby Ned of this, when he comes out?"

Another boy, smaller than Tony—so small that he might have been almost unobserved — came stealthily up, with a look of wistful desire on his pinched face.

Tony Nip, as soon as he espied him, slipped the sixpence back in its hiding-place, and putting on the most innocent look, said—

"What d'ye want?"

"I don't want nothing," the little boy said, timidly.

"You'd better take it, and go," replied Tony— who, besides being a glutton, was a bit of a tyrant when he had the power, albeit a rank coward.

"Lend us your broom?" the small boy asked plaintively.

"Shan't."

"You ain't going to use it."

"Ain't I?"

"No; you chucked it away."

"Did I? Well, you won't have it."

"Please let me have it, and stay till you come again," pleaded the little boy. "Mother's dying, and Mary and Jack havn't had nothing to eat this three days."

"What a whopper! That's a jolly tale to come out with—better try it on somewhere else."

"It's true, it is," the small boy answered, crying.

"What are you blubbering for?" asked Tony—

than whom no greater blubberer existed. "Hold your row, or else I'll hit you."

"I'm so hungry," the small boy muttered; "let me sweep till you come back. I won't go till you come."

"What d'ye want to sweep here for?"

"I might be as lucky as you."

"I ain't been lucky."

"Yes, you have. I seed the gemman give you sixpence."

As this was so palpably the truth, Tony Nip could not fairly deny it. He looked, however, very much inclined to bully; but after a while, with that magnanimity so truly characteristic of the great, he condescended to let the boy have the broom; and the little fellow, with very grateful looks, picked up the birch, and went to his post.

If it had been Nobby Ned who had been the recipient of the sixpence, and the witness to the small boy's woes, he would have given him a penny or two-pence to go home with, and have waited till he came back; but the greedy Tony Nip thought only of himself, and even had the selfishness to make a bargain with the poor little boy.

"Mind," he said, "you'll have to give me half of what you take; I shall know if you try to cheat me."

And he sulkily went his way.

But the hungry little fellow did not have the chance of taking any money there. As soon as Tony Nip had slunk off to buy a penny 'buster' and cram his greedy maw, a bigger, fierce-eyed boy, who had been watching the whole scene, ran across the road, and snatching the broom from the little one's hand, pushed him away from the crossing, where he ensconced himself, and was soon, by his pertinacious begging, gleaning a few halfpence; but the poor little fellow whom he had driven away, and whom nobody cared to see righted, sat crying on the kerb till a policeman drove him off, when he tottered back to his dying mother, and his starved brother and sister.

CHAPTER LXXI.

CHARLEY AGAIN MEETS WITH TONY NIP.

CRUSHER JEM, after lying concealed by the water side, and having, in the meanwhile, pulled his clothes to tatters, made his way along the back streets of Lambeth, acting the part of a cadger as he went.

By these means he escaped the vigilant look out of the police, and got to his old haunt, where he lay quiet for a week, and then went forth to recommence his career of sin.

He had made some alterations in his appearance; his eyebrows he had shaved off, and he allowed a stubbly beard to grow on his chin.

He had also varied the shape of his nose, by sleeping with it pinched in an iron clamp, the effect of which was to throw it all on one side, and give the rest of his face a very singular aspect.

Crusher Jem did not want to be taken. He wanted to settle off old scores.

"I'll choke that cub," he growled once or twice when he thought of Tiger Loo, "or cut her throat; and as for that kid, I'll stick him the first time I come across him."

But Crusher Jem did not carry out the last part of his threat, inasmuch as the first time he met Charley, the latter was in the company of Mr. Gloden, and Jem had no desire to place his neck in a rope after so narrowly escaping.

Neither Mr. Gloden nor Charley observed him, and the Crusher, after taking good notice of the house, was about to stalk off, when he saw a dirty and begrimed boy, who had been following at some distance behind Charley, creep up to the door-step where they had gone in, and, after taking a good look at it, sneak off again.

This interesting youth was Tony Nip, who was very much surprised, as he was making off, to find himself grappled by the ear, and be pulled back.

"I didn't do nothing," were the first words that came from his lips, as he looked in a frightened manner over his shoulder.

"Come here!" growled the Crusher, who had hold of him.

Tony Nip silently walked away with the Crusher, who, as soon as he got him round the corner, said—

"Now, my young nipper, do you want to go to quod?"

"Oh! don't—I didn't do it."

"What did you want at that house?"

"I was only follering him."

"Who?"

"Why, Nix Charley; didn't you see him go in with the old buffer? My eye, ain't he a swell!"

"Who told you he lived there?"

"Nobody didn't; I comed after him to see where he lived, acos the old bloke said the other day he'd do something for me."

A device had entered the Crusher's head. Mr. Gloden was rich, and no doubt his house contained booty that would reward a burglar's entry.

The Crusher saw a way, by means of Tony Nip, not only to get into the house, but to make suspicion fall on Charley, and get him turned out or imprisoned.

"Now," he said to Tony, "you get in with that kid soon; come here after. Don't let them do anything for you; if you do, I'll break your neck. I want you to do just what I tell you, and nothing else."

"Yes, I'll do it," Tony said, rather terrified at the Crusher's threats.

"Come along, then, and I'll tell you what to do."

The Crusher very soon initiated Tony into his part. He found him very pliable, and easily moulded to what he wanted. Tony brushed himself up a little, and loitered about Mr. Gloden's house till Charley came out, when he went up to him, and spoke.

Charley kindly greeted him.

"We've been looking for you," he said; "what made you go away?"

Tony made a grimace.

"Ain't I green?" he remarked.

"We have indeed," Charley answered, seeing that Tony did not put much faith in his assertion. "You should not have gone away. But come along in; Mr. Gloden's at home, and will be glad to see you here."

But Tony rolled his head aside in a negative manner.

"Musn't come in."

"Why not?"

"Musn't. Got any browns?"

"Mr. Gloden will give you some money and

clothes if you come in, he is such a kind gentleman."

"So it seems: my eye; ain't you dressed fine; but you've got some tin, ain't you? Let's have some: I won't come near you again."

"I don't want you to keep away; come along in."

"No."

"Do."

"Can't."

"You'll be so happy if you do; have new clothes, and be able to go to work and learn."

"You don't do no work, do you?"

"No; but I will soon."

For a moment the good of Tony's nature prevailed, and he felt inclined to accept the good that lay in Charley's offer. His eyes were already glistening at the idea, when he caught sight of the Crusher watching them from a distance.

The sight of that individual brought back all his fears, and made him shun the good that lay in his path.

As Charley was persuading him, Mr. Gloden came to the dining-room window and looked in surprise on the two boys.

The artful Tony no sooner saw him than he cried:

"The guvner's looking;" and made off.

Charley was so surprised that he stood looking after him in dismay, and did not hear the door open, and his kind benefactor come out on the steps.

Mr. Gloden called him in quietly.

"I have every faith in you, my dear boy," he observed quietly, "but I do not like the looks of that idler whom you were talking with. Why did he run away like a detected thief when he saw me?"

"I do not know," Charley answered, colouring, "I wanted him to come inside, but he would not."

"I am ready to carry out my promise to him," Mr. Gloden observed, "but if he is not willing to avail himself of it I hope you will hold no communion with him."

This visit of Tony Nip caused some pain and unpleasantness, which was not decreased when an evening or two afterwards he again came, but ran away as before when Mr. Gloden showed himself.

He did this two or three times, and one evening, after Charley had gone out he showed himself in front of the house and then went after him.

He overtook Charley before he got far.

"I say," he said when Charley turned and saw him, "ain't you ashamed to walk away and leave a cove in the lurch?"

"I did not leave you."

"Gammon, you did; but never mind; I want to speak to you."

"What is it?"

"I say."

"Well?"

"Ain't the guvner got some tin?"

He grinned as Charley looked at him in surprise.

"It's a shame he should have such a swag."

"He does good with all he has," Charley replied.

"Oh, yes; but we could do better."

"What do you mean?"

"Why, I say—oh, wouldn't it be jolly?"

"What?"

"Why, to coller the dose."

Charley looked very hard at him.

"Rob him?———"

"No, coller; he wouldn't miss it. I say we can do it fine; I know a bloke as will come, and you can let me in———"

"And would you have me rob him who has so befriended me and mine? I would die first; you are a bad fellow to think of such a thing."

"Oh, it's all right; we could do it you know; they couldn't think of your doing it; you'll have shares in the swag."

"Hush!" Charley interrupted, "don't speak like that."

A man in plain clothes passed them at that moment. He took a hard look at them both and then passed out of sight.

Out of their sight, but not out of sight of them.

He was a detective in plain clothes, and, having heard the words of Tony Nip, now stood watching them where he could not be seen.

"How could you think such wicked things?" Charley exclaimed; "some one has been putting you up to this. If you talk like it again, I will never let you speak to me."

Tony Nip put his great red knuckles in his eye, and began to blubber.

"I didn't mean it," he yelled, "don't hit me; I didn't mean it."

Charley looked at him to read if his tears were sincere.

"If I thought you were so wicked, I should beat you," he remarked; "but I don't."

"I ain't," blubbered Tony.

"Well, don't cry."

"You makes me."

"Here, take this shilling—I haven't got any more money. You can buy yourself something with that. Come to-morrow, and you'll have all sorts of nice things."

The man in plain clothes passed them again. Tony Nip, pocketing the shilling, looked slyly round, and, catching sight of a policeman in the distance, ran away as hard as his legs would carry him.

Charley was, of course, as much surprised at this as he was when Tony ran away before; but, persuading himself that it was merely the manner of the foolish boy, he went on his way.

He never thought that all this was part of the Crusher's plan, or that Tony could be so ungrateful and wicked as to do all this merely to get him into prison.

Nor did he know that the detective was noting down all that occurred.

CHAPTER LXXII.

HOW THE CRUSHER GOT INTO THE HOUSE.

"READY for the job to-night?" asked the Crusher of his pal, a lean-faced, vicious-eyed, costermonger-looking fellow.

"I'm all ready, Jem."

"Get the glim ready."

"Here we are."

"Here, give us that knife?"

"Ain't going to use it, are you?"

The Crusher grinned savagely.

"Perhaps I shall."

The other made no reply, but went on packing the implements necessary for a burglary.

"Think it's all right?" he asked, presently.

"Right as hell!"

"How are we going to get in?"

"I'll tell you when that whelp comes up."

The "whelp" referred to was Tony Nip, who came up, looking rather scared and nervous.

"Come here, you young thief," cried the Crusher, with an oath; "where have you been?"

"I ain't been nowhere."

"Ain't you; set off with you; wait till the Kiddy lets you in, and don't move till you hear me throw gravel up at the winder."

"I won't move."

"Come here. Don't go to sleep, and let us come and not make you hear."

"I won't."

"If you do I'll wring your neck when I come in, and you're a bit of a sleepy-head—so mind."

"I shan't be sleepy."

"And look here; if you'r took, if you don't say Charley let you in, I'll skin you alive."

"I ain't to be took, am I?" asked Tony, looking woefully at his master.

"Hold your jaw, and be off, or I'll break it."

Tony had before had a taste of the Crusher's fist and boot, so he made all haste to get out of the crib, and perform his part of the plot to ruin poor Charley, and strip the house of its valuables.

Mr. Gloden had gone from home that night. The Crusher had ascertained this before he fixed upon it for the burglary. Only one servant was there besides Charley, and he was standing by the window, looking out into the lighted street, when Tony Nip, looking stealthily about him, and seeming in great fear of being seen, made his appearance.

Although the room was darkened in which Charley was standing, Tony Nip could see him. Standing by the lamp, and on the edge of the kerbstone, so that he could be seen by every one who passed that way, Tony put his finger to his lips, and looking stealthily round, beckoned Charley out.

Charley wondered at the mystery affected by the homeless boy, but he left his place by the window, and coming to the door, opened it.

Tony, looking round again, slunk up the steps.

"May I come in?" he asked.

"Yes," Charley said, "you may."

Tony slunk in.

His eyes widened when he saw the magnificent antings in the hall, and the gilding of the ceiling.

"Oh, my!" he cried; "ain't it fine?"

Charley took him to his room, quite pleased that he had at last succeeded in getting him to come in.

"Sit down," he said, "and I will bring you something to eat."

The gluttonous maw of Tony opened.

"I'm jolly hungry," he exclaimed.

"You shall have some supper with me." The kind-hearted boy went away, and fetched a capital supper, of which Tony partook with greedy zest, his great eyes wandering about the room all the time.

"My!" he muttered, with his mouth full; "ain't you snug here? Is this your room?"

"Yes."

"All yours?"

"Yes."

"My!"

Tony could say no more! he stuffed his maw full of bread and meat.

"Shouldn't I like to live in a place like this? It must be jolly! You're jolly, ain't you?"

Charley sighed. He thought of Dick, by that time far away.

"I'm so hungry," Tony continued. "Ain't had no dinner."

"No dinner!"

"No, nor no breakfast neither."

"Here," Charley exclaimed, putting a large piece of meat before the lying young glutton; "have some more?"

"My!" spluttered Tony "ain't we having a tuck in?"

At that moment the thought of the Crusher came to his mind, and his jaws instinctively fell with a great gulp. A piece of meat that was in his mouth at once slipped down his gullet, and stuck half way there.

Charley saw the ragged boy's eyes distend, and heard the gurgling noise in his throat.

He jumped up, seeing that the young glutton was fast choking, and commenced thumping him on the back.

"Oh!—guk—oh!—guk," spluttered Tony, "Guk —I'll—tell—guk—all—oh!"

Here Charley, who was getting as frightened as Tony, hit him a hard blow on the nape of the neck, and shook the piece of meat down his throat.

Tony dropped to the floor, where he lay gasping.

"I thought I was choked. Oh, crikey! I ain't said nothing, have I—oh!"

"You're all right now," said Charley.

"Yes—what did I say?"

"You only said you were choking."

"I were wisht I—oh! I feel ill."

"Never mind, you shall stay here."

"Shall I?"

"Yes, and sleep with me."

"Oh! then I don't mind," rejoined the young traitor, delighted at the success of his wicked mission.

The two boys, the one so treacherous and ungrateful, the other so unsuspecting and good-natured, sat there together, talking of the time when they first met in the hole of the railway arch. Charley heard with sorrow that Nobby Ned had been taken up for stealing. He liked the generous boy, and believed that, like himself, he had been driven into practices that he would shun if once rescued from.

When the evening was well advanced, Charley went upstairs, and, bidding Mary good night, took Tony Nip to his bed-room. He little dreamed what a snake he was taking to his bosom.

Even that befriended glutton himself felt a little shame at what he was doing, and avoided Charley's eye when the grateful boy, with tremulous voice, spoke of Mr. Gloden's kindness to himself and Mary.

"He has acted the part of a true Christian," Charley said, "and I would die for him, if by doing so I could render him a return for what he has done for me and Dick."

"My!" said Tony, "ain't it a big house; and he's left you here with all the walleyables. Ain't you afraid?"

"Afraid, what of?"

"Why, bugglars—thieves."

"No," answered Charley; "I am not a coward,

and should not fail to do my best to defend the property of my benefactor."

He went across the room to a little shelf where some books stood.

Tony's eyes grew bigger when he saw him take down a pistol.

"Mr. Gloden left me this; he said he knew he could trust me how to use it, and if any one should enter I would shoot them.

Tony gulped down a cry of alarm.

"No, no. Oh, don't."

"I will not hurt you," Charley replied; "I only keep this for dishonest men who might come to rob my kind benefactor."

"He knows all about it," thought Tony; "he'll blow my brains out."

"I say," he said.

"Well."

"It ain't loaded, is it? It's only your gammon?"

"You can see."

Charley showed him the capped nipple.

But Tony drew back.

"Oh, criminy! put it back. I ain't done nothink, I ain't."

"Then you need not fear."

"Oh, but it might go off."

Charley smiled sadly, and put the pistol back.

Tony's eyes glistened, and his great cheeks puffed out, as he watched him.

He had made up his mind to have that pistol.

It was too horrible to think of being shot, if Charley should awake and detect him in the midst of his treachery.

Charley helped the wickedly-disposed boy to undress, and then, having said his prayers, leaped into bed.

Calm in the consciousness of an upright mind, he was soon asleep. Not so Tony Nip, who, tormented by an uneasy conscience, and fearful of going to sleep lest he should meet the Crusher's vengeance, lay still, and with his heart beating so violently that it frightened him, and his face breaking out into a cold sweat.

When he thought Charley was safely asleep he got away from him a little at a time, and then sidled out of bed.

He stood quaking by the side for a few moments.

Tony Nip was going to do a treacherous deed and *he was afraid*.

The room was very dark, and Tony began to grope his way about, with a terrified feeling that he would encounter somebody before he got to the shelf whereon lay the loaded pistol.

Dreadful instrument! Tony quaked nervously at the thought of taking it in his hand lest it should explode.

However, he got at length across the room, after beating his breath nearly out against the corner of a table, and coming in contact with a shelf, the sharp edge of which nearly knocked his eye out, and made him groan inwardly.

This was the shelf where Charley had put the pistol. He groped his hand along, his limbs shaking under him all the time, and at length touched the pistol.

But as the cold iron of the trigger was the first that came in contact with his fingers, he drew quickly back again.

Charley turned in the bed! Tony began to blubber; he was afraid of what he had to do.

Charley lay still again, and Tony took hold of the pistol.

He had just got his plump finger put round it when a strange, rattling noise sounded behind him.

A smothered cry came from his lips, and he fell back against the wall.

CHAPTER LXXIII.

ANOTHER PART OF THE PLOT.

THE Crusher, with his pal, was on his way to the house, when he met a man whom he had seen once or twice before, and had held occasional conversations with.

This personage was the reader's old acquaintance, Ralph Merton, who had made one or two bargains with the Crusher, and now came to see one carried out that he had planned respecting Mary.

The injuries he had received in his last attempt had, if anything, more strengthened his malevolence, and now that Dick was away he had less fear of being foiled.

He spoke but few words to the Crusher, and the two proceeded along the silent streets till they came to Mr. Gloden's dwelling.

The Crusher went in advance, and threw a few grains of gravel up at the window. That was the sound which Tony heard, and which had so frightened him.

He was sometime now before he recovered from his terror, and then he listened again to see if he could find out what had caused his fear.

He was not kept long in suspense; the Crusher, skilful though impatient, softly threw up a little more sand.

"Oh, it's him," Tony thought; "how shall I get down?"

He opened the door gently and crept out.

The landing and stairs were dark, and Tony felt anything but disposed to venture down. Nothing but the remembrance of the Crusher's threat induced him to make the descent. When he got down one or two of the stairs, the pistol, which lay like a heavy weight on his conscience, became very uncomfortable to hold.

Tony was haunted by a fear that it might go off and shoot him. His finger was always getting in the way of the trigger, and as he did not know much about the construction of the weapon, and only knew that it went off by pressure, he was so frightened that he felt for an odd corner, and carefully laid it out of the way.

Opening the door was a work of time and labour, for the Crusher had sworn to wring his neck if he made any noise, and, as he did not wish to have his neck wrung, he went to work silently and slowly.

At last it was opened, and the Crusher stepped in.

He gave Tony a look that made the treacherous boy feel his skin creeping over him.

A cab stood at the door.

Ralph Merton had engaged for a driver to meet him whom he could trust.

The three stood in the passage in the dark, when the Crusher turned on his lantern.

They then saw Tony, white as a sheet, and trembling all over.

Crusher Jem laid his big fist on the boy's nose.

"Make a row, and I'll smash you!" was his mild admonition.

Tony merely opened wide his mouth, and the three stole softly up the stairs.

"You get in his room," the Crusher said, "and don't let him move till the job's done."

Tony, glad to get away from the proximity of the Crusher, stole to Charley's room, and, creeping in, began to put on his clothes.

In the meantime, silently the night marauders went to their work.

Ralph Merton sought the chamber of Mary.

Crusher Jem and his pal commenced their investigations for booty.

In the calm trustfulness of security Mary was tranquilly sleeping; her thoughts were with Dick, on his weary journey; and she slept all the more soundly that her dreams brought him again to her.

Poor helpless girl; she heard not the light step of the prowling villain who entered her chamber.

She did not wake till he had thrown a cloak over her and lifted her in his arms, when the sudden shock of seeing herself in his power took away her senses, when she had most need of them.

And so he got her out of the house and into the cab, and away to his own den of sin, where he knew she would be in his power.

While he was successful in his work, the Crusher and his pal were not idle; they had already picked up a considerable quantity of spoil, and were eagerly hunting for more.

Up stairs Tony stood shivering and afraid, and praying that Charley might not wake till they were all gone.

But Charley did wake. He missed his bedfellow directly, and after calling him, slid out to the floor.

Then Tony, who was shivering with cowardice, sneaked to the door, and got out.

He was afraid to face Charley.

The latter, in strange surprise, was feeling his way about, and wondering where Tony had got to. When he could not find him anywhere, he began to dress—a strange feeling creeping over him that all was not right.

He had scarcely finished throwing on his clothes, when he heard a sound below.

In an instant he was on the landing.

The sound of a voice came.

It was low and stealthy.

But Charley recognised it.

It was the Crusher's.

How many emotions went thrilling through the brave boy's breast at this discovery?

That the Crusher was only there to plunder the house was very certain, and, resolved to do his best to defend his benefactor's property, Charley hastened down stairs.

His foot struck something on the landing. He picked it up. He had forgotten it till then, but he was glad to have it in his possession.

As he took it in his grasp, a figure glided by him, and went blundering down the stairs. Charley hurried down after him, but paused half way to open the staircase window, and call loudly for the police!

This cry created a sudden commotion in the house. A door shut, and the Crusher's voice was heard loudly cursing.

That they would make an attack upon him, and, perhaps kill him, he was well aware; but he planted himself in the way, determined to let none pass to the door while he had life to defend Mr. Gloden's property.

His cries for the police brought an answer from outside. A policeman's rattle rang on the morning air. The noise of the burglars showed that they were preparing for a precipitate retreat, and Charley got ready to stop the flight of one man—the Crusher.

He had stood there in the darkness. As a sudden light flashed for an instant, then disappeared, somebody rushed by him, pushing him to the wall, and hurrying to the door.

Charley felt sure it was the Crusher escaping: he strained his eyes where he saw a dark form fleeing, and, as the door was torn open, fired.

The flash and roar electrified the brave boy: he heard a cry of pain and the slamming of a door, then the fall of a body, and the hasty rush of feet: the door shut to again, and as the shriek of the alarmed servant rang through the house, Charley ran down the stairs and to the door.

He had hardly reached it when it was dashed open, hurling him back upon some huge body that he had passed without touching. A strong hand grasped him by the shoulder, and as a policeman's light was turned upon him, a strong, hard voice exclaimed:

"Don't try any games on, my young 'un: I've got you safe enough."

A policeman's rattle sprung.

He felt that he was taken.

The policeman held him fast, and turned the light of his lantern in his face.

"The very young customer I've been told to watch," he said. "Well: what,—murder!"

Charley looked down: the body of a policeman lay upon the floor of the hall. By his side lay Tony in a fit, where he had fallen on hearing the report of the pistol, just as he was escaping.

Another policeman came up at that juncture, followed by the detective.

Charley heard their words of accusation; saw them rise the wounded policeman, and struck as confounded—dumb—was not able to say a word in his own defence, or repel the charge that lay so black against him.

And that night he was dragged off to become again the inmate of a police station.

CHAPTER LXXIV.

THE CRUSHER AT THE FIGHT.

AFTER getting away snugly with his booty, the Crusher led a life of brutal jollity for several weeks, during nearly the whole of which time he was beastly drunk, and the terror of the people who lived in the same low street.

Every evening he turned out for his popular amusement of knocking about the first who came in his way, and, as his pugilistic prowess was well known, the police took no heed of his nightly brutality.

Flushed with cash, the Crusher had made up his mind to go down to see the international fight between Heenan and King for £2,000. Hitherto, when going to a fight, the Crusher's usual proceeding had been to fight his way to the train, and despoil some unfortunate victim of his ticket; but now he determined to do the thing in the right manner, and pay for his ticket like a swell.

He would not have been able to do anything else; as this time the managers of the affair had determined it should be free from those disgusting scenes which usually preceded a prize fight. No one was allowed down without paying his three pounds, those bright lads who had ensconced themselves under the seats, on the roof, or even under the carriages themselves, being dragged out, and bundled from the platf rm.

A large detachment of police was present in authority, and there was a still stronger reserve at hand, should their services be required.

The brutal fraternity were, on this occasion, completely foiled, and they hovered about in small groups, like baffled hounds, or stood sullenly looking on in the darkness upon visitors whom they would, but for the presence of the police, have almost torn to pieces like hungry wolves.

It was felt that the right "direction" had been discovered at last, and these miserable ruffians, so valiant when attacking the defenceless, slunk away hopelessly subdued by the tall figures of the police, whose bull's eyes were ever and anon turned on with suspicious sharpness upon certain characters.

Crusher Jem paid his money with a swagger, and walked in amongst the fraternity. He was well known by the members of the P.R., and when King came on the platform he walked up to him and told him if he did not lick the Yankee he would himself break his jaw.

Whereupon Jem Mace, who was with King, quietly said that not only would King beat Heenan, but that he himself would lick him after.

The Crusher growled his satisfaction and got into the carriage.

The train stopped at Wadhurst, beyond Tunbridge Wells, and the whole of the passengers, numbering over 1,000, having turned out, the ring was pitched after the usual delay.

In each corner was planted the American and English colours. At length all was prepared, and Tom King, amongst the enthusiastic cheers of his friends, threw his cap into the ring, and stalked into the centre in a proud, defiant manner.

Heenan followed within a minute afterwards, and, it is needless to say, he was welcomed with acclamation by his partisans.

Not the least interesting incident at this moment was the fact of Tom Sayers divesting himself of his coat, and in a yellow flannel waistcoat commencing his duties as second to Heenan.

During the period occupied in the selection of the referee, Heenan and King sat in their corners, wrapped up to their eyes in horsecloths, quietly awaiting the result, and occasionally stealing furtive glances at each other. Heenan won the toss for corners, and chose the eastern corner, with his back to the sun, while King had the parallel angle on the west side.

The American got impatient at last, and called out energetically to the other side—"Come on, I want to fight!"

Immediately the referee difficulty was removed, the men commenced to undress, Jack M'Donald and Tom Sayers being seconds of Heenan, while Jerry Noon and Bos Tyler esquired King.

Jem Mace was in King's corner on the outside of the ring, and during the progress of the fight was unremitting in his advice and attention to his former opponent. Sayers, though acting as second, left the chief business to M'Donald, but was particularly solicitous for Heenan whenever he required his services.

As soon as King had got his fighting boots on, he walked to the centre of the ring to try their elasticity and spikes, while Sayers, with his arms folded, and Heenan, lolling back in a chair, calmly contemplated the young Englishman. In Heenan's corner, on the outside of the ring, were his brothers—Tim and James—and the main bulk of the supporters of the American.

The men set-to in earnest, and after some sparring King attempted to reach Heenan's face, but was stopped, more accidentally than scientifically, and King's head coming within reach of the American's left arm the Englishman was in a moment drawn into "chancery," and there held as Heenan liked for more than a minute, until by a slip both went down, Heenan uppermost.

The fall was a heavy one, and when King was carried to his chair he seemed so like fainting that there were all round from the Americans cries of "It's all over." But it was nothing like all over, for when time was called for the second round King was up shortly after Heenan, and administered to that "bhoy" a severe blow on the jaw, which made the bones appear to give way. "Hit him again," growled the Crusher. But Heenan tried hugging again, and threw King heavily, "first blood" being accorded to King.

The fighting proceeded, nearly every round King administering a heavy facer, and nearly every round Heenan throwing King, without, however, doing the latter as much harm as the cutting blows did the former. But still King was being very badly hurt by the falls; and it is more than doubtful whether he would have been up to time on one or two occasions had not Mace, who was attending to his former opponent, entreated, pushed—nay, even threatened him.

Blood was flowing rapidly from Heenan, who was gradually growing weaker, while the later falls did not seem to hurt King nearly so much as the earlier ones.

The fighting was tremendous; there was no shifting on either side—Heenan relying more than anything on his wrestling, King on his blows.

In the 16th round, however, Heenan happened to get a good blow on King's face, which sent the latter falling into his corner; and as he did not fall directly, there was some dispute as to whether he did not go down without a blow.

In the next round both men were very weak, and in the 18th round, although King had far the best of the fighting, Heenan threw him again with such force that, but for violent restoratives, King could not have recovered the stunning of the skull. His hard head came with a bump on the ground, and only the sharp teeth of a well-known "bruiser" brought him to. So excited did the on-lookers become, that the ring was broken into, and the men had, during that round, to fight in the middle of a surging, seething crowd, when King, getting Heenan over the ropes, he punished the American just as he liked, and the ring resounded with cries of "King wins in a walk!"

In the 20th round, Heenan's face was nearly covered with blood from the cuts which his backers could not stanch.

In the next bout King delivered two terrific blows on Heenan's jaw and eye, cutting his lip as if with a knife. King then closed and threw Heenan, who from that moment had no chance. In the 22nd round, both combatants were drenched with water, and Heenan also with blood, which nearly blinded him.

From that time it was sheer barbarity to continue the fight, but both men were still willing, and the crowd, amongst whom the Crusher's gruff voice was prominent, would have it fairly out.

In the three next rounds it was simply setting up a dummy for King to do what he liked with, and in the last turn Heenan was only put up for the mere name of the thing, and that there might be a final knock-down blow, which came as a matter of course, for at the moment we do not believe Heenan could have brushed a fly from his nose.

So there were twenty-four or twenty-five rounds in thirty-five minutes, at the end of which remarkably speedy fighting Heenan was helpless, while King, when hailed as the winner of £2,000, was well able to return the greetings of his friends, and to even walk across the ring, and to take the hand of his late opponent, who was now a fearful object, his face being absolutely running with blood, while also swollen to an extent which can scarcely be imagined.

He was also punished internally, for he vomited so much that it was feared he was about to die; and it was only after a very considerable interval that he was brought in an open fly to the station at Wadhurst, where it was thought better he should remain for the day at least.

King returned to town in the special train which arrived at Bricklayers' Arms station at two o'clock.

King has proved his pluck and his growing skill; Heenan has, if a rumour of a broken jaw be true, been put definitively *hors de combat*.

Heenan would never have held out against Sayers if the latter had not been unlucky enough to lose the use of one arm; and that Sayers with only one arm left could keep the American at bay for an hour and a half ought to have shown that "The Benicia Boy" was not the man to take the belt from old England. Now a man who is a match for Heenan in point of size and weight, taken together, has beaten him easily in little more than half an hour.

The truth of the matter is that Heenan cannot fight.

He can wrestle, he can hug, he can bear down, but he cannot spar. His days as a boxer are over in this country, though he may aspire to fill the place in America of the far-famed "Yankee Sullivan." If he should have the temerity to meet Mace, the latter would cover him in blood or pound him into mincemeat in a quarter of an hour.

Such was the Crusher's expression of opinion, when after taking a good stare at Heenan's disfigured face, he caught King by the hand, and after giving him a hearty shake, turned round and asked, if there was any other Yankee that wanted licking.

No response being made, the Crusher swore he would lick any six of them, and stalked off to get to the train.

So ended this great fight—a fight witnessed by the upper ten thousand—peers, magistrates, clergymen, paying their money cheerfully to witness these two men pound each other till one had been knocked almost out of his senses, and after being brought to by a most disgusting process, beating his opponent till the American, one mass of crimson, bruised flesh and oozing blood, was laid on the ground, vomiting 'as if he were going to die,' from the battering he had received.

CHAPTER LXXV.

MISSING MARY.

Mr. Gloden came home, summoned thither by the news of the unexpected things that had occurred in his absence; came home, to find his house robbed, Mary absent, and Charley in custody, on the charge of aiding the burglars.

At first, Mr. Gloden was the first to go down and offer bail for his young protégé, whose guilt he could not then bring himself to believe; but when he heard the condemning evidence, his faith was shaken, and he began to think that he had been mistaken; that which people had told him was true; and that Charley was a mere artful hypocrite.

It was not till he had well digested all the circumstances that Mr. Gloden allowed this conviction to gain strength in his mind.

But it seemed to lay so clear against poor Charley.

There was the detective's evidence, who had seen Charley and Tony together, and had heard them talk of a projected robbery. He deposed, too, to Charley giving the other boy some money, all of which Charley could not but admit was true.

Then Mr. Gloden himself could not but remember the suspicious manner in which Tony and Charley had met before his house.

It was proved that on the night of the burglary Charley had let Tony secretly into the house; the policeman who had taken him deposed to finding him inside the house, with the exploded pistol in his hand.

The presumption then was clear that he had, in conjunction with Tony Nip, admitted the burglar, and had shot the policeman who first entered, in order to allow the other to escape, and would doubtless have escaped himself had he not been stopped by the constable who arrived second.

Such was the tenor of the case against Charley, and Mr. Gloden came to the grand conviction that his confidence in human nature was misplaced, and that Charley had met his kindness only with ingratitude and deceit.

It hurt Charley more than his captivity to be adjudged guilty by Mr. Gloden, for although with his wonted goodness Mr. Gloden refused to press the charge against him, as far as he was concerned, yet Charley could see by his manner that he had lost faith.

If it had not been for the charge of wounding the policeman, whom the bullet had grazed along the head, passing within an inch or two of the brain, but only stunning him, Charley would have been let off; but this remained to be answered, and in the meantime the police hoped to get out of Charley the confession of the truth, as it appeared to them.

Tony Nip had also been marched off to his cell,

and Charley very eagerly awaited his hearing, for he had no doubt that he would be able to convince the jury still of his innocence.

Judge, then, of his surprise, when, on being placed in the dock, side by side, Tony, in reply to Charley's interrogations, not only denied that he had gone to bed with him, but—primed by the Crusher, and in dread of his threats—swore that they had stayed up with the intention of letting in the others.

So far Tony was agreeable to confess, but all efforts to draw from him any intelligence respecting the burglar failed signally.

When pressed on this point he only put on the most stolid look of stupidity.

He preferred being sent to prison to having his throat cut, as the Crusher had vowed to do if he betrayed him.

Under all circumstances, and considering his suspicious antecedents, it is not to be marvelled at if a feeling of Charley's guilt should prevail: looking at the two as they stood in the dock, people believed them to be artful young sinners, and if they expressed sorrow at all it was that one so fair-looking as Charley should be so incorrigibly bad.

It seemed clear that they were both well-tutored rogues, for Charley's story was a direct contradiction to Tony's, and the latter, while implicating Charley, pretended not to be able to give any further account.

Charley did his best to explain the unhappy affair, but people shook their heads.

He told them how he had taken Tony into his room, and how, hearing the Crusher's voice, he had tried to prevent him escaping; but the evidence of the policeman and the detective was too much for him, and he was led away, committed for trial.

True to his nature, Mr. Gloden did all he could

No. 23.

for Charley: he visited him in prison, engaged a talented counsel for his defence, and had the boy, Tony Nip, sounded, in order to extort from him the truth, if he concealed anything.

But still, scared by the Crusher's threats, Tony stuck to his story, and Mr. Gloden was forced to confess that there appeared some truth in it.

Not so the lawyer: he deeply believed in the looks of the guilty and innocent—soon pronounced Charley innocent and Tony guilty; he saw the pale firmness and candour of the one and detected the shuffling prevarications of the other. He made Mr. Gloden happy by the expression of his convictions, and then set sharp agents to work to hunt up evidence.

A very curious fact came to light.

Two bullets had been found in Mr. Gloden's house!

One had passed out, after wounding the policeman, the other had lodged in the door.

This was a discovery made such able use of by the counsel for the defence, that Charley was acquitted, and left the court. Mr. Gloden warmly welcomed him, and again restoring him his confidence, took him home.

As for Tony, he was sentenced to a week's imprisonment and a whipping, both of which he literally received.

Mary's disappearance was the occasion of much grief and surprise, but Mr. Gloden set inquiries on foot which he believed would soon result in her discovery. As for Charley, he was inconsolable at the loss of her whom he had been appointed by Dick to watch.

Freed from the calamity that had threatened his own liberty, Charley might have been again in the position he was before, had not an unhappy accident deprived him of the protection of Mr. Gloden: that gentleman, in riding out one evening, was thrown and killed, and Charley lost the best friend he had ever had.

He lost more than this, for a relative came in with a rascally lawyer, and there being no will discovered, Charley was sent forth homeless and penniless by this grasping relation, who, by fraud and felony—for he had abstracted the will wherein Charley was named—took possession of the property.

CHAPTER LXXVI.

IN THE WIDE WORLD ALONE.

Charley went out alone again in the cheerless world. He had scarcely a shilling in his pocket; but he was young—well dressed; and if he could get any one to employ him, did not despair.

But he was broken hearted respecting Mary. No tidings had been heard of her.

She seemed lost for ever, and he knew not what answer he should make to Dick when he came back, and, asking for Mary, found her not.

Charley tried hard to get employment, but found it very difficult, and was wandering sadly along, when he saw before him one of his victims and acquaintances—Nobby Ned.

No sooner did this young gentleman perceive him than he indulged in some very queer movements.

First he stopped, put his tongue in his cheek, and stuck his cap on one side.

Then he put both hands on his hips, and took a hard stare at Charley.

Finally, he made a run up to him, and exclaimed—

"What! you turned up again! Well, if that ain't stunning. Lor, ain't you stylish. Where have you been getting them togs from?"

Charley explained what had befallen him.

"Why, you've been as unlucky as me," said his sympathising friend; but never mind. I'm jolly well up now, and don't do nothing for a living. Come on, you shall live with me; no railway arch jobs, though."

He essayed a laugh as he spoke, but Charley saw that it was a failure. He could not help noticing, too, that Nobby had changed since he last saw him. He seemed seven years older at the least.

In his present position, Charley did not long resist the kind offer of the good-hearted boy, and thus he again found himself trudging along by the side of the young boy, to share his bed and partake of his food, as he had done before.

"I'll break that Tony Nip's nose!" Nobby Ned cried, when Charley had told him his behaviour. "I didn't think he was such a blessed wretch as that; but I'll make him sweat for it, I will."

The room he took Charley to was one at the top of a very small and dirty house. A very few articles, and these of the commonest sort, comprised its furniture. It was, altogether, of most mean appearance, but Nobby Ned looked round with the air of a monarch, and said, proudly—

"There, it's a stunning crib, and I pay for it; you shall have half of it, and shan't pay nothing. I'm going to begin to make my fortune. I've heard of other boys that's done it—like Whittington, you know, of the bells, and I don't see why I shouldn't."

Charley warmly grasped the boy's hand.

"Will you make your fortune honestly?"

"I mean to try to."

"I am glad of that; and now we can be together, and if I earn a shilling you shall have the most of it."

A long while those two boys sat together in their little room, building up mutual resolutions that they would persevere to become great men, Nobby Ned declaring the inside of a prison should never be tenanted by him, and Charley glad to attest this vow of amendment and honest perseverance.

And then they went to bed, to wake in the morning and go forth to gain employment.

CHAPTER LXXVII.

MARY AND RALPH.

The reader will be wishing to learn what happened to Mary after her second abduction by Ralph.

She awoke from her swoon to find him leaning over her, and regarding her with a look that showed, too plainly, his infernal triumph.

She was in a room rather well furnished, but only dimly lighted. Gazing rapidly round at the walls, she saw, nearly opposite her, a large mirror, the reflection of which showed her herself, with her dress disarranged, and her breast partially exposed.

She leaped u to find herself firmly held by the constraining arm of Ralph.

"Don't think of going yet," he said, with his usual leer and mocking laugh; "we've got to be very happy together. You need only fancy me that fellow Warne, or Dick, and we shall be all right."

Mary drew her dress tight, and struggled from his arm. All the energy of her disposition was called into action by his evil intents, and when she spoke it was in a tone whose firmness astonished him.

"You have brought me here, bad Ralph, but do not think I am your victim. If I have been dishonoured by my trust in infamous men, I will not fall a prey to such as you. We are here alone; I can see that by your cunning looks. You think no one can aid me, and if I shriek you may stifle my cries; but you are mistaken. I have a defender you have not counted upon: that defender is myself. You are a man, and boast of strength; I am a woman, and much weakened by sorrow and suffering, but dare to attempt your wicked purpose and I will prove what a woman can do in her own defence."

Mr. Ralph was very much taken down by her calm words and bearing. Her arm seemed to take the firmness of iron as she pushed him off, and stood away. His sullen looks grew more malicious, and he answered, scoffingly,—

"I like to hear a woman talk like that, especially when I have her so completely in my power that I could carve her limb from limb without interference. Do not think I have taken my measures badly; I tell you, Mary, that I will make of you what I desire before you quit this room, and, if need be, you shall leave it afterwards not as you are now, able to speak and mouth against me, but in pieces, like Greenacre took his woman out!"

Mary felt her heart beating a little more violently at the cool villany of that man. She had no doubt now whose hand committed the murder at Parson Wordly's, and she sighed as she thought how she had wronged poor Dick.

"Bad, evil man," she said, as he came before her, "do not think to add this to your other crimes. Be careful not to dare me to meet you on your own terms."

Ralph smiled mockingly, and stood in her path. He was quite surprised when her small arm was put out, and he was thrust out of the way; in fact, it took him a few moments to recover himself, and then Mary was at the door.

He controlled the passion that was surging at his black heart, and tried the effect of milder words.

"You need not make so much fuss. I am not without money; stay here, Mary. You shall wear what you like, and do what you please."

"I will go now, and I dare you to oppose me!" Mary cried, snatching up a large-headed stick which stood by the door.

Ralph laughed scoffingly as he saw her take it. He thought those light fingers would lack the power to do any damage with the weapon. He was quite surprised then, in fact, completely stunned for the moment, when the stick whirled round in an uncertain kind of way, and, finally meeting his head, struck him in the centre of the forehead, raising on the instant a blue, big bump, and knocking him back.

Having struck this blow for her liberty, Mary, who was in a wild state of excitement, seized the lamp, and hurried down the stairs.

But Ralph made one or two stupid clutches at the air, and finally leant against the table for a few moments, to consider whether he was standing on his head or his heels.

The room was swimming round, and, though Mary had taken away the lamp, there were many lights flashing in his eyes.

Mary's little arm had struck remarkably hard.

But, after a bit, Master Ralph recovered. He heard Mary fumbling about down stairs, and, with a bitter curse, followed her.

Then Mr. Ralph took out of his pocket a large knife, which he coolly opened.

It was a large clasp knife, with a blade as keen and formidable as a bowie.

It had more than once tasted blood, and Ralph was in the humour to let it taste more.

He went down the stairs two or three at a time.

Mary heard him coming, and her nimble figure flew the faster. There were a number of fastenings in the door. Ralph liked to lock himself well in with his prey.

These fastenings now threatened to be Mary's destruction; for though she had removed two or three, there yet remained others, and Ralph, with the knife open in his hand, was already on the bottom flight of stairs.

Mary heard him mutter a fearful oath; she heard him leap to the floor of the passage, and her heart gave a great bound as he flew towards her.

By an instinct or accident she got back the last fastening, and as Ralph, swearing by many an oath that he would kill her, took her by the shoulder, and pressed the gleaming knife to her throat, she uttered a wild scream, and dashed the lamp full in his face.

Then, with a dash she had the door open, and flew out into the street.

The brasswork of the lamp struck Ralph just above the bridge of the nose, and besides causing him exquisite pain, made the blood spout out in a torrent, as if he had been in a mill with one of the "big 'uns."

Beyond that the blow did him no damage, and he only stayed a moment to get the key of the door, before he was in the street after Mary.

Reckless of consequences, he chased after her. She was flying nimbly, but he knew he should soon overtake her.

There were few people about. Ralph was glad to see this. He had but one idea now—the murderous intent of stabbing Mary to the heart, and leaving her weltering in her blood.

But in case he might be seen, he hid the knife. Mary was already losing breath. A woman is not so capable of endurance as a man, and her excitement, though at first enabling her to free herself from his power, was very rapidly weakening her.

All this Ralph saw with elate heart and murderous satisfaction.

It might be looked upon as impossible that any one should be afraid of being murdered in the open street, but unfortunately it too often occurs that such deeds are perpetrated when it would appear impossible for the murderer to escape detection. Mary knew there was no protection for her if once Ralph overtook her, and that very thought was helping to have that effect.

Ralph closed upon her. He laughed at her faint scream, and, chuckling, drew his knife.

As she tried to flee away, he grasped her shawl. Making a bound forward, Mary loosened her shawl, and let it go.

But Ralph, thus unexpectedly tricked, and hanging all his weight to the shawl, was thrown off his equilibrium, and on to the road.

He jumped up. A mist was before his eyes—vengeance in his looks. He saw a form dimly before him, and making a plunge forward, drove his knife, as he thought, at Mary's back.

There is a saying that "many a slip comes between the cup and the lip;" and there was a slip there. When Ralph had expected to feel his knife cutting through Mary's flesh, he, instead, found his arm knocked down by a tremendous blow, and in the next instant he was knocked on to the kerb by a second like visitation.

"'May I be blowed if that ain't a queer way to come across a feller,' as the whale said to the elephant."

In a voice which Ralph knew, Roving Rob exclaimed—

"Stand up again, and 'I'll see how quick you'll roll on your nob again,' as the bloke said when he knocked the ten dozen over one at a time."

Ralph did stand up again, but in a very confused and unsteady manner. He looked wildly round, his glance seeking Mary, who was not there.

She had fled away like a bounding fawn when released from the shawl.

Ralph was very white, and he shook slightly: he never knew when he was dispossessed of his knife, nor how it was taken, but he saw it in Roving Rob's hand.

The latter was turning it over in a curious manner, weighing it in his palm, and scrutinising all its perfections with an experienced eye.

"Ah, ah, a nice bit of steel it is," he said, " but it warn't made for what you was trying it on; solid and sharp, warranted to cut its own way out of a man's pocket—why, you varmint, was you going to stick this into her?"

A sudden gleam shot from Ralph's vindictive eyes, and he made a swift clutch at the knife.

But he was destined that night to make a mistake in everything he attempted, for in place of catching the knife, he caught Rob's fist, which, as the knife shot back, went quickly out and sent Ralph sprawling again to the gutter.

"'That's your game, is it?'" Rob cried, "as the downy bloke said to the poacher; but you don't try it on here. Just get up again, and I'll give you the dressing I have been longing to give you ever since that day in the village where Mary lived."

Ralph got up; he looked fierce, and inclined to do murder. He thought he might terrify Nobby by his looks, but he was quite out there. Rob coolly rolled up his sleeves, and after putting the knife in in his pocket, gave Ralph in less than three minutes such a thrashing that he left him on the step of a door, breathless, and one mass of bruises.

"He'll come round after a while," Rob muttered, as he walked coolly away, "and if he does'nt, why it'll not be such a over partiklar matter; wonder where that gal skipped to, and how he got hold of her; he! a purty little cheesetaster this is; why its edge is so sharp that it cuts you when you look at it. He wanted to stick this into purty Mary; if I come alongside of him again, if I don't give him worserer than I guved him now, my name aint noways Roving Bob, which it ar' what it used to be."

Leaving her shawl behind her, Mary fled, and slackened her speed only when she was obliged to lean, breathless, against the portico of a doorway. She was alone; alone in the great metropolis; alone in her misery and shame, yet with thousands around her, but none of whom cared whether she dropped where she stood, and died!

And, indeed, poor Mary felt much inclined to lay herself down and never rise again. She gazed wearily round, and then pressing her hand to her heart, went tottering on.

But she did not wander far before a deadly weakness again overcame her, and she sunk on the cold stone flags of a big inhospitable lane.

A policeman going to his work, and with some of the kindness of human nature, spoke to her gently, as he came up, and when he found that she did not desire to be interfered with, walked slowly away.

Another would have driven her harshly away from her hard-resting place.

So she sat there alone, while the cold stars went fading from the sky, and the darkness of coming morn grew intense.

And all that while her bitter tears were falling down her weary pallid cheeks.

She had fallen into a trance-like reverie, and was awakened by a voice strained and emphatic, addressing her in these words.

"Why, my dear, whatever makes you sit here in the cold, and without any shawl or anything. Deary me, you will be quite ill. Come, let me take you to my home, if you have not one of your own to go to."

Mary sadly raised her head; her glance rested on the course, and certainly not far from repulsive features of Mother Rawlings, who, passing by, had seen the crouching form of the poor girl, and judging by her neat garb that she was not one of those night wanderers who nightly make such places their resting-place, and seeing also that Mary possessed both good looks and a well-made form, her villanous mind was instantly made up to get the young girl into her power.

She helped her up, and even went so far in her strained kindness as to take an under shawl from her well-wrapped person, and placed it over Mary's shoulders.

The wretched girl burst into fresh tears at this seemingly generous act, and she suffered Mother Rawlings to lead her away, and conduct her to her home.

Mother Rawlings was very careful in her treatment of victims like Mary. She did not try to frighten them by abruptly putting before them the life she had inveigled them into.

But still, for all that, once within her establishment of vice, they never went forth again, except shorn of that self respect and virtue which they prize1 as true woman's rarest jewel.

Poor Mary, unsuspecting and weary, was as surely doomed as ever poor girl was, when taken in the snare.

The door of liberty was closed upon her, and she was in the power of those wretches whom Mother Rawlings led.

She was first taken to a neat little room, quietly furnished, and with nothing in it that might give any evidence of the nature of the house.

But this room was so well secured, that once in, it was impossible to escape.

Mother Rawlings took care that Mary should have every comfort. She had good reasons for this. In the first place, she wished the unhappy girl to contrast them with the miseries of street wandering; in the next place, in the mart of sin, Mary would fetch a better price, if her good looks were restored.

Naturally blooming and plump, Mary soon regained much of her former prettiness, and Mother Rawlings saw with pleasure the change in her appearance.

She had determined to sell Mary to some one of these unprincipled and titled villains who at her house bought women's virtue at a price—not as a fallen modest woman, but as one who had never deviated from the path of virtue.

Not but that her keen penetration had told her that Mary had already lost that bright honour.

Unsuspecting the evil to which she was ensnared, Mary remained in that house—remained there unsuspicious, whilst in rooms contiguous to her own, maidens inveigled there were being betrayed to the vicious sensuality of worthless men, and sold for a sum of money, like bartered sheep,—where the life of many an unhappy ruined girl was ruthlessly taken,—and where the dreadful flogging machine had its nightly victims.

Such things are in our great city.

Five days had passed, and now Mother Rawlings thought it time to commence her designs upon her young victim. So, having arranged with a wealthy peer, she informed Mary one night that she was about to introduce her to a gentleman who had been making many kind inquiries about her.

Although there was nothing in the manner of the bedizened procuress different from usual, Mary felt a strange thrill running through her.

A presentiment of evil came over her, and she answered her destroyer very indifferently.

It had struck her once before that, though meeting with so much attention, she was little else than a prisoner there, as, although she had once or twice expressed a desire to go out and procure a situation, Mother Rawlings had put her off with frivolous pretexts.

"You must know, my dear," said that bad woman, when preparing her for the introduction, "that this gentleman is most wealthy: I can assure you he has taken quite an interest in you, and when I told him you wanted a situation, he said I ought not to think of such a thing: but, then, when I told him you would be more easy in your mind, he said you might be comfortable like in his house."

"In his house?" interrupted Mary.

"Yes, my dear, don't look so straight. You see he has a young wife and two little children, and what he wants is a lady-like person, just as you are, to be a companion to his wife, and be with his little girls—for, of course, he doesn't like them to be along with common servants. And I think, my dear, it would be very nice for you, and you could be so happy with the dear little children; so you must mind what you say to the gentleman. But mind that you don't fall in love with him; for, I can tell you, he is very distinguished and handsome, and so wealthy!"

This was said with a cat-like smile, that was far from pleasing to Mary; she was silent, and Mother Rawlings went on,

"I ought not to forget to tell you, my dear, that this gentleman, though quite the lord, is very free in his manner. He is so used to be flattered, that you must take it quite a favour if he makes a little free with you; and be very choice, my dear, in how you answer him—for these real gentlefolks is so over-particular, that one don't know sometimes how one can speak without offending them. But I think, my dear, you can manage him nicely."

The depraved procuress tried the effect of a second smile, and hearing a sudden knock at the door, jumped up, and exclaiming, "Here he is, my dear, I declare!" left the room.

She returned in a short time, ushering in a tall, elegantly-dressed gentleman, whose countenance, despite its refinement, bore unmistakable evidence of the roué and profligate.

He looked with a bold glance on Mary, and, greeting her with a fashionable bow, took the seat which was near her.

Mary blushed under his unabashed gaze. She could only speak a few words in reply to his drawling, long-winded introduction, and then sat, silent and sad, her suspicions strengthened by every look and word of her visitor.

These timorous suspicions were not lessened when Mother Rawlings presently rose, and said, "Mary, dear; I will leave you for a few moments to entertain Mr. Herbert. I must attend to a little matter I had forgot. I shall not be long, however."

That cat-like smile spread half over her coarse features, and a significant look passed between her and the 'gentleman.'

It was an awkward moment for Mary. Whatever were her suspicions, she could not be certain that she was right, and to act in accordance with them might cause her to look very foolish.

But there was that in the complexion of the whole affair which gave her grounds for fear; and when Mother Rawlings moved to the door, she also rose.

"You will excuse me," she said; "I am but poorly able to interest Mr. Herbert."

"Oh, nonsense, my dear, I must insist—in a word, Mr. Herbert has a few words to say to you, and, although I am interested in all that concerns you, a third person is not always necessary."

She left the room before Mary could speak in answer.

Left the room, and shut the door.

Shut the door, and *locked it!*

Mr. Herbert was safely locked in with his victim.

As soon as they were alone, Mr. Herbert fixed his fascinating glance on Mary, and drew his chair a little closer to her.

He was well used to these affairs, and was not, therefore, bashful in his part.

"My dear young girl," he said, "Mrs. Rawlings has informed me of the whole circumstances of your sad position. Believe me, as one who looks forward to some day having grown-up daughters of my own, I feel deeply the—the—what you must have experienced. I—that is—my dear girl—"

He had drawn yet nearer, and was in the act of taking her hand, when Mary drew it away, and said,—

"Pardon me, sir; I am not accustomed—"

"To be made much of; no. Well, then, all I can say is, that you ought to be, and, dear one, you shall be. I—dear girl- forgive me, but I cannot resist; although I have a fair wife of my own I cannot help loving you—"

"Sir," Mary said, rising, her cheeks flushed, and her eyes kindled, "I was not aware of what object Mrs. Rawlings had in view in leaving me here to be insulted."

His arm slid forcibly round her waist.

"You don't go, by Jove; no. My dear girl,

believe me when I tell you that I love you, from this first meeting; early, I know, but, by Jove, I mean it; and I'm unalterable in that attachment, I can tell you, and you shall come with me. My wife won't suspect you a bit. We can—"

"Unhand me," Mary cried, as he more forcibly tried to place her on a seat.

"No, by Jove. I've got you, and I—"

Mary struck him, in her wildness, as he put his face to hers.

The look of Mr. Herbert changed immediately. He cast a spiteful glance on the brave, young girl, and flung his arm more tightly round her.

The scream that came from Mary's lips was very faint. She was weary of this constant struggling against an ever-pursuing destiny—tired with the world, that seemed so much the same in its wickedness wherever she went.

But she nevertheless resisted the smooth-tongued libertine, who was not chary of making his real intention known.

The door opened, and Mrs. Rawlings entered; she cast a spiteful cat-like look at Mary, but immediately smoothed her features.

As cunning as the feline animal before referred to was Mother Rawlings.

"Why, deary me," she said, "what means all this, Mr. Herbert? Goodness gracious! why Mary—"

Mr. Herbert quitted his hold of Mary instantly.

"A little play, Mrs. Rawlings," he said, stroking his moustache.

"Play, sir," Mary cried, bursting into tears, and moving nearer the door; "I have been ill used shamefully. I did not think when I entered your house that it was for that purpose."

"*Me*, my dear," echoed Mother Rawlings; "well I'm sure! Mr. Herbert, I can't think what you can mean by such conduct. If you have insulted the young lady you should apologise—"

Mr. Herbert took the hint.

"I must beg her pardon if I have been rude. I did not intentionally forget myself."

"But you've very much agitated the poor dear," rejoined Mother Rawlings, who had her part to play, and played it well. "You ought to do something to soothe her."

The profligate nobleman, for such he was, stepped nearer to Mary, but the young girl drew herself away.

"If any reparation I can make," he began.

"There, do leave us, sir—I'm sure it's so wrong of you: perhaps I may induce her to look over this——"

"Never!" Mary cried, as the so-far-baffled libertine left the room to wait the manœuvring of Mother Rawlings. "I know not, madam, if you are willing that I should be so treated."

"Do not say that, my dear, or I shall be more vexed than I am; I'm sure I wouldn't have thought —but it's what comes of having a pretty face. Still it's very provoking, though, if a gentleman does prefer you to his own wife, and wishes to dress you in silks and jewels: I'm sure ——"

Mary looked at her so steadfastly that her artful speech failed her.

But she soon recovered her customary baseness, and by such words of condolence, interlarded with stray illusions to the wealth of Mr. Herbert, and what he could do for her, tried to bring Mary round to the required point of easiness.

Mary was not so easily lulled; her suspicions were too well excited, and the libertine who was waiting in the next room, heard little that would give him encouragement.

The artful procuress, finding her words had no effect on Mary, all at once pretended to see that she was very pale.

"You are ill, child," she said, in well-affected alarm, "let me get you a glass of wine. Dear me! how stupid of me not to see you were so upset. 'Jane!'"

She touched the bell, and Jane appeared—a sharp-faced girl, very plainly attired.

"Bring me two glasses of wine—this young lady—"

"I thank you," Mary replied, "I do not desire any refreshment."

"Why, my dear, you are all of a faint now. Go, Jane!"

Jane departed, and soon returned with a tray, on which were a decanter of wine, and two glasses.

There could be no trickery about this, certainly, and the manner of Mother Rawlings was as unconstrained as possible when she induced Mary to sit down, and then took the stopper out of the decanter.

Two clear white glasses, glittering in the chandelier's light; who could suspect trickery in these?

Mary might have noticed, had she been very alert in her suspicious, that, when Jane brought in the tray, she turned one end towards Mary. Still, there could have been nothing in that, for Mother Rawlings, in the most off-hand way, slightly turned the tray, so as to place another of the glasses towards Mary.

Then she poured out the wine.

It bubbled clear and juicy into the glasses, and shone like liquid ruby, when she took one up, and handed it to Mary.

"You must take it—just a sip, you know; you are so faint, it will revive you."

She half emptied her own glass. Mary, disarmed of her suspicions by this act, sipped the wine that had been handed to her.

Mother Rawlings, who was all solicitude and anxiety, engaging her in conversation till she had drank it all.

Then, with a satisfied look on her coarse features, she poured herself out another glass of wine.

"Mary, my love—you will take another?"

"I would rather not, thank you."

Mother Rawlings put the stopper into the decanter.

It did not much matter that Mary had refused. That one glass was enough.

There had been just one drop of a clear liquid at the bottom of that glass from which she drank.

Only one drop.

But it was enough.

Mary was drugged.

The cat-like look of Mother Rawlings deepened when she saw the drug beginning to work upon Mary, whose eyes were growing heavy.

"You have been quite upset, my dear," she artfully remarked; "I think you will be glad when you get to your room."

"I shall be glad to get there," Mary answered.

"You will, I am sure, poor dear. Your eyes are quite swollen with agitation. I'm sure I don't see why you should not go to bed at once—that is to say, if you like."

"I think I should be better there."

"Then you shall. Jane!—yet no, I will accompany you to your room. You are far from well, and at such a time it is not well to have servants about one."

Mary rose very weak, and with her head whirling. She never suspected the treachery of that smooth-tongued procuress, and suffered her to lead her to her room.

Mr. Herbert, watching from behind a door, saw this progress with satisfaction.

He was impatient for his villany.

Poor Mary! unsuspicious of guile, she even thanked the base creature whose hand smoothed her hair after she had got into bed.

She was fast sinking into a dreamy, listless state, which she believed to be her weary drowsiness, but which, instead, was the effects of the drug.

She had not consciousness enough to know what occurred when another hand stole over her face. She was too far under the stupor of the drug to be aware of the cool villainy that was being perpetrated towards her. She sank into a dreamy, calm rest; and did not awake till the morning light was peering into the room.

Awoke to find another by her side—to know how foul a wrong had been done against her.

Awoke to realise that she was a prisoner there, despoiled of the last remnant of her honour, and doomed to undergo a fate of horror from which there was no liberation but death.

CHAPTER LXXVIII.

THE DOWNY COVE IN A NEW CHARACTER.

The escape of Crusher Jem had put the Downy Cove in a state of discomfort and alarm for his personal safety.

He, as well as Tiger Loo, were under the ban of the gang; and the Downy had no chance of standing on his own defence, if he were once brought up to be judged and sentenced by his criminal associates.

But the character of the Downy was remarkable for its mildness. He bore unrepiningly the buffets of fate, and though, as we have seen, he did not altogether relish the prospect of being hanged in Dick's stead, it was only from a desire to save the world from the loss it would sustain if he took so sudden a leap from it.

That same delicate consideration caused him to proceed with great caution, lest, in an untimely hour, he should find himself seized, and dragged before the dread tribunal.

But there are no limits to the chances of destiny; and after evading his associates for so long a period, he unexpectedly found himself called upon to thrust himself in upon their notice.

The case was this: Entering one evening to have his favourite pot of porter and pipe, in his favourite house, the Downy, on penetrating to the inner room, beheld two of those very individuals who, from such kind motives, were bent upon finding him.

His first impulse was to withdraw his head immediately, but his second was to boldly force his way in.

He had seen Tiger Loo.

She was sitting at a table, leaning her head on her hands, and evidently unconscious of the nearness of those members of the gang who were there to watch and take her.

When the Downy had stepped inside, he made his way to the same table where Tiger Loo sat, and ordered his pipe and porter.

Tiger looked up on hearing his voice, and spoke; the Downy answered her in his usual manner, taking no notice of those whose presence had given him such alarm.

Tiger Loo made a few remarks, which the Downy Cove took very quickly; his attention being engrossed by the two members of the gang; they were a leary-looking pair; slim, low-browed, and ruffianly; ready, as he could see, for any enterprise.

He was much surprised when they got up and, without glancing at himself or Tiger Loo, went out of the room.

"Them coves wants you," he said to Tiger Loo.

"Which?" the young girl asked, looking fiercely round.

"What's just gone out."

"What for?"

"About the Crusher."

"Jem?"

"The very same."

"And they want me?"

"That's just their game."

"Well; let them attempt anything; let them come on, I'll be ready for them."

Her face flushed a deep crimson, and her eye brightly glittered.

"Hi!" she called out, suddenly, "a quartern of brandy bring me quick."

The brandy was brought.

She tossed it off at a gulp.

"Another," she said.

"Don't try any more," urged the Downy.

"Bring the stuff."

A second quartern was tossed down her throat.

The flush deepened on her face.

Her eyes were more wild.

"Now," she cried, "I am ready."

She leapt up in excited haste.

"What are you going to do?" the Downy asked.

"Meet them," Tiger Loo answered.

"What; get in their way?"

"They are waiting, are they not?"

"Well, but that's no reason why we should get into their jaws."

"I'm not afraid," Tiger Loo cried, "if there are twenty instead of two. Come, if you are not."

"Oh, I'm not afeard," answered the Downy. "Who says I'm afeard? I'll take forty instead of twenty. Now, I'm ready for them."

The Downy Cove certainly did not look very heroic at the moment.

"Come," Tiger Loo exclaimed; "you know what they did to me once; they won't put me *there* again,"

The Downy got up, and went with her out of the house. No one suspicious was to be seen, but they had no doubt that they were being watched.

They were. The same two low-browed fellows stalked after them. They had been hiding out of sight, and now tracked the pair.

The Downy went on till he came to a much more quiet house, seemingly but little frequented.

"Let's go in here," he said.

But before they had time to enter, the two thieves came up.

Tiger Loo stood looking them boldly in the face; the Downy Cove drew back.

The thieves came quietly up.

A very brief look of recognition passed between them.

"Downy," the first one said, "you can take your hook."

The Downy knew what they meant.

They wanted to be left there with Tiger Loo.

Which the Downy didn't see.

"What's up?" he asked, in his most innocent tone.

"Want her."

He pointed to Tiger Loo.

"Does you? What for?"

"Want me?" Tiger Loo cried; "let one of you try to interfere with me. I'm going in here; come after me, if you dare?"

She went inside, and the Downy Cove followed. So did the other men.

They went into a small dimly-lighted room, where several men and women were drinking and talking, their conversation being the vilest slang, and full of oaths.

To this room a masonic sign of fraternity had admitted them, and it was easy to see by a glance of what class those were who were congregated there.

The vilest prostitutes and thieves.

The Downy, apprehensive of the worst, would have retreated, but Tiger Loo pushed forward, and he followed in her wake, very much after the manner of a little poodle trotting after its mistress.

The Downy was right. They were hardly inside before the two following gentlemen stepped towards Tiger Loo.

In an instant one had thrown a large muffler over her head, and drawn it round her neck.

This sudden act created a great stir amongst the thieves, while Tiger Loo began struggling, and the Downy rushed to her rescue. He was, however, instantly caught by the legs by the other one, and thrown on to his back.

Tiger Loo, dropping quickly to the floor, struggled herself out of the grasp of her assailant, but before she could free herself from the muffler, the pair had flung themselves on her.

But while they were holding her down, the Downy, who had slid off his back, walked behind them, and hitting each very sharply under the ear, knocked them over.

Then he liberated Tiger Loo, who, flushed and excited, no sooner found herself free, than she flew at the first one who had attacked her, and bearing him to the ground, as he was rising clenched her fingers tightly on his throat.

"Help!" howled the man, "I shall be strangled."

"That's what you were born for," the Downy observed, as he gave the other one a second tap with the boot, and upset him again.

The utmost confusion by this time had prevailed. With oaths and cries of the vilest nature, the low denizens of the place came crowding to the spot.

"Off," whispered the Downy, "you'll be limbo'd if you don't."

But Tiger Loo was too well occupied in squeezing the throat of her assailant to take any notice of the Downy's admonitions; it was only when she was by main force pulled away that she allowed the half-choked man to be taken from her clutches.

In the midst of the universal uproar, the second of her assailants addressed the other thieves.

He told them that she had peached against the Crusher, and had before escaped, after being thrust down the pit, and ended by calling upon them to assist in bringing her to the tribunal of the gang. This statement set everyone against Tiger Loo; above all, the members of that fraternity dread a "peach." They know they would have little safety if they had any amongst them who were likely to sell them to justice.

On this account Tiger Loo was, on the nature of her offence being known, greeted with groans from the male, and hisses from the female, portion of the assembly, many of the latter coming forward, as if to summarily inflict punishment.

"You'd better slope," the Downy again said.

"I'll not go," Tiger Loo answered.

She snatched up a large knife that lay on the table, and stood facing them all.

"What I did," she cried, "I'll answer for to Jem when I meet him; and mark me, when I do meet him I will cut his throat, or stick him to the heart. I am going away; stop me who can!"

By a swift movement she raised the knife, and stepped forward.

There were a number of swearing men and boasting women in front of her, but they fell back like a pack of wolves as she leaped in among them.

That bright knife brandished above their heads, and threatening to cut flesh and sinew in its track, intimidated the boldest, but those who were in the rear stimulated those in front to withstand her, they not being in imminent danger; but when the next instant she was making her tracks through them, the bright knife, dulled by the hue of blood on it, fell with a sharp sound on quivering flesh, they gave way like the receding waves, and Tiger Loo passed from amidst them.

She had what is popularly called, "run-a-muck," and never did furious cattle, dashing through crowded streets, create a greater commotion than did Tiger Loo. It was but a moment that she seemed to be in their clutches, and then she had passed away, leaving her opposers bleeding and yelling in pain and fear.

She was gone; for, though they rushed after her, she was not to be found.

Deprived of this one mark of their vengeance, their wrath now fell on the Downy Cove, who was in the act of sneaking quietly off, when a nimble young thief laid hold of him by the collar.

The Downy Cove was usually cool and prompt in his action, so, when he found himself thus seized, he lifted his foot, and hitting the man who held him in the stomach, knocked him backwards, feeling very sick and uncomfortable.

Whereupon the Downy Cove took advantage of the opportunity to slope.

But the whole rabble came following after him —not in a body, for that would have created a crowd—but by twos and threes, each party taking different directions in their pursuit.

After dodging them for a considerable time, and almost laid hold of, then slipping down some back alley, the Downy suddenly gave them the double by dropping into a theatrical outfitter's. The door was a little way open when he reached it, but the Downy quickly shut it to, and stood breathless and perspiring inside.

As soon as he could look round, he found himself confronted by a little man in almost every respect the counterpart of himself.

The little man regarded him with curiosity, and in a soft tone, said—

"Your pleasure, sir?"

The Downy stared at him, but could not speak.

"Aw—may I have—"

"Keep the door shut," exclaimed the Downy, falling down to the floor in terror, as some of his pursuers came rushing by. "Don't let them in; they'll rob you—they will."

The little man thought his visitor scarcely looked altogether honest, but he said nothing.

"I can serve you," presently he said, when the Downy rose.

"You can?" He grasped the little man's hands affectionately. "Be my friend—disguise—I'll pay—disguise me so that nobody won't know me."

The little man smiled, and said quietly—

"We can do that."

"My friend—"

"What style would you like?"

"Anything—anything. Make me a cart-horse—anything."

"We won't make you that," said the little man quietly, and he moved away.

In a very short time he returned, with the suit of an officer in the line, complete with sword, moustache, and everything requisite for the character.

"Now," he said.

"Eh?"

"Undress."

"What—put them on?"

"Yes."

"Make me a horsifer?'

"Yes."

"Why, I shall look a guy."

"Yes."

"But I ain't to wear them to gs?'

"Yes."

"Won't suit me."

"Yes."

"Well, if you think they will, of course—but I don't."

The little man quietly helped him off with his coat.

No. 24.

"Suit you well, when we get this moustache on, and a little colour on the face to match with the scarlet of your coat."

"Oh, my eye!"

"Yes."

The trousers and coat were by this time on, and the little man stood in front of the Downy to put on the moustache.

Now, the Downy thought this a very good opportunity of using his hands, and as there was a profusion of gold lace and ornamental weapons lying on the counter, he helped himself to a few of them.

"That's just your fit," said the little man.

"Yes."

He was fumbling for the pocket.

"Just the thing."

"Oh no, but it ain't" thought the Downy, who was fumbling in vain for his pocket.

Just then the little man turned for the powder-box and paint.

The Downy's hands went instantly behind him, when the whole of the booty found its way into the breech of his trousers.

He looked the very picture of innocence when the little man turned again to apply the colour to his face.

"There," he said, "you'll do now."

"Yes," said the Downy, who had just then lifted the handkerchief out of his trousers' pocket.

"Capital!"

"Glad to hear it."

"Quite distinguished."

"What's to pay?"

The little man named an exorbitant sum. The Downy Cove pulled a long face; but instantly recollecting himself, pulled the purse out of the little man's pocket without the little man being aware of it, and with mock honesty paid the amount.

The Downy glided to the door.

The little man bowed him out.

He had charged him six times the value of the articles, and so he thought he had made a good bargain.

The Downy Cove, on his part, was well satisfied. He had the better of the suit, and a purse of money by his visit to that shop.

The pair of quiet rogues bowed adieu to each other, and the little man went inside to his little room, to count over the profits of that little performance.

"But the Downy Cove "sloped" out of sight in less than no time.

To have remained longer in that neighbourhood might have led to very unpleasant results.

The leary gentlemen who had been on the Downy's track had all disappeared, and our hero, secure from danger, went swaggering about in an interesting style, displaying to advantage the magnificent attire which the clothier had given him.

Elated by his good fortune, and blessed with the superb abundance of cash, he sallied into several public houses on his route, imbibing at each a large quantity of ardent spirits, for which he paid like a lord.

When he was pretty well sprung this way, he determined on sauntering into the park to disport himself after the fashion of other gallants.

"They'll take me to be the officer of the Guards," he thought, as he staggered towards the Duke of York's Column.

Here he met with the first acknowledgment of his new character. The soldiers on guard, either being really taken in or intending a bit of fun, saluted him in a respectful manner as he passed.

The Downy was overcome by this deference; and, to tell the truth, he did not know how to return the salute. He was saved by a mischance of fate, for as he was raising his hand to his cap his foot slipped, and he went down several of the hard flint steps before he could stop himself.

After he had recovered from the effects of this downfall he staggered up the Mall, greatly to the amazement of the passers-by, the nursemaids especially making him the object of particular observation.

The Downy bore his greatness meekly. He lavished his smiles on every side, and made himself quite a distinguished object of attention for that day.

The last that was seen of him was when he was found by Policeman B leaning elegantly against a tree, trying to impress an idea of his dignity upon a troop of boys, who, having smelt him out, were indulging in no little trickery and shouting at his expense.

CHAPTER LXXIX.

MARY.

DESTITUTE now of the last hope of woman, poor Mary made up her mind to escape from her prison or die in the attempt.

Mother Rawlings had succeeded more than once in making her the victim of her infamous beating, and as there were so many means of overcoming the unfortunate girl, Mary had no chance of resisting her.

She was now destined for a worse treatment—the flogging machine was to hold her as the next victim.

Mary gleaned this shudderingly from the servant girl that attended on her, who took a malicious delight in preparing her for fresh misery. To-night she was to be tied up there, to undergo that frightful outrage.

"It shall never be," Mary said to herself; "if needs be I will die, but this I will not suffer."

A change had come over the girl's character; she was desperate and fierce where she had been diffident and gentle.

She resolved that night to make a vigorous attempt at escape.

For once fate seemed inclined to favour her. Sitting by a window, which, though well closed and secured, afforded a view of the street, she saw the pale face of Charley looking up at her.

A few tremulous signs, her fingers tracing some letters along the window, and the brave boy was made acquainted with her imprisonment and design of escape.

Charley hurried away, leaving her buoyed up by this new hope of liberty and encouragement.

Our youthful hero had been greatly excited at the sight of Mary, whom so long he had sought; but he had learnt enough of the ways of this metropolis to know that if he wished to get Mary away it would have to be secretly done.

Had he obeyed his first impulse, and summoned the police to break into the house and liberate

Mary, the poor girl would have been mercilessly disposed of by her pitiless jailors.

So the boy resolved on meeting them with stratagems and cunning.

Where Charley and his boy chum, Nobby Ned, lodged there lived a working man of kindly disposition and resolute character, but unfortunately addicted to habits of intemperance.

He was very much taken up with Charley, and would have done anything to serve him; so when the boy returned and told his story, he struck his fist on the table, and swore that he would be with them on that night's venture.

In this man they would have had an invaluable aid if he could only have kept sober, but unluckily the warmth of his honest indignation against Mary's persecutors caused him to go out and indulge in a little tippling, so that when the hour came for the start, he was as drunk as a fiddler and as independent as a lord.

Charley was very grieved when he came and saw this. The man's wife had been doing her best to sober her husband, but he was in anything but a yielding mood, and Charley began to fear that he would have to manage without him.

But Mrs. Luker, the man's wife, adopted a vigorous measure: coming suddenly behind her husband, she emptied a pail of cold water over his head, and so well soused him that he was half sobered almost at once.

He soon got over the fit of temper this occasioned, and, with many profound regrets for his shortcomings, staggered to his feet, and went forth with Charley and Nobby Ned.

When they got to the house it was as silent as if nothing of any import was going on there. No one would have suspected that so much of crime was being enacted therein.

Luker, who was a very dexterous locksmith, lost no time in getting to work; in two minutes he had the door open, and the trio noiselessly entered.

The house had been quiet enough up to that moment, but they were no sooner fairly inside than such a shriek arose as almost turned the wits of Luker upside down.

"I hear Mary's voice!" Charley sprung forward, but noiselessly. Guided by that sound of distress, they made their way to a room, and entered in time to discover Mary on her knees, being dragged across the room by Crusher Jem and his worthless accomplice.

The action of Luke the tinker was very prompt, and very effectual. Taking a small hammer out of his pocket, he quietly walked up to Crusher Jem, and, without any fuss whatever, deliberately struck him a strong blow under the ear. Crusher Jem fell in an instant like a poleaxed ox, and the tinker coolly put back his hammer.

"Now," he said to Charley, "get her out, and I'll keep the way clear."

Mary had sprung to her feet on the fall of the Crusher; she was by Charley's side in a moment; the Crusher's confederate was so completely surprised by the unexpected interruption that he had done nothing but stared stupidly on the scene.

He now made a brisk move forward, but receiving the foot of the tinker full in the pit of the stomach went reeling back, looking very sick and disgusted.

Fleeing to the door, Charley and Mary were confronted by Mother Rawlings, who had heard the unusual proceedings, and now stood looking wildly at them, and opposing their flight. Charley and Nobby Ned endeavoured to push her out of the way, but she gave them such a clip under the ear that sounded all over the room, and half stunned them.

She then gave a most uproarious alarm, and was in the flush of her outcry, when the indomitable tinker glided to her side, and with no more compunction than if he had been knocking down a bullock hit her full on the forehead with the renowned hammer.

It was a frightful hit; though given so easily, it told instantly. The iron end seemed to sink through flesh and bone; and as the crashing sound arose from the blow, the evil procuress fell bleeding and insensible to the floor.

"Now," said the tinker, "she's got her dose, and it's no more than she deserved. Come on."

To come on was not so easy a matter; the outcry had been raised, and two bully-looking vagabonds met them on the stairs.

Poor Mary! desperate and wild, clenched her little hand, and prepared to battle, if necessary, for her liberty: but it was not unaided; the famous hammer went swiftly out of the tinker's hand, and meeting the temple of one of the ruffians knocked him down the stairs. The other slid swiftly down after the hammer, and had just possessed himself of it, when Tinker Luker, who was in no wise particular in his manner of dealing with such gentlemen, jumped on his back as he stooped down a stair.

It jumped the life almost out of the ruffian; he groaned and lay writhing.

"I think that's broke his back," the tinker said quietly, as he picked up his hammer; "now, boys, let's be off."

They reached the door unmolested, though the door had opened through the house; but the tinker's process had so effectually disposed of the first lot that no one for a moment suspected that Mary was being got out of the house.

The little tinker was evidently satisfied with his night's work.

"I hope they won't none of them die," he muttered "not that I should fret; but I'd like them to live with their broken heads and backs also! What a pretty little tap I gave that ——. Served her right! They've served this poor lass out, I can see, in a wicked way. It's all right now though, and I'll get jolly drunk to-night."

And he did.

His wife took every care of Mary. Poor Mary! She wanted some comforting. The kindness of the tinker's wife was soothing after her many sorrows, and she was doomed to trespass much upon it.

A fever prostrated her, and for two months she lay between life and death, during all which time Charley worked gladly to provide for her wine and other necessaries, and glad enough was the noble boy when she was pronounced out of danger, and began to slowly recover. So soon as her health was well established, Mary insisted upon going into a situation which was offered to her, as companion to a widowed lady, who, with her remaining child, resided in a suburban mansion.

Under all circumstances this was the best thing that she could have done, as her duties relieved her mind of its preying thoughts; but this change in her fortunes was destined to bring her and our other characters into collision with events as startling and wondrous as have ever occurred even in our metropolis.

Following her and Charley's fortunes, now the reader will be introduced to the "Secret Band," a league of twenty youths, who, with their leader, carried on a system of desperate deeds, conducted with such skill as to baffle the whole force of police.

Some graphic and interesting particulars will now be disclosed of places familiar to many of our readers, amongst which will be the Haunted Houses of Stamford Street, shown here in characters totally different from any that have yet been ascribed to them.

We are confident there have never been disclosures so rich in the marvellous and thrilling as those we are about to give, nor which so fully give the keystone to the history of crime with which our mammoth city abounds.

Many a deed, for a long time shrouded in secrecy, will have the veil lifted from its dark features. Many a desperate act of violence and murder will find ample exposure in these pages.

CHAPTER LXXX.

THE PLOTTER AND HIS INSTRUMENT.

It was Saturday evening in the plebeian locality known as the New Cut, Lambeth; all the transpontine world was astir, and throngs of marketers passed in continuous streams along the streets, courts, and alleys leading to that great mart of low-priced goods.

There shopkeepers and shopmen were in the height of their business; shops were jammed tight with articles of trade and crowded by customers; piles of cheeses, hams, and pieces of bacon were propped up in the cheesemonger's window, or spread on shelves and boards; the grocers had their various goods displayed to the best advantage—sugar fresh sanded, raisins redolent with treacle, and tea that was never grown in China or Japan, were spread in wild profusion; the fronts of the butchers' shops were obscured by joints of meat of all sizes and of every quality, and bespattered by huge tickets; and before these arrays of legs and shoulders stood, greasy-haired, ruddy-faced butchers, dressed in blue suits, and armed with long bright knives, which they flourished wildly as they ejaculated furiously and incessantly the monotonous and peremptory demand of "Buy, buy!"

Furniture shops had their goods well furbished up and arranged to the best advantage, and hatchet-faced touters rushed furiously at any whom they detected glancing at their displayed wares, and dragging them by main force into the shops, so overwhelmed the victims with bargains and marvels of cheapness, that they were fain to purchase some gimcrack article before they had time to recover their breath.

Nor was the business confined to the shops: all along each side of the road stalls were posted up with every conceivable article of consumption, ornament, use, or useless. Side by side with the vendor of combs was one who sold sweetmeats; then came stalls of fish, of fruit, of vegetables, of incongruities; in short, of everything which could possibly be brought there, or for which there could be found a customer.

Little boys, with dirty faces and large mouths, were perched on the top of pyramids of cabbages, or ensconced behind barrels of fresh herrings, where a lamp-post intervened. The sellers of flash jewellery or porte-monnaies took up their position, and along the kerb, where a foot of space was available, stunted men, with unshorn chins and begrimmed features, arranged their stock of patched-up boots and shoes, or gentlemen of unmistakably Jewish countenances entrenched themselves behind a rampart of caps.

The evening was progressing and business flourishing, and the dense throng squeezed between the shops and stalls, or forced their way in and out of public houses. The lively members of several itinerant bands "tuned their footsteps to a march" of peculiar and disagreeable discordance.

A perfect Babel of sounds rent the air. Shopmen and shopboys shouted, touters persuaded, children cried, women joked, men swore, and the costermonger colony kept up their discordance of hoarse yells and multitudinous cries, with a persistency that showed that whatever might be their real grievances weak lungs was not to be reckoned amongst them.

The usual crowd of apple-munching boys stood before the entrance to the twopenny show, listening with open mouths to the cadaverous man with a whip in his hand, who was energetically holding forth upon the wonders to be seen inside, and of the astounding performance, "Never before witnessed," that was now about to commence for positively the last time that evening.

Numbers of women and men walked in the road to avoid the crowd or the pavement; but even here the throng was dense, and the horses and carts that occasionally passed had much ado in forcing a passage through the multitude of marketers, of all aspects, and dressed in every variety and style of costume were they; some slovenly dressed, others smartly attired; women with anxious, care-worn faces, inwardly calculating how to obtain the greatest currency for a shilling; dissipated creatures, hurrying to the crowded gin-shops; workingmen, tidily dressed men, and men out-at-elbows, all helped to form that living stream of people in search of Saturday night bargains, and goods that were more renowned for cheapness in price than for quality.

It was near eight o'clock when a man, evidently superior to the class frequenting the place, turned sharply from the Westminster-road, and, diving amidst the throng, made his way as quick as he was able through the crowd. He was a tall, upright man, with features at once harsh and arrogant. With the exception of a slight whisker, he was closely shaved, and as he petulantly passed along the road, his grey ferretting eye and aquiline nose, with the frowning brow, showed him to be a man whose disposition was not to be trifled with.

Muttering many an execration on the crowded street, he pursued his way till he arrived at a narrow dark turning near the centre of the place; here he paused, and, glancing along the line of stalls, eagerly scanned the features of the owners.

His glance at length rested upon a man who was attending a fruit stall, and apparently satisfied that he was the man he wanted, he, not without some difficulty, forced his way through the crowd to him.

The individual whom he thus appeared to recognise was a short, thickset man, dressed in corduroy trousers and fustian jacket; a fur cap adorned his head, and his bull neck was encircled by a yellow handkerchief spotted with white. In appearance he was repulsive and ruffianly. His hair was cropped short to his ears, which were large and flat; not a vestige of beard or whisker appeared on his sallow features; and as he hoarsely cried his goods, or uttered some coarse witticism to the owners of the stalls contiguous, his rolling, cat-like eyes seemed to express a brutality of the most coarse and determined kind.

The name of this interesting personage was Bill Simmons; he was, however, more popularly known as the Lambeth Bulldog—an appellation bestowed upon him in honour of his having once, in a street encounter, bitten his opponent's ear off, as well as on account of his tenacity and persistence, as displayed in the prize ring. where his prowess was both cherished and admired; for though now pursuing the peaceful and honest occupation of a vendor of fruit, this worthy was a noted pugilistic hero, and a notorious ruffian, combining the profession of costermonger with that of bird-fancier, dog-stealer, smasher, and housebreaker.

His friends were justly proud of him, for he had travelled as far as Botany Bay, at which place he had resided for some time, and had besides sojourned in several of the London prisons, where, to use his own words, "he lived like a gemman." Besides his travelling propensity, he was known to have kicked a policeman to death, for which playful amusement he received a week's imprisonment for manslaughter, had beaten in the face of a "swell," and knocked silly the last man he fought in the P.R.

He was also reputed a good runner, having at one time been seen to double at a remarkable pace when hotly chased by two policemen, he having unconsciously put his fingers into a gentleman's pocket, extracting thence his gold watch, which, in the hurry of the moment, he forgot to replace.

To this gentleman of many acquirements the tall traveller advanced, and passing by his stall into the road beckoned him to follow.

The visage of Bill Simmons fell somewhat on beholding the stranger, and he looked suspiciously round before he ventured to leave his stall. No active and intelligent officer in blue being near, and seeing no one with a detective cast of countenance anywhere by, he consigned the care of his fruit to a long, thin, cadaverous seller of cured haddocks, and hastened to join the individual who had summoned him to follow.

"I wonder wot's up now, Meg," said the vendor of haddocks, addressing himself to a poverty stricken, dissipated wench. with a discoloured eye, who occupied the next stall.

"Can't say," rejoined she, "who is the old buffer?"

"Never seed him afore," rejoined the long cadaverous party, who was known amongst his intimates by the not inapt sobriquet of "Long Tim."

"May be it's some copper togged out to nab him."

"No fear," returned Long Tim with an expressive grin, "Bill's too fly for any one to nab like that."

"Well, they're having a long confab," said Meg.

"Yes, rather; old chap wants him I 'spose; as Bill's a lucky one, I dessay he'll be flash with the shiners now."

"And flush of flimsies," returned Meg. "Penny a lot." The latter observation was addressed to a passer-by, and bore reference to sundry lots of vegetables arranged on the board before her.

While this colloquy was taking place, the "bulldog" had joined the stranger, and now stood awkwardly before him.

"You remember me, I suppose?" said the latter abruptly.

"Vell, I ain't forgot you," replied Simmons, glancing furtively round.

"You need not be uneasy," said the other, noticing the suspicious movement; "I have not come to betray you; I want your further services."

"All right, guv'nor; I'm your man if there's any shiners to be made. When do you want me?"

"Now. You must leave those things and come with me at once."

"*Must*, guv'nor?"

"Must, I said," rejoined the stranger significantly. The ruffian winced slightly.

"But how about them goods; I have only just begun to sell, and I shall lose a good profit if I leaves 'em.

"Pooh!" exclaimed the stranger petulantly, "have I not told you that I want your services? What is that paltry stock of apples in comparison with the money you will earn of me? Have you not always found me liberal?"

"Vell, guv'nor, I must say, pays well, but then you see I've done some ockard jobs for you."

"Silenee, fool; this is no place for such reminiscences; come, make arrangements for leaving the stall, and accompany me."

"Vot's the job this time?" inquired Bill, "any bloke to be settled ——"

"The task is easy," interrupted the stranger, "and is not one of bloodshed. We will talk of it elsewhere; conduct me to some house that you are *well* acquainted with, where we can sit in a room to converse without fear of interruption. You will be particular as to what sort of house you take me to," he added, noting a sudden sinister light in the evil eyes of the ruffian, "for, remember, I have no money about me; when on such expeditions as these I carry nothing with me but a loaded revolver. The reward you will earn will be paid when the job is accomplished."

"All right, guv'nor," rejoined Simmons, letting his glance fall before the steady gaze of the stranger, "I'll just go to Long Tim and be back directly."

"I will wait," said the stranger, and the bulldog, having made arrangements with Long Tim respecting the sale of his stock, returned to where he had left his employer.

"Lead on," said that personage, "I will follow closely; lead the way from this infernal Babel as soon as possible, and remember I am armed, but moneyless."

Grunting forth some inaudible reply, Bill Simmons led the way from the "Cut," and the stranger, drawing his hat more over his eyes, so as to screen his features, followed at a short distance from him.

"So, they're off," said Meg, looking significantly at Long Tim.

"Yes," returned that elongated specimen of humanity—"I wonder wot's the game there."

"He's a knowing old cove," said Meg, alluding to the stranger.

"Rather! And Bill's sure to bag some shiners. I should like to know where they've gone to. If

I'd only somebody to look arter the stalls," muttered Tim.

"You ain't likely to know," said Meg, who had only heard part of the foregoing sentence; "Bill's rather a close 'un; he don't tell more nor he's obliged to. He knows what's what, I'll wager.'"

The profundity of the last observations seemed to strike Tim, for he made no reply, but fell into a brown study.

The throng passed slowly on—fresh faces, a continued moving stream of human beings, engrossed by the mysteries and sublimity of marketing.

Meg plied a busy trade, for her voice was high and her vegetables were not, and she was in the act of cramming into a customer's basket (which already contained a shoulder of mutton, a pair of boots, and a pound of candles), a "lot" of vegetables, when a sudden exclamation from elongated Timothy startled her from her usual equanimity.

"I'm blowed if I don't!" said Tim, rousing from his deep reverie.

"Don't what?" inquired Meg, sarcastically. I'm blessed if I think you'll *sell*—here's every one near you selling out, and you haven't taken a penny since Bill went."

"Nay," said Tim, "I knows you're a good 'un to keep a secret, so you needn't say anything to Bill about this, but just look arter these things till I send young Wideawake to mind 'em."

Before the fair Meg had time to express the amazement that was depicted upon her countenance Tim had disappeared in the crowd, and in about five minutes his place was supplied by a ragged young urchin, with an old face on his young shoulders, who, winking familiarly at me, forthwith commenced to vociferate an incessant eulogium of his goods, interlarding his set phrases with such funny expressions as are best calculated to make people laugh and buy, viz.: "Here we are," "Sold agin an' got the money," "Now, mum, waiting for yer," &c. &c.; and so loudly did he bawl, and so briskly did he attend to his customers, that he seemed likely to sell out the contents of both stalls in a very short space of time.

"Ah!" muttered the hitherto mystified Meg, as a sudden light flashed to her mind, "I tumbles; Ha! Long Tim, I knows yer little game."

Having thus expressed herself, she glanced complacently at young Wideawake, and continued her avocation of yelling "Penny a lot, penny a lot!"

CHAPTER LXXXI.

THE SHADOW ON THE WALL.

THE world is much made up of rogues and fools. Of a necessity where one exists, the other is sure to be, and stultified and stultifiers abound in every grade of society, though, in some instances, the attendant circumstances may so glozen the act that roguery loses its nomenclature, and stupidity is modified to remissness. It has been said, too, that if there were no great rogues there would be no little ones. The distinction may, or may not, be obvious; it is a fine drawn line—a split-hair, in fact —for the polished exterior may conceal a greater scoundrel than is he of villainous aspect, whose roguery, though of small degree, is apparent.

But the accomplished rascal may make the meaner rogue his tool; therein lies the pith of the proverb, for the smaller rogue is led by the nose into the meshes of rascality, whilst the *great* rascal is well screened behind the curtain of society.

A spade is a spade, and should be called so. Not so with rascality. Society has different names for it; thus theft may be a mania; fraud, sharp practice; profligacy, indiscretion; and so forth. What is crime in the sweaty-browed, hard-fisted plebeian, is recklessness in the case of the white-skinned and interesting "Honourable," and the well-dressed scoundrel, whose plotting brain was teeming with villainy, pondered, as he strode after the ruffianly Bill Simmons, upon the probable fate of that hardened villain.

Doubtless had it been suggested to his mind that his rascality was as great, if not greater, than that of the murderous-visaged Bulldog, he would have scouted the idea as a ridiculous absurdity, not to be for a moment entertained. For his hands were white, and *he* had struck no blow when any had been smitten.

Swaggering on as if the whole place belonged to him, the accomplished Bill emerged from the "Cut," and, striking down a dark and narrow turning, soon left the noise and the glare of that fashionable spot behind.

His employer stalked steadily after him; no one looking at the two could have supposed that they had any dealings with each other, and, indeed, had the Bulldog stopped to greet any passing friend, the well-dressed rogue would have passed majestically on.

One hand rested lightly on the breast of his coat; there was a bulky something there that he wished to keep secure: one button of his coat was unfastened, in order that he might reach the article directly it was wanted.

In this manner several streets were traversed, and about half-an-hour's walking brought them to a dirty winding turning, up which Bill Simmons passed.

The houses were old and out of repair. Near the centre a lamp was supported by iron rods from the front of a house; one of the panes of glass was broken, and the remainder were dirty, and as the wind dashed through the broken pane the flickering ray but ineffectually illumined the surrounding darkness.

Opposite was an old wooden gate; the timbers were decayed, and several cavities enabled the beholder to see that it was the entrance to a disused shed. Three ragged urchins, with hair unkempt and faces unwashed, were tossing for half-pence by the light of the lamp.

The two worthies passed them. A little further on an open door revealed a den of misery and filth almost indescribable. In a small room, carpeted only by a thick layer of mud and filth, several half-nude human beings were huddled. A solitary rushlight, stuck in a broken image, illuminated the apartment, showing by its feeble glimmering a pallet of dirty straw, on what, at first sight, appeared to be a bundle of rags.

It was a woman in the last stage of sickness.

The other occupants squatted on the floor. They were an old woman, one much younger—but old by care, and perhaps dissipation—two young children, and a thin, wasted man.

Bill Simmons swaggered by. The stranger cast a momentary glance upon the apartment and its occupants; then his lips curled in scorn, and he too passed on: for in his heart he despised that scene of starvation and squalid misery.

As he passed the gaslight threw his shadow obliquely upon the wall of the wretched room.

The younger of the two women turned and glanced at the passer-by. His face, averted in scorn, still bore that expression of disdainful pride; and in the shade his features for the moment seemed truly satanic. A slight scream broke from the lips of the wan creature as she thus caught sight of his features; then her teeth set harshly together, and, laying her hand upon the man's shoulder, she pointed to the window.

The emaciated man turned; he, too, caught a momentary glimpse of that face. A slight colour rose to his cheeks, and he stood up.

"'Tis him," said the woman, speaking in a hoarse whisper as she, too, rose.

They walked to the door and looked out.

The two travellers still walked on; no sound had reached their ears, and the two trembling watchers, as they stood at the door, beheld them pause at a low ale house near the end of the street. It was an old-fashioned cottage, that appeared to have been built for centuries; an almost obliterated board announced that malt liquors were sold there, whilst a square signboard, that had equally experienced the effects of time and weather, bore an indistinct figure, something resembling a spotted dog.

Some letters underneath, however, explained that it was meant for a leopard. Some dingy red blinds were put up before the parlour windows, the shutters of which were still open.

The Bulldog walked up the steps that led to the interior, and the stranger, casting a searching glance up the street, followed him.

Then the thin, haggard man turned to the careworn woman who leant upon him. She had become a heavy weight, and seeing that she had fainted, he carried her into that abode of dirt and destitution. The sick woman feebly inquired what was the matter; the children moved round the fainting girl, and the old woman fetched some water to restore her to consciousness; but the man knelt by the inanimate form, and as he took the rigid hand his lips trembled, and his body shook, but from his eyes flashed a ray, fierce and malevolent, whilst a hectic spot burned on each cheek, as he seemed to breathe some terrible oath, to the fulfilment of which he had sworn.

CHAPTER LXXXII.

THE CONFERENCE AT THE "LEOPARD."

THE door of the "Leopard" slowly swung to, and the stranger and his willing aid stood before the bar.

The interior was small, and in keeping with the outside.

Some empty beer barrels were placed on end near the bar, and a low dirty form, in a very dilapidated state, was placed by the wall opposite. The walls were bare, except where, behind the bar, hung a few discoloured prints representing notorious fighting men or runners. From the centre of the ceiling hung a wirecage, in which was a grey parrot.

Behind the bar, talking to shabby men of somewhat sinister aspect, stood the landlady, a shrivelled woman of about fifty. Contrary to the generality of such ladies she was tall and gaunt; a few frizzled curls straggled from under her cap, her upper lip was adorned with a downy moustache, and a huge mole appeared on her right cheek.

Two men, somewhat similar in looks and dress to Bill Simmons, sat on the form before-mentioned, and as the stranger and his guide entered they eyed him with curious glances, and then glanced significantly at each other, while the man who was leaning over the bar stood up to gaze at the newcomers.

Neither the place nor the people were in the slightest degree prepossessing, and it was not exactly the sort of place the stranger would have selected for a confidential conference.

He was, however, not disposed to stick at trifles, and therefore awaited for his conductor to lead the way.

"Glad to see you, Mr. Simmons," said the hostess, forcing a grimace, intended for a smile, to her parchment visage.

"Thank you," said the respectable Bill; "but this gemman and me wants to have a little private talk. Can we go to your best room?"

"Oh, certainly, Mr. Simmons What shall I bring for you and the gentleman?"

The Bulldog looked inquiringly at the gentleman.

"Have what you please," said that personage, tartly; "I shall not take anything."

"Vell, let me have a pot of heavy, missis," said the thirsty Simmons; "and bring it up directly."

The hostess filled a pewter measure, and led the way up a ricketty flight of stairs, to a room directly over the bar. Having placed the beer upon the table, and lighted another candle, she retired, curtseying.

"No interruption, missis," said the lordly Bill; "me and this gemman wants to be private to ourselves."

"No one will disturb you," said the hostess, as she closed the door.

"That's all right," growled Simmons, as he half emptied the pot at a draught.

The stranger, who had all this time kept his hand upon his breast, now drew forth the "something" he had kept concealed there. It was a revolver, loaded and capped, and having seen that it was all right, he placed it before him on the table.

Bill regarded him in silence.

"Simmons," said the stranger, still keeping his hand upon the weapon, "you have, I believe, a wife."

"Vell, vife or voman, it's all the same, you know."

"Enough. Where does she reside?"

"Werry close to where yer honour found me."

"Has she any children?"

The Bulldog grinned.

"Not exactly," he rejoined.

"But she could take charge of one."

"Oh, yes; Moll's a good 'un for looking arter 'em," replied Bill, looking as if he did not quite see the drift of these questions.

"Listen," said the stranger; "you will to-night take a child to your home; your wife will attend to it under the instructions that I will give you."

"But where's the kid now?"

"At it's home; where you will have to go for it."

"Me!" exclaimed the bruiser, looking aghast. "Vell, that's a good 'un; as if any von 'ud give me a child to take care on."

"You will not ask their permission in the matter: you will have to steal it."

The brute's face brightened.

"That's a different thing; more my style," he said, as he emptied the pewter measure. "But the pot's out," he added, as he turned it upside down.

"Ring for more," said the stranger, looking at him in disgust.

The measure having been replenished the stranger continued, as he passed a slip of paper towards the ruffian,

"Repair to the house described on that paper, some time to-night, alone. Do you think you can find it?"

"Easy; but wich vay am I to get in?"

"I will tell you. At midnight all the inmates of the house will be asleep. At the rear of the house is a large garden. There is a watch-dog, but I will look to him. A ladder will be placed there; by its aid you can, with a little skill, mount to the back drawing-room window. All the fastenings will be unscrewed, so that a little force only will be required to gain an entrance. You will be able to pick any locks that may be in your way. Exactly over that room is the chamber in which the child sleeps with its nurse. You must secure the child without disturbing any of the household, for secrecy is required, and violence must be avoided. You understand?"

"It's all notched down; but suppose the nuss should vake?"

"The narcotic I will contrive to administer will cause her to sleep soundly: it will be your own clumsiness if you arouse any one else. The mother sleeps in the adjoining chamber."

"I shall have to quiet her."

"Not so," said the stranger, sternly. "You will have to use caution and adroitness. The servants all have arms within their reach: a slight alarm, and if you had a thousand lives, your chance of escape would be poor. For the rest, if any one is harmed by you, beware! for I would hunt you to your lair, and, at every risk, drag you to the scaffold."

The Bulldog looked dangerous for a moment, but the fingers of the strangers were compressed on the revolver, and the shining barrels pointed to him.

"I 'spose I must do the job," he muttered, "but vot's the terms?"

"The terms are conditional. If you succeed, as you will assuredly if you use caution and dexterity, if, I say, you convey the child unharmed, and without discovery, without also injuring any one in the house, to your abode, two hundred guineas will be yours. When the infant is safely lodged in the care of your wife, you shall receive the money. *Upon the death of that child* you will receive five hundred guineas, providing his death is *not* the result of ill-usage."

Simmons, who during the delivery of that sentence had exhibited on his brutal face the pleasure he felt, became somewhat crestfallen as he heard the concluding part of it.

"How's the kid to die?" he asked.

"The child will pine, and it must be brought up *by hand*, till it pines and dies."

Even the hardened ruffian felt that he sat before a most heartless scoundrel. To have brained or strangled the child would not have affected him in the least; but to take it from its mother—its nurse—and wait for it to pine to death; to feed the yearning little creature on such coarse food that, whilst clogging its stomach, could not satisfy its hungry cravings, there was a refinement — a subtlety of cruelty about the proposal that caused him to look askant at the speaker.

"Are the terms understood?" asked the stranger, speaking calmly and deliberatively.

"Vell I 'spose so; but ain't I to get nuffin' if I shouldn't get the child safe home?"

"Not a fraction."

The man of many accomplishments looked at him.

"But it might squall. Is it a young 'un?"

"One week old. Take a blanket from its cot and wrap it in, coward, fool!"

Again the dangerous look glittered in the eye of the Bulldog.

"Take a cab there, I suppose, to take the kid away in?"

"What for? To be tracked—discovered! No."

"But you don't think I should go far without being stopped if I had a brat in my arms at that time of night?"

The disdainful smile played round the stranger's lips as he replied—

"When I said you were to go alone, I meant unaccompanied by any male confederate; but your wife can wait near the house. An old shawl will wrap up the child, and you will pass the busy night force without exciting in their breasts the slightest suspicion. Is it all clear to you now?"

The Bulldog pondered a few moments, then, having drank the remainder of the beer, he said gruffly—

"I s'pose you'll give me something to begin with?"

"I tell you, not a penny shall be paid until the task is safely accomplished."

"But, now, if I won't do it?"

"Then you will not earn or get the money—that's all."

The bully half rose, but the steady eye and calm manner of the other awed his ruffianly nature, and he sank in his seat.

"Look here, guv'nor," he began; "I'll do the job, all right; but give us a taste of the shiners."

"I have before told you that I have no money with me."

"Yes, but that's gammon, we know."

"It is the truth," said the stranger, frowning as he rose, at the same time taking up the pistol.

"What—you havn't any money with you?"

"Not a farthing."

"Then who's to pay for the heavy?" and he pointed to the empty beer measure.

"Yourself."

"Me! That's a good 'un, too; and I havn't a coin about me."

"Your friend the landlady must give you credit, then," said the stranger, with provoking calmness. "And now that our conference is ended, and you have received ample instructions, we will hasten from this den."

"Vell, guv'nor," exclaimed the astounded Bulldog, "I allers did give you credit for being a cool chap, and may I be cursed if you ain't. But, howsomedever, as I knows you keeps your promises, and that the shiners is sure ven the job's done, vy I'll manage it and vy I'll pay the score down stairs."

An almost imperceptible smile played round the lips of the stranger, but he said nothing.

"But you sees," persisted Bill Simmons, "as how you've not been over cute, this slip of paper tells me where to go, and if ve hadn't parted friendly, vy, a course, I could a gone there and blowed on the whole business."

He looked significantly as he spoke.

"Despicable fool!" said the stranger, his features flushing with anger; "I will tell you why you could not do as you hint. Were you to present yourself at that house, where you are *known*, mind, your course would speedily be brought to a fitting close. Who, think you, would credit your improbable tale? You are known, remember, and every servant in that house would take a pleasure in driving a bullet through your skull. Come, let us have no further parley, we waste time that is precious."

He placed the pistol in its former place of concealment, and opening the room door motioned Simmons to precede him down the stairs. Arrived at the bar, the Bulldog, to the landlady's evident surprise, paid for the two pots of beer, and then, followed by the stern stranger, issued from the place.

The street was silent, and seemed forsaken; the doors were shut, and the lights extinguished, and they passed up the dark avenue without observing any human being. A famished dog only lay in their path, and the bully, with an oath, kicked it into the gutter. Once the stranger fancied he heard a door open; once, too, he thought he saw the shadowy form of a human being following

No. 25.

him; but all was still, and, leaving the dark alley, they wended their way back in the same order in which they had come, until they reached more populated streets, when the stranger, turning abruptly on his heel, whispered to Simmons to remember and be cautious, and hailing a conveyance rapidly left the neighbourhood.

"Vell," thought the Bulldog, as he prepared for his midnight expedition, "ve're a precious pair o' rogues, but I vonder vich is the biggest."

Having given vent to this philosophical speculation, he lighted a short pipe, and, having hastened to his abode, prepared the dutiful Dorothy for the forthcoming excursion.

CHAPTER LXXXIII.

A NIGHT'S WORK.

BEFORE Bill Simmons proceeded to the house whence he was to abduct the child he received a note, brought by a boy, which contained the following words:

"In the room where the child sleeps is a casket; in that you will find a gold chain with a locket attached; a similar chain and locket are round the child's neck. See that the one from the casket is preserved for me when we meet. The other must be left round the child's neck that I may recognise it when it is dead."

The note was from his employer, and when, after a long study, the ruffian had deciphered it, he tore it in pieces and made his way to the house.

This house was the very one where Mary lived as companion, and the lady, Mrs. Carvan, was the mother of the child Bill Simmons had to take away. She had lost her husband only a few months since, and before their child had been born.

His death had been sudden, and there were many dark suspicions, which at times filled the brain of the young widow—suspicions that her husband had been hastened out of the world.

A short history of the lady may give the reader some clue whether such suspicions were well founded or not.

She had been engaged to Mr. Carvan many years, but had, nevertheless, suffered much from his brother, who wished her to forego her engagement with him and become his wife.

These proposals she had coldly rejected, and the brother, John Carvan, had desisted from his persecution. But the young wife often thought she read in his eyes a look that told her he had not abandoned what she had before feared were his intentions.

After her marriage he went away for a year, but came back some time after, and was received with eager welcome by his brother Henry. But from that day the health of the latter sensibly declined, and at length he fell into that sleep from which he never more awoke.

John Carvan expressed much sorrow for his brother's death, but Mrs. Carvan, from some indefinable cause, suspected that his grief was only affected.

There were many valid reasons for her belief in his insincerity. Her husband had so fixed his fortune, that if he and she died their child was to be left to the brother's care; but, if they died childless, the fortune was to go to John Carvan at her death.

The young wife, when those sinister suspicions came to her mind, feared that her husband's death was only the prelude to a scheme for getting possession of herself and fortune.

It may be well conceived with what jealous care she cherished the child born sorrowfully at her husband's death. John Carvan had, it is true, never hinted at his former proposals, but she still suspected and feared him—feared him because he had a cold, calculating will, that, once resolved, was never turned aside till the accomplishment of its object.

Her suspicions were to some extent shared by many who, from the first, entertained a mistrust of John Carvan; she was the chosen confidant of the widow, and between them they took care of the child, never suffering it from their sight.

The reader may form his own conclusions when we state that John Carvan was the unscrupulous employer of Bill Simmons.

That night Mary slept with the child in a chamber adjoining Mrs. Carvan's: it was at one wing of the building, and easy of access from the ground.

When Bill Simmons came, he found no difficulty in reaching it from the ground, and the night being rather windy prevented the slight noise he made alarming the inmates.

The watch-dog, in which they reposed great trust, was not their friend this night, for John Carvan had dealt wit it, and it lay drugged in its kennel.

Bill Simmons was no novice in housebreaking. He entered Mary's chamber by the window without any alarming sound, and stepped to the bedside.

Lightly as he trod the sound disturbed her, and she awoke to find the ruffian bending over her.

Before he had time to deal with her, she uttered a low cry, but Bill Simmons instantly snatched the pillow from under her head, and held it pressed on her mouth till her struggles ceased.

"She'll come to by the morning," he muttered, as he flung aside the pillow, and took the babe from the side of the half-suffocated child.

The cry that Mary had uttered did not appear to have disturbed any one. Bill Simmons, by means of a phosphorus light, found out the casket, and as the readiest way of getting the chain put the whole affair under his arm.

As he turned he was surprised to see that the door had been noiselessly opened, and a shadowy form stood on the threshold.

A cold sweat oozed to the ruffian's brow at this unexpected and spectral sight. He was not, however, much given to superstitious fear, and when the first alarm had passed away he prepared himself to encounter some interference in mortal shape.

By the feeble light of his phosphorus lamp he could trace the outline of a man carrying something that looked like a heavy stick in his hand: while the ruffian was gathering himself for a spring on this half invisible foe, the light of a hitherto masked lantern fell upon him, and he saw that he was confronted by one of the men-servants carrying a gun.

There would have been enough in that to have startled him, but he recognised the man as one who had formerly given him a taste of his powers when he had entered that same house on an errand of burglary. The man recognised him instantly: a smile passed across his features, and he raised his gun.

"Come again, have you?" he said. "I am sorry to have to make a noise, but I must shoot you."

"You wouldn't do that Jack," cried Bill Simmons, "we was pals once."

"I know, which is more the reason why I should put you out of the way now I've got the chance."

The face of Simmons grew ashy white; he saw the long hollow tube levelled at his head, and knew enough of the temper of the other to know that the light in his eyes meant death: he crouched down suddenly as the finger of the servant rested on the trigger, but the pressure was too quick, and the lock fell.

There was a flash and a report, but Bill Simmons was unharmed.

As the bullet left the barrel a scream was heard from the adjoining chamber; a light figure passed between the two, and then fell heavily to the floor.

Bill Simmons sprang up with a laugh.

"You've hit her," he said, "and you'll have to swing for it."

He leapt to the window and escaped with the child and the casket before the servant, who stood rooted to the spot in dismay and horror, could recover himself to move forward to the being whom he had unintentionally shot.

Bill Simmons made his way quickly out of the place; the jaded, miserably-clad woman, who passed as his wife, was waiting shivering by the wall.

"Oh! Bill," she said, "I was afeard for you: what was up? I heard a gun fire."

"Take the kid, curse you," he growled; "do you want me to be took?"

"There's blood on your sleeve," cried the wretched woman. "Oh! what have you done?"

The only reply of the brute was to force the child into her arms, and to strike her a frightful blow in the chest, that sent her staggering against the wall.

"Take that with you and hook it," he growled savagely, "and look out that you don't drop the kid."

The poor woman was yet gasping for breath; but, being apprehensive of suffering from his further brutality, she tottered along, leaning, every now and then, for support against the wall, and spitting blood at every step.

The callous ruffian put the casket under his jacket, and made off in the opposite direction.

When he had gone about thirty yards he was brought to a stand by a hand being placed on his shoulder, and a voice, extremely soft and effeminate, saying—

"Stay: I want you, Bill Simmons."

The bully turned, with a savage look on his face, and glanced spitefully at his interrogator. This was a slim youth, whose frame and limbs were remarkable for their symmetry and fine proportions. His face, however, was fair, and quite delicate and beautiful enough for a woman's, but there was a stern firmness and strength about the lineaments more masculine.

"Where are you hurrying?" asked this youthful interrupter, as the bully stared doggedly at him.

"That ain't nothink to you, is it?"

"It is everything."

"I ain't obliged to tell you."

"Are you not? Come, no trifling—tell me."

"Vell, I'm going home."

"What are you going to do with that trifle you have under your jacket—take that home, too?"

"Yes; I s'pose I may do that, if I like?"

"You may do nothing unless I like."

"Mayn't I?"

"No; and in the first place you will not take that casket home."

"Von't I, though?"

"No."

"Vell, I'd like to know vy."

"*Because I want it.*"

The ruffian looked inclined to be dangerous, but there was something in the eye of the youth that seemed to awe him considerably.

The latter again spoke calmly.

"The casket."

"I can't give it you."

"Do not say that again, as I shall take it, and you know what will be your punishment for disobeying my commands."

"Look here," Bill Simmonds said savagely, "I don't see vy, if you does as you like with your own gang, you're to do as you like with me."

"Then I will tell you why: because I have a supreme command over those who will obey my dictates, whatever they may be. But enough. I was willing to relieve you of that burthen; now I shall compel you to bring it to me. Go; but remember, if in one hour's time you do not present yourself with that casket unopened at the house in Stamford-street, I will fix the ban of punishment against you."

Henry said this in a calm tone of voice. The youthful stranger walked coolly away, leaving Bill Simmons standing with the cold sweat thick on his face.

That smooth-voiced youth seemed to exercise a strange control over him, for after muttering many deep oaths he made his way towards the house in Stamford-street.

CHAPTER LXXXIV.

THE MYSTERIOUS MISSIVE.

The bullet which the manservant had discharged at Bill Simmons had not struck his mistress, as he had feared, and as the ruffian had thought.

It was her maid who, alarmed by the sound in the next chamber, rushed out in time to receive the fatal shot.

It had struck her in the breast, and she lay bleeding at his feet, when the rest of the servants rushed in at one door, and their mistress appeared from the other.

The first impression was, of course, that she had been shot by the manservant, and his attitude of horror and dismay confirmed the impression of his guilt.

He roused himself when Mrs. Carvan ran to the couch where Mary lay, and uttered a piercing shriek at the discovery that her babe was absent.

Then he let the gun fall from his hands, and with a moan of agony fell back, covering his face with his hands.

A policeman was speedily on the scene: he summoned assistance. The house was taken charge of, and while Mrs. Carvan was carried to bed in a fit, the servant, John Kellard, was taken to the station, to meet the charge of murder.

With the first blush of morn John Carvan arrived: he affected the greatest consternation at the events of the night, and after vainly endeavouring to console the bereaved widow, left the house to institute, as he said, inquiries for the missing babe.

Two hours after he had gone two other visitors arrived: they were Sir Ashleigh Morton, a middle-aged nobleman, much attached to Mrs. Carvan, and Arthur Brown, a young artist, whom he was doing his best to advance in the world.

They heard, with amazement, what had taken place; and, after a sorrowful look at the body of the unfortunate maid, sat down with Mrs. Carvan to plan the recovery of the babe.

Mary had by this time recovered; but the account she could give was very meagre, and the distress of the widowed mother grew every hour more poignant.

She could not rid herself of the idea that, in spite of his affectation of consternation, John Carvan was at the bottom of it; and as Sir Ashleigh was her fast friend, she communicated to him her surmises.

"He must be evil indeed if he is concerned in it," Sir Ashleigh answered; "but we will see what's to be done."

While they were deliberating the servant entered with a note, addressed to Mrs. Carvan. When she had broken it open, and perused its contents, she uttered a half-stifled sob, and gave the missive to Sir Ashleigh to read.

It was a note of peculiar form, and, in place of date and address, was headed by a blue dagger, on which, in red letters, were traced—

THE LEAGUE OF FATE.

Under this appeared the following words, written in a hieroglyphical sort of letter:—

"*The child you would seek for has been stolen by the connivance of the wolf whom, in sheep's clothing, you have in your midst. Trouble not to seek for it. In good time - if constancy and fidelity are still graven on your heart — if, in your hours of life you remember the dead, the babe shall be restored, and the wolf shall perish by its own fang. But for the proofs that were stolen with the child, let him who most deeply is your friend seek and gain them at the HALL OF HELL, the place of which is known to one who will not fail you if you show him this.*"

Sir Ashleigh read this mysterious *billet* two or three times, and then handed it to the young artist, who perused it attentively.

"An inexplicable note, is it not?" said the baronet.

"One part is clear," replied the painter, looking from Mrs. Carvan to Mary, whom he had fallen slightly in love with since the first time he had been introduced to her; "the place mentioned here is known to me, and it may be that I am the one referred to."

"What! you know the place?" cried Sir Ashleigh, while Mary and Mrs. Carvan looked up in amazement.

"Yes. A part of my history has, as you know, been mixed up with strange characters. I propose going to this place this evening."

"I will go with you, my dear fellow."

Mrs. Carvan looked more hopefully. This note seemed to throw open a clue which might lead to the discovery of her child.

"Be careful that it is not any snare to lead you into danger," she said timidly; "it is known that you are my two staunchest friends since my dear husband's loss, and if I were to lose you I should be helpless indeed."

"Fear not," the baronet answered tenderly, "we will do our best to unveil this villainy. As for the wolf in sheep's clothing, I think I can scent out who that is, and, if so, I shall know how to deal with him. This evening we will make our first essay, and something tells me it will be prosperous. By the way, I must insist upon sending you a boy in whom I have taken a great interest, and who was the means of rescuing poor Mary here from the villains that had her in their power. He is a brave fellow, and will be a faithful defender here."

It was Charley to whom he referred, and whom that afternoon he sent to remain in the house, with orders to watch the movements of John Carvan.

CHAPTER LXXXV.

THE HALL OF HELL.

THAT evening Sir Ashleigh was to present himself at the studio of his young friend the artist.

"We shall, I think, baulk the villains," he said as they were separating; "they will not expect us on the clue."

"No; we have a shrewd task before us," replied the artist.

"It would be as well to put a pistol in your pocket, as a last resort."

"Very well, then—I will be here at eight o'clock."

Taking leave of the painter, Sir Ashleigh returned to his hotel, where he dined, and passed the time as well as he could until the hour of the rendezvous arrived.

He then made his way to the house of his friend, where he found his artistic acquaintance impatiently awaiting him.

The painter had already metamorphosed himself by donning a greasy blue cloth cap, with a battered visor; a blouse, so stained that its original colour was purely conjectural, and a pair of rough, hob-nailed shoes.

A similar dress had been prepared for Sir Ashleigh, and, stepping behind a screen, he changed his toilet with marvellous celerity.

"*Bon!*" cried the painter, when Sir Ashleigh emerged into the studio. "You look like one of the people, you'll do."

All being ready, they descended to the street.

Upon walking some distance, Bruno stopped and spoke a few words to the driver of a hackney coach, into which they stepped, and were driven rapidly over the rough pavements for about half-an-hour.

Here the driver pulled up his horses, Bruno and his companion alighted, the former handed his fare to the hackman, and the man drove back to the stand.

They were now in an obscure and badly-lighted quarter of the city.

No brilliant gas jets, installed at brief intervals, imitated the light of day, but here and there a smoky oil-lamp was burning dimly in a lantern, swung on cord, suspended across the street.

"Does your heart fail you?" asked Sir Ashleigh's guide. "We are now in places where a man's throat is often cut for the sake of a few shillings."

"Put your hand on my wrist, Mr. Bruno, and see if my pulse beats regularly," was Sir Ashleigh's reply.

The painter did as he was bid, and exclaimed—

"It is as regular as clock-work. You might have served in the Grand Army. This way, then."

He suddenly turned to the right, and descended a long and narrow flight of stone steps leading to a low door.

At this he tapped three times.

"Who goes there?" cried a hoarse voice.

"Friends!" was the reply.

"Advance, one friend, and give the countersign," was the military rejoinder.

Bruno stepped forward, and whispered the word to the janitor.

The door was then cautiously opened, and the visitors were allowed to enter.

The porter scrutinized Sir Ashleigh sharply as he advanced, but the examination was apparently satisfactory, for he growled out, "Pass, friends," in as amicable a tone as his husky voice permitted him to assume.

No wonder the painter sometimes revisited his old haunts, for the scene that the adventurers now beheld was eminently picturesque—one that would have delighted the savage nature of Salvator Rosa.

The room was well lighted up by candles set in sconces fastened to the rough, slimy, and green stone walls.

In a huge grate burned a fire of coal that failed to dispel the dampness of the vault, though it emitted a powerful heat.

Tables of various dimensions were set out all over the floor, around which were gathered ruffianly groups of men, mixed with boys and women, all intent on eating or carousing.

Here a savage-bearded fellow, half famished, was cutting off huge slices of bread from a big loaf, with a knife that might have been used for more terrible work.

There a girl, once beautiful, was fast obliterating by deep potations every semblance of softness and intelligence from her besotted countenance.

Boys of tender age, but with features as hard and stern as men of fifty, candidates for the galleys and the guillotine, were drinking "blue ruin" in the company of remorseless men.

It was the undisguised saturnalia of crime.

One brawny ruffian, satiated with bread and beef, and saturated with brandy, was sprawling on a bench, with his back against the wall, recounting the details of a murder in which he had participated, pausing to add, by the aid of a short pipe, to the clouds of tobacco-smoke which formed a dense canopy overhead.

At a rude counter, a muscular, firey-faced woman, dressed in a blazing red silk, with a flaming turban, gold ear-drops, and a mass of rings upon her hard, short fingers, dispensed the burning liquids which formed her stock in trade.

Her vigilant eye noticed the new comers, and she called out—

"Hulloa, there! Come hither, my lad. It's a long time since my eyes have beheld you, my pearl of painters."

"Tip us your flipper, my pal!"

The painter extended his hand, and received a vice-like grip from the Hebe of the taproom.

Her sharp eyes now detected the presence of Sir Ashleigh, who kept himself a little in the background.

"So you've brought a pal with you, eh?" she grunted. "If he's one of the sort as *whiddles* and *peaches*" (blabs and betrays) "he's in the wrong box, my little spoiler of canvases."

"Madame Poison," said the painter, "I swear to you he is as trustworthy as myself."

"All right," said the lady. "Let me give the gentleman the grip of welcome."

Sir Ashleigh extended his hand, and the presiding genius of the cellar grasped it with great cordiality.

"That's the hand of an aristo, however," she said.

"An aristo!" cried a bull-necked fellow, in a blue blouse, with a scarlet neck-tie. "What business has an aristocrat here? To the devil with aristocrats!"

Three or four other ruffians caught up the cry, and sprang to their feet.

"Order, there—order!" cried Madame Poison. "Have you no respect for the presence of a lady?"

"Lady or no lady," said the fellow with the scarlet neck-tie; "I demand this—this *gentleman*" (he sneeringly emphasised the title) "to treat the entire company."

"Bravo, bravo!" cried the assembled ruffians.

"You will have to comply with the demand," whispered Bruno in Sir Ashleigh's ear.

"Do you hear?" roared the bully of the taproom, his face reddening with passion.

"What if I decline?" asked Sir Ashleigh, with perfect coolness.

"Then you will have to do with me," replied the bully.

"Hurrah for the Red Choker!" cried one of that gentleman's backers and cronies.

"It has never been my custom to yield to menaces," said Sir Ashleigh, with aggravating coolness, "and I do not propose to depart from it to-night."

"Then you will not comply with my demand?" asked Red Choker.

"I never comply with *demands*," replied Sir Ashleigh.

"Then look out for yourself, my fine fellow," roared the bully; "I shall soon spoil that smooth countenance, that looks as if nothing could ruffle it."

Sir Ashleigh quietly seated himself at a table, and deliberately pulled out a small silver-mounted pistol.

"I do not wish to create any uproar," he said, "but the first who attempts to interfere with me shall have the contents of this in his body."

Red Choker uttered a fierce menace, but drew back from the presented pistol.

"Pals," he said, "are we to be baulked by a d——d swell like this?"

"No, no!" was the cry which was yelled all round the room, the company pressing closer to the baronet and his friend.

There would, most probably, have been a serious *fracas* had not the woman interposed.

"Sit quiet lads, will you? The gentleman will treat you presently, as it's the rule, but not while you make that row."

"But will he treat us?" cried several.

"Hear me," said Sir Ashleigh, laying his pistol down on the table. "I am never frightened into anything, but I know your rules. As a stranger I should give liquor to the whole company. I may do so, but not while you are crowding round like a pack of cutthroats."

His quick manner and firm address had their effect. The men, growling discontentedly, distributed themselves about the "Hall," and waited till it should be the pleasure of their visitor to accord them the expected libation.

"A pretty crew," Sir Ashleigh said when he had given the order, and saw them all plying busily their potations; "but what can be the results of our visit here? Our mysterious communicant promised nothing."

"He never promises much, except it is fate."

"Indeed! You seem to know him — who is he?"

"One at whose uplifted finger all those you see brawling here would sink down like frightened apes—the chief of what is ominously called THE LEAGUE OF FATE."

"A strange thing."

"Terribly so. They go about secretly detecting crimes, and punishing them. In their prosperous hours many a guilty sinner of either sex receives death. But the most singular affair is that their leader, a youth of great beauty, is suspected to be a woman."

"A woman?"

"Yes; one of education and title, too."

"A lady, and mingle in such scenes—give orders for such deeds?"

"Yes; and execute them herself if needs be."

"You startle me. I shall be curious to meet her."

"You will do so, I doubt not. Let us hope it will not be when under the ban of her league. Before the baronet could make any comment two new comers entered the hall. In one could he recognise the atrocious Bill Simmons; the other was a tall, hard-featured man, with a restless look and ashy face.

He walked by the side of Bill Simmons till he got to the centre of the room, when, letting his glance rest a moment on the artist's face, he took six steps towards the end of the room, and then, retracing a step, walked two paces forward, as if about to speak to some one opposite, and then, turning again, took four steps in the opposite direction, and, pausing a moment, called for a glass of brandy.

"The sign of the dagger!" whispered the artist to his friend; "some one is menaced whom we know."

"We are in the midst of mysteries."

"Ay, and of dangers."

"I fear not."

"Good. If anything should occur be not too precipitate. The presence of that man is a sign that something is on the wing. He belongs to the band."

"Which band?"

"*The League of Fate!*"

The baronet looked hard at the first member of that mysterious fraternity.

"A resolute heart," he said quietly.

"It is so, indeed. I can give you an anecdote of him while we wait that will convince you of his character."

"Is he an Englishman?"

"Yes, but has not always spent his time in this country. But my story will tell you more."

Somewhere about the year 1855, William Bradway, a young man of five and twenty, then living in the interior of the State of New York, left his family, consisting of a wife and two small children, and went South on a tour of speculation.

He was absent nearly a year, and stated, on his return, that he had been successful, and had purchased a place on the Red River, whither he proposed to remove his family, and there settle, perhaps for life.

His wife, pleased with the novelty of change, readily assented to the arrangement, and, as soon as their northern affairs were properly settled, they set off for their new home, which, in due course of time, they reached in safety.

But Mrs. Bradway was sadly disappointed on finding the place so different from what she had pictured in her fancy.

The settlement was new, and everything was rough.

The houses, many of them, were built of logs, and even the best of them lacked the finish of her northern home, while the furniture was generally of the plainest and coarsest description, and scanty at that.

But worse than all the rest was the inhabitants. Composed principally of rough speculators, negro traders, gamblers, and outlaws from different quarters, with such females and children as looked to them for support, Mrs. Bradway, who had been well educated and brought up in refined society, sought in vain among them for suitable associates and companions, and, being a stranger in a strange land, soon became depressed and home-sick.

Under the peculiar circumstances she unguardedly made some remarks not complimentary to the place and its inhabitants; and these remarks being reported, with such additions and exaggerations as scandal-mongers generally use for embellishments, she soon found herself surrounded by open enemies, and subjected to such petty annoyances and persecutions as little, malicious minds delight to inflict upon those they secretly believe to be their superiors, and envy and hate for that cause.

Six months had not passed away ere William Bradway felt the necessity of removing his family from that unpleasant and lawless locality; and this he was preparing to do, when an awful tragedy occurred, which changed the peaceable man into a bloody avenger.

Some business, at a neighbouring settlement, called him from home for a couple of days; and on his return he found his house in ashes, and learned that his wife and children had all been murdered, under the most atrocious and aggravating circumstances—his poor wife, previous to her throat being cut, having been subjected to treatment worse than death, by the three ruffians concerned in the horrible affair.

To a fond husband and father this was a terrible blow, and for a day and a night William Bradway remained beside the still smoking ruins of his dwelling, some of the time walking slowly around them with his eyes bent on the ground, and some of the time standing and gazing at them with an abstracted air, as if he were recalling the past, or looking into the future. He had shown no violent sorrow even at the first, but had received the awful intelligence as one mentally stupified- as cne who could not clearly believe the facts and comprehend the whole extent of his loss.

It was observed that his features suddenly became deadly white, even to his lips, and then gradually changed to a livid hue, which remained, without alteration, and without being afterward tinged by even the slightest flush.

"Who did it?" he inquired, in a tone of unnatural calmness.

Three men were named George Harbaugh, James Fawcet, and John Ellery.

These men were known gamblers and desperadoes, and had been suspected of being robbers and murderers.

They did not live in the village, but had visited it occasionally, and one of them had, some time previously, had a quarrel with Bradway, and threatened revenge, though the latter little dreamed at the time that anything so terrible was meant as had been accomplished.

It is but justice to say, that though the Bradways, as previously mentioned, had made themselves very unpopular in the place, there were very few of the residents who openly sanctioned the horrid crimes that had been committed, and there were some who boldly expressed a hope that the vile perpetrators would yet meet with a just punishment; but though the ruffians had made no secret of their hellish deeds, and had even boasted of them before they left the place, no one had made any attempt to arrest or detain them, and they had gone, no one knew whither.

It was about ten o'clock in the morning that William Bradway first saw the ruins of his home, and heard the awful news of his irreparable loss; and all through the remainder of that day, and the night which followed it, he conducted himself in the manner we have described, seemingly taking no notice of the curious groups that gathered around him, and replying to none of the idle questions put to him.

The next morning he went into a neighbour's house and asked for something to eat, which was given him. He offered to pay for this; but the man of the house declined to receive any money, and, with expressions of sympathy, invited him to make his home there for a few days.

"No," returned Bradway, "I intend to leave the village to-day."

"You don't look as if you'd got strength to go far," said the man, in a kindly tone.

"I have that *within* which will sustain me!" rejoined Bradway.

He then inquired into the particulars of the awful tragedy, and the direction taken by the murderers—speaking calmly himself, and listening calmly to all the replies—his features the while retaining their unnatural, livid hue, and displaying no signs of emotion, save, perhaps, now and then a perceptible quiver of the bloodless lips.

As he passed through the village, after taking leave of this family, he was several times stopped, by different parties, who wanted to enter into conversation with him, and find out what he intended to do—but he gave them only evasive answers, and slipped off as quietly as possible.

It was about two months after this that George Harbaugh, late one night, was picking his way through the dark streets of Nacogdoches, from a gambling house to his lodgings, when a man came up to him, and quietly said—

"Good evening, sir."

"Who're you, and what d'ye want?" demanded the ruffian, in a gruff, surly tone, at the same time thrusting his right hand into his bosom, as if to draw a pistol.

"Do not be alarmed, sir," returned the stranger; "but permit me to ask you one or two questions. In the first place, is your name George Harbaugh?"

"Well, what of it, whether it is or isn't?" was the uncivil reply.

"If it is, I owe you something, which I wish to pay," returned the stranger, "and if it is not, perhaps you can put me in the way to find the person I seek?"

"What do you owe me for, and how much?" inquired the gambler, taking his hand from his bosom.

"I am right, then, in supposing I address George Harbaugh himself?"

"Yes, that's my name. What's yours? and where'd we ever meet before?"

"If I am not mistaken," pursued the stranger, "you, with two companions, were at the village of ...., on the Red River, on the night of the sixth of September last?"

"Ha! what's this?" cried the ruffian, springing back, and again thrusting his hand into his bosom.

He had not time for more, ere, with a flash and a crack, a ball passed through his breast.

As he staggered and fell, shouting murder, a sharp knife was drawn across his throat, and the name of William Bradway hissed into his dying ear.

It was the last earthly sound he ever heard.

He was found murdered, but his assassin was not found.

"During the winter following, James Fawcet went among the Choctaws to purchase horses.

"While trading with the Indians, he fell in with a small dealer, who, for a trifling consideration, offered to assist him in taking his horses to the settlement—some two hundred miles distant— where he expected to dispose of them at a heavy profit.

The bargain was struck, and, with fifteen horses, James Fawcet set off, with his assistant, through a long stretch of wilderness.

On the second night, as the gambler and murderer sat smoking before his camp fire, he was suddenly startled by finding a noose dropped over his head and shoulders, and drawn around his body, so as to pinion his arms.

In less than a minute, notwithstanding a vigorous resistance on his part, he was literally bound, hand and foot, and lay stretched on the earth as helpless as an infant.

"What's the meaning of this? do you intend to murder me?" he demanded, in a voice made tremulous by fear."

"I suppose you do not recollect ever having seen me before you met me in the Indian village?" said the man who had been acting as his assistant, as he now stood over his prostrate form.

"No, of course not; where'd I ever see you before?" replied Fawcet.

The other removed a wig of long hair, and a patch from one eye, and then quietly said—

"Do you know me now?"

"Well, it does seem more as I'd seen you before, but I can't tell where," said the ruffian.

"Do you remember the woman and children you helped to murder on the sixth of last September?"

"Ha! you're Bradway," cried the villain, in a tone of despair.

"William Bradway, at your service — the same in name as when you knew me, but not the same in nature; then I would not have harmed you, but now I would execute the vengeance of a wronged husband and father."

"Mercy!" gasped Fawcet.

"Did you show any?"

"You will not murder me?"

"You must die; I have sworn it — I have sworn it. I have followed you to rid the earth of a monster. Harbaugh fell by my hand; I shall not spare you; and then to hunt down John Ellery. Say your prayers, if you have any to say, for your minutes are numbered."

"Mercy! mercy!" gasped the terrified ruffian.

The avenger made no further reply, but deliberately proceeded to fasten a rope, with a noose, around the neck of Fawcet.

This done, he dragged him to a sapling, bent it over, secured the other end of the rope near its top, and let it go.

With a wild, unearthly yell, the second murderer was jerked up from the earth, and hung dangling, swinging, and struggling a few feet from the ground.

Bradway looked calmly on till the body became still in death; and then, mounting his own horse, he rode swiftly away, leaving the other horses, and the money on the person of the dead man, to whoever might find them.

It might have been six months after the terrible death of the ruffian just recorded, that two men sat in a private room of a gambling den in Natchez playing cards for money.

Piles of gold and silver, and rolls of bank-notes, were on the table between them, and each was staking his money freely, and apparently considering nothing but how to beggar the other by his superior skill or knavery.

"You know," said one of the two men, "that we are to play till one of us wins all?"

"Yes, I know," was the reply.

"Suppose we take another drink on it?"

"Agreed!"

A bottle and tumblers stood on a table just behind the first speaker, who got up and turned round and poured out two glasses—his companion, who had the deal, improving the opportunity, as well as he could, to stock or arrange the cards, so as to give himself a winning hand. The man who poured out the liquor now handed one glass to the gambler at the table, and held the other himself, ready for drinking.

"To the cholera!" he said, quietly nodding to the other—for this malady had at that time begun its work of destruction.

"To the cholera be it then, and let it do it's —— work!" cried the gambler, with forced bravado, turning somewhat pale, and tossing off his glass at a gulp.

The other drank quietly, replaced the two tumblers, and resumed his seat at the gambling board.

For a few minutes there was no remark made, except what concerned the game; and then the one who had partially stocked the cards, as he raked down a large sum he had just won, said, looking up, with an expression of alarm—

"By heavens! I feel very strange!"

"You look very pale," returned the other, "I think you are going to die."

"Well, you're a —— pretty comforter, I must say."

"I think you will find me so presently."

"Ah!" groaned the gambler, dropping the cards and clasping his stomach with both hands, "I am on fire inside."

"Of course you are!"

"How, of course? what do you know about it? have I got the —— cholera?" demanded the gambler, somewhat fiercely.

"Listen to me a few moments, and you will know and understand all.

"There were once three companions, named George Harbaugh, James Fawcet, and John Ellery. A little more than a year ago they murdered an innocent woman and two children, in the village of ...., while the husband and father, William Bradway, was away. When he returned and learned all the horrid particulars, he swore a solemn oath, that he would never rest in peace till he should have hunted them all down, and put an end to their guilty lives. George Harbaugh was assassinated in the streets of Nacogdoches, James Fawcet was hung in the wilderness, and John Ellery was poisoned in Natchez."

"But I am John Ellery!" cried the gambler, the very picture of horror.

"No need to tell *me* that, who have hunted you to your *death*," said the other. "I am William Bradway."

"Good God! am I then poisoned?" shrieked the wretched man, as new pangs seized him.

"Yes; beyond hope! In five minutes you will be a corpse!"

"Murder! help!" the dying man began to cry.

"None of that!" said Bradway, springing upon him like a tiger, and forcing a handkerchief into his mouth, which he held there till the man fell down in spasms, when he turned to the table, and quietly selected his own money from the gambler's, and put it in his pocket.

"The poison was quick and sure, and, in less than half an hour from his last drink of spirits, the murderer and gambler was a corpse.

"Waiting only to be certain of his death, Bradway went down stairs, and told some of the people of the house that his companion either had the cholera or had fallen down in a fit, and they had better go up and see to him.

"He then hastened down to the river, got upon the first passing steamer, and, before night, was many miles away from the scene of his last act of vengeance."

"Such a man were indeed desperate, and to be relied on," remarked the baronet.

"And that man," returned the artist, "is *there*.

THE FIGHT IN THE THIEVES' KITCHEN.

He does not now bear that name. He is called White Hand, and is dreaded more than any of the league."

The baronet fell into a reverie. Strange reflections occurred to him. He was rather mystified at the connection his young friend, the artist, had with such dealings, and at one moment almost suspected that he belonged himself to the League of Fate.

His patience lasted very well for some time, but at length he began to think he had waited long enough, and, nudging his young painter friend, he said—

"Well, Bruno; I must say I don't admire this style of waiting."

"Be patient," was Bruno's reply.

"Oh, I'll be patient; but I am stifled here."

Bruno pacified him into silence, and they sat quiet for some little while longer.

An incident then occurred which produced as much commotion as the hungry soul of the baronet could desire.

A tall individual, muffled and disguised, his face hidden by heavy whiskers, and his frame evidently altered from its original shape by padding and a strange costume, was shown into the Hall of Hell.

When the artist fixed his first glance on him, he fancied he beheld a face that, in spite of its disguise, was familiar to him.

The baronet also stared hard at the stranger, but, like the artist, kept quiet in his seat.

The stranger, having made a sign that satisfied the gang, took his seat at a corner table, and sat in deep thought. In two minutes, Bill Simmons, after looking stealthily round, staggered up to the same table, and sat down.

The other did not appear annoyed at this intrusion, but neither did he stay to get into conversation with the ruffian.

At this moment the keen eyes of the member of the League of Fate who had been pointed out to the baronet by his friend, fixed a searching glance on the pair, and then, folding his arms, leaned back in his chair, as if about to go to sleep.

"Something will presently occur," whispered the young painter; "be on your guard. At any moment a blow may reach you."

"That's comfortable," thought the baronet, as he felt for his revolver.

"Do not be over hasty," whispered the young artist.

At this moment Bill Simmons was observed to take cautiously out of his pocket a something wrapped in a piece of dirty rag, which the muffled stranger eagerly put out his hand to take.

But as his hand touched it he whom the young artist had pointed out as belonging to the secret League, stepped quickly across the room, and, seizing Bill Simmons by the arm, pulled him quickly out of the way.

Then, seizing the muffled stranger by the cloak, he pulled aside his disguise, and exclaimed—

"It is desired that the features of a villain be revealed."

The Baronet and his young friend started forward.

It was not he whom they expected. Not John Carvan.

At least it was not like him in features. But William Bradway seemed to see deeper than the two friends. Looking the astonished stranger full in the face, he said—

"The wolf is yet in his sheep's clothing, but the hour will come when his own fangs shall tear his heart: in the meantime the League of Fate send this."

As he held him with one hand he drew a sharp-pointed dagger with the other, and in a moment of time drew it across the stranger's breast twice, forming the two strokes of a cross. It penetrated through clothes and skin, and marked his breast with the red scar of a cross.

John Carvan—for he it was, though so well disguised by an invisible mask that the others had not recognised him—uttered a cry of horror and pain as the swift weapon cut into his breast; there rose, too, a terrible commotion for a second, amongst the inmates of that place, but it was stilled when they saw that dreaded sign marked on the breast of the victim.

Every one knew then that he was branded for doom; that this was only the mark they would affix upon him before decreeing his fate.

John Carvan stood agonised and writhing, and Bill Simmons had fallen back in evident fear; the member of the League of Fate now took Carvan by the shoulder and, pointing to the door, said, addressing himself to the artist and Sir Ashleigh—

"When you desire to unmask the wolf, you will know him by that bloody cross on his breast."

He pointed then to the door, and continued—

"Make way for him who has been marked with the bloody baptism; let him go through his remaining days of life branded as the first act of the League that adjudges him death."

The members of that criminal fraternity fell back as the wounded and bleeding villain, palsied by fear and eager to escape from what he looked upon as an impending death, staggered towards the door.

It flew wide open as he neared it—opened by unseen power; and, groaning in agony, the scheming man of crime passed out.

Then the door closed upon him.

Bill Simmons had all this time been standing aloof with the look of one expecting punishment, and he quailed in deadly fear when the man of Fate turned his cold eye upon him.

His knees began to give way when the avenger stepped to his side.

The denizens of that place gathered in expectant groups—apprehensive of some more terrible deed.

Bradway's voice was harsh and stern when he addressed the cowering wretch.

"Give me the chain."

Bill Simmons, in a trembling manner, unrolled the bit of rag and revealed a golden chain with a locket attached.

Sir Ashleigh, recognising it as the one that had been in the possession of Mrs. Carvan, uttered an exclamation, and sprang to the side of the hardened ruffian, the young artist following.

As Bill Simmons displayed the chain, Bradway took it quickly from his hand.

"You were bidden," he said, "to repair to the appointed house with a casket then in your possession; from that casket, despite the commands that were given you, you dared extract this chain: for that crime, perpetrated against the decree of the leader of our League, it is adjudged that you die—when and where may not be told you, but do not count upon one minute of life when you hear the words, 'It is time, your death will be on the wing.'"

Leaving the terrified ruffian mute with deadly fear, he handed the chain and locket to Sir Ashleigh.

"The lady who now is childless," he said, "will so continue till her faith and virtues are proved; should either fail, she will be childless through life. Should she remain firm to the memory of him whom she saw given to the grave, in good time she shall have her child restored to her; for this let her know that when she meets anyone with a chain like this round his neck, he will be her son; if her course has been fair she shall have him restored in honourable beauty; if she fail, she may meet him on his road to the gallows. Let her remember the gold chain soldered round his neck."

Sir Ashleigh took the chain, and was about to speak when the man of Fate spoke again—

"The purpose for which you were brought here having been accomplished, you are bound to depart at once; and beware that you do not look back before the door is closed upon you."

As he concluded, the door flew wide open; Sir Ashleigh would have stayed to speak, but the young artist, who appeared better used to the symbols of procedure adopted by that singular League, took his arm and led him hastily away.

They had barely reached the door when they heard the stern voice of the Man of Doom exclaim—

"It is time."

A yell of agony came from the lips of Bill Simmons, who had read his fate in those words, and had leaped back to escape death.

Then arose excited cries as the ruffian tried to

sneak behind the others. Sir Ashleigh, horrified by the indications of so murderous a business, would have paused and turned then, but another knew his danger, and pulled him out; and, as the door was closing, the shriek of mortal agony coming from the condemned ruffian showed that the Doom of Fate was being committed.

It was. Without the least appearance of discomfiture Bradway turned till he faced the crouching bully, when he gave one spring and leaped upon him.

As swiftly as he had sprang forward he went back. Those in the den thought that he had missed his spring, but when they looked Bill Simmons was seen lying on the floor deluged in his own blood.

The Dagger of the League of Fate was in his lungs.

CHAPTER LXXXVI.

MORE ABOUT THE MYSTERIOUS LEAGUE.

WITH all haste Arthur Bruno got his horrified companion from the Hall of Hell. The baronet was so appalled by the scenes he had witnessed, that he was a passive instrument in the hands of his young friend, who conducted him into a cab, and back to his own residence.

When they had arrived there Sir Ashleigh, for the first time, found speech.

"What horrors!" he exclaimed. "And you have dealings with this terrible league."

"No," answered the artist, sadly; "yet the secret of a life is bound up there. I have no affinity with the myrmidons of that association, but a horrible phantasy has linked my whole existence to despair and unrest.

The Baronet looked hard at his young friend, who presently said—

"I have before spoken of their leader—said to be a lady of title and beauty; but this being has two identities; in one you may behold her most beautiful, and enchanting—her loveliness veiled by a mask which at times is raised to disclose the glorious vision; in the other you gaze upon a being fair in all respects, but when you would raise her veil you would behold a grisly spectacle of terror—the head of death."

"How," exclaimed the Baronet, "if you have seen her in her beauty——"

"I have only seen her in visions."

"In visions?"

"Even so. I have believed she has been beside me—I have drank the rarest wines with her—have pressed my lips to hers—"

"Then she is real?"

"This was only in my dreams. At other times, when I have striven to press her lips, I have beheld what I have described, the frightful impersonation of death."

"But if these are only in visions, what matters it?"

"There I am uncertain," replied the artist, "and 'tis that incertitude which blasts my life. These dreams have seemed to me more than the phantoms of a disordered imagination. I have sat waking and found her beside me; for hours I have revelled in delirious joy, and yet it has afterwards seemed only a vision. I cannot tell if it be true or false, but one thing is certain, this mysterious being is linked to my destiny, and I must give my whole life to the elucidation of that which, undiscovered, is killing me."

Sir Ashleigh saw that his young friend's face was ashy pale, and pained by the agony of his feelings. He tried to rouse him from such disordered beliefs.

"It is useless," the young artist said, "I have not told you all. Continually, in mingling with society, do I meet this mystic being. Wherever I go she comes upon my sight, but always in some fresh name, and under different circumstances. At such times, though I would speak to her of her influence in my fate, she will not linger to hear my words, but as a stranger comes, as a stranger goes; but so surely as she is near me do I see her in my dreams, or it may be in reality; but under some potent spell that chains my faculties, and keeps me from the truth."

"My friend," said the baronet, when his young friend paused from agitation, "you are pursuing a phantom that will lead you to the grave."

"That will lead me to everlasting destruction, rather say; I know my fate, but cannot avoid it. On the contrary, I must blindly seek it; for by the heavens, never will I rest till I have ferreted out the secret. I will know whether her fairness is real, or if it but conceal that horrid face of death. I will know, too, what influence it is by which she chains me to this consuming destiny."

The features of the young artist became wildly excited, and Sir Ashleigh could see that his very heart was one mass of fire in its burning agony.

They spoke no more upon that subject; it was a topic too strange for present discussion, and the Baronet had seen too much recently not to know that there were mysteries in the heart of our great city that were undreamed of, and the unravelling of which would have appalled the world. They remained in silence for some time, and then took their departure to acquaint Mrs. Carvan with the principal events that had taken place.

By the time they reached her house, the young artist had recovered his serenity; his features bore no trace of that terrible secret passion that was killing him; and as with pleasant, though grave face he greeted Mary, Sir Ashleigh experienced the hope that the genial influence of the young girl might subdue his mind, and wean him from his mysterious idolatry.

It was not possible, yet Mrs. Carvan and the baronet would have been pleased to see Mary and the young artist united in marriage.

They, of course, did not know the whole of what Mary had endured, nor did they suppose her love for Dick was of that lasting nature which would prove firm against the temptations of a world.

But Mary was firm in her faith to poor Dick, and if she had been likely to swerve, there was Charley there to keep her in the right track.

The brave boy would have suffered no intrusion on his unhappy mate's love.

We now turn aside for a brief while to lay before our readers certain events which may help to give a clue to the mysterious nature of that singular creature who was the object of the young artist's passion, and whom he met under such wild circumstances.

We shall, also, unfold something more of that secret association whose decrees were potent in life and death—

THE LEAGUE OF FATE.

CHAPTER LXXXVII.

IN the course of the year, a crime, accompanied by very extraordinary circumstances, was committed in London. A magistrate, an individual enjoying general esteem and consideration, was found one morning assassinated in his bed.

The instrument employed by the murderer was a poignard, fashioned by the hand of a skilful artist, and the idea for its formation must have found its birth in an imagination that seemed to revel in the horrible. The handle represented a skeleton half-concealed by drapery. Upon the blade was read in damaskened letters the detestable pleasantry, *The blade gives the handle* (*i.e.*, causes death.) From the instrument of the murder, which remained implanted in the heart of the victim, was suspended, attached by a small chain of bronzed steel, an ebony label, on the black ground of which was inscribed, in red letters, the single word "Seducer." At the same time there was seen on the brow of the murdered man, a red stamp, bearing in the centre of a shield the figure 1. It appeared, as it were, the announcement of the first drawn number of a horrible series of assassinations.

These various circumstances, however, at once assumed a striking appearance in the eyes of justice, as well as in those of the family of the magistrate, whose public life the assassin thus accused; the most absolute secrecy was kept respecting the kind of death of death to which the unhappy man had succumbed. Another consideration, that of avoiding to spread alarm in the population, who might have thought themselves under the menace of a band of invisible bravos, led to the adoption of a secret investigation.

Several weeks passed away, during which all the researches of the police had remained fruitless, when a new crime and a new victim became known. A female enjoying a distinguished reputation for piety and virtue, and who for the recent loss of her husband had exhibited an inconsolable grief, of which it never entered the mind of any one to doubt the sincerity, was found dead in her bedchamber, struck while in the act of kneeling at prayer. The same stab in the heart, the same kind of poignard left in the wound, and attached to the murderous instrument a like ebony label, bearing the double epithet of "Adulteress and Poisoner;" in short, on the brow of the deceased the same red stamp, and in the centre of the shield the figure 2!

The reasons which had led to keeping secret the first crime, determined the most complete reserve as to the second; but the inquiry into this affair led to a serious complication. Attention having been drawn to the accusation thrown on the memory of the victim, justice urged its investigations in every direction, and while it remained without trace of the audacious murderer who numbered his crimes, it acquired the posthumous certainty that a female, in the opinion of the world considered as the model of wives, had, in fact, been led, under the excitation of an adulterous passion, to make away with her husband by means of poison.

It is unnecessary to detail the redoubled zeal which this discovery was calculated to impart to the magisterial researches already engaged by their duty and conscience in this inquiry. They now received the impulse of self-love. Was there not, in fact, for them an insolent defiance in the existence of a kind of secret tribunal, having its justice and executioners, and which public example remained unpunished or unknown. A month had scarcely elapsed since the drama—when, one evening, at rather an early hour, in the open street, and at a few paces from one of the great thoroughfares in London, as if the assassins had been desirous of attaining that notoriety which, until then, had not accompanied their crimes, an old man was stabbed to the heart. His was more than a mere reputation for probity: it was a striking celebrity for philanthropy, that the murderers had undertaken the task of extinguishing in blood Number 3, as the red mark imprinted on the forehead of the victim indicated, must have been, according to the table appended to the poignard, an INCORRIGIBLE USURER; and this accusation was, in fact, borne out by an examination into the state of his pecuniary affairs.

Nevertheless, the publicity which this secret justice seemed determined on obtaining, at any price for its executions, failed it once more this time. No newspaper was permitted to notice the event; and, as for a few oral details which might have been put into circulation by a small number of persons present when the corpse was removed, they were denied and treated as ridiculous fables. Towards the end of the same year, another adventure, surpassing in strangeness all the surprising facts laid before the reader, came to close the series of these mysterious crimes.

To the west of the metropolis is situated the entrance to a vast subterranean receptacle for human skeletons, galleries of which extend under several streets.

On the 24th of December, the wife of the keeper of this funereal *depôt* had invited some friends to celebrate with her Christmas Eve.

The repast was a gay one, as it may be generally remarked that these individuals, who live by means of the graveyard, are anything but given to melancholy.

The sparkling glass and the merry anecdote were circulating gaily, when, in the sombre empire of which he was the Cerberus, the keeper thought he could distinguish subterranean noises, and as it were an occasional burst of voices.

A superstitious terror immediately spread itself among the guests, for the residence of the keeper comprised the only entrance to these funereal galleries, and the latter thought he was certain that no one could have effected an entrance, or have remained there without his knowledge.

An old soldier, and minutely exact in the fulfilment of his duty, the guardian of the catacombs, notwithstanding the endeavours of his wife to the contrary, was determined on learning whence the strange noises that reached him proceeded; and as none of those at his table had the courage to accompany him, he descended alone into the vaults, armed with two pistols, and carrying a lantern, in order to find out what was actually going on there.

After some time his prudent companions heard

the report of two shots, and then all remained silent.

Several dreary hours passed without witnessing the return of this second Æneas, gone to visit the lower regions; and although night was at length succeeded by day, still the unfortunate man did not make his appearance.

The fact was made known to the police, and, having provided themselves with torches, a strong party descended to the galleries, endeavouring to discover the cause of the noises said to have been heard, and to assure themselves of the fate of him who had first commenced that exploration.

The result of these researches was terrible.

After a quarter of an hour they stumbled over the body of the unfortunate keeper.

At his side, and near to the still burning lantern, which had been placed on his breast, was found the two pistols discharged.

And here again appeared, with the eternal poignard, the red stamp, which this time marked No. 4.

Inscribed upon the label, the words "IMPERTINENTLY CURIOUS" assigned the reason of the murder, and led to the supposition of some frightful mysteries with which the unlucky guardian had had the misfortune to interfere.

As usual, no trace of the invisible assassins could be found; everything in this profaned asylum of death remained silent and in its habitual state, and notwithstanding the most minute researches, nothing led to a knowledge of the means by which these men of blood had introduced themselves into the underground galleries.

During several weeks frequent daily and nightly patrols vainly came to aid the very natural desire of justice to penetrate this black and seemingly unattainable secret; an impenetrable obscurity continued to veil it.

Besides, this crime was, more than the murders which had preceded it, carefully concealed from a knowledge of the public; for never had the defective power of the magistrates against these midnight assassins, whom it was their mission to discover, been so scandalously demonstrated.

CHAPTER LXXXVIII.

THE MASK OF DEATH.

ABOUT this time some colour was given to the artist's assertions by the rumour that a young lady had come over with a rich exile, her father; and that a certain misfortune afflicted the young lady to such an extent that, though the heiress of a wealthy father, she could get no one to marry her.

When inquiry was made about this singular affair it was found to be true: the young lady, indeed, existing under the affliction hinted at, but now discovered. She was doomed, indeed; for the most inveterate fortune hunters, shrank from the thought of an alliance with the *young woman with the death's head!*

She was, according to public rumour, a rich heiress, who placed her hand and an immense fortune at the disposal of the man courageous enough to look upon her without shuddering after she should have unmasked before him.

Now, this singular girl, desirous of getting married, whose existence, as will shortly be seen, was much less fabulous than many imagined it, was nothing more nor less than the daughter of the Marquis de Lupiano.

Accompanying her father into public places and assemblies she never exhibited herself without a mask of wax upon her face. But the cruel caprice of nature, of which she was the victim, seemed to have limited its attack to the charms of her visage; for she was tall and well shaped, exhibited a head of beautiful blonde hair, an admirable bust, and hands of matchless whiteness and form.

Nevertheless, whenever she gave expression to her thoughts, an exterior revelation of her infirmity might be detected in the sound of her voice, which, all prejudice apart, permitted something to be felt that was hollow and sepulchral.

Considering as serious the offer of her hand that this strange would-be bride was reported to have made to the first-comer, some simple-minded pretenders presented themselves at the marquis's hotel, and, according to the humour of the latter, they were either pleasantly mystified or rudely repulsed.

Nevertheless, M. de Lupiano did not attempt to deny the hideous deformity; on the contrary, he was the first to confirm a belief in it by the explanation which he himself gave.

According to this explanation, the marchioness, his wife, while *enciente*, was present at some archæological researches, and frightened by the turning up of a human skull, which rolled forth under the pickaxes of the workmen.

But, in supposing that celibacy should have been the only thought and unavoidable destiny of this poor creature, whom a cruel accident had deprived of all beauty, undoubtedly she was not reduced to the ridiculous matrimonial sale of which the report had been bruited abroad.

Possessing a magnificent marriage portion with which to dazzle the eyes of fortune-hunters, and with the remarkable mental superiority of which she afforded proof in conversation, she was yet a girl whom it was not difficult to establish in life, and on whom more than one lofty family in the aristocracy would gladly have conferred their name.

Sir Ashleigh saw the effect this being had upon Arthur when first he met her in public. He turned ashy pale, and kept his eyes fixed upon the mask she wore the whole evening.

She, on her part, seemed to take no notice of the excited young fellow, though once or twice a strange look glittered from the eyes that shone vividly from behind the mask.

Arthur tried to get an opportunity of speaking with the masked maiden, but this was not afforded him, and when she had departed it required all Sir Ashleigh's presence of mind to prevent his young friend from going off after her.

It was given out shortly after that the masked lady would not again be seen in public, and this turned out true; for Arthur, though he tried every method, could not get to see her, nor was it discovered where her father had taken her to, both having disappeared.

With the disappearance of the Lady in the Mask of Death as she was termed, arose the rumours of the "Red Maiden," a being whose history was quite as mysterious and terrible.

To our young artist her existence was more than these; for in the Red Maiden he believed there existed either the being who went by the name of the Masked Lady, or else that it was a twin sister of that mysterious personage.

Sir Ashleigh saw with grief that his young friend's mind was again excited to frenzy by these events, which had so powerful a hold upon his being, and he accompanied him in all his excursions after her.

They passed one day the establishment of one of those dealers in valuable second-hand commodities, when a distinguished-looking lady stepped forward, and walked away.

The moment he saw her Arthur became fearfully agitated.

"It is she," he cried, "my destiny. By Heaven I will know if she be life or death. I will follow her, and see what horrors are linked to such wondrous fancies."

Thus speaking, he had quitted the baronet's arm, and was about to follow the trace of the charming apparition, who was already almost out of sight.

"Not at all! not at all!" observed the baronet, in retaining his impetuous friend; "you are not going, like a simple student, to dog the heels of a pretty woman. This trader," added he, pointing to Madame Constantin's shop, "will assuredly inform us of all we wish to know."

And an instant after, followed by Arthur, he passed into the second-hand dealer's.

"Madame, we are desirous of seeing some lace," said he on entering, and with the air of one really intending to buy.

"English, Mechlin, or Alençon?" asked the dame, as much for the purpose of learning what they wanted with her, as to show off the extent of her assortment.

"Whichever you please," replied the baronet, "only let it be of the richest."

"Sir, here is a magnificent article, and, moreover, quite a bargain," said the dame, beginning to unrol several yards of Brussels point wound round a piece of cardboard.

Nothing seems misplaced at a second-hand dealer's, and chance sometimes wills it that everything may be found there, from a bridal robe to a pair of duelling-pistols. It need not therefore cause astonishment that the baronet should hastily shift from the article of the Brussels point to inquire what might be the value set on the bow and arrow of a savage, on which his eye had suddenly alighted in a corner.

"That, sir? It is real Indian," continued the dealer, in a soft, insinuating tone, which was equal to saying that, between the demand and the reply, the object which had in so unexpected a manner fixed the attention of the purchaser, had doubled its price.

"No," observed the baronet, who had travelled much and was a connoisseur, "that is not Indian; it is Caffre, from the Cape of Good Hope. But the question is not whence it comes; I ask you what you will let it go for?"

The dealer put on it an exorbitant price, which the baronet, without attempting to beat down, paid in gold, at the same time saying that he wished his purchase laid aside, and that he would send one of his people for it.

Having thus obtained the right of exercising his curiosity—"You had here," said he, a little while since, a very remarkable woman; do you happen to know her?"

"A very remarkable woman?" repeated the second-hand dealer, with an air of not knowing what was meant, which is indubitably the commencement of such conversations.

"Yes, a tall and handsome woman, who has just left your shop; one of your customers apparently."

"Ah! yes!" said Madame Constantin, recovering her memory; "a brunette, wearing a green cashmere? You are right, sir; in my opinion, she is one of the most charming women in London; and certainly it may well be said, that she is not in her proper sphere, the poor child!"

"What do you mean by not in her proper sphere?"

"That is to say, one who is not fortunate; you must be aware, sir, that there must always be many such people."

"But," interjected the Marquis, "in what consists this want of good fortune? It is surely something to be beautiful, and in London a handsome woman is rarely unfortunate."

"Really, if you imagine, sir, that to lose a rich admirer without there being any fault on your side, and to see oneself on the point of having one's furniture seized, be a subject of rejoicing, such is her position."

"The loss of one is the gain of another," remarked Sir Ashleigh.

"Hum! for Georgina," replied the dame, "it is not so very easy. There are words which destroy, do you perceive?"

"How words which destroy? You are fond of talking riddles, Madame Constantin."

"Yes, sir, such are men; and very frequently a wretched nickname is sufficient to destroy a poor woman in their estimation."

"Oh! as to that," continued the baronet, in order to draw forth more particulars, "this damsel, Georgina, must then be a light giddy sort of person."

"In that, sir, you are wrong! Georgina is a quiet, steady girl, gentle as a lamb, fond only of her own home, incapable of deceiving or of having words with any one; but it seems to be her destiny, that's a fact!"

"What! to lose her admirers?"

"Yes, sir; to see them all depart, one after another, but not in an ordinary way, or by ceasing to admire her. Her misfortune is to be thus deprived of them by death, and always by horrid frightful deaths. Thus, for instance, she will have an admirer to-day who will be killed in a duel; to-morrow, another in making a promenade with her in the Mall, will be thrown from his horse, and never move again from the spot; the week after, it is some foreign nobleman, who, without rhyme or reason, commits suicide in her boudoir, and destroys her Persian carpet. There are some also who come to an end through politics and conspiracies."

"In truth, her's is indeed a singular destiny," remarked the artist, a spasm of anguish passing over his features.

"And in consequence of all these disasters, what is then," demanded the baronet, "this disagreeable surname conferred upon her?"

"Some young fellows have taken it into their heads," mysteriously replied the second-hand dealer, "to call her the *red maiden*, from the famous romance you must know, sir, in which there is a *nun*. The name has taken effect, and I do not impose upon you in saying so; at this very time of day, I know sensible men, magistrates, peers, bankers, in short, men of knowledge and capacity, who, through a dread of their lives, would not dare even to nod to Georgina in the street!"

"Eh, what! the *red maiden!*" said the baronet, exchanging a glance with his young friend.

"Yes, certainly," observed the latter, as if entering into his idea; then addressing the dealer, "But, I say, tell us, if you please," added he, "the residence of this very sanguinary beauty; for in fact, one should positively avoid even to approach her neighbourhood."

Madame Constantin assumed an air of considering the question as a mere pleasantry, and in place of replying to it, "Well," said she, in an insinuating tone to Sir Ashleigh, "you will not make me an offer for my Brussels point?"

"Certainly I will," hastily exclaimed the baronet; "it is you, my dear lady, who do not inform me of the price."

Sir Ashleigh having once more paid very dearly, and without seeking to lower the extortionate demand, "Your pardon, gentlemen," said the dealer in cast-off stuffs; "I forgot a matter of business that presses." And at the same time placing herself at the entrance to her backshop, "Ernestine!" she cried to her assistant, "there is a cashmere that must be carried to Miss Georgina's, at her old address in Piccadilly; she is not to change her lodgings till after to morrow."

Having thus ingeniously communicated the information desired, "Madame, I wish you a very good day," said the nobleman, directing his steps to the door, followed by the artist.

"Shall I cause these things to be carried home, sir?"

"No, that is unnecessary; as I have already informed you, they will be sent for." And the two friends withdrew.

Sir Ashleigh still held his young friend by the arm; the face of the artist was wildly convulsed, and was beaded with cold sweat.

"Do not hold me," he cried. "Since I have gained this intelligence, I will not rest till I have faced her and stripped her of this terrible secret."

The baronet vainly strove to hold him; he broke furiously from his grasp, and dashed madly towards the house in Piccadilly.

The house of the mysterious Red Maiden, to love whom was *death!*

CHAPTER LXXXIX.

THE QUEST OF THE MASK OF DEATH.

THAT evening passed, and the artist did not return. The next day being in like manner unaccompanied by his return, the baronet began to entertain uneasy fears.

At nightfall, after an interview with Mrs. Carvan and Mary, he started for the house in Piccadilly, his mind now quite filled with misgivings respecting his young friend.

He knew not, indeed, how to fathom the mystery that warped Arthur's existence; the identity of the Red Maiden and the lady with the mask of death was a matter he could not make out by any process of reasoning.

That one and the same person should be seen under such strange circumstances—now beautiful as a Hebe, then frightful as the dead—was incomprehensible. That she could be seen under such various characters was another mystifying subject.

Certain it was that, whatever might be her nature, she exercised a fascination over Arthur that could only lead him to ruin.

If the baronet had been a prey to forebodings before he started, what were his anxieties when he reached the house in Piccadilly?

It was closed and tenantless.

He rang the bell and knocked loudly at the door; but the sounds he awoke showed too plainly that the house was empty.

Here was a fresh mystery: yesterday this house had been the abode of that young girl, and now it was stripped and forsaken.

What, then, had become of his young friend the artist?

Had he gained admission to that inscrutable being, and had she lured him to some appalling doom—or taken private vengeance upon him for troubling her with his presence?

The baronet could only fear that some such calamity had attended the young artist.

He repeated his summons at the door, until he could not but be convinced that the house was destitute of human beings.

"Some foul play has taken place," he soliloquised; "but whatever power this being of mystery may possess, I will meet it in the search of my friend: I will have this house searched thoroughly as a preliminary, and failing to discover anything here, inquiries shall be instituted all over the kingdom."

Sir Ashleigh's first act was to seek out the agent who had the letting of the house: from him he learned that he had been equally surprised by the receipt that morning of a note enclosing the balance of the year's rent, and intimating that the house being no longer required, he could at once take possession.

To Sir Ashleigh's request that the house might be searched, he gave a ready assent, and they started the same hour to look over the house.

There was nothing to give them any clue; the house presented merely the desolate appearance of a place suddenly denuded of furniture and occupants; and after minutely examining every room, they came to the conclusion that nothing was to be gained there.

But just as the baronet was about to retire, he perceived lying at his feet, stuck into the boards by a small, thin dagger, not two inches long, a scrap of paper.

He rapidly plucked them from the floor, and read what the scroll contained.

There were merely these words:—

"Who treads on my track must prepare to face death."

The words were written in a peculiar manner and appeared inscribed in blood.

A horrible supposition took possession of Sir Ashleigh on reading this scroll. What if his young friend had there met his death, and this had been written in his heart's blood?

He grew sick at the thought; mentioning his suspicions to the agent, the pair recommenced their search, scanning eagerly every spot that looked like a trace of blood.

They saw no such sign, however, and after peering into all the cupboards, and pulling open places where a dead body might be secreted, they shut up the house and left.

Many were the anxieties and perplexities of the baronet as he wended his way home, who was this inexplicable being, who, under so many identities acted in such a mysterious way: what gave her that influence over Arthur, an influence which, if it had not so now, must at some time be his doom.

Lastly, what had become of the young artist? That the Red Maiden was connected with his disappearance was plain enough, but in what manner that disappearance had been effected, could not be penetrated.

There was another question the baronet asked himself.

Who were the members of that mysterious League of Fate, whose decrees, given in secret, were executed more surely than the law of the land; and who seemed to have power to present themselves anywhere at the desired moment; entering dwellings and taking possession of the realms of the dead, that they might give forth and accomplish their judgments against man?

Sir Ashleigh could get no sleep that night: he lay restlessly scanning the singular events in which he had become involved, and when he did dose off, for a moment, his mind was harassed by visions of the Red Maiden, beautiful in features, but steeped in the blood of her lover; and changing as he looked at her, from the beauty of features to the hideous mask of death.

In the morning the baronet rose early, and having hastily dressed himself, and made a slight repast, went out to institute further inquiries respecting his young friend and the RED MAIDEN.

CHAPTER XC.

THE RED MAIDEN.

IN order to give some clue to the disappearance of the artist, we must briefly relate a little of what befel him after he left the baronet, to seek the Mystery, whose existence held so terrible an influence over his fate.

He reached the house in Piccadilly, as a female figure ascended the steps, convinced that this was the being he sought, he by a few bounds brought himself to the steps, and stood panting by her side.

She was about entering the house, when his sudden approach and gasped word 'stay,' caused her to turn round on her breathless pursuer.

She was closely veiled, but the shining eyes gleamed luridly on him with a light that he had seen before.

He put his hand out and grasped her mantle.

"Being of my destiny " he cried, "speak to me."

The veiled female turned herself and shook off his feeble grasp. Then without a sound, she was about passing in at the doorway, when again he arrested her.

This time her eyes flashed more vividly, and her tones were thrilling, as she said quickly the one word—

"Forbear."

Raising her arm she waved him back, and stepped into the hall.

Pausing a moment to collect his scattered senses, Arthur Bruno the next instant precipitated himself against the door.

It had closed quickly in his face, but on his third bound against it, flew wide open, and he dashed into the hall.

Immediately the door closed swiftly behind him, and he found himself in total darkness.

Thrilled by a feeling that swept over his frame, he commenced groping his hands about; while so engaged a soft arm glided a moment round his neck, and a face, warm and delicate, rested against his cheek. Entranced by the delirium of this sensation he flung out his arms to grasp the object so near him, but in an instant the figure had glided away, and his hands swept only the empty air.

Dashing madly from side to side of the hall, he felt in all parts of it, but the being he sought was not there: and, after a fruitless quest, he sprang towards the stairs, a light sound having reached him from above.

At the top the door of a room stood slightly open, and he bounded wildly in; his wild rush was brought to a stop by the sight of a figure standing in the centre of the room: the figure of a female, the same that he had followed, but now standing motionless, where a blaze of white light fell full upon her, displaying her dazzling robes and falling on her white arms, her warm and beautiful neck, and on the small white veil that hid her face.

It was only for an instant that he stood arrested by this vision, and ere one could count twice he had sprang towards the object of his wild enchantment.

"Being of earth or other worlds," he cried, " I have followed you as my Fate, and you shall not again elude me, except by death."

"If I am your Fate," coldly replied the veiled figure, "tempt it not; there is doom in every look that gleams from my hidden eyes."

" If there be ten thousand dooms I will meet them: I have followed you long enough as a chimera, but now I hold you in my grasp will and unmask the charms that are veiled from my sight, but not from my vision."

Imperceptibly as he spoke she moved from before him; when he had leapt to the spot where she had a moment before stood, it was vacant, but she was a few yards behind him.

"Be warned," she said slowly. "Forbear, it is your Fate that speaks."

"I care not what terrors lie buried in my destiny," replied the young artist, maddened to excitement; " I will know who and what you are."

"I am called 'the veiled figure,' " she replied, and she laughed awfully as she spoke; " that which most you should dread—the Red Maiden."

" Then by the Heavens I will make you reveal who and what else you are."

" Forbear—tempt not Destiny."

" I will tempt and dare it," he exclaimed, springing again towards her. But as his arms were out to grasp her, a something, like a pillar of stone, rose suddenly between them; a vice-like grip seized him by the throat, a band of iron pressed rudely against his brow; he saw beautiful Mystery gliding away as his senses failed him, and with his life, as it seemed, squeezed out of him by that grip, he fell senseless to the floor.

* * * * *

When the young artist came to his senses, he was lying in the hall on the cold marble and in the

DICK'S FIGHT WITH THE BOATMEN.

darkness; an oppressive feeling of silence and desolation was upon him as he raised himself, and with benumbed limbs tried to stand.

Accomplishing this, at length he realised where he was and what had befallen him, and as a rush of feelings came to his brain, he started forward.

"Being of Fate," he cried madly, "whether for life or death,—aye, for eternal torment,—I will discover the mystery of your life."

A hollow sound, like the moaning of the wind, answered him; he groped his way to the stairs and ascended them.

But the room above was empty.

A light came in at the window—it was daybreak —and showed him that the place had been stripped of every article of furniture; he rushed from room to room, but found each was in the same condition, and with his faculties benumbed by this fresh mystery, he staggered back to the empty hall.

Here his foot touched a hard substance, which he at once picked up; it was the skeleton of a human jaw, and held between its closed teeth a scrip of parchment.

Arthur flung open the door, and letting the light fall upon the scrip, read—

"If life is bitter, follow and meet a more bitter destiny."

"I will follow," he muttered between his set teeth, "to the end of the world, if needs be."

He pulled the door to behind him, and ran from the house.

His wild appearance in the street caused the few stragglers who were about to bestow curious looks on him, but unheeding them, he hastened from the place, with the parchment and the human jaw yet in his hand.

"Only the jaws of death," he muttered, "shall keep me from this terrible mystery of fate and doom."

At a period approximating to that in which had taken place the unexplained departure of the mysterious lady, nothing was talked of in the city of Bordeaux save the charms of a London lady, who had recently alighted at the Grand Hotel de Guienne in company with her husband.

In order to produce so great a sensation, it was necessary to suppose in this lady, who moreover had already passed the age of early youth, a beauty in fact miraculous, for it is well known that the females of Bordeaux pique themselves on their charms, whilst the male part of the population, with a southern gasconade which has made the political fortune of many among them, would willingly persuade strangers that in their native city a Venus de Medici and a hunting Diana were to be met in every street.

What, moreover, contributed to bring out in bolder relief the splendid attractions of the London belle, was, perhaps, the contrast of a husband already on the decline, and who did not compensate by any species of exterior advantage for the cruel disproportion in age which at a first glance was remarked between them.

This striking difference had even commenced by attracting to every step made by the amiable stranger a host of ardent admirers, to whom the mean exterior of the husband had not acted as a trifling encouragement; but we must not forget to add that, in less than a week, this grand competition, and compact and palpitating crowd were very considerably diminished.

Rendered, it would seem, extremely jealous by the consciousness of his want of personal attractions and evident venerableness in point of age, the husband, in whom these two aggravating circumstances did not appear to have lessened the muscular vigour of his arm, commenced by killing in a duel one of these pretenders to his Penelope.

Another adorer had been found one evening stabbed at the corner of a street, without the smallest proof, it is true, of the direct or indirect participation of the ferocious Othello, but also without this tragical adventure presenting any other possible explanation than the indiscreet ardour of the proceedings and sighs to which the victim had addicted himself.

These two murders, it will be readily comprehended, had sufficed to draw round the handsome dame an imposing sanatory cordon; so that, the husband left out of the question, there yet remained the difficulty of gaining the lady's attention.

Now, the latter showing herself rather disdainful, and far more indifferent than eager to receive homage, the gentlemen contented themselves with admiring at a distance, and outside the railing that encircled the shrine; the devotion of which she remained the object was a kind of realisation of the popular caricature—*Look, but touch not.*

Although they had arrived with post horses, and occupied the best apartments in the first hotel in the city, this lofty couple were not accompanied by a single servant, a circumstance which left the less chance for the ultimate gratification of that curiosity of which they were the object.

They were rarely seen at the theatre or on the public promenades, and almost their only amusement appeared to be for the wife to change her dress several times a day, and for the husband to watch every movement in the harbour, either in walking along the quays or in observing from the elevation of a balcony the numerous vessels arriving or setting sail.

As to the way in which the two spouses passed their time together, so far as could be learned, it was singular. Never did this husband, so terrible a guardian of his honour, address a kindly or tender expression to his wife, and he treated her with a coldness not at all equivocal, if not with a certain disdain.

On her side this beauty, so proud and repelling did not seem even to except her gracious lord and master from that freezing indifference with which she had the air of honouring the entire masculine sex.

Moreover, abounding in wealth, and possessing in one of the banks of the city credit to a considerable amount, not taking their repasts at the general table of the hotel, never receiving any one, and avoiding with marked attention everything that could lead to the forming of either friendship or acquaintance, the more this singular couple excited curiosity the less they appeared disposed to satisfy it.

The only circumstance that could be learned with certainty of the mysterious strangers was that they had come from Paris, and were called Monsieur and Madame Lelouard, a revelation due to their passport, which without the slightest hesitation they had handed to the proprietor of the hotel the very day of their arrival.

Another matter, which was not known to the inhabitants of this vicinity, would have created further comment and have introduced more curiosity, which was that this pair had been followed from London by a young gentleman who, not coming directly in their track, had, by assiduous diligence, ferreted out and followed the various stages of their journey.

Few who had known this individual a few weeks previous would have recognised the young artist, Arthur Bruno. He was so changed as to be but a remnant of his former self. His eyes were wild, his cheeks haggard, his limbs effeminate. He had all the signs of a man who had passed through some terrible crisis in a more terrible destiny.

Why had he followed on the track of this couple? Why was he here when they sojourned in their isolation here?

Because in that veiled female, the wife of this ancient husband, he believed he followed the mysterious being who was at once his destiny and ruin.

He had followed, determined to see and be with her; to gain access to her chamber in spite of the ferocity and coldness of her lover-killing husband; he could but die, and if he died in discovering the secret that, unknown, ate up his existence, it were a willing death.

After all he might be mistaken, for although the rumour of her beauty had spread far and wide, there were few who could boast of having seen her features, inasmuch as she kept them usually concealed by a veil of extraordinary richness and beauty, and as she seldom entered into society where she would be required to lay aside this covering—herself and her husband maintaining such seclusion, there was no occasion for her to risk that display which she evidently avoided.

It might be that the report of her beauty was merely a rumour, brought about as the fact of her keeping her face so continually hid, but this the impetuous young artist did not pause to consider. He would seek access to her chamber by any means, and then and there alone discover that which his restless passion prompted him to make known.

To get to her chamber was no easy task. His eagerness would not suffer him to attempt, by working on the cupidity of her *femme de chambre*, to get that way of admission.

He glanced at the height of the window, scanned the difficulties of the ascent, and prepared for the perilous adventure that night,

He had watched the old man, her husband, go out, and when the streets were wrapped in the shadow of night, he began an ascent that every inch of the way opposed obstacles which threatened to send him with violence to the ground, there to be dashed to pieces.

But with the prowess of excitement he gained the sill, threw open the window, and sprang into the room.

The lady sat on an easy lounge near the couch: she was dressed in evening attire, but the veil was before her features.

She manifested neither fear nor surprise at the entrance of the intruder, but maintaining an immovable position, fixed those winning eyes upon him.

He cast himself quickly at her feet.

"The first part of my vow is accomplished," he cried; "I have tracked and found you, and am here to tear the veil from your face and behold what phantom houri or voluptuous beauty lingers beneath."

"Madman!" the lady said; "for your temerity and folly it were well that I caused your exit by the way you came. Back, those impious hands! I, whom you have constituted your Fate, would more than wither your existence if you dared gaze on my features. Back! and tell me why you seek me here."

"Because," he replied, springing to his feet, "a secret link of nature binds our destinies, whether for good or evil. I have seen you often in dreams that have seemed reality, and have felt that same warm pressure of your arm and cheek that you gave me ere last you left me! I am in bondage—bondage of soul unto eternity—to what you make of me! You are here——"

"With my husband——"

"I could laugh at such a word," he rejoined. "Seen in so many characters, I believe in none. He holds no husband's right whom you sojourn with here. No male habiliments are in this chamber; besides, I have seen your shadow on the blind —*one* shadow, never *two*."

"You are true in judgment," she returned, coldly. "He is not my husband, nor dares do what you have done—enter my chamber. And now, having told you this, I bid you begone."

"Never, till I have seen your face."

"Back! Were you to look thereon you would wither away in horror."

"Answer, then, that I may so wither, if there is such horror in your gaze."

"Never! yet, stay: you would gaze on that which is awful as the brow of Fate—more grisly than the cheeks of death; have your wish, but not now. When you are beckoned by the sign of a dagger with three stars, or hear these words spoken, follow, you will have to pass more terrors than the mind conceives, but pass them all, and there is one greater to behold—and I am that one. You who look on this rounded arm, these shoulders, white as alabaster, know not the graveyard horrors dwell on my face. You have heard; quit me now with this hope, or stay and perish unmercifully."

She opened wide the door.

"Obey my bidding, for I am your destiny."

Her eyes flashed fire upon him and an odour like the air of a vault crept to his nostrils obeying that inexplicable feeling, he stepped silently back, and found himself on a staircase that led to the hotel passage.

"Let none see you here, nor see you depart; be secret, and in three days you shall behold enough of mysteries."

She closed the door.

"Three days;" his brain was reeling, his limbs were filled with wildfire, he dashed madly from the hotel, and wandered he knew not whither.

Three days, at the end of which time he was to behold the Red Maiden remove the veil, and let him look upon the Mask of Death.

CHAPTER XCI.

THE CARNIVAL AND THE MYSTERIOUS BOX.

REVEL ran riot in the City of Paris. Carnival time had come, the period when gaiety, debauchery, and crime, mingle with harmless sport.

Here was a young student who had once or twice joined our adventurer, Arthur Bruno, and on the first morning of the Carnival, he sat in his room prepared to join in the day's excitement.

Amaulé was the name of this individual.

On that morning, Arthur Bruno had received a missive, bearing the dagger and the stars inscribed upon it, and bidding him present himself at the *fete* where Amaulé was that day to be.

The student, disguised and masked, had called in upon Arthur, and thrown him a lawyer's bag, in which the missive had been placed.

Leaving him to discover and peruse it, he went to other houses, playing such pranks as the day justified.

A sober bishop was startled out of his wits by his frolics.

A harlequin and a Turk of his friends, three-fourths of whose doors he had greatly damaged under pretext of awaking them, next received his visit, and that of his lively companion; and the *sextuor* completed by the adjunction of a clown and a fish-fag.

After a preliminary and ample breakfast, they picturesquely grouped themselves in an open caleche, the hire of which they had arranged to pay by a joint contribution.

The day passed away in driving processionally along the Boulevards.

The youths had dined at the Cadran Bleu, and night being come, after having provided themselves with torches, they commenced a round of all the places having any claim to notoriety at which the carnival was being fêted.

Amaulé proposing to leave his friends about eleven o'clock, in order to proceed to the ball given by the attorney who inhabited the Faubourg St. Germain, the joyous band had for an instant entered the Salon de Mars, Rue de Bac, and for a last trip had fallen back upon Vauxhall, frequented by the lowest class, and which was then situated on the Quai Voltaire, in the abandoned church of an ancient religious community, from whence arose, by a rather singular alliance of words, the name of Bal des Théatins, conferred on this indifferently famed spot.

The artist mingled with the throng of revellers, and was for some time accompanied by Amaulé, who followed him very pertinaciously; in the midst of the excited revelry a female masquerader in a red domino stood beside Arthur.

Before she spoke—before her whisper reached him—instinct told Arthur that it was his mysterious Fate.

The voice thrilled to his heart when she said, in a whisper—

"Follow in silence and unobserved." Instantly she made her way from the crowd, and the artist passed after her.

A few paces from the place a carriage was waiting; the domino, turning for a moment to place her finger on the lower part of her mask, enabled Arthur to see that she beckoned him to enter with her.

He was in the act of obeying when a heavy hand was laid on his shoulder; as he turned, a voice exclaimed,

"Madman, to follow there will be to follow Fate—to follow death—she is the Mask of Death—the *Red Maiden!*"

Arthur turned quickly.

"Who are you to interfere with me," he asked.

"I am the Duc de Berle, and I bid you beware; the *woman with the death's head* lures only those whose doom is sealed,"

Before the young artist could reply the domino stepped from the carriage.

"The Duc de Berle can speak of what he has seen, *when he has the power*," she remarked, in a significant tone.

"Assassin!" cried the Duke, uttering a sharp cry, and falling backwards.

The hand of the masked female was instantly placed on Arthur's shoulder, and, without looking round, he found himself persuaded into the carriage.

He had not thus observed the Duke fall, nor knew, as the vehicle swiftly hove away, that the nobleman lay helpless on the ground.

He only had attention for that mysterious being with whom he at last sat and was in contact.

No one looked in at the carriage window. Was it well?

There was a redness in the fair wrist of the masked woman that was not caused by the red domino she wore.

She put her hand once out of the window, and raised it as two cloaked men went by.

They hastened towards the fallen noble.

The young artist in ecstatic rapture got closer to his mystic companion.

"Whither are you taking me?" he once asked.

"To meet your ——," was the significant response.

The carriage bore them away.

Silence reigned in the street. Then a number of men came trooping by, and an outcry was raised.

The Duc de Berle was found with a dagger in his breast.

And on the dagger-hilt were three stars.

* * * *

Sir Ashleigh came to Paris as the Carnival commenced. He had received a mysterious intimation that he would find the young artist there.

The letter, which was written in red (as if in blood), and marked with the dagger, as usual, told him that he would be near his young friend, when he saw brought to the Carnival a large box.

Sir Ashleigh went to the carnival. He followed the student, Amaulé, whom he at first believed to be the artist, and only discovered his error on whispering his name.

Amaulé soon after went away.

Sir Ashleigh had gained tidings of his friend, and sought him in every part of the building.

In despair he sat himself down, and all at once felt a note slipped into his hand.

It contained the familiar crest and these words:—

"The mysterious box is on its way with its burthen. Open it and seek. He whom you seek has left to seek his fate."

Alarmed by this note, the baronet made every inquiry, and soon learned that a masked gentleman, in every way answering the description of the artist, had been seen to leave with a female masquerader.

"It is she," thought the baronet; "and she has led him to his fate."

He quitted the assembly, not knowing whither to wander in search of his misguided and lost friend.

In the meanwhile, the fête which Amaulé had quitted, seemed to get on very well without him.

It had already reached its highest degree of animation, when the attention of the attorney was all at once attracted by the noise of an animated discussion, or rather by a quarrel, of which his antechamber had become the scene.

Having proceeded to learn the cause of this scandalous proceeding, the host ascertained that it was occasioned by a kind of porter carrying a chest of considerable weight and dimensions.

In this grotesque disguise, which he called his costume, this singular guest, notwithstanding a lively opposition on the part of the domestics, insisted on penetrating to the ball-room, and presenting his homage to the mistress of the house.

At sight of the mask worn by the blusterer, the host concluded that the whole affair was merely some Carnival joke, and without considering the pleasantry as one founded on the best taste, he took it in better part than his servants had done.

After some little discussion the mystery was cleared up, and under this burlesque equipment, which formed the subject of debate, Amaulé finished by being discovered.

In the first moments, the very natural manner in which he played the part of a drunken porter had rendered the detection of his person impossible by the inmates of the mansion.

At the period in question the fashion had not as yet reached the hideous and half-naked disguises which since then have had such wonderful success; the attorney was, however, but indifferently satisfied with the style of dress, something more than negligent, of his guest, and drawing largely on the right of censure delegated to him by the father of the young man, he rebuked him sharply touching the wretched choice and unsuitableness of the dress under which he had thought fit to present himself.

Nevertheless, at the conclusion of some rather

lengthy explanations, it was decided that, in spite of his costume of ticket porter, the adventurous youth should, at his proper risk and peril, have access to the saloons; but on the chapter of his great box, the host was inexorable, and it was doomed to remain with the pelisses and great-coats in the ante-chamber, in spite of the persistence and protestations of Amaulé, who exclaimed in despair, that he should thus be altogether made to fail in his début.

"The freak of the student had in the meantime occasioned some noise in the ball-room, and some joyous surprise was generally suspected to be concealed, and was looked for in the interior of that gigantic box which he had taken the trouble of carrying on his shoulders, and upon which the puritanism of the notary had placed an interdict.

"On every side the pretended porter was therefore pressed with questions, but, assuming a mysterious air, he gave them to understand that a drama, an entire history, like that of the old Trojan horse, lay hid within this chest; and to some ladies, whose curiosity persecuted him with untiring ardour, he had finished by replying, 'That the mystery was one of those which could not with propriety be spoken in the ears of angels.'

"While this was going forward the moment of supper arrived.

"The ladie passed into the refreshment-room, where, conformably to the usage in all great réunions, they alone sat down.

Amaulé had now become pretty well besieged to tell the story of the box, and he was in the act of commencing when Sir Ashleigh entered, and without preface commenced making inquiries respecting Arthur.

"If you mean a young artist," said Amaulé, "I believe I can tell you something about the matter, though very little."

"I am eager to hear," the baronet replied.

"Well, then," said Amaule, "I myself was a little interested in him, and should have had much pleasure in forming his acquaintance; indeed, I followed him at the fête for the purpose, and was on the eve of speaking when I saw him beckoned to by a domino, whom he at once quitted the place with."

"An hour afterwards, while envying him his good fortune, I perceived facing me a charming black domino, who from under her mask shot lightning glances at me, and beckoned to me to come after her.

"I did so, and outside in silence gave her my arm: I was about then to call a diligence, when my charmer intimated that her carriage was waiting for her a little distance off.

"Whereupon I accompanied her joyfully; we entered, and the handsome vehicle rolled off.

"'You have a friend, whom you saw lately led away,' said the lady.

"'One whom I should have been happy to make my friend,' I replied, 'convinced that he was suffering from some terrible grief, my heart was drawn towards him.'

"'You may make acquaintance with him under circumstances unexpected by you both,' she answered, and her words were at the time vehement, as if a tigress had spoken in human voice.

We proceeded for some time, and as long as the coachman chose, for I cared little for what was passing outside, occupied as I was in endeavouring to lift the mask of my adored, but which I owe it to truth to declare, she prevented me from effecting.

All at once, however, the carriage stopped, and what is not usually the case both the coach doors were at the same time thrown open with a bang: "What a terrible misfortune!" then exclaimed the domino, while leaping out at the door on the left. I, however, did not attempt to leave by either one of them, but I looked out, and with an astonishment that may be easily conceived, I found myself in a spot dark as night, for the precaution had been taken to extinguish the carriage lamps. I also particularly recollect that I breathed an odour of stable dung, and of a poultry-yard, which led me to suppose myself in a straw-yard or some other filthy and rural locality, and then, by way of additional satisfaction, I heard some one undo the chain of a watch-dog, which he had the honor presenting to me under the gracious appellation of Tiger, and I could perfectly figure to myself the size and cut of this playful monster by one or two powerful bass notes which proceeded from its throat in the form of a bark to celebrate, amid the profound silence of the night, its first moments of liberty; upon which, continuing to hold the coach-door open, "Are you not going to alight, sir?" inquired the negro, respectively.

"No, by heavens! I am not going to alight. What is the meaning of all this? and whither have I been led?'

"'You cannot, sir, sleep in the carriage.'

"'I tell you that nothing shall compel me to alight. I am here in a cut-throat-looking place: but, if it must be so, I will sustain a siege.'

"'Take away!' now exclaimed the villanous black, and instantly, as it were by magic, the imperial of the carriage divided itself into two, and left me exposed to the heavens. At the same instant I felt myself seized round the waist from behind; in front a running knot encircled my legs, and, in spite of the vigorous manner in which I plied my arms for the purpose of disengaging myself, I was rapidly transported into a room on the ground floor, where, in shutting me up, my jailor begged in the politest terms that I would have the goodness to wait a little.

"A romance writer would have experienced no difficulty in describing this room; for furniture it presented nothing more or less than the four walls, and it was only lighted by a night-lamp, formed of a chipped drinking-glass, placed in a corner on the ground.

"If I had been overcome by wine, as my impertinent acquaintance had pretended, there was here, by my faith! wherewithal to have sobered me; and it must be confessed that, in the first moments, my reflections were anything but rose-coloured.

"Cursing the duplicity of women, and my stupid belief in flattering intrigues, I now foresaw only the most sinister denouément, and found that, though joyously commenced, the Carnival would terminate most villanously for me.

But with the word carnival there presented itself to my mind a more consoling idea.

At Paris, I finished by saying, people are jovially disposed; we are in the season of mirth and frolic; my adventure began at a ball, and will it not ultimately turn out that I am simply the object of a farce?

I did not deceive myself.

The next moment I heard a "hist! hist!" and

then under the doorway was thrown a scrap of paper, which I picked up.

Hastily written with a pencil, it contained—

Here Amaulé drew from his pocket, as a justificatory proof of his assertion, a piece of paper folded in four, and read as follows:—

"'Dear Sir,—I am in despair at what has happened to us; it is a practical joke intended to be played off on you, and which, far from being able to prevent, I am forced to take part in; otherwise I should be compelled to declare that you are not the person you have been taken for, and that I returned to the house with an unknown individual.

"'I, moreover, beseech you, for the interest of my safety, on no account to quit your mask, and to soften your tone of voice as much as possible.

"'If you are desirous of again seeing me, you must, in order to get over all suspicion, do without fail whatever may be required of you, and which will appear more absurd than difficult of execution.

"'Do not be grieved for the strange place in which you find yourself; it was for greater security that I caused you to be brought through the outhouses and stables, and shortly it will be a very different matter, seeing that these detestable jokers are about to make you descend into the cellars.

"'Here is, moreover, my name and, the address of the house in which you now are.

"'One more test; lend yourself to it willingly, and fear nothing.

"'To-morrow, at as early an hour as may suit you, present yourself at my house.

"'I shall impatiently expect you, were it only to offer, with more ample explanations my excuses and regrets.'

"By the light of the lamp," he continued, resuming his recital, "I had just finished reading this consolatory epistle, when the second act commenced.

"I saw enter two individuals, masked and strangely attired in loose black and red robes, in the style of those worn by executioners on the stage.

"One of these savage-looking personages, in whom I observed a portly rotundity of form, held a white handkerchief, rolled up so as to serve as a bandage, the other a kind of running knot, doubtless destined to alarm me in case I exhibited symptoms of resistance, and with the greatest affability and attention to forms, these would-be jailers invited me to follow them.

"Whilst I was undergoing the formality of suffering my eyes to be bandaged over my mask—

"'It is I; do not be alarmed,' said to me in a whisper the charming executioner, who at the same time found the means of pressing my hand significantly.

"We then made about twenty steps out of my prison, when I was told to take care, as we were about to descend.

"This was, in fact, the order of the programme, the staircase leading to the cellar which had been announced.

"In order to lead me to a belief that I was penetrating into the bowels of the earth, my guides did not set about it in the least ingenious manner. We at first descended a certain number of steps, which I should not have failed to count had I imagined myself engaged in a serious adventure. I was then made to walk straight forward, next to descend, then to mount again, until I began to feel fatigued with the exercise; but at length, reaching the level ground, the bandage was removed, and although forewarned of the purely facetious turn which the encounter was to assume, I must confess it, the lugubrious appearance of the place into which I had been introduced did not fail in greatly astonishing me.

"Figure to yourselves a long gallery, very imperfectly seen by means of a reddish and sepulchral light.

"On the side by which I had entered it was closed by immense red hangings descending from the vaulted roof to the ground.

"On the right and left the wall appeared covered with painted cloth, representing in frightful relief long ranges of death's heads and human bones.

"At the other extremity, bounded solely by the profound obscurity, this terrible hall had an air of infinity; but towards the spot where the light ceased to act, the eyes were attracted by a species of throne surmounting a platform, and crowned by a dais or canopy.

"On each side of the platform was ranged a number of seats.

"I counted a dozen; ten only, besides the throne, were occupied by a kind of phantoms, who wore red masks, red gloves, and red cloaks with hoods. This flaming colour was also that of the entire furniture, and decidedly appeared to be the favourite tint of the establishment.

"My two conductors, who never lost sight of me, after having placed me near to the platform, made to the president a silent and profound salutation, and then placed themselves a few paces behind me, one on each side.

"Then, speaking in a hollow tone—

"'Sir,' said the high functionary to me, 'I would fain believe that, agreeably to my instructions, you have been treated with the greatest respect. I nevertheless owe you an apology relative to the species of violence which must have been employed in bringing you here.'

"'Not at all, president,' I replied; 'to kidnap people by means of a pretty woman is, on the contrary, very flattering and gallant.'

"'Nothing could please me more,' observed my grave interlocutor, 'than your self-possession in a situation where many others would feel alarmed perhaps by the apparent danger. Your gaiety proves that we have to do with a man of courage, and that we could not have made a better choice for the important mission which it is our desire to confide to you! nevertheless, we are here for the purpose of occupying ourselves with serious interests, and like me, perhaps, you will find it suitable to treat them seriously.'

"This kind of reprimand brought back to my recollection the recommendation of the beautiful Spaniard, who had keenly solicited me to play naturally my part of dupe; at the same time softening down my voice to the flute stop, in order to observe the tenor of the instructions she had communicated to me.

"'I am in your hands, sir,' replied I; 'say what it is you wish me to do?'

"'As you may readily perceive by the mystery with which we surround ourselves,' was the reply, 'we are a secret association, and, what is more, a political association. It is enough to say that, under a Government the enemy of liberty, we can only assemble together in the midst of the greatest peril. Hunted for a long period by the police, we are at the present moment sold and betrayed by a traitor. In consequence of his information, the place of our meetings, where it is thought we must surely be surprised, is this very night to be surrounded by an armed force, and we are here assembled for the last time.

"'That's a pity, 'pon my soul!' I could not hinder myself from replying, forgetting, for a moment the nature of my own part; 'the hall is spacious, commodious, well ventilated and decorated with especial taste.'

"'We shall not want for space,' replied the president, with increased solemnity; 'and to form for us an asuylm, there remains for us the entire wealth, over which extend the innumerable ramifications of our association. But to-day, momentarily forced to disperse, we are about to set out while pre-occupied by a grave interest—that is to say, the safety of our archives. None of those here present can undertake to provide for their safe keeping; for at this moment, each of the members of this assembly is preparing to start for a different and distant point of the globe.'

"'I understand,' I hastened to say, in interrupting him; 'the affair in hand is, as one may say, to lend a help in finding another locality for these papers.'

"'You have said it, and trust that our gratitude—'

"'Gratitude—I shall be flattered by it; but, on the other hand, the gentlemen of the police and the Attorney General?'

"'It is precisely the peril that constitutes the service; for if the question merely regarded the carrying of an ordinary burden, the first ticket porter in the street could render us that good turn, and we should have no need of the special individual upon whom we have cast our eyes.'

"'Enchanted with the preference; nevertheless, permit me to have the honour of observing that—'

"'President,' now hastily exclaimed one of the assessors in rising, 'this person hesitates, and we are losing with him precious moments. I demand that another decision be come to, after, however, getting rid of this poltroon, who has come here only to possess himself of our secret.'

"'Do not alarm yourself, brother,' replied the president; 'between the prudence which weighs a danger, and the baseness which declines it, there is some distinction to be made; and I shall entertain so much the more confidence in the resolution of our accomplice that he shall have well reflected upon it, and calculated its extent.'

"'That's what I call speaking,' exclaimed I, 'while the other gentleman is desirous that I should take and adopt a resolution before it has even been explained to me what the nature of the proceeding is which this honourable association expects from me.

"'You see that object yonder,' said the president, directing my attention to a corner in which was a box of large dimensions, upon which the words WITH CARE were written many times in large and legible characters. 'In that are contained all the documents of our chancery.'

"'I would rather have bet on its being porcelain, so often is it indicated to touch it with precaution.'

"'You must,' continued the scarlet gentleman, 'take that box upon those shoulders, which, heaven be thanked, you possess both large and strong.

"'Thus loaded, by favour of the darkness you will proceed without hindrance, according to all appearance, to the Rue Notre Dame des Victoires, where is situated the office of the diligence, which starts to-morrow morning at four o'clock for Bordeaux.

"'Taking the first name that presents itself as the sender, you will have the box registered to the address which it bears on the lid.

"'That accomplished, your labour will have terminated; and in a few days the society, without considering itself capable of worthily recompensing so important a service, will nevertheless cause to reach you a testimonial of its high satisfaction.'

"'But, president,' I took it upon me to observe, 'am I to carry that enormous box on my bare shoulders?'

"'All has been provided for,' replied, with an important air, the lofty dignitary, who, in fact played his part in the most natural way imaginable.

"'You will there find a knot and a porter's dress complete, the ticket included, in case of your being accosted by a patrol, or a body of police making their rounds.

"'You can have no possible objections to make, unless it be that your heart fails you at the moment of proceeding to act.'

"What a charming fellow, this dear president, with his *no objections to make!*—there would have been a cart-load of them, provided that one had been disposed to examine curiously his amiable proposition.

"For instance, he might have been told that in this hasty removal there appeared something much more perilous than he chose to make believed, since in fact no member of the distinguished society possessed sufficient enthusiasm to take charge of the unwieldy box.

"One might even, in taking the commission for what it really was, that is to say a practical joke, have hinted to the gentlemen mystificators that their farce was not skilfully got up, nothing bearing less resemblance to the truth than their having accorded their confidence for so ill-favoured a job to the first individual picked up in the street.

"But it was not my part to play the debater.

"I knew the solution of the enigma.

"The pleasantry consisted in forcing me to walk through Paris for a longer or shorter period of time with the ridiculous burden upon my back; and, unquestionably, when I reflected that, as the price of this complaisance, I assured to myself the kindly regards of the charming Spanish lady, who, to say the truth, ran strangely in my head, I do not very well see how any one can prove to me that I made a bad bargain.

"Pretending, therefore, to be deeply hurt by the doubt implied by the last words of the president as to my courage, in the twinkling of an eye, and with the assistance of my two conductors, I assumed the dress fitting the occasion.

"Next came a second edition of the bandage formality, which was more than repaid me by a renewed and more energetic pressure of the hand from my beautiful conquest, and another recommendation given in a whisper to be punctual and exact in the execution of my mission.

"But at the moment of my departing I was surprised by the strange emphasis of her words when she said—

"'You will be met by one who is seeking your

friend: bid him not to send too far when he is unbidden: the artist, whom you have *nearer you than you think*, has sought and found his fate.'"

"I should have stopped to reply to this, but I was hustled and turned about, and directly after, with two of the associates preceding us carrying the box, we now were ascending the staircase.

"Having regained the stable-yard, I was told to take my place in a carriage; but there was no question this time of the magnificent equipage; and a tilted cart, of which, as if nothing were the matter, my hand slyly felt the covering, gave me to understand that, like a criminal, my evasion was to be operated in the humblest of vehicles.

"Having for travelling companion the red and black gentleman who, in his quality as master of the ceremonies, had served to introduce me, we continued our route for some time with the slow and uneven pace usually exhibited by heavily loaded carts.

"My conductor at length begged me to alight, and having done the like himself, he assisted me in adjusting the knot, on which he installed the box; then leaping back into the cart, which instantly set off at a rapid trot, he wished me 'good luck!' and authorised me to undo the bandage.

"The handkerchief removed, I turned round to learn where I was, and the first thing which presented itself to my eyes was, to my surprise, the dome of the Invalides!

"The villanous jokers, because I was considered to have business near the Place de la Bourse, had caused me to be conducted to and abandoned on the Banks of the Seine, opposite the Esplanade of the Invalides.''

As Amaulé concluded, Sir Ashleigh sprang up.

"This box," he cried, "where is it? What terrible meaning may be attached to the words of this fiend; good Heavens! if by having him nearer than you thought, she meant that you carried his body in that immense box."

"Impossible!" Amaulé cried, aghast at the question.

"I submit," said Sir Ashleigh, "that the box be immediately examined; there has evidently been foul play abroad, and my poor young friend may at this moment lie murdered near us."

"I have sent for the notary," the host said, "and he will presently be here. Till he comes, I dare not take upon myself the responsibility of having the box opened."

At this moment a servant opened the door of the closet in which this grave deliberation was being held. Thinking it was the magistrate whom he had sent for, the host hastily advanced to meet him, disposed beforehand to show all the attention and politeness which one never fails in exhibiting to the dispensers of justice when not without apprehension of getting entangled in the meshes of the law.

But the servant did not announce the commissary; and the amazement will be easily imagined, when the individual who had entered set about informing him, with an air of alarm.

"Sir, it must be that your house is taken for a waggon-office—four other boxes and four more porters have just arrived!"

At these words Sir Ashleigh and Amaulé looked at each other as if to consult on what was to be concluded from this new and curious turn in the affair, in which decidedly the carnival seemed to engross a larger share than politics; but this mute exchange of thoughts bringing with it no lucid explanation, it was decided to proceed upstairs immediately.

When the attorney reached the ante-chamber, the brawny-shouldered individuals whom he proposed to lecture roundly, notwithstanding all that had been said to the contrary, had got rid of their burdens; and now, ranged by the side of the box brought by Amaulé, four others of nearly similar dimensions, imparted to the invaded apartment the appearance of a warehouse or the yard of the diligence-office.

Closely questioned as to the origin and destination of these huge boxes, the porters replied, in a discordant concert of Auvergnian *patois*, that a well-dressed gentleman had come to their lodgings and awakened them from their slumbers; that he had paid them liberally, in consequence of the unseasonable hour at which he claimed their service.

He had then conducted them to a waggon-office near the Jardin des Plantes, and directed them to carry in all haste these four boxes to their addresses, which, as might be seen written on the lids, was that of M. B——, attorney, Rue de l'Université, Faubourg St. Germain, to whom a M. Britannicus, of Bordeaux, had sent them.

If, previous to this burlesque incident, Amaulé had given himself the trouble of reading the address on the box which he had brought, and especially if, making use of his head, he had been capable of comparing two things together, he would on the instant have been struck by a circumstance sufficiently remarkable, that is to say, that he himself had been charged to send to M. Britannicus at Bordeaux, whilst now it was M. Britannicus of Bordeaux who was sending to M. B—— in Paris.

But in the midst of the attorney's indignation, and the almost unintelligible explanations of the porters, exposed to the cross-fire of a hundred questions put by the guests, whom the noise had succeeded in drawing from the saloons, and who, all at the same time, were desirous of learning the facts, it would have been impossible for a mind gifted with the most scrutinising powers to have retained sufficient self-possession for the enregistering a remark of that temerity.

Finishing by ranging himself on the side of Amaulé, who now declared the fact of the quadruple invoice the incontestible suite and continuation of his own adventure, the host, in order to cut short the ridiculous situation in which he found himself placed, imperiously ordered the porters to remove what they had brought, and instantly to relieve the apartment of their presence.

Although they at first refused obedience to the mandate, the Auvergnians, who from a certain bantering and jovial air might be supposed better informed on the matter than they pretended, effected nevertheless their retreat with some promptness, and they had been gone from the premises for more than ten minutes when the comissary arrived.

Informed of the manner in which the suspected box had been confided to Amaulé, the magistrate was far from adopting the student's opinion.

The fact of the cavern and the *gentlemen in red* instantly recalled to the mind of the functionary that audacious series of crimes which we have already stated; for in his quality of officer of the judicial police, he had been called on to act in some of these affairs, with the details of which he had been made acquainted.

particular, the strange invasion of the porters
...ed to him highly worthy of attention and
...ignificant; and he blamed the attorney for
...ing them to remove the boxes.
...uspicion flashed to the mind of Sir Ashleigh
... notary spoke.
...at if the invasion of the boxes had been only
...ed that they might carry off the first box
... contained a clue that might lead to the clear-
...f this incontestible mystery.
... suspicion, so far, was right; the porters
...ht four boxes and they took four away.
... one of the boxes they left there was not the
...ought by Amaulé.
...re you aware of what has just happened?"
... the notary, with increased seriousness and

severity. "His royal Highness the Duc d
Berle has been assassinated!"

"Really!" replied the student. "Who has
been trumping up such a story?"

"The gentleman here brought the news of the
frightful event; and he has every reason to believe
his information but too correct, since a little time
since, on leaving a house in which he had been passing the evening, he met within a short space of
each other the Duc d'Angouleme and the Count
d'Artois, proceeding in all haste to the theatre of
the crime, which was committed at the masked
ball which took place this evening at the opera.

"He was found just outside with a dagger in his
breast."

"As a means towards the clearance of these

No. 28.

events," Sir Ashleigh exclaimed, "let us see opened and examined this box."

"I am afraid," the notary observed, "it is *too late*."

His words were verified. The box, on being opened, was found to be filled with stones and rags.

"We have been cheated," cried Sir Ashleigh, furiously; "but before I return I will have this dreadful matter cleared up, or I, too, will fall a victim to this woman of death."

CHAPTER XCII.

THE FIRST NEWS OF THE ARTIST.

Sir Ashleigh put himself in immediate communication with the secret police; he advertised also largely for information respecting the porters, whom he was well assured were made up to their part.

For some time he could gain no information; but the first that came was contained in a parcel that was forwarded to him, and which, on opening, he found to contain the following statement of a man who signed himself a spy, and said he would shortly come to give further evidence, if he gained any, and claim the offered reward:—

Sir Ashleigh impatiently perused the report.

It contained a summary of the spy's proceedings during the fatal evening of the 13th.

The writer first attended a ball given at a banker's, and frequented by political partisans.

On leaving this species of club he went to pass a quarter of an hour at the Duchess de N.'s, better known for its devotional habits than for dancing.

Here he gleaned the anecdotes and *bon mots* which were passing current.

Finally, he attended the fancy dress ball at the attorney's, with what result will be known on perusing the following extract:—

"A perquisition by the magistrates had just been made; and whilst the crowd of guests, before separating, were indulging in commentaries such as you may suppose, I hastened to take my leave, in order to draw up in writing the result of my various observations during the evening, when, passing before a hackney coach standing in the vicinity of the house.

"I distinctly heard a female voice saying, in an animated tone, to the coachman,

"'Yes, the Englishman begs the porter of the house to tell him that there is a lady inquiring for him, and that he is requested to come down immediately.'

"Hearing the name of the Englishman, which was that of the artist, my attention was instantly awakened.

"Then at the same moment recognising that the lady who claimed the young man presented herself masked, and in a domino, my first movement was to have had her arrested, in order that, through her means, might at last be obtained the solution of the murder of the Duc de Berle.

"I advanced towards the mysterious dame, and, with a perfectly simple and natural air, I hastened to say to her—

"'You are desirous of speaking with the Englishman? I believe he is still within; and if you will permit me to become your ambassador, I will inform him that he is waited for.'

"Had the beautiful mask shown ever so little embarrassment, I should have called for aid, and forced her to alight, whatever might have been the consequence; but not the slightest objection was offered to confiding to me the commission for which I presented myself; on the contrary, I had excuses and thanks showered on me.

"I encountered the young artist upon the stairs, and made known to him the good fortune that awaited him.

"He gave me a thousand thanks, and ran off.

"I mounted my cabriolet, and instantly followed their traces; for, after a very short colloquy, the hero of the adventure had seated himself by the side of the lady, and immediately the rumbling machine was set a-rolling.

"We thus traversed together the Rue du Bac and the Pont Royal, and it appeared to me that in a very short time I should be in possession of the address of the charming domino.

"Where, in fact, could the pair be proceeding?

"At the hour it then was, and in consequence of the sinister news already spread abroad, all the public places and balls had shut their doors.

"On the other hand, they were not proceeding to the student's quarters, for I had been informed that he resided in the Pays Latin, upon which we had now turned our backs.

"Having arrived in the neighbourhood of the Palais Royal, all at once the carriage stopped, turned back, and at length terminated its course in the Rue d'Argenteuil, before a house of mean appearance, where, the coachman having been paid and sent away, the parties entered.

"After having sent away my cabriolet I set about considering this residence, the aspect of which afforded me matter for reflection; but a recollection which flashed on my mind suddenly explained the resolution adopted by the mysterious pair of seeking an asylum there.

"Without being what may be called disreputable, the house before which I then stood was of somewhat suspicious character for intrigue.

"The greater part of this dwelling was occupied by workmen, and free from the inconvenient watchfulness of a porter or door-keeper; and the second floor, to the best of my recollection, had for occupant a certain lady, *widow of a colonel*, who had experienced the usual misfortunes.

"In the sad state of money matters to which she saw herself reduced, Madame Grisa carried into execution the idea of engaging and furnishing an extensive suite of rooms, of which she had reserved for her own use only a very small portion.

"The remainder, comprised of several rooms, which were so happily disposed as not to interfere with each other, formed a species of asylum for embarrassed friends, who, for various reasons, might be desirous of occasional quiet and retirement.

"On this hospitable floor a light was not long in showing itself in two windows, which previously had remained in darkness.

"I thereupon no longer remained in doubt as to the happy inspiration of my recollections.

"From that moment all hesitation was at an end.

"Finding without much trouble the secret by which the outer door was opened, I groped my way up stairs, and decided on knocking at the complaisant widow's, exercising, however, every possible discretion in order not to frighten the turtle-doves from their temporary retreat.

"After some little hesitation, and a few words exchanged through the key-hole, Madame Grisa decided on admitting me, and I began by placing a in her hand, and begging, with a degree of solemnity, a private conversation.
ece I mysteriously confided to my incorrupt'ble ow that her two *proteges* were strongly suspected of a participation, more or less intimate, in the great political crime which had just been committed; but, instead of yielding obedience to this species of requisition, the cunning jade took advantage of this sad intelligence I had given her, she burst into the most immoderate explosion of grief.

"It was necessary, however, to bring the affair to a close, and my ultimatum was thus laid down:—

"If I continued to meet a refusal of the prompt and devoted aid which I had a right to demand from by the refractory dame might from the following day expect that her conduct should be revealed to the prefect of police, and there would be reason to inquire how far her manner was compatible with the rigour of the laws laid down and observed in like cases.

"Attacked in this fashion, Madame Grisa no longer exhibited a shadow of hesitation, and she immediately introduced and installed me, with the least possible noise, into a room admirably adapted for becoming an observatory.

"Left alone, and aided by a few holes effected in the partition by means of a gimlet, which habitually I carry in my pocket, I considerably increased my chances of correct information, and thenceforward it only remained for me to bring my eyes and ears into play.

"Between the young man and the domino, who until then had not unmasked, everything, let us hasten to declare, had passed with the strictest attention to decorum.

"They were now conversing in a genial manner; the Englishman was earnest and impassioned, nevertheless the lady's face I could not see in consequence of her mask, but her eyes were glittering strangely through it.

"'Mysterious one,' I heard him say, 'reveal me this secret: I have dared much to learn all.'

"'Ah! let us talk of more serious matters,' said the domino, avoiding to reply more directly to the observation; 'if I have risked all to see you again, it was to make known to you the perils which surround you, and not to give ear to the expressions of your folly.'

"'Nonsense, the peril!' replied, like a real lover, the young Englishman; 'when it presents itself, we shall see it approach;' and speaking thus he endeavoured to loose the mask of the amiable domino.

"'At all events,' replied the lady, while defending her mask, 'I shall not suffer you to see my face, being daily exposed to meet you in society; and now, believe me, sir, lose no time in withdrawing yourself from the vengeance of these terrible associates; they have sworn to make of you a fearful example; and did you but know the power of these people—ah! sir, you cannot imagine what they are capable of, and it is simply your life which is now in question.'

"That is a reason the more, for in the meantime drowning it in pleasure;" and the artist indicated an intention of becoming more enterprising for the future.

"In fact," remarked the unknown dame, "this house is perhaps for you the best place of refuge, therefore I am about to leave you here, and in a few hours I shall send you all the indications necessary for your safety; but the first step you must understand—the most indispensable, in fact,—will be to quit Paris, and that, too, without delay."

"Not while you, who are my destiny, linger here," he cried, passionately. "Come, I must look upon your face."

"Not yet," she said quickly, and standing up: "let us not be slaves to folly; I perceive you are faint; I will obtain some wine and other refreshments, over which we can better converse."

"With a smile she left the room. An instant after she returned, bringing the results of her inroad on the hostess's larder. "We are not very fortunate," said she; "I have only found some ham, a bottle of claret, and part of a bottle of Madeira."

"Counting on the effect produced by the stronger wine, the Englishman was desirous that the claret should remain untouched; but his companion insisted on drinking no other, and she even mixed it with two-thirds water. He, on the contrary, applied himself wholly to the Madeira, and at the end of a quarter of an hour his exaltation had reached the highest diapason. In that situation of mind, become audacious even to impertinence, he was desirous at any price to see the countenance of the amiable domino, and advancing towards her, by a sudden movement he succeeded in undoing the mask.

"What he then said I, from the position of the lady, was unable to discern; but it was enough to extort from him an exclamation and start of horror; I saw, too, that he fell back pale and shuddering.

"Had the pretended beauty, whose features he had succeeded in uncovering, been no other than the famous young woman *with the death's head*, with whose name rumour had been busy in Paris for several months, he could not have been more horrified.

"The lady herself was thrown into a high state of excitement.

"Taking advantage of the surprise and terror into which the artist naturally found himself thrown by her hideous aspect—

"'You are a wretch!' she exclaimed; 'but you shall pay dearly for this'

"And at the same time rushing out of the room, she double-locked the door.

"Almost at the same moment a like ceremony was performed at the door of my chamber, in which I had suffered to be revealed the presence of an *inhabitant* by foolishly neglecting to withdraw the key.

"That double precaution taken, the domino tranquilly left the apartment, and in a few seconds she was safely out of the house.

"Thus encaged, the artist began to make a continuous noise; it lasted, however, but for a short time.

"The matron (whether in connivance with the young woman who had left the house, or whether the noise had not succeeded in awakening her) appeared to have heard nothing, and without budging suffered the Englishman to exhaust his fury.

"The latter soon began to yawn, stretch out his arms, and at length appeared as if struggling against a violent attack of stupor.

"He afterwards went and threw himself on a bed placed in an angle of the room, which was not long in resounding with his harmonious snoring.

"On seeing him so rapidly assailed by sleep, my first idea was that the Madeira had been drugged with some narcotic, although at the same time all might be explained by the heady nature of the wine of which he had made too free a use.

"On my side, also, I was deprived of liberty.

"My reclusion was anything but agreeable; but making a disturbance in order to obtain my deliverance would probably attract the attention of the student, and consequently lead him to the knowledge of my having watched his steps.

"After waiting a mortal quarter of an hour, this ridiculous situation was crowned by a sorrowful termination.

"To the powerful snoring of the sleeper which I had at first heard, low groans and inarticulate sounds succeeded; I then beheld him turn and twist himself on the bed, and at last exhibit all the symptoms of serious indisposition.

"Struck by this circumstance with a horrible idea, I no longer thought it necessary to act with a prudent caution, and by the tremendous hubbub which I made at my door I finished by attracting the attention of the landlady, who restored me to liberty.

"Rushing instantly to the young man's chamber, I found him pale, exhausted, and suffering greatly from vomiting.

"I thereupon ordered the matron, who, by the unaffected expression of her terror, seemed to protect herself against every suspicion of complicity, to give the patient warm water to drink, and taking the address of the nearest physician, I ran to awaken and bring him back with me.

"When we arrived the poison appeared to have taken its course to the intestines, where it exercised the most frightful ravages.

"My attention was no longer necessary to the patient, and I had a pressing duty to perform, that of informing justice, and more especially my dear director-general, that of rendering you the present account.

"Nevertheless, before quitting the place, I was anxious to have the opinion of the doctor, and asked him what decidedly he considered the nature of the case to be.

"'In similar circumstances,' he replied, 'we are never quite sure; it is, above all, necessary that the liquids should be analysed; but there is, unfortunately, here the strongest appearances, and my opinion, until better informed, is that the unhappy young man has been poisoned.'

"My own convictions tended this way, and I resolved to return speedily; but when I came back with officers of justice, the house was closed and empty—the keeper, the doctor, and the Englishman were absent; and though the secret police have been on their track, no trace has yet been discovered of them beyond this.

"A labouring man passing by in the dead of the night saw two persons, the one veiled and the other cloaked in disguise, leaving the house to enter a diligence.

"They carried, assisted by the driver, a large trunk, very long, and apparently heavy.

"But he took little further notice of them, and no clue has since been discovered."

Here the communication ended, and Sir Ashleigh sank back with a groan.

"It is too true!" he cried; "in that box must have been the body of my poor young friend, fallen a victim to the rage and malice of that deadly woman. But it shall not rest here. I will set fresh men on the track, and never rest till I have avenged him."

CHAPTER XCIII.

DICK'S STRUGGLE WITH THE BUSHMEN.

WE return to Dick—Dick, the unfortunate Dick, the convict—unjustly made criminal—unjustly immured from the sight of his kindred, and shut up with men of the lowest depths of infamy.

Time had worked favours in Dick's condition. The privilege which the intercession of good old Mr. Elsden had failed to obtain was accorded by the humanity of the chaplain of the gaol, who recognised in Dick, not the hardened ruffian whose crimes required that he should be caged like a wild beast, but the victim of an illegal and outrageous persecution.

Yes, Dick had been liberated, and on a Ticket-of-Leave.

But not with this did he gain his liberty. He was not yet suffered to return to England. His respite was only given on terms that further galled his heart. He was to remain in the colony for one year.

So, cast on the world in a strange land, Dick, without resources, without friends, was left to find for himself a means of honest living.

Honest livelihood, with the stigma of a convict attached to his name; the taint of a poison clinging like a foul garment to his every act.

Dick panted for pure air. He hated the sight of hard walls and close rooms.

He had been entombed long enough.

Drinking in the fresh air, by deep inspiration he started towards the wilder regions, the regions of danger and excitement, where the bushman prowled, and the gold fiends lurked.

The country expanded gloriously to his view. He left the habited towns behind him.

Here and there, through the vast wilderness which, a century since, stretched to the westward, were erected block-houses for the protection of the surrounding settlements.

At these were sometimes collected a number of hardy rangers and hunters, who continually made through the forests in quest of game; and, drawn on by irresistible fascination, sought out the wily Red man, and engaged him in the deadly hand-to-hand encounter.

That day, in the summer, a runner had arrived at the block-house at the mouth of Munika River with the intelligence that the aborigines were congregating in large numbers in the Munika valley, and evidently making preparations for a campaign against the settlers.

They were engaged in throwing the hatchet, shooting at a mark, and indulging in athletic exercise, such as invariably presaged offensive operations on their part.

The Munika block-house at this time was not in the best condition for defence, and the little garrison heard these tidings with considerable apprehension.

To make certain of the matter, it was arranged that a guard should be kept out in the woods, so as to apprise the settlers upon the approach of the aborigines, when they were to retire within the stockades, and defend it to the last.

While these precautions were being taken, two rangers, Waller and Barnup by name, were sent out to reconnoitre the valley, and to bring back definite information of the number, strength, and intentions of the enemy.

These comprehended all their instructions.

As to the manner in which they were to be carried out, and to the time occupied, the spies were left entirely to themselves.

All this Dick learned, before he had proceeded many hours' journey, from a settler who encountered him in his march, and, against his will, kept in his company.

Irksome to him at first, the companionship of this bold ranger became, after a time, agreeable to Dick's feelings; the prospect of something to excite his blood stirred up his spirits, and long before the ranger had finished his story, he was heart and soul in the expedition; and by the time they met the other rangers he was eager for the coming fray.

On this beautiful sunshiny day these rangers left the block-house, and set out on their perilous undertaking.

Moving stealthily and rapidly through the wood, enveloped in all the fiery beauty and sombre gloom of autumn, they at length reached a singular eminence now known by the name of Point Joyful.

The western termination of this sheer precipice was more than three hundred feet in height.

Climbing to its extreme summit, the rangers saw the broad valley spread out for miles before them, the Munika River winding lazily through its centre as it swept off to the westward.

It required barely a glance to show that the rumours which had reached the block-house were well founded.

Right beneath them the eagle-eyed hunters observed hundreds of dusky natives congregated upon the open prairie, running foot-races, engaged in horse-racing, leaping, throwing the hatchet, and performing the war-dance, with all its horrible accompaniments of yells, screeches, and whoops.

Fresh war parties were constantly arriving, until even the rangers, great as was their experience, expressed their astonishment.

"Courage!" muttered the latter, as he peered over the edge of the cliff; there's a powerful lot of the dogs. What a scrimmage we might get up if we could coax a half dozen of 'em out on one side where the rest wouldn't interfere!"

The eyes of the brother ranger sparkled as, removing his coon skin cap, he gazed down into the valley.

Then replacing it, he rolled upon his back, and holding his hand over his mouth, kicked both feet, into the air with a vigour that at times fairly held him for the instant upon his crown.

"What ails you?" asked Barnup, in astonishment.

"I was just thinking what a chance there will be for some fun. Them fellows down thar mean fight, and as that is what we mean down at the block-house, what's to hinder us from having a real old-fashioned—"

"Sh! down!"

From his look-out, the other had detected a company of aborigines coming toward the bluff, and he felt pretty certain they intended to ascend it.

They, therefore, lost no time in concealing themselves in one of the numerous fissures, from which they witnessed the savages less than a dozen yards distant.

Finally they withdrew, and the two were left to themselves again.

Dick and the rangers now consulted together, and agreed to remain in this spot until they had ascertained pretty definitely the destination of the savages.

For their food they relied upon a quantity of jerked venison in their possession, while numerous indentations in the rocks afforded them considerable quantities of rain water.

During the cold autumn nights they drew their blankets around their shivering forms, and nestled down among the leaves and stones, not daring to strike a spark from their flint and tinder, nor even to discharge a rifle, for fear of attaching suspicion to themselves.

After spending several days in this manner their supply of water was out, and they were reduced to the necessity of either giving up their enterprise or of searching for more.

Waller resolved upon the latter, and with a couple of canteens slung over his shoulders, and a rifle in his hand, he cautiously descended to the prairies skirting the hills on the north.

Under cover of a dense thicket he reached the river, and, turning a sharp point, came upon a celebrated spring of water, still famous in that neighbourhood.

Filling his canteens he returned in safety to his companions, who had anxiously watched his approach.

It was determined that they should alternate with each other in obtaining the precious element, and, accordingly, the next day Barnup, in charge of the canteens, descended from the point, and set out in quest of the spring.

He met with equal success, having successfully avoided every enemy upon his return.

This was kept up for several days, until it once more devolved upon Barnup to perform the duty.

He had reached the spring, filled his canteens, and was seated upon the ground, gazing dreamily at the water as it bubbled upward through the silver sand, when his ear caught the sound of footsteps.

Turning quickly around, he saw two squaws within a few feet of him.

The eldest, the instant she caught sight of the ranger, gave utterance to a whoop that resounded against the cliffs and far out into the woods.

Barnup comprehended his imminent peril at once.

To save his own life it was necessary to slay the two beings before him.

The lithe and powerful ranger inflicted a noiseless death upon the elder squaw, and springing into the water with the younger, endeavoured to drown her.

She resisted powerfully, and while endeavouring to force her under, to his amazement she addressed him in his own language.

Now, for the first time, he noted that she was white like himself.

A few words explained all.

Years before she had been taken prisoner by the savages after they had slain nearly all of her family.

"Do you want to go with me?" asked the impatient ranger.

"I will do anything to reach my friends again."

"Then foller."

With this he plunged away in the direction of the mount, the girl speeding rapidly after him.

They were yet a considerable distance away when an alarm cry reached their ears.

He understood the cause at once.

The body of the squaw, floating down the stream, had been discovered by some of the warriors, and an instant attempt to avenge her death was certain.

Hurrying forward, they at length reached the mount, where, as well may be supposed, Waller and Dick anxiously awaited them.

Barnup had barely time to explain matters, when his brother ranger assured him that their hiding place was discovered, and that twenty warriors at that moment had reached the eastern slope of the mount, taking care to keep their persons under cover.

Shortly after the spies distinguished the swarthy enemies leaping from tree to rock, until they were completely surrounded, except upon the eastern side, which, as will be recollected, was a steep precipice of immense height.

All chances of escape were therefore cut off, and the determined hunters resolved to defend themselves to the last.

Assuring the girl of their impending doom, they advised her to escape to the aborigines, and tell them that she had been taken prisoner.

But she replied she would meet death a thousand times before returning again to her terrible captivity, and that, if they would get her a gun, she would show the savages that she understood the use of it as well as they.

The adventurers, feeling certain she would not escape being a prisoner again in case she remained, still remonstrated with her, but she positively refused, and they gave over their useless task.

In approaching the hiding place of the rangers the savages were compelled to pass in single file over a narrow neck, a sort of backbone to the summit, where they were exposed for a moment to the rifles of their foes. Beyond this neck they were secured by the shelter of the trees and rocks in advancing; but in springing from one to the other they afforded opportunity for skilful marksmen to pick them off, and not knowing how many whites were in ambuscade they became exceedingly cautious as they approached the narrow neck to which we have alluded.

For several hours the unerring rifles of the whites kept the savages at bay.

So sure as a tufted head appeared for an instant upon the upper ridge, or a part of the person was exposed in leaping from one shelter to another, it was pierced by the bullet, and the savage rolled, dying or dead, to the earth.

This species of warfare was kept up until, convinced they could accomplish nothing by it, the savages resorted to a new expedient.

On the southern side of the hill was an isolated rock, from which a rifle, aimed at the spies, could not fail of reaching them.

It offered a chance of a flank movement, which could not but prove successful.

This rock, once gained, would bring the whites under point blank range, without the remotest chance of escape.

The Australians, comprehending the advantages it afforded, attempted to reach it, and the rangers, understanding their deadly peril, did their utmost to prevent it.

Dick had just discharged the rifle which the ranger had given him when Waller saw a huge savage stealing towards the sheltering rock.

He was fully a hundred yards distant, and, in passing to the cover, could not avoid exposing an inch or two of his person.

The rock, once reached, it was all over with the whites; and, with a full consciousness of the responsibility that rested upon him, the dauntless woodman raised his gun, and coolly awaited the critical moment.

A second later the tawny hide of the savage was discerned, gliding like a snake behind a flat rock.

Shading the sight with his hand Dick drew a bead that he felt sure would do the deed.

Gently touching the trigger, down came the hammer, breaking the flint into a dozen pieces without emitting a spark!

"Wagh! that's bad, as that redskin will get to kiver afore I can fix another," muttered the ranger, with perfect nonchalance, as, taking the rifle from Dick, he unscrewed the flint, and produced another in its place. "As it's sartin he'll reach it for all me, I'll jist watch him."

Keeping his eye upon the savage, he saw him stretching every muscle for the leap.

Like a crouching panther he bounded far outward; but instead of striking the rock, he uttered a yell while in mid air, and rolled headlong down the steep into the valley below.

The amazement and fury of the savages were no greater than the astonishment of the rangers at the unexpected occurrence.

A rifle from some unseen hand had done it.

Still furious and determined another savage made the attempt; but while in the very act of leaping, he was shot precisely as his predecessor—the rangers being so occupied with the attack in front that they had no time to attend to him.

This second defeat cast dismay among the Australians, and they withdrew to devise other means for dislodging their dangerous enemies.

The respite came most opportunely to the whites, who had kept up the defence for several hours, and they now began to converse as if there were some possibility of escape.

At this juncture they noted, for the first time, that the girl was by their side, with a rifle in her hand.

During the excitement of the attack, she saw a warrior fall, who had advanced some distance ahead of his companions, and stealing up to him, she possessed herself of his gun and ammunition.

With the eye of the huntress, she had noted the fatal rock, and it was by her hand that the two savages had fallen.

By this time night was at hand, and the sky gave every appearance of an approaching storm.

The distant mutterings of thunder came nigher, the darkness seemed fairly palpable in its intensity, while the rain fell in torrents.

After a brief consultation, the hunters decided upon their plan of action.

The girl, whose knowledge of the neighbourhood was so accurate that she could not go amiss, took upon herself the duty of guide, and they cautiously followed her.

They had gone scarcely a hundred yards when she encountered two bushmen sentinels.

Her perfect knowledge of their tongue enabled her to deceive them, and, after the most painful and laborious toil, the entire number of spies were passed.

Once in the woods again, the three took a direct course for the river, and after three days' travel the vicinity of the block-house was safely reached.

The rangers were not backward in congratulating Dick upon his readiness with the rifle. As for the young girl so strangely found, they were loud in their unreserved admiration of her prowess.

She took their praise quietly, and seemed to give her whole attention to Dick, upon whom her dark eyes were fixed with an expression of interest and sympathy.

The hunters, conversing busily together, walked on ahead, and thus Dick found himself left to the company of a young creature towards whom he, who had so long been shut out from all sympathy and love, could not but feel strangely attracted.

A very beautiful girl she was, still young, and exceedingly docile. Her life amongst the aboriginals did not appear to have taken from her interesting and intellectual manners, and it was quite clear that, from the first moment of seeing Dick, she had taken, not a mere liking, but a strong fancy to him.

The rangers, deep in their friendly discourse, passed on, and were soon out of sight. Dick and the young girl thus found themselves entirely together.

At first they did not perceive the absence of the rangers, but, after proceeding some distance, Dick said that they were nowhere in sight.

He was thus placed in rather a delicate position with regard to his fair companion. Although they were near to the settler's place of abode, they were ignorant of the way to it, and the spot where they were was extremely lonely and cold.

Perhaps it was this sense of her loneliness with him which induced the young girl to lean more affectionately on his arm, and look into his face with those beaming eyes—eyes that spoke volumes by a single glance.

Hitherto moody with his own thoughts, Dick had paid little attention to the feeling which was growing upon him, but now, as he turned his gaze on the beautiful countenance of the heroic girl, his heart seemed drawn to her, and he suffered his arm to press hers, which rested on his own.

It was not that he was deficient in his allegiance to Mary, or that she had passed from his mind. He believed that she was still awaiting his return, and that when they met it would be in the meeting of love.

But he had been so long lonely, so long uncared for, unsoothed by any word of tenderness, that the confiding trust of this heroic being, whom chance had given so strangely to his care, gave him a brotherly kind of love for her.

He broke the silence by remarking upon the adventures she must have gone through with the savages; and the flow of dialogue thus brought about, she told him of her troubles and perils, drawing from his honest heart many a fervent wish that he had been by her to aid her, when she required some such help.

He did not fail to compliment her upon the bravery with which she had helped to repel the attack of the savages, and though she seemed pleased at the terms in which he eulogised her acts, she modestly avoided his manly flattery.

She talked with him of her former life, and told him her name. Her father, it seemed, had been unjustly accused of a crime, and sentenced to a term of imprisonment, from which he escaped, and was now, as she believed, with the bushrangers.

This statement further awoke Dick's sympathy, and he suffered the young girl's head to rest rather near his breast as they went on together.

Before they could attract the attention of the rangers the gloom of night began to fall, and Dick, fearful lest they might be lost in that region, went forward to see if he could discover some sign of the settlement.

Not that he was very much charmed by the prospect of passing the night there with his fair companion, but he knew it would not be well for her to remain there; and, besides, he was but mortal, and she seemed so far attracted towards him as to have made it extremely dangerous for them to be there the rest of the night together.

So he went forward to explore the scene.

It cannot be said that Mynna, such was the young girl's name, displayed much anxiety at the idea of being left out there with him: on the contrary, her large eyes beamed with an expression that might have been construed significantly by any one with a less regulated mind than Dick.

She remained silently awaiting his return; and when some few minutes had elapsed, and the darkness so deepened that the surrounding landscape became obscured from the gaze, a look of curious pleasure and diffidence came to her young face.

A footstep falling near her aroused her from her reverie. Supposing it to be Dick she stepped forward gladly to meet him; but her surprise was as great as her disappointment when, in place of Dick, two men presented themselves, whose appearance was quite enough to create alarm in her mind.

They were two rough, hairy, burly fellows, dressed after the fashion of the notorious bushrangers, and having monstrous pistols and bowie knives in their belts.

Uttering a coarse exclamation at the sight of Mynna they came boldly before the young girl, their ruffianly countenances expressive of the worst villainy.

Mynna stepped back hastily, and cast her glance round for Dick. The fellow observed her startled glance, and laughed brutally at her expressed fears.

"Oh! you needn't be afeared on us," one of them said, a hideous grin distorting his features; "we shan't eat you after finding such a pleasant girl in such a silent spot."

"No, no," chimed in the other, "we'll look after her comfort for this night."

The meaning looks of these wretches, their gestures, and the vile intent their words implied caused Mynna more apprehension than she had experienced during her sojourn with the savages of the soil.

As one of the ruffians put his arm forth and tried to take hold of her dress, she sprang back and, defiantly facing them, said—

"Keep off, scoundrels. I am not alone. You will repent if you dare attempt violence."

"Ho! ho!" laughed the ruffians. "The bird is skillish; we must take her in our arms and hold her while she flutters to get away."

So saying they threw themselves upon her.

The bushes impeded Mynna's flight, and already as she moved back she found herself clutched by these unscrupulous men.

One of them had taken her arm in his rude grasp, and was holding her dress; the other had flung both arms round her body, and was dragging her off her feet.

In this position it only remained for Mynna to make the best use of those faculties which were still left her, namely, her voice and her hands.

These she did not fail to make the most of. Her voice sent a succession of shrill calls for help, and her hands, armed with long sharp nails, plied pretty nimbly up and down the sensual ruffians' faces, drawing from them oaths and curses of the vilest, while they rudely attempted to settle the struggle at once by flinging her to the ground.

But Mynna had not learned patience or humility in the time that she had been amongst the wild Australians.

Her feet were planted firmly on the ground, and while she resisted all attempts to drag her down her long sharp nails scarred in deep gashes the faces of the scowling bushrangers.

"Curses!" growled one, swearing, as she laid his cheek open across; "hold her, man—down with her   Devils!—furies!—she will tear us to pieces!"

"Over with you, cat!" shouted the other, as he flung her off her feet.

But before she had reached the ground, Dick came with a swift bound from amid the bushes.

He cast himself on them at once, and with one blow of his powerful arm struck the first one to the ground; the next he had grappled with in an instant, seizing him round the throat and dragging him back.

The bushranger whom he now attacked was a powerful ruffian, with a frame of iron and limbs like those of a young gladiator.

He gripped Dick in return with a hold as forcible, gliding his arm round his throat, and, struggling to throw him to the earth, beat him with his huge, brawny fist.

At the first attack Mynna had, on finding herself released, sprang clear of the two ruffians. The one who was laid prostrate by the stroke of Dick's arm, on recovering from the effects of the blow rolled over towards Mynna, intending to deal violently with her while his companion settled scores with Dick.

The better to aid him in this laudable design he had drawn a terrific-looking knife, with a broad, huge blade, and an edge as keen as a razor; this he brandished murderously as he neared the young girl, whom he intended to make his victim.

While she was stepping back to avoid his blow, the struggle between Dick and his assailant was growing fast, deadly, and furious.

The bushranger forced back, step by step, by Dick, and finding himself being beaten in the wrestling match, now fought desperately to get his arms free.

He also had a large knife in his pocket, and his intention of drawing it to sheath in Dick's body was pretty manifest.

By dint of sheer perseverance he got his hand free and his knife out.

To find his wrist grasped by Dick, and his arm forced back till the point of the blade entered his flesh.

The ruffian groaned out a deep oath as he was pricked in the side, and slung his body away.

The knife had been slowly entering his flesh.

He fought hard now to draw his hand away, trying to drag the knife through Dick's hand, and to slash him along the arm, in both of which generous resolves he was thwarted by the determined courage of Dick.

It was now all in Dick's favour; he had got the hilt of the knife in his grasp, and was in the act of getting total possession of it.

The bushranger called on his companion to help him, and growled out his bitter curse between his teeth at the stalwart young Englishman whose mettle had proved so good.

His ruffianly comrade, hitherto thwarted by the quick movements of Mynna, no sooner heard the other calling him to his help than he sprang back, and attacked Dick with the ferocity of a savage.

His eyes glistened with deadly hate.

His teeth were set closely together, and his murderous knife shone in the air as it circled in its stroke of intending death.

He had aimed at Dick's back.

Dick was in deadly jeopardy then. His own attention was taken up by his man.

There seemed no hope for Dick.

In one moment more he must have fallen dead at the feet of his assailant.

But the true devotion of the young girl saved him.

With one light, graceful spring she came in front of the burly ruffian.

Her eyes looked wildly into his.

Her breast heaved, and her cheek was pale as ashes.

But her lips were firm, and her hand steady.

She struck the ruffian with her little hand so full a blow in his coarse, burly throat that for the moment it stopped his breath, and sent him back reeling.

Then would have been the moment to have possessed herself of the deadly knife, but the excitement of the hour drew her attention to Dick, and she came nearer to save him if he needed help.

This act afforded the other ruffian the opportunity of again leaping to the attack.

With more deadly purpose than before he had sprung forward, and thrusting Mynna out of the way with a violence that forced her almost to the ground, he raised the deadly weapon and let it fall full at Dick's back.

The gallant fellow was pretty well hampered with his own assailant, and as the knife fell with such vengeful fury, Mynna shrieked and ran forward.

She saw him turn, writhing, as it seemed, and the blood gushed forth in a deluging stream.

But not from Dick.

The bold Englishman had seen the coming of his assailant, and with a quick movement he turned and thrust the knife full at his breast in time to keep off the blow aimed at himself and transfix the man.

The blow was as unexpected as it was furious; it struck the ruffian almost to the heart, passing by one dash through the flesh and sinews of his breast, and touching his very backbone ere it passed quivering and bloody.

The fellow gave utterance to a frightful groan.

A groan that seemed torn with his life blood from his heart.

Then he brought his hands swiftly to the bleeding gash, and writhed in mortal agony as he went back reeling.

Then Dick plucked the knife from the wound.

The ruffian fell like a block of lead.

His body quivered for a few moments.

His limbs drew up and down.

His hands clutched the hard earth.

Then he lay stiff and still.

He was dead.

The unexpected turn in affairs was a relief to Mynna.

She had fancied it was Dick, whose life blood was gushing out.

Hence her scream of wild agony.

Hence her sudden, horrified leap to his side.

No. 29.

Hence it was that she had taken his arm in her grip before she could realise that he was safe.

The momentary cessation of their struggle had given the other ruffian a little breathing time, and now the fury with which he tried to break away from Dick caused the latter to shake off Mynna's grasp, and turn himself anew to this conflict.

The stroke which had been the *coup-de-grace* to the other had been one of those dexterous lunges that sometimes enable a man in some such conflict to save his own life and rid himself of his adversary.

But his hands were not free enough for him to do as he wished with his present antagonist.

And, truth to tell, that gentleman had no desire to be disposed of in any such manner as his tall comrade had been.

He was stricken by the swift doom that worthy had met, and to prevent sharing a like fate, he suddenly leaped up in the air, carrying Dick with him, and descending with a force that shook them off each other, and caused Dick to drop the reeking knife.

It lay right between them as their mutual fury forced them apart.

The eyes of the bushranger glared like those of a panther as he saw the deadly weapon within his reach.

Dick, more intent upon seizing his enemy omitted the thought of the knife.

His more wary opponent saw his chance, and as Dick again came on to renew the attack, he jumped aside.

Then he gave one bound to where the knife lay.

Dick saw his error.

But it was too late.

The weapon, with its stain of blood, was within the grasp of his foe.

With that in his possession, Dick knew that his chances would be almost gone.

He heard the wild cry of triumph as the bushranger clutched at the knife.

He saw the red blade showing still on the earth.

Then came a low, faint cry.

An oath, terrible and bitter, had succeeded it.

The ruffian, at the moment of victory, had found himself thwarted.

And by a woman,

Mynna, the valorous, heroic girl!

She had seen the danger to Dick if the knife lay in the power of the bushranger.

She it was who, lithe and agile as an Indian maiden, glided in between him and the weapon at the moment when his fingers touched it.

Her arm it was that thrust him back, her hand that grasped the blood-imbued steel, and plucked it from the grasp of the cursing assassin.

Her low cry it was that Dick heard as proudly and defiantly she faced the angered villains.

Their murderous eyes gleamed savagely at her as he bounded to her and put out his powerful arm to crush out her life.

Dick, hurrying to the rescue, stumbled over the prostrate body of the dead man, and was thus out of the way of aiding Mynna.

It lay between the ruffian and herself.

But she was true to her nature.

Undaunted by his look of savage hate. Unfaltering when her fingers tightened on the weapon that trickled its gore drops on to her dress.

Unflinching when the next moment seemed to threaten her death.

Brave and steady she met the fellow's rush: her little arm was thrust out with the deadly knife.

Headlong in his own fury he came full upon it.

It checked him with a sudden stop, as the broad point cut through his flesh.

He gripped the arm of his slayer with the involuntary instinct of death agony.

A ghastly pallor came to his face.

His limbs shook.

Still the young girl never moved.

After that first measured lunge she held herself perfectly motionless.

Her eyes flashing.

Her features flushed.

Her bosom panting.

Her arms extended.

The knife, red and reeking, in her opposer's breast.

A hollow groan escaped his lips. He gazed into her face with the look of a demon.

An instant, and all the deadly passions of his nature seemed concentrated in one fell effort for her destruction.

Then his looks relaxed in their fury.

His limbs failed.

A film came to his glazing eyes.

A sigh of wild agony came from her lips.

The wind came rushing with his heart's blood from the gaping wound.

Then, with a swift collapse, he dropped to the earth.

Never a move came from her limbs after he fell.

Never a sound.

Not one twitch of pain or convulsion.

He lay as still as if he had been dead for hours.

And Mynna stood, Judith-like, bending over him.

Then another form glided to her side. Dick stood beside her.

He passed his arms round her frame.

She was trembling from head to foot. Her little fingers were tight upon the knife.

And her gaze was fixed upon the face of the dead man.

She shivered when Dick took the knife from her hand, and fell sobbing on his breast.

CHAPTER XCIV.

RALPH WARNER CONCOCTS FRESH VILLANY.

BAFFLED for a time in his designs against Mary, Ralph Warner, now recovered from the deserved punishment he had received, and failing in finding out where Mary was, turned his attention towards getting in his power some new victim.

About this time he received a letter from his father, requiring his presence; and thinking this a good opportunity of getting into the old Squire's favour, so that no *contretemps* might shut him out from the good gentleman's will, he determined on complying.

There was another reason.

There lived at the village a young girl named Jenny Wade, whom he had long marked out for his victim, and whom he now resolved to make his own.

So he went down to the house of his father.

Mr. Warner was scarcely altered; he looked a little older, but that was all.

He welcomed his son gladly, and was quite overcome with joy to see the attention which the base hypocrite affected in his conduct.

The restraint which Ralph was obliged to put on himself, in order to keep up the favourable impression which he had made was extremely annoying; but it was at length removed by the old gentleman himself, who, fearful that their monotonous life might weary his son, proposed, that as the shooting season had commenced, he should take his gun and try if the famous county still deserved its long-established reputation for game and moor-fowl.

Ralph needed no pressing to such a tempting proposition, and started next morning by rise of sun.

Returning after a good day's sport, he passed the cottage of John Wade, the wood-ranger, whose lovely daughter attracted his attention, as she sat within the porch plying her needle, and humming a rustic ballad.

In sooth it was a pretty picture.

Jenny Wade was little more than sixteen; but, though a child in years, she was exquisitely lovely.

Her sylph-like figure, which the simplicity of her attire set off to the utmost advantage, accorded perfectly with the character of her sweet, ingenuous countenance.

Her soft blue eyes, shaded by long dark lashes, shone with the bright pure imaginings of her innocent mind; her fair hair, unconfined by band or comb, curled in natural ringlets; while her delicately-chiselled mouth and ruby lips encased small, pearly teeth, the whitest and best formed in the world.

She was Nature's fairest child; and as she sat on her rustic seat, embowered in the woodbine and jasmine that wound their graceful tendrils round the quaint porch of the cottage, she looked like some fairy that had paid earth a visit to make man dissatisfied with his own dull sphere, and lure him to weal or woe wherever she might lead.

So, at least, thought Ralph, as he stood transfixed with wonder and delight, contemplating her surpassing beauty.

"Can it be possible," he thought, "that this fair creature is Jenny Wade—the same with whom I used to play when a child; and who, two years ago, though then pretty, gave no promise of such heavenly beauty? She must be mine. No clownish arms shall encircle that perfect form—no vulgar lips shall taste that sweet mouth—not, at least, until I have gathered the first fruits."

And he entered the garden.

Ralph advanced towards the unconscious girl, who had not yet perceived him.

As he approached she raised her head, and immediately rose to welcome him; for, though she remembered him not, she knew at once that he could be no one else than the young Squire.

With a winning smile that he knew well how to assume, the libertine, in the gentlest accents, inquired for John Wade, saying that he could not pass the cottage without calling to see him.

Jenny answered that her father was from home; and Ralph, pleading fatigue, requested permission to rest himself on the rustic bench.

Half-pleased, half-frightened at such unlooked-for condescension, Jenny fetched some home-brewed cider and a home-baked cake, which she placed on a small table before her unexpected guest.

While partaking of the refreshment, which his long ride rendered not a little acceptable, he entered into conversation with his fair entertainer.

Jenny had her weak points—she was ambitious, and she was also a most enthusiastic admirer of personal beauty.

Ralph appeared intuitively to comprehend these traits in her character, and proceeded forthwith to avail himself of his penetration.

He saw at once that though she was pleased at his notice, yet that her pleasure sprang chiefly from the knowledge of who he was, and that a stranger, or one less favoured in point of personal advantages, would have failed in so readily winning her attention and good opinion.

He saw that, lovely as she was, she was not vain; and he thus felt that flattery—that is, direct flattery—would excite her suspicion and distrust.

He felt, also, that his handsome person, his faultless figure, his commanding air, and his aristocratic descent, spoke volumes in his favour; and that if to their influence he added the insinuating tones of his musical voice, and the courteousness of a condescension more implied than expressed, he would bind a coil round the poor country maiden from which she could hardly escape.

This evening, therefore, he contented himself with admiring her flowers, praising the order of her garden, and talking of her father and his father's gentle sister, of whom Jenny spoke in raptures, she having been often permitted to visit at the manse as a sort of humble companion to that lady.

"I was not aware, sweet Jenny," said Ralph, "that you knew my dear aunt, as I always called her—that is, not so well as it appears you did."

"Oh, yes," answered the young girl; "your aunt was so kind as to send for me frequently, and I have much to thank her for. She taught me almost all I know, and when she was taken ill I thought myself too happy in being permitted to attend her."

"Well, I am sure it would," rejoined the artful profligate, "have been a great relief to my mind had I known she had so kind—so gentle—a nurse; and you must not be surprised, my dear friend—for such permit me to call you—if I sometimes come to see one to whom I owe so much."

Jenny, overpowered by these kind words and the gentleness with which they were spoken, could not reply; and the arch-hypocrite, respectfully kissing her hand, departed.

On reaching home Ralph found his father already in the dining-room, and accounted for his late return by mentioning his visit to the wood-ranger's cottage, but of his long *tete-a-tete* with Jenny he said nothing.

He was much chagrined to learn that he had so great a difficulty to contend against as the watchfulness and jealousy of an accepted lover; but he had no doubt of ultimate success, as, resolved not to be foiled, he pursued his plans with a steadiness and zeal worthy a better cause.

Not a day was allowed to pass without a visit to the cottage; and yet his manners were so easy, and his attentions so respectful and natural, that the most jealous eye could have detected nothing to censure.

Then he was careful to time his visits to Jenny, so that he never encountered her lover, and but seldom the father of the devoted girl; while to the latter his behaviour was so guarded, that he had insinuated himself deeply in her thoughts before she was aware that she had forgotten the impassable gulf that existed between them.

He sent her books, selected so judiciously, that, while they contained nothing positively offensive to delicacy, they yet left on the mind an impression; and by these and other crafty methods the wily destroyer made his way to the inducing of her mind to him.

One day as they sat side by side on the rustic bench, Ralph, emboldened by her silence, ventured to look up, and, taking her hand, drew her to a seat beside him; then, in his own low, soft tones, that fell like sweetest music on her charmed ear, he told her his tale of love.

He painted in such vivid colours the sufferings he had already endured—the wreck he should be if he lost her, and the happiness they should enjoy if united; at the same time artfully referring to her own elevated position as his wife, that, inflated by the dazzling prospects, his importunities at length won her to relinquish her humble lover, and accept himself instead.

Determined to bring the affair to a close, especially as the new house was almost finished, he at every succeeding visit pressed Jenny to consent to an elopement, assigning as a reason the impossibility of obtaining his father's sanction to their marriage; but representing to her that if they went to London, they could there be immediately united; and that when the deed was done past recal, his father would be easily induced to forgive them.

Her scruples at leaving her father were much more difficult to remove than he had anticipated; but he was gradually overcoming them, when one evening, as she sat in the little parlour listening to his dangerous pleadings, to which she was on the point of yielding, the garden-gate opened, and her village lover, pale and breathless, rushed up the path towards the cottage porch.

The guilty libertine sprang from the room, and hastened away by the back entrance, while Jenny with difficulty recovered presence of mind sufficient to face her much-wronged lover.

The agitation of the deluded girl passed unobserved by her admirer, who, leading her back into the room, informed her that a rumour which he had heard respecting herself and the Squire's son had brought him there in such agitation.

What could the young girl say?

Her guilty mind was abashed; but her lover, mistaking the cause of her silence, believed that he had offended her, and earnestly entreated forgiveness for what he had said.

Poor Jenny! she was on the point then of disclosing all, and in tears imploring *his* forgiveness; but pride, and the feelings with which Ralph had inspired her, kept back the confession; and some time after, when he left her, her thoughts were faithlessly wandering to the oily-tongued flatterer, whose libertine attentions were rapidly overcoming her virtue.

He came again that evening; her father was out, and the young damsel, won from her prudence by his crafty blandishments, forgot her respect for herself in his embrace, when he strained her to his breast, and vowed that she should be his only for ever.

At first, indeed, when his persuasions passed the limits of modesty, she resisted and struggled against the temptation; but his masked deceit, his hypocritical show of tenderness at last prevailed, and before the night had come on she was indeed *his* eternally.

Exultant over his conquest, the reprobate libertine soothed her remorseful regrets, and departed, leaving her still beguiled by his oily flatteries.

He came again and again; in secret she met him —in secret she wandered out with him in the woods; yielding herself to his persuasive entreaties, and learning to love him more deeply with each day that passed.

For a time she was confirmed in her trust in him, but gradually, when the charm of her sacrifice wore away, and he began to tire of her, his manners altered, until at length he threw off the mask, and left her, with a satanic sneer upon his lips, and his laugh of triumph ringing in her ears.

That night, when the moon was high in the heavens, a deed was committed that added a fresh crime to his already burdened soul.

Poor Jenny Wade, deceived, dishonoured, and deserted, grew rash in her thoughts, and gave herself to the waters of the stream that flowed near her father's cottage.

They found her in the morning pale, placid, and beautiful; none suspected, when they gazed on her sad face, how she had been foully wronged; none thought that the tabernacle which looked so pure had been sullied by a villain's infamy.

Yet they marvelled why she should have given herself to that cruel death.

They carried her to the home she had left so desolate, and left her for her broken-hearted father and her distracted lover to mourn over.

It might have been thought that the miscreant who had been the cause of this young girl's early death would have experienced some remorse for her fate, but he took no heed of the tragic deed—in fact, proving himself so heartless, that while they were laying her in the grave his evil mind was watching how he might lure to infamy with him other victims on whom he had set his libertine eyes.

These were two sisters—each young and beautiful —and so much resembling each other that at first sight it was difficult to determine one from the other.

They were twins, were equally kind and affectionate in their disposition—trusting, and untaught in the world's wickedness.

To them the world appeared what they dreamed it, and thus, in their unconscious innocence, they were ready victims for a designing profligate of the stamp of that villain who had resolved upon not the destruction of one, but of both.

Minnie and Ruth, the twin daughters of Sir Arden Blakely, had at this period just completed their eighteenth year.

It was on the occasion of their coming out that Ralph first beheld them; and as he gazed with admiration on their lovely and innocent countenances, his impure spirit felt a more villanous impulse.

Determined to become known to these girls, he lost no time in obtaining an introduction to Sir Arden, who courteously invited him to his house where the handsome person and fascinating manners of the accomplished libertine insured him a welcome reception, and he became, as we have seen, a constant visitor.

Cold-blooded, deliberate destroyer of innocence! What misery does the companionship of such a man bring to the hearts and homes of the unsuspecting!

Before his introduction to the family circle, Mr. Calcroft, a man of high honour and worth, had been paying very marked attention to Minnie.

In the judgment of her parents there appeared but one objection to his addresses: Mr. Calcroft being thirty-two years of age, they feared the disparity was too great.

Minnie had never shown any predilection in the suitor's favour, and her intimacy with Ralph soon decided the matter; for though the attentions of the latter were paid equally to the sisters in society, he found abundant opportunities of privately convincing Minnie that she was the sole object of his affection.

As soon as he found he had made the impression he wished on the unsuspecting girl, he commenced a course of treachery and duplicity.

He vowed that without her life would be valueless to him; but that his father, on whom he was entirely dependent, having compelled him to engage himself to a rich old maid, his interest and honour called for the concealment of their mutual attachment.

He begged her to rely on his love and management to break the hateful engagement into which he had been forced, and the burthen of which he never felt till admitted into her dear society.

"I am convinced," he would often say, "that if once we were married my father would soon become reconciled to my beautiful wife. But we must be wary—we must be prudent; so, dearest, prove your confidence in me by permitting the attentions of Mr. Calcroft, in order to divert from us the observations of those around us, and leave me to clear our path of the only obstacle that stands between us and happiness."

In an evil hour the misguided girl consented to participate in his duplicity, and thus paved the way for her ruin and unending misery.

Short is the path from virtue to vice!

It is the first step from rectitude that betrays us—that taken, we follow the downward steep with comparatively little hesitation or compunction.

It was so with her, like poor Jenny, caught in the toils, she never realised her hazard till the fatal moment came, when she yielded herself to the cursed arts of her seducer.

Having succeeded in ruining this innocent girl, Ralph turned his attentions to her sister, whom his carnal mind also resolved to make his prey.

Meanwhile, in compliance with the wishes of Ralph, Minnie did not repulse the respectful attention of Mr. Calcroft, though her natural delicacy made her shrink from encouraging them.

The compact into which she had entered with her deceiver forbade her seeking the sympathy of her sister, from whom she had hitherto never concealed a thought.

She was thus thrown completely into the power of her artful destroyer.

One evening feeling particularly depressed, Ralph having departed for the country the day before, she declined accompanying her mother and father out, glad of a quiet hour for sober thought.

After their departure, she seated herself in the drawing-room, and was soon lost in mournful retrospection; suddenly the door opened, and unannounced, her lover entered the room.

Joy at his unexpected appearance superseded the surprise she felt at his return, and when he came, and sitting beside her, passed his arms round her waist, and drew her lips to his, she passively gave herself to the embrace his solicitations mutely desired.

While she was thus suffering him to clasp her fair form to his breast, the door was suddenly burst open, and Gilbert, the rustic lover of poor Jenny Wade, rushed into the room.

He heeded not the disordered confusion of Jenny, who with a scream of fear and shame, leapt from her seducer's guilty arms, and stood ashamed and colouring, wishing almost that the earth would open to swallow her—sprang towards Ralph, whom he clutched desperately by the throat, and dragged to the middle of the room.

There was a look of deadly fury in his face that warned the villain that he was in danger, and he tried in vain to break away.

But the other's grip was like an iron bond, and, with the deep ferocity of a roused panther, he tightened his iron grip.

"Devil," he hissed through his teeth, "I have you now, your heart's black blood shall pay the penalty, and by all most sacred and terrible, the poor lost girl you so foully betrayed shall be avenged."

There was no mistaking his deadly purpose; all the time he was speaking his strong hand, clutched on the seducer's throat, was tightening almost to the point of strangulation.

Ralph tried again to burst away, but he tried in vain. All the outraged feelings of the other's soul were concentrated into the fearful grip he held on the libertine's throat, and, with choking voice and starting eyes, Ralph Warner struggled and fought madly for his life.

"Help," he gasped, "oh! help, I shall be murdered!"

Gilbert smiled grimly.

In the savage exultation of his revengeful power, it gladdened him to see the man who had robbed him of his lover writhing in agony.

There was no help near.

The girl, abashed and terror-stricken, had retired in confusion. No one was near to hear her loud cries. She feared to go again into the room, and so the libertine and the avenger were alone.

The strong hand upon his throat still held and crushed the soft, delicate flesh. He felt the life breath struggling vainly to escape, with a sense of suffocating pain that became insupportable. His starting eyes, and his face with all the blood forced into a black tide, that dyed it through like the dark flood at his heart, would have brought a thought of mercy to a heart less wronged and less revengeful.

But Gilbert had no mercy—no remorse—no mercy for the man who had blighted the joy of his life, and sent to death in shame an innocent girl—innocent and pure till she met the base destroyer, and was lured by his devilish tongue to disgrace.

Sullied in mind, polluted in body, she had died, wept and mourned by her early lover, whose heart had never ceased to cherish her in tenderness: he had known her in her purity and beauty—known her ere dishonour set its blistering mark on her brow—known her when she loved him alone.

And now he stood face to face with her destroyer—face to face with the man who had marred the prose of her young life—broken her truth—her innocence—her heart—and withered out the happiness of his.

No mercy then for Ralph.

No mercy for the deeply-dyed man of blood and crime—nothing left but to have revenge.

Revenge—

Life—blood.

That was the revenge.

Such revenge was most satisfactory to the feelings of the man who now sought it, and laughed to have it in his power.

"Let go!" gasped Ralph, again; "I am dying!"

The hard, grim smile again lit the features of the other.

"Not before your time," he said, with quiet determination. "You have lived long enough—done too much of evil in a career as brief as villainous—devil!"

He took one hand from Warner's throat, and struck him heavily on the face.

Ralph fell.

The heavy blow had cut his white skin, and the blood oozed out slowly.

He lay prone upon the floor on his back, his arms extended and his face upturned, his swollen, distorted form growing white again, as the blood ebbed back—growing red and gory as the blood trickled down.

"He is not yet dead, I hope," said Gilbert, as he gazed upon the prostrate form, "not killed so suddenly, I hope; I have not told him half I had to say."

Another dark look he gave at the fallen man; then, taking a jug of water, dashed it over his face.

It brought no sign of life.

He knelt and placed his hand upon his heart.

It beat.

Very faintly—yet there was still life within.

"Not dead," said Gilbert, "not dead—so, mark this; had I the power to give him the tortures of a hundred deaths, he should know them all."

He paused and regarded the still senseless libertine, then muttered again—

"Poor lost Jenny, you shall be well avenged; the base, ruthless destroyer who now lies so helpless at her foot shall do full expiation for his coward, brutal wrong, fair and sweet flower as thou wert, so bruised, so stricken, and so withered, blighted by his scorching breath, stricken by his polluting touch. Let your destruction and death be the last crime with which his bloody soul shall be charged—no other shall he live to strike—no other shall he live to wrong."

He dashed more water in Ralph Warner's face, then stood back and waited the result.

Not in mercy did he this, only as the ministers of the ancient inquisitions took their senseless victims from the rack that they might live to undergo greater tortures.

Warner breathed, and a faint groan broke from his lips.

Gilbert smiled.

A hard, grim smile—it was full of bitters and hate, and more bitter exultation as he watched the man his strong arm had stricken to the dust.

Warner's chest heaved slow and heavily as he still lay panting beneath the gaze of his deadly foe; consciousness coming dimly back awoke him to a dreamy sense of danger which he did not realise until his glance fell again upon the features of his deadly foe.

Then he knew what had come to pass.

In the very moment when he might have succeeded in his lawless design he had been seized and stricken down by the man he had wronged.

That man stood before him now, waiting with savage patience to see him rise, only that, after torturing his heart by torturing words, he might strike him down again.

To death this time.

No endeavours to bring him back to life after Gilbert had sated his vengeance, by reverting first to his crimes, then dealing deadly punishment.

The libertine slowly raised his head, half in fear lest another blow should strike it back again; his heart quaking with inward terror lest the penalty of his misdeeds should be inflicted then.

But it was not so.

The other stood with folded arms, regarding him in silence, until rising from the floor and cowering back as he rose Ralph Warner stood up over him.

Then Gilbert spoke.

"We have met," he said, his deep, strong voice quivering with concentrated passion; "we have met at last; and now we will say what is to be said, and do what is to be done."

Ralph shuddered.

Too well did he know what the words implied.

"Mercy!" he gasped again; "mercy!"

Gilbert laughed.

"Mercy!" he repeated.

Then laughed again.

He was not savage by nature.

There was nothing in his heart but what was true and honest; yet so wrung and stricken had he been by the villain before him that he could look without remorse upon a deed of blood.

Ralph saw it in the deadly gloom of his dark eye.

So weak the villain was, so cowed by the blow he had received, that now, though he stood in such deadly peril, he could not battle in his own behalf.

This Gilbert saw, and the dark smile deepened on his lip.

It was retribution, stern and just—revenge, true and well deserved.

Warner shuddered inwardly as he looked at him.

What an end to his career of lawless pleasure—his profligacy, and pleasant vice!

To die!

Swift and sudden, and, to all, a sudden breaking from the earth with all its beauty—a sundering from the pleasures he had drowned, and whose consummation was so near.

To perish—strangled, perhaps!

Perhaps stabbed through and through by some murderous weapon that, perchance, the other's coat concealed.

To die then, perhaps. Some few minutes hence he who was so full of life, whose face was so handsome, form so symmetrical; he whose tongue had the power to charm with such destructiveness; whose heart had all the will to dare, and was so ruthless that he recked not for the misery his lawlessness might bring; he, the handsome, accomplished scoundrel, who had hitherto been so successful in all things of crime, libertinism, murder—he would, perchance, die there a few minutes hence, a quivering, dabbled corse, bloody, stark, and limp, with the death sweat upon his brow, and the death agony strong in his distorted face.

Horrible to contemplate.

Horrible to be in such peril.

Horrible to be alone with a man, whose look of ferocity showed that he could do all that; and, more horrible still, that he had not sufficient left of strength to fight against a fate so appalling.

He stood back, cowering almost to the wall, staggering round and away from the other, who, now for the first time since Ralph had risen, moved from his still motionless position.

Away he moved, putting up his hand and wrenching his wrist aside in a futile attempt to guard it from the iron grasp that was again coming upon it.

But all to no purpose.

The strong hand forced his down like reeds, and the steel-like fingers renewed their grasp.

Ralph tried to shriek.

Still purposeless.

His throat was being impressed more tightly, and the sense of suffocation was coming back when Gilbert said, again—

"Not yet?"

"Not yet."

Ralph repeated the words mentally.

Were they words of hope? or were they words of doom?

Did they mean that the merciless revenge was but prolonging his life to end it in greater agony.

Or was his intention but to torture him with words and violence?

"Then let him live."

They were in jest, perhaps.

In that thought there was hope, and Ralph did not struggle again.

"Do not strangle me!" he said, imploringly; "spare my life!"

Again the ferocious glitter of the eyes, and the smile that gave no hope of mercy.

That was his only reply.

"Let me live," he said again; "I will be a better man."

"You could not be a worse one."

"Let me live!"

The other ground his teeth.

"Ask me to take my foot from off the poisonous head of a serpent, whose sting rankles me."

He struck his breast, then went on again—

"Ask me to take my hand from the throat of a rabid dog, whose vicious bite is agonising death!—you might as well, as to ask me to let you live now, when for her, who but for me, you would have made a wanton. We are alone!"

He shook the libertine like a reed in his grasp, and cry after cry of terror came from Ralph Warner.

Each cry, as it was given echoed on the frail heart of her who loved the scoundrel in spite of all.

At first she had fled—prompted so to do by shame—but the recollection of the danger in which she had left him—the thought of the hand that gripped his neck in a grasp that threatened death —overcame her sense of shame, and she returned to see them as they stood now.

Gilbert did not see her, or his look of utter despondency might have touched his heart; as it was he only saw the betrayer of loving woman.

There was quite enough in that to blind his sense to all else, and he spoke once again ere he proceeded to the last act of the terrible drama he had arranged.

"Listen," he said, "and listen well, for it is the last time a human voice will ever fall upon your ear. You have lived through a life of sin—crime the blackest—deeds the most devilish. To all that you have done there could not have come a darker culmination than that in which, with deliberate ruthlessness, you plotted against the innocence of Jenny Wade. I can well understand your cold-blooded, brutal lasciviousness of nature. You saw her as she was—full of all the lithe grace and supple charms of early womanhood's beautiful dawn; she was innocent, and guileless, gentle, and trusting as a child, and—God help me and her—loved me; that, too, you saw; and bloodless scoundrel as you are—imbued with the callous hatred and contempt that is borne by the aristocrat against his humbler brother, you thought it no wrong to breathe your subtle eloquence into her ear—and broke her heart—dead to me. She listened, poor girl—believed you; for whom, not knowing your scoundrel's soul, would think you the thing you are! She listened—believed you—trusted—and fell. Her unsophisticated nature was not strong enough to withstand the infernal wiles of a practised seducer. She was yours—a toy—a thing of wanton shame—polluted, sullied—the beauty of her life destroyed, and her reputation withered. Yet she was beautiful, even while tainted with dishonour; and until every sense was sated and your passion palled, you made her happy by delusive promises. But at last you tired of them—threw the mask full off, and let her go whither the storm of life might let her. She had then lost all—her own self-respect—destroyed an honest heart—mine, to which, had you not stepped between, she would have been clasped in pride and love. There was no hope for her on earth—nothing in the future but misery and degredation. Even you, to whom she clung to in spite of all, turned from her and left her desolate. Then, seeing what a lost thing of shame and guilt she had become—she died."

He paused.

A tear gathered in his eye, but he checked it back, and a lurid light seemed to dry it away; his broad chest heaved, and fell with heavy pain; but he stifled it all back, and continued, while Ralph stood, held dumb with terror, and the girl stood breathless, scarce giving credence to the evidence of her own senses.

"You heeded not that: it was not much to you that her life went out in misery, or that I, her betrothed husband,—her lover—was kept a dreary mourner for the lost one. She was only another victim added to the list of many; there was nothing in the fact of her death to give one thrill of remorse to your black soul. She died, and was out of the way—taken by her own act from your path —and so you have no need of further trouble on her account. But I, when I stood by the brink of the village stream, by the side of which we have so oft sat together and listened to the music of the waters, never dreaming that our love would be so shattered —I, when I took her poor, pale form in my own, and laid her on the mossy sward—registered a deep and fearful vow that I would have revenge. I swore it beneath the solemn sky while the stars twinkled down on her sweet, fair form, hushed plaintively into the deep repose of death—I swore it while pushing back the damp tresses from her pallid brow—and I swore it while kissing the pale lips as pallid and as cold. The oath was borne to Heaven on the evening wind that wafted her stricken spirit to the stars, and an oath so sworn must be fulfilled. Now take your last look on earth, for your time has come. You are to die! There is no help near—no second villain's hand to aid you—no pitying aid above to listen to your prayer for mercy. Your time has come. You struggle, but you might as well try to break from the angry grasp of a lion! There is in my heart a spirit of retribution that prompts me to this deed. You cry for mercy, but it is too late; and thus—thus do I avenge the misery and death of Jenny Wade."

Slowly and remorselessly he raised the shrinking, panting wretch in his strong arms, and bore him to the open window. It was a fearful depth to look upon—more fearful to descend; but Gilbert recked not that. The cowering, trembling form rose high in air, and as the girl behind, overcome with terror, fell senseless to the floor, Warner gave a loud shriek, and Gilbert hurled him down.

Down, down he went—the avenger watching his descent with a calm smile of vengeful satisfaction—watching him till his head struck the hard ground with crushing force, and he lay as he had thought, limp, quivering, and bloody — crushed almost dead, and writhing in agony.

CHAPTER XCV.

HOW DICK AND MYNNA PASSED THE NIGHT.

NIGHT had come on.

Night that had been heralded by such deeds of blood.

The two adventurers whom fate had destined to meet under such thrilling circumstances gazed upon the scene.

The sunlight had died away.

The blackness of night lay upon the earth.

They turned their gaze upon the spot where, prone in death, the two bushrangers lay.

Powerful, full-bodied men they had been; men of strength and sinew; men of energy and violence.

They had gone through a career of crime; many an innocent victim's last hour had they gloated over.

Now they lay still and stark—food for worms.

Mynna was recovering now from the shock to her system; she leaned for support on Dick's breast, and nestled her face to his shoulder.

"Come,' Dick said, "you are trembling, Mynna; are you unstrung by the death of these wretches?"

"I was tempted for your sake," Myna replied.

Dick drew her closer to him.

"You have saved me from death."

Mynna looked fervently in his face.

"I would have died to have seen you safe."

"I know it," Dick answered; "you are a brave, beautiful girl, and a true woman."

He raised her head, and kissed her as he would have kissed a sister.

"You do not think harshly of me, then?"

"Harshly, Mynna!"

"My hands are stained in blood."

"She died in my defence, Mynna, and so cease."

"It is in our profession to be concerned in deeds of death."

"It is unavoidable," Dick replied, gallantly, "but come, we must not stay here; night has come already, and we know of no shelter here."

Mynna's eyes beamed fervently.

"I should not fear the night," she said, "if you were with me."

This was a delicate hint; but Dick did not take it.

"You would suffer from the damp air," he remarked.

"I am accustomed to it," she said, proudly. "I have been forced to make the earth my bed, and the night dew my mantle, very often when I have been bondaged to those savages. Think you, then, I should shrink from sharing such a couch with you?"

Dick gazed into her face as she spoke: her words were bold, but when he looked on her features he saw that their expression was one of ingenuous confidence.

She seemed to regard him as one whom she could trust, and Dick, after a little wondering, had convinced himself that there was no chance while the night lasted of discovering a way to any settlement.

Under such circumstances there was nothing left for them to do but to make the best of their position.

Dick, whose scruples against sleeping by the side of a young and pretty girl were fast disappearing, set about finding out a nook where they could make a snug resting place for the night.

While he was purposing this, Mynna stood apart wistfully gazing at the rising stars of night.

When he had made a couch of leaves and moss he returned, and with more gallantry than might have been expected fom him led her to the spot.

"I have done all I can," he said. "Let me wish you good night."

"Good night," she said, inquiringly. "Are you going?"

"Should I stay?" Dick asked.

"Ah! have I cause to fear you will misconstrue my words?"

"I shall not, Mynna."

"Then let me be near you this night. I have no dread of you, if you have none of me, except that I love you beyond all judgment."

This was more than only half murmured, and when she had concluded Dick had led her gently to the primitive couch.

There was no sin in their hearts. In innocence and truthfulness Mynna lay down in the protection of Dick, and he, keeping a little distance between them, gave himself to sleep.

He dropped off suddenly, fatigued by the incidents of a day. He was eager for sleep, and the quick manner in which he sank into slumber proved that no eager feeling of love were swaying his passions.

Was it so with Mynna?

No.

Her eyes did not close immediately in sleep.

A long while she lay with her eyes open, her

gaze fixed intently on the honest countenance of the sleeper beside her.

She could see that he had suffered in the calm of his sleep, for a sadness spread over his features, and his lips were pressed together.

Long after his breathing sounded regularly did she remain passive as a babe.

But after a while, when it seemed that he was fast in slumber, she approached her face to his, and let her lips meet his in a stolen, fervent kiss.

Then the little arms stole round his broad form, and closer she drew herself, till lying in this pure embrace a sweet expression of satisfaction settled on her face, and she too dropped from her wakefulness.

Perhaps she had slept two hours when she was disturbed.

She knew not what had occurred to awaken her but an indefinable feeling of alarm held her in its thrall.

She looked towards her companion.

He still slept.

She listened.

All was still.

No sound of stealthy tread.

No rustle of a leaf.

And yet there thrilled through her heart a subtle sense of danger that caused her to strain every faculty to discover if there was anything near them inimical to their safety.

She glanced at Dick; his face was placid and serene.

Whatever it was that had disturbed her appeared to exercise no influence over him.

No. 30.

She looked up, but without stirring.

She was too well trained in the arts of back-wood life to so betray herself.

The moon was gleaming coldly down.

Its pale light streamed from the sky and over the dim landscape.

Cautiously she turned her gaze, but saw nothing to justify her fears.

Still, though fancying her fears had been caused by her arousing from a deep sleep, she resolved to lie awake, for fear of prowling evil.

This resolution held good for a time—but for a time only.

Imperceptibly a drowsiness overcame her, and she sank again into dream-land.

She was in that half-unconscious state, between sleeping and waking, when she fancied something passed over like a sheet of mist, and then she fancied she was gazing on some dark form that had taken the place of Dick.

Without moving a limb she thoroughly aroused herself, and wildly opened her eyes to see a spectacle that called all the energies of her mind and body into existence, and almost caused a shriek of horror to burst from her lips.

There was a form there beside Dick.

It was one of the aboriginals of the previous day's skirmish.

He was bending over Dick, with a glittering knife in his hand.

The first effect of this vision was to hold Mynna paralysed: the next to make her spring swiftly from the ground and encompass with her small white arms the savage who was in the act of thrusting his knife into Dick's body.

The surprise of the savage at being arrested in that very delightful process was as great as Dick's was when, on opening his eyes at that moment, he obtained a view of the scene.

He did not remain long to consider how matters stood, but at once stood erect and ready for his foe.

But the aboriginal, with a quick glide, slipped from Mynna's grasp, and fled into the darkness.

"Mynna," Dick said, "again you have saved my life."

"You have had a near escape," she replied tenderly.

"I had. The scoundrel would have butchered me. But how came he here?"

"They seek me."

"Do they?"

"Their vengeance will never be appeased till they have slain us both."

"They shall not slay you while I live."

"Hush!" said the young girl, "more foes come."

Dick stepped back with the speaker as the dry click of a snapping twig reached his ear.

"It is so," he muttered; "we are being surrounded, and I have no means of defence. If I had only a rifle here," Dick mused.

"Your own! what became of it?" asked Mynna.

"The rangers carried it with them," replied Dick moodily. "We are beset, and have not a chance of defending ourselves."

As Dick spoke the dusky form of one of the savages appeared amongst some stunted copswood a little to their right: he was creeping stealthily along, and they could see that he carried a rifle.

He was on his belly on the ground, and his rifle was underneath him.

Now arose a chance of defending themselves if this man came alone, as was probable, the nature of the aborigines leading them to undertake such expeditions where glory might accrue.

Dick gave Mynna a warning glance, and, pretending to look in a totally different direction to that in which the savage was creeping, he drew his knife—the knife that had already been so well whetted with the blood of his assailants.

The Australian was now within six yards of them; his left hand held the barrel of his rifle, his right clasped the hilt of a powerful knife, on which the moonlight flashed now and then as he came nearer and nearer.

His vicious-looking eyes could be seen in their malignity glaring upon the pair whom, one after the other, it was his intention to sacrifice.

Dick let him get a little nearer.

Mynna, fixing her dark eyes elsewhere, began to fear for the result.

All of a sudden, the savage having measured his distance, made a bound from the earth, and leapt to where Dick stood.

This was exactly what Dick wanted.

Swift as lightning his arm went out, and his knife buried itself in the breast of the savage.

Without a groan the latter fell, stabbed to the heart.

Mynna no sooner saw him fall than she flew to him and possessed herself of his rifle.

This she handed to Dick.

It was loaded, and would save them from at least one foe.

But Dick was not satisfied with this: he turned the dead savage over, and found, as he expected, a pouch of powder and some bullets of rough manufacture.

Armed with these a brighter look beamed from his eyes, and Mynna nestled to him in fuller confidence.

A mysterious silence succeeded the fate of the scout.

The two adventurers, listening for the coming of their enemies, were at a loss to understand why they were not attacked.

Where they stood was in a secluded hollow, well defended by the natural, cone-like formation at the back, and with a line of brushwood in the front.

This was a security so long as they had ammunition to defend themselves and were not attacked from above.

But they were undecided whether to venture out or remain.

Half an hour passed, and there was no sound of any approaching foe.

Mynna listened breathlessly and in patience.

But Dick began at last to grow tired of waiting.

"We had better quit this seclusion," he remarked. "In facing my foes I don't care how many there are, but I cannot say I admire this slow work."

"We are safe here," was Mynna's answer, "for a time at least. If we move we may expose ourselves to a bullet."

Hardly were the words out of her lips when the sharp crack of a rifle echoed through the place, and a bullet whistled within an inch of Dick's temple.

Mynna drew him quickly aside.

"Said I not that the savages lurked here?" she said; "they are subtle in their warfare, and if there are many our death is as sure as that the dawn of day will come."

Uttering this comfortable speech in an impressive manner, Mynna flashed her dark eyes upon Dick with a look that spoke as plain as words that if they died she would be content to die there with him.

Now dying together is something very heroic and all the rest of it, but it is not always the most pleasant thing to look forward to.

To Dick especially it was far from welcome.

He had only just began to taste the sweets of liberty, and although he was ready for any adventure, and did not shirk danger in any form, still he wanted to get the best of the day, and live after vanquishing his enemies.

That was the real, unromantic truth of it, and it was under this influence that he suffered Mynna to pull him behind a friendly stump, whence, unperceived by the enemy, and secure from their bullets, he might take aim at the first dusky carcase that showed itself.

The young girl pulled him by the sleeve, as he aimed his gun from behind the tree.

"Be careful," she said; "if the moon shines on the barrel, they will know where to fire."

"I will," Dick replied. "They shall have no chance of popping me off until I have had first hit."

"They come stealthily," the young girl answered, "but they will soon be as active as the devil seeds of the arrow tree."

As Dick did not know to what she referred he held his peace. But her remark had some meaning in it.

The remarkable seed to which she alluded grows on a tree called the *yerba de flecha*, or arrow tree.

When placed on the ground, or on a table, it immediately begins to move in all directions, sometimes travelling over considerable space by series of convulsive jerks.

On breaking a leaf or twig of this tree a milky juice exudes, which is used by the aboriginals for poisoning the points of their arrows. The results of a wound from one of these poisoned barbs are fearful. The person wounded is seized with convulsive tremblings, and death ensues in from fifty to sixty minutes.

In a short space of time after death the body becomes swollen like that of a drowned animal, and turns to a livid, bluish-green colour.

The *yerba de flecha* is a tree of moderate height, with leaves resembling those of the laurel; it is common throughout many countries.

So venomous is it that a gentleman, seeing another holding it in his hand, expressed his surprise at the rashness, averring that no money would tempt him even to touch it.

He stated that it was held in the greatest abhorrence and fear by all on account of its deadly properties, and no one acquainted with them would touch the leaf or a seed on any account.

He said the seed was "Diablo le Miraclos," or the miraculous devil.

A more miraculous-looking article was certainly never set eyes on; it is suggestive of spiritualism, odic force, and other abstruse powers.

It is well known that a ball made of the pith of elder may be so charged with electricity, by means of friction, that it will jump about for a considerable time.

The only possible explanation of the extraordinary movements of the miraculous devil seed is, that it is naturally charged with a vast quantity of electric fluid, which keeps it continually in motion.

Now some of the aboriginals had with them arrows poisoned in this very juice, and the point of one inflicting a mere scratch would have been quite enough to have settled Dick's business.

It must not be supposed from what has transpired that the natives were distinguished by an unflinching ferocity. In the present case they wished to avenge their fallen companions. But that they are as capable of using their strength as boldly in a nobler cause the following touching story will prove.

Among various methods of getting gold practised by the gold thieves was the following:—When a very successful miner came down to the diggings, they tracked him from the city in the direction of the place to which he returned, and as surely as he came near the city the next time, so surely was he stopped and never suffered to enter it. The quantity of gold brought down by a family of the name of Rawlinson was so unusually large that one of the gold thieves' friends, to whose knowledge it had come in the way of business, mentioned it to him as something extraordinary, especially as he knew they had arrived from England but a short time. This information was not thrown away upon Norris (such was the fellow's name), and two of the gang were sent after them, not to molest them in any way, for the fact that they had left the city with a train of ten mules raised the presumption that they had discovered a mine of gold, which it might be better worth their while to take possession of than to murder the Englishmen for the sake of what ten mules could carry.

Like bloodhounds plodding along a cold scent the two ruffians slowly followed the Rawlinsons, keeping far behind all day, but approaching very close to them at night. The journey was longer and more wearisome than they had expected, but at last they entered the gorge.

The train of mules was out of sight, and but for the traces they had left, the spies would not have known whether to turn to the right hand or to the left. The pines enabled them to continue their pursuit without much risk of being seen by persons who had spent days without seeing a human being and to whom it never occurred to suspect their presence.

The Rawlinsons had just dined, and were lying under the shade of the trees, talking of friends at home in England, and the surprise and pleasure they would feel at seeing them return so rich. An aboriginal they had with them was smoking a cigar, and watching the countenance of each speaker with the intenseness of a man totally deaf, who tries earnestly to understand the speaker's meaning from the motion of his lips and the expression of his face, while Rawlinson's daughter was wading about in the stream a hundred yards off.

Suddenly they were all startled by hearing the child scream fearfully, and all got up to see what was the matter, and to their utter astonishment they saw her in the midst of a party of men, and struggling with all her little strength to get free.

Geoffrey, one brother, rushed to rescue her without staying to arm himself, and his father and Arthur, the other, ran into their encampment to get their rifles. Geoffrey's strength and impetuosity was such that he easily pushed his way among them, took the little girl in his arms, and after addressing them in a few words, he turned to leave them, when several of the ruffians drew their revolvers and shot him in the back, killing the child at the same time.

Arthur and his father, on seeing the murder of

Geoffrey, fired at his murderers, and had just time to throw down their rifles and snatch up a revolver before the rest of the party were upon them.

There was a fearful struggle, for the Englishmen were strong, and fought with the fury inspired by the sight of Geoffrey's blood, and the feeling that they had themselves no other fate to hope for if they were beaten; but it was hopeless against the number opposed to them.

Arthur was shot to death, and his father, after receiving several wounds, fell to the ground, and was bruised and trampled upon till he was insensible.

The gang of murderers suffered severely, as much, very likely, from each other's shots as from those of their victims, and it took the survivors some time to bind up their wounds, before they could begin to collect and load the mules.

When all this was done, and they were prepared to start, they took the elder Rawlinson—who had in the meantime recovered his senses—and putting a rope loosely round his neck, they drew him up a little way from the ground, and fastening the end of the rope securely to the branch of the tree, they left him hanging there, with his hands tied to his heels, to increase the torment of his position; first raking the embers of the fire beneath him, and throwing on some wood. They were apparently so certain that nothing could save him that they did not even wait to see if the wood took fire. Being full of turpentine when it took fire it blazed furiously, but, from not being exactly beneath him, or from the current of air running along the valley, the body of the flame did not touch him, and he was still further protected by being clothed in flannel. A tongue of flame, as probably everybody knows, is susceptible of being drawn out of a perpendicular line by the presence of a body near it. It was so in this case; but not quite reaching the head, which was inclined towards the opposite shoulder, it kept darting at intervals round the cord by which he was suspended until it sank lower and lower and gradually burnt itself out. The cord, however, had been kindled, and the fire slowly ate its way nearly through, until it became too weak to sustain the sufferer's weight, when it gave way and he fell to the ground, the side of his face lying on the red-hot embers. He was unable to move an inch, and, to add to his sufferings, the cord continued to burn like a fusee, and he had to lie there while the fire crept round his neck like a serpent.

His having to lay there for several hours after the fire had gone out may, while it increased his sufferings, have assisted his recovery, for he simply states that, on being released from his bonds, the aboriginals who found him tied cloths round his head and neck, first laying ashes on the wound in the latter, his face being already thickly coated with them, and nothing else was done that he mentions.

As no mention is made of the aboriginal having been concerned in the fight, it is to be understood that he ran away on the first onset.

It was, perhaps, well that he did, for it may have been owing to his going off to fetch his friends that Rawlinson escaped with his life and lived to assist at the punishment of the murderers of his children.

His recovery was slow, but he did recover, and as soon as he was able to walk he made signs to the aboriginals that he wished to go in search of those who had wounded him.

They understood him with a readiness which showed what their own feelings would have been in such a case, and, giving him his rifle and dividing the rest of the arms among them, they set out.

The father of the murdered girl walked always first, and as though travelling a road with which he was familiar, and subsequent events would seem to prove that he had tracked the ruffians to Norris's house, for it was to that place he directed his companions.

It was a misfortune that Rawlinson could not comprehend their language nor they his, and he was quite staggered when the aboriginals led him up a little hill and pointed to Norris's house, for he could scarcely believe the murderers lived there, and he fancied their intention was to attack the house as a measure of retaliation.

There was only one way of setting his mind at ease, and this was by seeking some of the inhabitants, for he had a perfect recollection of the faces of some of his assailants—and those seen in a life or death encounter are never forgotten.

The aboriginals hid themselves to await his return, as he supposed, and he walked cautiously towards the house and hid himself among the shrubs near the entrance.

First he recognised one of the murderers, then another, and then others, and the first moment he could get away without risk of being seen he made his way back to the aboriginals.

In his impatience he made signs to them to begin the attack at once, but they easily made him understand that they would wait until after sunset.

It was a dark night out of doors, but there was no want of light in the dining-room and billiard-room, where Norris and his associates were enjoying themselves, never thinking of the Nemesis that was so close at hand.

The very precautions they had taken to make the house defensible, viz., by closing every window and opening with iron bars, and having but one way of ingress or egress—the door which opened in the front directly into the billiard-room—made the certainty of their destruction more complete.

The attack of the aboriginals was so sudden and so overpowering that the whole band of murderers were struck down without resistance; the very man with the cue in his hand, preparing to make his stroke, had not time to straighten himself, but sank down upon the table as if smitten by apoplexy.

From the billiard-room the greater part of the aboriginals rushed into the dining-room and continued the butchery; none were spared, not even their fair but abandoned companions.

When all were stretched upon the ground, the aboriginals spread themselves about the house and took possession of everything which excited their admiration. The pillage was soon finished, and at a cry from one of those who kept the door the last straggler left the house.

Two or three then returned and set fire to it in different places, and the entrance was choked up with fagots and likewise set on fire.

The wings being nearly all wood, and desiccated by the hot sun, blazed like paper, and before the aboriginals had retreated a quarter of a mile the whole building appeared one huge flame, and the dead and the living (if there were any) were reduced to ashes together.

Appeased by this vengeance, Rawlinson, rendered melancholy by the fearful loss he had sustained, wandered away, and, as no tidings were heard of him, his friends became anxious, and whilst his brother came into the township to make inquiries, Mr. Parkins and his mate, two old friends, in their solicitude for the missing man, went to look for tracks of him around some deserted shafts on the contiguous reef.

Passing near an old hole, which, like many others, was "caved in" a good deal with the surface drainage and late heavy rains, one of the men had a narrow escape of falling down, through the earth under his foot breaking away.

To prevent others from incurring the same risk, the two men broke down with their heels the rest of the overhanging dirt, which fell to the bottom with a heavy sound.

Almost instantly they heard a faint "cooey" proceeding from an old shaft near where they stood, and hastening to the top of it, they were soon assured that there was a human being below.

Ropes and assistance were procured, and eventually the missing man was brought to the surface, after forty-six hours' confinement in what had well-nigh proved his grave.

Wet, faint, and exhausted, he was borne to his tent, where restoratives were immediately administered.

The account he gave of the occurrence was as follows:—

On his way to his brother's he had occasion to pass by the shaft above-mentioned, the total depth of which was 160 feet, including about ten feet of water.

Walking close by the logs, with his hands in his pockets, he felt the ground give way under his feet, and, before he could attempt to save himself, he slid, with the dirt, underneath the logs, and was precipitated down the shaft.

In an almost miraculous manner he fell feet foremost on to an old stage, about forty feet above the water, and, with the exception of a few scratches, sustained not the slightest injury.

This, of itself, was a most remarkable occurrence, but more remains to be told.

There were old ladders left attached to the sides of the shaft, and one or two old skids, fastened in the usual way, to prevent the buckets striking the sides.

Thinking with these aids he could ascend to the surface the poor fellow made the attempt, and, after various struggles, had the extreme pleasure of finding himself within ten fet of the top.

Here he rested a moment, and then started up the last ladders, congratulating himself, doubtless, on his wonderful escape, when, horrible to relate, the ladder he clung to gave way, and, together with a quantity of earth, fell crashing down the shaft. The stage which had previously caught him, on being again struck with the accumulated weight, gave way, and, in the midst of all this wreck, poor Rawlinson was plunged into the water beneath. Still he instinctively clung to the ladder, and, though stunned, bruised, and his eyes filled with sand and dirt, so that for a time he was quite blind, he managed to extricate himself from the mass of timber, and get his head above water. And now the ladder, late his treacherous foe, became his support and only hope of safety.

Thirsty with pain and excitement he drank heartily of the water in which he was standing (on the ladder) up to his thighs. The water, being contaminated with the decaying carcases of one or two goats, made him very sick and giddy, but, luckily vomiting the rubbish from his stomach, he felt much relief.

And here we have to relate another of the many instances of presence of mind Rawlinson exhibited. He managed to extricate his knife from his pocket, hollowed out from the rock a hole sufficient to catch the clear water dripping from the surface; from this he drank, and to this he probably owes his final safety.

The situation of the poor fellow may be better imagined than described, as he hung on to the ladder two nights and one day, with the earth continually falling from the top; sometimes a piece large enough to kill him grazing his face as it fell, and ever and anon small pieces of rock and stone striking his unprotected head. But a danger almost as great was also perceptible; he felt the water gaining on him.

The falling earth and surface drainage was gradually raising it, and slowly but surely it crept up and up from his thighs to his waist, and it became a question as to whether starvation or drowning would finally deprive him of life. Add to this the plainly audible picks and hammers of the men at work in the roof scarcely a hundred yards from him, and we think a situation more horrible can scarcely be described.

He had cooeyed repeatedly, and was almost in despair, when, on Saturday, the earth falling in a hole near to him attracted his attention, and with all his remaining strength he sang out, and, by the great mercy of Providence, he was heard and rescued.

But if the aboriginals had shown themselves under the control of an Englishman, they were not so now. Dick, peering from his shelter, saw form after form of his dusky foes creeping round.

When he thought the foremost one was near enough he levelled his gun.

The hand of his female companion stayed him.

He followed the direction of her finger, and saw, not ten yards from him, the body of a savage wriggling along the ground, and in the act of preparing for his deadly spring.

As he rose Dick pulled the trigger.

The flash lit up the scene. It showed them the discovered savage falling back, with the red gash riven in his dusky breast.

It showed them their swarming enemies springing to the attack.

Then arose a discord of frightful yells; guns flashed, arrows whizzed through the air, and Dick clubbed his gun to defend himself to the last, as his tawny foes came screeching for vengeance and death.

But in the moment when death seemed so near a lurid flash shot before then, and half their swarthy enemies fell dead.

"Hurrah! rescue!" were the sounds that told Dick he was saved, and he was about to advance to join them when his female companion, catching sight of the face of one, uttered a suppressed shriek, and drew him away, not allowing him to pause till they had left the combatants far behind them.

CHAPTER XCVI.

DICK'S FRESH ADVENTURES—THE EXPLANATION OF HER SINGULAR ACT IS GIVEN.

Dick and Mynna were seated beneath a branching tree on the gentle slope of hill that commanded the extensive plain stretching far and wide beneath them.

The sun was going down, and his slanting rays glancing over the broad plain lighted up the tinted crests of the far-off mountains, and glittered upon the gleaming chain of pools that patched the dry and barren plain with little oases of verdure.

They had travelled far that day, and they were very weary.

Dick had killed a bird of the pheasant kind, which the girl had cooked for him in the primitive but efficient style peculiar to the natives, by covering it over with a soft clay, and then placing it in a hole dug in the ground, and surrounding it with burning wood and peat till the coating became hardened, and when removed left the fowl denuded of its feathers, and cooked to perfection.

Dick had some hard biscuit in his wallet, and they made no despicable repast.

The freshening breeze of the pure, free air, fanned the bronzed cheek of the convict, and the mildness of the evening scene—the unbounded freedom of the far-stretching landscape—the kind and gentle companionship of Mynna—all seemed to inspire his tried and blunted heart with new vigour, peace, and hopefulness.

A year—it was not much to a free man—the all-engrossing employments and adventures of one just liberated from the harsh restraint and degrading monotony of penal captivity—would soon bring round the time when he should be at liberty to return to his native land, to seek out his true girl, his constant and devoted Mary, to earn in the higher and less polluted atmosphere of society a position and a home for her who had borne so much for him, who had been so constant —alas, he knew not all that she had suffered —he did not foresee the long train of dangers and temptations that time, so short to his far-reaching thought, must comprise; but as he sat there—no longer watched by the stern turnkey, no longer under the threat of the soldier's musket, no longer garbed in the livery of a felon and a slave, but free to contemplate the beauteous panorama of Nature, free to breathe the pure air of, and to revel in, the glad light of heaven—free in his own rough way to exchange kind words and sympathies with fellow-man and woman; he could not doubt, he could not despond; the brand was still upon him, he was still, though so unjustly, a stigmatized pariah of society, a punished felon, a *Ticket-of-Leave;* but time might wear off the stamp of his infamy. The support of his clean conscience, his manly fortitude, his indomitable will, his inspiring trust in her he loved so tenderly, the pleasant sympathy of friends whom his own worth would attach to him, and, perhaps, some remembrance of the great and good Being whose grand creations now tuned his soul to such an exalted tone of peace and quietness, for he would wait and hope and work, and Heaven was no respecter of persons. God gave the sweet sunlight, the clear water, the cool shade, the strength of frame, the glow of health, and the charm of beauty, to the poor peasant as well as to the proud aristocrat. As poor Dick thought of all these things, his eye brightened, and he smiled unconsciously.

Mynna, with woman's jealous watchfulness, kept her soft, dark eyes, fixed on the expressive features of our simple, but manly hero.

After a little while she spoke to him.

"Your thoughts seem pleasant ones, if I can read them in your face," she said, softly. "But then," she added, with a slight sigh, "they seem to be roving very, very far away."

"You may say that, lass," replied Dick, with a frank laugh; "but you are not quite right to say my thoughts are over pleasant, for it's hoping against hope like. Woe to the man or the woman that once, either right or wrong, gets a chalk against 'em, and to hear the parson fellows how they preach up about forgiving seventy times seven, and not casting the first stone, and all that sort of thing; there's heaps of honour paid 'em in the way of tabernacles and 'broidered slippers, but devilish little in regard to the heed given to their teaching, I take it. No, for a man or a woman that falls, or, as most likely, is dragged down, it's very hard lines indeed.

"And you—good as you are—have suffered unjustly from oppression or scandal, perhaps?" said the girl, with a look of confidence and sympathy.

"Perhaps yes, perhaps no," replied Dick, gloomily; "but we'll not talk of these things, Mynna, it gives me the blues. We're not far from the block-house, when we've once turned the corner of yon ridge, and as 'tis such a lovely evening we might as well rest a bit longer; and if you will, Mynna, I should be right glad for you to tell me your story. It must be strange to live so many years among such a queer set as those tawny-skinned thieves we found you with."

"It is but a simple story," replied Mynna. "My father was a settler on the Munika river. He farmed many acres of land. He was a man well to do, and generally respected. His only children were myself and a younger brother. My parents had gone to Melbourne upon business, and I and Ernest were left at home in the charge of the overseer. One night, when all was quiet and we had laid down in confidence to sleep, the whole household was startled by a sound like the rustling of leaves. We leaped from our beds and looked from the windows, and perceived that the fold-yard, the stables, the paddock, and the home field, swarmed with a dense crowd of furious natives. Their yells were appalling. They had bundles of lighted furze in their hands, and they hurled their whistling boomerangs and long spears through the windows. A desperate fight ensued. There were not many rifles among the assailants, and our men were hardy fellows—strong and determined; but nothing could withstand the overwhelming force of numbers: the barbarous savages prevailed, after a fierce struggle. Many of the men were killed; others escaped. The overseer was among the missing. Whether he was killed, or wounded and carried off, could never be ascertained. The house was ransacked and fired. My brother Ernest was dragged away, and probably murdered at once. They carried me off, and for nine years I have lived a close prisoner amongst them. Within the last few months, however, I have enjoyed more liberty, as they had long ceased to suspect me, and I was permitted to accompany the king on his excursions against the whites; for I must tell you that I was a queen in the tribe.

"Do you know," she said, suddenly breaking off, "that more than once I think I have seen my father's overseer, who was thought to have been killed: it may not be, but the likeness is very striking. He is called in the tribe by a strange word that cannot be fairly translated. It means one who is neither black nor white, in allusion to his utter want of fealty either to the settlers or to the natives, as he is as ready to sacrifice the one as the other to his own interests. This man is known among the Europeans, I believe, by the name of Lawson. If he be identical with the former manager of my father's farm, he must be a great villain, as I will show you by-and-bye; but look, here comes your friends."

Mounted on strong and well-bred horses, the two rangers, Waller and Barnup, accompanied by a man whom Dick had not before seen, also well-mounted, came galloping up. They hailed our hero cheerily.

"Bravo!" cried Waller. "Just the fellow we want. Why the devil didn't you keep pace with us on the way to the Block. We're out on a ticklish job, but one that's worth looking after. If we have luck it will be as good as a gold find. A resolute chap as you've shown yourself, you'll be worth a Jew's eye. But you have no horse. Why the blazes didn't you keep pace with us?"

The last sentence was uttered with a vehemence of impatience and precipitation that caused a general laugh.

"Don't you see there's a lady in the case?" said Waller, looking from Dick to Mynna, with a quaint smile.

"Well, I ain't agin a fellow being gallant to the ladies, specially to such a charmer as the one present—excuse me for the remark,"—said the rough fellow, with a good-humoured laugh: "only every minute's a half hour in present circumstances. What's to be done, eh?"

The third man rode up. He was a most extraordinary fellow. Over six feet in height, thin as a lath, and quite as upright. His features were cast in a peculiar mould, but their expression was not unpleasing, even though there was a lurking fierceness about the curve of his thin lips, and a depth of determination in his large eyes. He could scarcely be called ugly, though his features were so grotesque: and even if he were, his plainness would be redeemed from repulsion by the beauty of one feature, his dark, lustrous, full eyes.

This worthy rode up, and leaped off his horse, which Dick at once remarked was the finest of the three.

"What's the good of all this palaver? Get up mate. Take this Australian Wenus before you, and ride into the Block as if the devil's sheriffs were after you, and ask the first man you see for 'Silken Jenny,' and tell him the Kangaroo wants her."

Dick laughed heartily at these orders, so queerly expressed, and especially at the appropriate cognomen of the speaker. The other men applauded the expedient. Lightly flinging Mynna into the saddle, Dick, who was a pretty fair rider, leaped up behind her, and, neck-or-nothing, dashed away.

Soon he rode back, bringing with him a beautiful mare, of rich chestnut colour, whose glossy coat had worthily earned her the epithet of "Silken."

"All right," said the Kangaroo, mounting her. "She's much too good for this sarvice. I shall ride her myself, because, mate, if you takes into your head to slope with the t'other, 'taint quite so much matter."

With this reason for his choice, complimentary to Dick, he curvetted with his thorough-bred mettlesome steed some paces in advance. Her garnish, fine eyes looked across the wide plain, and her flanks trembled, as she seemed impatient under the checking bridle, and restless to fly free like a bird, skimming the ground across the wide plain.

"And where are we off to?" naturally inquired Dick.

"No time to clack now, mate," returned Waller, curtly, as he reined his horse round for a start. "The night will clap down on us like a mush on a glim afore we've gone half a league; and then, if the antholes or the swamps don't chouse Jack Ketch of a job with some of ye, never trust me. Come, we'll have a race. First man four dollars; last in stand brandy smash all round. Handicap—I backs myself for a place. Off. Taroo!"

And away the party rattled, at a tremendous pace.

For a few yards the race was well-contested, but "Silken Jenny" forced ahead, and soon distanced her competitors by many a length.

CHAPTER XCVII.

MISERY'S HOME.

In a wretched abode, situated near the New Cut, and in a vile and filthy alley that in its dirt and squalor is a disgrace to the pretensions of this vast and costly metropolis, a miserable creature was sitting by the dusty hearth, in which a few pieces of rotten wood and half-consumed ashes were feebly struggling for existence. It was a woman. The tears were slowly trickling down her stained cheeks, that were untimely decayed by disease caused by privation of the common necessaries of life, and excess in the cursed stimulus of fiery liquids.

A study for the philanthropists, and the founders of utopias—the sensual face of that wretched being.

Not even the callousness of despair, or the recklessness of utter self-abandonment, the pinch of intense poverty, the bravery of vice—each and all of them so heart-breaking in their woeful aspect—are so impressive as the listless, inane look of patient and stupid indifference that sat on features regular and comely, though distorted by license and brutality, and spoke of a mission of suffering and degradation, only to increase in multifold measure till it dragged its victim through dark and obscure places to an unhallowed and obscure grave.

The wretched creature was Moll Fleming, to whom the miscreant, Bill Simmons, had alluded, when questioned by his villain employers, as his "woman."

She sat before the languishing fire in her dirty and wretched kennel, if even that word be not too good for the description of such a dwelling.

Across her knees a sweet and tender babe was lying, faintly wailing for the breast; the little bit of pure gold, the motherly instinct that, like a tiny but bright spark, still glowed in the centre of her heart, so much perverted and polluted by the contamination of evil fellowship, ill usage, and misery, yearning to the frail and feeble innocent, and she rocked it gently to and fro.

The shrewish voices of some of the matrons of the neighbouring houses, mingled with the growls and blasphemous oaths of the "roughs," their husbands or paramours, with whom they were desperately quarrelling, caused her to start and tremble; not that the occurrence was unusual, but that she thought she distinguished the heavy, sullen tread of the "Bulldog," and she quailed as she remembered in what surly mood she had left him, and how certain it was that, on his return, he would "carry on."

Her left cheek bore a purple stain, and her eye was bloodshot, the effect of a late domestic disturbance.

The "row" continued for an hour; every sort of invective in every pitch of shrillness was bandied from doors and windows by a dozen throats, all pouring forth the fiend-like and despicable malice of their ungovernable tempers at once. At last, *crescendo, crescendissimo*, the brawl grew louder and shriller, till there was a sound of brutal blows, the deep cursing of men, the piercing screams of women, the sobbing of children, and the yelping of curs. It sounded as if all the furies in Pandemonium were engaged in a pitched battle.

And yet that woman sits before the fading fire as the white ashes fall dustily through the rusty grate, listlessly rocking the hungry and moaning infant, and thinking only whether her "man" will come home *too* drunk to be able to do her much injury, and hoping he may.

Truth to say, she scarcely hears the riot; the sounds of hellish discord, the ribaldry of filthy vice, are so familiar to her ear that she heeds them no more than the Belgravian grandee notes the rattle of his neighbours' chariots as they roll by his door.

Is this so? Is there so much misery and pollution in our very midst, within a few roods of the mansions of ease and opulence?

If any paterfamilias, in the quiet and cheerful seclusion of his comfortable household doubt the fact, let him penetrate the "back slums" and study human nature in its most humiliating aspect. Mind, he must not walk his round and content himself with a cursory glance as if he were inspecting a caravan of wild beasts; many things will be concealed from his eyes, for there is an English pride that is good in the very surliness of the poor in their reticence: they are not fawning lazzaroni, but English "hearts of oak," with all their national faults of roughness and unpliability and all their national qualities of steadiness and soundness, only that their sap is dried up by the frost of neglect, and their growth stunted by the ill weeds of evil communication, and the hardness and barrenness of the soil in which they are misplanted.

But, say you, these pariahs must work their own redemption. *Give them the chance;* open the labour market; reward as well as punish; restrain their wickedness by *severe* but paternal enactments, that will not hopelessly plunge them back again into a deeper depth of crime and shame, instead of purifying them for better things. Let the paltry spirit of caste distinction, so unworthy of the high-souled nationality of our chartered kingdom, be swept away as a disgrace. If the noble and the rich would preserve their distinction, and enforce the deference of their less fortunate brethren, let it be done by helping to raise them above the dark sphere of helplessness and rebellious discontent; give them " whereon to stand," and you shall see that " they will move the earth." This is not to be done by the expensive means of pecuniary distributions, however excellent these may be in their temporary effects, but by giving every man that is willing to work the means of gaining a livelihood, and by supporting the friendless who are unable to labour for themselves.

Whether human legislation will ever be able to accomplish all this remains to be seen; but, doubtless, in God's good time the world will be happier, better, and wiser; policy more Christian, and punishment less degrading and more corrective—honest poverty less bitter and humiliating; old things will be done away, and an era of regeneration will commence. But, in the meanwhile, Heaven have pity on the branded poor, who struggle long and hard for steady employment, and die broken-hearted and beaten at last!

With the reader's pardon for this long but involuntary digression, we will return to the woman who is waiting for him who will never return.

The stern, gruff voice of a policeman had, after some opposition, allayed the storm without, and had awed the belligerents into a conditional and hollow truce, so that the street was tolerably quiet, though the sounds of loud and angry discussion indoors might still be heard through the thin partitions on either side of the squalid chamber.

The night was closing, for, be it remembered, the events narrated in this chapter took place on the day succeeding that on which the burglar and assassin had met his doom from the vengeance of the inexorable LEAGUE OF FATE.

A firm but light rap at the door caused the woman to start to her feet.

"That ain't him," she muttered, breathlessly, covering the infant's mouth with her hand and dirty fingers to hush its plaintive wailing; "should'nt wonder as he's lagged. What shall I do with the child?"

She hastened to a door on one side of the room, and placed the infant in a bed within a little recess, and covered it over with the clothes: it ceased crying.

She then stood in the centre of the room irresolutely.

Another rap.

"Come in, mum, if it's you, Mrs. Finighty; I'm all alone," she said, assuming a confidence she did not feel.

A slight and graceful youth of pale but beautiful countenance stepped into the room.

"I am sorry to be intrusive," said the stranger, in a sweet but thrilling voice, " but I have come on important business. You said you were alone. Is that so?"

"There's nobody in the house, sir, but myself—leastways the lodgers is all out, sir, I know, and my husband is gone to work."

The stranger smiled slightly.

"Then I may communicate what I have to say without the fear of impertinent listeners or intruders?—that's right."

With this the stranger carefully examined the place, opened the door, and hearkened for an instant.

The woman dusted a chair, and, looking at her guest furtively and timorously as the youth placed it near the fire.

"I'm sorry as the place is so untidy like," she apologised, "but you see as—leastways my husband is out to work late, and as I've allus got my hands full of one thing or t'other, as specially as we've seen better days, things ain't all as they should be."

At this little display of a lingering sense of propriety, a shade of sarcastic pity passed over the face of the youth, as he seated himself, replying:

"Pray don't apologise now, Mrs. Simmons; be seated, I want to talk to you very seriously."

"You does know me, then!" exclaimed the woman; "leastways you knows *him*."

"*I knew* him very well, Mrs. Simmons," returned the youth, gravely, "but ——"

"Lord above, sir, you don't go to say it!" said the woman, in a hurried whisper of alarm. "What's the matter; 'as the crushers nabbed him?— or——"

"You must not be too much grieved when I tell you that he is dead; he died a violent death, and I must say he deserved no better fate; we must not speak of him now please, as my time is very precious, and you are in danger."

The woman took no heed to this last warning, but, hiding her face in her grimy apron, she sobbed piteously.

"They say he ill-treated you very much," the youth said, softly; "and you must not give way in this fashion."

"But he was my man for all that, and he is dead —dead," sobbed the woman.

"Yes, it is sad, but there is no time for inactive

grief now; perhaps you remember the affair of the old lady who had been a housekeeper, and retired with her savings to the lone house on the flats."

"Oh God, sir," cried the woman, suddenly starting up white and trembling, "what do you know about that?" and then recovering her presence of mind, she added, "not as I knows what you're speaking on."

"It was Bill Simmons' work. You were only an accomplice after the act; but you are none the less likely to be placed in an unpleasant position;" and the youth went on calmly and coldly; "but don't look so frightened. I have not come to threaten but to save you; and if you consent to the easy conditions I am about to propose, I will put you in a home of peace and comfort for the remainder of your life. Do you observe me?"

"I'm listening very attentive, sir," said the woman, submissively.

"Do so. You have a child here?"

"A child, good sir? but what should I do with a child as ain't got none o' my own, and don't want to be bothered with 'em?"

"Don't try to deceive me. I know the babe is here."

"How do you know sich things? and for that matter, how do you know as Bill Simmons really be done for?" asked the woman warily.

The youth answered with a peculiar smile.

"And how should I know the particulars of that little affair of the old housekeeper, who was—"

"Well, sir; and suppose I *have* got a child to nuss?" interrupted the woman, flinching, "What then?"

"Does any one of your neighbours yet know that you have an infant in charge?"

"Lor, no, sir. My man had a-murdered me if I had split—"

"Let me see it."

The woman rose, and stood hesitating.

"I will fetch it myself," said the youth, springing up with a smile, and, walking towards the recess, he pulled back the dirty patched curtain that concealed the bed, and brought out the child in his arms.

The woman stood looking at him with wonderment and deference.

Holding the sleeping babe tenderly in his hands, the youth reseated himself, and looked gently and pityingly upon its fresh and innocent face. His voice, murmuring soothingly, sank into a melody of strange and womanly softness.

Presently he looked up, still holding the child with an unconscious care that contrasted strangely with the cold firmness that glittered in his large eyes.

The woman looked down.

"I suppose as you wants the little one restored to where he came from?" said the woman, sullenly.

"Not exactly: but we are not getting on at all with the business in hand. Will you enter my service? I will pay you liberally, and ask of you nothing more than an honest woman might perform. If you are silent and faithful you will have nothing to fear, and everything to hope for; if otherwise, remember, *I know all*. I would be the last to threaten, but should be the first to punish any disobedience or treachery."

"Werry well, sir. Now he's gone, I don't know where to turn for a crust for us. *I'm known.* Even the workus won't have anything to do with me, and I should have to starve, or get lagged for cadging, or wuss."

"Well, then, it's settled. How will you manage about this place and the furniture?"

"Well, I s'pose I'll have to tell the landlady as poor Bill is in the jug, and give her the sticks for the rent as I owes her."

"Do so. I will give you no money now, as you might display it and betray yourself. When can this be done?"

"Well, sir, as you seems to mean business, p'raps it would be as well to settle it at once, if you likes."

"It must be so. And you will be true?"

"I never yet peached on anybody as was good to me—no, nor bad neither, 'cos it ain't my way," replied the woman, with evident sincerity.

"Look you, then. I will take the child to the corner; no one will see it under my heavy cloak. I shall expect you at the corner of Waterloo Bridge in half an hour."

"Afore then. If you walks on slowly when you gets off the Cut, I'll overtake yer. If any of the folks here sees yer, I'll say as Bill's in trouble and you're his doctor" (counsel for defence).

"Well, arranged—at the corner of Waterloo-bridge in half an hour."

"Werry well, sir."

With this the woman threw the youth's cloak over his shoulders and adjusted it carefully, so as to conceal the sleeping child, and, cautiously letting him out at the front door, watched him till he had turned the corner of the street and disappeared.

She then descended into the subterranean abode in search of her landlady.

Having settled the business and bade her adieu, true to the minute, the woman walked to the foot of Waterloo-bridge.

A small and unostentatious carriage was awaiting her.

The driver got off the box as she approached.

He was a firm-set man, enveloped in a huge flapped driving-coat.

In spite of his disguise our readers might recognise in his stern, dark face the person of Bradway, that redoubtable member of the recent and terrible league of Fate.

When Mrs. Fleming got into the carriage she found the youth seated, with the infant still sleeping in his encircling arms.

At a sign she pulled down the blinds.

The carriage drove off, yet the youth did not offer to relinquish the child.

Moll Fleming thought this rather strange, but she did not make any remark.

CHAPTER XCVIII.

WE here take the opportunity of inserting a few lines concerning an event which we are sure every one of our readers will feel much interest in—the birth of the royal babe.

It had been intended that the confinement of her Royal Highness should take place at Marlborough House, and the Princess was to have left Frogmore for London in about a fortnight. For several days previous the Princess had been slightly indisposed, and was suffering from catarrh and cold, and it is stated that Dr. Browne, of Windsor, who attended her Royal Highness, judging from the symptoms of the Princess, had intimated that the delicate event might occur earlier than was anticipated. The Princess, however, had so far recovered from the indisposition under which she had been suffering as to feel no hesitation in being present at the skating party on the Virginia Water, on Friday. On returning to Frogmore her Royal Highness soon became so unwell that the Prince of Wales forwarded a telegraph to the Queen, at Osborne, respecting the condition of her Royal Highness.

The symptoms of an approaching birth continued to increase, and the Prince deemed it advisable to despatch a messenger forthwith, and requesting the immediate attendance of Dr. Browne, who arrived about seven o'clock in the evening of Friday, and, at the time already stated, her Royal Highness was safely delivered of a healthy prince. Messages were also sent for the medical men who were appointed to attend her Royal Highness, and for Sir George Grey. Dr. Sieveking, the physician to the Prince of Wales, was the first to arrive from London. He was followed by Dr. Farre and Dr. Gream, and later by Sir Charles Locock; but the confinement had taken place long before they could reach Frogmore.

The arrival of the little stranger was wholly unexpected, and as the Prince and Princess were staying at Frogmore, and not at Marlborough House, no arrangements had been made for his reception. There was no nurse in attendance; but the maternal experience of the Countess of Macclesfield, the lady in waiting, was of inestimable value in extemporising such articles of comfort and clothing as were necessary for the young prince.

A telegram was despatched to her Majesty immediately after the arrival of Dr. Browne, and the happy birth of the prince was also communicated by the same means. The Queen arrived at Windsor about noon, and immediately paid a visit to the Princess.

It may be gratifying to our readers, who are curious in these matters, to learn that the exact weight of the infant Prince after his birth was nine pounds.

The royal babe is now a month old, and we are happy to be enabled to state that the health of the Princess is most satisfactory, and that there is no reason to suppose that the infant prince will display hereafter any sign of his premature birth more than was shown by his Royal Highness's great grandfather, George the Third, who was said to have been born prematurely.

Having paused in our story to make this brief chronicle of so important an occurrence, we now resume our record of adventures.

CHAPTER XCIX.

DOWNY'S ASSIGNATION.

OUR readers will remember that we left the Downy in the Mall, leaning against a tree, with supercilious grace, trying to impress plebeian juveniles with due respect for his "attributes of awe and majesty," and, truth-compelled, we were forced to admit that his efforts to obtain deserved appreciation were not so successful as could be wished. Indeed, the shameless urchins, with the sharp sight and intuitive instinct of that most audacious, astute nondescript genus, London street boy, too plainly discerned the "lion-hide," and called the wearer accordingly.

Even the awful authority of Policeman B scarce sufficed to disperse the sparrows that twittered their derision around this stray falcon; and as they ran off they cast many a lingering look behind, and exchanged many sarcastic inquiries as to the name and local habitation of the gentleman's "hatter," and in earnest solicitude for information as to "who turned him out."

It was a dark evening—dark and misty—and the policeman turned his bull's-eye full in the Downy's face.

"Hillo," said the man in office, with a low whistle, "I think I knows you, young covey."

The Downy's stupified senses partially recovered from their numbing lethargy, and at once recovered their natural *acumen*.

"Aw—vewy pwobably—wo'al know among the awistocwacy," he replied with languid carelessness. "But I say those infernal boys, gweat boaws, devilish good fellah, policeman, here's a demi-quid—aw, I mean a half sovewing for you—pwaps you could inform me which is the way to the guawds, it's so dawk, and I wather fear imbibed too much clawet at the Duke Flimsy's.

The policeman looked at the money, slipped it into his pocket, and respectfully gave the requested information.

"Devilish good of you, 'pon my soul, policeman, good night, aw," and twirling his military scarf with the most approved *nonchalance*, the noble aristocrat swaggered away.

When he had got out of sight of the constable, he rubbed his eyes.

"Come, this here won't do," he said; "it won't do to get muddled in this boggery. I must steady myself somehow, or I shall soon get stopped at this little game."

With this timely reflection, the Downy turned out of the Mall, passed through the Court-yard of St. James's, and, entering a public house, called successively for two bottles of soda-water. After a while he emerged into the cool damp air, the little fright he had had, the effervescence of the antidote he had swallowed, and the chill mist sweeping against his hot forehead, had their wished-for effect, and he re-entered the Mall comparatively sobered.

As he stood under a lamp near Buckingham Palace, and contemplated his gorgeous array, the idiosyncracy for speculation grew strong within this light-fingered gentleman, and he was revolving in his mind a dozen schemes for the gratification of his eccentric propensity.

While he was ruminating he felt a touch on his arm.

At first he thought he was addressed by one of the "fair and frail," and was about to make a speech of mock gallantry; but on turning he perceived a young woman, pretty indeed, but modestly and plainly dressed, and evidently respectable.

"If you please, sir," she said, with a slight blush, "am I addressing Captain Adolphus Thesiger? My lady sent me with a message to that gentleman, and I was to see him at this spot, and seeing you in military uniform I made bold to speak."

"My eye, here's a go," mentally ejaculated the Downy; "I ain't agoing to do this moult for nothing, paying such a jolly price too" (rather a cool reflection, considering how he came by the money). "Blow me if I don't try it on. Aw, yaas, my love," he said, aloud; "quite correct. I am Captain—aw; Captain What's his name, very happy to attend to your communication."

"Well, sir, Lady Penelope Oldborough desired me to say——"

"Aw, yaas—exquisite young creature."

"*Young* creature! Well, that's a good one," said the girl, with a slight laugh.

"Aw, beg pardon, venerable matron," answered the Downy, in some confusion.

"She wouldn't like to hear you call her that, sir, any how."

"Estimable female of a certain age!" exclaimed the Downy, in a tone of desperation; "she desired——"

"Me to tell you that if you are really, as you stated in your note, languishing for a final interview, she will receive you for the last time at her residence in Curzon-street."

"'Pon my life—quite wavished—cull a hansom and get over the base length of gwound that sepewates me from my pwiceless tweasure in a few moments. Will you do me the honour—aw?"

He extended his left arm with ineffable grace.

"La, sir," said the girl, with great surprise and no little pleasure, "it is not proper—a real gentleman and me only a lady's maid, what *would* the people say?"

"Say," exclaimed the Downy gallantly, "Captain—what's his name—luckiest fellah in Belgwavia!"

The maid lightly touched his arm, and unconsciously tossing her little head, her heart beating exultingly, she strutted along arm in arm with the patrician.

As they were passing the open space before the Palac a tall, grim-looking gentleman encountered them, but in spite of his plain dress, there was something in the cool, searching glance of his grey eye and the inscrutability of his stern, compressed lips that bespoke him a detective.

This personage stood right in their way and narrowly eyed the Downy.

The *costumia's* rouge was true to its allegiance when the treacherous natural colour stole away from the cheek of the gallant officer. The moustache too was unusually adhesive, and did not fall off at the critical moment as it is too often prone to do.

The gentleman of the force seemed satisfied and passed on.

"Who ever is that?" said the girl indignantly, what a rude fellow, how he stared. I wonder who he is."

"M. P. for Tottlefields, my dear," returned the Captain carelessly, "devilish disagreeable fellah—aw—Colonel Walker of ours wanted me to call him out, but the fellah's no shot, and so the meeting would have been such a bore; but we don't speak; I avoid the fellah, though he's always intruding his odious company."

They reached Buckingham gate, a cab was called from the stand, the officer handed his fair companion to her seat, jumped in by her side, and ordered cabby to drive to Curzon-street.

The maid thought that the gentleman became more abstracted and taciturn as they proceeded, and was a little piqued and disappointed, especially as he seemed absorbed in some engrossing reflections that did not permit his paying the attention to her passing remarks that politeness might demand, and she ordered the cabman to set them down at the corner of the street.

The Captain paid him, and he drove off.

The maid led [the] way to the door of the house, and, opening it with a key, ushered the officer up the richly-carpeted staircase, opened the door of a handsomely-furnished drawing-room, and, lighting a splendid moderator lamp in ormolu that stood on the table, prayed him to be seated till her ladyship came down.

Left alone the Downy inspected the costly furniture and ornaments in a bewilderment of admiration. In a corner of the room, by the side of the magnificent pier-glass, was a beautiful inlaid armoire. It was empty, and either the key had been lost and the complicated Bramah lock had been taken off by some skilful workman, and lay near upon an ebony and pearl-chequered chess table. With an eye to the future the "'cute" and far-seeing cracksman assured himself that he was unobserved, and then, drawing from his pocket a little box of prepared wax, took a mould of the lock. Closing the box he re-pocketed it.

His next act was to take all the most costly ornaments he could lay hands on from the drawers and tables, and arrange those he was forced to spare in such a manner that his spoils might not be missed.

This labour of love accomplished he abandoned himself to the pleasure of contemplating his own handsome person—so expensively "got up"—from all points of view in the numerous and splendid mirrors that adorned the apartment.

While thus engaged he heard the rustle of a heavy silk dress.

He did not turn round, wishing to take his first impressions of his *inamorata* from the mirror.

The reflection showed him the figure of a woman, whose beauty was rather of the autumnal type; she was tall and buxom; had keen eyes of a bluish colour, but assuredly not cerulean; her hair was faultless and luxuriant, as it ought to be at the price. Like her new admirer, she did not think it superfluous to "paint the lily," as the crimson hue on her cheek might testify.

She spoke in a girlish simper, but not in girlish melody of tone.

"Adolphus, you foolish and infatuated creature, have you come to hear words which have already told me are poignards in your heart? Must you needs give me the pain of telling, and yourself the agony of hearing, that my proud heart is steeled to the assaults of love, and that we can never be united."

The gallant turned round.

She gave a slight scream.

With professional instinct the Downy clapped his hand over her mouth, effectually to gag her.

Then he recollected himself, and softly and affectionately let his arms fall to her buxom waist, and looked yearningly into her eyes.

"Aw—my adowable," he exclaimed. "Am I then at last blessed with the chance of telling you——"

She looked up into his face. Horror inexpressible to her delicate frame—wonder inexplicable that she did not sink into the earth! She was in the arms of a stranger, and not of her ardent admirer and tantalised slave, Captain Adolphus Thesiger.

She looked up into his face. The clear and brilliant lamplight perfected the illusion of his tinted cheeks and his sublime moustache. The Downy might have passed for Beau Brummell or the Count D'Orsay.

A faintness overwhelmed her, but she did not sink to the floor.

"But you—who are you? You are not Adolphus."

"Aw—no, I isn't."

"You isn't," cried the lady, suddenly starting up; "you isn't—what grammar!"

"It's not a crammer, my dear madam—aw," replied the Downy, rather taken aback. "I am not Captain Thrasher; but—aw—I am Lieutenant Leary, the companion of his mess—aw—and, I must confess it, decidedly a twaitor."

"A traitor?"

"Yaas, madam—to my fwriend. Cos vy, madam. I saw you, and I adored you; and I wesolved that I would thwow myself at your feet, and implore your mercy; for, madam, I love you."

With this the Downy flung himself upon his knees, and kissed the plump and jewelled fingers with extravagant devotion.

"Sir—rise! I beg of you to rise. You are a stranger to me, and, besides, it is mean of you to take advantage of a nature too generous and susceptible."

"Madam—take advantage! Why, if I were not going abwoad for ever, I would never have had the presumption——"

"Going away; to be an exile for my sake! Ah, I did not mean that!"

"I am a fwiend, madam, of Captain; you know, and I know; I saw you; and I thought to myself the adowable being is too high for me—too wich—I must forget her; she is loved by my fwiend, and I'll act square, if I dies for it."

"What an extraordinary expression; and the grammar most atrocious!"

"Aw—that gwammer! such a deblish common thing; every officer in our mess talks gwammer awful bwoad; but, as I was saying, madam, I had seen you, and I loved you, and I wesolved to go away to the west, far—far upon the sea—that I might learn to forget you for ever; but, before I sells my commission, I will go to the adowable being, and I will tell her everything. Oh, madam, may I speak?"

"It would be discourtesy to refuse you," replied Lady Penelope, reclining in the setter. "Speak," she said, majestically and pathetically; "but let your explanation be short as it ought to be forcible, to excuse your madness and temerity in intruding upon my seclusion.

The Downy had a long hour's hard work, and many a pitfall he narrowly escaped that was laid by his evil genii of Ignorance: however, by the exertion of unwonted eloquence, he finally persuaded the weak and vain old lady that he was indeed fellow in arms with Captain Thesiger, whom, with matchless impudence, he most shamefully scandalized, saying that he did nothing but make fun of her ladyship, and declaring that he only sought her for her money; he offered to challenge the miscreant, and this the amiable lady vehemently urged him to do.

Finally, with the air of a heart-broken lover in a melodrama, the Downy walked towards the door.

"And I must leave you for ever!"

"Ah, do not say so," cried Lady Penelope, with touching sweetness, "Lieutenant Leary; or, at least, tell me the reason for such a resolve."

"You do not love me!"

"But I may; hope—love never despairs," said the charming dame, with a bantering smirk.

"But worse—I am pursued. Since I have known that such a being as yourself existed I have thought of nothing but you. My serwants have wobbed me—my twadesmen have swindled me; and now, for the sake of two hundred pounds, I must fly from England, home, and beauty, or see myself nailed, lagged, and imprisoned. Farewell!—farewell! Wemember me!"

And, waving his hand in an agony of despair, the interesting Lieutenant Leary approached the door.

"Stay—stay, I beseech you stay," cried her ladyship. "You nor no man must be ruined for loving me, however much I may disapprove of this mode of paying your addresses. I will give you four hundred pounds. Clean yourself. Go, and forget me."

"And do you think I would accept this favour if I knew I must see you no more, though you are too beautiful for me, and too noble, too?"

He was going to say too young, but he thought that rather too strong, and supplemented,

"Too good."

"Absurd creature, romantic suitor, treacherous friend. And do you really know poor Thesiger?"

"Think as thieves. Reg'lar chum—aw—I mean companion in arms. We fought for glory in India—aw—"

"He was in India?"

"Of course he was. Knew him from infancy."

"You mean he knew *you* from infancy?"

"Aw—ya-as," a little staggered. "A reg'lar old buffer. But ah! my precious idol. Must I leave you for ever?"

Once more the Downy flung himself upon his knees, by the side of the Lady Oldborough.

For another half-hour he laboured hard, exhausting almost all his eloquence, and severely testing his powers of invention.

The charming maiden was thoroughly convinced of the necessity of all he said about his uncle's immense wealth—his own proximity to a high title. By subtlely extorting little admissions from the amorous lady, and skilfully making the most of them, he related amusing anecdotes of Captain Thesiger, and the lady was completely taken in.

She rose and approached an escretoire, and opened it with a small key.

The Downy had followed her.

She drew forth a roll of notes and placed in her—

"Lieutenant Leary," she said, in a voice of tragic affectation, "I have received you, perhaps, with unmaidenly imprudence. I have trusted you like a silly, confiding girl as I am. Go!—but if you are mercenary, and have heartlessness enough to deceive me, I will forgive your perfidy."

She laid her plump cheek on his shoulder.

The gallant lieutenant flung his arms round her fainting form in a rhapsody of gratitude, and his fingers were busy in the escretoire—he gently closed it.

Sinking on one knee he supported his tender susceptible, and trusting fair one.

"Madam," he said, "I'm fly, and to the end of my life I shall never forget this night; and I very well know what all this has cost your poor feelings."

With this and a gallant salute the noble Lieutenant Leary fled from the room, leaving the charming lady reclining on an ottoman, lone and disconsolate.

The lady rose, and, glancing into the mirror, arranged her finely-fashioned curls with a modest air.

"Strange and mysterious creature," she murmured; "in form and feature how God-like! In language and manner how vulgar, and common singular eccentricity. No doubt his *tout ensemble* is merely assumed."

"Oh, crickey!" chuckled the Downy gleefully, as he rushed up the street, crushing the precious pieces of paper in his lithesome, well-trained fingers. "Blow me tight, if the old gal isn't a reg'lar stunner!"

The roll of carriage wheels causes Lady Aldborough to approach the window.

A loud knocking and ringing at the door.

The maid entered.

"Lor, my lady," she said, quite surprised, "another gentleman, who calls himself Captain Thesiger."

"Admit him, Matilda. Yes, yes," she exclaimed, in romantic abstraction—"the moths will fly to the flame; but Captain Thesiger is *not* Lieutenant Leary!"

A short gentleman, on the shady side of forty, neatly but expensively dressed in plain clothes, and evidently got up by his valet and *perequier* in a masterly style, hurriedly enters the apartment.

"My dear Lady Oldborough," he began nervously, as he threw himself at her feet. "I waited in the Mall for your messenger. No one came. Wearied out with impatience and anxiety, I am here to hear my fate from your lips!"

"The fiat of that fate has gone forth," said the interesting lady, in a solemn tone. "Adolphus Thesiger, I can never be yours."

"And why, my dear Lady Penelope—why; do not add reserve to your cruelty?"

"Because, why should you force me to use a subterfuge, or to confess the secret of my heart."

"Oh, I implore you."

"And who—who is the scoundrel?"

"You do well to traduce a brave and gallant companion in arms!"

Captain Thesiger could scarcely restrain a laugh, as he thought of all the "chaff" he had suffered from his messmates in the score of his love affair.

"Yes, Lady Oldborough, and who has dared"—

"Lieutenant Leary—who the deuce is he?"

The question was not answered, at least by Lady Penelope, for there was a startling rat-tat at the door.

The lady's maid entered, her eyes wide dilated and her hands upheld in inexpressible amazement; "Laws, my lady, here are three more gentlemen, *and they're officers.*"

She had scarcely spoken when three stern-faced men in dark clothes entered.

In the tallest and keenest-looking of the three the maid at once recognised the M.P. for Tottlefields.

"Madam," said this gentleman, "I am sorry to intrude upon your privacy, but my name is Harker. I am a detective officer, and these gentlemen are my assistants. A daring and expert thief in some disguise has invaded your house, and, no doubt, has robbed you to a considerable extent."

"Lieutenant Leary for a thousand pounds!" cried Captain Thesiger.

Her ladyship gave an hysterical scream and sank upon a couch.

The detectives, in a business-like manner, began to search the apartment.

Her ladyship started up, and flew wildly from the tables to the chiffionier, from thence to the escretoire, and lifted her jewelled arms with a piercing shriek.

"My silver pilagree *mignonne* coffee-cups; my exquisite darling pug-dogs; my cameo signet; the Augustan coins in the ivory case; the Partici enamels; the antique rosary in gold and relics; the gems and notes in the escretoire; *and I lent the villain four hundred pounds!* Captain Thesiger, monster as you are! why did you betray me? Heartless detective, why did you not save my treasures? Where is that worthless Matilda? Send her at once. I swoon—I expire—I perish!"

CHAPTER C.

THE BUSHRANGERS.

WE are in the woods at night, in company with Dick and the hardy rangers.

Following each other in Indian file, the worthies are slowly and cautiously exploring the intricate windings of the low-browed woods; the party have given the rein to their tired horses, which follow sagaciously the beaten track that resembles rather the run of some wild animal than a pathway for travelling men.

Yet such it is. On either side, pioneers and path-finders have blazed the trees, *i.e.*, sliced off with their axes patches of bark for a guidance, and many rude but intelligible hireoglyphics are scored on the these rude, natural sign-posts.

The moon is shining brightly, though her beams are obstructed by the mingling branches.

At last they emerge upon an open space in the middle of the silent forest.

It is a wild spot, moist and sedgy, on the brink of a wide and slushy morass.

The muddy, slimy soil is thickly covered with a luxuriant growth of docks, flags, and other weeds peculiar to such localities.

Here Waller, who seemed to take the lead in this expedition, pulled up.

Dick rode to his side.

Barnup and the Kangaroo closed up behind them.

"Now, mate," said Dick; "seeing that we've had a pretty long ride, and this is a rum sort o' place to be in at supper time, perhaps you'll spare a moment to tell a fellow what the job in hand may be."

"The question's only nat'rel," returned Waller, and then sinking his voice to a whisper, he went on; "you see, mate, we're in a service as is not uncommon in these parts, but is infarnal unpleasant for all that; we're sent out for the recovery of———"

"What?"

"The corpse of a poor fellow as has had his throat cut by the cussed bush rangers."

"Good Heaven!"

" 'Tain t nothing, only you see we're in charge to foller the track of the infernal cusses, and that's rather a chary business; but there's no time to be wasted in gabbling, hi, Kangaroo."

The Ranger rose up alongside.

"You're a young 'un at this game," continued Waller looking doubtingly on our hero, " you ain't troubled with shivers no how?"

Dick smiled grimly.

"Waal, I don't doubt that you're game, mate," said Waller, "but I had my turn myself when I first had to probe a cussed long stick into the black stinking pools to fumble for the bloated carcase of a feller creetur'. Ugh, I don't favour the job now; I'd rather have a stand-up fight with a hundred of the murdering blackguards than be sneaking about in the dark to clear away their bloody work—the wretches. Waal, you go with Kangaroo—you'd be running counter, like a young dog as ain't broke on the first false trail the leary thieves have laid for yer; and a strong arm's no pertection from a shot behind a thicket. Me and Jem goes this way—' Mind, no jaw; silence, or death's the consequence,' for it ain't improbable that the wood's alive with 'em. If we meets in the dark the word is—' Sticks in a bundle,' and the answer, ' Don't break.' "

They dismounted, tethered their horses, and parted—Walter and Barnup skirting the stagnant pool in one direction, while Dick and his companion proceeded in the other.

Presently the Kangaroo halted, and, kneeling down, examined the state of the ground.

Dick leant over him, and perceived that the muddy soil was deeply indented with footprints.

Evidently there had been a struggle near the place.

A piece of dark stuff that might have once been part of a pilot-coat was fluttering upon a thorny shrub.

The ground seemed beaten by stamping feet.

Here and there were sprinkled at intervals dark crimson spots.

A dull red stain appeared on the edge of the oz er-tangled pool.

It might be one of those ruddy smears so often seen on the damp surface of swampy grounds: it might be—blood!

Kangaroo raised himself, and, touching Dick on the shoulder, pointed to a part of the muddy pond.

The moonlight flooded it with a silver blaze.

At the point indicated by the ranger, Dick perceived that the mire was puffed up, like a rising crust, into a sort of mound, and that little air-filled bubbles of water rose through and burst at the top.

"*He's there!*" said the Kangoroo in a thrilling whisper.

It was a weird place.

The frogs were croaking with a loudness and harshness that astounded our hero.

Strange birds were screaming in the woods.

The brave Dick, who had acted with such manly courage in his encounter with the natives and the Bushmen, was now ghastly pale, and his knees trembled. The Kangaroo gave three low calls, in excellent imitation of the note of some wood-bird.

He was answered in the same way by Waller, on the other side of the pool, whom they could not see for the long reeds and oziers.

Presently he and the Barnup joined them.

They held their rifles poised in their hands.

In silence the Kangaroo pointed to the swollen surface of the mud.

Waller nodded his head.

Barnup dragged the branch of a fallen tree from among the bushes. He thrust it out, and plunged it beneath the black mire.

A dreadful stench arose.

He seemed to have met with some obstacle; he raised his arm so as to make a lever of the pole, and——

A thrill of horror brought the beads of cold sweat to Dick's forehead.

His more tried companions looked very white.

Slowly rising to the surface, and bursting through the filthy shroud, appeared the purple, bloated, and unrecognisable features of the corpse, already in the last stage of dissolution.

Dick had much to do to restrain a cry of horror and disgust.

Let us pass over details too sickening for relation.

The body was dragged up on to the drier ground.

In awful silence, the men stood contemplating it.

The corpse appeared to be that of a man who had met his shocking fate in the prime of life.

He was dressed in a blue flannel shirt and a pilot-coat, and about his breast was a broad and heavy belt, from the edge of which depended the remains of a long leathern lining that plainly had been cut off by a bowie knife, and probably had contained the money of the murdered man; the belt had been put back on the body after the horrid deed had been committed, *for a purpose*. To it was attached a large and weighty stone.

A short consultation decided the men that the body was in such a fearful state that it was impossible to remove it to the Block.

Their next care was to inter the unfortunate victim of the bloodthirsty avarice of the lawless and remorseless felons, whose track they unanimously resolved to follow through fire and flood, though it should lead them on to a doom as terrible as his over whose appalling remains they were standing in horror.

Selecting as dry a spot as they could find, they hollowed out the ground with their hatchets.

They softly and reverently laid the body of the murdered man in its last resting-place.

They covered it over with turf and brushwood, and marked the spot by blazing the trees.

They did not, however, forget to retain the belt, thinking it might be of value in leading to the identification both of the victim and his murderers.

This duty performed, they next proceeded to re-inspect the spot where the struggle had taken place, and Waller soon declared his conviction that he had found a clue to the mystery, and asked his companions' opinion as to the number of the villains who had perpetrated the brutal deed.

The Kongaroo held up three fingers.

Barnup also declared that he could swear to the fact that there had been three concerned in it.

Even with his small share of experience, Dick felt justified in expressing the same opinion.

But whither had the atrocious ruffians betaken themselves?

Their track had been carefully concealed.

But four resolute men had sworn, at all risks, to bring them to justice.

On one side of the marsh some green and slimy stones form a sort of ford. The Kangaroo stole off to examine these. Presently he gave a low whistle.

The moss on these stones was at intervals crushed, and now and then they could distinguish a slight stain of blood.

Waller declared that he did not believe this to be the blood of the murdered man, but that of one of his assassins.

Upon reaching the end of the line of stones, they found the footmarks of *two* men—deeply impressed and staggeringly scattered stains of blood on either side of them.

The cause was plain.

The two ruffians had carried off their companion, wounded and bleeding.

As they were eagerly pushing their way through the brambles, like dogs on full scent, Dick suddenly started back.

What caused him to recoil?

Seated upon the ground, his head leaning against a tree, enveloped in a cloud of carrion-flies, was the loathsome object of a dead man, the top of his head blown completely off, and his brain smattered on the trunk.

Whose work was this second foul murder?

Had this been done in the fight with the traveller?

No, for the terrible evidence was there that he had been killed where he was now reclining.

The gash on his breast he probably received from the hands of the victim, but that wound was bandaged, and in his hands he yet held a bowl half full of water.

The treacherous companions of his guilt had dragged him thus far, and then, either weary of the charge, or fearful of their own safety, had blown his brains out, while he sat unsuspectingly at rest.

Proceeding further, the indignant rangers came full upon the clear track of three horses, and they resolved at once to remount, and follow the bloody wolves in full cry.

Toilsomely they retraced their steps. They reached the tree where they had tethered the animals.

They looked in each other's faces, mute and aghast with terror.

The horses were gone!

"I thought so," exclaimed Waller in a low tone, looking around him as if he discovered an enemy in every tree. "I thought as we could not trust that snivelling cuss that brought the news to the block, some of the gang has taken him and he's blown on us; what's to be done?"

"First of all, we must get out of the trap if we can," said the Kangaroo, "even if it was no worse than losing the horses we should have a hungry walk afore we reached home, but if they takes us they'll have to pay a pretty smart reckoning, I fancy."

"Silken Jenny, too," cried Waller plaintively, "a hoss that was more than a hoss, one of the devil's lot will get off any how, for there aint a animal as can catch her."

"We had better be off at once," said Barnup, nervously; "shall we disperse?"

"No, no, mate; let's stick together," said Dick, "let's die together, if need be. No separating. We're not over strong as it is; no need to weaken our strength by parting."

"Hem, hem," said Walter; "'sticks in a bundle don't break.' No more whinings, but look to your primings. Brace up and follow me. Where the devil's Kangaroo?" he exclaimed, suddenly turning round.

He was gone.

A shot was fired in a neighbouring thicket.

Kangaroo leaped over a bush in a style that justified the appropriateness of his cognomen.

"Run!—run!" he said; "I've done for one of the hounds. We're beset."

But there's a chance still.

With this he rushed past them, and plunged into the wood.

Closely they followed him.

A shout rang in their ears.

But as yet no enemy appeared.

Turning in and out, up and down, through the dense brush and over the uneven and broken ground they hurried on.

Just as they reached the skirts of the wood, looking before them they perceived in the centre of a little plain a large and branching tree, near it their horses tethered together, and from one of its extended boughs depended four ropes, each with a running noose at the end.

An instant, and loud, rough laughter rung in their ears, and they were surrounded by a score of desperate-looking ruffians, all with rifles in their hands, and a complete armoury of revolvers and bowie-knives in their belts.

CHAPTER CI.

MARY FLEMING.

In an apartment, furnished with every appliance of ease and comfort, at a table covered with books and papers, is seated a stern and sinister-looking man.

His face bears the traces of pain of body and mind—perhaps of both. He seems to be recovering from a severe illness.

Slowly he rises, and moodily paces the floor——

"Yes," he mutters; "I will break this terrible spell! I will lay these phantoms that haunt me sleeping and waking; I will exorcise this terrible devil of terror that is rending my heart; foiled in my dearest schemes, robbed of the prize for which I have toiled, and bartered sweet peace of mind, and, maybe, my soul's salvation — branded with a bloody mark in open day—doomed to death by a mysterious and all-powerful society that seems omnipresent and all-knowing—existing, in this advanced century, in the midst of the world's metropolis—the League of Fate! But I will lift the curtain that conceals this band of assassins. I will make a full and clear revelation of all their monstrous atrocities. Matters now hushed up and kept close shall be made patent as the noon-day. I will do this; for I cannot be in worse peril than I am. I will do this, though it cost me my life."

Our readers will recognise John Carvan.

A servant entered the room.

"Sir, a gentleman wishes to speak with you; he sent up this note."

John Carvan broke the seal, read the missive, and crumpling it in his hand flung it into the fire.

"Good," he said; "tell the gentleman I attend him."

The servant bowed, and left the room.

Presently a tall, stern man entered the chamber.

"Mr. Gower, you are very welcome; pray be seated. Have you been able yet to obtain any clue to this mysterious affair?"

"I think I have, sir; but I do not like to be premature in any assertion on that score. I have taken a minute detail from you of all that bears upon the subject, and judging from the intelligent description you have given me of the person, and hearing of the supposed president of this secret tribunal, I think he or she is not unknown to me.

"You do not say so!"

"Yes; and if my scheme prospers, I trust that he or she will soon be in the hands of the police authorities."

"Impossible!"

"By no means. Would you like to know by what means I have attained some knowledge of the whereabouts of one whose attributes are almost supernatural?"

"I burn to know."

"Well, then, you recollect—for we must begin at the beginning—that you sent for me at a time when you were very ill, and evidently enduring great agony of mind and body. You had heard of my alleged skill as a detective, and had therefore sought my advice and assistance to help you in your strange dilemma.

"You told me that you went in fear of your life, and you have reason enough to do so, for you are under the ban of a set of wretches quite insensible to every motive of fear or remorse. Eager was I to engage in this service of danger. For once before I had been baffled in my attempts to unravel this dread secret. So I proceeded—first to the penetration of thieves' kitchens. I mingled among the most desperate characters. I went into places where, had I been recognised, I should have been murdered at once. At last, in my official capacity, I laid hands on a wretch accused of a great crime, who has promised in exchange for his liberation to give me every information that can lead to the detection and conviction of this band, which sets at defiance the laws of every European empire."

"Capitally done. But is the fellow trustworthy?"

"Trustworthy? No. I would not trust him a hair's-breadth; but he is anxious—rather excusably, considering all things—to save his neck, and I am sufficiently used to dealing with such characters. Well, he has directed me to another of the *band* who is chafing under the fearful restraints put upon its members by the conditions of the fatal League. This man is known to me—he can be trusted."

"And who is he?"

"You will never guess."

"No. Why do you not tell me?"

"Because you know him."

"Indeed — I —it is possible. I have mixed in strange company in strange places."

"But he is known in your own domestic circle."

"Indeed—and he is—"

"A kind warm-hearted gentleman, and a skilful physician."

"A physician!"

"Yes, he attended your brother in his last illness. Dr. Rushton."

John Carvan gasped. He turned his eye wildly upon the calm inscrutable countenance of the detective.

After a moment's pause he said,

"And can it be possible that a gentleman so noted for his benevolence can be in any way connected with such villains?"

"How that may be he will explain. I said that he was chafing under the restraints of the compact, but I did not mean that he was actually one of the members of the secret association. It seems that his interest in the strange being who instituted this League of Fate, induced him to trust himself within the vortex of this whirlpool, and now he is fighting hard to get out of the reach of its influence. I have told you all I know at present, and I have done all that can be done without your assistance."

"Mine!" returned Carvan, with a start; "you know in what deadly peril I stand from the terrible machinations of these midnight assassins. If you can bring to justice this dreadful gang you will claim my warmest gratitude, and most liberally will I reward you. You will, at the same time, confer a boon on the nation at large. If you are not successful, you will still claim my reward and thanks for your good intentions. But—"

"I *shall* be successful if you will aid me."

"But wherefore I?"

"Dr. Rushton will explain all. It is arranged that we are to meet at the house in Bloomsbury, with what purpose you will then know."

"But why not inform me now?"

"Because I cannot. If you do not trust the doctor do not go."

"I have no reason to mistrust him."

"Certainly not. Your conscience is clear; will you come? Remember the doom that hangs over your head, think of the glory of unravelling the Gordian knot that all the police authorities could not untie, think of walking free and feeling the ban removed, and as you see the cruel sign upon your breast, think sternly how much better it would have been for your ruthless torturers to have driven the poignard home to your heart."

"Well, I will come."

"Spoken bravely! I will write the address."

"He did so."

"And the time?"

"To morrow at dusk—say seven o'clock, the nights are dark."

"I will be there."

"Good, Mr. Carvan. I have the honour to wish you good morning. I rely upon your promise."

"I will not fail."

"And the world will soon hear the last of the League of Fate."

Gower descended the stairs, and the servant opened the door; as he did so the detective gave him a peculiar look.

The servant bowed his head, and made a sign on his hand with his fingers.

The detective smiled, and saluted him courteously as he passed out.

"*He, too, is one of us!*" he murmured.

When he reached the corner of the street he was joined by a well-dressed man, who was closely muffled in a cloak.

It was Bradway.

"Is all well?"

"Yes; he will come," returned Gower, "but we have had enough of him; he must be removed; he is getting dangerous."

"His time is at hand," returned his companion, sternly.

CHAPTER CII.

It would not be easy to describe the delight felt by Mrs. Fleming when she found herself duly installed in a small, but neat, well-furnished cottage in the rustic and lovely village of Barnesdale. The youth who had exercised such a strange influence over her destiny had treated her with courtesy and kindness, and had very liberally paid for her submission to his wishes.

The woman who was by nature mild and gentle, and hardened to a life of vice and misery only by a long and cruel apprenticeship, improved so much in health, looks, habits, and manner that she was scarcely recognisable as the dirty and degraded paramour of the ferocious Bill Simmons.

At first she found the restraints of the calm and quiet country life extremely irksome; she felt as if she were a prisoner, debarred from the stimulus of drink, abandonment, and truculent society, things which seemed to become essential to her very existence, for, like the chameleon, man takes his tone from the objects around him. But she had learned patience in a hard school; she considered herself bound to obey her imperious young master, and the place and substantial comfort of her new life soon reconciled her to its disagreements, which, in truth, wore off altogether in a few weeks, and she then looked back with fear and horror on the dark vistas of her past life, and would not have returned to it for untold treasures.

The child had not been confided to her.

A young farmer and his wife took charge of it. Their infant had died, and Janet Miles soon became fondly attached to her little foster child.

The year passed round with its changing seasons—the fresh and child-like spring, the beauteous maiden summer, the mature and wealthy autumn, and the hoary winter.

Away—far away—from the sin, gloom, and suffering of the polluted city, like a withering flower removed from a dark and loathsome cellar to the pure air, the poor woman grew younger and healthier, as if the shadow on the dial had gone backwards.

One day, as she sat at the door of her cottage, knitting, and humming a sweet village tune, and thinking of the wondrous change that had taken place in her fortunes, a tall gipsey-looking fellow stood before her.

He was dressed in a long and shabby grey coat, a red kerchief was tied about his neck, his wild, dark, gipsey eyes were fixed upon the woman with a strange scrutiny.

"Good den, dame. Can you give a poor wayfarer a cup of water? and if you could spare a piece of bread you wouldn't lose by the act of charity."

The stranger spoke in a clear, ringing voice, and with an air of boldness unusual to those of his class.

The woman rose at once, and, laying by her work, entered the house, and presently returned with a glass of ale and some bread and meat, which she placed on the window-sill, and, re-seating herself, took her work up again.

The man thanked her for her kindness.

"Do you know, dame, it is strange, but I think I have seen your face before."

"Perhaps you have. Some of your people encamped near this place a while ago," returned the woman, carelessly.

"Nay, but this is long ago. Have you always lived in this place, dame?"

A shade of pain flitted over the woman's face, and she slightly sighed as she replied, with a little taint of her ancient craftiness—

"It is my first home."

"And that is strange, too," he said. "Do you remember a man called Hazael, the gipsey?"

'No," returned the woman, after reflection.

'Nor such a man as Reneike Varner?"

The woman started—the blood came to her cheek—it died away.

"I tell ye," she said, almost fiercely, "I know ye not! I have lived in this place long enough to forget that I ever had another home!"

"God forbid that I should remind you of things that you want to forget when the bread of your charity is in my mouth. But, look ye, dame; I am a friend and a foe, and I am come to tell ye of a danger that hangs over one who is, or ought to be, very dear to ye."

"Of whom do you speak?"

He went on without heeding her question.

"I have walked many a weary mile to tell you this, because he that is dead was kind to me when I had no other friend under heaven, and there shall be no evil fall on his offspring that I can avert. I have been wild, and have known nothing of self-control. I am a fool in many things, but not in all; and it shall go very hard if I do not foil one villain in the mischief he designs."

"And what is this villain's name?"

"John Carvan."

"The woman shuddered. She had heard Bill Simmons curse him by name.

"And does he know that the child is here?"

"No."

"Then—but if you are seeking to entrap me? and it is base of you, for I never did you harm."

"Do not speak if you are afraid of my hearing anything to compromise ye. Let me alone speak."

"But are you really Reneike Varner?"

"No other."

"But you are much changed."

"They say so. I have suffered from every sort of infliction that can wear any man out—body and brain."

"They used to say that you were transported somewhere in foreign parts."

"Yes; I have been a *forcat* at Cayenne. I was engaged in the riots caused by the *coup d'etat* in '48. But you know nothing of these things, and it's well you don't."

"But I have seen misery enough in my time, God knows, and now I am removed from it it seems the more awful like, for it must be very good to be born in the country. I hate towns now. I think that herding so many poor wretches together in close and dirty streets seems dreadful. Poverty is cleaner and lighter out here in the fields, ain't it?"

"Yes," replied the gipsey, "I love the country, too. It is there alone that one can breathe freely and walk like a man, there looks the sun full in the face, and ever reads in the changeful pages of nature's book something to solace, something to delight one. The happiest nights that I have known have been slept out under a tent or beneath the starry canopy of heaven alone. But we must not talk of this now, dame, for I have a mission to fulfil, and, as I must have your confidence, look me in the face and say if you can trust me."

Physiognomy, a science she had never heard of, was the daily study of the woman's suffering life in former times.

In those days she expected to find an enemy in every stranger, and in forming a new connection she always looked hard into the face to discover how much she had to bear or to contend against.

She glanced keenly at the gipsey.

She gave vent unconsciously to the expression.

"He's square!"

The simple words struck harshly on her sense.

She had left off all her slang phrases. It was wonderful how quickly and how completely she had accommodated herself to the manners of the society in which she was now placed.

Varner smiled.

"Yes, whatever my faults and weaknesses may be, I am loyal to my friends. But enough of this. What have they done with the child?"

"It is nursed by a young wife in the village."

"Is it a boy or a girl?"

"A boy."

"Good. How old?"

"A year and some weeks."

"Do you know from whence the babe was stolen?"

"Well enough, Varner, well enough."

"But is it not cruel as well as criminal to keep this child from its widowed parent?"

"What is it to me?" said the woman, resignedly. "If my master has arranged it so I cannot interfere, even if I wished to. Besides, the child will not be bred in the cursed city. His mother has been encouraged by those who have charge of the babe, whom they call the ward of the League of Fate."

"But how do you know all these particulars?"

"How do I know?" said the woman, with a quiet and subtle smile, "how do I know anything?"

"But it is death to be too wise in some things," said the gipsey, gravely.

"And what woman would not run the risk of death to satisfy her curiosity? But I have told you all I know."

"Has *he* been here lately?"

"No, but I expect him shortly."

"How soon?"

"In a few days."

"Does he write?"

"Yes."

"Let me look at the letter."

The woman produced an envelope.

The gipsey eagerly opened it, and drew out the note.

He pushed it back in disgust.

It was written in a large "expressionless" clerkish hand, and contained only a few commonplace words to the purpose that her employer would see Mary Fleming such a date.

The gipsey mused for a moment.

"Won't you come into the cottage?" she asked.

"Yes, for a moment, and perhaps you will lend me ink and paper."

He entered and seated himself at the table.

She produced the implements for writing.

The gipsey traced some lines in a strange and secret character.

"When the master comes give him this; in the mean while let no one else see—"

"I understand, and I'll be careful."

"I know you will, Mary Fleming. Good bye, we may meet again."

"Good bye, and Heaven guide you. But stay, you are hungry and are poor. Perhaps, as I have money by me, a little would help you."

The gipsey smiled. "No, thank you, I am not poor. My poverty is a part of my disguise. Fortune was tired of ill-using me, and, like a wayward woman, has flown to my arms when she found me unconquerable. Perhaps, some day, I may tell you all my adventures since we last met.

CHAPTER CIII.

THE MASKED HORSEMAN.

We left the doughty settlers and the luckless Dick in the hands of the savage bushrangers. Our readers will remember that the party had been surrounded by an ambuscade of these cut-throats, when, after they had discovered the body of the murdered traveller, they were preparing to mount their horses, in order to give chase to the brigands who had perpetrated the atrocious deed.

It was rather premature to say that they were *in the hands* of the dastardly wretches who were crowded about them to the number of thirty or more. For though their chance of ultimate escape was so small, they were yet four desperate men, and armed to the teeth.

They formed themselves in a square, and presented their gleaming barrels each in an opposite direction.

The ruffians fell back, for it was a dead certainty of destruction to four at least of their number who might dare to advance.

"Look ye, mates," cried Dick, firmly, to the bushrangers, "it seems to me that it will cost you more to take our lives than it's worth your while to lay out on that article. Suppose you come to terms, and give us a free road. Don't stir there. By the Lord! I'll fire."

A scowling miscreant sneaked back, revolver in hand.

"Come on," shouted a tall, red-haired savage, brandishing a murderous knife in one hand, and cocking a pistol in the other. "Don't be flabbergasted by the swines' bristles. Curse their limbs. Down with 'em peaching snipes. We'll stop their clap-traps with a hemp-cravat. They'll be for blowing on our little game, will 'em? Have to make their reports to the devil's commission in the infernal Tartary, I'm thinking. Come on, and see me wring this blustering cock-of-the-woods' neck."

There was a hoarse laugh.

And the freckled, squint-eyed buffoon swaggered up towards the gallant little band.

"Stand back, I tell ye," shouted Dick, fiercely, "if you've any respect for your mottled skin. I don't use to say the same thing twice, and I've given you due warning. You'd better stand back, lad."

"I'm of my friend's opinion," said Kangaroo, jerking his piece ominously. "If you don't want your skin riddled as well as raddled you had better sheer off."

This sally and its allusion to the peculiar personal embellishment of the fiery-faced, flame-winged bushranger, caused a coarse and hearty laugh among his fellows.

Enraged beyond prudence, the ruffian flung himself upon Dick.

The latter, with admirable presence of mind, took a step backwards, and, whirling round his rifle, struck his assailant such a crushing blow with the butt end of his gun that the fellow staggered back, and sank to the ground like a felled ox.

"I told you you had best not venture. Next time you'll have something from the other end."

As the stunned man lay quite motionless this speech elicited another gruff laugh from the group of savages, among whom the defeated did not appear to be a reigning favourite.

After a pause, another ruffian spoke, at the same time advancing a step.

"Whose a goin' to be bilked in this way by four cursed spies and regulators when there's enough on us to quelp the whole tarnel crew of crushers in the colony. Look here, friend, we means hanging on you. Better men nor you has danced without music; but if you don't surrender at discretion, I'll be cussed if we don't brile you at a slow fire, or bury you alive. We ain't no ways pertickler, my covies."

"You may do your worst," replied Dick, without blenching, "and we'll do the same; but I don't stand threatening. My man, I've marked you."

The robber gave a coarse laugh, and turned, with a foul oath, to his comrades.

"Curse it all, if you can't stand, fire agin. Pour on 'em with enough barkers to blow a little nation to almighty smash. I'm ashamed o' sich company, and I'll undertake the job on my own hook."

So saying, he turned round, and deliberately levelled his piece at Dick's head.

"Look here, mates," said our hero, addressing the gang, "fair play's a jewel. Don't none of you fire till we've settled this little affair betwixt ourselves like gentlemen. One on you might give us the signal."

The bushrangers laughed again.

"All right," shouted one. "Odds on the reg'lator."

"Done," cried another. "Three to one, if you like?"

"All serene. Bill will drop the hankercher."

A man stepped forward with a red neck-tie at the end of a revolver.

Dick's companions, interested in this strange turn in events, began to relax their vigilance to watch proceedings.

"For God's sake look to yourselves," whispered Dick; "they'll take you off your guard, and you're dead men for a certainty."

Thus admonished, the three rangers kept a wary eye on their foes, while our hero stepped out of the square, and stood with his gun on his shoulder, waiting for the storm of angry dispute among the betters to subside.

The worthy Bill waved his red flag.

There was a sudden hush.

Dick's bright, clear eye took the measure of his opponent.

The latter looked rather cowed and sullen, but stepped out with as much manfulness as he could muster.

"Ready!—present!"

The deadly barrels were each levelled with fatal aim.

Before the word "fire" could be half uttered, the dastardly bushranger had forestalled the command.

He blazed away, and, but for his nervous haste, would have put his antagonist *hors de combat* for ever. As it was the bullet grazed Dick's cheek; and the light of anger and malice sparkled in his eye for a moment, but he quelled his indignation.

There was intense silence.

Dick coolly and carefully took aim, and before the ruffian could take to his heels, which he seemed inclined to do, dexterously knocked off his cap with the charge.

"There, lad, let that teach you fair play," said Dick, calmly running his ramrod down the barrel of his gun. "With your permission, gentlemen, we'll begin again."

There was a roar of applause.

"Let him bide. Sheep's liver's had enough," shouted several men, with a derisive laugh.

With hisses and yells they saluted their comrade as he sneaked to their rear.

A man advanced, after a little consultation with the rest.

"Mate, I'm commissioned to tell you that, in consideration of your pluck, we don't mean to spile your appetite with a rope choker—a painful duty we has to perform towards your pals. We don't know you. You're a new 'un, and we means to make you one of us. So, if you choose to save your life, you've only to step over here while we settles them. We've set our mark on Waller and Barnup—lagged a pal of mine—and we owes the Kangaroo rather a long reckoning. So come out of their company afore they spiles your morals."

"I'm much obliged to you, mate," said Dick, with his own frank smile; "but I hope you're not such fools as to spoil a good mind by excepting my companions from mercy. "To 'settle' us will cost you four lives, perhaps more, and there's no need to have recourse to such extreme measures as hanging us. At all events, all I've got to say is, that I don't understand deserting my friends when they're in danger."

"Go, Dick. You may live to revenge us," whispered Waller.

"Specially when they're willing for me to leave them to save myself. So you'd better come to some terms at once, and save all further unpleasantness."

"Well, my cove, you have had your chance, and it's over. We'll swing you like a cat. So look out for yourself."

A general rush upon the little party would have followed at once.

But every member of the gang stood suddenly spell-bound by the vibrations of a whistle that thrilled through the leafy arcades of the wood.

A horseman came galloping from out the bush, and rode furiously up to the party. As he advanced he pulled down from his low slouch hat a black crape mask, which completely shrouded his face. The men fell back as he approached, and, grounding their muskets, stood in silence and expectation.

The man who had made an offer of pardon to Dick, stepped up to the side of the rider, and, touching his hat, gave some explanations, in a low tone.

"Good," said the new comer, tersely. "I have seen it all. Where is John Rhodes?" The defeated duellist sneaked forward. "A man who is a coward, and who cannot stand fire in a fair fight, is useless in our band—dangerous to its safety—and must be removed."

"O, God, captain!" cried the wretch, falling upon his knees.

Without another word, the masked horseman deliberately drew a revolver and blew the man's brains out.

A cry of horror burst from the rangers.

The gang recoiled with scowling glances at this summary execution.

"Take him out of the way," said the horseman, replacing his revolver in the holster. "Disarm that man, and hang the rangers."

Some of the fellows who have anticipated this order had sidled up to the men, and suddenly flinging themselves upon them, after a struggle, in which several guns were discharged in the air, succeeded in securing them.

"You have but a few moments to live. If you wish to pray you can do so."

"Hear me speak," said Dick. "If you mean to spare me, I wish to tell you that I don't want your mercy, and won't accept it. Let me live or die with my companions."

"Your companions!" said the horseman, with a bitter sneer. "What have you to do with these? Are they not as truly your sworn enemies as they are mine? Would they not as gladly track you to your ruin or your death for blood money as another? They are your enemies as naturally as the wolf is the destroyer of cattle. Only you have served out one term of your life of degrading punishment and slavery, and you are free to struggle on till scorn, hunger, and temptation, drive the loosed wild beast back to his den, and his keeper—yet no, eternity of freedom is before you with the light condition that you must—*starve!* What have you to do with regulators and officers of justice when you know not how soon some officious knave may rob you of the bread you eat, the home you cherish, and the good name you toil for, by denouncing you to scandalised humanity, as a convicted thief, a returned transport—a 'Ticket-of-Leave!'"

Poor Dick buried his honest face in his hands and groaned.

"Not true, Dick. No convict. Give the dirty blackguard the lie," cried his companions simultaneously, forgetful, for the moment, of their own position of danger.

"Aye, mates, it's true enough; but I am an innocent man, for all that."

His comrades instinctively, perhaps unconsciously, removed from his side.

"Do ye mark them—their heads in the noose—they have enough pride and self-respect to sheer off from a branded felon?" cried the Captain of Outlaws with a triumphant laugh. "Well, Dick, the biter must sometimes get bit; and you'll have the pleasure of seeing these bloodhounds dangle from that tree in the same fashion as they would like to see such as you and us swing off the drop. Zounds! but it's a mighty pity we can't do the thing in the right style—such a shabby gallows, no St. Sepulchre toll, no white-faced parson, no black-coated Calcraft, no sheriffs, no crammed windows, no death-gloating mob, not even a cold Monday morning; but though the 'wretched men' must take their last look at earth among the calm, green woods in the silver night, without bell or burial service to the edification of such a poor company, they will suffer as cruel a pang of suffocation, they will present a spectacle as ennobling to humanity, as if they had 'suffered' in the first style at the Old Bailey; and our revenge will be just as sweet though we do not try them by jury."

"Away with them."

Dick rushed forward, and furiously seized the horse by the bridle.

The mettlesome steed reared, and curvetted and plunged fearfully.

Several rifles were levelled at our hero.

The captain lightly waved his hand.

"Stand back! I can defend myself. What is it Dick?" he said soothingly. "Are you mad? I am your friend?"

"Devil and tempter," cried Dick, "you would drive me mad. You have denounced me as a convict in sheer malice. You would spare me till you had sullied my soul that death would be eternal; and then you would butcher me as pitilessly as you murdered your miserable follower."

With this he strove to drag the outlaw from his saddle.

But he was pulled away by the bushrangers.

"Dick," said the strange rider, calmly, "that cowardly bully was a spy as well as poltroon, and he who would have hanged you so willingly has his pocket full of money in earnest of a reward for betraying the band. You see I know all these things. Nothing is hidden from me. I am at war with society, and have learned to know whom to distrust and whom to confide in. I find many of the former, few of the latter. I like you, Dick, and I mean to save you. In return, tell me this. If I let you go free, what will you do for a living?"

"Work."

"Who will employ you?"

"Many, for I am strong and willing, and no one will be mean enough to split upon me."

"*I* was mean enough."

"You are a villain."

"They will not know my disgrace."

"*I* knew it, Dick. You have had many keepers and fellow prisoners who, when they see you prosperous and happy, will feel no envy, malice, or uncharitableness, and would scorn to betray you. Of course they would; human nature, criminal human nature is *so* magnanimous."

"You wretch," cried Dick, between his clenched teeth. "Were my hands free I would tear your black tongue from your teeth. Hang me—murder me—but do not torture me to death."

"Truth is mostly painful. But look, Dick, you are a good fellow, and not a fool; and you are not so refreshingly innocent as to fancy you will be able to gain a position of competence and happiness with a ticket-of-leave in your pocket as a recommendation. Be one of us. Waller is a married man, so is Barnup. The Kangaroo is a fine fellow. They are your friends. If you will be one of us I will give them to you. Hang them or free them at your pleasure. If you refuse, they shall swing in five minutes, and you will remain my prisoner till I can bring you to reason."

The ferocious bushrangers at these words looked at each other with dissatisfaction strongly marked on their stern and sullen faces.

"Don't turn thief to save me," said the Kangaroo.

Waller and Barnup did not speak.

Dick folded his arms, and for a few moments remained silent. At length he looked up.

"No. I have suffered much to keep my conscience clean, and if I must put my hand in my pocket, and find it empty, if I must see the sneer on the lips of rogues at liberty, who despise me, a poor Ticket-of-Leave, who never wronged man nor woman in my life, I will, at least, lay my hand on my heart and say that there is nothing there to reproach or to make me feel ashamed. Let us shake hands, mates, and die like men. For I know that neither of you would buy your lives by selling me to these villains."

"Hurrah!" shouted Kangaroo. "I, for one, mate, honour and respect you, and would rather die a hundred times than see a good, brave lad like yourself join this gang of cut-throats. I don't doubt you are innocent, and have been cursedly ill-used."

"*You* don't think I am a thief?"

"No more than myself, Dick. In your own words, lad, let the devils do their worst."

The savage bushrangers, with looks of brutal pleasure, stood ready to lay hands on their victims.

The horseman sat seemingly absorbed in thought.

Not that he was wavering as to his resolution. To his stern, strong nature vacillation was unknown. But he seemed pondering and moralising on this turn in events. He held up his hand.

"Let the hounds die," he said; "hang the mean spaniel, too, that fawns on the hand that abuses him. I am sick of the hypocrite."

The bushrangers gave a deep growl of delight, and two of the wretches placed the ends of a long broad slip of wood upon two rough block pieces beneath the dangling nooses.

Deadly pale, but with firm-set lips, the four men

were marched up to the fatal spot, they mounted the stand, and the nooses were placed round their necks.

The masked horseman rode up and addressed our hero,

"I give you a last chance. Will you swear into our ranks? Speak! 'No' will be your last word."

"Must I recant, mates?" said poor Dick, in a thick voice to his comrades.

"No," roared the Kangaroo. "We'll die game."

"No," murmured Waller.

Barnup tried to utter something, but terror held him speechless.

Several men knelt down, and placed their hands on the board ready to push it away.

Their Captain reined his horse backwards.

"Dick, I have one last proposal to make. If I give you life and liberty—yourself and your comrades—will you swear, by all that you hold sacred, that, when the ungrateful crew have spurned you from amongst them, when all your honest endeavour fails to wash away the stain so unjustly fixed upon you, when you are starving for want of employment, you will join me?"

"Swear that, Dick," whispered Kangaroo, excitedly; "it will never come to that."

"I swear it; and more, that I will be the biggest thief among ye."

"Loose them. Let them get down," said the Captain.

The men sullenly obeyed the order. Wonder and joy almost deprived the rangers of their senses, thus snatched from the jaws of death.

The Captain made a sign to the gang, who bowed their heads in token of acquiescence, and disappeared into the thicket so suddenly and noiselessly that they seemed to " have melted into air."

The Captain held out his hand to Dick, but the latter drew himself up proudly, and did not respond to the salute.

"Well, well," said the Captain, with a strangely good-humoured laugh, " the day is coming when you will grasp this hand as the hand of your only friend. You will see, Dick; you may try to keep square, but it won't answer. Adieu! *Au revoir!*" which means, " *Till we meet again!*"

Another moment and the click of his horse's hoof was heard dying in the distance.

CHAPTER CIV.

THE ACTOR AT HOME.

LET us return to England. Let us enter a house in one of the eastern suburbs of the metropolis, and inspect the strange and motley appointments of the first floor of a large, dirty, dreary-looking house in one of the dreary, ghastly-genteel streets that abound in the neighbourhood.

Sparely accommodated with the ordinary effects, the room is rich to repletion in a curious sort of wealth.

Though there are but a table, three chairs, a truckle bed, and toilet conveniences, the walls are hung with coats of armours, velvet mantles, feathered hats, and a few tawdry prints; portraits of popular actors and ravishing *danseuses*; stage boots, shoes, and stockings of various colours; collars, buckles, bells, frills, ruffles, gauntlets, wigs, foils, pistols, and other theatrical properties, are lying about on boxes and on the floor.

Before a smouldering fire sits a pale, slim man, with large, dark eyes—a mass of black hair, sensual lips, and regular features.

By the light of a glaring candle he is conning his part from a dirty little pamphlet he holds in his hand. By his side is a bottle of rum, and a glass of ditto slightly diluted with hot water.

This gallant is no other than Mr. Dudley Mortimer, an eminent tragedian at one of the minor theatres in this oriental district.

He is reading aloud in that sonorous and measured tone now raised to a hectoring pitch—now lowered to a "stage whisper"—and broken at intervals by a burst of "stage" laughter, or a diapason of stage groans.

A loud knock at the door causes the actor, for a while at least, " to be heard no more."

" Come in!" he shouts, and then proceeds, hastily, to fling a royal robe over the glass and bottle on the table.

A stout, burly-looking woman enters the apartment, her face lighted up with a gleam of withering sarcasm, and her arms akimbo.

"Good morning, madam."

"Good morning to *you*, sir. I hope Mr. Dudley Mortimer will pardon my intruding, but I am really obliged to trouble him *once* more concerning the little trifle of rent that is owing."

The landlady curtseyed repeatedly with commendable reverence.

"Ah, my dear madam, the immortal Shakespeare won't pay your rent. You're all of the same bad lot, and all rogues together."

" ' Who steals my purse steals trash.' "

"That I werry well believe. But I'd have you know, sir, that I'm not agoing to be paid any longer in fine speeches and fine promises. If you cannot produce the seventeen and sixpence, due the last Monday as ever was, out of my house you goes, and I sticks to the things."

"But, my charming and indulgent fair, did you not promise that I should hear no more of all this until Saturday? You know that I have just succeeded in obtaining an engagement, and shall now have wealth untold at my disposal."

The landlady now seated herself with an air of defiance and determination.

"You know as you promised me faithful that when you got this engagement you would pay me up to the last penny, and give me something handsome besides; and here you have been three weeks receiving a good salary."

"A guinea a week, and find my own properties."

"That ain't my business, and I won't be contradicted by sich deceitful wretches; and all I've got to say is, that you don't touch none of these properties till I see the colour of your money."

With this the amiable creature snatched up a bundle in which poor Didley Mortimer had tied the properties made for the part he was to perform that very night.

"Inexorable woman," cried the actor, starting up in great alarm, "you would not, surely, take away the prop that doth sustain my life? Deprived of that precious parcel I am a ruined man. How can I appear without fleshings? As you are strong, be merciful."

"Don't think it; unless you settles my little bill this moment, I'll not only keep your rubbish, but I'll throw it on the fire, there now."

And with this the virago strode across the room towards the fire-place to put her threat into execution.

In great agitation the luckless player followed her, and caught her by the arm, imploring forebearance.

"Oh you wretch, and so you'd murder me would you, a poor lone woman? I'll let the neighbours know of your pretty goings on, you villain."

With this the injured and defenceless fair uttered a piercing shriek.

There was a long and loud knocking at the street door.

"Thank goodness! that's the police. Now we shall see if a lone woman is to be abused and assaulted in her own house."

With this she darted from the room, taking the bundle with her.

Presently she returned in some hurry and excitement.

"Mr. Mortimer, a gentleman wishes to speak with you," she said, in a tone strangely modified; "he seems a perfect gentleman, and is in a 'ansom."

"Won't he come up, madam? Must I go down to him?" asked the actor, in some surprise.

"Here he is, sir," said the landlady, instinctively dropping a curtsey as the stranger entered.

Most imposing was the presence of the new comer.

His hair was carefully curled, his huge moustache was black as jet, and trained to a perfection of symmetry. He wore a black velvet coat and waistcoat, the latter adorned with gold buttons as large as sixpences; more than one gold chain glittered across his breast; a glass was screwed in his eye, and in his elegantly gloved hand he held a gold-mounted walking-cane.

The stranger bowed gracefully.

Dudley Mortimer looked at him long and inquiringly.

"Beg pardon; 'pon my word, if I come *malapropos*—slight domestic *fracas*; such things will occur in the best-regulated households. Perhaps I had better postpone"—

"Oh, sir—indeed, sir," began the landlady, apologetically. "Any friend of Mr. Mortimer's is allus welcome to my humble dormitory (let us hope the good lady meant domicile), only the rates and the taxes is so enormous in this neighbourhood; and as we lives upon our lodgers, in course rent and breakfasses for six weeks *is* a consideration to a poor lone woman."

"Ah, I see. It's a small difficulty of a pecuniary nature. May I ask you, ma'am, what the little amount may be?"

"Four pound, fourteen, and tenpence three-farthings."

The distinguished personage, with a shrug and a pitying smile at the paucity of the amount, drew out his *porte-monnaie*, and took therefrom a roll of bank notes. Selecting one, he delicately handed it to the landlady.

"It's a fiver, that is, ma'am; a five-pound note. I trust it will suffice to discharge all present claims."

The actor and his merciless janitress both looked their astonishment.

"And now, ma'am, perhaps you will have the goodness to cut your st—that is aw—to slope—as I have a little business to settle with my friend Mr. Mortimer."

The landlady bustled about the room, dusting the chairs, and running on in a strain of glowing compliments and lively thanks, but seemed little disposed to leave the apartment.

The dignitary kept following her movements with his basilisk eye-glass till he fairly stared her out of the room.

Still chattering, she passed through the door, which she closed after her.

In another moment the visitor re-opened it, and perceiving her still lingering on the landing, again fixed a glassy glare upon her, which drove her down five or six stairs. Again she halted, and in some confusion proceeded, in a most pains-taking manner, to dust the ballusters.

The exquisite reclined in an attitude of statuesque grace, but still kept a stony stare upon all the manœuvres of the inquisitive and officious dame, who, finding the foe invincible, suddenly gave up the contest, and made a hurried retreat to the regions below.

Assured that she was out of eye-shot, and concluding that she had taken permanent refuge from his formidable glance in the nether "impenetralia," the distinguished personage re-entered the room, and, placing a chair by the side of the fire, motioned the actor to be seated, and then smoothing his luxuriant moustache turned round and thus addressed him—

"And so you don't know me, dear boy? That *is* strange. I always notice when a man gets a rise in the world that the memories of his pals and doxies is 'stonishing freshened, and then think of all sorts of good turns they have done, which he has quite orgotten; and crikey ain't they just astounded as they should have passed in the street with glumpy looks—when their poor hearts was yearning after him like a mother snivelling for her lost kid? Look here, my covey," he went on exultingly displaying a handful of sovereigns, "don't you know me now?"

"You are very much altered, and your 'get up' is admirable; but if I don't mistake, you are the Downy."

"The individual, sir, his mother's only son, at least, I was, for you see I'm going to make a fresh chalk and begin another dance, and you must help me."

"But you have been very prosperous," said the poor actor with a look of annoyance on his face, as he wonderingly scanned the elegant figure of his visitor. "It is rather hard of you, Downy, to invade my privacy and tempt my wretchedness by this display of money and toggery, when you know I can never run in the same harness with yourself on any account, for, whether it is wisdom or folly, I cannot swerve from honesty and further than poverty drives me against my will, as incurring a few beggarly debts that I cannot pay, and the like, God knows I've had a sad run of ill-luck lately." The actor put his hand to his forehead and pushed back his dark hair, while a shade of pain crossed his face. "It is hard," he said bitterly, "it is damnably hard—that with my unblemished character, my earnest striving, I can do nothing better for myself than I am doing now—that I should be spurned and degraded, while you thrive so much better by waging war with society. It makes me feel almost ready to foreswear all my good resolutions, and take up the gauntlet rown down by the pitiless world. But, no—no! though even the loved of my heart despises me for my poverty and misfortunes—though I have learned to look upon myself as a sort of criminal deservedly shunned and contemned—I will cling to the firm trust of my heart, that when I have lost all I shall save myself, and that if I die a pauper, they may write on my grave—a man who struggled through a weary life to die honest!"

The Downy yawned.

"Well—I s'pose there's a vacancy for a chaplain in one of the jugs, and you're a rehearsing for the sitivation. But I say, my chum, where's the bell—lets have a drain and a weed, and talk over our little affairs comfortable."

The actor smiled, and was about to leave the room in search of the "sedatives," when he paused—

"Downy," he said, "you know I must be at the theatre in an hour—suppose we adjourn to some quiet place, and there we can compare notes at our ease—or, if you like, you can come with me behind the scenes."

"I'm game—only, my covey, you ain't ashamed of my company?"

"Why should I be ?—you have been kind to me when every one else turned their back upon me—if you are at issue with the law, it is not my affair."

"Oh, Lord, Ned! if I had but your larning—see how you can turn a speech. If the crush has got their eye upon a leary cove—if you are's issue with—dear boy, *do* say it again! Oh, t larning!—but that's the very thing I have come

No. 33.

talk to you about. Ned, I've had a legacy; I'm going to give up the pilching lay and take to kite-flying and the higher branches, and I want you to give me some lessons in larning."

The actor laughed heartily.

"Cos vy?" the Downy went on, in no wise disconcerted; "fine feathers make fine birds; but a nobby rig out ain't much good if a fellow has no grammar. Nearly bilked myself for want of sich things in the last little game that turned out so stunning. But come along, I'm as thirsty as a Arab in the deserts of Sarah. We'll carry out mugs to the boozing-ken, and then I'll put you up to a move that will make you open both eyes without winking."

Dudley Mortimer threw on a cloak, beneath which he placed his little bundle of properties, and they sallied forth together.

"I'll tell you what, dear boy," said the Downy to his companion, "I can't see you agoin' on in this way; every chap has got some sort of fad or fancy, and you're for living on the square. Well, seeing as how we were brought up at the national expense—in the work—the Temple of Charity (damme, that's a good turn for it!)—it does you a deal of honour, and I think I can put you up to a thing that'll keep you out of the reach of the beaks and crushers, and yet turn you in flimsies enough to build a monument. Cos vy? You can act—have got larning and the gift of the gab. But let's come this way; there's the Beauchamp down yonder, and I want to meet an aristo cove that frequents it; he uses me, and comes down with the shiners handsome."

Turning off from the street they were passing they crossed over to a large and handsome tavern on the other side of the way.

Selecting a quiet department of the bar they entered.

The Downy called for glasses of brandy and water and cigars.

They sipped the stimulants and smoked for some moments without further interchange of conversation.

The actor appeared a little depressed and abstracted.

The Downy was evidently carefully maturing some plan that had suggested itself to his mind.

The door opened—a tall, burly-looking personage entered.

He was well and plainly dressed, and there was that indescribable stamp of caste in his demeanour that proclaimed him a gentleman.

He looked searchingly from beneath his thick and heavy eyebrows upon the young tragedian, and then slightly nodded to the Downy.

"Have you executed my commission?" he said, in a tone bland, yet imperative.

"Aw—yaas—my—sir; with every care and superinspection," returned the Downy, with a vile attempt at self-posesssion and carelessness, "I think you will be perfectly satisfied with the result of my negrociation."

The poor *illiteratus* gasped, and then dusting his sleeves with his silk banana, stood erect, and looked magnificent.

"Will he meet me? or will he write?"

"Right you are," replied the Downy, with a grisly smile at his atrocious attempt at a joke.

"What do you mean?" asked the gentleman testily.

"Why, sir—he writes."

"Good. And the other affair?"

"All square and comfortable."

"Good. Are you prepared to start for Norfolk?"

"Up to any thing."

"Well—"

The gentleman pondered awhile, and then looked up suddenly, and said—

"Hold yourself in readiness for another commission. I have changed my mind; I shall not send you thither."

"Werry good, sir."

"I think I owe you something. Take this. But stay—with this gentleman's kind indulgence I will speak to you at my carriage for one moment as I am in a hurry."

Lifting his hat, in a graceful salute to the actor, he left the bar, followed by the Downy.

Presently the latter returned, and on his re-entrance heartily slapped Dudley Mortimer on the shoulder.

"Damme, Ned," he cried exultingly, "your fortune's made. Did you notice the cut of the real swell that's just left us? Who is he, dear boy, eh?"

"No idea."

"Why he is the Earl of ———, but warhawks, I'm getting precious wide-jawed lately. But you've got the fidgets, what's the matter?"

"I must be off; it's a benefit night, my boy, and I must don the sables, for I am going to play Hamlet."

"The devil you are. I know the cove—sees ghosts—poisons the grave-diggers and plays with somebody's skull. 'To be or not to be,' comes on, goes mad, and sings about valentines. I'm down to it you see. Lord, I fancy I should make a stunning actor myself in my own room—by jingo! I have had practice enough. *I* had a benefit t'other night. Played Lieutenant Leary to the tune of six hundred—fact, 'pon my soul. But we won't walk, it's so deuced vulgar. Hi, Hansom!"

The Downy called a trim cab from off the stand and leaped in, beckoning his companion, who took a place by his side, and rattled off, lighting his perfumed Havanna.

A strange disenchantment in the aspect of things behind the curtain. The flare of lurid gas; the squalid daub of patchy scene-smearing; the tawdry tinsel and coarse cotton velvet; the thick plastering of cheeks with chalk and hectic rouge; blear eyes; thick voices; profane words; pewter pots; paper-capped shifters and stage carpenters; the beery, gunpowdery odours; the searching draughts of chill air; the narrow entrances; the break-neck traps; and, dreariest of all, the haggard, painted faces of the graceful fairies, "translated" from the glamour of their borrowed loveliness to the squalor of their real unseemliness—little of beauty, little of fascination in bare reality. But we won't moralise. The Downy mingles in strange company; drinks "humble" with the "royal Dane;" chats with the ghost; cracks broad jokes with the queen; kisses the chaste Ophelia; and very nearly comes to a row with the fiery Laertes.

The Downy is standing at the wing, and, with a silent group of other watchers, is, for a while, enthralled by the fervour and pathos with which poor Dudley Mortimer, in his transformed identity, utters, in heart-prompted bitterness, that grand enumeration of the stinging ills and scorns of restless, thankless existence:—

"'The oppressor's wrong; the proud man's contumely;
The pangs of despised love;
The law's delays; the insolence of office;'
And all the spurns that patient merit takes of the unworthy!'"

The Downy hears a little gush of excitement and admiration, and turns his head.

By his side a young girl is standing.

He has not noticed her before.

She heeds him not; her eyes are fixed intently upon the poor player, who, wafted by the sublime enthusiasm of his glorious art, soars far above the poor surroundings and the depressing associations, and walks, and feels as the grand, irresolute, human prince, whom the poet has for ever ennobled and immortalised.

The Downy can watch her beautiful and expressive features without fear of his scrutiny being observed.

She is finely moulded—a fay, indeed—her cheek is not disfigured with the loathsome rouge, but glows with nature's rosy tinting. Her bud-like lips pout childishly, and her little white teeth flush chastely; her large, dark, soft eyes, fringed with long, silken lashes, beam clear, and soft, and deep; her hands are clasped upon her heaving bosom in an attitude of unconscious but faultless grace.

The Downy looks upon her for a moment in an ecstasy of admiration, and then, in gawkish bashfulness, lowers his glance.

His erring and degraded nature is awed by her Una-like beauty and purity.

Mortimer leaves the stage.

With a faint smile he joins his companion.

The girl stepped backward as he advanced.

"Lotty, how charming you look to-night," said the actor, affectionately; "and how is your mother, dear?"

"She is better, thanks, Mr. Mortimer. The doctor says if I could only take her into the country, when the spring is a little more advanced, she would be likely to recover; but my engagement will be over soon," she went on, with a little sigh, "and we cannot always do what we wish in this world."

"And yet you have had several offers recently, Lotty."

"Yes, but they have been conditional," she said, with a deep blush; "but there are no folks in the world so generous and kind-hearted as our high-class managers, and I trust I shall soon hold a permanent position at a West-end theatre. But I am to play in your new piece, Mr. Mortimer."

"Yes, dear, and thereby insure its success."

"Ah, you are a sad flatterer. Oh, I wish I could speak as well as I can dance!" she exclaimed, with a burst of naive and charming vanity. "And I am to be your heroine! I tremble at the thought. I have read your play, and the verses. Oh, Mr. Mortimer, they are so suggestive—so sweet and tender in their pathos. Oh, if all the world thought of you as I do, what a great man you would be!"

The actor smiled with that exquisite pleasure that is the effect of every gratification of personal vanity, and he replied—

"The good opinion of all the world could not add one charm to the delight I feel at having gained yours, Miss Lotty; but, the curtain is up."

The girl smiled, and airily tripped away. Presently she burst upon the stage with a graceful bound, and in a quaint dance, in which she displayed an agility and a refinement of grace that brought down thunders of applause.

After having performed her enchanting dance and exquisite *poses*, she curtseyed to the audience with simple dignity, and flushed and lovely from the exertion tripped up to Mortimer and his companion.

The curtain had fallen for the last time, the performance was completed, and the heated and exhausted actors severally betook themselves to their respective homes.

Young Mortimer offered to escort Miss Lotty Meroyn to her mother's lodging, which was situated in Pimlico.

As they were threading the streets on their way thither Lotty chatted gaily and pleasantly, and the Downy exerted all his powers to ingratiate himself with the young *danseuse*, while Mortimer, who looked pale and fagged, walked on listlessly without joining in the conversation. They left Lotty at the door of her house, and then retraced their steps.

As they were crossing a large and bustling thoroughfare they were suddenly stopped by a little crowd obstructing the pavement, a body of ladies in ball costume, and gentlemen in full dress were pouring out from the door of some mansion and hurrying into their respective carriages, which were ranged in a long line that extended far down the street.

A tall, showy-looking gentleman, handsomely dressed, was handing a beautiful, fair girl down the steps, a light opera cloak was thrown around her, and she stepped daintily over the pavement.

When Mortimer saw her he stepped back, an ashy paleness overspread his fine countenance, and unconsciously he clutched the column of the portico.

The fair girl was murmuringly conversing with her companion, her eyes bent on the ground, tracing the way for her fairy feet, and her golden tresses glowing richly in the lamp-light.

Suddenly she raised her eyes, and her glance fell full upon the young actor.

She started, the rosy tint deeply suffusing her fair cheek and her moulded neck, and then her large blue eyes glared with strong coldness upon him, and an expression of chilling disdain sat on her arched lips as she swept into the carriage.

Mortimer did not speak. They passed on; but his sudden emotion had not escaped the notice of the Downy.

"What's up? Know that gal, Ned?—a regular empress, and no mistake. But what's the good of being a genius with a fine phiz and a noble heart if you're without a stiver? 'Put money in your purse.' It was a werry wise man as preached that philosophy. 'Put money in your purse,' Ned, and the Chief Justice will lift his hat to you. I had a flash gal myself once—a reg'lar model. Her father was a fence and a seller of ducats (duplicates of goods illegally pawned). He was in a werry good way of business, and she was werry high-minded; but while I was flush with swag she worshipped me like a Injin idol, and as soon as I got into trouble and the funds were low she spurned me like a stray cur. But I didn't bear her any spite; 'cos vy?—it's natur'."

Young Mortimer stopped suddenly, and, disengaging his arm, raised his hand to his head.

"She may well despise me," mentally ejaculated the young actor. "Oh, how low my fall has brought me!—the companion of a thief, and he my only friend!"

The Downy looked at him for a moment in surprise, and then held out his hand.

"Tip us your flipper, my pall," he said; "and take my davy for what I'm going to tell you:—I wouldn't see you what *I* am for all the swag in the Bank of England. I'm going to put you into a snug berth where you can do everything on the square, and perhaps if I don't happen on any ill-luck I'll retire myself. Look ye, Ned; once where I puts you you must forget as we ever met, only don't think too hard of a poor chap as had no way of keeping out of the jug but by doing the Downy."

CHAPTER CV.

THE BLOCK ON FIRE.

DICK and the Rangers have returned to the Block-house. In a few words they narrated their adventures.

It had been pre-arranged that no reference should be made to the subject of Dick's antecedents.

Waller, Barnup, and the Kangaroo had severally and collectively sworn eternal gratitude and friendship to our hero.

Mynna's joy at the return of her deliverer was without bounds, and in her natural openness and simplicity she took no pains to conceal it.

She was now located at the block with the wives of the rangers.

She soon became an object of universal affection and esteem.

Her gentle and winning manners: her fearless self-possession, and her pretty face had gained her an enviable popularity.

Entirely devoted to Dick Parker she paid no regard to the advances made to her by many a well-to-do landowner or official in the little regiment.

One fellow, a fierce and sinister-looking man, who possessed a little money and a great deal of impudence, offered her marriage, and earnestly strove to persuade her to abandon the little military settlement for his farm and plantation.

She refused his offers with much modesty and kindness. He seemed to take his answer as decisive, and from that time ceased to show any marked admiration for his charmer.

He was, however, a dangerous fellow; his vanity was deeply wounded, and he resolved at any cost to be avenged for his slight and disappointment.

With this intent he spent much time in our hero's company, and strove hard to elicit some account of his whereabouts, &c.

Dick was extremely careful not to commit himself in any way, especially as one of the officers of this Volunteer Service had told him that three fine fellows had been refused admission into the regiment on account of its being known that they had served a term of penal servitude, and were now at large on a ticket-of-leave.

Our hero had found in the Kangaroo a valuable ally, for the latter was entirely devoted to him ever since their expedition in search of the murdered man and their adventure with the bushrangers.

One evening Parker and his comrade were returning from a day's hunting, well laden with spoil, when, as they came within a mile of the Block, their attention was attracted by the appearance of a strange red light that flickered in the distant sky.

In the position in which they were then standing they could not distinguish the rampart-mounds, the cabins, nor even the clump of trees that surrounded the Block.

The place was concealed by a long low hill.

Yet still the red glare intensified and spread over the deep purple.

"Fire—Dick, God—the Block is in flames—run—run." With this the Kangaroo threw down the game that he held in either hand and the small deer that he carried on his shoulder, and flew up the hill.

Dick followed him hard, but had much ado to keep alongside.

The Kangaroo strode along with long leaping strides as if his legs had been encased in the "seven-league" boots.

When they had gained the brow of the hill they could discern the bright flames shooting up from the roof, and a dense cloud of smoke curling and bellowing upwards to pollute the clearness of the pure blue sky.

Men and women were running about, and cattle were rushing wildly down the steep sides of the eminence on which the Block stood.

"Injins?" asked Parker, as he reach his long-legged companion, and gasped for breath.

"No."

"Bushrangers?"

"No. Accident;—bad job, though. Timber's green at this season, and it's a devil of a piece of work to raise such a fort as that, I can tell you. The worst is that we shall be like unearthed foxes without a hole to hide in. But come along, put the steam on, we may be wanted."

Without another word the tall fellow flew down into the valley below as if his feet were winged.

Dick followed as close as he could, but was forced to make terrific exertions to keep within distance.

When they had reached the middle of the valley, the Kangaroo stopped so suddenly that Dick, who was following close at his heels, was almost thrown backwards.

Before them were several ridges of briars and brushwood, that had been cut through to make a narrow foot-way.

A sort of pool, one of the chain that stretched across that part of the country, and in the flood-time formed a wide and rapid river, was before them. It was thickly clogged by pollards and stunted willows.

"Hist!" said the Kangaroo. "Down, Dick; some of the cussed bushrangers in the 'plant' (a name by which such places are called.) Let us watch their devilish manœuvres before they claps eyes on us"

The companions stealthily crawled from tree to tree, and concealed themselves beneath a tall and flowering shrub. At a little distance they perceived two ruffians, whose faces they at once recognised as belonging to individuals of the party who had made them prisoners on the occasion of their expedition into the marshes.

"I owes that infernal cuss a reckoning that I means to get a receipt for," whispered the Kangaroo. "That's the cove that put the hemp round my neck. I'll spoil his hand for running slip-knots, cuss him."

"And the other rascal I knows myself," returned Dick, in the same tone. "I knew him at the hulks for a cursed sniveller, that barneyed the chaplain till he thought him a blessed martyr, damn him. Those sort are the very worst; 'cos a cove must be infernal bad when he can come that business. Shall we rush on 'em, and square up at once."

"No, Dick, that would be a fool's trick. There may be an army on 'em. But where's all our chaps?" asked Dick. "When we were on the top of the hill I didn't see above a dozen among the cabins, only the squalling women and the brats; which is always plentiful."

"A large gang of 'em are up at Fort Wilson at the new road; but I don't think as the cusses are up to a general assault, for I heard as a regiment of real soldiers was acoming to the fort to investigate that infernal affair of poor Dodd's murder, and the burning of the Leigh farms at Wymandale. Take a fool's word for it, mate, there's treason in the camp."

"But who—"

"Hush—don't gab, and keep down; one of the devils is startled. I don't want to chalk either on 'em till they have played their little game out and I have seen their cards."

A fierce and bearded bushranger stepped over the crackling briars, and, shading his eyes with his hand listened intently.

The two rangers held their breath, crouched close to the ground, and remained as motionless as logs of wood that lay scattered about them.

"Don't be gaping about like a pig. All the ruck in 'em are up at the Fort and the coast's clear," said one of the fellows in a gruff voice.

"Don't you shut your eyes like a stupid owl when there's something in the wind; get up, you skunk, and help me to beat the bush," returned the other gentleman with equal suavity.

The two fellows stood with a look of roused attention on their faces.

"I tell you I heard a voice," said one.

"Werry like, mate,"

"Some cussed mocking bird. I wish I could wring their infernal necks, they're always deceiving a fellow."

They waited for a moment to reassure themselves, and then returned to their former position.

"Here he comes," said one of them, starting to his feet.

As he spoke a man on horseback came bounding along from the direction of the Block.

Dick and his companion immediately recognised in him the person of Dan Sullivan, the ranger, who had had paid such attention to the pretty Mynna. He was a tall and swarthy fellow of about thirty, with a malicious eye, and a wild, profligate look.

"It's done," he said, briefly; "you may tell him, as there'll be no quarters for the red coats, no forage for their horses. He may come when he likes after to-morrow—that is, if he be strong enough; best at nightfall. There's old Spencer's 'plant' and homestead up beyond the river: might set fire to it, and carry off the hay that's just cut. One amongst us here—say Jackson—might give a thrilling account of the affair, and make out as the whole gang was engaged in it; so that would create a diversion."

"All right; a good plan. You ain't suspected Dan, no ways, are ye?"

"No, mate; leastways, I don't see any sign on it. But it's an infernal dirty trick of him to put me on the cussed spy business, after the narrow chance I had with the reg'lators last time."

"Well, he got you out of that quandry, anyhow; and give the devil what's his due. He is a royal stunner at doing the handsome when you does serve him to his mind."

"How's things at the Island?"

"Don't mention it—awful wuss! but he's never there hardly; summut takes up his attention in another quarter. Know anything about that planter's gal?"

"What, Mynna?"

"Yes; they say she's broke away from the aboriginals. One of the blacks told me."

"Did Lawson hear on it?"

"Yes; infernally riled."

"And the - what did he say?"

"Laughed."

"There won't no good come of it."

"I should like to see that snivelling Methodist cur ousted out of his cuckoo's nest."

"Curse it all, Jem, there ain't a usefuller man in all the gang than he be."

"You'll see, my nab, he'll turn out an infernal peach arter all."

"Well, it's getting devilish hot for all on us."

"I thinks of selling out."

"Well, Bill, you had best not jabber about that."

"But he says as any one as don't like the looks of things may take his share of the swag and go."

"Go," rejoined the other, with a derisive laugh, "ah that's to save funeral expenses. Go!"

"How far? Just to the brink of your own grave, I calculate, and never a step farther, back'ards or for'ards."

"That's right," said the other ruffian; "looking at Sam Brewster."

"But that cove was a blasted pinch, he deserved all he got."

"No matter for that; I tell you he sets his mark on whoever leaves the band, whatever he may say about their liberty of striking; and I would'nt advise you to try it on, my pal, and I don't like to listen to such like palaver."

"Well, it's time I was off any how," said Sullivan, reining his horse, and looking round impatiently. "Do you see, mates, how the flames is roaring. I pretty well fancy we've unkennelled these bloodhounds any how."

"Shall we meet again, Dan?"

"Aye, to-morrow."

"Where?"

"As good here as any where else, as I knows on."

"Come along?"

"No, Jackson and I have got a scheme."

"What is it?"

"You'd like to know."

"I should. Curse it all you can trust us."

"About as much as I can trust anybody, I dare say gem'men."

"'Spose there was a accident with the gunpowder, eh?"

"Awful calamity! I twig; does they store it?"

"In course; there's a big hut o' purpose. Might take fire!"

"To-night?"

"No, not till the lobsters are in season. Judge

Wharton wrote to the head-quarters for ammunition, and the baggage trains is loaded with enough powder for another Guy Fawks' treason plot."

"Well, that's a bang-up idea."

"Yes, and you must ask him what he thinks on it."

"We will."

"And now, as I ain't got no more to say, I'll just skedaddle; for it'll be rather ockard if I'm missed."

"Good night, Dan."

"Same to you. Look out for some of the rangers as be gone abroad after the game, for, if they lays hands on you, you'll have a good night's rest, I'm thinking."

"Blast 'em. If they comes within our range—"

"You'll be within their'n, which you'll find unconvenient."

"We'll look to it."

"Do. You'll find it better."

"To-morrow night, then?"

"Yes."

"Here?"

"I said so. Same place—"

"When?"

"Same time."

"All right. If anything happens you'll send us word."

"Yes. By Jackson."

With this Dan Sullivan struck his heels into the horse's side, and rode off towards the Block.

Dick cocked his musket and crept, and was moving towards the two bushrangers, who were turning to depart.

The Kangaroo hastily caught Dick by the arm.

"Hold! for God's sake, mate, let 'em go. You'll spoil our sport entirely if you hallo the birds afore they're netted. Let 'em go; we know all their precious plans, and we'll be ready for them; 'and as for that sneaking cuss, we'll brile him."

Dick acquiesced in the justice of this remark, and forebore to fire.

They lay close.

The bandits passed very near them, engaged in a conversation that entirely absorbed their attention. Presently they passed away out of hearing, and our hero and the Kangaroo emerged from their hiding place.

Finding the coast clear, and perceiving that they were unobserved by the bushrangers, they ran up the ascent and beheld the fire raging with uncontrollable fury.

They made all speed to reach the Block. Upon their arrival they found everything in confusion.

Men were shouting, women screaming, children yelling and getting in everybody's way.

The beeves and sheep released from the fold-yard and pens were running about unheeded.

The horses stood, their necks outstretched with widened nostril and starting eyes, trembling and neighing shrilly in their terror.

Among those most active in passing buckets from the well they perceived the treacherous Sulivan.

A long *cordon* of men had been formed and pails of water were handed down the line.

Men on the roofs of the fort and the outhouses were vainly striving to assuage the fury of the devouring element.

The red glare brilliantly illuminated the fear-stricken faces of the crowd.

The smoke soared sublimely aloft with a shower of lurid sparks and pieces of burning wood.

The dashing and hissing of the water seemed only to make the thick smoke still more dense, and to aggravate the heat and rage of the unquenchable conflagration.

Apart from the crowd, giving quick and sharp orders, stood Judge Wharton, the chief magistrate of the little community.

He was a short, good-humoured, yet determined-looking man.

Great respect was apparently paid to his authority.

His brief but sensible orders were obeyed with alacrity by the excited rangers.

Some of the party were dragging the hayricks down with their forks, and removing tables, benches, beds, and other furniture out of the reach of the fire.

Among the most active of the party were Waller and Barnup.

Those men hailed the coming of the Kangaroo and Dick Parker with much satisfaction.

All at once there was a shout. The large house in the centre of the clearing was perceived to be in flames.

This was rather extraordinary, as it was not near any of the other buildings.

The rangers stood for one moment in an agony of horror at this new disaster.

A hoarse murmur ran through the little cluster of hardy men who had rushed into the court-yard.

A sudden conviction seemed to take possession of them that this terrible accident was not the effect of mere chance, but that there was treachery.

Dick Parker, the Kangaroo, Waller, and Barnup approached Judge Wharton.

The old man listened to their words with a dark frown.

He replied.

Several men joined the group.

A bitter oath burst from them.

At this moment Dan Sullivan drew near, with a bucket of water in his hand.

Three of the men immediately rushed upon him, and before he could give utterance to his surprise and terror held him secure.

Others gathered around.

"Mates, tear the sheep's skin off that bloody wolf," cried the Kangaroo, pointing to the captive. "It is he has betrayed us to the cussed bushrangers. He has fired the Block."

There was a moment of ominous silence.

It was the calm that precedes the storm.

With looks of rage and vindictiveness the rangers drew their bowie knives, and were about to fall upon the traitor.

"No, lads—stand back I charge you—keep off your hands. If the prisoner is guilty of the horrid crime laid to his charge he shall pay the penalty in full; but he shall have a fair trial. The consternation of this moment shall not lead you into injustice. Stand back I tell ye, lads; he is my prisoner, and not one of you strikes him but through my heart."

It was Judge Wharton that spoke; he stood between Dan Sullivan and his infuriated comrades.

It was well for the treacherous villain that he did so.

The little mob, however, showed no disposition tamely to endure being deprived of the satisfaction of summary vengeance.

Dick, whose love of order and discipline had been acquired in a severe school, lent his aid to protect the prisoner.

The Kangaroo, who never thwarted our hero in any way, followed his leading in this instance.

Yet nothing would have saved the disguised bushranger from being hacked to pieces by the sharp knives of the settlers, had not their attention been suddenly diverted by a pealing scream from the upper windows of the central building, the lower part of which was constructed of hewn stones

Dick and the Kangaroo, assisted by some others, took this opportunity to drag off the miscreant.

He was tightly bound, and thrust into a log hut.

The door was secured.

A man, with loaded rifle, stood sentinel, with orders to shoot him dead if he contrived to get out.

Dick then returned to the burning fort.

He at once saw that a girl was on the roof, running wildly about among the lurid flames and the suffocating pillars of smoke.

It was Mynna.

Thrusting aside all who stood in his way, Dick made for the spot, where a little knot of the rangers, with pale and anxious faces, were gazing upwards.

Ladders had been placed.

Judge Wharton had offered a considerable reward to any one who was bold enough to risk their lives and rescue the girl.

Several daring fellows had successively mounted the ladder; they had been driven back by the jets of flame and smothering clouds that spurted out from the windows.

The upper part of the house was completely enveloped in a shroud of fire.

Calmly and resolutely Dick approached the foot of the ladder.

"Don't try it, mate, no go. Poor girl, it's all over with her, she's past saving."

Dick paid no heed to these discouraging words, but, picking up an axe firmly, he rapidly ran up the ladder. When he reached the top of the ladder he began clambering along a narrow ridge in the wall.

The crowd below were silent and breathless with excitement.

Reaching a little window with much difficulty, the gallant fellow thrust himself in.

No sooner had he entered than a groan burst from the horror-thrilled spectators.

A tongue of flame and a wreath of black smoke spurted out, as from the mane of a fiery dragon that had horribly consumed his hapless prey.

A moment of agonised suspense.

A dark form looms through the choking cloud that veils the roof.

It is Dick; he has gained the summit.

A roar of delight and admiration rings from below.

Mynna hangs on his left shoulder, his axe flashes glowing red in his right hand.

The red-hot wooden coping gives way, and with a loud crash thunders down into the yard below, leaving a shower of sparks sparkling the air like the trail of a rocket.

"Throw me a rope—for Heaven's sake be quick," shouted poor Dick.

A coil of rope swept through the air. Dick clutched at it.

It eluded his eager grasp, and was received as it fell with a cry of regret.

Again it was projected by eager hands; he this time was far out of reach. Those at a distance could see Dick, and cursed those who were closer to the wall for their clumsiness.

But these, as is often the case in such accidents, did not deserve any blame, for so dense were the drifts of smoke from the intervening windows that it was only occasionally that they could catch a glimpse at poor Dick.

The roof was rocking beneath his feet.

The heat and suffocation were getting unbearable.

Once more the rope unrolling whirled in the air.

Dick watched its progress, and snatched at it just as it was sinking down.

He bound it hastily round a chimney stack, and cautiously lowered himself over the parapet.

He hung suspended in mid air.

His fair burden lay still and unconsciously over his strong arm.

Twisting his legs firmly about the rope he began to descend.

Just as he had reached the lower window and placed his foot upon the sill he thought that the rope was giving way; jerking it to try whether his fear was well-founded, the rope spun down, bringing with it red-hot bricks and splinters of burning wood.

The people below stood as if they had been struck to stone by the Ægis of Perseus, so intense was their excitement and horror.

The Kangaroo placed a ladder, and rapidly mounted.

The position of Dick and Mynna, at that moment, was one of deadly peril.

It was an awful moment.

The gallant fellow cried out to his comrade below in a firm and manly voice—

"Never mind me, mate; I'm nothing. Save her."

Gently he lowered the unconscious girl to the ranger.

The latter carefully passed her down to another, and soon she was safe, rescued, and carefully tended by the women.

For Dick, his peril was still imminent.

The ladder did not reach so high as his window.

His foot-hold was very precarious.

A loud crash.

The roof had fallen in.

Part of the wall came toppling down.

The crowd receded as a wave of the sea draws back from the shore.

Kangaroo kept his post.

Dick leaped down—it was a fearful venture.

But it was horrible—death—to pause.

His faithful comrade caught him in his arms.

The ladder was almost upset.

It was saved from below.

Another moment poor Dick is lying on the ground, his head resting on the knee of the ranger—pitying and admiring faces around him.

He smiles faintly—his eyes close—his face loses all expression—he has swooned.

CHAPTER CVI.

THE BARONET'S PROTEGE.

IN a private room, sumptuously furnished, and in a small but handsome house in Mayfair, two persons are seated before the fire.

We will at once inform the reader that one of these was the Downy Cove, the other the aristocratic personage who had conversed with that respectable individual, the night previously in the private bar of the tavern near the Strand.

Sir Oswald Mordaunt was sitting, with a look of interest on his face, listening to a relation of the struggles and trials of Mr. Edward Dudley Mortimer, the young actor with whom, under the distinguishing auspices of the immaculate Downy, we have already made acquaintance.

"Mortimer and Dudley! Well, it is very strange, too; but are you quite sure that you are not deceiving me? for, remember, such a tale as you are trying to foist upon me will only defeat your own purpose. The person whom I select to carry out my designs must be a *low-born man*—that is, a *sine qua non* in our arrangements. Tell me, fellow, are you sure you are not trying to deceive me?"

"S' help me never!" cried the Downy, with a burst of virtuous indignation, "if it ain't enough to make a cove enter a action for defamation—as if a man of 'onour, as is known for sich in the highest circles, should be wounded on his tenderest pint because a work'us brat happens to have a fine name, and gets found swabbed in a broidered handkercher, which is not at all peculiar. Cos vy? Oh, very likely his mother filched it."

"It may be, truly, that the wretched creature who was burdened with this child might have dressed him with unwonted care, and gave him a 'fine name,' as you call it, from motives of female vanity, whose subtle vagaries there is no accounting for," replied the Baronet, thoughtfully.

"As for being low born," said the Downy, but half appeased, "I mean to say my pall is as good as anybody in that perticklar. Vy, he wasn't even found on the crib, but in the gutter. If that ain't being low born we must look out for a heligible coal mine."

"His appearance is all I could wish."

"Reg'lar flash."

"And it seems he is well educated?"

"The three R.'s — reading, 'riting, and 'rithmetic. Patters all the lingos of Babel, acts the Idiot witness, and sings like a piping bullfinch."

"He seems, by his physiognomy, to be of a poetical and impressionable temperament."

"Ain't got no *temper* at all; mild as a sucking lamb."

"And he has no relations living?"

"Vell; If you makes him rich they'll spring up like musherooms arter a shower. I allers thought I had none—but ven fust I had that little legacy as was left me, I discovered my grandfather had ten sons and ten daughters, and each on 'em had just a dozen kids apiece, and the affectionate creatures all wanted to board and lodge with me and to keep up the family party till I was kind enough to turn up my toes and leave 'em my old slippers. But though I'm reg'lar affectionate I didn't see it no how."

"Ha! is it not possible there may be some reason all this tomfoolery? Maybe some of his low kindred may turn up, but that can not happen yet and when I have done with him it will be all the better."

"But your honour won't be offended if I asks what you means by 'have done with him'? I hopes you don't mean to do the shabby, and when poor Ned has served your purpose, give him the slip and leave him just where he was afore?"

"And if in the meantime, during the term of our engagement, I pay him liberally, where's the injustice? You have been employed by me—how have I treated you?"

"Vy, your honour, I must say, has allers done the right thing."

"Be content then—and be assured that Mr. Edward Dudley Mortimer shall be well provided for, if he will only implicitly follow my wishes in all things."

"Vell, he's a young colt, and 'clined to be skittish, and it's allers his principle to 'keep square'—and I means to have him stick to it, so if you wants him to do anything in *my line*, vy all I can say is, just vot the managers writes on his tragedies—'Declined with thanks.'"

The Baronet looked at the Downy Cove with a searching look and an ironical smile on his lips.

"I should like to know whether you are sincere in your desire to keep him in the right path from which you have so widely wandered."

"And vich your honour is so anxious to bring me back to," returned the Downy with a sly leer, "I is—look here, I vas born on the eighth day of the week, in a little street down no vere; my father's name was Walker, and I cadged for ha'pence afore as I was half as high as the broom I used to sweep the crossings vith. Vell, I got legged for a wagrant, vas flogged for priggin' a loaf ven I had dined off the steam of the cook-shop vinders for several days. Ven they'd worked me, and frowned at me, and frightened me, and whipped me, they let me go; and as edication and a good trade is werry necessary to them as can live like the Frenchman's horse, and them gold fishes what nobody feeds, I believe; so I was dedicated accordin'. I learned the finding lay, set up as a area sneak, and did a werry good thing. But a intelligent officer spoilt my little game for a while, during vich I was employed in a light capacity in a Government office. Ven I vos discharged I got no knowing that I vos honoured by the interesting flash name—the Downy Cove. So, you see, it's all nat'ral, this sort of thing to meet; but still in my heart I feels a sort of hankering arter keeping square even now, and since I have knowed Ned Mortimer I've taken my davy to keep him out of bad company.

"The feeling does you honour. Well, you may make your mind easy that I shall not require him for any than lawful purposes, and how I should like to see him."

"All serene, your honour. He's awaiting for your orders. I'll go and fetch him, and bring him up."

"Let him come alone."

"Werry good, sir."

The Downy left the room.

The baronet remained, lost in thought.

"It is very strange," he murmured, "that such a wild thought should enter my brain. No doubt the foolish apprehension is quite groundless. But still, it will persistently thrust itself upon me. But he shall be a tool by which I will blind and dupe the haughty dowager, and tame the cursed pride of the hated family. Through him I shall secure the estates to myself, and shall reach the goal of my ambition by a bloodless path. And it is well that I have such means to do so; for, were it otherwise, so strong are my motives of interest and of hatred, that I should stick at nothing—no, not even at— but there is no need of that; there is no need to sully my soul with the mere thought of it. All will be mine; and through my instrument, I shall triumph. Young, ardent, handsome—used to the sound of an honourable name—a poet, an enthusiast, a scholar, and a fool—oh, he will do bravely!"

The subject of these reflections modestly opened the door.

The nobleman rose and saluted him courteously.

"Mr. Mortimer, I presume. Pray, sir, be seated. I am glad to see you. I have sent for you, Mr. Mortimer, to ask you if you would like to accept a position as secretary and agent to myself. You are aware that I am a 'member,' and I am overwhelmed with business, and greatly require the assistance of one in whom I can implicitly confide."

"But I almost fear that my attainments are not sufficiently high nor my abilities sufficiently tested to enable me to undertake a post so responsible."

"Never mind; I can teach you all that it is needful you should learn. I know something of you, Mr. Mortimer."

"Indeed, sir," said the young man, the blood flushing his cheek. "If you have formed a favourable opinion of me from any communication you may have had with those I served formerly I am very grateful to them for their kindness towards me."

"No, I have not communicated with any one in the matter, nor do I wish to do so. I have seen you play."

"Is it possible?" said the young man, his vanity aroused and his eye beaming with solicitude.

"Yes, in your own line, that is in parts adapted to your natural temperament, you are excellent indeed, but you have one fault."

"And it is?" asked young Mortimer breathlessly.

"You are too sincere."

"Indeed, can that be possible?"

"Yes, truly, for a good actor will identify himself with his part irrespective of his own disposition and prejudices, and will depict vice as faithfully as virtue."

"Then I am no actor at all," said poor Mr. Mortimer, deeply chagrined in spite of his good sense.

"You are born for better things. I trust I shall be able to secure you in a social position, and shall give you the means of following pursuits quite congenial to your taste."

"Oh, sir, you are good indeed."

"Not at all. I expect you to serve me faithfully; and now to touch upon pecuniary arrangements. I was thinking that I might name your salary at five hundred pounds a year, but of course you will not suffer yourself to be inconvenienced at any time.

CHAPTER CVII.

TRIAL OF THE SPY—ARREST OF DICK—DENOUEMENT.

IT will be remembered that the treacherous Dan Sullivan had been placed in confinement within one of the store-huts of the little settlement.

The night and its horrors were passed.

The house of Judge Wharton had been burned to the ground.

Yet though the sun was rising high in the heavens dense smoke still billowed upwards from the charred and scattered ruins.

In mute agony, but with assumed composure, the worthy magistrate mingled with the rangers, and strove to console them for the heavy losses they had sustained, and to inspire them with energy and patience to remedy the evil. His greatest difficulties were, on the one hand, to induce them to sink all selfish regrets and individual solicitudes in the momentous claim for general combination in their present critical position; and, on the other hand, to prevent the enraged settlers from taking summary and cruel vengeance upon the author of the terrible disaster.

He urged upon them the necessity at this conjuncture of preserving rigid discipline and order, and tried to convince them that as a fair trial would doubtless end in the conviction and punishment of the miscreant, it would be foolish and dangerous as a precedent if they did not await the result of an impartial examination of the culprit.

The rangers, however, were clamorous that immediate justice should be done upon the culprit.

Only one of the larger buildings remained entire.

This was the canteen, and its large adjoining room, which was used as a place for convivial assemblies during the week, and as a meeting-house on the Sabbaths.

A large group of men and women were assembled around the door of this erection with fierce and eager face, thirsting to see the criminal brought in to receive sentence.

Another and even fiercer party prowled around the hut in which Dan Sullivan was imprisoned.

The wretch was crouched down in one corner among some loose straw, his face overspread with deathly pallor, his limbs quaking, and his fingers passing convulsively through his unkempt hair.

The agonies of death had laid their hold upon him.

His eyes were strained, his lips parched, and his ear intently listening to sounds of fearful boding.

Terrible his mental suffering as he heard the curses not loud, but deep, that were breathed by his outraged fellow-rangers, thirsting for his blood.

He lay powerless, disabled by a palsy of terror.

The time passed slowly and horribly, and his tortured brain realised in its most hideous form the struggles and throes of a painful and shameful death.

At last the door was opened.

The glorious sunshine poured in, and a thrilling shout rang around his prison. A dozen furious faces peered in at the door.

Two strong and grave-looking men entered.

There was nothing but judgment and condemnation in their cold and pitiless looks.

As they drew near him he drew himself closely together in his corner, and hid his pale face in his trembling hands.

They sternly bade him rise.

He did not respond to the command.

The rangers bent over him, and dragged him from his sanctuary.

They lifted him to his feet.

The craven sank upon his knees, and cried wildly for mercy.

"Oh, God! Mates, do not kill, pray, pray, do not kill me. I am a guilty man—you will kill my soul. Give me a little while to repent—only a little while. Save my life, and I will save you all. I can show you worse than myself among you; there's Morris, and Reilly, and lots more. Oh, Lord God, be merciful! They led me on. It wasn't my fault. Only spare me—a poor wretch, mates, that hopes upon your mercy—and you shall have all the gang in irons afore to-morrow. By Heaven's light you shall."

One of the rangers, faithful to the judge, barricaded the doorway, to prevent the indignant mob from bursting in and tearing him to pieces.

Alternately whining and shrieking for mercy, the miserable wretch was dragged forth.

He was close pressed on all sides; instant death on all sides threatened him, from uplifted bowie knives and levelled rifles.

The yells and execrations that accompanied these deadly threatenings were fearful indeed. In an instant he would have been hacked to pieces; but the rangers commissioned to bring him to judgment stoutly defended him.

They interposed themselves between their prisoner and the infuriated mob.

Their peril was not slight.

An indiscriminate slaughter of the prisoner and his custodians seemed likely to ensue.

One of the men who had hold of his arm looked around him, shook his head deprecatingly, and then pointed significantly to the meeting-house.

This well-timed motion pacified the crowd.

The deep and ominous silence that followed was even yet more awful than the preceding storm for blood.

Knives were sheathed, revolvers replaced, and with a dumb sternness the rangers tramped along by the side of their victim.

The long shed—for the structure deserved no better name—was densely crowded. Upon a platform at one end Judge Wharton, with other influential men, was sitting at a rude table.

On one side stood Dick, the Kangaroo, Waller, and two others, the little group of witnesses.

On a rough bench sat twelve men, the jury of this rude and primitive tribunal.

When the prisoner was brought into court, a hundred scowling faces lowered upon him.

Respect for the occasion and for the Judge restrained the cry of rage that would have otherwise found vent. As it was, the criminal was greeted with a deep, but half-suppressed, groan of fury.

So terrified was the poor wretch, that had he not been supported by one of his warders, he must have sunk to the ground.

The charge against him was read somewhat hurriedly, and the witnesses were called upon to give their evidence.

The Kangaroo and Dick Parker in turn gave theirs, describing the prisoner's interview with the bushrangers, which they had witnessed in the "plant."

The others gave information of certain circumstances which clearly showed that Sullivan was the incendiary who had caused the terrible calamity that had left the little settlement defenceless, and placed the rangers, with their wives and families, in a position of imminent peril.

Judge Wharton calmly and moderately summed up, exhorting the jury to remember that, though removed from the seat of Government, they were not the less responsible for their verdict, and exhorted them, as faithful men and true Christians, not to allow themselves to be biassed by any remembrance of the horrible disaster that had befallen them, nor by any intimation of popular prejudice, but to give their decision impartially, and according to their conscience.

Things had reached this point when from without was heard the sound of a bugle.

Every one started.

A man hastily entered the court.

He was immediately passed to Judge Wharton.

He whispered something to the magistrate.

A cry of joy rang around the place.

The soldiers were come!

The little colony was safe.

Mary rushed out of her hut.

For a moment the prisoner was disregarded.

A dark man with a large black beard, in officer's uniform, entered the room.

He was accompanied by several subalterns.

He was greeted with joyful and enthusiastic cheers, to which he responded with a graceful bow.

Wharton arose, and heartily shook hands with the new-comer.

The latter at once produced his papers.

The Judge glanced over them with an air of satisfaction.

The rangers looked on with curiosity and interest as the two superiors conversed in an under tone.

Wharton started; a shade of annoyance passed over his face.

"And are these your orders, Captain Roslin?"

"My imperative orders, Judge Wharton! Here is the despatch which conveys them from head-quarters."

"And I must, then, surrender this prisoner, and place the men, bearing the names herein set down, under close arrest?"

"More than that, Judge Wharton: they must be delivered up to me for removal to Fort Munika."

"If such are your commands, Captain, there is no course left to me but to see them obeyed; but truly I am very sorry."

The rangers began to understand a little of the purport of the conversation.

They began to perceive that in all probability their victim would be rescued from their hands.

They were not at all disposed that any such thing should occur.

With stern faces they instinctively crowded to that part of the hut where Dan Sullivan stood.

Upon the entrance of Captain Roslin, the wretched man who stood arrayed for his atrocious offence looked up hurriedly.

His eye brightened slowly, the colour stole back to his pallid cheeks, and his lips trembled with eagerness.

A withering glance from the officer quelled him at once, and he stood with his eyes bent on the ground in abashment and silence.

Judge Wharton turned towards the assembly, and held up his hand in token for silence.

All eyes were turned towards him.

Captain Roslin stood at his right hand, leaning upon his sword.

"I am sorry to tell you, my men, that Captain Roslin is the bearer of positive orders for the deliverance of our prisoner into his hands; but perhaps it is well, as we are thereby saved the onus and responsibility of carrying out the law; but I am grieved, indeed, to tell you that this gallant officer has further orders to arrest Richard Parker and Michael Bourne, known as the Kangaroo."

A cry of surprise and indignation burst from the rangers, and they immediately rallied around Dick and his companions, as if to defend them.

"Don't let the red coats have 'em; what have they done? A sight truer men than the skulking feather-beds, that let the infernal bushrangers burn plants and murder innocent settlers while they were diverting themselves. No martial law here— it won't wash."

These and other similar expressions of general disgust and dissatisfaction rung round the place, mingled with deep growlings and hisses."

"My men," said the officer, with calm authority of manner, "you cannot more truly regret seeing your comrades placed under arrest than I do the unpleasant duty of obeying distasteful orders; but you are not so unjust and unreasonable as to blame me for a measure taken for the safety of every member of your little community. I am only the instrument in carrying out the commands of others whom, you all know, I am bound to obey. Therefore, I shall not meet with any opposition from you. No doubt the men are worthy of your sympathy; and if, as I am willing to believe, they are innocent of the grave offence charged against them, they will have every means of clearing themselves, which they, no doubt, will be able to do. For Richard Parker—he is, as I suppose you know, a felon, who has been liberated on a ticket-of-leave."

"No, no," cried the crowd, turning towards our hero, in full expectation of an indignant denial of this statement.

But poor Dick did not reply. His face blushed scarlet, and he clenched his teeth in agony.

"Speak up," cried some amongst them; "stick up for your own honour, Dick. Give him the lie like a Briton; we'll protect you."

"Mates, it is true enough. I have served my time as a convict, but I am as innocent as the best among ye of the crime for which I was sentenced. What I have done that I should be hurried and hunted like a wild beast, God knows. I have my license in my pocket, and will not surrender with my life to any of the cursed wretches, who are in league to persecute me without cause. I rely upon you to defend me."

But there was no response to this appeal.

Deep silence prevailed.

"If you are conscious of innocence, Richard Parker," said Wharton, gravely, "you will not be disturbed by the prospect of being placed in a position for proving it. I am truly sorry that I have no alternative from giving you up to Captain Roslin. At the same time it is only my duty to avow that, whatever your antecedents might have been, during the time you have lived amongst us your conduct in every sense has deserved the highest praise. You assert that you were innocent of the crime for which you suffered punishment, and, if my good opinion is of any value, I can assure you I firmly believe your assertion, and look upon you as an injured man."

"God for ever bless you for those kind words, sir," cried poor Dick, with passionate fervour "and now I am ready to go whither they choose to take me, to endure all they choose to inflict upon me, and I would serve out a dozen lives of servitude for the pleasure of doing you one good turn in token of my gratitude. God bless you, sir."

With this our hero stepped manfully from his place, and approached the officer.

The Kangaroo followed him in silence.

The door was opened—a sergeant and a dozen soldiers, with muskets on their shoulders, entered the room.

Dick, the Kangaroo, and Dan Sullivan were placed between.

"Surely, Captain Roslin, you are not going to depart in such haste. You see that from the natural effects of our late calamity things are in terrific disorder. But you'll stay at least to partake of some refreshment before you start?"

"Thanks, Judge, but I cannot stop. My orders are imperative. I must return to head-quarters without a moment's delay."

"And when may we expect your regiment, which is to secure us from the attacks of the murdering bushrangers?"

"To morrow at latest. They will bring with them such succour as the state of this luckless settlement demands; and I trust they will be no unwelcome visitors."

"Take care of your prisoners."

"Never fear."

"The fellow Parker is an honest man. He bears the impress of integrity in every feature. I could swear he is honest."

"I do not doubt it, Judge, but I must not allow you to induce me to another moment's protraction. I must depart at once. Adieu."

"Honour and success lie in your road," returned Wharton, smiling.

The escort, with their prisoners, left the meeting. The soldiers were supplied with ale and spirits; Dick and his fellow-prisoners swallowed a little brandy, and the party left the Block.

There was a very faint cheer from the rangers.

Descending the hill the officers mounted their horses, and the party filed away along the winding road, and were soon lost to view in the heavy screen of the "plant."

An hour's march brought the captors and the captives to a lonely spot, beyond a wild range of low, blue hills. As they defiled into this valley, Dick's companions perceived that, among the low and stunted trees that were thickly scattered over the rugged and briar-cumbered soil, little turf huts had been erected. Fires were burning; there was a strong odour of cooking meat, and the air was not a little impregnated with the smell of brandy and gunpowder.

Ticket-of-Leave himself, however, observed none

of these things. Moodily and sullenly he tramped along, his eyes bent on the ground, his heart deeply chagrined, and bitterly brooding over his wrongs, and revolting against the tacit repulse he had sustained from the men who were his comrades, and whom he had served so well.

The Kangaroo seized his arm, for neither of the men were bound.

"My God, Dick!" he exclaimed, "we are trapped."

Loud laughter, cheers, and shouts made the hills reverberate.

They stood in the midst of a strong party of the bushrangers. It seemed that the whole gang was assembled.

The soldiers drew off from the side of their prisoners, and stood at a little distance, in a circle, leaning upon their muskets, indulging in their long-pent hilarity.

There was a roar of laughter as Captain Roslin pulled off his great black beard and held out his hand to Dick.

"Right welcome, son of my adoption," he said with a smile; "I am sorry you should have constrained me to come and fetch you. I hoped you would have been amongst us of your own free will. You will see that I am not Captain Roslin, of her Majesty's Service, but Captain Regan, of my own."

"We need recruits like you; and I think I have shown you to-day how utterly fruitless your efforts of re-establishing yourself by honest means will prove. Even your rough comrades turned their backs on you when you told them you were a Ticket-of-Leave; but I cannot stay to talk to you now. Till my return you must remain a prisoner. Bradley, see that these men are secured, but well cared for. Sullivan, follow me."

The captain of these daring freebooters rode his horse towards a sort of tent, that stood at a little distance.

Dick and the Kangaroo looked at each other inquiringly.

Their looks bore testimony to the similarity of their opinions.

Resistance was useless—escape hopeless.

With a dogged resignation, therefore, they followed their companions, who led them away towards the side of the hill, and ushered them into a sort of cavern, the entrance of which was through a narrow and winding passage hewn in the rock.

The floor was strewn with rushes; there was a rude table and benches, and, in one corner, a couch, composed of heather and long grass, covered by a rough blanket.

The place was lighted from above.

A fire was burning under a hole in the roof.

Upon their entry Dick threw himself down on one of the benches, folded his arms, and gazed vacantly before him.

The Kangaroo laid his hand upon his comrade's shoulder, and spoke in tones of encouragement.

"Look up, Dick. It's hard upon you, a brave, good lad as you are; but never say die, man. If we're in the hands of the Philistines we must bide our time, and sleep with one eye open till we can spy a chance of escape."

Two of the bushrangers entered the little cave.

One of them placed a large loaf and some "savoury meats" upon the table, and the other produced a bottle of rum and a drinking horn.

"Here's your health, gemmen," said the fellow, with a rough laugh; "glad to see you amongst us. You might be in worse quarters, I can tell ye. The Captain acts royal where he takes, and he's quite spooney on you, Dick Parker. You're in a snug berth, both o' yer; and I'd advise yer to let well alone, for if you try a skeddadle you'll find yourselves bilked, I take it. There are three men without who will administer a blue pill to soothe your restlessness, if you get up to any mouching capers. Good-bye; enjoy yourselves, mates. There's a box of the Captain's best cigars, accordin' to order. I shall just take half-a-dozen as proper perquisites, and we'll be here again in an hour to see if you wants anything."

With this the two fellows decamped.

Half famished, Dick and the Kangaroo paid their *devoirs* to the meal provided, drank pretty freely of the rum, and, sitting down before the fire, lighted their cigars, and began to feel more resigned to their position.

"Dick," said the Kangaroo, "it won't do for chaps like us to give way to the hump. I don't see any mortal good in grizzling. We have done a bad feed, and arter all it's better to be here than to be brow-beaten by some cuss of a beak, and locked up in detention, even if we got off clear at last, which, accordin' to your own case, ain't sure to follow. If you'll leave off looking vicious, I'll spin you a yarn concerning a fellow of your stamp, who had a sudden turn in luck which made a man on him. *He* was a 'Ticket,' and as good a chap as ever drew breath. Shall I tell you the story?"

"Aye, do, lad," returned Parker; "it will distract my thoughts, for at this moment I feel the devil in my heart dragging at the strings, and trying to pull it away from its honesty and foolery to Regan!—gold and revenge! Do, lad, tell me this story."

They re-filled their horns, re-lighted their cigars, and the Kangaroo began in the following strain.

CHAPTER CVIII.

THE KANAROO'S STORY.

"It was in this wise, Dick: Frank Wilton was a sort of relation of mine, and, when we were boys, we went to school together.

"Now, you see, mate, I never took to book learning, and that's about all I have got to thank my stars for.

"I was mighty fond of Frank. He was a pale and sickly boy, mild and gentle as a girl; he was a pretty, genteel lad, and I was a rough one. But though young Frank was soft and quiet-like, he had a will of his own, and was noways sneakish. When he did get in a fury the bigger boys were quite scared at him; but he was so forgiving and so patient when he was not provoked that some of the scampish lads used to like to try how far they could tease him, but, I'll warrant you, they always stopped when they found they were going too far. I liked young Frank, as I said, Dick, and young Frank liked me. It was queer, too; the lad couldn't climb at all. In some things he was as nervous and timid as could be—he could not jump nor fling a stone, nor turn a summersault; and yet at his books he was surprisin'. I never could learn, and I cost my master enough canes to make a sugar plantation. It was all no use. What with playing the wag, robbing the orchards, and hunting after birds' nests I had too much on my mind to attend to the spelling book; and, perhaps, I was stupid."

"In a year or two young Frank had learned all that the master could teach him; and then he took to music, and used to play the organ in the village church.

"He was growing a fine fellow now. He was very orderly and methodical in his ways, and used to study so many hours, and then he would walk out into the woods and the fields; but he was studying even then—nat'ral history, you know, and all that sort of thing. Bless you, mate, he could tell you such fine names for every bit of paltry grass or weed he picked up in the lanes as you never heard on.

"Well, the old schoolmaster died, and young Frank applied for his place; and in a little while he became dominie. For a bit he got on well enough; but though the people thought him the best fellow alive, and an excellent teacher, yet, somehow, he was too far ahead of his bumpkin scholars, and being bodily delicate, he had not the nerve and strength to lug 'em up to his own mark; and as for thrashing on 'em, unless it was for lying or bullying, he would not and could not do it. And the young vagabonds took advantage of him, you may believe. He began to wear out; he had no time for his own studies, and the work was too much for his weak constitution. Our parson and the squire recommended him to a merchant in London; he became a clerk in the office of the gentleman, and well he prospered, Dick. I went to see him in London, and in a fine place he was, and a lot of books he had: yet he received me as kind and hearty as if he had never risen an inch above me. Now this young chap, Dick, you must know, was a sentimental sort of fellow, and, somehow or other, contrived to fall head over ears in love with the sister of one of his fellow clerks. But the brother of the girl turned out a black scoundrel—embezzled the governor's money and committed forgery; but for the sake of the gal—the sister, you know—poor Frank hushed and muddled it up in some sort for a while. But the gap wanted filling up; poor Frank was too generous to save much, and so, as you may guess, it all came out at last, and, as it often happens in such cases, poor Frank got transported, and the precious brother of his girl only got a few months' imprisonment, and was greatly pitied as being 'led on' by a designing villain. But there, Dick, I must give the rascal due credit, for he did do the 'snivel' most beautiful. Frank was away two years. He returned to England, tried to get work—but you know all about that from experience."

"And the girl," said Dick; "was she true to him?"

"As the stars—a reg'lar angel. Wanted to run off with him, in spite of father and mother, and all, but he wouldn't have that. He was full of hope about getting a little home for himself and his beloved girl, where they might forget all past troubles, and grow old together in love and happiness. It was very natural, Dick."

"Poor fellow!" returned our hero, with a heavy sigh.

"Well, he found it all no use; and at last, worn out with trying to get employment, he resolved to try his luck at the gold diggings in California.

"Now I ought to have told you that there was a young boy as she had taken a fancy to, a poor, dirty little urchin, that begged of him in the streets. The lad had been put in prison for cadging, and could not do anything for a living. This youngster took on so about losing Frank, one day, when the poor chap told him how he was going out to the gold diggings to seek his fortune, that Frank offered to take him with him. The boy was an orphan, there was no tie to bind him to this country, and he was overjoyed to go anywhere with his only friend. When they got to California, they joined in with a party of rough fellows, and went to work for gold in the fields in California. Precious little luck they had—all sorts of troubles and disappointments. Sometimes they would find some dust or a little nugget, but it's value was but poor pay for their loss of time and heavy labours. At last sickness broke out among them, and cut off the best of them. Out of spirits, and woeful poor, the remainder left the field on which they were working, and travelled on to a distant and dreary part that had never been worked before. The things went awful bad. There was no water to speak of, and what there was was unwholesome. Game was scarce, and nothing seemed to grow—it was a reg'lar wilderness. Well, they scratched, they dug, they washed, and riddled, but it was all no use; they could not find enough stuff to gild a farthing. At last one day they all resolved to give it up and make their way home as well as they could. That very morning the poor street boy that Frank had brought over with him died, blessing his kind friend, who had nursed him as tender as a mother for weeks, and given him all the food that he could get, till he left himself as lean as a herring. The boy was dead, and poor Frank leaned over him with a bleeding heart, and felt himself quite lonely and friendless. He asked his mates to stay for a while, and help him to bury the poor fellow, but they were surly fellows, and were out of patience, as poor Frank had coaxed them, day after day, to remain, for he knew that the poor boy could never bear removing. The oxen were yoked to the wagons, and every preparation had been made for the start. They would not stay, but told Frank if he liked to follow he might overtake them, and so they left him. Poor Frank, left alone with the dead, gave way for a little time, but then roused himself. Taking his spade, he wandered a short space to find a pleasant spot in which to bury the poor boy. As he threw up the earth he paused from time to time, and looked across the plain, and saw the oxen and the vans crawling along on the edge of the sky, no bigger than so many small beetles, and presently they disappeared entirely. He nerved his arm to the sad work, and dug away. Presently his spade struck against something hard; it was a large nugget of gold—one of the largest ever found; all around him were scattered smaller pieces. He was digging for the boy he had so nobly protected, and of whose frail remains he was so piously careful, a grave of gold. Fancy, Dick, the joy of his return, for he found yet more in the neighbourhood. He concealed his treasures in his little travelling wagon, and, escaping all dangers, returned to Old England a wealthy man."

"And did he find his sweetheart still true to him?"

"Yes; and, before I left England, I went to see him. He and his wife lived in the country. He had taken to writing books, and the like, and mighty well he was doing. And so you see, Dick, that it is never too late to hope; things mostly take sudden turns for good luck or bad."

"It is so," said Dick; "and I will seek a new life elsewhere. I will away to the coast, and the first ship that comes shall bear me away from here for ever. When I return to England, it shall be with a name, or not at all."

THE END.

NOTICE TO OUR READERS.

NEXT SATURDAY WILL BE PUBLISHED THE FIRST TWO NUMBERS OF

THE BOY PIRATE,

OR,

LIFE ON THE OCEAN,

Commencing the daring history of a British Boy, who, born to wealth and rank, cast upon the wide world of adventure, created for himself a name that will be handed down as the Terror of Wrong, the Champion of the Defenceless, and the Scourge of the Seas.

This remarkable and thrilling Tale will be made more interesting by the family records in the possession of the writer, and will be read with intense excitement by every boy in the United Kingdom, as proving that the lion-like courage which, in the days of the immortal Nelson, was the dread of our foes, still exists in the breasts of our British Boys.

The story will be written by

CAPTAIN LYONS,

who has already gained celebrity for his nautical romances, of which, we can assure our readers, this will prove the best.

This work will be of a larger size than the Ticket-of-Leave Man, the type will admit of more reading, and the illustrations will be of a superior style.

One Penny Weekly.—Order No. 1.—No. 2 will be presented Gratis, in a Coloured Wrapper.

The further adventures of Dick Parker will be given in the course of the work. Our readers will, therefore, please to see that they next week receive instead the two numbers of the BOY PIRATE, in the wrapper, for One Penny.